The Works of Mark Twain

VOLUME 15

EARLY TALES & SKETCHES

VOLUME 1 (1851–1864)

Editorial work for this volume has been made possible by a generous grant from the Editing Program of the National Endowment for the Humanities, an independent federal agency.

THE WORKS OF MARK TWAIN

The following volumes in this edition of Mark Twain's previously published works have been issued to date:

ROUGHING IT
edited by Franklin R. Rogers and Paul Baender

WHAT IS MAN? AND OTHER PHILOSOPHICAL WRITINGS
edited by Paul Baender

THE ADVENTURES OF TOM SAWYER
TOM SAWYER ABROAD
TOM SAWYER, DETECTIVE
edited by John C. Gerber, Paul Baender, and Terry Firkins

THE PRINCE AND THE PAUPER
edited by Victor Fischer and Lin Salamo,
with the assistance of Mary Jane Jones

A CONNECTICUT YANKEE IN KING ARTHUR'S COURT
edited by Bernard L. Stein
with an introduction by Henry Nash Smith

EARLY TALES & SKETCHES, VOLUME 1 (1851–1864)
edited by Edgar M. Branch and Robert H. Hirst,
with the assistance of Harriet Elinor Smith

The Works of Mark Twain

Editorial Board

JOHN C. GERBER, *CHAIRMAN*

PAUL BAENDER

WALTER BLAIR

WILLIAM M. GIBSON

WILLIAM B. TODD

Series Editor of
The Works of Mark Twain
and
The Mark Twain Papers

FREDERICK ANDERSON

The Works of Mark Twain

EARLY TALES & SKETCHES

VOLUME 1
1851-1864

Edited by
EDGAR MARQUESS BRANCH and ROBERT H. HIRST
With the Assistance of
HARRIET ELINOR SMITH

PUBLISHED FOR
THE IOWA CENTER FOR TEXTUAL STUDIES
BY THE
UNIVERSITY OF CALIFORNIA PRESS
BERKELEY, LOS ANGELES, LONDON
1979

CENTER FOR EDITIONS OF
AMERICAN AUTHORS

AN APPROVED TEXT

MODERN LANGUAGE
ASSOCIATION OF AMERICA

UNIVERSITY OF CALIFORNIA PRESS
BERKELEY AND LOS ANGELES, CALIFORNIA

UNIVERSITY OF CALIFORNIA PRESS, LTD.
LONDON, ENGLAND

PREVIOUSLY UNPUBLISHED MATERIAL BY MARK TWAIN
COPYRIGHT ©1979 BY THE MARK TWAIN COMPANY
ORIGINAL MATERIAL COPYRIGHT © 1979 BY
THE REGENTS OF THE UNIVERSITY OF CALIFORNIA
ISBN: 0-520-03186-5
LIBRARY OF CONGRESS CATALOG
CARD NUMBER: 75-46045

DESIGNED BY HARLEAN RICHARDSON
IN COLLABORATION WITH DAVE COMSTOCK

MANUFACTURED IN THE UNITED STATES OF AMERICA

ACKNOWLEDGMENTS

OUR FIRST thanks must go to the American taxpayers for their willingness to finance this and other efforts to preserve our national heritage. Editorial work for this collection was largely supported by a generous grant from the Editing Program of the National Endowment for the Humanities, an independent federal agency. It was begun under a contract with the United States Office of Education, Department of Health, Education, and Welfare, under the provisions of the Cooperative Research Program.

Mr. Branch was assisted in his work on the collection by a grant-in-aid from the American Council of Learned Societies in 1969, by a senior fellowship from the National Endowment for the Humanities in 1971, and by the continued support of the administration and the Faculty Research Committee of Miami University. Mr. Hirst was assisted by generous support from the Faculty Research Committee of the University of California at Los Angeles. Financial assistance for production costs was provided by the Graduate College of the University of Iowa. We are deeply indebted for all this support of a long and difficult project.

Finding, identifying, and annotating Mark Twain's early work has been a collaborative enterprise among scholars of the last three generations. We would like to acknowledge contributions from Frederick Anderson, Howard G. Baetzhold, Ivan Benson, Minnie M. Brashear, George H. Brownell, Louis J. Budd, Roger Butterfield, Paul Fatout, Walter Francis Frear, John Howell, Franklin J. Meine, William C. Miller, Henry Nash Smith, Franklin Walker, and Dixon Wecter. Other scholars have helped lay the foundation for the textual history of the early sketches: Dewey Ganzel, M. E. Grenander, Hamlin Hill, and Dennis Welland. We have profited from the continuing efforts of all these scholars to enlarge and define the canon of Mark Twain's works.

All our efforts would be in vain, of course, without the unfailing patience and inflexible kindness of many libraries and their staffs. Two of these have borne with us longer, and therefore more patiently, than the rest. We would particularly like to thank the staff of The Bancroft Library, University of California at Berkeley: James D. Hart, John Barr Tompkins, Helen Bretnor, Irene M. Moran, Peter E. Hanff, William M. Roberts, Alma Compton, Robert H. Becker, Suzanne H. Gallup, Vivian C. Fisher, and Cecil Chase. We would also like to thank the staff of the Edgar W. King Library at Miami University: Donald E. Oehlerts, Leland S. Dutton, Peter Flinterman, Sarah C. Barr, William A. Wortman, Mary D. Stanton, C. Martin Miller, Jr., Richard H. Quay, Helen C. Ball, Valerie Edwards, Susan W. Berry, and Joann D. Olson. None of the work published here would have been possible without the unstinting help of these dedicated men and women.

We have made fewer but no less crucial demands on the following persons and institutions, who have our thanks: Donald C. Gallup, Marjorie B. Wynne, Kenneth M. Nesheim, and Anne Whelpley of the Beinecke Rare Book and Manuscript Library, Yale University; Floyd C. Shoemaker, Kenneth Holmes, and Alma Vaughan of the State Historical Society of Missouri, Columbia; Robert D. Armstrong of the University of Nevada Library, Reno; Anne Freudenberg and Kendon Stubbs of the Clifton Waller Barrett Collection, University of Virginia Library, Charlottesville; Lola L. Szladits, curator of the Henry W. and Albert A. Berg Collection, The New York Public Library; Allan R. Ottley and Mabel R. Gillis of the California State Library, Sacramento; Doris A. Foley, Karl Kiedaisch, Jr., and Shirley Dick of the Keokuk Public Library; Barbara LaMont and Frances Goudy of the Vassar College Library, Poughkeepsie, New York; James de T. Abajian of the California State Historical Society Library; Yetive Applegate and James E. Vale of the Los Angeles Public Library; Marion Welliver and L. James Higgins, Jr., of the Nevada Historical Society; Ralph Gregory of the Mark Twain Birthplace Memorial Shrine; Helen S. Giffen and Dolores W. Bryant, Society of California Pioneers, San Francisco; Felix Pollak and Lloyd W. Griffin of the University of Wisconsin Memorial Library, Madison; Mary Isabel Fry and Herbert C. Schulz of the Henry E. Huntington Library and Art Gallery; Opal Tanner and Barbara Bublitz of the P. M. Musser Public Library, Muscatine, Iowa; the staff of The Houghton Library, Harvard University; Connie B. Griffith of the Special Collections Division, Tulane University Library; Anna H. Perrault of the Rare Book Room, Louisiana State University Library at Baton Rouge.

We are particularly indebted to the following institutions and persons for permission to photograph, copy, and reproduce documentary material in these volumes: Norman Franklin of Routledge & Kegan Paul, Ltd., London; Norah Smallwood and Ian Parsons of Chatto & Windus, London; Donald D. Eddy, Department of Rare Books, Cornell University Library; John Payne of the Humanities Research Center Library, University of Texas at Austin; Donald C. Gallup of the Collection of American Literature, Beinecke Rare Book and Manuscript Library, Yale University; Maureen Duffany of the Estelle Doheny Collection, The Edward Laurence Doheny Memorial Library, St. John's Seminary, Camarillo, California; Alma Vaughan of the State Historical Society of Missouri, Columbia.

A number of graduate assistants have contributed to our work. We would particularly like to thank Jill Root, Randall Mawer, and David Wykes for their help; and for briefer but no less essential contributions, Kathleen Harrick, Larry Rosenthal, Margaret Standish, and Margaret Bonner. Harlean Richardson has been a patient and invaluable designer. We are grateful to Jan Benes for his skill in producing the charts and drawings in the textual material. We would also like to thank several colleagues for help above and beyond ordinary courtesy: Louis J. Budd has promptly and selflessly shared his research findings with us; Howard G. Baetzhold and Frank Jordan have made repeated contributions to our work; Henry Nash Smith has given us the benefit of his experience and his uncommonly common sense. Hershel Parker inspected the collection for the Center for Editions of American Authors, and has been an invaluable critic and resource throughout the later stages of this work. The editorial board has read and criticized portions of the editorial matter, and we are grateful for their assistance.

The present collection was begun some seventeen years ago by Mr. Branch, who was joined in 1971 by Mr. Hirst. For the last eight years we have both had the benefit of the exceptionally talented and dedicated staff of the Mark Twain Papers at Berkeley. The collective editorial skills of this unusual group have been brought to bear on the historical and textual materials of this early work, and the collection has profited in countless ways from the standard of excellence which this group makes possible. Frederick Anderson generously granted access to the resources of the Mark Twain Papers and offered us many valuable suggestions for improving the editorial matter. We are particularly indebted to Robert Schildgen for his careful collation of relevant printings on the Hinman collator, and to Dahlia Armon, Robert Pack Browning, Jay Gillette, Paul Machlis, Kate Malloy, and Lin Salamo for checking, collating, proofreading, and lending expertise of all kinds. Victor Fischer, Michael B. Frank, and Kenneth M. Sanderson have given us the benefit of their extensive experience, timely information, and selfless advice throughout the project.

Two friends and colleagues have made exceptional contributions to the collection which we would like to acknowledge here. Bernard L. Stein has for many years acted as the general textual editor of The Works of Mark Twain. His unfailing acuity, rigor, and patience, and his wisely tempered enthusiasm, have made him a silent benefactor not only of this collection, but of the edition as a whole. Harriet Smith has facilitated, assisted, organized, and improved the editorial work of the collection in so many ways—as researcher, copy editor, proofreader, indexer, and logician—that we acknowledge her invaluable work on the title page. We, and the reader, are permanently and deeply indebted to both of these scholars.

Finally, we would like to thank our wives, Mary Jo and Margaret, for their encouragement, their understanding, and their remarkable endurance.

                                                               E.M.B.
                                                               R.H.H.

CONTENTS

ABBREVIATIONS

THE FOLLOWING abbreviations and location symbols have been used for citation in this volume. (For the lists of works cited in the explanatory notes by a shortened title, see pp. 443 and 454–455.)

AD	Autobiographical Dictation
Bancroft	The Bancroft Library, University of California, Berkeley
Berg	Henry W. and Albert A. Berg Collection, The New York Public Library, Astor, Lenox and Tilden Foundations
Berkeley	Charles Franklin Doe Memorial Library, University of California, Berkeley
CWB	Clifton Waller Barrett Library, University of Virginia, Charlottesville
Doheny	Estelle Doheny Collection, The Edward Laurence Doheny Memorial Library, St. John's Seminary, Camarillo, California
Harvard	The Houghton Library, Harvard University, Cambridge, Massachusetts
Iowa	University of Iowa Library, Iowa City
MoHist	State Historical Society of Missouri, Columbia
MS	Manuscript
MTP	Mark Twain Papers, The Bancroft Library, University of California, Berkeley
PH	Photocopy

Texas   Humanities Research Center Library, University of
             Texas, Austin

TS   Typescript

Vassar   Jean Webster McKinney Family Papers, Francis Fitz Ran-
             dolph Rare Book Room, Vassar College Library, Pough-
             keepsie, New York

Yale   Collection of American Literature, Beinecke Rare Book
             and Manuscript Library, Yale University, New Haven,
             Connecticut

                            WORKS CITED

BAL   Jacob Blanck, *Bibliography of American Literature* (New
             Haven: Yale University Press, 1957), vol. 2

CL1   *Mark Twain's Collected Letters, Volume I (1853–1869)*,
             ed. Lin Salamo (Berkeley, Los Angeles, London: Univer-
             sity of California Press, forthcoming) [*Quotations are
             from the printer's copy for all three volumes of letters;
             the texts as published may vary slightly.*]

CL2   *Mark Twain's Collected Letters, Volume II (1869–1870)*,
             ed. Frederick Anderson and Hamlin Hill (Berkeley, Los
             Angeles, London: University of California Press, forth-
             coming)

CL3   *Mark Twain's Collected Letters, Volume III (1871–1874)*,
             ed. Michael B. Frank (Berkeley, Los Angeles, London:
             University of California Press, forthcoming)

CofC   *Clemens of the "Call": Mark Twain in San Francisco*,
             ed. Edgar M. Branch (Berkeley and Los Angeles: Univer-
             sity of California Press, 1969)

LAMT   Edgar M. Branch, *The Literary Apprenticeship of Mark
             Twain* (Urbana: University of Illinois Press, 1950)

MTA   *Mark Twain's Autobiography*, ed. Albert Bigelow Paine,
             2 vols. (New York: Harper and Brothers, 1924)

MTAm   Bernard DeVoto, *Mark Twain's America* (Boston: Little,
             Brown, and Co., 1932)

MTB   Albert Bigelow Paine, *Mark Twain: A Biography*, 3 vols.

(New York: Harper and Brothers, 1912) [*Volume numbers in citations are to this edition; page numbers are the same in all editions.*]

MTBus   *Mark Twain, Business Man*, ed. Samuel C. Webster (Boston: Little, Brown, and Co., 1946)

MTCH   *Mark Twain: The Critical Heritage*, ed. Frederick Anderson (New York: Barnes and Noble, 1971)

MTE   *Mark Twain in Eruption*, ed. Bernard DeVoto (New York: Harper and Brothers, 1940)

MTEnt   *Mark Twain of the "Enterprise,"* ed. Henry Nash Smith (Berkeley and Los Angeles: University of California Press, 1957)

MTH   Walter Francis Frear, *Mark Twain and Hawaii* (Chicago: Lakeside Press, 1947)

MTHL   *Mark Twain–Howells Letters*, ed. Henry Nash Smith and William M. Gibson, 2 vols. (Cambridge: Harvard University Press, 1960)

MTL   *Mark Twain's Letters*, ed. Albert Bigelow Paine, 2 vols. (New York: Harper and Brothers, 1917)

MTLP   *Mark Twain's Letters to His Publishers*, ed. Hamlin Hill (Berkeley and Los Angeles: University of California Press, 1967)

MTMF   *Mark Twain to Mrs. Fairbanks*, ed. Dixon Wecter (San Marino, California: Huntington Library, 1949)

MTMR   Allan Bates, "Mark Twain and the Mississippi River" (Ph.D. diss., University of Chicago, 1968)

MTNev   Effie Mona Mack, *Mark Twain in Nevada* (New York: Charles Scribner's Sons, 1947)

MTSM   Minnie M. Brashear, *Mark Twain: Son of Missouri* (Chapel Hill: University of North Carolina Press, 1934)

MTTB   *Mark Twain's Travels with Mr. Brown*, ed. Franklin Walker and G. Ezra Dane (New York: Alfred A. Knopf, 1940)

MTVC   Paul Fatout, *Mark Twain in Virginia City* (Bloomington: Indiana University Press, 1964)

N&J1   *Mark Twain's Notebooks & Journals, Volume I (1855–
            1873)*, ed. Frederick Anderson, Michael B. Frank, and
            Kenneth M. Sanderson (Berkeley, Los Angeles, London:
            University of California Press, 1975)

N&J2   *Mark Twain's Notebooks & Journals, Volume II (1877–
            1883)*, ed. Frederick Anderson, Lin Salamo, and Bernard
            L. Stein (Berkeley, Los Angeles, London: University of
            California Press, 1975)

N&J3   *Mark Twain's Notebooks & Journals, Volume III (1883–
            1891)*, ed. Robert Pack Browning, Michael B. Frank, and
            Lin Salamo (Berkeley, Los Angeles, London: University of
            California Press, 1979)

SCH   Dixon Wecter, *Sam Clemens of Hannibal* (Boston:
            Houghton Mifflin Co., 1952)

TIA   *Traveling with the Innocents Abroad*, ed. D. M. McKei-
            than (Norman: University of Oklahoma Press, 1958)

TJS   *The Adventures of Thomas Jefferson Snodgrass*, ed.
            Charles Honce (Chicago: Pascal Covici, 1928)

WG·   *The Washoe Giant in San Francisco*, ed. Franklin Walker
            (San Francisco: George Fields, 1938)

INTRODUCTION

THIS COLLECTION brings together for the first time more than 360 of Mark Twain's short works written between 1851, the year of his first extant sketch, and 1871, when he renounced his ties with the Buffalo *Express* and the *Galaxy*, resolving to "write but little for periodicals hereafter."[1] In October 1871 Clemens and his family moved to Hartford, where they would live until 1891. No longer a journalist, he was about to complete his second full-length book, *Roughing It*. The literary apprenticeship that he had begun twenty years before in the print shops of Hannibal, and pursued in the newspaper offices of Virginia City, San Francisco, and Buffalo, had at last come to a close.

The selections included in these volumes represent a generous sampling from Mark Twain's most imaginative journalism, a few set speeches, a few poems, and hundreds of tales and sketches recovered from more than fifty newspapers and journals, as well as two dozen unpublished items of various description—the main body of what can now be found of his early literary and subliterary work, though by no means everything written during those twenty years of experimentation. The selections are ordered chronologically and therefore provide a nearly continuous record of the author's literary activity from his earliest juvenilia up through the mature work that he published in the *Galaxy*, the Buffalo *Express*, and many other journals.

It is part of the plan for The Works of Mark Twain to reprint the author's short works in five distinct collections. The editors of these collections have cooperated to assign each piece to an appropriate category: (1) religious and philosophical works; (2) social and political commentary; (3) literary, theatrical, and art criticism; (4) travel writings; and (5) tales and sketches, broadly defined to include some

---

[1] "Valedictory," the introductory paragraph to "My First Literary Venture" (no. 357), first published in the *Galaxy* 11 (April 1871): 615.

speeches and poems as well. The editors recognize that a number of selections might, with reason, be assigned to more than one category. But their consistent aim has been to present the short works in a manner that would effectively highlight their closest kinship with each other and record the author's literary development along generally recognized lines of interest. Thus, the series of American travel letters (1866–1868) will be kept intact, even though these letters contain many items that might legitimately be called tales or sketches. On the other hand, several sketches that contain at least some political or social commentary have been incorporated in the present collection. In every case the consensus of the collection editors, the series editor, and the editorial board has been followed. And only one exception has been made to the overall plan just outlined: some twenty sketches originally assigned to one or another of the first four categories have been included here because they complete the roster of sketches that Mark Twain revised and reprinted between 1867 and 1875, when he published *Sketches, New and Old.*

It is perhaps needless to say that the terms "tale" and "sketch" are not precise. The author himself used "sketch" loosely, at times to signify all of his miscellaneous short writings (including some speeches and poems), and at others to indicate what we would call a "tale," as when he described "Jim Smiley and His Jumping Frog" (no. 119) as a "villainous backwoods sketch."[2] The collection includes that one, and several other genuine tales, or imaginative narratives: "Ghost Life on the Mississippi" (no. 27), "Cannibalism in the Cars" (no. 232), and "Journalism in Tennessee" (no. 252) to name only the most ambitious. The great preponderance of short items, however, are sketches—and these range from ambitious magazine articles several thousand words long to short, hundred-word trifles tossed off by the newspaperman during a working day. The sketches include comic letters to the editor, hoaxes, exaggerated accounts of the author's personal activities, burlesques of many kinds, comic or satirical feuds with fellow journalists, ingeniously contrived self-advertisements, commentary in a light and personal vein, descriptive

---

[2]Clemens to Jane Clemens and Pamela Moffett, 20 January 1866, *CL1*, letter 97. Insignificant cancellations in letters have been silently dropped from quotations throughout.

reporting, reminiscences of past pleasures and adventures, and so on—but neither this nor any other list can easily be exhaustive. Sketches have been extracted from all kinds of sources, and we have occasionally isolated them from mundane material (such as lists and routine news) without any literary interest. No effort has been spared to locate the first printing (or manuscript) of every item. It is of course too much to hope that nothing remains to be found, but we have fully explored every resource available to us.

Our purpose throughout has been to recover and preserve this largely uncollected work: with few exceptions, every item is reprinted as the author first composed and published it, whether or not he later revised or dismissed it. In fact Mark Twain revised about one-third of the items—sometimes slightly, sometimes elaborately and repeatedly—and the story of revision and reprinting is fully told in the textual introduction; all known details of authorial revision are recorded in the textual apparatus.[3]

Historical annotation is supplied in two forms. Headnotes to each item discuss problems of authenticity; circumstances of composition and publication; dating; and real persons, places, and events mentioned in the sketch. Additional historical data are given in the explanatory notes section at the back of each volume. These notes contain information of more detailed and usually less essential character: identification of literary allusions, persons, places, and events not covered in the headnote. Every effort has been made to explain obscurities, but the absence of any note is allowed to stand for our failure to find an explanation. Literary allusions are identified even when they are well known, in the hope that the information will contribute to our knowledge of Clemens' literary background. In general, only first references have been annotated; the index at the back of each volume should be consulted for later references or for the first, annotated one.

Items are arranged chronologically by their date of publication, when this closely followed composition, or by the date of composition, when the text was either unpublished or published posthumously. The date appears below the title in the headnote. Since all

---

[3]For further details see the textual introduction, especially pp. 655–657.

items are numbered sequentially throughout the collection, the numbering sequence corresponds to the sequence of composition, with the following exceptions:

(1) Closely related sketches have occasionally been grouped together. These groups are organized chronologically within themselves, but they usually interrupt the overall sequence of items. For instance, the last sketch in the group about the San Francisco earthquake (nos. 120–123) did not appear until November 1865, yet it is followed in this collection by a sketch that was published in October 1865—a sketch that resumes the main sequence where the group about the earthquake interrupted it. The headnote numbers of all items within a group of this kind are preceded by a symbol (§) to warn the reader that he may be temporarily outside the main chronological sequence of the collection.

(2) Some sketches were published as much as a month after their date of composition, as in the case of pieces sent from San Francisco to New York for publication, and the sequence of their printing here may therefore conflict with the order in which they were written.

(3) When the date of a sketch remains uncertain, we have conjectured inclusive dates for it—for example, 17–22 February 1863, March–April 1863, or simply June 1868. Items with such dates appear in the sequence at the *earliest* possible point. Thus a sketch known to have been published on 19 February 1863 is made to follow one that is conjecturally dated February 17–22, even though a more precise knowledge might reverse their order.

(4) Sketches published in monthly journals are placed in the chronology at the beginning of the month on the issue, because actual publication invariably preceded the first day of the month. For example, the May *Galaxy* always appeared sometime in late April; sketches published in that issue may therefore actually predate work that was published after the magazine appeared in April.

Most of the items in this collection pose no problem of authorship: they were signed or appeared under known conditions of Clemens' journalistic employment. When the evidence for his authorship is less certain, the procedure for establishing it is always discussed in the headnote. In general, we have required two independent pieces of objective evidence for a positive attribution, and in no case have stylistic traits—however persuasive or characteristic—sufficed by themselves. In fact, the body of the collection excludes many imaginative pieces that we and other scholars have attributed to Clemens, but that lack such corroboration of their authenticity. Appendixes in each of the volumes therefore reprint attributed items that in our opinion deserve special consideration by anyone interested in establishing the full canon of Clemens' works.

The narrative that follows here recounts the known history of the circumstances of composition and first publication for these 365 short works, including the conditions of Clemens' employment and the growth of his reputation. The sketches are divided into four sections: (1) Hannibal and the River: 1851–1861; (2) Nevada Territory: 1862–1864; (3) California: 1864–1866; and (4) The Midwest and East Coast: 1866–1871. The narrative takes up each section in turn and concludes with a brief characterization of Mark Twain's work and overall literary development during this twenty-year period.

1. *Hannibal and the River: 1851–1861.*   Ten years elapsed between the publication of "A Gallant Fireman" (no. 1), which Clemens composed in Hannibal when he was fifteen years old, and "Ghost Life on the Mississippi" (no. 27), written early in 1861 toward the end of his career as a pilot. These twenty-seven selections comprise a motley group of works: the author's juvenilia in Hannibal newspapers, articles from a few eastern journals, the river columns of New Orleans and St. Louis newspapers, and a few unpublished manuscripts preserved by his contemporaries, including his sister, Pamela. They provide some insight into the author's earliest command of his native talent, but they do not suggest an unwavering interest in literature or in publication. For well over a decade Clemens published only sporadically, as opportunity—or an especially appealing occasion—presented itself.

Clemens was probably introduced to newspaper work in the office of Henry La Cossitt's Hannibal *Gazette* during the fall of 1847 (several months after the death of his father), where he worked as printer's devil and jack-of-all-trades. During the next five years he served first as an apprentice on Joseph P. Ament's *Missouri Courier* and then, probably in January 1851, joined his brother Orion Clemens' Hannibal *Western Union* (later the *Journal*). It was in the *Western Union* that he published "A Gallant Fireman," a piece that was in all probability produced by the young compositor while he stood at his case setting it into type. The piece epitomizes the close connection between Clemens' training as a printer and his impulse to write. Indeed, most of the juvenilia reprinted here were stimulated by his early experience on a country newspaper.

Clemens' newspaper work had a more general influence on him as well. In his role as amateur reporter and subeditor under Orion he learned the rudiments of journalism—the value of using local names for concrete interest, for example, a sound principle that he later applied with great originality. He was exposed—through the institution of the newspaper exchange—to a wide variety of writing, including humor, fiction, short essays, local doggerel, sentimental poems, instructive commentary, letters from other towns and cities, and even correspondence from distant points like the Sandwich Islands and the Holy Land. Orion reprinted this kind of newspaper work, and we may be sure that Clemens helped search for appropriate material in magazines like the recently founded San Francisco *Golden Era* and the long-established Boston *Carpet-Bag*. Eventually, of course, Mark Twain would try his hand at all of these forms.

Certainly the idea of publishing something of his own in such journals occurred rather early. By May 1852 Clemens had succeeded in placing two brief items in the eastern press: "The Dandy Frightening the Squatter" (no. 2) in the Boston *Carpet-Bag*, and "Hannibal, Missouri" (no. 3) in the Philadelphia *American Courier*. These two sketches appeared within a week of each other, and are almost certainly the pieces that in old age he mistakenly remembered having published in the Philadelphia *Saturday Evening Post*, another weekly. Although he mistook the place of publication, there is no reason to doubt what he told Albert Bigelow Paine about his reaction: "Seeing them in print was a joy which rather exceeded anything in that line I have ever experienced since."[4]

This youthful "joy" shortly prompted new essays, for within a few months Clemens had discovered another, albeit less challenging, way to publish his work. In 1871, looking back on his early career, he recalled that in September 1852 his "uncle" (in reality, Orion) had left Hannibal "to be gone a week," placing him, the apprentice, in

---

[4]Quoted in *MTB*, 1:90.

charge. Clemens wrote, "He . . . asked me if I thought I could edit one issue of the paper judiciously. Ah, didn't I want to try!"[5] In Orion's absence Clemens wrote and published at least four items in the Hannibal *Journal*, including the ambitious "Historical Exhibition—A No. 1 Ruse" (no. 7) and two irreverent jibes at J. T. Hinton, local editor of the competing Hannibal *Tri-Weekly Messenger:* "'Local' Resolves to Commit Suicide" (no. 5) and, one week later, "'Pictur'' Department" (no. 6). The last two sketches, in their personal and altogether shrewd satire, raised more of a commotion than the young author anticipated. Although Orion returned to smooth things over with Hinton, the damage had been done. Clemens recalled in 1871 that he thought both pieces "desperately funny" and was "densely unconscious that there was any moral obliquity about such a publication."[6]

Hinton's impassioned but somewhat dull-witted response may have temporarily chastened the youthful satirist, for from November until the following May (1853) he seems not to have returned to print. Then while Orion was away again Clemens took charge of the paper (by then a daily) and wrote and published still another "feud," this time a week-long imaginary dispute between three correspondents ("Rambler," "Grumbler," and "Peter Pencilcase's Son, John Snooks") about a poem's subtitle, "To Miss Katie of H———l" (nos. 11–16). Even though Orion professed dismay on returning home, he was wise enough to value such work and to continue to publish it: "Oh, She Has a Red Head!" (no. 18) and "The Burial of Sir Abner Gilstrap" (no. 19) are some of the most interesting products of this period, and they show Clemens' early eclectic bent.

Orion belatedly promoted his brother to "assistant editor" and gave him his first regular writing assignment, "Our Assistant's Column," which Clemens filled until the end of the month. But such a privilege was not sufficient to keep the young man at home, and late in May 1853 he left Hannibal for St. Louis, where he worked briefly as a printer before traveling to other jobs in New York, Philadelphia, Washington, and once again the Midwest, eventually resuming work under Orion in 1855–1856, this time in his brother's Ben Franklin

---

[5]"My First Literary Venture," *Galaxy*, p. 615.
[6]"My First Literary Venture," *Galaxy*, p. 615.

Book and Job Office in Keokuk, Iowa. From mid-1853 until Clemens left for Nevada in mid-1861 we have little concrete evidence of his literary interests, but we do know from the eight pieces written during this period that he continued to explore his talents. In November 1870 he recalled in the *Galaxy* a youthful upsurge of literary ambition that must have overtaken him when he first worked in St. Louis:

When I was sixteen or seventeen years old, a splendid idea burst upon me—a bran-new one, which had never occurred to anybody before: I would write some "pieces" and take them down to the editor of the "Republican," and ask him to give me his plain, unvarnished opinion of their value! Now, as old and threadbare as the idea was, it was fresh and beautiful to me, and it went flaming and crashing through my system like the genuine lightning and thunder of originality. I wrote the pieces. I wrote them with that placid confidence and that happy facility which only want of practice and absence of literary experience can give. There was not one sentence in them that cost half an hour's weighing and shaping and trimming and fixing. Indeed, it is possible that there was no one sentence whose mere wording cost even one-sixth of that time. If I remember rightly, there was not one single erasure or interlineation in all that chaste manuscript. (I have since lost that large belief in my powers, and likewise that marvellous perfection of execution.) I started down to the "Republican" office with my pocket full of manuscripts, my brain full of dreams, and a grand future opening out before me. I knew perfectly well that the editor would be ravished with my pieces.[7]

Clemens went on to explain, however, that as he approached the newspaper office his self-confidence gradually disappeared, and a mere word from the editor put him to flight, the manuscripts still in his pocket.

This is an interesting recollection, even though it is probably hyperbolic. Clemens' characterization of himself as both ambitious and confident is balanced by the recognition that he was also "green and ignorant, wordy, pompously-assertive, ungrammatical, and with a vague, distorted knowledge of men and the world acquired in a back-country village." The would-be author, Clemens recalled, had reached out for fame, naively unaware that beginning writers must first submit to "the same tedious, ill-paid apprenticeship" required of beginners in other professions.[8]

---

[7]"A General Reply" (no. 332), first published in the *Galaxy* 10 (November 1870): 732.

[8]"A General Reply," *Galaxy*, p. 732.

The recollection coincides with another memory of himself at this time which Clemens set down in 1876—a response to a letter from a boyhood friend, J. H. Burrough:

As you describe me I can picture myself as I was, 22 years ago. The portrait is correct. You think I have grown some; upon my word there was room for it. You have described a callow fool, a self-sufficient ass, a mere human tumble-bug, stern in air, heaving at his bit of dung & imagining he is re-modeling the world & is entirely capable of doing it right. Ignorance, intolerance, egotism, self-assertion, opaque perception, dense & pitiful chuckle-headedness—& an almost pathetic unconsciousness of it all. That is what I was at 19–20.[9]

His callowness and self-righteousness are perhaps exaggerated in retrospect, but they may have contributed to still another unsuccessful effort to publish his work, this time in Philadelphia. Paine reported in 1912 that Clemens said only that his efforts at this time "were not received with approval."[10] Still, before returning to St. Louis Clemens dispatched several travel letters to the Muscatine *Journal* published by his brother Orion, and in 1856 he published the "Thomas Jefferson Snodgrass" letters in the Keokuk *Post*, earning five dollars apiece for his work.[11]

Four items in the present collection were written in 1855–1856, and three of them were clearly never intended for publication: poems written in the private autograph albums of his sister-in-law Mollie and of a young friend, Ann Virginia Ruffner, who was visiting Keokuk ("To Mollie," no. 21; "Lines" and "To Jennie," nos. 22 and 23). A fourth item, "Jul'us Caesar" (no. 20), was almost certainly designed to be published; it survives in the author's manuscript in part because he never printed it. "Jul'us Caesar" bears some evidence of Clemens' youthful callowness. It offers a satirical portrait of a young country bumpkin whom the author and a companion lure into putting on airs—first as a "writer" and then as a "painter." The sketch has several flashes of talent—including a wonderful parody of conventional nature poetry ("The Storm")—but it falls short of those sketches that the author would publish while he worked as a pilot on the river.

---

[9]Clemens to Burrough, 1 November 1876, Kent Library, Southeast Missouri State College, Cape Girardeau.

[10]Quoted in *MTB*, 1:98.

[11]See *CL1*, letters 7 and 9–12, and *TJS*. These letters are all scheduled to appear in the collection of travel writings in The Works of Mark Twain.

In April 1857 Clemens abandoned his work as a printer and apprenticed himself to a Mississippi steamboat pilot, Horace E. Bixby. Bixby recalled that as a young pilot Clemens "was always scribbling when not at the wheel,"[12] but this memory, though certainly plausible, is borne out only to a limited extent by letters and manuscripts, and by known published work. In fact, during the four years Clemens spent on the river he produced only four known sketches, three of which drew on his experience as a pilot. Of these four pieces, two remained unpublished. It seems likely that there was little time for literature during his initial months as a cub pilot, for as Clemens told his brother on 9 March 1858, he could not write to the newspapers because "when one is learning the river, he is not allowed to do or think about anything else."[13]

The most famous of Clemens' three river pieces appeared in May 1859, shortly after he received his pilot's license. "River Intelligence" (no. 24) was published anonymously as part of the daily river column in the New Orleans *Crescent* and was well received by at least one portion of the very specialized audience at which it was aimed—Clemens' fellow pilots. The sketch was widely reprinted in newspapers in 1871–1872, when Mark Twain began making a national reputation, and he himself acknowledged it in chapter 50 of *Life on the Mississippi* and, implicitly, through Paine's remarks in the biography.[14] "River Intelligence" exemplifies the author's early fascination with vernacular eccentrics and it is a minor masterpiece of satirical burlesque on the smugly omniscient manner of Captain Isaiah Sellers, an old and experienced river pilot given to pontification. Like Clemens' earlier satirical target, J. T. Hinton, Sellers appears to have taken the sketch rather more seriously than the author anticipated, and in 1883 Clemens declared that he regretted the severity or at least the public character of his remarks:

It was a great pity; for it did nobody any worthy service, and it sent a pang deep into a good man's heart. There was no malice in my rubbish; but it laughed at the captain. It laughed at a man to whom such a thing was new and strange and dreadful. I did not know then, though I do now, that there is no suffering comparable with that

---

[12]*MTB*, 1:149.

[13]Clemens to Orion and Mollie Clemens, 9 March 1858, *CL1*, letter 17.

[14]*MTB*, 1:149–150, and 3:1553–1556.

which a private person feels when he is for the first time pilloried in print.[15]

This was to be an important lesson of Clemens' apprenticeship, but it was one he did not thoroughly grasp until he had left Nevada and California.

Although Clemens had earlier lost his nerve on the threshold of the St. Louis *Missouri Republican*, he did publish his second river piece in that journal: "Pilot's Memoranda" (no. 26) appeared in the river column in August 1860. This unique burlesque was, like "River Intelligence," written for his fellow pilots, and it depends even more heavily on their intimate technical knowledge of the river to achieve its humorous effects. It is aimed quite broadly at the self-important style of pilots' newspaper reports—their tendency to boast or to report the obvious—and as such it pokes good-humored fun at their idiosyncrasies while it invites them to smile at a joke that only they can share. Perhaps more significantly, it anticipates one of Clemens' most promising and fruitful techniques: mixing the truth with fiction in a way that makes the work neither a tall tale nor a hoax, but something in between.

The only attempts at straightforward fiction which Clemens is known to have written at this time both survive in manuscript and were, like "Jul'us Caesar," left unpublished by the author. "Ghost Life on the Mississippi" (no. 27) depends to some degree on technical knowledge of the river, but its intended audience is manifestly larger than the pilot brotherhood. Clemens' niece, Annie Moffett, recalled hearing him recite or read the sketch in St. Louis around the time he left for Nevada (1861), and this suggests that it was a self-conscious literary effort deriving from oral tradition on the river. The sketch is surprisingly mature in its narrative technique and in its creation of suspense, though at the same time it has several small structural flaws.

A closely related sketch, "The Mysterious Murders in Risse" (no. 25), was written in the summer of 1859, just after "River Intelligence." It is a gothic tale of murder and revenge, cast in the fictional towns of Risse and Lun, Germany, and although the young author's handling of his material is sometimes wooden and awkward, the tale shows him struggling to control the basic tools of narrative and suspense.

---

[15]*Life on the Mississippi*, chapter 50.

Like "Ghost Life," it suggests that even without a regular opportunity to publish his work the young pilot continued to nurture some kind of literary ambition.

2. *Nevada Territory: 1862–1864.*   The impending Civil War closed down steamboat traffic on the Mississippi and threw Clemens out of work: despite a persistent—and eventually productive—nostalgia for his pilot days, he never returned to the wheel. For a while he lived in St. Louis with his mother and sister, Jane Clemens and Pamela Moffett, and his sister's family. There in the spring of 1861 he watched the intensifying hostilities between North and South and the secession of the Confederacy. His own political sympathies wavered, but that summer he and some Hannibal friends of "Secesh" persuasion organized the Marion Rangers and briefly went to war—a story that he recounted in "The Private History of the Campaign That Failed" (1885). Having soon had his fill of warfare, Clemens agreed to accompany Orion, and to assist him, in his recently won appointment as secretary of the Territory of Nevada. President Lincoln had signed Orion's commission on 27 March 1861, but it was not until June 26 that the secretary's instructions were dispatched to him.[16] Exactly one month later—only a few days after Bull Run—the two brothers left St. Joseph by overland stagecoach, arriving in Carson City on August 14.[17]

It has recently been shown that one of Clemens' earliest activities in Nevada was to serve his brother as clerk during the first session of the Territorial Legislature—from October 1 through November 29. He earned eight dollars a day—a significant supplement to his brother's small income—and he also became acquainted with Washoe politicians, men like William M. Gillespie and William H. Barstow. Having completed his clerkship, Clemens acknowledged payment on December 4 and turned his full attention to the problem of striking it rich.[18] Even before this his letters home told of timber claims on the

---

[16]William C. Miller, "Samuel L. and Orion Clemens vs. Mark Twain and His Biographers (1861–1962)," *Mark Twain Journal* 16 (Summer 1973): 2.

[17]Orion Clemens ("Carson") to St. Louis *Missouri Democrat*, written 19 August and published 16 September 1861, reprinted in Franklin Rogers, *The Pattern for Mark Twain's Roughing It* (Berkeley and Los Angeles: University of California Press, 1961), pp. 47–49.

[18]Miller, "Samuel L. and Orion Clemens," *Mark Twain Journal*, p. 3.

shores of Lake Tahoe and speculation in mining stock (or "feet").
By late January 1862 he was feeling sanguine about success, which he
predicted would come by the following July: "I think that by that
time some of our claims will be paying handsomely," he told Orion's
wife, Mollie, "and we could have a house fit to live in—and servants
to do your work."[19] He himself engaged in arduous prospecting, both
in Humboldt and Esmeralda counties; he and several friends formed
the Clemens Gold and Silver Mining Company, and he eventually
held stock in, and claims to, a number of mining ventures[20]—all of
which came, finally, to nothing.

Clemens' reminiscences in later life suggest that when mining failed
him he drifted more or less unwillingly and by chance into newspaper
work. But contemporary documents show that well before he was
forced to abandon the search for gold he was contributing letters to
the newspapers and was actively interested in becoming a regular
correspondent. On 30 January, 20 March, and 10 May 1862 he wrote
three long, wonderfully humorous travel letters that were published in
the Keokuk *Gate City*.[21] And probably in April he had begun sending
letters signed "Josh" to the Virginia City *Territorial Enterprise*.
Clemens recalled in chapter 42 of *Roughing It* that at the time he had
amused himself "with writing letters to the chief paper of the Territory," and that he "had always been surprised" when these were
actually published. "My good opinion of the editors had steadily
declined; for it seemed to me that they might have found something
better to fill up with than my literature."[22] Yet this diffidence is
clearly facetious, and there were, moreover, other signs of his re-
awakened interest in writing. On May 12 Clemens told Orion that
he had helped his mining partner, Horatio Phillips, write a letter to
the Carson City *Silver Age*; and he indicated that he, or his partner,
would "drop a line to the 'Age' occasionally" in the future, adding
that he supposed Orion saw his "letters in the 'Enterprize.'"[23]

---

[19]Clemens to Mollie Clemens, 31 January 1862, *CL1*, letter 39.

[20]Clemens to Orion Clemens, 11–12 and 17 May 1862, *CL1*, letters 52 and 53; "Still
More Mining Companies," San Francisco *Evening Bulletin*, 3 May 1863, p. 3.

[21]The letters are reprinted in Rogers, *The Pattern for Roughing It*, pp. 29–45. They
are scheduled to appear in the collection of travel writings in The Works of Mark
Twain.

[22]*Roughing It*, ed. Franklin Rogers and Paul Baender (Berkeley and Los Angeles:
University of California Press, 1972), pp. 266–267.

[23]Clemens to Orion Clemens, 11–12 May 1862, *CL1*, letter 52.

Clemens' association with the *Enterprise* came about through one of the men he had met during the first session of the legislature: William H. Barstow, who worked in the business office of the *Enterprise*. Barstow not only accepted the "Josh" letters and knew that Clemens was their author, he apparently wanted to reprint the letters of the young correspondent to the *Gate City*. On May 17 Clemens wrote Orion that he hoped Barstow would "leave the 'S.L.C.' off my Gate City letters, in case he publishes them."[24] By late June, however, Clemens had ceased to correspond with the *Gate City*, allegedly for want of time. Even so, the "Josh" letters to the *Enterprise* continued to appear, and Clemens was anything but indifferent to their publication. On June 22 he complained with some bitterness to Orion, "Those Enterprise fellows make perfect nonsense of my letters—like all d—d fool printers, they can't follow the punctuation as it is in the manuscript. They have, by this means made a mass of senseless, d—d stupidity out of my last letter."[25] This is not the sentiment of an author who was chagrined to see his work published.

While Clemens claimed lack of time to write to the *Gate City*, he was in fact aiming at still other professional writing commitments. William M. Gillespie, another acquaintance from the legislature, was evidently planning to begin his own newspaper—and had invited Clemens to write for it. On June 25 Clemens wrote Orion: "If Gillespie gets up a large paper, it will suit me exactly to correspond for it. I shall not refuse pay, either, although $4 or $5 a week could hardly be called extensive when you write by the 'column,' you know. I am his man, though. Let me know further about his paper."[26] The project was still alive on July 9, when Clemens again wrote his brother from Esmeralda: "Gillespie talks reasonably now, and I shall try and be ready for him as soon as he starts his paper. Tell him not to secure a San Francisco correspondent for the winter, because they do nothing here during the winter months, and I want the job myself. I want to spend the winter in California. When will his first number be published, and where?" Clemens reiterated that he was tempted to "write a correspondence for the 'Age,' " but that "want of time" would "not permit it."[27]

---

[24]Clemens to Orion Clemens, 17 May 1862, *CL1*, letter 53.
[25]Clemens to Orion Clemens, 22 June 1862, *CL1*, letter 56.
[26]Clemens to Orion Clemens, 25 June 1862, *CL1*, letter 57.
[27]Clemens to Orion Clemens, 9 July 1862, *CL1*, letter 58.

The aspiring correspondent did not get to spend the winter in California—at least not that year—but it is clear that by June 1862 he had already formulated plans to write regularly for some newspaper. Gillespie's project failed to materialize, however, and Clemens apparently never did correspond for the *Silver Age*. But in late July, when his debts mounted and his capital was exhausted, he applied in earnest for newspaper work. He asked Orion on July 23 to recommend him to "the Sacramento Union folks," to whom he was almost certainly known through their political correspondent, Andrew J. Marsh. "Tell them I'll write as many letters a week as they want, for $10 a week—my board must be paid. Tell them I have corresponded with the N. Orleans Crescent, and other papers—and the Enterprise. . . . If they want letters from here, who'll run from morning till night collecting materials cheaper[?] I'll write a short letter twice a week for the present for the 'Age,' for $5 per week."[28]

Orion did write a letter to the Sacramento *Union*, but before any reply could be returned Clemens received a concrete offer from Barstow, his friend at the *Enterprise* office. "I hope you will receive an answer right away," he told Orion about the *Union* application, "because Barstow has offered me the post of local reporter for the Enterprise at $25 a week, and I have written him that I will let him know next mail if possible, whether I can take it or not. If G. is not *sure* of starting his paper within a month, I think I had better close with Barstow's offer."[29] On August 7, evidently still without hearing from the Sacramento *Union* or Gillespie, Clemens told Orion that he had accepted the *Enterprise* job. Barstow had renewed his offer and Clemens had replied: "I wrote him that I guessed I would take it, and asked him how long before I must come up there. I have not heard from him since."[30] There was, evidently, no special urgency—and Clemens did not begin work until sometime in late September. The first extant articles that he probably wrote as a salaried reporter (see Appendix B1, volume 1) appeared in the October 1 issue; the first that he indubitably wrote—"Petrified Man" (no. 28)—appeared in the *Enterprise* on October 4.

The Virginia City *Territorial Enterprise* had been owned by

---

[28]Clemens to Orion Clemens, 23 July 1862, *CL1*, letter 59.
[29]Clemens to Orion Clemens, 30 July 1862, *CL1*, letter 60.
[30]Clemens to Orion Clemens, 7 August 1862, *CL1*, letter 61.

Joseph T. Goodman and Denis E. McCarthy for about one year; it was published daily (except Monday) and was rapidly becoming both a popular and a financial success. Rollin M. Daggett, twice editor of the *Enterprise*, recalled in 1893 that in these early years "there was probably no paper in the West that exerted so great an influence as the *Territorial Enterprise.* . . . It occupied the same field in Nevada as did the Sacramento *Union* in California."[31] Despite this influence, which was just beginning when Clemens joined the paper, the *Enterprise* evinced a youthful and often irreverent nature, largely because of Goodman's influence (he was twenty-four in 1862). "Original, forcible, confident, mocking and alive with the impulses of an abounding and generous youth, the *Enterprise* was to Goodman a safety-valve for his ideas rather than a daily burden of responsibility," according to Arthur McEwen. "There never has been a paper like the *Enterprise* on the Coast since and never can be again—never one so entirely human, so completely the reflex of a splendid personality and a mining camp's buoyant life."[32] Even allowing for a pardonable exaggeration here, it is clear that the *Enterprise* offered Clemens an extraordinary opportunity in 1862—one that he fully and promptly exploited. By August 1863 he could "boast of having the widest reputation as a local editor, of any man on the Pacific coast."[33] And when he finally left Virginia City behind him in May 1864, this reputation had grown still more formidable.

The *Enterprise* owners were interested in Clemens for several reasons: they had been pleased with his volunteer "Josh" letters, which demonstrated his superior humorous talents; they would soon need someone to replace their local editor, Dan De Quille (William Wright), who was planning a trip back East; and finally they knew that Clemens had been the gregarious "clerk" who served his brother, Secretary Clemens, in the first session of the legislature—a fact that might make him a good political reporter and would almost certainly make him a political influence.

In 1893 Rollin Daggett recalled that one "Josh" letter had been

---

[31]Rollin M. Daggett, "Daggett's Recollections," San Francisco *Examiner*, 22 January 1893, p. 15.

[32]Arthur McEwen, "In the Heroic Days," San Francisco *Examiner*, 22 January 1893, p. 15.

[33]Clemens to Jane Clemens and Pamela Moffett, 19 August 1863, *CL1*, letter 75.

particularly suggestive of Clemens' powers as a humorist:

I first heard of him through a bogus Fourth of July oration purporting to have been delivered near Owens's Lake, where Mark was engaged in prospecting. The oration was sent to the *Enterprise* for publication and Goodman showed it to me. It was written in Twain's best vein and it was decided at once that the writer was a man worth cultivating. He was offered a place on the local department of the *Enterprise,* which he accepted.[34]

Neither this "bogus" oration nor any other of the "Josh" letters is extant, but in 1906 Clemens recalled the events referred to by Daggett in a way that illuminates what these early *Enterprise* contributions must have been like.

Chief Justice Turner came down there and delivered an oration. I was not present, but I knew his subject and I knew what he would say about it and how he would say it, and that into it he would inject all his pet quotations. I knew that he would scatter through it the remark about somebody's lips having been sweetened by "the honey of the bees of Hymettus," and the remark that, "Whom the gods would destroy they first make mad," and the one which says, "Against the stupid even the gods strive in vain." He had a dozen other pet prettinesses and I knew them all, for I had heard him orate a good many times. He had an exceedingly flowery style and I knew how to imitate it. . . . I didn't hear his speech, as I have already said, but I made a report of it anyway and got in all the pet phrases; and although the burlesque was rather extravagant, it was easily recognizable by the whole Territory as being a smart imitation. It was published in the *Enterprise,* and just in the nick of time to save me. That paper's city editor was going East for three months and by return mail I was offered his place for that interval.[35]

The mock oration seems to have been in the same vein of burlesque that informed Clemens' earlier sketch on Isaiah Sellers ("River Intelligence," no. 24)—a "smart imitation" of the judge's all too predictable style, offered as a transparent hoax at his expense. However, Clemens simplified events somewhat. Dan De Quille was indeed

---

[34]Daggett, "Recollections," San Francisco *Examiner,* 22 January 1893, p. 15.

[35]AD, 2 October 1906, *MTE,* pp. 390–391. Miller has plausibly suggested that L. O. Sterns, not Chief Justice George Turner, was the object of Clemens' ridicule. Sterns did give a Fourth of July oration in Esmeralda in 1862, and Clemens later burlesqued his oratorical style in a letter to the *Enterprise.* (See Miller, "Samuel L. and Orion Clemens," *Mark Twain Journal,* pp. 7–8, and *MTEnt,* pp. 94–95.)

planning a trip back East, but we now know that he did not actually leave Virginia City until December 27—about three months after Clemens joined the staff. The record indicates that Clemens must have worked with Dan for part of September and all of October, learning the ropes as local editor. This phase of his apprenticeship was interrupted, however, when the paper sent him to Carson City to cover the second session of the Territorial Legislature, which convened on November 11 and did not adjourn until December 20. Clemens' previous experience with the legislators, as well as his relationship to Secretary Clemens, were obvious assets, despite his inexperience as a political reporter. He was, for instance, almost certainly instrumental in securing for the *Enterprise* a lucrative contract to publish the laws of the session—a contract that had previously been held by the rival Virginia City *Union*.[36]

Clemens did not return to Virginia City until late December 1862. When Dan departed by overland stagecoach, Clemens took over the sole responsibility for the *Enterprise* local columns—a job that he filled, with several interruptions, until Dan returned to join him early in September 1863. Clemens' first contribution in his new capacity, "The Illustrious Departed" (no. 32), a humorous farewell to his friend Dan, is the first of eight short imaginative local items reprinted here. All eight appeared in the *Enterprise* column during the brief period before Clemens publicly adopted the name "Mark Twain" early in February 1863.

Although Clemens wrote almost continuously for the *Enterprise* between September 1862 and June 1864, our knowledge of what he wrote is severely limited: there is no extant file of the paper for those years. The office files owned by Goodman were destroyed in the 1875 fire that leveled Virginia City; two other complete files, both in San Francisco, were destroyed by the earthquake and fire which struck that city in 1906.[37] Even Clemens' own records—the "coffin of 'Enterprise' files" that Orion sent him in March 1870 as he began writing *Roughing It*[38]—have been, for the most part, either lost or destroyed. Thus the forty pieces reprinted here have been gleaned

---

[36]Miller, "Samuel L. and Orion Clemens," *Mark Twain Journal*, pp. 8–9.

[37]Richard G. Lillard, "Studies in Washoe Journalism and Humor" (Ph.D. diss., University of Iowa, 1953), pp. 104–105.

[38]Clemens to Jane Clemens et al., 26 March 1870, *CL2*, letter 177.

from a wide variety of anomalous resources: a few family scrapbooks (what remained of the "coffin") which came to light in 1954; scattered clippings in the William Wright Papers; scrapbooks in the Beinecke Rare Book and Manuscript Library at Yale; a few stray copies of the *Enterprise* in western libraries; nineteenth-century histories and anthologies compiled before 1906; and contemporary newspapers and journals in California and Nevada, which frequently reprinted items from the *Enterprise*. It seems clear that, under such limiting circumstances, some of Clemens' political writings from Carson City, some of his out-of-town newspaper letters, and most of his routine reports and daily local items have vanished with the *Enterprise* itself. Certainly none of our present resources is anything like exhaustive: each contains items not to be found in the others.

Still it may be hoped that none of Clemens' most ambitious work failed to be preserved in one way or another, for Dan De Quille was probably correct when he recalled in 1893 that while Mark Twain worked on the *Enterprise* "he wrote no long stories or sketches for that paper."[39] Indeed, only four *Enterprise* sketches collected here assume the aspect of humorous fiction: "Ye Sentimental Law Student" (no. 44), "City Marshal Perry" (no. 49), "Mark Twain—More of Him" (no. 64), and "Washoe.—'Information Wanted'" (no. 75). These are probably as close to being fully developed literary sketches as anything he published in that paper.

The chief interest of what Clemens did write, however, lies in the way it anticipates his fiction, exhibiting with marvelous nonchalance his native gift of phrase, his talent for assimilating and appreciating slang, and of course his inexorable drift toward humor. Four routine reports included here—"The Spanish Mine" (no. 29), "The Spanish" (no. 30), "Silver Bars—How Assayed" (no. 43), and "Examination of Teachers" (no. 48)—show numerous small touches of humor, even in the face of the implacably factual. The same tendency is present in the briefest local items, like "Due Notice" (no. 38) and "Our Stock Remarks" (no. 33). And the capacity for humorous fiction is of course present in comic hoaxes like "Petrified Man" (no. 28) and "A Bloody Massacre near Carson" (no. 66), as well as in the running, good-

---

[39]Dan De Quille, "Reporting with Mark Twain," *California Illustrated Magazine* 4 (July 1893): 176.

natured "feuds" he carried on with the Unreliable (Clement T. Rice of the Virginia City *Union*) and later with his *Enterprise* partner, Dan De Quille.

McEwen recalled in 1893 that the local department of the *Enterprise* as conducted by Mark Twain and Dan De Quille was "noble" in its "indifference to 'news.'"[40] Even judging from the few surviving items, unevenly winnowed by time and chance, we can see that this "indifference to 'news'" amounted to a style of reporting—a style at which Clemens was particularly adept, and to which he contributed his own personal characteristics. Consider, for example, two brief—wholly inconsequential—squibs that appeared in the columns of the *Enterprise*, the first one shortly after Clemens teamed up with Dan in September 1862, the second shortly after he took over on his own later that year:

A GALE.—About 7 o'clock Tuesday evening (Sept. 30th) a sudden blast of wind picked up a shooting gallery, two lodging houses and a drug store from their tall wooden stilts and set them down again some ten or twelve feet back of their original location, with such a degree of roughness as to jostle their insides into a sort of chaos. There were many guests in the lodging houses at the time of the accident, but it is pleasant to reflect that they seized their carpet sacks and vacated the premises with an alacrity suited to the occasion.[41]

[FREE FIGHT.—] A beautiful and ably conducted free fight came off in C street yesterday afternoon, but as nobody was killed or mortally wounded in a manner sufficiently fatal to cause death, no particular interest attaches to the matter, and we shall not publish the details. We pine for murder—these fist fights are of no consequence to anybody.[42]

Although the assertion cannot be proved, Clemens almost certainly wrote both items. The first belongs to the western tall-tale genre (variety, "Washoe zephyr"), even though it is apparently based upon fact. Its deadpan account of an occurrence of some seriousness—and probably of some embarrassment—to the "guests" moves it out of the

[40]McEwen, "Heroic Days," San Francisco *Examiner*, 22 January 1893, p. 15.

[41]Reprinted in the Oroville (Calif.) *Butte Record*, 11 October 1862, p. 2. The reference to "Tuesday evening (Sept. 30th)" indicates that the item appeared in the *Enterprise* on October 1.

[42]Reprinted in the Marysville (Calif.) *Appeal*, 9 January 1863, p. 2, which attributes the story to the *Enterprise* of January 6.

realm of pure news and into that of humor. The second item, which cavalierly dismisses a street brawl in order to comment ironically on the insatiable public appetite for "a man for breakfast," is less an item of news than a philosophic observation. Each item, moreover, employs diction and techniques and even subjects that Clemens would use again and again in more ambitious items. "Frightful Accident to Dan De Quille" (no. 73) is a fine example of a comic disaster loosely based on the facts; and "A Duel Prevented" (no. 56) highlights the reporter's alleged disappointment when a duel is stopped by officers of the law—the genre of the "missed item." "A Gale" and "Free Fight" show us that the routine work that Clemens produced daily for nearly two years was not entirely perfunctory: it formed a seed bed for later, maturer work much more like his fictions.

The "indifference to 'news'" also gave rise, as Clemens himself noted, to the outright hoax. In *Roughing It* he said that "stirring news . . . was what a paper needed, and I felt that I was peculiarly endowed with the ability to furnish it."[43] Before that, in February 1868, he asserted that purely fictional "news items" were often included in his columns:

To find a petrified man, or break a stranger's leg, or cave an imaginary mine, or discover some dead Indians in a Gold Hill tunnel, or massacre a family at Dutch Nick's, were feats and calamities that *we* never hesitated about devising when the public needed matters of thrilling interest for breakfast. The seemingly tranquil ENTERPRISE office was a ghastly factory of slaughter, mutilation and general destruction in those days.[44]

Clemens' carefully contrived hoaxes, including "Petrified Man" (no. 28) and "A Bloody Massacre near Carson" (no. 66), eventually became his most infamous contributions to the western press, but it is clear that both were written within a subliterary tradition that permitted and even encouraged an indifference to news.

Although in February 1863 he had been serving as local editor for only about one month, Clemens persuaded Goodman to grant him a week's vacation in Carson City. From there he sent three long comic

---

[43]*Roughing It*, ed. Rogers and Baender, pp. 269–270.
[44]"Mark Twain's Letters from Washington. Number IX," Virginia City *Territorial Enterprise*, 7 March 1868, p. 1. See "Horrible Affair" (no. 52), another one of Clemens' hoaxes.

letters (nos. 40, 41, and 42), signed for the first time "Mark Twain." Although these letters conveyed some news, their chief import was a relaxed, informal kind of humor—personal narrative, the genre that became Mark Twain's chief literary form. On February 9 "Isreal Putnam" wrote to tell Clemens that John Nugent, a close friend of the late John Phoenix (George H. Derby), had inquired of him "who Mark Twain was, and added that he had not seen so amusing a thing in newspaper literature in a long while as your letter in the Enterprise this morning."[45] Clearly Nugent's favorable response was widely shared. On February 16 Clemens, by then back in Virginia City, told his family that his employers "haven't much confidence in me now. If they have, I am proud to say it is misplaced." He added, "I am very well satisfied here. They pay me six dollars a day, and I make 50 per cent. profit by only doing three dollars' worth of work."[46] As this letter indicates (and as he later recalled in chapter 44 of Roughing It), Goodman had made his salary "forty dollars a week," a significant raise above the original twenty-five.[47]

Mark Twain had achieved sufficient stature with the Enterprise by May 1863 to earn a more extended vacation, this time in San Francisco. He and Rice spent May and June there, and Clemens apparently wrote only very occasionally to the Enterprise. On June 4 he told his family that he had "lived like a lord—to make up for two years of privation, you know," and that he had not "written to the paper but twice. . . . I have always got something more agreeable on hand."[48] Both of these San Francisco letters are reprinted here (nos. 53 and 64).

Despite the paucity of his Enterprise correspondence, he was about to enter upon an important contract with the San Francisco Morning Call. In mid-May he told his family, "They want me to correspond with one of these dailies here, & if they will pay me enough I'll do it. (The pay is only a 'blind'—I'll correspond anyhow. If I don't know how to make such a thing pay me . . . who does, I should like to know?)"[49] When he returned to Virginia City early in July he sent the first of ten letters to the Call: portions of four are reprinted in

[45]"Isreal Putnam" to Clemens, 9 February 1863, MTP. The newspaper letter referred to is almost certainly "Letter from Carson" (no. 42), published on 8 February 1863.
[46]Clemens to Jane Clemens and Pamela Moffett, 16 February 1863, CL1, letter 65.
[47]Roughing It, ed. Rogers and Baender, p. 277.
[48]Clemens to Jane Clemens and Pamela Moffett, 4 June 1863, CL1, letter 71.
[49]Clemens to Jane Clemens and Pamela Moffett, mid-May 1863, CL1, letter 69.

this collection, and they record an important step in Mark Twain's career—the first effort to amuse a sophisticated city audience with his yarns. " 'Mark Twain's' Letter" (no. 59), for instance, contains his first version ("A Rich Decision") of "The Facts in the Great Land-Slide Case" (no. 286), a sketch that would eventually find its way into *Roughing It*. At this time Clemens also made contact with the San Francisco *Golden Era*, a literary weekly to which he would contribute several sketches in the fall of 1863: "How to Cure a Cold" (no. 63), "The Lick House Ball" (no. 65), and "The Great Prize Fight"; all are signs of his ambition to move beyond the local columns of the *Enterprise* into more genuinely literary work.

The *Golden Era* sketches began to appear when Clemens returned to San Francisco on September 6—shortly after Dan De Quille arrived back in Virginia City from the East. It was presumably these contributions that Fitzhugh Ludlow (another *Era* contributor) had in mind when, in November 1863, he publicly praised their author: "In funny literature," he wrote in the *Era*, "that Irresistible Washoe Giant, Mark Twain, takes quite a unique position. He makes me laugh more than any Californian since poor Derby died. He imitates nobody. He is a school by himself."[50] This was high praise, and it was soon endorsed and amplified by yet another major American humorist when he visited Virginia City in mid-December 1863: Artemus Ward. Early in January 1864, after telling his family that Ludlow had "published a high encomium upon Mark Twain, (the same being eminently just & truthful, I beseech you to believe,) in a San Francisco paper," Clemens continued: "Artemus Ward said that when my gorgeous talents were publicly acknowledged by such high authority, I ought to appreciate them myself—leave sage-brush obscurity, & journey to New York with him, as he wanted me to do. But I preferred not to burst upon the New York public too suddenly & brilliantly, & so I concluded to remain here."[51] Despite this diffidence, Mark Twain was persuaded to send some of his work to the New York *Sunday Mercury* by Ward's promise to intervene with the editors on his behalf. By mid-January 1864 he had sent two sketches that were accepted by the *Mercury*: "Doings in Nevada" and "Those Blasted Children" (no. 72). Clemens' plans to write occasionally for the

---

[50]Fitzhugh Ludlow, "A Good-Bye Article," *Golden Era* 11 (22 November 1863): 4.
[51]Clemens to Jane Clemens and Pamela Moffett, 1–9 January 1864, *CL1*, letter 76.

Mercury, however, failed to materialize: it would not be until he moved to California that he would again successfully venture into the eastern press.

One aspect of Clemens' development in this two-year period in Nevada deserves special notice: the emergence of Mark Twain as a public figure whose way of reporting the news, whose peculiar expressions ("so to speak," "they shoved," "infernal humbug," "from hell to breakfast"), and whose very comings and goings were themselves news.[52] Because from the beginning of his Nevada journalism Clemens wrote about himself, and because his talents as a writer and as a public speaker—what Paine called his "matchless gift of phrase"[53] —were manifestly out of the ordinary, he became the object of considerable attention in the press, a combination of celebrity and journalist. Mark Twain was a highly adaptable, partly fictional version of Clemens himself. Shortly before he adopted the pseudonym, for instance, he presented himself as a brash, socially inept reporter whose supposed obtuseness and awkward predicaments supplied the real interest of his amusing report "The Sanitary Ball" (no. 37). This bumbling figure assumed much greater autonomy and complexity when he adopted the name "Mark Twain." In his more exuberant moods he exhibited an extraordinary capacity for ridicule and vituperation, but above all for exaggeration of all kinds. This last element—the reporter's supposed inability to keep the facts straight or to report anything without comic elaboration—became the most prominent element of his public character. The reporter who could be forgiven for making up items about hay wagons and pack trains (as he recalled in *Roughing It*) soon became one who wrote more pointed hoaxes, and then in turn one who explicitly assumed the role of yarn spinner and teller of tall tales.

The disposition to elaborate was part of Mark Twain's mask, but we may be sure that the disposition had its origins in Clemens' own character, even as a boy in Hannibal. In 1906 he recalled that Jimmy McDaniel "was the first human being to whom I ever told a humorous

[52]Clement T. Rice, "Notice," Virginia City *Territorial Enterprise*, 3 April 1863, p. 3: "If the Madison have no ledge, then those gentlemen have taken an extension on the *north end of nothing*, and with that action we are content; and if they are dissatisfied, why don't they go into Court and settle the vexed question, whether they do really own, as Mark Twain would say, 'from hell to breakfast.'" See also *CofC*, p. 4.
[53]*MTB*, 1:213.

story, so far as I can remember. This was about Jim Wolfe and the cats; and I gave him that tale the morning after that memorable episode. I thought he would laugh his remaining teeth out. I had never been so proud and happy before, and I have seldom been so proud and happy since."[54] The facts here suffered their usual transformation, no doubt, and it was not until 1867 that Clemens (writing for the *Mercury*) rendered his earliest tale in truly professional form through the voice of Simon Wheeler. Still, the disposition toward "yarning" clearly preceded his ventures into print. Calvin Higbie, Clemens' Aurora mining partner in 1861, recalled that the story-telling impulse was evident in Clemens even before he began writing to the *Enterprise*, and that it compelled friendship despite his proverbial laziness. Higbie remembered that Clemens would do no physical labor around the cabin (certainly an exaggeration), but—"He could tell stories!"

In that humorous drawl of his, that made him a favorite with practically everyone he met, he would spin yarns by the hour. . . . He tried me sorely many times, and I seriously considered ending it all by pitching him and his belongings out of doors. But I never did it.

   The truth was, I found his yarns so rich that I soon got in the habit of letting wood, water and fire go to the dogs. I would sit down spellbound and just listen, first lost in admiration and then roaring with laughter at the beauty and quaintness of his stories.[55]

This native talent fully informed Clemens' work as an *Enterprise* reporter, whether the subject was mining, politics, or the latest street brawl.

   Indeed, in December 1862, when Clemens first became an official reporter of the Territorial Legislature, his fellow reporter Andrew J. Marsh of the Sacramento *Union* recorded that a member of the house introduced a resolution "highly complimentary to the powers of imagination possessed by one of the reporters for a Territorial paper, and after a thrilling discussion, which jealousy prevents me from reporting verbatim, the resolution was laid on the table. Sic transit, etc." In the unpublished manuscript "Journal Proceedings of the House, 1862," the inventive reporter is identified as Samuel Clemens

---

[54]AD, 16 March 1906, *MTA*, 2:213.
[55]Quoted in Michael J. Phillips, "Mark Twain's Partner," *Saturday Evening Post* 193 (11 September 1920): 69.

"of the *Territorial Enterprise*," who was asked to "restrain his imagination and confine himself to the truth" when reporting the words
of "members on this floor."[56] The impulse to embroider the facts was,
even at this early date, recognized as Clemens' distinguishing idio-
syncrasy. In Nevada Mark Twain's reputation for elaboration was
sometimes criticized—he was unfavorably compared to Ananias—but
his inability to keep fact and fancy apart eventually became a permanent part of his professional literary equipment: "Mr. Mark Twain
. . . he told the truth, mainly." Clemens' apprenticeship on the
Enterprise was in this specific sense a preparation for his career as an
author of fiction; even when his work is most like conventional journalism, we find his humorous sensibility coloring the report and
dominating the interest of these ephemera.

3. *California: 1864–1866.*   On 29 May 1864 Clemens left Nevada by
California stagecoach, turning his back on a bitter quarrel with
James L. Laird of the Virginia City *Union* over the integrity of pledges
made to the United States Sanitary Fund. The controversy provided a
strong impulse to leave his berth on the *Enterprise* and, although he
did not plan it this way, to make a new start in San Francisco. Apparently Clemens first intended to remain in California only a few weeks
while he sold his mining stocks, but he eventually stayed for most of
the next two and one-half years. At first he roomed in luxury at the
Occidental Hotel—"Heaven on the half shell"[57] to the harried reporter, fresh from the anxiety and the alkali of Washoe. But when
the depression in stocks worsened, and the value of his own holdings
seriously declined, he resolved to stay on, take a job, and work long
enough "to make 'a stake.'"[58]

About June 6, within a few days of his arrival in San Francisco,
Clemens became the local reporter (at forty dollars a week) on the
San Francisco *Morning Call*, which had solicited his letters from
Virginia City the previous year. He remained on the *Call* staff just four

---

[56]Andrew J. Marsh, *Letters from Nevada Territory: 1861–1862,* ed. William C. Miller,
Russell W. McDonald, and Ann Rollins (Nevada: Legislative Counsel Bureau, 1972),
pp. 582, 713 n. 564.

[57]" 'Mark Twain' in the Metropolis" (no. 77).

[58]George E. Barnes, "Mark Twain as He Was Known during His Stay on the Pacific
Slope," San Francisco *Morning Call,* 17 April 1887, p. 1.

months, until the end of September, although the "fearful drudgery, soulless drudgery"[59] of the job led him to accept in his final month a reduction in salary to only twenty-five dollars a week in return for shorter working hours. Working for the *Call* was much more taxing than working for the *Enterprise*, where he had shared the burden with other reporters and had enjoyed the same pay with much more freedom. Even so, the job kept him professionally active and, to a considerable degree, creatively alert. He ventured local items, for instance, that truly tested the limits of editorial permissiveness, as in "No Earthquake," published on 23 August 1864:

> In consequence of the warm, close atmosphere which smothered the city at two o'clock yesterday afternoon, everybody expected to be shaken out of their boots by an earthquake before night, but up to the hour of our going to press the supernatural boot-jack had not arrived yet. That is just what makes it so unhealthy—the earthquakes are getting so irregular. When a community get used to a thing, they suffer when they have to go without it. However, the trouble cannot be remedied; we know of nothing that will answer as a substitute for one of those convulsions—to an unmarried man.[60]

This squib belongs to the same genre Clemens practiced in his *Enterprise* column (it is a variation on the "missed item"), but it is a shade more subtle and certainly more risqué. In general, Clemens handled his daily reporting for the *Call* with undiminished inventiveness and flair ("supernatural boot-jack") which is the more remarkable because it was so much more anonymous. The nine *Call* sketches (as distinct from letters) reprinted here are not wholly representative, but they are all good examples of his capacity for humorous reporting that verged on fiction. "What a Sky-Rocket Did" (no. 81) belongs to the family of hoaxes he began in Nevada, although it did not cause the same kind of commotion. "Inexplicable News from San José" (no. 87) is a brief, thoroughly fictional account that may have originally been intended for the *Golden Era*. And four brief items (nos. 82–85) on the new Chinese Temple in San Francisco show Mark Twain at his genial best.

Although Clemens published hundreds of items in the *Call*, it is

---

[59]AD, 13 June 1906, *MTE*, p. 256.
[60]San Francisco *Morning Call*, 23 August 1864, p. 1, reprinted in *CofC*, p. 41. A clipping of the article is preserved in Scrapbook 5, p. 41, MTP. For a sampling of *Call* items attributed to Mark Twain, see Appendix A in volume 2.

apparent that in July and August 1864 he was seriously questioning his career as a writer. John McComb recalled a conversation with him in 1864, when Clemens was "city editor of the *Morning Call.*" According to McComb, they met at the corner of Clay and Montgomery streets and Clemens said, "Mac, I've done my last newspaper work; I'm going back East." He had secured an appointment to act as a government pilot on the Mississippi, for a salary of $300 a month, and he planned to take the job. McComb, who "conceived a high regard for his literary ability," urged against this radical step:

Sam, you are making the mistake of your life. There is a better place for you than a Mississippi steamboat. You have a style of writing that is fresh and original and is bound to be popular. If you don't like the treadmill work of a newspaper man, strike up higher; write sketches, write a book; you'll find a market for your stuff, and in time you'll be appreciated and get more money than you can standing alongside the wheel of a steamboat. . . . No, Sam, don't you drop your pen now, stick to it, and it will make your fortune.[61]

After listening carefully to this admonition, and thinking it through, Clemens is reported to have told McComb, "Now, Mac, I've taken your advice. I thought it all over last night, and finally I wrote to Washington declining the appointment, and so I'll stick to the newspaper work a while longer."[62]

Clemens did more than "stick to the newspaper work." In late June and early July he had continued his earlier connection with the *Golden Era*, publishing two wonderfully comic sketches: "The Evidence in the Case of Smith *vs.* Jones" and "Early Rising, As Regards Excursions to the Cliff House" (nos. 78–79). But, prompted by McComb's encouragement, he soon made other arrangements as well. On September 25 he wrote his family:

I have engaged to write for the new literary paper—the "Californian" —same pay I used to receive on the "Golden Era"—one article a week, fifty dollars a month. I quit the "Era," long ago. It wasn't high-toned enough. I thought that whether I was a literary "jackleg" or not, I wouldn't class myself with that style of people, anyhow. The "Californian" circulates among the highest class of the community, & is

───────────
    [61]Quoted in Will M. Clemens, *Mark Twain: His Life and Work* (Chicago and New York: F. Tennyson Neely, 1894), pp. 56–59.
    [62]Clemens, *Life and Work*, p. 59.

the best weekly literary paper in the United States—& I suppose I ought to know.[63]

Three days later he told Orion and Mollie that while the *Californian* only paid him twelve dollars an article, it had "an exalted reputation in the east, & is liberally copied from by papers like the Home Journal." And in this same letter he indicated that he would soon begin work "on my book," presumably an early experiment to work up his western experiences.[64] Clemens seems, in other words, to have taken McComb's advice to "strike up higher" in all seriousness.

Although Charles Henry Webb had founded the *Californian* on 29 May 1864, Bret Harte, the editor in September 1864, was almost certainly the one who solicited Clemens' work. "A Notable Conundrum" (no. 91) appeared on October 1, and after that the *Californian* became Mark Twain's chief literary outlet for the rest of 1864 and again during the spring and summer of 1865. Although later in 1865 and in 1866 he continued to appear occasionally in its columns, it was at intervals of much greater length. The present collection reprints twenty-five contributions to the *Californian* from these years: self-consciously wrought, and (to Clemens' great satisfaction) meticulously printed, they constitute his most deliberately literary work of the period.

The routine of Clemens' urban existence was broken in early December 1864 by a three-month stay in some of the played-out mining camps of Tuolumne and Calaveras counties. On December 4 he arrived at Jim Gillis' cabin on Jackass Hill and, for the most part, remained there and at nearby Angel's Camp (the latter from 22 January to 20 February 1865) until he returned to San Francisco on February 26. There he found, as he wrote in his notebook, "letters from 'Artemus Ward' asking me to write a sketch for his new book of Nevada Territory travels which is soon to come out." He added, "Too late—ought to have got the letters 3 months ago. They are dated early in November."[65]

But the brief moratorium he had enjoyed in those three months away from San Francisco would have extraordinary literary conse-

---

[63]Clemens to Jane Clemens and Pamela Moffett, 25 September 1864, *CL1*, letter 91.
[64]Clemens to Orion and Mollie Clemens, 28 September 1864, *CL1*, letter 92. See also *CofC*, p. 19.
[65]*N&J1*, p. 82.

quences for him. At Jackass Hill he heard Jim Gillis and his partner Dick Stoker tell yarns he later turned to superb literary use. He recorded tag lines in his notebook to remind him of memorable incidents and characters, anecdotes, turns of phrase, and personal mining experiences in Nevada—material that eventually found its way into *Roughing It, A Tramp Abroad,* and *Huckleberry Finn.* But for immediate value, the most important thing he heard was the germ of the "Jumping Frog" tale, an anecdote told by Ben Coon at Angel's Camp in early February. It was not until mid-October 1865 that Clemens succeeded in writing his most famous tale (addressed to Ward), but in the intervening months he tried several times to make use of material from the mining camps. When he returned to San Francisco he continued to publish work in the *Californian:* "An Unbiased Criticism" (no. 100), which appeared on 18 March 1865, used a vernacular narrator, Coon, obviously inspired by mining-camp storytellers. Coon was an early version of Simon Wheeler, who first appeared in another *Californian* sketch in June 1865: "Answers to Correspondents" (no. 107) contained his enthusiastic endorsement of "He Done His Level Best." And, of course, Wheeler reappeared as the narrator in "Jim Smiley and His Jumping Frog" (no. 119), published by the New York *Saturday Press* in November 1865. Moreover, we now know that in addition to these three sketches Mark Twain wrote two preliminary efforts in which he exploited Wheeler's narrative powers. Presumably these were completed and abandoned before he sent the finished "Jumping Frog" sketch, belatedly, to Ward: they are published here for the first time and include "The Only Reliable Account of the Celebrated Jumping Frog of Calaveras County" (no. 117) and "Angel's Camp Constable" (no. 118).

When Clemens resumed his contributions to the *Californian* in March 1865 he began to pursue other outlets as well. Probably by mid-June he had begun a correspondence with the *Enterprise* that soon developed into daily letters, for which he received $100 a month; this arrangement continued into 1866. Because no file of the *Enterprise* is extant, relatively few of these letters survive. Our knowledge of the *Enterprise* letters of 1865 and 1866 derives from one scrapbook in which Clemens preserved part or all of some twenty letters, and from California and Nevada papers that sometimes reprinted excerpts. These excerpts range in length from substantial sketches to merely ephemeral and pungent squibs that give only a fragment of the original letter, as in the following paragraph reprinted in the *Call:*

FEELS SOMBER.—"Mark Twain" feels lugubrious over the depression in stocks, and the consequent financial wrecks he finds floating around San Francisco. "Out," he says in a recent letter to the *Enterprise,* "out upon these vain theatricals, these tinsel trappings of folly! Bring us shrouds, and coffins, and the tolling of bells, and the waving of sable plumes, and the solemn pomp of the passing funeral! What are the poor vanities of this world unto this people, who 'called' their persecuted Washoe with 'two pairs and a jack,' and she answered with a 'king full?' They digged the props from under Washoe, and she fell on them."[66]

Fortunately for us, Mark Twain was considered "good copy" even in so slight a paragraph as this.

When Clemens came to California he was well known as a newspaper humorist and enjoyed at least a local reputation (in Nevada) as a witty speaker for select occasions. The first and last pieces from the California section record successful talks before San Francisco audiences, but they also provide a measure of how rapidly and how fully his reputation grew in that two-year period. The first talk was a "presentation" speech before a group of appreciative males ("Parting Presentation," no. 76); the last was a celebrity's farewell to the population at large ("'Mark Twain's' Farewell," no. 200). As we have seen, this transformation from local editor to traveling celebrity occurred gradually. Clemens was widely recognized as an outstanding contributor to the *Golden Era* and then to the *Californian;* the Gold Hill *News,* for instance, asserted in July 1865 that he was a major reason for the superior quality of that "most excellent weekly newspaper," the *Californian.*[67]

Indeed, in mid- and late 1865 there was a rising tide of appreciation to which Clemens was certainly attentive. On September 9 the New York *Round Table* broadly characterized American humor and surveyed native humorists in general:

The enterprising State of California, which follows as closely as she can upon the steps of her older Eastern sisters, has produced some

---

[66]San Francisco *Morning Call,* 22 December 1865, p. 1.

[67]"Letter from San Francisco," Virginia City *Evening Bulletin,* 24 September 1863, p. 1; "The Californian," Gold Hill *News,* 5 July 1863, p. 2.

examples of our national humor which compare favorably with those
already mentioned. They are but little known in this region, and few,
if any, have yet appeared "between covers." The foremost among
the merry gentlemen of the California press, as far as we have been
able to judge, is one who signs himself "Mark Twain." Of his real
name we are ignorant, but his style resembles that of "John Phoenix"
more nearly than any other, and some things we have seen from
his pen would do honor to the memory of even that chieftain among
humorists. He is, we believe, quite a young man, and has not written
a great deal. Perhaps, if he will husband his resources and not kill
with overwork the mental goose that has given us these golden eggs,
he may one day take rank among the brightest of our wits.[68]

This is an important commentary, in part because it came well before
Mark Twain published the "Jumping Frog" story (the *Round Table*
editor must have seen things reprinted from the *Californian*, as
Clemens himself had anticipated), and in part because we may be sure
that the comment encouraged Mark Twain to pursue his career as
a writer. The editors of the San Francisco *Dramatic Chronicle* republished the *Round Table* comment in a brief squib, "Recognized," on
October 18. The next day Clemens wrote Orion and Mollie, in an
extraordinary letter, that he had at last resolved to "drop all trifling,
& sighing after vain impossibilities, & strive for a fame—unworthy
& evanescent though it must of necessity be." He told Orion:

You see in me a talent for humorous writing, & urge me to cultivate
it. But I always regarded it as brotherly partiality on your part, &
attached no value to it. It is only now, when editors of standard literary papers in the distant east give me high praise, & who do not know
me & cannot of course be blinded by the glamour of partiality, that I
really begin to believe there must be something in it.[69]

The letter is particularly significant because Clemens was again discouraged, as he had been in 1864, about his career. "Utterly miserable," badly in debt, and believing "that there is a God for the rich
man but none for the poor," he promised "pistols or poison for one—
exit *me*" if he could not reverse his luck within three months.[70]

There are several material signs that Clemens set to work in earnest
at this time. "Jim Smiley and His Jumping Frog" was almost certainly

---

[68]"American Humor and Humorists," *Round Table,* 9 September 1865, p. 2.
[69]Clemens to Orion and Mollie Clemens, 19 October 1865, *CL1,* letter 95.
[70]Clemens to Orion and Mollie Clemens, 19 October 1865, *CL1,* letter 95.

completed as part of this renewed campaign,[71] and he submitte(
Great Earthquake in San Francisco" (no. 123) to the prestigious
New York *Weekly Review,* which published it on November 25.
Moreover, as Clemens told Orion and Mollie, he would begin "next
week" to work for the San Francisco *Dramatic Chronicle* ("$40 a
month for dramatic criticisms"), in addition to his daily *Enterprise*
letter, in an effort to pay off his debt.[72] On October 17 the *Chronicle*
published his brief "Earthquake Almanac" (no. 122). Over the next
few weeks it also published a number of unsigned commentaries on
various topics (see Appendix B in volume 2), and his contributions to
the column "Amusements," which contained the theater notices.
Beyond this, in November and December Mark Twain published
three letters in the Napa County *Reporter.* These contained some
news, and three sketches reprinted here: "The Guard on a Bender"
(no. 138), "Benkert Cometh!" (no. 139), and "Webb's Benefit"
(no. 141).

The notice in the *Round Table* and then the enormous success of
the "Jumping Frog" story called forth a great deal of public comment.
In a letter dated 1 November 1865, Charles Henry Webb wrote the
Sacramento *Union:*

To my thinking Shakspeare had no more idea that he was writing for
posterity than Mark Twain has at the present time, and it sometimes
amuses me to think how future Mark Twain scholars will puzzle over
that gentleman's present hieroglyphics and occasionally eccentric
expressions. Apropos, of Twain, who is a man of Mark, I am glad
to see that his humor has met with recognition at the East, and that
mention is made of him in that critical journal, the *Round Table.*
They may talk of coarse humor, if they please, but in his case it is
simply the strength of the soil—the germ is there and it sprouts good
and strong. To my mind Mark Twain and Dan Setchell are the wild
Humorists of the Pacific.[73]

The hallmarks of Clemens' colloquial humor—"she didn't keep up
her lick" and "they shoved"—were frequently noticed in the press,[74]
and to one Nevada journalist his humor seemed a "blaze of fun"

[71]See Edgar M. Branch, "'My Voice is Still for Setchell': A Background Study of
'Jim Smiley and His Jumping Frog,'" *PMLA* 82 (December 1967): 591–601.
[72]Clemens to Orion and Mollie Clemens, 19 October 1865, *CL1,* letter 95.
[73]"Letter from San Francisco," Sacramento *Union,* 3 November 1865, p. 2.
[74]"Amusements," San Francisco *Dramatic Chronicle,* 7 November 1865, p. 3;
"Fenians, Beware!" ibid., 25 April 1866, p. 4.

compared with which "'Artemus Ward's' slight gleam is as a farthing rushlight to the sun."[75] On December 10 Podgers (Richard L. Ogden) wrote from New York in his regular letter to the San Francisco *Alta California*:

Mark Twain's story in the *Saturday Press* of November 18th. called "Jim Smiley and his Jumping Frog," has set all New York in a roar, and he may be said to have made his mark. I have been asked fifty times about it and its author, and the papers are copying it far and near. It is voted the best thing of the day. Cannot the *Californian* afford to keep Mark all to itself? It should not let him scintillate so widely without first being filtered through the California press.[76]

In late January 1866 a colleague on the *Chronicle* affirmed that "'Mark' is bound to have a biographer one of these days—may it be a hundred years hence!"[77]

On January 20 Clemens could boast to his family that he was "generally placed at the head of my breed of scribblers in this part of the country."[78] Clearly aware of his mounting reputation, and determined to capitalize on his new eastern fame, he soon published more sketches in the *Weekly Review* and the *Saturday Press*: "An Open Letter to the American People" (no. 181) on February 17, "The Mysterious Bottle of Whiskey" (no. 186) on March 3, and "A Strange Dream" (no. 189) on June 2. By the end of 1866 the *Saturday Press* had published three major sketches, and the *Weekly Review* had printed (or reprinted) eight.

The sudden swell of popularity, especially in the East, persuaded Clemens to consider or reconsider plans for various kinds of books. On January 20 he told his family that Bret Harte had asked him to collaborate on a book of sketches to be drawn from his *Enterprise* and *Californian* contributions. The two men also contemplated writing a burlesque of "a book of poems which the publisher, Bancroft, is to issue in the spring. We know all the tribe of California poets, & understand their different styles," he gloated, "& I think we can just make them get up & howl." Neither project was ever completed, but

---

[75]"Amusements, Etc.," San Francisco *Dramatic Chronicle*, 27 September 1866, p. 3.
[76]"Podgers' Letter from New York," written 10 December 1865, published in the San Francisco *Alta California*, 10 January 1866, p. 1.
[77]"Biographical," San Francisco *Dramatic Chronicle*, 23 January 1866, p. 2.
[78]Clemens to Jane Clemens and Pamela Moffett, 20 January 1866, *CL1*, letter 97.

Clemens was entertaining still another idea at this time—what he called a "pet notion of mine"—a book of "about three hundred pages, and the last hundred will have to be written in St Louis, because the materials for them can only be got there."[79] The reference suggests an early concern with material that would eventually become "Old Times on the Mississippi" (1874–1875). This conjecture is reinforced by a report dated March 4 which appeared in the Unionville (Nev.) *Humboldt Register*. That paper's San Francisco correspondent had been talking with Mark Twain, who had told him "last night he would leave, in a few days, for the Sandwich Islands, in the employ of The Sacramento Union. Will be gone about two months. Then will go to Montana for same paper, and next Fall down the Missouri river in a Mackinac boat—he's an old Mississippi pilot—to New Orleans; where he intends writing a book."[80]

Clemens did sail to the Sandwich Islands on March 6, employed by the *Union* to write "twenty or thirty letters"[81] in a month-long visit. The excursion eventually lasted five months and produced twenty-five travel letters—and what is most important, still more material suitable for a book. When Clemens returned to California in August 1866 the editors of the *Californian* publicly urged him to revise and collect his Sandwich Island letters into a book: their "intrinsic interest and value" would make the book "both a literary and a pecuniary success."[82] Clemens worked on this project in late 1866 and early 1867, and he must actually have submitted a completed manuscript to the New York publishers Dick and Fitzgerald before deciding to withdraw it: "It would be useless to publish it in these dull publishing times," he rationalized to his family.[83]

Although none of these projects reached immediate fruition, Clemens' stay in California proved to be one of the most productive periods of his life. One year after he had made his resolve in the letter to Orion, a fully revitalized Clemens gave his first—and wholly triumphant—Sandwich Islands lecture at Maguire's Academy of

[79]Clemens to Jane Clemens and Pamela Moffett, 20 January 1866, *CL1*, letter 97.
[80]"Letter from San Francisco," Unionville (Nev.) *Humboldt Register*, 10 March 1866, p. 1.
[81]Clemens to Jane Clemens and Pamela Moffett, 5 March 1866, *CL1*, letter 99.
[82]*Californian* 5 (25 August 1866): 1.
[83]Clemens to Jane Clemens et al., 7 June 1867, *CL1*, letter 137.

Music in San Francisco. One week later Bret Harte wrote, in a letter
to the Springfield (Mass.) *Republican*, that Clemens' talent was so far
superior to Artemus Ward's that it heralded "a new star rising in this
western horizon." Mark Twain's humor, Harte added, was "of the
western character of ludicrous exaggeration and audacious statement,
which perhaps is more thoroughly national and American than even
the Yankee delineations of Lowell." His faults were "crudeness,
coarseness, and an occasional Panurge-like plainness of statement."
But his satirical power, his shrewdness, and his hatred of shams
promised to "make his faculty serviceable to mankind. His talent is
so well based that he can write seriously and well when he chooses,
which is perhaps the best test of true humor."[84]

Just as the Sandwich Islands letters provided a trial run for the
forthcoming letters from the *Quaker City*, so Mark Twain's successful San Francisco lecture opened up an area of incalculable importance to his writing. Hastily arranged lecture tours into the interior
of California and Nevada permitted him to experiment with techniques of oral storytelling, and they established his self-confidence as
a public lecturer while reaffirming that Mark Twain was a distinct
public figure. Five days after a final San Francisco lecture on December 10, Mark Twain sailed on the steamer *America* for New York
City, serving as the special correspondent for the *Alta*, which expected him to circumnavigate the globe and return in triumph. The
parting words of that paper, possibly written by his faithful supporter
John McComb, were:

"Mark Twain" goes off on his journey over the world as the Travelling
Correspondent of the ALTA CALIFORNIA, not stinted as to time, place
or direction—writing his weekly letters on such subjects and from
such places as will best suit him; but we may say that he will first
visit the home of his youth—St. Louis—thence through the principal
cities to the Atlantic seaboard again, crossing the ocean to visit the
"Universal Exposition" at Paris, through Italy, the Mediterranean,
India, China, Japan, and back to San Francisco by the China Mail
Steamship line. That his letters will be read with interest needs no
assurance from us—his reputation has been made here in California,
and his great ability is well known; but he has been known principally

---

[84]"From California," Springfield (Mass.) *Republican*, 10 November 1866, quoted in
George R. Stewart, "Bret Harte upon Mark Twain in 1866," *American Literature* 13
(November 1941): 263–264.

as a humorist, while he really has no superior as a descriptive writer—a keen observer of men and their surroundings—and we feel confident his letters to the ALTA, from his new field of observation, will give him a world-wide reputation.[85]

Clearly Clemens was considered a man of note in his profession, but more importantly one who would soon transcend journalism as an author of books.

One hundred twenty-five pieces written in California are collected in these volumes, almost twice as many as are preserved from the first thirteen years of Mark Twain's apprenticeship. The disparity is even greater when measured in sheer number of words. As a journalist in Nevada Clemens was employed by a single newspaper on which his main assignment was to write up local events. In California, by contrast, he was essentially a free-lance writer, barring the four months he spent on the *Call* and the two months he worked on the *Chronicle*. Although his daily correspondence for the *Enterprise* in 1865 and 1866 eventually became a chore, the newspaper letter form was flexible enough to permit extraordinary freedom in choice of subject and mode of expression. Thus Mark Twain's fundamental inclination toward literary tales and sketches based remotely on the facts was supported and encouraged by the conditions of his employment, and even by the periods of leisure that he enjoyed in the mining camps. The need to earn a living by journalism, by keeping him in touch with events, affected the form and the content of all his work—scarcely a single piece does not derive from some news event, however trivial—but his relative freedom from the more confining type of journalism gave his imagination the working room it required.

It is hardly possible to give an adequate characterization of so many diverse sketches—but it may be noted that Clemens continued to indulge in the running newspaper "feud," this time with Fitz Smythe (Albert S. Evans); that he showed an exuberantly anti-romantic taste for satire and burlesque, finding an enormous number of forms and styles to parody; and finally that he experimented consciously and with great inventiveness with the various poses he took as Mark Twain, as well as with an alternative technique of some

---

[85] " 'Mark Twain's' Farewell," San Francisco *Alta California*, 15 December 1866, p. 2.

importance—using a figure like Mother Utterback, Coon, or Simon Wheeler to give the narrative in full vernacular. From the standpoint of his reputation, as well as from that of his skills as a writer, the California period was enormously rewarding.

4. *The Midwest and East: 1866–1871.*   We have already traced Mark Twain's interest in writing a book from as early as September 1864 up through the first months of 1866—an interest that blossomed when his reputation grew and when the various forms open to him (extended parody, sketch books, travel narrative) multiplied. In the five years between his departure from San Francisco and his move to Hartford in October 1871, Clemens published three books and planned several more. The Sandwich Islands book was completed but set aside as unpublishable in early 1867; *The Celebrated Jumping Frog of Calaveras County, And other Sketches* (1867) was published in collaboration with his California colleague Charles Henry Webb; *The Innocents Abroad*, which was based on the *Quaker City* letters, took almost two years to write and publish, but when it finally appeared in mid-1869 was a phenomenal best seller that soon established the author's national and international reputation; finally, *Mark Twain's (Burlesque) Autobiography and First Romance*, a slight pamphlet of little significance, appeared in March 1871.

The story of Clemens' efforts to publish books, especially sketch books, is fully treated in the textual introduction to this collection. What needs to be stressed here is that the energy which went into these projects, especially *Innocents*, naturally had a corresponding negative effect on his production of brief sketches. Only thirty-five items in the present collection were written between the time of his arrival in New York in January 1867 and the completion of *Innocents* in July 1869: his travel correspondence with half a dozen papers, his various lecture tours, and his courtship and marriage, not to mention the extensive job of redacting his *Alta California* and *Tribune* letters for the book, all combined to minimize the production of short works. Following the publication of *Innocents*, however, he would assume a new role as editor of the Buffalo *Express* (August 1869), and within eight months he would also contract with the *Galaxy* for a monthly column, "Memoranda," into which he planned to funnel various short works. Of the one hundred sixty-five items included in this portion of the collection, forty-eight first appeared in the *Express*, sixty-seven in the *Galaxy*, and thirty-two in a variety of other journals; eighteen additional selections, some of them intended for the *Express* or *Galaxy*, he left unpublished. They are collected here for the first time.

Clemens arrived in New York on 12 January 1867. He promptly began to work with Webb on the *Jumping Frog* book, and perhaps tinkered with the Sandwich Islands manuscript, while he also contributed at least one letter a week to the *Alta*. Late in February he must have reached an agreement with the New York *Sunday Mercury*, the paper that had accepted "Those Blasted Children" (no. 72) in February 1864: on March 3 the *Mercury* published "The Winner of the Medal" (no. 203), the first of seven articles by Mark Twain which would appear there in early 1867. Also in March the paper published "A Curtain Lecture Concerning Skating" (no. 204) and "Barbarous" (no. 207).

Clemens must have written these pieces in February and early March, since he left for St. Louis by train on March 3 to visit his family—the first time he had seen them in six years. While in the Midwest he lectured twice in St. Louis and, in early April, in Hannibal, Keokuk, and Quincy. In mid-March he published a series of three comic articles on female suffrage in the *Missouri Democrat* and, somewhat later, advertised his St. Louis and Quincy lectures by two elaborately devised newspaper pieces: "Explanatory" (no. 206) and "Mark Twain and John Smith" (no. 208). Despite these uninspired efforts, he seems to have been stimulated by his return to boyhood haunts, for he produced two sketches for the *Mercury* which drew directly or indirectly on that energy: "Jim Wolf and the Tom-Cats" (no. 212) and "A Reminiscence of Artemus Ward" (no. 211), the former being a boyhood memory narrated through Simon Wheeler. Both tales appeared in July, after he had sailed on the *Quaker City* in early June.

Clemens returned from St. Louis to New York in mid-April, made final arrangements for his *Quaker City* voyage, saw Webb bring out the *Jumping Frog* book, and lectured three times before large audiences. The lectures were popular but not financial successes, and the *Jumping Frog* book failed to sell as expected. Nevertheless, Clemens'

reception by influential easterners continued to be encouraging, as
he had recently suggested in a letter to his family: "James Russell
Lowell ('Hosea Biglow,') says the Jumping Frog is the finest piece of
humorous writing ever produced in America."[86] Three weeks later
Clemens' new friend Edward H. House, who worked on the New
York *Tribune* as a drama critic, published a lecture review which
Clemens later praised and which shows us how New York perceived
this newcomer. House recalled Clemens' "Jumping Frog" tale in the
Saturday Press as a sketch

so singularly fresh, original, and full of character as to attract prompt
and universal attention among the readers of light humorous literature. Mark Twain was immediately entered as a candidate for high
position among writers of his class, and passages from his first contribution to the metropolitan press became proverbs in the mouths
of his admirers. No reputation was ever more rapidly won. . . . Subsequent productions, however—most of them reproduced from
California periodicals—confirmed the good opinion so suddenly
vouchsafed him, and abundantly vindicated the applause with which
his first essay had been received.[87]

Despite this warm reception, Clemens declined to lecture again, pleading his journalistic commitments: "I am one magazine article & eighteen letters behindhand (18 days to do them in, before sailing.)" By
June 1 he was "wild with impatience to move—move—*move!*"[88]
And on June 8, in possession of a sound reputation of modest dimensions, this writer of "light humorous literature" sailed for the
Holy Land under contract to correspond for the *Alta California*
and the New York *Tribune*. He did not return to New York until
November 19.

In August Clemens agreed to become Senator William M. Stewart's
private secretary. Two days after disembarking at New York he was on
his way to Washington, D.C., to take up his new duties, hoping to
make the position "one of the best paying berths in Washington" and
eventually to secure a government job for Orion.[89] December 1867
through January and February 1868 was an extraordinarily busy period
for him. Besides working for Senator Stewart (an arrangement that did

[86]Clemens to Jane Clemens et al., 19 April 1867, *CL1*, letter 125.

[87]"Mark Twain as a Lecturer," New York *Tribune*, 11 May 1867, p. 2.

[88]Clemens to John Stanton (Corry O'Lanus), 20 May 1867, *CL1*, letter 134; Clemens
to Jane Clemens et al., 1 June 1867, *CL1*, letter 135.

[89]Clemens to Jane Clemens et al., 9 August 1867, *CL1*, letter 146.

not long endure) he may have served briefly as a clerk to a Senate committee, and he maintained an enormous variety of newspaper correspondence. He was a member of the New York *Tribune* Washington staff—an "occasional"—and he wrote regular letters to the *Alta California*, the *Enterprise*, the Chicago *Republican*, and possibly the New York *Herald*.[90] Clemens recalled many years later, moreover, that he and William Swinton worked together at this time on "the old original first Newspaper Syndicate on the planet. . . . We had twelve journals on our list; they were all weeklies, all obscure and poor and all scattered far away among the back settlements. . . . Each of the twelve took two letters a week from us, at a dollar per letter; each of us wrote one letter per week and sent off six duplicates of it to these benefactors."[91] Although most of his regular letters written at this time for the daily newspapers mentioned above will be collected in other volumes of The Works of Mark Twain, the present collection prints several items that either appeared in or were probably designed to appear in the "syndicate" of weeklies: "General Spinner as a Religious Enthusiast" (no. 222), "Mr. Brown, the Sergeant-at-Arms of the Senate" (no. 214), and "Interview with Gen. Grant" (no. 215).

While pursuing an active career as a journalist Mark Twain also became convinced that the influence of Senator John Conness of California and Justice Stephen J. Field could secure his appointment as San Francisco postmaster, and he was momentarily tempted to return to the West Coast in that capacity. He eventually decided against it. In fact, Clemens was at this time routinely turning down invitations to lecture at $100 a night, and he rejected his friend Frank Fuller's insistent pleas to launch a lecture tour in the provinces. To his family he confided: "Am pretty well known, now—intend to be better known. Am hob-nobbing with these old Generals & Senators & other humbugs for no good purpose."[92] His purpose was, in fact, to build a reputation "that shall stand fire" and then to "make a bran new start in the lecturing business, & I don't mean to do it in Tuttletown, Ark., or Baldwinsville, Michigan, either."[93] But by December 10 he was writing a lecture, having become convinced that he was al-

[90]Louis J. Budd, "Did Mark Twain Write 'Impersonally' for the *New York Herald?*" *Duke University Library Notes*, no. 43 (November 1972), pp. 5–9.

[91]AD, 3 October 1907, *MTE*, p. 352.

[92]Clemens to Jane Clemens et al., 25 November 1867, *CL1*, letter 159.

[93]Clemens to Fuller, 24 November 1867, *CL1*, letter 157.

ready better known than he had thought. To Fuller he admitted, "I
should be tempted to receive proposals from Young Men's Christian
Ass.'s & such like. Because I am already tired of being in one place so
long."[94] Nevertheless, he spoke first in Washington, D.C., on January 9. His lecture, billed as "The Frozen Truth," was his first on the
Holy Land excursion. Three days later, praised as "the distinguished
humorist,"[95] he gave his famous mock eulogy on women ("Woman—
An Opinion," no. 218) before the Washington Correspondents' Club
and happily wrote home that Speaker Schuyler Colfax said it "was the
best dinner-table speech he ever heard at a banquet."[96] A profitable
lecture tour into "the provinces" now became a distinct possibility.

But two powerful inducements temporarily kept him in the East
close to his home base. "Charlie Langdon's sister . . . (beautiful
girl,)"[97] was one: he had met her in late December 1867 and on New
Year's Eve had escorted her to a public reading by Charles Dickens.
The other inducement was his book, then tentatively called "The
New Pilgrim's Progress." As early as December 2 he reported to Mrs.
Fairbanks that he had received "several propositions from the book
publishers" for a volume about the *Quaker City* trip, and it now
seems obvious that long before he embarked in June he fully understood the potential for embodying his account of the voyage in a book.
He told Mrs. Fairbanks that he liked the proposal from the American
Publishing Company at Hartford "much the best,"[98] and he wrote to
Elisha Bliss the same day, asking in detail what was required and
what would be offered in return. But Bliss was slow to respond, and
not especially forthcoming about his terms, so Clemens took matters
in hand and went to see him. "This great American Publishing Company," he told his family on January 24, "kept on trying to bargain
with me for a book till I thought I would cut the matter short by coming up for a *talk*."[99] The matter was settled to his satisfaction, and
he returned to his heavy newspaper duties in Washington.

His first impulse was to maintain this extensive correspondence
while also writing the book: "I shall write to the Enterprise & Alta

[94]Clemens to Fuller, 13 December 1867, *CL1*, letter 171.
[95]"Annual Banquet of the Correspondents' Club," Washington (D.C.) *Evening Star*,
13 January 1868, p. 2.
[96]Clemens to Jane Clemens et al., 13 January 1868, *CL1*, letter 179.
[97]Clemens to Jane Clemens and Pamela Moffett, 8 January 1868, *CL1*, letter 174.
[98]Clemens to Mary Mason Fairbanks, 2 December 1867, *CL1*, letter 164.
[99]Clemens to Jane Clemens and Pamela Moffett, 24 January 1868, *CL1*, letter 181.

every week, as usual, I guess, & to the Herald twice a week—occasionally to the Tribune & the magazines (I have a stupid article in the
Galaxy, just issued), but I am not going to write to this, that & the
other paper any more."[100] But these ambitious plans were soon abandoned, and he asked Bliss for a $1,000 advance, cut back severely on
his correspondence, and began steadily turning out book manuscript.

Yet having made this step toward the life of an author and away
from that of a journalist, Clemens was no longer tied to the East Coast.
And when he learned that the *Alta* was planning to republish his
letters on their own, he seized the opportunity to return to San Francisco, leaving on March 12 and arriving on April 2. "A business call
in any given direction is a most comfortable thing when your inclina-
tions call you powerfully in the self same direction," he explained.[101]
He was welcomed by the *Call* as "the world-wide known 'Mark
Twain'" but "still the same old 'Mark.'"[102] He lectured in San Francisco on April 14 and 15, then for the remainder of the month toured
the interior, lecturing from Sacramento to Carson City. Everywhere he
was welcomed back with great enthusiasm and some ceremony. Conrad Wiegand, a Virginia City assayer, presented him on April 28 with a
polished silver brick bearing the inscription "Mark Twain—Matthew
v; 41—Pilgrim," alluding to the verse "And whosoever shall compel
thee to go a mile, go with him twain."[103]

Early in May he returned to San Francisco where, after some debate,
John McComb and Frederick McCrellish of the *Alta* soon granted
him exclusive rights to his printed letters. On May 5 he wrote Bliss
from his favorite San Francisco hotel, the Occidental, "I am steadily
at work."[104] For the better part of two months he diligently revised
his letters and added material to his copy, which he submitted to
Harte for suggestions. Despite this heavy work schedule he found time
for social activity, and his very presence in San Francisco continued
to make news. The *Dramatic Chronicle* reported his meeting with
Charles Warren Stoddard, James F. Bowman, and Prentice Mulford

---

[100]Clemens to Jane Clemens and Pamela Moffett, 24 January 1868, *CL1*, letter 181.
The article was "General Washington's Negro Body-Servant. A Biographical Sketch"
(no. 220), his first contribution to the *Galaxy*.
     [101]"Letter from Mark Twain," Chicago *Republican*, 19 May 1868, p. 2.
     [102]" 'Mark Twain,' " San Francisco *Morning Call*, 3 April 1868, p. 2.
     [103]"Mark Twain Bricked," San Francisco *Dramatic Chronicle*, 9 May 1868, p. 3;
"Theatrical Record," San Francisco *Morning Call*, 10 May 1868, p. 1.
     [104]Clemens to Bliss, 5 May 1868, *CL1*, letter 202.

"with the view of improving the tone of his morals and if possible, shaking off the prejudices against orthodoxy, acquired by reason of the enforced contact and consequent martyrdom while in the company of his fellow pilgrims to Jerusalem."[105] On May 17, the very day the *Alta* published his last *Quaker City* letter, he attended a Baptist church and simmered while the minister, unaware of his presence, excoriated at some length "the letters of this person, Mark Twain, who visits the Holy Land and ridicules sacred scenes and things. The letters are sought after and eagerly read, because of his puerile attempts at wit, and miserable puns upon subjects which are dear to every Christian heart."[106] Loftily Clemens dismissed all such incidents: "It is only the small-fry ministers who assail me."[107] The *Chronicle* was particularly disposed to champion his work. Even before he returned to San Francisco it had linked his writing with that of Oliver Wendell Holmes[108] and had defended his *Quaker City* letters against the strictures of Calvin B. McDonald, formerly the "triple-thunderer" of the San Francisco *American Flag*. McDonald had characterized the letters as the "disgusting literary truck" of a "mountebank grimmacing and gyrating through a country which the whole world of civilization regard[s] as classic, sublime and holy."[109] Such reactions were the inevitable penalty for bringing his humor into a larger public context than that of Virginia City or even San Francisco. Although Mark Twain claimed to be indifferent to them, we now know that he wrote at least one manuscript—"I Rise to a Question of Privilege" (no. 227)—designed to respond humorously to charges of irreverence. In "Remarkable Sagacity of a Cat" (no. 228) he also seems to have experimented briefly with western material that would prove productive indeed within a year; the sketch was written in June 1868 but would remain unpublished until he prepared a fuller version for his "Around the World" letters in December 1869. The preparation of *The Innocents Abroad* clearly took most of his time. With the manuscript completed, Clemens gave a farewell lecture on July 2 and sailed from San Francisco on July 6, arriving in New York

[105]"Good Results," San Francisco *Dramatic Chronicle*, 26 May 1868, p. 2.
[106]"Mark Twain at Church," San Francisco *Morning Call*, 20 May 1868, p. 1.
[107]Clemens to Mary Mason Fairbanks, 17 June 1868, *CL1*, letter 207.
[108]"Pinchbeck Literature," San Francisco *Dramatic Chronicle*, 20 March 1868, p. 2.
[109]"After Mark Twain," San Francisco *Dramatic Chronicle*, 5 March 1868, p. 2.

on July 29. The months of transition that saw him change from a senator's secretary to an author engrossed with his first major book are noticeably barren of short imaginative pieces.

During the year following his return to New York City from San Francisco Clemens distributed his time among three projects: the manuscript and proofs of *Innocents*, his courtship of Olivia Langdon, and a rigorous schedule of lectures in the Midwest and East which lasted from 17 November 1868 through 3 March 1869. This extraordinarily successful tour demonstrated his stamina and his drawing power on the platform, where he took rank as the most popular American humorist of the day. But of more immediate concern to Clemens was his ability to earn a steady living at some respectable profession. In fact, to make his marriage to Olivia more acceptable, he felt that he should "get located in a newspaper in a way to suit me."[110] What he had in mind was partial ownership and partial editorial control of an urban, eastern journal—a natural step to someone who had spent the last eight years as a fully professional but itinerant journalist. "I want to be permanent," he wrote, "I must feel thoroughly & completely *satisfied* when I anchor 'for good & all.'"[111]

Among the several alternatives that Clemens considered was to accept the post of political editor on the Cleveland *Herald*. But the terms Abel W. Fairbanks offered proved unsatisfactory, and he eventually declined the job. To Mrs. Fairbanks he explained, "It just offered *another* apprenticeship—another one, to be tacked on to the tail end of a foolish life *made up* of apprenticeships."[112] Shortly before August 12, relying on funds borrowed from his fiancée's father, Clemens purchased a one-third interest in the Buffalo *Express* from Thomas A. Kennett for $25,000. To Bliss he wrote, "It is an exceedingly thriving newspaper. We propose to make it more so."[113] Soon his hope was "to make this newspaper support me hereafter,"[114] thus avoiding the necessity of lecturing. The choice of the *Express* was a sound one: it is doubtful whether he could have been his own man on the Cleveland *Herald* to the extent that he could on the *Express*.

---

[110]Clemens to Jane Clemens et al., 4 June 1869, *CL2*, letter 66.
[111]Clemens to Mary Mason Fairbanks, 10 May 1869, *CL2*, letter 48.
[112]Clemens to Mary Mason Fairbanks, 14 August 1869, *CL2*, letter 84.
[113]Clemens to Bliss, 12 August 1869, *CL2*, letter 82.
[114]Clemens to Henry M. Crane, 8 September 1869, *CL2*, letter 103.

He formally assumed his position on August 14, by which time he had also seen the first copies of *Innocents.*

The year had afforded him little opportunity for short newspaper or magazine work. In late 1868 he had published "Cannibalism in the Cars" (no. 232)—his first publication in an English journal; he had written "A Mystery" (no. 233), published in the Cleveland *Herald;* "A Wicked Fraud" (no. 234) had appeared in a New Jersey paper; and he had written three sketches for *Packard's Monthly,* two of them reprinted in this collection: "Mark Twain's Eulogy on the 'Reliable Contraband' " (no. 235) and "Personal Habits of the Siamese Twins" (no. 237). On 4 June 1869, speaking as a literary journalist and characteristically stressing his "idleness," Clemens noted that the number of his current publications had drastically fallen off because of his preoccupation with Olivia, his lectures, and his book: "In twelve months (or rather I believe it is fourteen,) I have earned just *eighty dollars* by my pen—two little magazine squibs & one newspaper letter—altogether the idlest, laziest 14 months I ever spent in my life."[115] So spoke the man who was still in the midst of one of the most demanding years of his life. He would soon admit, "When I got to counting up the irons I had in the fire (marriage, editing a newspaper, and lecturing,) I said it was most too many, for the subscriber."[116]

Albert Bigelow Paine characterized Clemens' responsibility on the Buffalo *Express* as that of "a sort of general and contributing editor, with a more or less 'roving commission'—his hours and duties not very clearly defined." It was expected, Paine added, that Mark Twain's "connection with the paper would give it prestige and circulation."[117] Clemens soon established the pattern for his major contributions to the paper: a featured article each Saturday. With few exceptions he observed that schedule from 21 August 1869 through 29 January 1870, immediately before his marriage on February 2. No Saturday features appeared in February; he wrote Bliss on February 23, "I don't go near the Express office more than twice a week—& then only for an hour. I am just as good as other men—& other men take honey-moons I

[115]Clemens to Jane Clemens et al., 4 June 1869, *CL2,* letter 66.
[116]Clemens to Bliss, 15 August 1869, *CL2,* letter 86.
[117]*MTB,* 1:386–387.

reckon."[118] After this his interest in writing for the paper declined: in the next three months (March through May) only five featured articles appeared in the *Express*, and thereafter only four, the final one coming on 17 September 1870 ("Fortifications of Paris," no. 323).

In addition to his Saturday features, Clemens also compiled the daily column "People and Things" from 17 August until 27 September 1869, when he wrote to Bliss: "I like newspapering very well, as far as I have got—but I adjourn, a week hence, to commence preparing my lecture, & shall not be here again till the middle of February. After a few days, now, I shall be *in Elmira till Nov. 1. Recollect.*"[119] While on tour in New England and New York from 1 November 1869 to 21 January 1870 Clemens presumably mailed his weekly features to the *Express*, but he found it impractical to continue "People and Things." This column was a miscellany of comments—breezy, skeptical, or merely comic, ranging from single sentences to miniature essays—on news events and oddities evidently gleaned from the newspaper exchanges. Clemens had always been attracted by the endless procession of "extraordinary but true" items so amply furnished by the newspapers, and although he occasionally found material here for sketches, his tenure on the "People and Things" column shows that he welcomed the opportunity to wisecrack at will, to pass judgment whimsically or severely on the most ephemeral matters. His comments were usually brief, epigrams really, and they remind us that he would return in the 1890s to writing Pudd'nhead Wilson's maxims. At the same time, some of the longer items look back to his experiments in the local columns of the *Enterprise* and the *Call*. Some samples from the column of August 18 follow:

—A pig with a human head is astonishing South Carolina. Are they rare, there?

—A Wisconsin girl has swallowed forty percussion caps and is afraid to sit down.

. . . .

—A human skull, wrapped up in a piece of brown paper along with a brick, has been found in a marsh near Milwaukee. The proprietor

---

[118]Clemens to Bliss, 23 February 1870, *CL2*, letter 165.
[119]Clemens to Bliss, 27 September 1869, *CL2*, letter 108.

can recover it by applying to the Milwaukee authorities. It will not be easy to identify it, because so many like it have been lost—it was empty.

. . . .

—In Nevada, a man with the consumption took the small-pox from a negro, the cholera from a Chinaman, and the yellow fever and the erysipelas from other parties, and swallowed fifteen grains of strychnine and fell out of the third-story window and broke his neck. Verdict of the jury, "Died by the visitation of God."[120]

This collection reprints thirteen items from "People and Things," all of them paragraphs of more than usual length and development.[121]

A week after Clemens began his winter lecture tour of 1869–1870 he told his sister, Pamela, "They flood me with high-priced invitations to write for magazines and papers, and publishers besiege me to write books. Can't do *any* of these things."[122] Nevertheless, by January he had decided to write another book, was planning to bring out a new collection of sketches, and was thinking about his "Noah's Ark book," which would, he said, "be several years" in completion.[123] Later that year he began to get excited about a collaboration with J. H. Riley—a book about the South African diamond mines which was intended to "sweep the world like a besom of destruction."[124]

The overriding concern of this period turned out to be "the big California & Plains book."[125] In the *Express* for 16 October 1869 Clemens had published the first of his "Around the World" letters, six of which gave highlights of his Nevada and California days. Later sketches in the *Galaxy* also reverted to his western experiences, and on 15 July 1870 he and Bliss signed the contract for *Roughing It*. Certainly it is not surprising that with all these projects on hand his contributions to the *Express* tapered off. In a March 1870 letter to Olivia's parents he said, "I shall write one or two sketches a month for

---

[120]"People and Things," Buffalo *Express*, 18 August 1869, p. 2.

[121]Clemens' third responsibility on the *Express* was to write occasional editorials on current social and political questions. Sometimes he pooled his efforts with his co-editor, J. N. Larned, to produce "patch-work editorials" (Clemens to Olivia Langdon, 21 August 1869, *CL2*, letter 90). Editorials clearly identifiable as Clemens' work are scheduled to appear in the collection of social and political writings in The Works of Mark Twain.

[122]Clemens to Pamela Moffett, 9 November 1869, *CL2*, letter 116.

[123]Clemens to Bliss, 22 January 1870, *CL2*, letter 153.

[124]Clemens to Riley, 2 December 1870, *CL2*, letter 259.

[125]Clemens to Bliss, 24 January 1871, *CL3*, letter 10.

the Express, & I have an idea that for a good while I shall do nothing else on the paper."[126]

Early in March 1870 Clemens was approached by the proprietors of the *Galaxy* magazine to write a monthly column. On March 11 he wrote Bliss:

A first-class New York magazine wants me to edit a humorous department in it. They want ten pages a month. They offer twenty-four hundred dollars a year for the service, & then they want a publishing house there to have the privilege of issuing the matter in book form at the end of the year . . . & pay me a royalty of 20 cents on each copy sold. I have just written them that you would have to have a bid in the matter. I also wrote that I would do the editing only on condition that I *own* the matter after use in the magazine & have the privilege of doing just what I please with it. All this had better be kept still for the present.[127]

Apparently his offer was accepted, and the *Galaxy* "Memoranda" column became a major preoccupation for the rest of the year. William C. and Francis P. Church, the owners of the *Galaxy*, were trying to make it the leading literary journal of the middle Atlantic seaboard. They paid well for such writers as Henry James, Whitman, Trollope, and De Forest. On March 26 Clemens reported that he had signed the contract: "The berth is exceedingly easy & the salary liberal."[128] From May 1870 through April 1871, with the notable exception of two months when family troubles forced him to limit his contribution to a single sketch, Clemens packed his ten-page installments with fun making and satire, ranging in length from brief anecdotes to sustained sketches and tales.

Like all of his work at this time, the *Galaxy* pieces were written under the strain imposed by the illness and subsequent death of his wife's father on August 6, the death of Olivia's friend Emma Nye in the Clemens home on September 29, and the continuing illness of Olivia herself following the birth of their first child on November 7. Through all these domestic afflictions Clemens persisted as best he could. At first he valued the freedom and the prestige afforded by his *Galaxy* assignment. Soon, however, he found himself in "a terrible

[126]Clemens to Mr. and Mrs. Jervis Langdon, 27 March 1870, *CL2*, letter 178.
[127]Clemens to Bliss, 11 March 1870, *CL2*, letter 172.
[128]Clemens to Jane Clemens et al., 26 March 1870, *CL2*, letter 177.

whirl with Galaxy & book work,"[129] the more so as the pressure to
finish *Roughing It* increased. By mid-January 1871 he had decided to
"draw out of the Galaxy with the April No. & write no more for any
periodical—except, at long intervals a screed that I happened to dearly
want to write."[130] Two months later, when Orion and Bliss were
pressing him for contributions to Bliss's trade magazine, the *American
Publisher*, they elicited the following emphatic declaration:
"There isn't money enough between hell & Hartford to hire me to
write once a month for *any* periodical."[131] This aversion coincided
with a growing distaste for Buffalo (and presumably for his work on
the *Express*). On March 3 he told Riley, "I have come at last to loathe
Buffalo so bitterly (always hated it) that yesterday I advertised our
dwelling house for sale, & the man that comes forward & pays us
what it cost a year ago, ($25,000,) can take it. . . . I offer the Express
for sale also, & the man that will pay me $10,000 less than I gave can
take *that*." After reiterating his determination to "write no more for
any periodical," he added: "Shall simply write books."[132] On March
18, with Olivia "on a mattrass,"[133] he moved his family to Elmira,
leaving their Buffalo residence for the last time.

    Roughing It would soon become Mark Twain's sole literary pre-
occupation: he himself realized that he had come to the end of twenty
years of apprenticeship. In his penultimate contribution to the *Galaxy*
(April 1871) he published "My First Literary Venture" (no. 357),
justifying the sketch with these words: "As I shall write but little for
periodicals hereafter, it seems to fit in with a sort of inoffensive ap-
propriateness here, since it is a record of the first scribbling for any
sort of periodical I ever had the temerity to attempt."[134] To be sure,
Bliss coaxed a few sketches from him in July and September 1871 for
the *American Publisher*, but these were chiefly to gain advertising
for *Roughing It*.

    Like his work in California periodicals, many of Clemens' tales and
sketches in the *Express* and the *Galaxy* were topical, their kernel
found in the daily telegraphic news summaries and the newspaper

---

[129]Clemens to Mary Mason Fairbanks, 13 October 1870, *CL2*, letter 234.
[130]Clemens to Webb, 14 January 1871, *CL3*, letter 6.
[131]Clemens to Orion Clemens, 11 and 13 March 1871, *CL3*, letter 32.
[132]Clemens to Riley, 3 March 1871, *CL3*, letter 28.
[133]Clemens to Bliss, 17 March 1871, *CL3*, letter 38.
[134]"My First Literary Venture," *Galaxy*, p. 615.

exchanges. "A Comfortable Day's Work" (no. 250), for instance, embellished a newspaper item about the discovery of a large gold nugget in California. As he wrote to Olivia, he valued such components of his "People and Things" column because "they are excellent, as texts to string out a sketch from."[135] Similarly, many of his imaginative items in the *Galaxy* arose from his editorial reading: "The Judge's 'Spirited Woman' " (no. 300) derived from reports of the trial of Prince Pierre Napoleon Bonaparte. And "Human Nature" (no. 297) arose from an editorial in the Toronto *Globe* about a contemporary disaster at sea. Occasionally the topical element entered his imaginative construction in a more tangential way: "The Legend of the Capitoline Venus" (no. 272) is a "condensed novel" that grew out of rumors of the Cardiff Giant hoax, the author's memories of Rome from his *Quaker City* voyage, and deeply repressed feelings about his courtship of Olivia Langdon.

The *Express* and the *Galaxy* gave Clemens a forum in which to exercise his talents freely, whether he wished to comment tartly on a news event or write an extravagant burlesque. As a proprietor of the *Express* and sole editor of "Memoranda," Clemens enjoyed a degree of freedom greater than any he had achieved as a contributor to the *Californian* or even the *Enterprise*. When he signed on with the *Galaxy* he told Mrs. Fairbanks:

I just came to the conclusion that I would quit turning my attention to making money especially & go to writing for enjoyment as well as profit. I needed a *Magazine* wherein to shovel any fine-spun stuff that might accumulate in my head, & which isn't entirely suited to either a daily, Weekly, or *any* kind of newspaper. . . . I can make a *living* without any trouble, & still write *to suit myself*.[136]

He paid tribute to such friends as J. H. Riley and Henry Ward Beecher, and he obviously felt free to follow his satiric impulses—to attack the treatment of the Chinese in America ("Goldsmith's Friend Abroad Again," no. 326), for instance—something that had been forbidden to him on the *Call*. He castigated "The Meanest Railroad" (no. 242), and he ridiculed the reasoning of paleontologists ("A Brace of Brief Lectures on Science," no. 362) no less vigorously than he satirized

---

[135]Clemens to Olivia Langdon, 7 September 1869, *CL2*, letter 101.
[136]Clemens to Mary Mason Fairbanks, 22–24 March 1870, *CL2*, letter 176.

romantic ideas about the American Indian ("The Noble Red Man," no. 320). His contributions elicited letters of praise from many readers, including one who called him "a national benefactor,"[137] and another who deplored "the stilted sentiment of the time" that had stifled all humor "excepting Mr. Dickens' works . . . until your appearance in the Galaxy."[138]

Even this apparent freedom soon became hateful to Clemens, for although he was more or less unfettered in what he chose to write, he was obliged to write regularly and to meet weekly and monthly deadlines. Especially when these duties came in conflict with his desire to finish *Roughing It*, he rebelled and eventually cast off the obligations completely. Moreover, a number of sketches reprinted in these volumes indicate that he was growing dissatisfied with the institution of journalism itself. "A Protest" and "A Wail" (nos. 282 and 283), "The Editorial Office Bore" (no. 312), and "The 'Present' Nuisance" (no. 339) were all about various difficulties connected with his editorial role on the *Express*, and although he exaggerated for the sake of humor, the real abuses clearly rankled. A more serious matter was the way newspapers generated and perpetuated myths, which he attacked in "General Washington's Negro Body-Servant" and "Interviewing the Interviewer" (nos. 220 and 277). In other sketches he ridiculed the newspapers' confusion ("Where Governor Hoffman Is," no. 251), their inflamed rhetoric ("Journalism in Tennessee," no. 252), and their sensationalism ("The 'Wild Man' 'Interviewed,'" no. 259). His attitude was generally one of impatience with the profession and seems to reflect his ambition to rise above it.

On the other hand, much of what he wrote for the *Express* and *Galaxy* formed a valuable part of his apprentice work, and some of it survived to be incorporated into *Sketches, New and Old* and even *Roughing It*. He continued to develop a literary repertoire of extraordinary range: from the anecdote to the sustained humorous narrative, from the miniature essay to the ambitious set piece, and from explosive denunciations of specific abuses to burlesques of popular literary and journalistic forms as different as medieval romances and newspaper interviews. He also continued to experiment with various

---

[137]Laura E. Lyman to Clemens, 2 January 1871, MTP.
[138]A. C. Walker to Clemens, 23 August 1870, MTP.

poses for the character Mark Twain: the naive, romantic inquirer ("A Day at Niagara," no. 241); the sly poultry thief ("More Distinction," no. 307); and especially the hapless victim—whether of celebrating Englishmen, a lightning rod salesman, a barber, or a watch mechanism and the technicians who professed to regulate it. He experimented freely with other narrators too, such as the judge in "The Judge's 'Spirited Woman'" (no. 300) and the undertaker in "A Reminiscence of the Back Settlements" (no. 331). In several sketches he began to create a kind of comic mythology of his own childhood and to probe his immediate past in the West. He touched on several themes that would occupy his later work: intellectual pretentiousness, callousness toward one's fellow man, pride rooted in family or status, the problem of identity, and the uses of the vernacular character.

5. *"The Artifice of . . . Partial Incoherence."*   On 19 October 1875 William Dean Howells wrote to Clemens about his forthcoming review of *Sketches, New and Old:* "You can imagine the difficulty of noticing a book of short sketches," he apologized, "it's like noticing a library."[139] The 365 items collected in these volumes do indeed constitute a kind of library—one that records the humorist's development over a period of twenty years—and it is a library of immense variety that resists simple characterization. In part this difficulty arises from the sheer volume of Clemens' apprentice work. If, in addition to the pieces printed or reprinted here, one counts his early social and political commentary; his early theatrical, art, and literary criticism; his legislative reports in Nevada; his unsigned local news items and general commentary for the Virginia City *Territorial Enterprise,* the San Francisco *Morning Call,* and the San Francisco *Dramatic Chronicle;* his many travel letters, notably to the Sacramento *Union* and the San Francisco *Alta California;* his out-of-town correspondence to the *Enterprise,* the Chicago *Republican,* New York *Tribune,* and New York *Herald;* and the squibs to be found in the Hannibal *Journal* "Our Assistant's Column" and in the Buffalo *Express* "People and Things" as well as the brief items in the *Galaxy's* "Memoranda," the sheer number of words is staggering, and the number of separate

---

[139]Howells to Clemens, 19 October 1875, *MTHL,* 1:106.

pieces easily three or four thousand. Clearly, before 1871 Clemens found ample opportunity to indulge his well-known preference for the short forms and to experiment with them.

From first to last the apprentice writer was intimately involved with nineteenth-century journalism in a variety of capacities. He was type-setter, local reporter, out-of-town correspondent, free-lance and feature writer, contributing editor to the *Galaxy*, and owner-editor of the Buffalo *Express*. The compiler of "People and Things" on the *Express* read the exchanges as regularly as "Our Assistant Editor" had done many years earlier on the Hannibal *Journal*; and in those exchanges Clemens found basic models for the short forms he practiced and developed—and also burlesqued, taking aim, it sometimes seems, at every conceivable target. Whether he wrote an account of his descent into the Spanish mine for the *Enterprise*, a burlesque "Answers to Correspondents" for the *Californian*, an epigram for "People and Things," or a mellow reminiscence for the *Galaxy*, his writing re-veals a thorough familiarity with the preferred modes of nineteenth-century journalism and a readiness to appropriate all its resources. His approach was radically eclectic.

So was his imagination, which ranged widely to invent new and quite idiosyncratic forms of humorous expression, as may readily be seen even in his simplest local items. He freely combined disparate or incongruous elements to produce sketches that were entirely unpredictable—true originals. "Bob Roach's Plan for Circumventing a Democrat" (no. 124), for instance, somehow merges details of San Francisco election returns, a Mississippi River memory recast as a yarn, and oblique political satire into a thoroughly delightful but pointed whimsy. Similarly, when Clemens adopted the daily or weekly newspaper letter as a mode of expression, he followed the accepted custom of mingling news with gossipy commentary, but he improved upon this mode by introducing an informal chronicle of his own doings and thoughts—a kind of rambling personal narrative—and by incorporating brief tales, miniature essays, fantasies, burlesques, scathing denunciations, or any of these in combination.

Throughout his apprenticeship, in fact, Clemens deliberately mixed literary impulses with his journalistic tasks, and this was an unfailing source of novelty leading to unique effects and even entire sketches that still defy categorization except under the term of "humor." For example, an early *Californian* piece, "Whereas" (no. 94), joins a genteel, essaylike reflection on love with an extravagantly cynical burlesque of sentimental conventions. In "An Unbiased Criticism" (no. 100) a casually introduced parenthetical aside blossoms into a brilliant comic monologue by Simon Wheeler, and in the "biography" of "City Marshal Perry" (no. 49) the author's free association takes over and engulfs the rhetorical pattern that the reader has been led to expect. Such techniques remind us of Clemens' reliance on the appeal of variety, and they typically produce a coherence less formal than personal. At times the autobiographical impulse in this early work— whether it reflects Clemens' own character or one of his quirky alter egos—may so fully inform the piece that it seems to be governed only by unpredictable whim, sheer gaiety, or critical animus.

Clemens' better short works exert a special fascination, not only because when read in chronological order they demonstrate his considerable growth in craft, but also because they tell us a great deal about his rather mysterious and unpredictable mind. Their artistry lies—as his best readers have always felt—in the seeming ease with which he imposes fiction on reality, shapes incongruities into a unique coherence, or generates an indescribable effect, "doubling and turning upon itself" as Howells noted, "till you wonder why Mr. Clemens has ever been left out of the list of our *subtile* humorists."[140] Many of Clemens' best efforts resemble a one-man jam session in which he improvises dazzling solo performances on all the instruments.

This effect is pervasive in his tales, his sketches, and his oral performances. It was well recognized by his contemporaries as a characteristic of the man himself. Calvin Higbie, his Aurora mining partner, once described the way Clemens danced at a frontier ball:

In changing partners, whenever he saw a hand raised he would grasp it with great pleasure and sail off into another set, oblivious to his surroundings. Sometimes he would act as though there were no use in trying to go right or to dance like other people, and with his eyes closed he would do a hoe-down or a double-shuffle all alone, talking to himself and saying that he never dreamed there was so much pleasure to be obtained at a ball. It was all as natural as a child's play. By

---

[140]Review of *Sketches, New and Old, Atlantic Monthly* 36 (December 1875): 749–751, reprinted in *MTCH*, p. 52.

l set, all the ladies were falling over themselves to get him
_er, and most of the crowd, too full of mirth to dance, were
standing and sitting around, dying with laughter.[141]

Both Higbie and Paine were naive in thinking this sort of performance "as natural as a child's play," although one may suspect that the
art of appearing natural sprang from the deepest sources of Clemens'
personality. Edward H. House, who reviewed Clemens' Sandwich
Islands lecture in May 1867, was in some ways closer to the truth.
House wrote of his technique at that time:

The scheme of the lecturer appeared to be to employ the various
facts he had gathered as bases upon which to build fanciful illustrations of character, which were furthermore embellished with a multitude of fantastic anecdotes and personal reminiscences. The frequent
incongruities of the narration—evidently intentional—made it all
the more diverting, and the artifice of its partial incoherence was so
cleverly contrived as to intensify the amusement of the audience,
while leaving them for the most part in ignorance of the means
employed.[142]

This talent for controlled incoherence was, as House recognized, a
fundamental comic tool—one which Clemens cultivated throughout
the literary apprenticeship and which came to its first full flower in
The Innocents Abroad. Howells said of that book that "almost any
topic, and any event of the author's past life, he finds pertinent to the
story of European and Oriental travel, and if the reader finds it imper-
tinent, he does not find it the less amusing. The effect is dependent
in so great degree upon this continuous incoherence, that no chosen
passage can illustrate the spirit of the whole."[143] It is in the light of
Clemens' preoccupation with journalism and with developing this
disarming comic technique that the early short works are best appreciated. These interests led Clemens to disregard most traditional
genres—except to burlesque them—and they made his work difficult
to categorize, even for contemporaries. His early work is almost always
surprising and delightful—but it is also impossible to divide into neat
and precise generic divisions. For an effective narrative from his pen
might yield political implications, and an article aimed at exposing

---

[141]Quoted in *MTB*, 1:195.

[142]"Mark Twain as a Lecturer," New York *Tribune*, 11 May 1867, p. 2.

[143]Review of *The Innocents Abroad*, *Atlantic Monthly* 24 (December 1869): 764–
766, reprinted in *MTCH*, p. 30.

social or journalistic abuse might employ an amusing literary sketch. Skillful analysis of plodding or humorless writing might balloon unexpectedly into fantasy, and of course the travel letter could always include anything and in any order. The selections collected in these volumes offer the chance to study that eclecticism, that growing technique in the earliest years of Mark Twain's development as a writer.

E.M.B.
September 1977

Miami University

SECTION 1

Hannibal and the River

1851-1861

1. A Gallant Fireman

16 January 1851

"A Gallant Fireman" is "the first known venture of Sam Clemens into print."[1] It is a brief anecdote that appeared in his brother Orion Clemens' Hannibal *Western Union* not long after Clemens had joined its staff subsequent to his apprenticeship on Joseph P. Ament's Hannibal *Missouri Courier*. The "fireman" of the brief sketch is Jim Wolf (or Wolfe), an apprentice printer in Orion's shop. For a while Jim roomed and boarded at the Clemens home, where he became a favorite target for the practical jokes of Clemens and his brother Henry. He is also the subject of Clemens' 1867 sketch "Jim Wolf and the Tom-Cats" (no. 212).

In the early morning of 9 January 1851 a fire broke out in A. C. Parker's family grocery store next door to Orion's printing office. Discovered "by the hands of this office, while returning home from their 'nightly labor,'"[2] the fire was quickly extinguished, but not before Jim had removed some utensils from the endangered print shop. More than half a century later Clemens described the then lost sketch to Albert Bigelow Paine, remembering that "Jim in his excitement had carried the office broom half a mile and had then come back after the wash-pan"[3]—a surprisingly accurate recollection of the "precious burden" Jim had rescued from the shop.

---

[1]*SCH*, p. 236.
[2]Hannibal *Western Union*, 16 January 1851, p. 3.
[3]*MTB*, 1:92.

A Gallant Fireman

At the fire, on Thursday morning, we were apprehensive of our own safety, (being only one door from the building on fire) and commenced arranging our material in order to remove them in case of necessity. Our gallant *devil*, seeing us somewhat excited, concluded he would perform a noble deed, and immediately gathered the broom, an old mallet, the wash-pan and a dirty towel, and in a fit of patriotic excitement, rushed out of the office and deposited his precious burden some ten squares off, out of danger. Being of a *snailish* disposition, even in his quickest moments, the fire had been extinguished during his absence. He returned in the course of an hour, nearly out of breath, and thinking he had immortalized himself, threw his giant frame in a tragic attitude, and exclaimed, with an eloquent expression: "If that thar fire hadn't bin put out, thar'd a' bin the greatest *confirmation* of the age!"

2. The Dandy Frightening the Squatter

1 May 1852

"The Dandy Frightening the Squatter," Clemens' first humorous tale of moderate length, was published in the Boston *Carpet-Bag* with the by-line "S.L.C." Very possibly it is one of the two pieces that Clemens mistakenly remembered having contributed to the Philadelphia *Saturday Evening Post* early "in 1851."[1] Like much of his later apprentice writing, it appeared in a weekly newspaper that catered to popular forms of comic literature. "Its material," Bernard DeVoto remarked, "is the characteristic frontier life of Hannibal. It is typical of the newspaper humor of the South and Southwest."[2] Exactly how typical is suggested by the analogues and similar themes scholars have discovered in contemporary American humorous tales. Although the writing of the sixteen-year-old author is at times understandably amateurish, the tale nevertheless begins to focus on much that proved essential to his most successful fiction.[3]

---

[1] *MTB*, 1:90.

[2] *MTAm*, p. 91.

[3] For additional discussion of the tale and its literary background, see Walter Blair, *Native American Humor (1800–1900)* (New York: American Book Company, 1937), p. 154 and *passim*; *LAMT*, pp. 7–10; *MTAm*, pp. 90–91, 244; Franklin J. Meine, introduction to *Tall Tales of the Southwest* (New York: Alfred A. Knopf, 1930), pp. xxx–xxxi, and foreword to *Mark Twain's First Story* (Iowa City: The Prairie Press, 1952), pp. 3–14.

The Dandy Frightening the Squatter

ABOUT THIRTEEN years ago, when the now flourishing young city of Hannibal, on the Mississippi River, was but a "wood-yard," surrounded by a few huts, belonging to some hardy "*squatters*," and such a thing as a steamboat was considered quite a sight, the following incident occurred:

A tall, brawny woodsman stood leaning against a tree which stood upon the bank of the river, gazing at some approaching object, which our readers would easily have discovered to be a steamboat.

About half an hour elapsed, and the boat was moored, and the hands busily engaged in taking on wood.

Now among the many passengers on this boat, both male and female, was a spruce young dandy, with a killing moustache, &c., who seemed bent on making an impression upon the hearts of the young ladies on board, and to do this, he thought he must perform some heroic deed. Observing our squatter friend, he imagined this to be a fine opportunity to bring himself into notice; so, stepping into the cabin, he said:

"Ladies, if you wish to enjoy a good laugh, step out on the guards. I intend to frighten that gentleman into fits who stands on the bank."

The ladies complied with the request, and our dandy drew from his bosom a formidable looking bowie-knife, and thrust it into his belt; then, taking a large horse-pistol in each hand, he seemed satisfied that all was right. Thus equipped, he strode on shore, with an air which seemed to say—"The hopes of a nation depend on me." Marching up to the woodsman, he exclaimed:

"Found you at last, have I? You are the very man I've been looking
for these three weeks! Say your prayers!" he continued, presenting his
pistols, "you'll make a capital barn door, and I shall drill the key-hole
myself!"

The squatter calmly surveyed him a moment, and then, drawing
back a step, he planted his huge fist directly between the eyes of his
astonished antagonist, who, in a moment, was floundering in the
turbid waters of the Mississippi.

Every passenger on the boat had by this time collected on the guards,
and the shout that now went up from the crowd speedily restored the
crest-fallen hero to his senses, and, as he was sneaking off towards the
boat, was thus accosted by his conqueror:

"I say, yeou, next time yeou come around drillin' key-holes, don't
forget yer old acquaintances!"

The ladies unanimously voted the knife and pistols to the victor.

3. *Hannibal, Missouri*

8 May 1852

This highly selective sketch of Clemens' home town, dated 25 March 1852 and signed "S. L. C.," appeared in the Philadelphia *American Courier* exactly one week after the publication of "The Dandy Frightening the Squatter" (no. 2).[1] It may well be the second piece that the author, as an old man, believed he had contributed to the Philadelphia *Saturday Evening Post* nearly sixty years earlier.[2] Published as "Original Correspondence" in a regular column called "The Topographist," the sketch foreshadowed a large body of newspaper writing Clemens produced during the succeeding two decades. Like "The Dandy," it was carefully constructed. Hannibal is "located" with reference to its Indian past, its commercial enterprise, eastern attitudes, and its greatest natural wonder, the cave. The author's evocation in the opening paragraph of the vanished "children of the forest" (the kind of sentiment he would gleefully burlesque within ten years) is balanced by his vignette of the civilized easterner. The writing of the youthful correspondent already reveals what proved to be his constitutional drift away from mere factual reporting and toward imaginative invention and the human drama.

---

[1] In 1967 it was reprinted in photofacsimile by the Antiquarian Booksellers Association of America, with an introduction by Roger Butterfield.

[2] *MTB*, 1:90.

Hannibal, Missouri

DEAR COURIER—

The first house was built in this city about sixteen years ago. Then the wild war-whoop of the Indian resounded where now rise our stately buildings, and their bark canoes were moored where now land our noble steamers; here they traded their skins for guns, powder, &c. But where now are the children of the forest? Hushed is the war-cry—no more does the light canoe cut the crystal waters of the proud Mississippi; but the remnant of those once powerful tribes are torn asunder and scattered abroad, and they now wander far, far from the homes of their childhood and the graves of their fathers.

This town is situated on the Mississippi river, about one hundred and thirty miles above St. Louis, and contains a population of about three thousand. A charter has been granted by the State for a railroad, to commence at Hannibal, and terminate at St. Joseph, on the western border of Missouri. The State takes $1,500,000 of stock in the road; the counties along the route have also subscribed liberally, and already more than one-third the amount requisite for its construction has been subscribed. The manner in which the State takes stock is this: for every $50,000 that the company spends in the construction of the road, the State gives her bonds for that amount, until the $1,500,000 is paid.

Within this year a plank-road will be built from Hannibal to New London, a small town in the adjoining county of Ralls, and about twelve miles from here. Every dollar of stock in this improvement has already been subscribed.

Your Eastern people seem to think this country is a barren, uncultivated region, with a population consisting of heathens. A man came out here from your part of the world, and in writing home to his friends, made the following remark:—"This is the queerest country I ever saw; a little cloud will come up, about as big as your hat, and directly a clap of thunder will knock the bottom out of it, and, Jerusalem! how it 'ill rain!"

Among the curiosities of this place we may mention the *Cave,* which is about three miles below the city. It is of unknown length; it has innumerable passages, which are not unlike the streets of a large city. The ceiling arches over, and from it hang beautiful stalactites, which sparkle in the light of the torches, and remind one of the fairy palaces spoken of in the Arabian Nights. There are several springs, rivers, and wells, some of which are of unknown depth. Directly over one of the narrow passages, and supported merely by two small pieces of stone, which jut out from the main walls on either side, hangs an immense rock, end down, which measures ten feet in length by three feet in diameter.

Yours, &c.,

S. L. C.

HANNIBAL, MO., March 25, 1852.

4. A Family Muss

9 September 1852

"A Family Muss," by "W. Epaminondas Adrastus Perkins," is the earliest substantial piece of writing in Orion's Hannibal *Journal* which can be confidently attributed to Clemens. One week after its publication the young subeditor altered "Perkins" to "Blab" and, with his brother safely distant in St. Louis, filled several columns of the *Journal* with his creative efforts. "A Family Muss" is altogether more modest than those later sketches by Blab. Its routine subject called for no more than a local item of a few lines, but the young reporter dressed up his information in the garb of a narrative and festooned it with comic Irish dialect. Thus "A Family Muss" affords a preview—as do "The Dandy" (no. 2) and "Hannibal, Missouri" (no. 3) in their different ways—of the fictionalizing that the journalist Clemens would often practice in Nevada and California.

A Family Muss

On the side of "Holliday's Hill" there is a small house, occupied by an indefinite number of very large families, chiefly composed of Dutch, Irish, Scotch, Americans, English, &c. The paternal head of one of these families took it into his head on Tuesday, to take holyday, and with this laudable intention, he left his work at an early hour in the day, and depositing a large "brick" carefully in his hat, he cleared for his "highland home." After arriving without damage at his journey's end, the idea struck him that he was very much in want of exercise; and that the said house full of humanity, was in the same fix, so, procuring himself a good stout cudgel, he commenced thumping the heads of his astounded neighbors promiscuously; and the way the gentleman made the "furriners" fly around was decidedly amusing. After diverting himself in this manner until he felt that his health was greatly improved, and also feeling somewhat fatigued from his patriotic exertions, he came down in town to rest himself.

When he thought his limbs sufficiently recruited, he laid in another "brick," and about supper time, returned to the scene of his labors. This time, he commenced on his wife, and after administering to her a sound beating, he took his stick and leveled a fellow lodger, and while waiting for the fallen gentleman to regain his perpendicular, he was amusing himself by tapping over the women and children, when Marshal Hawkins "grabbed" the unlucky offender, and marched him off to the Calaboose, and one of his female victims, groaning under the effects of his harsh discipline, expressed it as her wish that—

"If yees iver git 'im thar, I hope ye'll hould 'im tight. Och! he's the dreadfulest man I *iver* see. Oh, me, I'se scairt to death, I is, an' I'll niver git over it in the worl'. Och'! the bloody divil!"—

We managed to hear that much above the din that assailed our ears on every side. We then decamped. The above is a *"striking"* example of what a man can do, when he's "half seas over."

Yours,
W. Epaminondas Adrastus Perkins.

[THE DOG CONTROVERSY]

§ 5. *"Local" Resolves to Commit Suicide*

16 September 1852

§ 6. *"Pictur'" Department*

23 September 1852

These two sketches were installments in the first of Clemens' journalistic "feuds" and were made possible by Orion's absence in Tennessee. They appeared in two successive issues of the September 1852 Hannibal *Journal* (a weekly): "'Local' Resolves to Commit Suicide" on September 16, and "'Pictur'' Department" one week later.

Writing as "A Dog-bedeviled citizen" Orion had apparently complained about the noise of stray barking dogs sometime in mid-August 1852. His complaint had been answered by J. T. Hinton, the "local" for the Hannibal *Tri-Weekly Messenger* and a town newcomer, on August 24:

A fierce hater of the canine race pours out his vials of wrath, as if to add a fresh stimulus to our worthy dog-exterminator, whose active exertions have already silenced the plaintive wail and mournful howl of many a pugnacious cur and ferocious mastiff. "A Dog-bedeviled citizen" must surely be a man of nervous temperament, else why so pitiful a dirge over an annoyance to which a long familiarity has made us accustomed. . . . To men of such extreme sensibility as the writer in question, barks-canine naturally prove annoying, but to those composed of firmer materials they only prove a source of solace, giving to them security during their midnight slumbers. The faithful watch-dogs deter miscreants from making inroads upon the property of our citizens, then surely, if music be their humor, they may be permitted to engage in vocal concerts, leaving it to the option of nervous gentlemen to place cotton in their ears, ere they retire to their pillows.[1]

Orion evidently declined to answer this sarcastic notice, but when Clemens was left in charge of the paper he boldly took up the challenge as a pretext

---

[1] "Two 'Richmond's in the Field!'—Any Chance for a 'Richard?' " Hannibal *Tri-Weekly Messenger*, 24 August 1852, PH from Yale.

for his satiric attack on Hinton. The real occasion for the satire, at least as Clemens remembered it almost twenty years later, was Hinton's attempt to commit suicide by drowning himself in Bear Creek because he had been jilted. According to Clemens, the attempt failed when the love-stricken editor changed his mind and waded ashore: "The village was full of it for several days, but Hinton did not suspect it."[2]

Clemens, perhaps taking his cue from a recent issue of the Boston *Carpet-Bag* containing a cartoon of a man wading in a stream with his "pocket pistol" showing, illustrated his first sketch with a crude but quite intelligible picture of "Local," walking stick and lantern in hand, cautiously wading into Bear Creek. To mock Hinton's defense of "barks-canine" Clemens drew him with the head of a dog. Hinton's response to this rather personal assault was to be outraged and at least momentarily vengeful: "This newly arisen 'Ned Buntline,'" he warned, "shall be paid in his own coin, even if we incur the risk of being set down as a sap-head for taking notice of a writer who has not the decency of a gentleman, nor the honor of a blackguard; yet, as he has attempted to turn the laugh against us by caricature, we will retaliate, basing our likeness, however, upon, at least, a semblance of the truth."[3] Two days later, perhaps realizing the youth of his opponent, he thought better of his threat:

PERSONAL.—Not desiring to carry on a personal controversy of so low and contemptible a nature as "A Dog-be-deviled Citizen" has clearly convinced the community is his own natural element, we have given over our intention of adding to the correspondent's disgrace by exhibiting him in his true light through the means of wood cuts. Such controversies are adapted only to those whose ideas are of so obscene and despicable an order as to forever bar them against a gentlemanly or even decent discussion, either in conversation or with the pen; and we have too much respect for ourself, and the paper with which we are connected, to ever be guilty of any act that might place us on an equality with a writer of this character.
In justice to the Editor of the Journal, we would take this occasion to remark, that we believe him innocent of intentionally doing us an injury, and absolve him from all censure.[4]

Clemens' response to this diatribe was to publish "'Pictur'' Department," which he embellished with two additional, equally crude portraits of "Local."[5]

---

[2]"My First Literary Venture" (no. 357), first published in the *Galaxy* 11 (April 1871): 615.

[3]"Lo! He's Howled Again," Hannibal *Tri-Weekly Messenger*, 16 September 1852, PH from Yale.

[4]"Personal," Hannibal *Tri-Weekly Messenger*, 18 September 1852, PH from Yale.

[5]Clemens recalled that he had made the "villainous cuts" by engraving "the bottoms of wooden type with a jack-knife" ("My First Literary Venture," *Galaxy*, p. 615).

In 1871 Clemens recalled that the object of his ridicule "threw up his situation that night and left town for good."[6] This is an exaggeration, but it is apparent that Hinton took the whole matter rather seriously—even though he knew that the "Editor" (that is, Orion) was not responsible. In the same issue that carried " 'Pictur'' Department" (September 23) Orion tried to smooth over hurt feelings: "The jokes of our correspondent have been rather rough; but originating and perpetrated in a spirit of fun, and without a serious thought, no attention was expected to be paid to them, beyond a smile at the local editor's expense."[7] Hinton was not easily mollified, however, and could not forbear further comment that evening:

☞ We have but a few words to say in reference to the picture gallery furnished in the Journal of this morning. The author, throughout the entire piece, displays an amount of egotism, that is a universal characteristic of all blackguards—they depend upon gross and insipid personalities to gain that which they could not do in a respectable or decent manner; and they have not the manliness to make a direct assertion, but deal in implication, so that they may have a loop-hole through which to escape, if things should take a more serious turn than they desire.

"Thinks it best to stop the controversy!" well that [is] impudence of the first order! We never have nor never will stoop to a controversy of so contemptible a nature as is 'A-dog-bedeviled-citizen's' delight, and if he sees fit to swallow the truth in such warm doses as we have given it, we shall not object, and shall pass his illustrations by as the feeble eminations of a puppy's brain.[8]

Although Hinton appears to have the last word, it is certainly clear that the sixteen-year-old "puppy" emerged from the scuffle victorious. The extraordinary gift of satire which these pieces manifest, and the energy of the response they elicited, remind us that the apprentice author would eventually find other, bitterer feuds to fight in the newspapers.[9]

---

[6]"My First Literary Venture," *Galaxy*, p. 616.

[7]"The Dog Controversy," Hannibal *Journal*, 23 September 1852, p. 2.

[8]From the column "Miscellaneous Matters," Hannibal *Tri-Weekly Messenger*, 23 September 1852, PH from Yale.

[9]For further discussion of Clemens' controversy with Hinton, see *MTSM*, pp. 109–116, and *SCH*, pp. 249–251.

"Local" Resolves
to Commit Suicide

'LOCAL,' disconsolate from receiving no further notice from 'A DOG-BE-DEVILED CITIZEN,' contemplates Suicide. His 'pocket-pistol' (i. e. the *bottle*,) failing in the patriotic work of ridding the country of a nuisance, he resolves to 'extinguish his chunk' by feeding his carcass to the fishes of Bear Creek, while friend and foe are wrapt in sleep. Fearing, however, that he may get out of his depth, he *sounds the stream with his walking-stick.*

The artist has, you will perceive, Mr. Editor, caught the gentleman's countenance as correctly as the thing could have been done with the real *dog*-gerytype apparatus. Ain't he pretty? and don't he step along through the mud with an air? 'Peace to his *re*-manes.'

'A DOG-BE-DEVILED CITIZEN.'

"Pictur'" Department

"LOCAL" discovers something interesting in the *Journal,* and becomes excited.

["LOCAL," determined upon the destruction of the great enemy of the canine race, charters an old swivel (a six pounder) and declares war. *Lead* being scarce, he loads his cannon with *Tri-Weekly Messengers.*]

"LOCAL" is somewhat astonished at the effect of the discharge, and is under the impression that there was something the matter with the apparatus—thinks the hole must have been drilled in the wrong end of the artillery. He finds, however, that although he missed the "DOG-BE-DEVILED CITIZEN,"* he nevertheless hit the man "who has not the decency of a gentleman nor the honor of a blackguard," and thinks it best to stop the controversy.

———————————

MR. EDITOR:

I have now dropped this farce, and all attempts to again call me forth will be useless.

A DOG-BE-DEVILED CITIZEN.

———————

*Who walks quietly away, in the distance, uninjured.

7. *Historical Exhibition—A No. 1 Ruse*

16 September 1852

"Historical Exhibition" is one of three features written by "W. Epaminondas Adrastus Blab" for the Hannibal *Journal* of 16 September 1852, the issue that Clemens edited in his brother's absence.[1]

No doubt the most famous "sell" described in Clemens' writings is "The King's Camelopard or the Royal Nonesuch," performed by the king and the duke in Bricksville, Arkansas (chapter 23 of *Huckleberry Finn*). By comparison, the youthful "Historical Exhibition" is a diffuse and mannered tale. Like the Royal Nonesuch, to which "ladies and children" were not admitted, Abram Curts's exhibition attracts the young and curious by offering something vaguely sexual: the "bony part" crossing the rind is typical country-store phallic humor. But the handling of the tale is somewhat unsure, and the ending flat, probably because Jim's embarrassment and Curts's gloating are drawn out a little too long.

Nevertheless, the tale is evidence of Clemens' early impulse to write realistic fiction. It is his initial attempt to draw individualized characters, rather than stereotypes like the Dandy, and the yarn it tells is obviously based foursquare on a local event and real people. Curts, who dodges responsibility for the "sell" with all the agility of Flem Snopes in Faulkner's *The Hamlet*, was a partner in the dry goods and grocery firm of Curts and Lockwood, and a perennial candidate for city marshal of Hannibal.[2] "Jim C——" may have been Clemens' Hannibal friend James H. Collins, whose name is recorded in Clemens' 1855 notebook and also appears, as does Clemens', on the roster of the Hannibal Cadets of Temperance compiled about 1850.[3]

---

[1] The two others—"Editorial Agility" and "Blabbing Government Secrets!"—are scheduled to appear in the collection of social and political writings in The Works of Mark Twain. The latter is reprinted in *MTSM*, pp. 117–118.

[2] *LAMT*, p. 273 n. 21.

[3] *N&J1*, p. 33.

Historical Exhibition—
A No. 1 Ruse

A YOUNG FRIEND gives me the following yarn as fact, and if it should turn out to be a double joke, (that is, that he imagined the story to fool me with,) on his own head be the blame:

It seems that the news had been pretty extensively circulated, that Mr. Curts, of the enterprising firm of Curts & Lockwood, was exhibiting at their store, for the benefit of the natives, a show of some kind, bearing the attractive title of "Bonaparte crossing the Rhine," upon which he was to deliver a lecture, explaining its points, and giving the history of the piece, the price being "one dime per head, children half price." Well, the other day about dusk, a young man went in, paid his dime, "saw the elephant," and departed, apparently "with a flea in his ear," but the uninitiated could get nothing out of him on the subject; he was mum—had seen the varmint, and that was the full extent of the information which could be pumped out of him by his enquiring friends.

Well, everybody who saw the sight seemed seized with a sudden fit of melancholy immediately afterwards, and dimes began to grow scarce. But pretty soon Jim C——, with a crowd of eager boys at his heels, was seen coming down the street like half a dozen telegraphs. They arrived at the store, gasping and out of breath, and Jim broke out with:

"Mr. Curts—want—to see—that—show! What's—price!"

"Oh, we let boys see it at half price—hand out your five cents."

Jim had got done blowing by this time, and threw down his money in as great a hurry as if life and death depended upon the speed of his movements, saying:

"Quick! Mr. Curts, I want to see it the worst kind."

"Yes, Oh yes; you want to see 'Bonaparte crossing the Rhine,' do you," said Abram, very deliberately.

"Yes, that's it—that's what I want to see," said Jim, who was so anxious to see the show that he could scarcely stand still.

"Well, you shall see it," said the worthy exhibitor, with a wise look, at the same time dropping the five cents into the money drawer, "and I hope by this show to impress upon your young minds, this valuable piece of history, and illustrate the same in so plain a manner that the silliest lad amongst you will readily comprehend it."

The juvenile audience was now breathless with expectation, and crowded around with eager looks, and not the slightest movement on the part of the learned lecturer was overlooked by them, as he drew from a drawer a piece of bone about three inches long, and holding it up before the wondering boys, he slowly and deliberately commenced his lecture, or explanation:

"My young friends, you now perceive——"

"Yes sir," interrupted Jim with mouth, eyes and ears wide open.

"As I was saying," continued Mr. Curts, "you now see before you the 'Bonaparte'—the 'Bony-part,' you understand, the 'bony part' of a hog's leg (house shakes with laughter from the crowd which had now assembled, but Jim did not join in the general merriment, but looked very sober, seeming to think there was very little about it to laugh at, at least on his side) yes, boys," said Abram, as grave and solemn as a judge about to pass sentence, "this is the bony-part of a hog's leg."

"Is-is a-a-that all!" gasped poor Jim, beginning to look blue about the gills.

"Oh no," said the lecturer, "this is merely a part of the exhibition," and he took from a shelf a piece of meat skin about as large as a piece of paper i. e. the size of a dollar bill, and presenting it to view he proceeded with the lecture.

"Now, my young hearers, this you see is the 'Rhine'—yes," he continued, as solemnly as before, "this is the 'Rhine,'—properly speaking, the hog's rind—a piece of hog's rind."

When the laugh had subsided, Mr. C. again went on with the explanation:

"Now, young gentlemen, draw near and give me your attention a moment, for this is the most interesting part of the exhibition," and old Abram looked and spoke, if possible, still more wise and solemn than before; then slowly passing the piece of bone back and forth across the skin, he said, "you see, boys this is the 'bony part crossing the rind,' very lucidly explained—yes, (drawing his bone across again with the most imperturbable gravity imaginable, amid the roars of laughter) this sir, is, I may be allowed to say, a *very* apt illustration of that noted event in history, 'Napoleon crossing the Rhine.' You have now learned a valuable lesson——"

"Yes!" broke in Jim "I have that, but it's the last one you'll ever learn me—(laughter) you're nothing but an old swindler, anyhow—(renewed laughter, which somewhat riled our hero) yes, this is a swindling shop and a swindling show, and you don't do nothing but swindle people."

The laugh now became so universal, that poor Jim had to force a laugh and a "don't care" look, as he continued:

"I don't care, laugh, jest as much as you please—I ain't particular about the money, nohow; I know'd it was a swindle, 'fore I come down (a piece of knowledge which Jim, in the excitement had before unfortunately forgotten that he ever possessed,) yes I knowed it, and I jest come down for devilment—but I don't care, you can keep the money, I ain't particular about it (Jim seemed particularly anxious to impress this important fact upon the mind of the lecturer)—cause I know you need it worse'n I do, when you can swindle a feller out of it that way."

The crowd now laughed till they were completely exhausted, and Jim's face slowly relaxed from the ludicrous expression it had worn for a time. He now looked as if he had been suddenly bereft of every relation he had in the world—his face became lengthened to an alarming extent, and upon the said countenance the most woe-begone look settled, mingled with a most "sheep-stealing" expression; he was now in a profound reverie, seemingly entirely unconscious of the jeers cast at him by the company. But Abram now broke in upon his meditations, and although he too had been enjoying his joke with a hearty laugh, he immediately assumed his former solemn look and grave tone, and thus addressed the cheap-looking "seeker after knowledge under difficulties."

"Young man, you have now learned an important historical lesson, and are no doubt well pleased with it. I am anxious, however —ahem!—I am anxious, as I before remarked, that you should be entirely satisfied with the exhibition—if you did not understand it in its minutest details—if the illustration was not sufficiently lucid, and everything has not been exhibited to your entire satisfaction, I beg of you, my friend, to make it known; and if it has met with favor in your eyes, I shall hold myself under the greatest of obligations, (with a profound bow,) if you will use your influence in forwarding the cause of learning and knowledge, (another bow,) by inviting your friends to step in when they pass this way. What, may I ask, is your opinion of the exhibition?"

Poor Jim! He seemed not to have heard a word that had been spoken; but, with his eyes bent steadfastly upon some object that wasn't there, he moved not a muscle for the space of a minute, when, opening his lips, he slowly ejaculated the few, but significant words "Sold!—cheap- -as- -dirt!"

And striding out of the house he marched down the street in a profound fit of mental abstraction.

Since the above occurrence, if any one speaks to Jim, or asks him a question, he merely mutters "Bonaparte crossing—sold!"

Mr. Curts told one of Jim's companions to say to him, that his exhibition was merely an agency—that a noted wholesale firm of this city were the proprietors of the concern, that the apparatus belonged to them, that if Jim did not think his money well spent, they would in all probability refund it—but that being himself merely an agent, he did not feel authorized to do so.

                               W. Epaminondas Adrastus Blab.

8. [Blab's Tour]

23 September 1852

In this letter, published in the Hannibal *Journal*, "W. Epaminondas Adrastus Blab" announced his final appearance in that newspaper. Glasscock's Island, in the Mississippi River across from the mouth of Bear Creek, became "Jackson's Island" in *Tom Sawyer* and *Huckleberry Finn*.

[Blab's Tour]

MR. EDITOR:

I believe it is customary, nowadays, for a man, as soon as he gets his name up, to take a "furrin" tour, for the benefit of his health; or, if his health is good, he goes without any excuse at all. Now, I think my health was sufficiently injured by last week's efforts, to justify me in starting on my tour; and, ere your hebdomadal is published, I shall be on my way to another country—yes, Mr. Editor, I have retired from public life to the shades of Glasscock's Island!—and I shall gratify such of your readers as have never been so far from home, with an account of this great island, and my voyage thither.

W. EPAMINONDAS ADRASTUS BLAB, Esq.

9. *"Connubial Bliss"*

4 November 1852

This sketch was published in the Hannibal *Journal;* its last sentence is taken as sufficient evidence of Clemens' authorship. Like "A Family Muss" (no. 4), the piece springs from the rowdy actions of an Irishman living on Holliday's Hill. But this time the former Cadet of Temperance prefaces his report with a miniature moralistic essay on "the bloated, reeling drunkard," in a manner, as Dixon Wecter wrote, "to win approval from that cold-water crusader Orion."[1]

---

[1]*SCH*, p. 253.

"Connubial Bliss"

Wʜᴀᴛ ᴀ ᴡᴏʀʟᴅ of trouble those who never marry escape! There are many happy matches, it is true, and sometimes "my dear," and "my love" come from the heart; but what sensible bachelor, rejoicing in his freedom and years of discretion, will run the tremendous risk?

Preachers of temperance do not look for warning examples among moderate drinkers; but they point to the bloated, reeling drunkard; he who sleeps in the gutter at night, and cannot tell to-day, where his crust of bread is to come from to-morrow; who is a reproach to his relations; a terror to his family; a fugitive from the post given him by God in this life, a hastener to his grave, flying to the "ills we know not of;" relentlessly, mercilessly pursued, in sight of his last resting place, by serpents, and by horrid monsters in every shape, created and living in his own fiery imagination—imaginary, fancied and unreal to all else—to him a terrible reality. Temperance men point to examples such as these, and say beware! beware!! beware!!! lest you come to *that*. So we pass by the lesser squabbles of married life, and hold up to view an example of an extreme case of matrimony.

A squalid family living on the side of 'Holliday's Hill' is under the 'protection' of a big fellow who once in a while, say about every afternoon, gets drunk and "cuts up" considerably. Sometimes he gathers the baby and goes staggering and stumbling and pitching about over the hill, to the great dismay of his wife. Having amused himself in this manner till tired, he lays down the child, and "lams" its mama; and if the unwashed, tow-headed boarder, who stands by with his hands in his pockets, offers to interfere he "lams" him too. Within a few days past, his amusements of this sort have been charmingly varied:—such as taking sheets and dresses from the clothes line, and tearing them into ribbons; smashing up the cooking stove; throwing a brick at his wife's head, and chasing her around the house with a ten foot pole. Quite a contrast, doubtless the poor woman thinks, when her mind wanders back to the courtship and the "honey-moon!" Well, we are all subject to change—except printers; they never have any spare *change*.

10. The Heart's Lament

5 May 1853

Almost two months after Orion began the Hannibal *Daily Journal* in conjunction with the *Weekly Journal*, Clemens reappeared as "Rambler"—first a reporter of local events and then a poet. "The Heart's Lament" was written for the *Daily Journal* and was dedicated to "Bettie W———e, of Tennessee," who has not been identified. It is the first of three utterly conventional sentimental love poems by Rambler to appear in the Hannibal newspapers within one week. They suggest an acquaintance with Thomas Moore's love songs and ballads or other poems in a similar vein.

The Heart's Lament

TO BETTIE W————E, OF TENNESSEE.

I know thou wilt forget me,
   For that fond soul of thine
Turns boldly from the passionate,
   And ardent love of mine.
It may be, that thou deemest it
   A light and simple thing,
To strike with bold and nervous arm,
   The heart's lone mystic string.

Thou wilt not deign to hear the strain,
   Thy own dear hand hath woke;
It matters not if ne'er to thee
   Its troubling echoes broke.
I know—ay, well, thou wilt forget
   I ever dreamed of thee;
Thou lovest not, thou carest not,
   My fettered soul to free.

Tho' gay and gifted crowd thee around,
   The beautiful are thine—
Then how canst thou, Oh! lofty one,
   Kneel at a lonely shrine?

I ask it not; Oh, never more
    My soul's cry shalt thou hear—
My heart shall learn in bitterness,
    To hide its love so dear.

RAMBLER.

§ 11. *Love Concealed*

6 May 1853

§ 12. *[First Letter from Grumbler]*

7 May 1853

§ 13. *[First Letter from Rambler]*

9 May 1853

§ 14. *To Rambler*

10 May 1853

§ 15. *[Letter from Peter Pencilcase's Son,
John Snooks]*

12 May 1853

§ 16. *[Second Letter from Rambler]*

13 May 1853

[THE "KATIE OF H———L" CONTROVERSY]

Clemens himself recounted the story of "The 'Katie of H———l' Controversy" in April 1871 in "My First Literary Venture" (no. 357). This piece conflated his experiences in 1852 and 1853 on Orion's Hannibal *Journal*, but the portion of his remarks that applies to these six items—published in the *Daily Journal* on 6, 7, 9, 10, 12, and 13 May 1853—deserves to be quoted here:

> Next I gently touched up the newest stranger—the lion of the day, the gorgeous journeyman tailor from Quincy. He was a simpering coxcomb of the first water and the "loudest" dressed man in the State. He was an inveterate woman-killer. Every week he wrote lushy "poetry" for the "Journal" about his newest conquest. His rhymes for my week were headed "To MARY IN H—L," meaning to Mary in Hannibal, of course. But while setting up the piece I was suddenly riven from head to heel by what I regarded as a perfect thunder-bolt of humor, and I compressed it into a snappy foot-note at the bottom—thus: "We will let this thing pass, just this once; but we wish Mr. J. Gordon Runnels to understand distinctly that we have a character to sustain, and from this time forth when he wants to commune with his friends in h—l he must select some other medium than the columns of this journal!"[1]

This recollection captures the sense of the controversy, without recapitulating its details: Clemens had no copies of his *Journal* pieces, and he was deliberately writing autobiographical fiction.

Albert Bigelow Paine, probably reflecting testimony from the author himself, implied that Clemens, rather than a "journeyman tailor from Quincy," wrote the poem "addressed 'To Mary in Hannibal,'" whose "title was too long to be set in one column, so he left out all the letters in Hanni-

---

[1]First published in the *Galaxy* 11 (April 1871): 615.

bal, except the first and the last."[2] And in April 1871 Clemens c
implied that he wrote the rest of the items, although they were obviously
longer than the "snappy foot-note" to which he alluded. In fact, it seems
safe to say that, like a one-man band, Clemens orchestrated the medley and
played all the instruments—first as "Rambler," then as "Grumbler," and
finally as "Peter Pencilcase's Son, John Snooks." Rambler's poetry is as feeble
as in "The Heart's Lament" (no. 10), and the raillery of all hands is crude,
but vigorous. In the subtitle to "Love Concealed" Clemens may be echoing
Robert Burns's poem "To Mary in Heaven" as well as Burns's frequent use
of the name "Katie" in his songs. In the garbled syntax of John Snooks's
letter, he was employing for the first time a technique that he later developed
and perfected in such pieces as "The Facts Concerning the Recent Trouble
between Mr. Mark Twain and Mr. John William Skae of Virginia City"
(no. 116) and "A Reminiscence of Artemus Ward" (no. 211).[3]

---

[2]*MTB*, 1:90. The subtitle was not in fact too long to be fully spelled out in the newspaper column: see the photofacsimile in *MTSM*, facing p. 122.

[3]For further discussion of the "Katie of H———l" controversy, see *MTSM*, pp. 119–
126, and *SCH*, pp. 258–259.

Love Concealed

TO MISS KATIE OF H———L.

Oh, thou wilt never know how fond a love
    This heart could have felt for thee;
Or ever dream how love and friendship strove,
    Through long, long hours for mastery;
How passion often urged, but pride restrained,
    Or how thy coldness grieved, but kindness pained.

How hours have soothed the feelings, then that were
    The torture of my lonely life—
But ever yet will often fall a tear,
    O'er wildest hopes and thoughts then rife;
Where'er recalled by passing word or tone,
    Fond memory mirrors all those visions flown.

For much I fear he has won thy heart,
    And thou art but a friend to me;
I feel that in thy love I have no part,
    I know how much he worships thee;
Yet still often will there rise a gleam of hope,
    Wherewith but only time and pride can cope.

HANNIBAL, May 4th, 1853.   RAMBLER.

[First Letter from Grumbler]

MR. EDITOR:

In your yesterday's paper I see a piece of poetry addressed "To Katie in H—l" (*hell*). Now, I've often seen pieces to "Mary in Heaven," or "Lucy in Heaven," or something of that sort, but "Katie in *Hell*," is carrying the matter too far.

GRUMBLER.

[First Letter from Rambler]

POOR GRUMBLER! are you so ignorant as not to be able to distinguish "of" from "in"? Read again—see if it is not "of" H—l (Hannibal), instead of "in" Hell. Now, did you suppose that there was another such an idiot as yourself in the city of Hannibal, one who, like yourself, would as soon address a person in "hell" as upon earth, you are widely mistaken. Poor fellow, I much fear that some Lunatic Asylum will have to mourn the absence of a fit subject until you are placed in a straight jacket and sent there. From the remotest depths of my heart I pity you, nor will I again condescend to notice you, for it ill becomes a rational man to engage in a controversy with one who has placed upon his shoulders a head without either eyes, brains, or sense. Now, Grumbler, one word of advice (and I leave you to the torture of your ignorance), don't, for the sake of your friends, (if any you have) expose yourself any further. I am done with you, so I wish you a safe arrival at that place for which only you are a fit subject—the Lunatic Asylum.

RAMBLER.

To Rambler

MUST APOLOGISE. I merely glanced at your doggerel, and naturally supposing that you had friends in "H—l," (or *Hannibal*, as you are pleased to interpret it,) I just thought you seemed to need some one to take care of and give you advice, and considered it my duty, in a friendly way, to tell you that you were going too far. However, you turned it off into "Hannibal," very well, and I give you credit for your ingenuity.

You "will not again condescend to notice me," you say. Cruel "Rambler!" thus to annihilate me, because I cannot appreciate your *poetry!*

> Resp'ly,
> Your Friend,
> And Admirer,
> GRUMBLER.

[Letter from Peter Pencilcase's Son, John Snooks]

MR. EDITOR:

Several articles have recently appeared in the Daily Journal, over the signature of "Rambler" (truly appropriate).

It is really amusing to every intelligent and intellectual mind, to see how consequential some coxcombs are. The parlor is too remote a place, and not conspicuous enough to reveal the overflowing affections of the H-e-a-r-t. In (yes too obscure) the columns of the public presses are resorted to, by the venerable writer, as being in keeping, with, and a more appropriate way of infusing the sentiments of an *all loving* h-e-a-r-t into the mind of one of the Misses of the city of Hannibal, from the tone of the above writer. It is desired, that the world should awake from its slumbers, and learn that there is one loving heart extant. "Vanity of Vanities!" such may be the custom from whence he hails, but I can assure Mr. "Rambler," that the above course will never win the affections and admiration of the young Misses in this latitude; such a course is not congenial to their nature.

PETER PENCILCASE'S SON,

JOHN SNOOKS.

HANNIBAL, May 12, 1853.

[Second Letter from Rambler]

MR. EDITOR:

In your paper of yesterday I find that I have attracted the notice of a
—— fool. I had fondly hoped that I would not again be troubled with
that class of individuals. But alas for me! I was doomed to be
disappointed. Here, now, comes poor pitiful "Snooks," charging upon
me. I am wholly unable to comprehend his "pitiful" article. It has
been subjected to the criticism of several, and none have been able to
make "sense" of anything he has said. He calls me a "Cox-Comb." I
will not say that he belongs to that long eared race of animals that have
more head and ears than brains. It is the custom from whence I hailed
for a man to act just as I have, without having every "puny puppy" that
runs the streets, whining at his heels. His piece is couched in
exceedingly bad taste.

RAMBLER.

17. *Separation*

12 May 1853

Unlike Rambler's first two poems ("The Heart's Lament" and "Love Concealed," nos. 10 and 11), both of which were published in Orion's Hannibal
Daily Journal, "Separation" appeared in the rival town newspaper, the
Hannibal *Missouri Courier.* This oddity casts some doubt on Clemens'
authorship of the poem: it is conceivable that the "Rambler" who signed the
verses in the *Courier* was someone who wished to take advantage of the
success of the *Journal's* columnist. Unfortunately, none of the three poems
contributes any evidence to solve this problem.

Separation

The sweetest flowers alas! how soon
   Will all their hues of brightness wither!
The loveliest just bud and bloom,
   Then drooping fade away forever.

Yet, if as each sweet rose-bud dies
   Its leaves are gathered, they will shed
A perfume that shall still arise
   Though all its beauteous tints are fled.

And thus while kindred bosoms heave,
   And hearts at meeting fondly swell,
How soon, alas! those hearts must breathe
   The parting sigh, the sad farewell.

Yet, from such moments, as from flowers,
   Shall friendship with delight distil,
A fragrance that shall hold past hours
   Embalmed in memory's odor still.

RAMBLER.

18. *"Oh, She Has a Red Head!"*

13 May 1853

Liberally flavored with dashes of western hyperbole, this mock paean by "A Son of Adam" glorifies redheads—people like the fiery Jane Clemens and her son Sam, who were proud of their auburn hair. The source of the title, perhaps a song, has not been identified, nor has the precise occasion for the sketch, which appeared in the Hannibal *Daily Journal*. The author may have been chastising one or more brunettes for criticizing the color of his hair; but his cocky tone and uninhibited claims for the pristine beauty of the color red are appealing. As Dixon Wecter remarked, the resulting sketch was unusually "polished."[1]

Neither Clemens nor Albert Bigelow Paine mentioned this sketch as one of Clemens' early productions. But the belief (shared by Minnie Brashear, Wecter, and others) that Clemens was indeed its author may be justified on a number of grounds. The publication of the sketch along with Rambler's last letter (no. 16) when Orion returned to Hannibal points to Clemens' authorship. With mock gruffness, Orion remarked under the masthead that "'Rambler' and his enemies must stop their 'stuff.' It is a great bore to us, and doubtless to the public generally." But he added, "All our red headed friends should read the article over the signature of 'A son of Adam.' We like the racy humor of his style of writing, and invite him to continue his correspondence for this paper."[2] Ten days later Clemens began "Our Assistant's Column." Orion also alluded with possessive praise to this sketch on 9 June 1853, noting that it had "afforded much comfort to the red-headed portion of the community" and that several other papers had reprinted it,

---

[1]*SCH*, p. 260.
[2]Hannibal *Daily Journal*, 13 May 1853, p. 2.

although without crediting the *Journal*.[3] The interest in red hair, moreover, and the preoccupation with Adam (who also intrigued "W. Epaminondas Adrastus Blab" in the political sketch "Blabbing Government Secrets!" on 16 September 1852) also point to Clemens. Notable, too, are the fanciful mock-heroics of the sketch, its comically single-minded accumulation of grandiose associations with redness—a comic rhetorical technique that Clemens perfected in later sketches like "City Marshal Perry" (no. 49) and other western burlesques.

---

[3]*SCH*, p. 260.

"Oh, She Has a Red Head!"

Turn up your nose at red heads! What ignorance! I pity your lack of taste.

Why, man, red is the natural color of beauty! What is there that is really beautiful or grand in Nature or Art, that is not tinted with this primordial color?

What gives to the bright flowers of the field—those painted by Nature's own hand—the power to charm the eye and purify the mind of man, and raise his thoughts to heaven, but the softening touches of the all-admired red!

Unless the delicate blushes of the rose mingle upon the cheek of youth—though the features be perfect in form and proportion, and the eye beam with celestial sweetness, no one will pronounce their possessor beautiful.

And the flag under which the proud sons of American sires find protection in every nation under heaven, is rendered more conspicuous and beautiful by the red which mingles in its sacred "stars and stripes."

The Falls of Niagara are never seen to advantage, unless embellished with the rainbow's hues.

The midnight *storm* may howl, and the thunders loud may roar; but how are its grandeur and beauty heightened by the lightning's vivid flash?

Most animals are fond of red—and *all children*, before their tastes are corrupted, and their judgments perverted, are fond of red.

The Romans anciently regarded red hair as *necessary* to a beautiful lady!

Thomas Jefferson's hair was red—and Jesus Christ, our Savior— "The chief among ten thousand, and altogether lovely," is said to have had "auburn" or red hair—and, although it is not stated in so many words, I have but little doubt that Adam's hair was red—for he was made of "red earth" (as his name indicates), and as the name "Adam" was given to him *after* he was made, it is pretty clear he must have had red hair! And the great probability is that Eve's hair was red also, she being made of a 'rib' from Adam, who was made of a lump of "red earth."

Now, Adam and Eve before they sinned, are generally supposed to have been the most lovely and beautiful of creation, and they, in all probability were both "red headed."

But you, O ye deteriorated black headed descendants of an illustrious stock! have no more taste than to glory in the evidence of your departure from original beauty! I'm ashamed of you; I don't know but you'll repudiate your ancestry, and deny you are descended from Adam next.

A SON OF ADAM.

19. The Burial of Sir Abner Gilstrap, Editor of the Bloomington "Republican"

23 May 1853

This satire upon Abner Gilstrap was part of the first installment of "Our Assistant's Column," a new feature that Clemens wrote for the Hannibal *Daily Journal* shortly before he left home for St. Louis and eventually the East Coast. Clemens parodied Charles Wolfe's "The Burial of Sir John Moore after Corunna" (1817), a poetic tribute to the British lieutenant general who died in 1809 from wounds received at the battle of Corunna, Spain, during the Peninsular War with Napoleon's armies. Thirteen years later, in October 1866, Clemens parodied the poem again, this time in his twenty-fourth letter from the Sandwich Islands.[1]

Recalling his original experiment, Clemens wrote in "My First Literary Venture" (no. 357): "It struck me that it would make good, interesting matter to charge the editor of a neighboring country paper with a piece of gratuitous rascality and 'see him squirm!' I did it, putting the article into the form of a parody on the 'Burial of Sir John Moore'—and a pretty crude parody it was, too."[2] Minnie Brashear has shown in detail that Clemens' satire was actually part of a long-simmering quarrel between the *Journal* and Abner Gilstrap, editor of the Bloomington (Mo.) *Republican* and a candidate for the legislature.[3] Bad feeling had arisen when Bloomington lost the fight to be chosen as the terminus of what eventually became the Hannibal and St. Joseph Railroad (hence Clemens' reference to the "Iron Horse" in the penultimate stanza). On May 11 Gilstrap had published his latest contribution to the feud—some verses of satirical dialogue between

---

[1]Sacramento *Union*, 25 October 1866, p. 1, reprinted in *MTH*, pp. 411–412.
[2]First published in the *Galaxy* 11 (April 1871): 615.
[3]*MTSM*, pp. 135–139.

the *Republican* and the *Journal*.[4] "The Burial of Sir Abner Gilstrap," introduced by a brief prose comment, was Clemens' response. The author's memory that it was "a pretty crude parody" is borne out when we compare it
with Wolfe's poem: Clemens closely followed Wolfe's first four stanzas and
his last.

---

[4]The verses, apparently printed in the *Republican*, are not extant. They were mentioned in "A Modern Shakespeare," Hannibal *Daily Journal*, 13 May 1853, p. 2.

The Burial of Sir Abner Gilstrap, Editor of the Bloomington "Republican"

🖙 WE HAVE PONDERED long and well over the Bloomington Republican's mysterious rhymes in that paper of the 11th, but can't discover what the editor was driving at, or what he intended to mean, and don't suppose he knows himself. We could guess better at the meaning of Egyptian hieroglyphics than his verses. However, we'll reply with a random shot of the same sort:

The Burial of Sir Abner Gilstrap,
Editor of the Bloomington "Republican."

A PARODY ON "THE BURIAL OF SIR JOHN MOORE."

"Not a drum was heard, nor a funeral note,
As his corse to the ramparts we hurried;
Not a soldier discharged his farewell shot,
O'er the grave where our hero we buried."
—[*Burial of Sir John Moore.*

Not a sound was heard, nor a funeral note,
    As his carcass through town we hurried;
Not e'en an obituary we wrote,
    In respect for the rascal we buried.

We buried him darkly, at dead of night—
    The dirt with our pitchforks turning;
By the moonbeams' grim and ghastly light,
    And our candles dimly burning.

No useless coffin confined his breast,
    Nor in sheet nor in shirt we bound him;
But he lay like an Editor taking his rest,
    With a Hannibal Journal around him.

Few and *very* short were the *prayers* we said,
    And we felt not a pang of sorrow; ·
But we mused, as we gazed on the wretch now defunct—
    Oh! where will he be to-morrow!

The "Iron Horse" will snort o'er his head,
    And the notes of its whistle upbraid him;
But nothing he'll care if they let him sleep on,
    In the grave where his nonsense hath laid him.

Slowly, but gladly we laid him down,
    From the field of his fame fresh and gory;
We carved not a line, we raised not a stone,
    To mark where we buried a tory.

20. *"Jul'us Caesar"*

1855–1856

The text of "Jul'us Caesar" is taken from an undated holograph preserved in the Jean Webster McKinney Family Papers, now at Vassar. The sketch has not been published before.

The period referred to in the sketch is 1853–1854, a span of several months when Clemens, while rooming with "an Englishman named Sumner," set type in Philadelphia.[1] Although the date of composition remains uncertain, it may be tentatively given as sometime between mid-1855, when Clemens had become acquainted with phrenological terms,[2] and late 1856, when he left Keokuk, Iowa, for Cincinnati and eventually the Mississippi River.

Longer by far than anything that Clemens succeeded in publishing at this time, "Jul'us Caesar" provides striking evidence that he was exercising his literary talents, at least in private. It contains an excellent parody of conventional nature poetry ("The Storm"), and it develops two fairly vigorous characters: Jul'us himself and his vociferous landlady. Alan Gribben has noted the resemblance of Clemens' portrait of Jul'us to his later depiction of Pet McMurray, a journeyman printer Clemens knew in Hannibal.[3] But one may also surmise that his characterization reflects his interest at this time in the writings of Charles Dickens: in some respects Jul'us is similar to Tommy Traddles in *David Copperfield.*

---

[1]*MTB*, 1:98.

[2]*N&J1*, pp. 11–16.

[3]Alan Gribben, "Mark Twain, Phrenology and the 'Temperaments': A Study of Pseudoscientific Influence," *American Quarterly* 24 (March 1972): 55.

"Jul'us Caesar"

Don't imagine, now, that you are to have a learned dissertation upon the life of the Caesar of history. No: *our* Caesar trod the humbler paths of life; our Caesar wielded a hammer instead of a battle-axe; war had no charms for him; but, on the contrary, his soul delighted in peace, penny cigars and lager-bier.

Our Caesar stood about five feet eight inches in his stockings (or somebody else's, for, according to his regular weekly complaint, his washerwoman *never did* bring back the same clothes she took away with her,); very thick heavy build; long, fiery red hair, and large, round, coarse face, which looked like the full moon in the last stage of small pox. Jul'us Caesar was a ship-smith, and worked at the Navy Yard in Philadelphia; and the name which heads this sketch was bestowed upon him at our boarding house because, when anything astonished him, instead of exclaiming "The mischief!" or "The Devil!" as gentlemen usually do, he brought out an emphatic "Jul'us Caesar!" in a voice by no means remarkable for its sweetness—the manner of speaking the two words showing at the same time, that his great mind was not in the habit of spending its force upon trifles, such as correctness of punctuation, &c.

Jul'us Caesar, on ordinary occasions, wore an ancient high crowned hat, a check shirt without a collar, and a very long black cravat wound round his neck three times and the extreme ends tied in a very small knot at his throat; a black satin vest, gracefully fringed in front, from having its lower edge gradually worn away; an old black coat, which had once borne a very dandified appearance; pants which *had* been gray, but now changed to a dingy brown from long service; and brogan shoes of prodigious size and weight. In the morning, when he would rise to a sitting posture in his bed (with his everlasting cravat wound round his neck, and which he only removed once a week,) and lazily rub his big, round eyes, he was a picture to look at—a theme for naturalists to study—with his sparse red moustaches, which *would* persist in growing the wrong way, do what he would; his big red face bigger and redder than ever, and his long hair, caked and matted together with grease, spread abroad and standing out like a turkey gobbler's tail. Then, with a "Jul'us Caesar! ain't it cold!" he would spring into the middle of the room, and commence jerking on his clothes in as great a hurry as if the house was on fire and five seconds the time allowed him to save himself in. After washing, he would devote half an hour to drumming up and restoring to their proper place his wandering locks of hair; and in arranging this portion of his toilet he had a method peculiarly his own—parting his head covering on both sides, and combing that which grew above the lines, into a huge roll on top of his head, said roll extending from his forehead back to the crown, and looking like a great wave, giving his upper story the appearance of a sandy beach when the tide is coming in. If it were a week-day, he would stride down street with his hat leaning the slightest mite in the world to the western side of his head, (on Sundays it occupied the *extreme* western side) and his hands thrust into his coat pockets and then brought round and crossed in front, thereby stretching the garment very tightly behind; and as he always walked very erectly, and maintained a most rigid perpendicular, this afforded one an excellent opportunity of seeing and admiring the graceful motions of his muscles.

"Jul'us Caesar" was a phrenological curiosity: his head was one vast lump of Approbativeness; and though he was as ignorant and as void of intellect as a Hottentot, yet the great leveller and equalizer, Self-Conceit made him believe himself fully as talented, learned and handsome as it is possible for a human being to be. He was decidedly literary, after a fashion of his own, and the gems which find their way before the public through the medium of the "Flag of our Union," and "Boston True Flag," together with such instructive and entertaining books as "The Black Avenger of the Spanish Main," "Jack Sheppard," &c., &c., were food and drink to his soul.

My friend Sumner, and myself thought that by good management, we might draw some amusement from this apparently barren subject. Having decided to make the effort, we proceeded, by slow and careful advances to instil into his mind a notion that he could write *poetry*. To accomplish this undertaking successfully, was no small labor; for, to sit down, and tell such a block of wood that he could write *poetry*, and do it, too, with a sober face and a truthful air—why, the self-complacent look which would settle on his countenance as he listened to and believed it all, was so irresistibly ludicrous that it was almost impossible to carry the thing through without laughing, which would of course have spoiled all. However, after a week of earnest application to our great work, our labors were at last crowned with success. As we stepped in one Sunday morning, the great Caesar approached us with a most important stride, and drawing from his pocket a folded sheet of paper, handed it to Sumner without saying a word, and then stepped aside with a very exalted air to watch the result. Sumner opened and glanced at it, and being taken so much by surprise, he could not control his risibles; so, to prevent an explosion and also the ruin which would follow the same, he bit his lip, handed the paper to me, and stepped into the entry, where he could work off his surplus laughter without causing any damage to our scheme. I had to reassure the poet, (for the paper contained an effusion,) who looked somewhat puzzled at Sumner's behavior, by quietly telling him "Sumner was sick—had been very sick at the stomach all the morning." I spread out the foolscap, and my vision was refreshed with the following pearl, written under the inspiration of the awful and the sublime, awakened by a thunder storm the night before:

` [There were originally six verses, but I can remember only four— which four, at least, I will rescue from oblivion:]

"The Storm.

"Just see the lightning's lurid glare!
Just hear that thunder's crash!
Behold that riven stable there:—
Oh, what an awful smash!

"And every time it lightens,
   The thunder charges round,
And everybody frightens,
   And some knocks on the ground.

"The oyster stalls are thinning now,
   The engine houses filling,
Old *Borus* sweeps from street to street—
   Oh, ain't such weather killing?

"And now the hail begins to pelt
   On hill and vale and level,
And now the rain comes pouring down
   Just like the very devil!"

————————

How we enjoyed ourselves, Sumner and I, over this morsel, it is impossible to say on paper; how we praised and flattered and fooled the author; how we patted him on the back and told him to persevere—it was the decree of fate and destiny that he should be a poet; how we praised him to each other when he lay upon his bed apparently asleep—though we knew he was not; how he turned poet *all* over, in nature, in action, and in sentiment; how he talked nonsense with a poetical air, walked with a poetical gait, and eat with—*not* a poetical appetite; how he reclined languidly, smoked spasmodically, and uttered his favorite ejaculation tragically (three essentials to a poet's second nature); how he kept on writing till we were handsomely bored, and the rooms flooded with "poetry"; how he might have *kept on* writing till Doomsday perhaps, if Sumner had not told him in the most approved English that he was a fool, an idiot, and never would be able to write poetry, and advised him to waste no more paper; and how Sumner—who was angry when he said it,—begged his pardon and said he didn't mean half he said; how all this happened, and a great deal more, is matter sufficient for an article much longer than I care about writing, and therefore I shall leave that portion of my sketch to be imagined.

"Jul'us" laid by the pen, but after a good deal of persuasion and a
large amount of flattery, we succeeded in convincing him that he
could at least draw and paint. We took this course, after discovering
upon a sheet of paper several nondescript figures, with their names
underneath, in Jul'us's own handwriting—there was no mistake as to
the chirography, for its style was to be met with no where else. One
figure, which upon a first view we took to be a representation of a
carpenter's work bench, proved, upon reference to the inscription
beneath, to be "a hors;" by the latter method of proceeding, we also
discovered that what at first appeared to be a shovel and tongs, was "a
man and woman." These things he had evidently displayed purposely,
and was doubtless very proud of them. It was sharp work this time to
impose upon the ex-poet, and we had almost concluded to give it up,
when we noticed, one morning, the slightest tinge in the world of red
upon a tea cup on the mantel piece, and a little yellow spot on the
corner of the washstand. If these spots had been white, they would
have awakened no suspicions, for the room had been lately
whitewashed: but no, the marks were paint, and put there by "Julus
Caesar," and no one else—for who but him would be so careless as to
daub it over everything? and moreover, he must certainly intend to
take us by surprise again, or why would he keep the matter so secret?
These were the thoughts that flitted across our minds, and we looked
anxiously for the first efforts of this newly awakened genius, confident
that they would be of the most *brilliant* character. Our landlady was
one of the most terrible of her sex when her temper was ruffled, and as
she had a most unqualified contempt for "Julus," she was particularly
severe upon him when ever he did anything to displease her—nor was
she at all choice in the epithets she selected for his benefit. We were all
sitting in the parlor one afternoon, when Mrs. C. flourished into the
room with an air which left no room to doubt that her blood was up.
Without any unnecessary preliminaries, she at once commenced,
while our astounded genius listened in silent awe:

"That everlasting fool has been at some more of his nonsense! Oh, it
was you, you insignificant 'natomy, for no body else in all Philadelphia
has got that little sense! Oh, you needn't say a word (now "Julus" had
not the remotest idea of attempting such a thing,) you puddin'-headed
ignoramus! To go and do it, too, just after I had the room all nicely

whitewashed. Oh-h! (and she ground the words out from between her teeth as she shook her fist at poor "Julus,") I've a *good* mind to scratch your eyes out! Come up here, every one of you, and see what the idiot has been doing"—and she wheeled around with a jerk that made her dresses rustle like a small tornado, and flourished up stairs. As soon as the assembled boarders had recovered from the almost fatal fit of laughter which the lady's speech and "Julus's" mortification had thrown them into, we all proceeded up stairs, followed by the crest fallen poet, and there, on the white wall, over Sumner's bed and mine, was a sight to make a saint laugh. First, there was a caricature of the stars and stripes or a rain bow,—it was impossible to tell which,—but whatever it was, it had colors enough; next was another "hors," of huge proportions, with a red body and green legs; and lastly,—the crowning effort—was "a firemen," in a pugilistic attitude, with one leg a great deal smaller, and a great deal shorter than the other one, a gaudy red hat on the side of his head, green shirt, with sleeves tucked up, and intensely yellow pants and blue boots—the picture happily relieved by a tailless yellow dog with brilliant green and blue spots on his sides. The yell that went up from our little crowd would have put a band of Comanche indians to the blush, and drowned for a moment the landlady's harangue, but she soon got under way again, devoting her speech, as before, to our artist:

"Ugh! you great calf, you ought to be ashamed of such childishness. Who raised you? Where in the name of sense did you come from? Who taught you to make a fool of yourself? But I pity you, indeed I do. (Another glance at the picture) If you belonged to me, I'd whip you if you were a hundred years old. I never saw such an outrageous block-head in all my life. Why don't you go to school and learn something? I've seen a good many geese with clothes on in my time, but never, till I saw you, did I think a man could be made *entirely* without brains. Why don't you learn to behave yourself like a Christian? Ugh! you poor miserable——"

The old lady, although addressing her remarks to "Julus," had started down stairs when she commenced, and her voice gradually died away in the distance, till the remainder of her last exclamation was lost to us.

With this much of the veritable and wonderful history of the great modern "Julus Caesar," I will now leave him, and

> "No further seek his merits to disclose,
>   Nor draw his frailties from their dread abode,"

hoping, some day, when time and opportunity shall offer, to be able to continue the history of, and do justice to, this great man. I must say, though, that though his faults were numerous; though his manners were unrefined and his speech rude; though his mind was uncultivated, and his vanity made him unpleasant—yet he had a kind and generous nature, and his failings were those of the head, and not of the heart.

21. To Mollie

20 April 1856

This utterly conventional poem is addressed to Clemens' sister-in-law, Mary Eleanor (Mollie) Stotts Clemens, who had married his brother Orion on 19 December 1854. The text is preserved in the author's holograph in Mollie's memory book, now owned by Dorris B. Schmidt of Lincoln, Nebraska.

To Mollie

All the earth with buds is teeming,—
   Bursting into life and light,—
The morning sun is kindly beaming,
   And lingering Winter takes his flight.

Long absent Spring, to Earth returning,
   Is welcomed by the *bowing* trees,
While soaring birds, the forest spurning,
   Are greeting her with songs of praise.

Green is the earth, and cloudless is the sky—
   Peace reigns within the hearts of men;
Clouds and Winter, vanquished, fly—
   Oh, may they ne'er return again!

Years of sorrow and trouble will over you pass,
   And the ties of your Earth-home be riven,
But your *Winter* of Woe will give place at the last,
   To a *Spring* everlasting in Heaven!

                              S.C.

KEOKUK, April 20th, 1856.

22. "Lines

Suggested by a Reminiscence, and Which
You Will Perhaps Understand"

Early May 1856

This poem and the next one ("To Jennie," no. 23), both addressed to Ann
Virginia Ruffner, were inscribed by Clemens in her autograph album. The
text of "Lines" is taken from a printing in the Hannibal *Evening Courier-
Post* for 6 March 1935 because the autograph album itself is not now
available.

Both the title and the text show that Clemens was writing a gentle take-off
on Wordsworth's "Lines written a few miles above Tintern Abbey, on re-
visiting the banks of the Wye during a tour." According to the article in the
Courier-Post, Miss Ruffner was visiting Keokuk early in May 1856, where
she met Clemens, who was then working in Orion's Ben Franklin Book and
Job Office.

There were many gatherings of the young people of Keokuk that spring
when Miss Ruffner visited there. She met Sam Clemens frequently, and no
doubt he was her partner several times in the stately party games of that
bygone day.

They also went to church on Sunday nights in company with other young
people. It was an amusing incident that happened when they were coming
home from church one night which Sam Clemens made the theme of a
poem.

The party consisted, evidently, of Miss Ruffner and Clemens, and the unidentified Miss Iowa Burns and "Cal." "A rain storm had come up during
the sermon and in the darkness of the rainy night the group of young people,
chatting vivaciously as they walked home, found themselves walking off

the crude sidewalk into a muddy ditch." Clemens evidently added "an explanatory note, 'long meter,' " in the margin of the last, rather free stanza.[1]

---

[1]"Young Sam Clemens Tried Hand at Poetry," Hannibal *Evening Courier-Post*, 6 March 1935, p. 9C. The account in this article is evidently based in part on the memories of Mrs. M. W. Spencer, daughter of Ann Virginia Ruffner Hixson.

"Lines
Suggested by a Reminiscence, and Which You Will Perhaps Understand"

Long days have passed since last we met,
(Last Sunday night, you know.)
Yet in my heart your image reigns,
(It rained some then, you know.)

An eventful night was that, my friend,
It still in my memory burns:
It lingers in Cal's memory, too,
And in that of Iowa burns.

A thunder and lightning sermon we had,
Aye, a sermon of lightning and thunder.
We caught thunder and lightning going home.
(But Cal heeded naught save his blunder.)

For consolation poor Cal came to me,
I did for him all I could do;
"I've made such a fool of myself," said he,
(And I kindly assented thereto.)

"A fool! a fool! a perfect fool! I'll go and drown myself."
("Indeed! Goodbye, my friend, goodbye")
"Blow out my brains and cut my throat!"
("I'll hold your hat," said I.)

S. L. C.

Now Ginnie, don't forget that night,
Nor fire and brimstone lecture,
And deign to pity my sad plight,
After tumbling into that abominable gully,
Which incident may be attributed to neglect of duty,
On the part of the street inspector.

SAM C.

23. To Jennie

7 May 1856

Like the previous poem, this one was inscribed in the autograph album of Ann Virginia Ruffner. The text is taken from a photofacsimile of the holograph reproduced in the Hannibal *Evening Courier-Post* for 6 March 1935.[1]

Dixon Wecter mistakenly dated this poem in 1853, conjecturing that it was written on the occasion of Clemens' departure from Hannibal in that year.[2] The manuscript, which Clemens signed with his initials and dated, indicates that it was written on 7 May 1856 in Keokuk. The article in the *Courier-Post* makes it clear that the occasion was, in fact, Miss Ruffner's departure from Keokuk. Nevertheless, Clemens' allusion to "destiny" in the first stanza may suggest that his plans for sailing to the Amazon were well formed at this point.

---

[1]"Young Sam Clemens Tried Hand at Poetry," Hannibal *Evening Courier-Post*, 6 March 1935, p. 9C.

[2]*SCH*, p. 264. The opening stanza was first published by Julian Street in *Abroad at Home* (New York: The Century Company, 1916), p. 252.

To Jennie

Good-bye! a kind good-bye,
  I bid you now, my friend,
And though 'tis sad to speak the word,
  To destiny I bend.

——————————

And though it be decreed by Fate
  That we ne'er meet again,
Your image, graven on my heart,
  Forever shall remain.

——————————

Aye, in my heart thoult have a place,
  Among the friends held dear,—
Nor shall the hand of Time efface
  The *memories* written there.
                    Good-bye,
                       S. L. C.

KEOKUK, IOWA, May 7, 1856.

24. [River Intelligence]

17 May 1859

During the six years following Clemens' departure from Hannibal, his publications were limited to several out-of-town "travel" letters written for Orion's newspapers in Hannibal and Muscatine (Iowa) and three Thomas Jefferson Snodgrass letters in the Keokuk *Post*.[1] The two-year period Clemens devoted to learning the river proved especially barren in writings. But less than six weeks after he became a licensed pilot on 9 April 1859, Clemens published "River Intelligence" in the New Orleans *Crescent*. This satire on Isaiah Sellers was perhaps the most ambitious of his prewestern imaginative pieces. It was his first extended prose burlesque, a mode he freely experimented with in later sketches and in travel writings and novels. Furthermore, Clemens' Sergeant Fathom anticipated a host of loquacious eccentrics he created in years to come—men who revealed their idiosyncrasies through a seemingly unrestrained flow of words.

Isaiah Sellers, the original of Sergeant Fathom, was a pilot and captain on the Mississippi River for almost forty years: he began his career in 1825, when he was twenty-two or twenty-three years old, and he died on 6 March 1864. Although he was known as an unusually safe pilot, he nevertheless for many years held the record for the speediest run between New Orleans and St. Louis. His unequaled experience qualified him as an authority on the river—its history, commerce, landmarks, and hydrodynamics—and as Clemens recalled, he used to contribute "brief paragraphs of plain practical information about the river" to the New Orleans newspapers.[2] While writing *Life on the Mississippi* in 1882, Clemens said of Sellers that "out there he was 'illustrious.'"[3] And both in that book and in his autobiography (1906)

---

[1]These letters are scheduled to appear in the collection of travel writings in The Works of Mark Twain. They are reprinted in *TJS*.

[2]*Life on the Mississippi*, chapter 50.

[3]Clemens to James R. Osgood, 19 July 1882, *MTLP*, p. 157.

Clemens recalled the jealousy of his fellow pilots toward Sellers, whose experiences easily overshadowed their own, making "their small marvels look pale and sick."[4]

But there may have been more personal reasons for the animosity that fueled Clemens' lampoon of Sellers, just as three years later his hostile feelings toward Judge G. T. Sewall lay behind the hoax "Petrified Man" (no. 28). A recently discovered account of Sellers' career, written in 1880 (three years before *Life on the Mississippi* was published), relates an occurrence that specifically connects Sellers with Clemens:

Sellers was a tall, fine looking person, as straight as an Indian, and carried a distingué air. He was a man to attract attention anywhere, and he also had his peculiarities and mannerisms. One of the latter was a passion to sleep, and that oft-times a little beyond the middle watch when the other pilot of the boat was compelled to do more than his share of duty because of Sellers' somnolent appetite. Mark Twain, in those days an apprentice or cub pilot on the same boat, and the opposite watch to Sellers', used to be sent on repeated errands to arouse the heavy sleeper. On one occasion 'tis said Twain was suddenly struck square on the nose by a heavy boot, and he didn't like it much.[5]

The anonymous writer (who knew some details of Henry Clemens' death in Memphis and so may be reliable) then mentions that "some time later" Clemens retaliated by publishing a lampoon of Sellers in the New Orleans *Crescent*. If the described incident actually occurred, Clemens' resentment of Sellers probably struck deep and continued to rankle. In line with this supposition, Allan Bates has presented evidence showing that the remorse Clemens expressed in chapter 50 of *Life on the Mississippi* about the cruelty of his satire "was only a pretense, or at least was not permanent."[6]

It is possible that Clemens served on the *William M. Morrison* in July 1858, when Sellers was pilot of that boat.[7] After the death of his brother Henry on June 21, Clemens was temporarily without a berth because of the destruction of the *Pennsylvania*, and so may have signed on the *Morrison* as a clerk. On July 2, the day the *Morrison* left St. Louis on its regular run to New Orleans, the *Missouri Republican* listed a "Clemens" as third clerk along with the regular clerks, Moore and Garbutt.[8] Two weeks later, when

---

[4]AD, 10 September 1906, *MTE*, p. 229.

[5]"Big Tows—Mulberry Sellers," Cincinnati *Commercial*, 29 January 1880, p. 7.

[6]*MTMR*, p. 268.

[7]Sellers is identified as one of the officers, presumably the pilot, in "River News," St. Louis *Missouri Republican*, 11 June 1858, p. 3.

[8]"River News," St. Louis *Missouri Republican*, 2 July 1858, p. 3; see also Dewey Ganzel, "Samuel Clemens' Correspondence in the St. Louis *Missouri Republican*," *Anglia* 85 (1967): 402–403.

the *Morrison* returned to St. Louis, "Walsh" had replaced "Clemens" as third clerk.[9]

Clemens' *Crescent* burlesque was obviously written for his fellow pilots, who must have been familiar with Sellers' contributions of "river intelligence" to the newspapers, and who may have been directly responsible for having the burlesque published.[10] Judging from the date of Sergeant Fathom's letter ("May 8, 1859"), the immediate occasion for Clemens' burlesque was a letter from Sellers, accompanied by an editorial preface, which was published on May 7 in the "Steamboat and River Intelligence" column of the New Orleans *True Delta:*

Our friend, Capt. Sellers, one of the oldest pilots on the river, and now on the WM. M. MORRISON, sends us a rather bad account concerning the state of the river. Capt. Sellers is a man of experience, and though we do not coincide in his view of the matter, we give his note a place in our columns, only hoping that his prophecy will not be verified in this instance:

STEAMER WM. M. MORRISON. ⎱
VICKSBURG, May 4, 1859. ⎰

The river from your city up to this port is higher than it has been since the high water of 1815, and my opinion is that *the water will be in Canal street* before the 1st day of June. Mrs. Turner's plantation, which has not been affected by the river since 1815, is now under water.

Yours, &c.,
ISAIAH SELLERS.[11]

Clemens recalled in *Life on the Mississippi* that Sellers' letter "became the text" for his burlesque, in which he strung his "fantastics out to the extent of eight hundred or a thousand words."[12] His memory was quite accurate: the burlesque is closely modeled on the preface and the letter, parodying their language as well as their content. Clemens introduced "Our

---

[9]"River News," St. Louis *Missouri Republican*, 18 July 1858, p. 3.

[10]Clemens recalled in chapter 50 of *Life on the Mississippi* that he showed his "performance to some pilots, and they eagerly rushed it into print in the 'New Orleans True Delta.'" He misremembered the paper—the piece was published in the *Crescent* —but there may be some truth in his recollection about the other pilots. Paine reported that Clemens' friend Bart Bowen had "insisted on showing it to others and finally upon printing it" (*MTB*, 1:150). This report is confirmed by contemporary evidence: the editor of the *Crescent* explained on Thursday, 19 May 1859, that "the letter which appeared in the river column of the Crescent of Tuesday morning was handed to us by Mr. B. W. S. Bowen, pilot of the steamer A. T. Lacey" ("River Intelligence," New Orleans *Crescent*, 19 May 1859, p. 7).

[11]"Steamboat and River Intelligence," New Orleans *True Delta*, 7 May 1859, p. 8.

[12]*Life on the Mississippi*, chapter 50. Sellers' *True Delta* letter was not reprinted with Mark Twain's burlesque in the *Crescent*, although the appearance of the two together in Albert Bigelow Paine's *MTB* has misled some readers into believing that the Sellers' item was used as Clemens' epigraph. Paine did not have Sellers' original text from the *True Delta*, so he reprinted it from the footnote in chapter 50 of *Life on the Mississippi*, where Mark Twain had reprinted it from "the original MS" (*MTB*, 3:1593).

friend Sergeant Fathom," who sent a "bad account concerning the state of the river," at even greater length than the *True Delta* had done, and he greatly elaborated his accomplishments, charm, and fame in order to mock them. His preface was in turn followed by a parody of Sellers' letter, written from the "R. R. STEAMER TROMBONE," and featuring a grand disquisition on "high water."

Both Sellers' original letter and the parody reflect real conditions on the river. Late in April, high winds, heavy rains, and a strong tide at New Orleans had combined to flood the upper and lower steamboat landings; water surging over the levee had turned streets into rivers. The river opposite Vicksburg was reported in the *True Delta* "as being *twenty inches and a half* above the highest water of last year, and *eighteen and a quarter above* the water of 1850. The water of 1828 was the highest ever known in Vicksburg until this year—the river now being sixteen inches above that."[13] By the first week of May the ominous rise at Vicksburg had reached New Orleans, and the river, swelled by continuing rains, was flooding the city streets more seriously than before.[14] Sergeant Fathom's comparison of this situation with the *real* "'high-water' years" and his prediction that the river would soon "cease to rise altogether" should be read in this context.

But Clemens' parody also drew upon still another communication from Sellers to the *True Delta:* extracts from his journal published six weeks earlier on 22 March 1859 in the same column, "Steamboat and River Intelligence." The following extracts illustrate the distinctive combination of pedestrian observation, antiquarian memory, and far-fetched speculation that characterized Sellers' writings, and that made him a good target for ridicule:

> While the upper river was at this low stage, the towboats Post Boy and Grampus towed to sea the packet ship Oceana, drawing 21 feet; a fact confirming the theory that low waters above tend to increase the depth of channels at the mouths of the Mississippi.
>
> Further confirmation is found in the condition of the river during the years 1839 and '40, the average of which was very low, so much so that the lakes and ponds in the vicinity of Bolivar, Miss., and Helena, Arkansas, dried up and all the fish died. . . .
>
> After 34 years of careful and constant observation, I am clearly of opinion that the changes so frequently occurring in the channel of this river, at certain points, are solely the result of the action of currents at extreme stages of high and low water on the banks and bed of the river. I notice that where the river is narrow, and the current strikes the bluff at right angles, there is invariably a shoal place immediately above. . . .

---

[13]"Steamboat and River Intelligence," New Orleans *True Delta*, 28 April 1859, p. 8.

[14]"Overflow Uptown," New Orleans *True Delta*, 27 April 1859, p. 5; "Steamboat and River Intelligence," ibid., 3 May 1859, p. 8.

The river in 1858 was 18 inches higher at Island 18, 70 and 71 than it has been since 1815. This is on record. During the latter year, the water was checked by the bluff above Walnut hills and backed up some fifty miles. . . . In 1828, 1844 and 1851, the river was backed up from the same point, varying from 30 to 50 miles.[15]

By combining elements from Sellers' original letter and from this journal, Clemens mocked the captain's public image as "one of the oldest pilots on the river" and a "man of experience."

Moreover, Sellers apparently talked the way he wrote, a fact suggested by the report of "C. C.," writing from Cairo "On Board Steamer Wm. M. Morrison, June 16, 1858," a time of extremely high water: "I have just learned from Capt. Sellers, who was piloting in '28, that the average width of the river from Cairo to Vicksburg now, is 300 feet more than it was at that time; and from Cairo to Memphis there remains scarcely a land-mark, standing at that period; and this fact reduces the decision as to the comparative height of the river then and now to something of an uncertainty."[16] Even without his personal and professional animus, Clemens would always find such characters ripe for satire.[17]

---

[15]"Steamboat and River Intelligence," New Orleans *True Delta*, 22 March 1859, p. 8.

[16]"From the Lower Mississippi," St. Louis *Sunday Republican*, 20 June 1858, p. 2.

[17]Clemens' most important remarks about Sellers and "River Intelligence" may be found in *Life on the Mississippi*, chapter 50, and *MTE*, pp. 228–229. For discussions of "River Intelligence" see Ernest E. Leisy, "Mark Twain and Isaiah Sellers," *American Literature* 13 (January 1942): 398–405, which reprints the entire Sellers journal passage reproduced in the 22 March 1859 *True Delta*; *MTMR*, pp. 214–224; and *LAMT*, pp. 44–47.

[River Intelligence]

OUR FRIEND Sergeant Fathom, one of the oldest cub pilots on the river, and now on the Railroad Line steamer Trombone, sends us a rather bad account concerning the state of the river. Sergeant Fathom is a "cub" of much experience, and although we are loth to coincide in his view of the matter, we give his note a place in our columns, only hoping that his prophesy will not be verified in this instance. While introducing the Sergeant, "we consider it but simple justice (we quote from a friend of his) to remark that he is distinguished for being, in pilot phrase, 'close,' as well as superhumanly 'safe.' " It is a well-known fact that he has made fourteen hundred and fifty trips in the New Orleans and St. Louis trade without causing serious damage to a steamboat. This astonishing success is attributed to the fact that he seldom runs his boat after early candle light. It is related of the Sergeant that upon one occasion he actually ran the chute of Glasscock's Island, down stream, *in the night*, and at a time, too, when the river was scarcely more than bank full. His method of accomplishing this feat proves what we have just said of his "safeness"—he sounded the chute first, and then built a fire on the head of the island to run by. As to the Sergeant's "closeness," we have heard it whispered that he once went up to the right of the "Old Hen," but this is probably a pardonable little exaggeration, prompted by the love and admiration in which he is held by various ancient dames of his acquaintance, (for albeit the Sergeant *may* have already numbered the allotted years of man, still his form is erect, his step is firm, his hair retains its sable hue, and more than all, he hath a winning way about him, an air of docility and sweetness, if you will, and a smoothness of speech, together with an exhaustless fund of funny sayings; and lastly, an ever-flowing stream, without beginning, or middle, or end, of astonishing reminiscences of the ancient Mississippi, which, taken together, form a *tout ensemble* which is a sufficient excuse for the tender epithet which is, by common consent, applied to him by all those ancient dames aforesaid of "che-*arm*ing creature!") As the Sergeant has been longer on the river, and is better acquainted with it than any other "cub" extant, his remarks are entitled to extraordinary consideration, and are always read with the deepest interest by high and low, rich and poor, from "Kiho" to Kamschatka, for be it known that his fame extends to the uttermost parts of the earth:

R. R. Steamer Trombone,⎫
Vicksburg, May 8, 1859. ⎭

The river from New Orleans up to Natchez is higher than it has been since the niggers were executed, (which was in the fall of 1813) and my opinion is, that if the rise continues at this rate *the water will be on the roof of the St. Charles Hotel* before the middle of January. The point at Cairo, which has not even been moistened by the river since 1813, is now entirely under water.

However, Mr. Editor, the inhabitants of the Mississippi Valley should not act precipitately and sell their plantations at a sacrifice on account of this prophesy of mine, for I shall proceed to convince them of a great fact in regard to this matter, viz: That the tendency of the Mississippi is to rise less and less higher every year (with an occasional variation of the rule), that such has been the case for many centuries, and finally that it will cease to rise at all. Therefore, I would suggest to the planters, as we say in an innocent little parlor game, commonly called "draw," that if they can only "stand the raise" this time, they may enjoy the comfortable assurance that the old river's banks will never hold a "full" again during their natural lives.

In the summer of 1763 I came down the river on the old *first* "Jubilee." She was new, then, however; a singular sort of a single-engine boat, with a Chinese captain and a Choctaw crew, forecastle on her stern, wheels in the center, and the jackstaff "no where," for I steered her with a window shutter, and when we wanted to land we sent a line ashore and "rounded her to" with a yoke of oxen.

Well, sir, we wooded off the top of the big bluff above Selma—the only dry land visible—and waited there three weeks, swapping knives and playing "seven up" with the Indians, waiting for the river to fall. Finally, it fell about a hundred feet, and we went on. One day we rounded to, and I got in a horse-trough, which my partner borrowed from the Indians up there at Selma while they were at prayers, and went down to sound around No. 8, and while I was gone my partner got aground on the hills at Hickman. After three days labor we finally succeeded in sparring her off with a capstan bar, and went on to Memphis. By the time we got there the river had subsided to such an extent that we were able to land where the Gayoso House now stands. We finished loading at Memphis, and engaged part of the stone for the present St. Louis Court-House, (which was then in process of erection) to be taken up on our return trip.

You can form some conception by these memoranda of how high the water was in 1763. In 1775 it did not rise so high by thirty feet; in 1790 it missed the original mark at least sixty-five feet; in 1797, one hundred and fifty feet; and in 1806, nearly two hundred and fifty feet. These were "high-water" years. The "high waters" since then have been so insignificant that I have scarcely taken the trouble to notice them. Thus, you will perceive that the planters need not feel uneasy. The river may make an occasional spasmodic effort at a flood, but the time is approaching when it will cease to rise altogether.

In conclusion, sir, I will condescend to *hint* at the foundation of these arguments: When me and DeSoto discovered the Mississippi, I could stand at Bolivar Landing (several miles above "Roaring Waters Bar") and pitch a biscuit to the main shore on the other side, and in low water we waded across at Donaldsonville. The gradual *widening* and *deepening* of the river is the whole secret of the matter.

Yours, etc.,
SERGEANT FATHOM.

25. [The Mysterious Murders in Risse]

1 August 1859

The text of this untitled sketch is taken from a holograph preserved in the Jean Webster McKinney Family Papers, now at Vassar. The sketch has not been published before.

The manuscript is written in pencil and is marred by two lacunae: one small (only a few words) and one large (perhaps as many as 400 words). The small lacuna occurs in a sentence that Clemens squeezed between the lines of the first and second paragraphs: his tiny letters, the smudged pencil, and the folds in the paper make some of the words impossible to recover, and they are indicated here by ellipsis points. The large lacuna occurs late in the manuscript where a leaf has been lost. Clemens originally wrote on three folded sheets containing four pages apiece: the first two pages of the third folder are now lost, and the missing material is again indicated by ellipsis points.

"The Mysterious Murders in Risse" is, of course, pure fiction. Although Wittenberge and Reutlingen are real places in Germany, Risse and the town mentioned later in the sketch, Lun, are not. Clemens is not known to have written anything else at this time remotely like this romantic, gothic tale of murder and revenge, and the present sketch suggests that he was not entirely comfortable with the conventions of the genre. His natural bent toward humor emerges somewhat incongruously throughout—for example, in his allusion to Von Muller's "impassioned tale of love, wrought in chaste and unpronounceable German" and in his sniping comments on the timidity of "policemen in general." The story itself is given a rather wooden handling, and the modern reader might have derived as little suspense from the original tale as from the now incomplete one.

The story, in the form of a newspaper letter addressed to "Dear Editors," was obviously intended for publication: a cancellation underneath that greeting reads "Missouri Repub," suggesting Clemens may have intended to publish it in the St. Louis *Missouri Republican*. Of course, the allusion in the penultimate paragraph to Robert Montgomery Bird's *Nick of the Woods; or, The Jibbenainosay* (1837) suggests Clemens' most immediate source for his tale. Indeed, it will be recalled that in chapter 55 of *Life on the Mississippi* Mark Twain recounted his boyhood memory of the carpenter who had frightened him with stories of assassination: "This ass [had] been reading the 'Jibbenainosay,' no doubt, and had had his poor romantic head turned by it; but as I had not yet seen the book then, I took his inventions for truth, and did not suspect that he was a plagiarist." The present sketch was written when Clemens was twenty-three, and represents his own attempt to get a literary effect out of Bird's compelling fantasy of murderous revenge.

[The Mysterious Murders in Risse]

REUTLINGEN, KINGDOM OF WITTENBERGE,
August 1st 1859.

DEAR EDITORS:

The phlegmatic depths of this usually quiet old town have just been stirred to the very bottom; its slumbers have been rudely disturbed, and at this moment it is rubbing its sleepy eyes in amazement—in a word, the staid and dignified city of Reutlingen hath been betrayed into an excitement. In the streets, on the *Spaziergang*, at the hotel, around the fireside, nothing is thought of, nothing is talked about, but the Mysterious Murders in Risse. The knees of the community, to the very last man, are shaky with terror, and their haggard countenances are capable of but one expression—viz: unmitigated astonishment, modified by a pleasing cast of intense horror. Even stout kneed . . . go not abroad often.

Risse is a small village situated a short distance north of this place. Indeed, said distance is so short that Risse is looked upon as a suburb of Reutlingen. Risse basks in the warm light of two notable honors—to wit: a fine old Cathedral, worthy of the pride which is felt for it (over its great altar hangs the famous portrait of John the Evangelist, concerning the origin of which all records have been lost—lost, ages ago—but it is reverently whispered that the picture was the work of a divine miracle,) and the ancient seat of the Counts of Von Muller, which lies just on the western verge of the town. Under the Cathedral is a great dark vault, where repose in state many a departed Muller, whose dreamless slumbers are watched over by their own stern effigies clad in brave suits of armor, rusty and dusty, and festooned with the cobwebs of centuries.

But I must get back to my subject. It seems that two years ago, a handsome girl of sixteen or seventeen, respectably dressed, stopped, late one evening, at the little hotel in Risse, where she remained several days, conducting herself properly, paying her board promptly, and minding her own business, whatever it was. She seemed entirely unattended, and this fact seemed to call for an investigation into her private affairs, which investigation was immediately undertaken by several kind-hearted village matrons. The information gained was only this: the girl's name was Katrina Lieber; she was a music teacher; she had traveled alone from Heidelberg, in the Grand Duchy of Baden, where her father was still living; she had only lately become a teacher of music; her family was highly respectable, and had been wealthy, but a financial calamity had suddenly reduced them to want. This was all. The investigating committee returned a verdict of Guilty of—Poverty—with a recommendation to mercy, and discontinued the examination.

Katrina obtained employment in the family of Herr Wahlner, a retired merchant, and shortly after, sent for her father. They rented a small cottage within a stone's-throw of the castle, and settled themselves down to live as comfortably as they had any right to, considering the Verdict that had been rendered against them. The father was a haughty man, with mighty muscles, a huge frame, a long gray moustache, which was twisted and curved till the two ends stood up straight and stiff beneath his cold, unforgiving eyes, like the horns of an ox. He seldom came out of the cottage, and when he did he never spoke to any one, but strode moodily along, taking no notice of anything, and never seeming disturbed when those natural physiognomists, the children, fled in fear before his stately tread.

Katrina was pretty, and gentle, and unassuming, and made friends with everybody. No one was afraid of her soft blue eyes, except, perhaps, the spruce young beaux of Risse. And yet the young Count Ritter Von Muller feared them not, but even liked right well to be near them, although they beamed less kindly upon him than upon the children of the hamlet.

Ritter never went to the cottage, but he often met her, and accompanied her part of the way on her long walk home from Herr

Wahlner's, and on these occasions he poured into her ear an impassioned tale of love, wrought in chaste and unpronounceable German. His suit found no encouragement. Katrina was distressed. She told the neighbors that she always trembled with fear when walking home with him after night. They counseled her to acquaint the stern old Lieber with her troubles—but she only started, and shook her head.

One day Katrina said she had forbidden the Count to speak to her again—the acquaintance must end at once and forever. Katrina never entered the cottage again. Late at night, old Lieber, unmindful of the rain, and unheeding the lightning and the thunder, marched through the deserted streets to Herr Wahlner's house, and knocking furiously at the door, demanded his daughter. Madame Wahlner fainted with terror when she learned that Katrina had not reached the cottage. The Wahlners only knew that she left their door alone, just after nightfall—that it was raining a little at the time, and very dark—that they had thought nothing of her going home without company, as she had often done it before. Lieber's face grew dark. He swore a fearful oath that if Katrina had met with foul play, the guilty ones should learn the strength of a father's wrath, and the weight of a father's hand. And muttering curses, he stalked out into the storm, banging the door after him till the house shook again. The bellman's melancholy cry was heard after that, and heavy feet on the sidewalks; and lanterns glimmered here and there in all the rainy streets. But nothing came of it.

The next day, a woman said that early the previous evening she heard three piercing screams, and then a man's voice exclaimed, in German, "Put her in the carriage, quick—and gag her!" and the next moment a vehicle of some kind drove rapidly by. She could see nothing, owing to the density of the rain and mist. In the afternoon, a handkerchief marked in the corner, with Katrina's initials, was found near the castle, and near it a bracelet which old Lieber identified as her property.

Day and night, without resting, the poor old father searched for his lost child, but without success. He suspected that Count Ritter Von Muller was concerned in her disappearance, and so did the neighbors. The young nobleman's character was none of the brightest, as all were free to acknowledge—in a whisper. Lieber had the Count arrested, but nothing could be proven against him, and he was discharged. Then Lieber demanded that the Castle should be searched. This was granted, but not a vestige of the missing girl came to light.

At last, on the tenth morning after Katrina's disappearance, the body of the unfortunate girl, weltering in blood, was found in the midst of a dense wood, some three or four miles from Risse. Her throat had been cut from ear to ear. Near the corpse a bloody knife was found. A slip of paper was discovered, concealed about her clothing, containing these words, written in pencil:

"I charge Ritter Von Muller with my abduction. And I charge Carl Ohlman, Frederick Uhr, Heinrich Schmidt, and Johannes Mehler with aiding him. As God is my witness, I have spoken truly.

Katrina Lieber."

The note bore the date of the night of Katrina's abduction. There were many footprints in the vicinity of the body, but only one of them was well defined. This one seemed to have been made by a small, well-shaped shoe, and near the toe of it appeared the impression of three tack or nail-heads, in the shape of a tri-angle.

At the inquest, Lieber stood rigid and silent, with folded arms and tearless eyes. At the close, Herr Wahlner tapped him on the shoulder:

"What will you do now?"

"Nothing!" ejaculated Lieber, almost fiercely.

"Nothing?" said Herr Wahlner. "Is it thus that you intend to keep your threats? The law must deal with this matter."

"What! These men (glaring at the note,) are sons of noble and wealthy families, every one of them. My girl was poor. I am poor. Will the law hang Count Von Muller? Will the law imprison Count Von Muller? Stuff!" and he turned on his heel and became stone again.

Old Lieber followed his murdered child to the grave, and after placing a simple tombstone at the head of it bearing the single word "Katrina," went away, no one knew whither.

Count Von Muller, Carl Ohlman, Frederick Uhr, Heinrich Schmidt and Johannes Mehler were arrested, charged with the abduction and murder of Katrina Lieber. As Lieber had said, they were all of noble and wealthy families, and no one expected the trial to amount to anything of a serious nature. And so it turned out. A shoe was produced in Court which had been found on Frederick Uhr's premises, and certain witnesses swore that said shoe fitted exactly, and corresponded in every respect with the peculiar track noticed at the scene of the tragedy. But that was nothing. If any person had ever seen that shoe on Frederick Uhr's foot, that person was not forthcoming at the trial. And besides, Frederick Uhr proved, by witnesses of lawful age, that he was confined to his bed by sickness during the entire night of the murder. The Court decided that the dead girl's note was no evidence at all, and the matter ended with an honorable acquittal of the five young noblemen.

Nearly two years had elapsed since the occurrence of the events which I have just recorded, and during that time no one had seen or heard of Lieber. Poor Katrina was almost forgotten. About two months ago, cries of murder were heard issuing—strange circumstance—from the vault of the old Cathedral, and that, too, at the dead hour of midnight. The Risse watchmen, after the manner of policemen in general, rushed bravely to the rescue just as soon as ever they were sure that the noise had entirely ceased. They broke open the church doors, and then broke open the entrance to the vault. All was dark. But a flood of light from a "bull's-eye" showed them a sight that made their knees knock together. It was nothing more nor less than the body of the young Count Von Muller, with his life blood, warm and smoking, welling from a dozen ghastly stabs in his breast, and flooding with its crimson tide the tombs of his knightly ancestors. The Count was dead. But the strangest thing about the fearful tragedy was, that a hideous cross had been cut in the centre of the Count's forehead with some sharp instrument. Near the body was found an extinguished lantern, the wick in which was still hot. Not a vestige of the murderer could be found; and to this day, the question of how he and his victim got into the vault through barred and bolted doors, and how he afterwards escaped so suddenly, are unfathomed mysteries. Searches for secret passages about the old church are still carried on. The Count was bound hand and foot, and he had also been gagged, but the fastenings of the gag were broken. At the inquest, the porter of the castle testified that about two hours before the murder was committed, he met the Count in the outskirts of the town, followed by three men, one of whom was a large man, and carried a lantern. The suspicion was soon whispered abroad that the large man must

. . . .

This paragraph appeared:

"MYSTERIOUS.—Yesterday morning, the body of a young man was found in the public road, a few miles north of the city, stabbed in a dozen places, and bearing upon the centre of his forehead the form of a cross, apparently cut with a knife. A dagger was sticking in the body, and fastened to its hilt was a slip of paper on one side of which a note had evidently been written, but the words were all obliterated except these:

"'* charge Ritter * * * * abduction * * * Frederick Uhr (or Uber,) * * * * Johannes Mehler with aiding * * * *.'

"On the other side of the slip were these words:

"'This dagger took away the blameless life of Katrina Lieber—peace to her ashes! It hath also slain Count Ritter Von Muller, Carl Ohlman, Frederick Uhr, Heinrich Schmidt and Johannes Mehler. I leave it as a legacy to their noble houses.'

"Papers found on the body led the jury to suppose that this was Johannes Mehler. The cross upon the forehead of the murdered man, as well as the note attached to the dagger, indicate that this deed was performed by the mysterious Lun assassin."

Now you have the sanguinary story, Mr. Editor, and you can discern why it is that Lun and Risse have shaken off their torpor and undignifiedly given way to an excitement.

The blood-stained dagger and the note are on exhibition at the office of the *Burgermeister*, and trembling crowds come daily to gaze upon it. I fear me these people will never sleep quietly again unless the death of the terrible Lieber is speedily compassed. What an acquisition to the ancient Brotherhood of Assassins the man would have been! Yea—and what a genial companion to our own "Nick of the Woods" (from both parties he probably borrowed an idea or so.)

I shall say no more at present, as the mail will close presently.

Yours, &c.

SAM

P.S.—The town has gone wild with the news of Lieber's arrest. The people are overjoyed, although the rumor is not perfectly well authenticated.

26. [Pilot's Memoranda]

30 August 1860

The impulse to burlesque evident in almost every detail of Clemens' "River Intelligence" (no. 24) is present more subtly in "Pilot's Memoranda," published over a year later in the St. Louis *Missouri Republican*. A typical pilot's memoranda[1] of the time might record the main events of a steamboat's trip: when and where other boats were met or passed and observations of noteworthy river occurrences and conditions. In May 1860, for instance, a memoranda signed by Clemens and Wesley Jacobs, copilots of the *City of Memphis*, appeared under "River News" in the *Missouri Republican*. Although the memoranda is brief and limited mainly to one kind of information, in tone and style it is not uncharacteristic of many others:

From the Western Boatmen's Benevolent Association. Memoranda—
Steamer City of Memphis left St. Louis, Thursday, the 14th at 3 P.M., $7\frac{1}{2}$ feet; found $10\frac{1}{2}$ feet at Barrack's crossing, 12 do at Marramee, $9\frac{1}{2}$ do at Bridgewater, 8 do at Crawfords, 8 do scant at Tea Table, 8 do at Vancil's, 8 do at Devil's Island; took on 1,000 bbls of lime at Cape Girardeau, which made us draw 7 feet 9 inches; had 7 feet at Power's Island—rubbed very hard; 8 feet at Goose Island—rubbed very hard; $10\frac{1}{2}$ feet at Buffalo Island; 12 feet at head of Dog Tooth Bend.

> Wesley Jacobs,
> Sam'l Clemens, Pilots[2]

Clemens left the *City of Memphis* and joined the new "tramp" steamer *Arago* on 28 July 1860. His burlesque memoranda, also signed by his copilot, J. W. Hood, appeared one month later. It gives highlights of the *Arago's*

---

[1]In contemporary usage there was no singular "memorandum."

[2]"River News," St. Louis *Missouri Republican*, 27 May 1860, p. 4; quoted by Dewey Ganzel in "Samuel Clemens' Correspondence in the St. Louis *Missouri Republican*," *Anglia* 85 (1967): 393.

trip from New Orleans to Cairo between August 22 and 28, mentioning landmarks and islands passed on the voyage up river. But unlike ordinary memoranda, this one interlaces facts with comic inventions, real landmarks and steamers with fictitious ones. Indeed, "Pilot's Memoranda" anticipates the more subtle blend of fact and fiction that Clemens would achieve in his correspondence with Nevada and California newspapers. But because he wrote it almost exclusively for his fellow pilots, the humor depends heavily on their intimate technical knowledge of the river and its hazards. The explanatory notes to this sketch are therefore essential in following the rather private joke he published for their benefit.[3]

---

[3]For a detailed consideration of the *Arago* burlesque memoranda and Clemens' service on that steamer, see Allan Bates, "Sam Clemens, Pilot-Humorist of a Tramp Steamboat," *American Literature* 39 (March 1967): 102–109.

[Pilot's Memoranda]

STEAMER ARAGO, ⎫
CAIRO, August 28th ⎭

Pilot's Memoranda—Steamer Arago left New Orleans on Wednesday, August 22, at 3 P. M. In port and loading for St Louis, steamers Sovereign and Great Western. 23d—Met Minne-ha ha at Port Hudson, Wm. M. Morrison at Palmetto Point; passed the Tommy-whack at Dead Mare, and the Yahoo at the Cotton Gin. 24th—Met John Walsh at Rodney, Sky Lark at Vicksburg; passed the Skylight and the Twilight and the Daylight at Mud Bar. These boats are said to be *fast*, and so they may be, under *ordinary* circumstances. 25th—Met Dan'l G. Taylor at Lake Providence, Planet at No. 76, South Wester at Napoleon; found the Saltpetre hard aground at Seven-Up, North Wester pulling at her; passed the Don Cæsar de Bazan at the Wood Pile. 26th—Met J. C. Swon at Old Town, D. A. January and Emma at Friar's Point; found the Tycoon aground at Boomerang; they were lighting her off by removing her cargo, consisting of railroad iron, from the main deck to the hurricane deck. Capt. Bladders intimated to the pilots of this boat confidentially, that in his opinion if he did not stay there long, he would probably get off shortly. Capt. is an experienced steamboatman, and what he even intimates may be depended on. Passed the Grand Duke of Kiho at John Battese's. 27th—Met City of Memphis at Greenock, John H. Dickey at No. 36, J. D. Perry at Ashport, Edw. J. Gay at Forked Deer. Also, met the Gladiator above New Madrid, with the "pilot factory" in full operation. Passed the Kangaroo Belle at Blackjack.

Mem—The agents in New Orleans informed the pilots of this boat that "they considered the fact that freights were not so rotten property, as pretty well established." Amen! Nothing doing at Natchez—provisions and things scarce, at least the pilots of this boat were told so. Plenty new crop cotton on the banks. A heavy rise is reported in the Arkansas river—so the everlasting pilots of this boat were informed at Napoleon. Notice to Pilots—Run the crossing at Helena lower. Steamer Choctaw still broken in two at Island 34, and pretty much sunk. A great part of her freight had been put ashore and covered with tarpaulins. A diving bell boat was along side of her, and somebody informed the pilots of this boat that "they'll raise her if nothing but the bottom's knocked of her," and we cheerfully indorse the sentiment.

P. S.—Found Edward Walsh loading at Cairo.

P. S. No. 2—We have not mentioned all the boats we passed—we only take "cognizance" of the fast ones.

P. S. No. 3.—We, the pilots of this boat, saw on board the Ed. J. Gay our distinguished fellow-citizen, Major General Sobeisky Jolly, on his way to Japan. Col. Joseph Bryant and several other members of Congress were also on board the same boat, going out to "look at the river."

P. S. No. 4—"Adoo."

Respectfully submitted.

SAM. L. CLEMENS,

J. W. HOOD,

Pilots of this boat.

27. [Ghost Life on the Mississippi]

January–June 1861

"Ghost Life on the Mississippi" was probably written in 1861 before Clemens took the overland stage to Nevada in July. Annie Moffett, his niece, remembered having heard her uncle tell or read this tale—or a version of it—when she was a little girl in St. Louis.[1] The untitled manuscript, which Clemens probably left with the Moffetts when he went West, is preserved in the Jean Webster McKinney Family Papers, now at Vassar. The sketch was published by Samuel C. Webster in 1948, but the present text has been reedited from the manuscript and restores a number of readings inadvertently omitted from Webster's text.

As Allan Bates has shown in a thorough analysis, "Ghost Life" is a milestone in Clemens' early career as a writer.[2] Despite certain inconsistencies and weaknesses in the narrative handling, the tale reveals a growing literary maturity and a distinct ability to construct serious fiction of some length. In it Clemens shows demonstrable growth in craft over "The Mysterious Murders in Risse" (no. 25), in particular through sophistication in establishing credibility, creating and maintaining suspense, and dramatizing the action through the effective use of details. Neither the third-person narrative nor the dialogue achieves the ease and seeming simplicity of his later vernacular style, but the author has taken long strides beyond the stiffness of his earlier works, and he has taken an important step toward assimilating material from his own experience.

---

[1] *MTBus*, p. 48.
[2] *MTMR*, pp. 234–245.

[Ghost Life on the Mississippi]

THE RECENT DEATH of an old Saint Louis and New Orleans pilot has brought the following strange story to light. I shall not attempt, by any word of my own, to secure the reader's belief in it, but I will merely relate the simple facts in the case, as they fell from the lips of a dying man, and leave him to form his own opinion. Fictitious names, however, will be used throughout the narrative, in accordance with the wishes of certain actors in the mysterious drama who are still living.

Joseph Millard, the pilot referred to, was a master of his profession, a good man, and a truthful man; and this tale, coming from his lips, while in a perfectly sound state of mind, and stretched upon his death-bed, leaves but a small field for the cavilings of the incredulous. Until that hour the whole thing had been kept a profound secret by himself and the other witnesses of the horrible affair. And now for the facts.

A number of years ago, a Saint Louis and New Orleans packet, which I will call the "Boreas," was on her way up the river, and at about ten o'clock at night, the sky, which had before been clear, suddenly became overcast, and snow commenced falling soon afterwards. The boat was near the head of Dog Tooth Bend at the time. The Captain stepped out of the "Texas," and said to the pilot on watch:

"Well, I reckon Goose Island would n't be a very safe place for the Boreas to-night, Mr. Jones. So, if it keeps on snowing at this rate, I reckon you had better bring her to at the first wood-pile you come across near the head of Dog Tooth or Buffalo Island."

The little narrow bend around Goose Island is called the "Grave-Yard," because of the numerous wrecks of steamboats that have found a tomb in it. Besides these obstructions, a great many large snags stood directly in the way at the time I speak of, and the narrow channel being very "shoal" also, the best of piloting was necessary in order to "run" Goose Island in safety, even in daylight.

Mr. Jones passed the wood-yards in silence, and held his way up the river through the driving rain; for that very day he had declared that Goose Island "had no terrors for *him*, on any kind of night," and had been laughed at by several other pilots, who jestingly called him the "King of Pilots." He was still angry and sullen, and occasionally, as he thought of the jest, he would grate his teeth and mutter that "he would show them that he *was* the king of pilots in reality."

At about half past eleven the other pilot came up, having been called too soon, through a mistake on the part of the watchman, and noticing that the boat was approaching the foot of Goose Island, he said:

"Why, Jones, surely you are not going to run this place on such a night as this?"

"I'll take her through, if the Devil seizes me for it in five minutes afterwards!"

And through those hidden dangers,—and shrouded in that Egyptian darkness—the steamer plowed her way, watched by an unerring eye and guided by a master hand, whose nerves trembled not for a single instant! And snags and wrecks remained untouched.

"*Now*, who is king of pilots!"

And those were the last words of William Jones, pilot.

Then he gave up the wheel and left the pilot house, and when the four o'clock watch was called, he could not be found. There was blood upon the "nosing" of the starboard guard, and a fireman said, the next day, that a man fell from the boiler deck in the night, and he thought his head struck that place, but that the watchman only laughed at him when he mentioned it, and said he had a fertile imagination.

When the Boreas arrived at Saint Louis she was sold, and lay idle the balance of the summer, and fall, and finally left for New Orleans in the dead of winter, with an entirely new set of officers—Joe Millard and Ben. Reubens, pilots.

One cold, raw night, as the boat was approaching Goose Island, snow commenced falling, and it soon became almost too dark to run. This reminded Joe of the almost forgotten Jones; and he determined to try and get the boat up into the little bend as far as the "Shingle Pile," and lay up till morning, as he preferred having the balance of Goose Island in daylight.

He had just gained the foot of the bend when the snow commenced falling so densely that he could see nothing at all—not even the trees on the shore at his side. He stopped the engines, of course.

At that moment he felt conscious that he was not alone—that some one was in the pilot house with him—although he had bolted the door on the inside, to keep it from blowing open, and that was the only mode of ingress! Yes, he was sure he could distinguish the dim outline of a human figure standing on the opposite side of the wheel. A moment after, he heard the bell lines pulled—heard the handles strike the frame as they fell back to their places, and then the faint tinkle of the answering bells came up from below. In an instant the wheel was jerked out of his hands, and a sudden gleam of light from a crack in the stove pipe revealed the ghastly features of William Jones, with a great piece of skin, ragged and bloody, torn loose from his forehead and dangling and flapping over his left eye—the other eye dead and fixed and lustreless—hair wet and disordered, and the whole body bent and shapeless, like that of a drowned man, and apparently rigid as marble, except the hands and arms, which seemed alone endued with life and motion!

Joseph Millard's blood curdled in his veins, and he trembled in every limb at the horrid vision. And yet he was a brave man, and held no superstitious notions. He would have left the accursed place, but he seemed bound with bands of iron. He tried to call for help, but his tongue refused its office; he caught the sound of the watchman's heavy tramp on the hurricane deck—would *no* signal draw his attention?— but the trial was vain—he could neither move nor speak,—and aid and comfort almost in a whisper's reach of him. Then the footsteps died away and the desperate man was left alone with his fearful company.

Riveted to the spot he listened to the clashing engines and the moaning of the frosty wind, while that ghostly pilot steered the vessel through darkness such as no human eye could penetrate. Millard expected every moment to hear the timbers crashing against wreck or snag, but he was deceived. Through every danger that infested the way the dead man steered in safety, turning the wheel from one side to the other calmly and quietly as if it had been noonday.

It seemed to Millard as if an age had passed over his head, when he heard something fall on the floor with a slight clatter on the other side of the wheel; he did not know what it was—he only shuddered, and wondered what it meant. Soon after, by the faint light from the crack in the stove-pipe he saw his ghostly comrade moving silently towards the door—saw him lean against it for a moment, *open it*, and disappear.

Millard mustered strength enough to stop the engines, and at the same moment he heard the voice of his partner at the door. He stepped back to open it, and found that it was *still bolted on the inside!*

Poor Millard was now utterly confounded. He felt qualified to swear that he had seen the shape—no matter what it was—man or ghost or devil—go out at that very door—and yet it was still bolted! and so securely too that he hardly had strength enough left to unfasten it. But when the feat was at last accomplished, he sank down exhausted, and trembling from head to foot like a man with the palsy.

"Why how is this, Joe?—out in such a snow-storm, when one can't see the chimneys, let alone the derricks and jackstaff! You're beating Jones himself, Joe. Where are we, man?—where are we?"

"God only knows! Land her, Ben, for Heaven's sake, if you can ever find the shore."

During a momentary lull in the storm, Ben felt his way to shore, and rounded to under Philadelphia Point. And then he proceeded to question Joe.

"Swear that you will never mention the matter during my life, and I will tell you what I have seen this night; but on no other terms will I open my lips—for if the story should get abroad, Joseph Millard would become the laughing stock of the whole river, Ben."

Reubens wondered much at Millard's strange conduct; his curiosity was raised, however, and he took the oath. And quaking and shuddering, his comrade told the fearful tale.

Reubens was silent for a moment, after Millard had finished.

"You spoke of something that fell and rattled on the floor, Joe—what do you suppose it was?"

"It startled me when it fell, but I have no idea what it was, Ben."

"Well, I'll go after a lantern, and we'll soon find out."

"What! and leave me here by myself! I would n't stay here alone five minutes for a dozen steamboats."

So they both went, and soon returned with a light. Near the foot-board, on the starboard side of the wheel, they saw a glittering object, which proved to be a silver watch, lying open, with the crystal detached and broken in half. The break seemed recent. Neatly engraved, on the back of the watch, were these words.

"WILLIAM JONES—PRESENTED BY HIS FATHER."

SECTION 2

Nevada Territory

1862-1864

28. Petrified Man

4 October 1862

The first printing of "Petrified Man" in the Virginia City *Territorial Enterprise* is not extant, but at least three contemporary newspapers reprinted the complete text. Two of these papers attributed the piece to the *Enterprise* for 4 October 1862 and gave the title Clemens used in a letter to his brother Orion on October 21: "Did you see that squib of mine headed 'Petrified Man?'"

In the same letter Clemens went on to explain the motive behind his hoax: "It is an unmitigated lie, made from whole cloth. I got it up to worry Sewall. Every day, I send him some California paper containing it; moreover, I am getting things so arranged that he will soon begin to receive letters from all parts of the country, purporting to come from scientific men, asking for further information concerning the wonderful stone man. If I had plenty of time, I would worry the life out of the poor cuss."[1] The reasons for Clemens' dislike of G. T. Sewall remain obscure. Sewall had been a resident of Humboldt County since 1853 and had received his commission as judge of that county from Governor Nye in December 1861. Sewall was also active in mining. By October 1863 he was general superintendent and in charge of all mining operations of the Atlantic and Pacific Gold and Silver Mining Company, which controlled five mines in Humboldt township and aggressively claimed in its prospectus the rights to "all unclaimed or 'blind ledges' they may strike."[2] Sewall's status in the district is indicated by his accompanying the nationally famous scientist Benjamin Silliman, Jr., on Silliman's much-

---

[1]Clemens to Orion [and Mollie] Clemens, 21 October 1862, *CL1*, letter 64.

[2]*Prospectus of the Atlantic and Pacific Gold and Silver Mining Co. Together with the By-Laws* (New York: Latimer Bros. and Seymour, 1864), p. 12.

publicized inspection of the Humboldt and Reese River mines in September 1864.[3]

It is unlikely that Clemens really enlisted "scientific men" in his project, but entirely plausible that he sent Sewall the California reprints. In 1870 Clemens recalled that for "about eleven months . . . Mr. Sewall's daily mail contained along in the neighborhood of half a bushel of newspapers . . . with the Petrified Man in them, marked around with a prominent belt of ink. I sent them to him. I did it for spite, not for fun." In fact, the number of California papers that reprinted part or all of the hoax—at least ten are extant, the last appearing on 8 November 1862—suggests that Clemens had an ample supply to draw upon. "I hated Sewall in those days," he explained, "and these things pacified me and pleased me. I could not have gotten more real comfort out of him without killing him."[4]

Presumably Clemens and Sewall became acquainted while Clemens was prospecting in the Humboldt mining district in 1861–1862. In view of Sewall's aggressive policy toward "unclaimed or 'blind ledges' " they may have clashed over mining rights. But Clemens' southern sympathies may also have been offensive to the Humboldt County judge. Seven months before this sketch appeared Clemens wrote from Carson City to his friend William Clagett: "I have heard from several reliable sources that Sewall will be here shortly, and has sworn to whip me on sight. . . . I don't see why he should dislike me. He is a Yankee,—and I natural[l]y love a Yankee."[5] However, it is not known whether political differences were the source of the animosity Clemens felt. Whatever caused the hard feelings, he was still plugging the hoax more than a month after its publication. He reported that "Mr. Herr Weisnicht" had brought "the head and one foot of the petrified man" with him to Virginia City, and that the remains could "be seen in a neat glass case in the third story of the Library Building."[6] And he retained enough animus toward Sewall in July 1863 to needle him in a letter to the San Francisco *Morning Call:* "Mr. Sewall is the profound Justice of the Peace who held an inquest last Fall at Gravelly Ford, on the Humboldt River, on a petrified man, who had been sitting there, cemented to the bed-rock, for the last three or four hundred years. The citizens wished to blast him out and bury him, but Judge S. refused to allow the sacrilege to be committed."[7]

[3]"Over the Mountains," San Francisco *Alta California,* 10 September 1864, p. 1.
[4]"A Couple of Sad Experiences" (no. 299), first published in the *Galaxy* 9 (June 1870): 858–861.
[5]Clemens to Clagett, 8 March 1862, *CL1,* letter 43.
[6]"The Petrified Man," reprinted from the *Enterprise* by the Oroville (Calif.) *Butte Record,* 15 November 1862, p. 2, quoted in *MTVC,* p. 17.
[7]" 'Mark Twain's' Letter," San Francisco *Morning Call,* 15 July 1863, PH from Yale.

Nevertheless, in 1870 Clemens recalled that his desire to annoy Sewall had been merely an incidental motive for the hoax. Instead, he claimed that he had wanted to "destroy" what he called a growing mania among newsmen for reporting "extraordinary petrifactions and other natural marvels. One could scarcely pick up a paper without finding in it one or two glorified discoveries of this kind."[8] An examination of surviving files of Nevada and California newspapers published just before October 1862 fails to substantiate his claim, almost certainly because so few papers are extant. As early as 1831 a Mississippi paper printed an account of an "ossified man," who became "all bone, except the skin, eyes and entrails" because he incautiously fell "asleep in the open air during a state of perspiration."[9] And examples of similar marvels, usually reported seriously, crowd the local columns of western papers after 1862 when the files become more numerous and more complete. There are many reported discoveries of skeletons and fossils, petrified beehives and plums, and such artifacts as mummified bodies or bodies turned to solid marble, a silver man, living frogs encased in sandstone, monster serpents, and showers of fish. It seems implausible that such items did not also appear prior to 1862.

Obviously such reports of "marvels" shade off into deliberately tall stories and hoaxes. In fact, Clemens' piece was not the first western hoax about a petrified human being: an article entitled "Extraordinary and Shocking Death of Miner" was published four years earlier (1858) in the San Francisco *Alta California* and widely reprinted as "Extraordinary Account of Human Petrifaction." This piece is unusually detailed and studded with technical terms, and is thus more akin to the scientific tall tales of Dan De Quille than it is to the seemingly legitimate reports of petrifaction that Clemens' hoax parodied. It purports to be a letter from Dr. Friedrich Lichtenberger, M.D., Ph.D., who describes the rapid silification of Ernest Flucterspiegel, a miner in the Frazer River area, who broke open a geode and incautiously drank the "water of crystallization" it contained. Within two and one-half hours Flucterspiegel was "inflexible." Describing his dissection of the corpse, Dr. Lichtenberger found that the heart "strongly resembled a piece of red jasper. . . . By means of a small hatchet, I separated the heart from its connections with the aorta, pulmonary artery and vena cava and with some difficulty was able to break it in pieces. . . . The larger blood vessels were all as rigid as pipe stems, and in some cases the petrified blood could be cracked out from the veins, exhibiting a beautiful moulding upon the valves of the latter." The silicic acid in the geode water had reacted with "the

---

[8]"A Couple of Sad Experiences," *Galaxy*, p. 858.
[9]"An Ossified Man," Woodville *Mississippi Democrat*, 12 March 1831, p. 2.

conjugated acids of the bile, (acting as an alkali) and with the albuminose of the ingesta" and had formed a "silicate of albumen" with the blood. The doctor announced his intention to send specimens of the body to the Academy of Natural Sciences at Philadelphia for examination.[10]

Clemens recalled in 1870 that "as a *satire* on the petrifaction mania" his piece had been a "disheartening failure; for everybody received" the petrified man "in innocent good faith." He remembered that the hoax was widely reprinted in newspapers across the country, until it "swept the great globe and culminated in sublime and unimpeached legitimacy in the august 'London Lancet.'"[11] Of course, this is certainly an exaggeration—but it contains an element of truth. Of the twelve California and Nevada papers that are known to have reprinted "Petrified Man," eight of them gave no sign whatever that they doubted the truth of the story. San Francisco newspapers were shrewd enough: the *Alta* called it a "sell" and the *Evening Bulletin* "A Washoe Joke." But the Sacramento *Bee* asserted more tentatively that it was "probably a hoax," and the *Bulletin* reported that "the interior journals seem to be copying [it] in good faith."[12]

---

[10]"Extraordinary and Shocking Death of Miner," San Francisco *Alta California*, 19 July 1858, p. 1.

[11]"A Couple of Sad Experiences," *Galaxy*, p. 859.

[12]DeLancey Ferguson, in " 'The Petrified Truth,' " *Colophon* n.s. 2 (Winter 1937): 189–196, points out the exaggeration in Clemens' account, but does not recognize that the hoax in fact deceived the editors of some local papers.

Petrified Man

A PETRIFIED MAN was found some time ago in the mountains south of Gravelly Ford. Every limb and feature of the stony mummy was perfect, not even excepting the left leg, which has evidently been a wooden one during the lifetime of the owner—which lifetime, by the way, came to a close about a century ago, in the opinion of a savan who has examined the defunct. The body was in a sitting posture, and leaning against a huge mass of croppings; the attitude was pensive, the right thumb resting against the side of the nose; the left thumb partially supported the chin, the fore-finger pressing the inner corner of the left eye and drawing it partly open; the right eye was closed, and the fingers of the right hand spread apart. This strange freak of nature created a profound sensation in the vicinity, and our informant states that by request, Justice Sewell or Sowell, of Humboldt City, at once proceeded to the spot and held an inquest on the body. The verdict of the jury was that "deceased came to his death from protracted exposure," etc. The people of the neighborhood volunteered to bury the poor unfortunate, and were even anxious to do so; but it was discovered, when they attempted to remove him, that the water which had dripped upon him for ages from the crag above, had coursed down his back and deposited a limestone sediment under him which had glued him to the bed rock upon which he sat, as with a cement of adamant, and Judge S. refused to allow the charitable citizens to blast him from his position. The opinion expressed by his Honor that such a course would be little less than sacrilege, was eminently just and proper. Everybody goes to see the stone man, as many as three hundred having visited the hardened creature during the past five or six weeks.

§ 29. The Spanish Mine

Late October 1862

§ 30. The Spanish

12 or 22 February 1863

When the Ophir claim was located on the Comstock Lode in June 1859, Emanuel Penrod and Henry Comstock, two members of the Ophir Company, were allotted an extra one hundred feet on the lead. The company gave them this either in return for water rights under their control or, as Penrod later said, because he, supported by Comstock, had identified the ore-bearing quartz lead. Later that year Penrod and Comstock sold their one hundred feet for $9,500 to Gabriel Maldonado and Francis J. Hughes, who formed the Mexican Company and began to work the Mexican, or Spanish, mine.[1] It soon became one of the most productive and valuable mines on the Comstock Lode.

In late October 1862 and again in mid-February 1863 Mark Twain descended into the Spanish mine and published two closely linked accounts of his visits. The first, called "The Spanish Mine," was published in the Virginia City *Territorial Enterprise* sometime in October, but is extant only in the Oroville (Calif.) *Butte Record* for 1 November 1862, which reprinted the *Enterprise*. The second, which is entitled "The Spanish," survives in an *Enterprise* clipping; it fulfilled the author's promise in the first sketch to speak at a later date of the "steam hoisting apparatus now in process of erection by the Spanish Company."

Neither piece was signed, but circumstantial and stylistic evidence combine to show that Clemens wrote both of them. The first sketch is, for instance, remarkable for its irresistible drift toward humor. The author played

---

[1]Myron Angel, ed., *History of Nevada* (Oakland: Thompson and West, 1881), pp. 56–57; Eliot Lord, *Comstock Mining and Miners* (Berkeley: Howell-North, 1959), p. 61. In his "Around the World. Letter Number 6" (no. 268), first published in the Buffalo *Express*, 8 January 1870, pp. 2–3, Clemens gave a condensed version of the origin of the Spanish mine which he later repeated in chapter 46 of *Roughing It*.

with the notion of nearing "the confines of purgatory—so to speak," and visiting "the infernal regions." The complex timbering prompted him to wonder "where the forest around [him] came from, and how they managed to get it into that hole." He compared descending through these square-set timbers to "falling through a well-ventilated shot-tower with the windows all open." And he casually mocked his own guided tour of a local marvel: "keep on going until you come to a horse."

Dan De Quille, the mining expert on the *Enterprise* staff, was sharing the duties of local reporter with Clemens in October 1862. Dan was capable of such playful reporting, but a number of circumstances show that he did not write these two sketches. The style of each is unmistakably Clemens': the use of the phrase "you know" and of "waltz" as a slang verb of motion are both practically signatures. But beyond this, the implicit sense of naive wonder that pervades the first sketch is not consistent with Dan's expertise.[2] And he certainly could not have written the second one (forecast in the first), because he had by then left Nevada for Iowa, and Clemens was writing all of the local items by himself. The first sketch must, in fact, record Clemens' earliest exposure to mining techniques, such as Philip Deidesheimer's square-set method of mine timbering, and the relatively primitive methods of descent—a winding staircase, and a bucket at the end of a rope.

Moreover, many of the details mentioned in the first sketch were used in other descriptions of mine interiors that were demonstrably written by Clemens. In a letter probably written early in 1863 to his family, Clemens said that if Pamela were to visit a mine, she would see "great, dark, timbered chambers, with a lot of shapeless devils flitting about in the distance, with dim candles flickering in the gloom; and then she could look far above her head, to the top of the shaft, and see a faint little square of daylight, apparently no bigger than one of the spots on a chess-board."[3] And in late May 1868, while visiting Virginia City on his western lecture tour, Clemens wrote a newspaper letter in which he recalled visiting the mines:

In those old days, when we reporters went dangling down a dark shaft at the end of a crazy rope, with a candle in our teeth, to the depth of two or three hundred feet, we felt as if we were getting into the very bowels of the earth. We prowled uncomfortably through muddy, crumbling drifts and tunnels, and were happy no more until the man up at the bullet-hole that showed us a far-off glimpse of blue sky, wound us up with his windlass and set us in the cheerful light of the sun again.[4]

---

[2]For instance, Dan probably wrote "Mexican Mine," a detailed article describing the mine's steam-powered hoisting apparatus, reprinted from the *Enterprise* by the Oroville (Calif.) *Butte Record*, 29 November 1862, p. 2. This highly technical account of the machinery is absolutely humorless.

[3]Clemens to Jane Clemens, [ca. February–March 1863], *CL1*, letter 66.

[4]"Letter from Mark Twain," Chicago *Republican*, 31 May 1868, p. 2.

We may compare these passages with references in the first sketch to "work-men poking about in the gloom with twinkling candles," "bottomless holes with endless ropes hanging down into them," and "hot candle-grease" and the chance to "get your clothes dirty," and particularly to the anxiety to return to the daylight above.

External circumstantial evidence also corroborates Clemens' authorship. In January 1870 he reminisced about the Spanish mine and its sudden rise in "market value": "I was down in it about that time, 600 ft under the ground, and about half of it caved in over my head."[5] "About that time" could mean either 1862 or 1863. Another factual detail, moreover, seems to link Clemens with the first sketch. The mine superintendent mentioned late in the sketch, Harvey Beckwith, was evidently known to Clemens in 1862, when the piece was published: in January 1868 Clemens wrote a letter of recommendation for him in which he said that Beckwith was "a first-rate man in every way—steady, faithful, smart & particularly energetic. . . . God never made two such men. . . . I have known him six years."[6]

The *Enterprise* clipping from the local column that included the second sketch is in the Grant Smith Papers. Above it someone has penciled "Mark visits the Mexican mine, Enterprise Feb. 2, 1863." This date cannot be correct, however, because February 2 fell on a Monday that year, and the *Enterprise* did not publish on Mondays. Moreover, Clemens was in Carson City from January 29 until at least February 7 and so could not have visited the mine "yesterday," if publication occurred in the first week of February. Still, February 1863 is a plausible time for it to have appeared. Clemens was then busily feuding with Clement T. Rice (the Unreliable), whose head, we are told in the second sketch, was "filled with oysters instead of brains." And early in 1863 heavy rains caused flooding in some of the Comstock mines, a condition alluded to in this account. It therefore seems likely that whoever annotated the clipping in the Grant Smith Papers mistook the date by one digit, and we have conjectured it as either February 12 or 22.

---

[5]"Around the World. Letter Number 6," Buffalo *Express*, pp. 2–3. This recollection seems to conflate Clemens' memories of his visits to the Spanish mine with those he made to the Ophir in July 1863, shortly before and shortly after the Spanish mine caved in to a depth of 225 feet with a force that damaged the bordering Ophir down to the fourth gallery. For Clemens' account of his descents into the Ophir see " 'Mark Twain's' Letter," San Francisco *Morning Call*, 15, 18, and 23 July 1863, PH at Yale. His story in the *Enterprise*, "An Hour in the Caved Mines," must have appeared about the same time; it was reprinted at the end of chapter 52 in *Roughing It*, probably from an *Enterprise* clipping.

[6]Clemens to Stephen J. Field, 9 January 1868, *CL1*, letter 176. Harvey Beckwith is listed as foreman of the Spanish mine in J. Wells Kelly, *Second Directory of Nevada Territory* (San Francisco: Valentine and Co., 1863), p. 173.

When Clemens wrote this second sketch he had obviously learned more about mines and mining than he had known in the fall of 1862, when he wrote the previous one. Sometime between 17 and 22 February 1863 he also published "Silver Bars—How Assayed" (no. 43), a rather wide-eyed account of what he had recently learned of the assay process. And the first item in his column for February 19 was also devoted to mining news.[7] But like other "experts," including the officials of the Spanish mine, he did not foresee the seriousness of the damage caused by the flooding. Water from the spring thaw further weakened the mine's timbering and caused a major cave-in on July 15.

---

[7]See Appendix B8, volume 1.

The Spanish Mine

THIS COMPRISES one hundred feet of the great Comstock lead, and is situated in the midst of the Ophir claims. We visited it yesterday, in company with Mr. Kingman, Assistant Superintendent, and our impression is that stout-legged people with an affinity to darkness, may spend an hour or so there very comfortably. A confused sense of being buried alive, and a vague consciousness of stony dampness, and huge timbers, and tortuous caverns, and bottomless holes with endless ropes hanging down into them, and narrow ladders climbing in a short twilight through the colossal lattice work and suddenly perishing in midnight, and workmen poking about in the gloom with twinkling candles—is all, or nearly all that remains to us of our experience in the Spanish mine. Yet, for the information of those who may wish to go down and see how things are conducted in the realms beyond the jurisdiction of daylight, we are willing to tell a portion of what we know about it. Entering the Spanish tunnel in A street, you grope along by candle light for two hundred and fifty feet—but you need not count your steps—keep on going until you come to a horse. This horse works a whim used for hoisting ore from the infernal regions below, and from long service in the dark, his coat has turned to a beautiful black color. You are now upon the confines of the ledge, and from this point several drifts branch out to different portions of the mine. Without stopping to admire these gloomy grottoes you descend a ladder and halt upon a landing where you are fenced in with an open-work labyrinth of timbers some eighteen inches square, extending in front of you and behind you, and far away above you and below you, until they are lost in darkness. These timbers are framed in squares or "stations," five feet each way, one above another, and so neatly put together that there is not room for the insertion of a knife-blade where they intersect. You are apt to wonder where the forest around you came from, and how they managed to get it into that hole, and what sums of money it must have cost, and so forth and so on, and you wind up with a confused notion that the man who designed it all had a shining talent for saw mills on a large scale. He could build the frame-work beautifully at any rate. Whereupon, you desist from further speculation, and waltz down a very narrow winding staircase, and the further you squirm down it the dizzier you get and the more those open timber squares seem to whiz by you, until you feel as if you are falling through a well-ventilated shot-tower with the windows all open.

Finally, after you have gone down ninety-four feet, you touch bottom again and find yourself in the midst of the saw mill yet, with the regular accomplishments of workmen, and windlasses, and glimmering candles and cetera, as usual. Now you can stoop and dodge about under the "stations," and get your clothes dirty, and drip hot candle-grease all over your hands, and find out how they take those timbers and commence at the top of the mine, and build them together like mighty window sashes all the way down to the bottom of it; and if, after coming down that tipsy staircase, you can by any possibility make out to understand it, then you can render the information useful above ground by building the third story of your house to suit you first, and continuing its erection wrong end foremost until you wind up with the cellar. You will also find out that at this depth the lead is forty-six feet wide, with its sides walled and weather boarded as compactly and substantially as those of a jail. And here and there in little recesses, the walls of the lead are laid bare, showing the blue silver lines traced upon the white quartz, after the fashion of variegated marble —this, in places, you know, while others, where the ore is richer, the blue predominates and the white is scarcely perceptible. From these various recesses a swarm of workmen are constantly conveying wheel-barrow loads of quartz to the windlasses, of all shades of value, from that worth $75 to that worth $3,000 per ton—and if you should chance to be in better luck than we were, you may happen to stumble on a small specimen worth a dollar and a half a pound. Such things have occurred in the Spanish mine before now. However, as we were saying, you are now one hundred and seventy feet under the ground, and you can move about and see how the ore is quarried and moved from one place to another, and how systematically the great mine is arranged and worked altogether, and how unsystematically the Mexicans used to carry on business down there—and you may get into a bucket, if you please, and extend your visit to the confines of purgatory—so to speak—if you feel anxious to do so; but as this would afford you nothing more than a glance at the bottom of a drain shaft, you could better employ your time and talents in climbing that corkscrew and seeking daylight again. And before leaving the mouth of the tunnel, you would do well to visit the office of Mr. Beckwith, the superintendent, where you can see a small cabinet of specimens from the mine which has been pronounced by scientific travelers to be one of the richest collections of the kind in the world. We shall have occasion to speak of the steam hoisting apparatus now in process of erection by the Spanish Company at an early day.

The Spanish

W<small>E SLID DOWN</small> into the Spanish mine yesterday, to look after the rich strike which was made there lately. We found things going on at about their usual gait, and the general appearance of the mine in no respect differing from what it was before the recent flood. A few inches of water still remain in the lower gallery, but it interferes with nobody, and can be easily bailed out whenever it may be deemed necessary. Every department of the Spanish mine is now in first class working order, owing to the able management of the general Superintendent, Mr. J. P. Corrigan: the slight damage done by the inundation having been thoroughly repaired. In the matter of bracing and timbering the mine, an improvement upon the old plan has lately been added, which makes a large saving in the bill of expenses. This improvement consists in building the stations wider and higher, and filling up a wall of them here and there with refuse rock. Expenses are not only lightened thus, but such walls never rot, are never in danger of caving, need never be removed, and are altogether the strongest supports that a mine can have. Intelligent people can understand, now, that about a hundred dollars a day may be saved in this way, without even taking into consideration the costly job of re-timbering every two or three years, which is rendered unnecessary by it—and by way of driving the proposition into heads like the Unreliable's, which is filled with oysters instead of brains, we will say that by building these walls, you are saved the time and labor of lowering heavy timbers 300 feet into the earth and hoisting up refuse rock the same distance; for you can leave the one in the woods, and pile the other into boxed-up stations as fast as you dig it out. However, it is time to speak of the rich strike, now. This charming spot is two hundred and forty feet below the surface of the earth. It extends across the entire width of the ledge—from twenty-five to thirty feet—and has been excavated some twenty feet on the length of the lead, and to the depth of twenty-one feet. How much deeper it reaches, no man knoweth. The face of the walls is of a dark blue color, sparkling with pyrites, or sulphurets, or something, and beautifully marbled with little crooked streaks of lightning as white as loaf sugar. This mass of richness pays from eight to twelve hundred dollars a ton just as it is taken from the ledge, without "sorting." Twenty thousand dollars' worth of it was hoisted out of the mine last Saturday; about two hundred and fifty tons have been taken out altogether. The hoisting apparatus is about perfect: when put to its best speed, it can bail out somewhere in the neighborhood of a hundred and fifty tons of rock in daylight. The rich ore we have been talking about is sacked up as soon as it reaches the surface of the Territory, and shipped off to the Company's mill (the Silver State) at Empire City. The Silver State is a forty-stamp arrangement, with a thundering chimney to it, which any one has noticed who has traveled from here to Carson. Mr. Dorsey is the superintendent, and Mr. Janin assayer.

31. The Pah-Utes

13–19 December 1862

The text of "The Pah-Utes," reprinted from the Virginia City *Territorial Enterprise*, survives in the Marysville (Calif.) *Appeal* for 21 December 1862. It recorded Clemens' fanciful greeting to the Pi-Utes, a newly formed organization of Nevada pioneers limited to those who had come before the mining rush of May 1860.[1] The *Appeal* prefaced its extract as follows: "The old citizens of Nevada Territory are getting up a Pioneer Association, to be called the 'Pah-Utes.' The Carson correspondent of the Virginia City *Enterprise*, thus moralizes thereupon." Clemens was the *Enterprise* correspondent in Carson City, where he was covering the sessions of the second Territorial Legislature of Nevada, which met from 11 November through 20 December 1862. His surviving *Enterprise* letters from that period through 1863 reveal his familiarity with the Pi-Utes.[2] And in one letter, dated 12 December 1863 and signed "Mark Twain," he echoed his final comment below by referring to himself as a relative newcomer: "only an ignorant half-breed" as compared to "a blooded Pi-Ute."[3]

---

[1] *MTEnt*, p. 35.
[2] *MTEnt*, pp. 38, 99; "Letter from Carson" (no. 41).
[3] *MTEnt*, p. 99.

The Pah-Utes

AH, WELL—it is touching to see these knotty and rugged old pioneers—who have beheld Nevada in her infancy, and toiled through
her virgin sands unmolested by toll-keepers; and prospected her unsmiling hills, and knocked at the doors of her sealed treasure vaults;
and camped with her horned-toads, and tarantulas and lizards, under
her inhospitable sage brush; and smoked the same pipe; and imbibed
lightning out of the same bottle; and eaten their regular bacon and
beans from the same pot; and lain down to their rest under the same
blanket—happy, and lousy and contented—yea, happier and lousier
and more contented than they are this day, or may be in the days that
are to come; it is touching, I say, to see these weather-beaten and
blasted old patriarchs banding together like a decaying tribe, for the
sake of the privations they have undergone, and the dangers they have
met—to rehearse the deeds of the hoary past, and rescue its traditions
from oblivion! The Pah-Ute Association will become a high and honorable order in the land—its certificate of membership a patent of
nobility. I extend unto the fraternity the right hand of a poor but
honest half-breed, and say God speed your sacred enterprise.

32. *The Illustrious Departed*

28 December 1862

Dan De Quille (William Wright) left Virginia City by overland stagecoach on 27 December 1862 for a nine-month visit to his home in Iowa. "The Illustrious Departed," written as a mock eulogy, is Clemens' farewell to him, and it survives in an undated clipping from the *Territorial Enterprise*, now in the William Wright Papers. Since Clemens says that Dan "left for Carson yesterday," the item must have appeared on December 28. With the exception of a brief period in early February 1863, and again in May and June of that year, Clemens took over Dan's chores as editor of the local items column in the *Enterprise* until he returned in September.[1] The heading **"Daily Territorial Enterprise,"** at the top of the clipping, shows that it began the first local column that Clemens wrote. Appropriately, the sketch records the transfer of responsibility: Dan "said '*Et tu Brute,*' and gave us his pen."

"The Illustrious Departed" is followed in the present collection by seven more local items (ending with "Territorial Sweets," no. 39)—a selection of unsigned pieces retrieved from the columns Clemens wrote between 28 December 1862 and 29 January 1863, just before he assumed the name "Mark Twain." Some of these items are taken from original *Enterprise* clippings, others from reprintings in California newspapers whose editors apparently were struck by the vigorous originality of the new *Enterprise* "local."

Dan De Quille had already become a close friend and helpful colleague of Clemens', and when he returned in the fall, the two men became still better

---

[1]"Gone Home," another clipping in the folder containing this sketch (carton 1, folder 120, William Wright Papers, Bancroft), reprints a notice from the San Francisco *Police Gazette* which gives the date of Dan's departure and says that during his absence "his position will be filled by that inveterate Carson Valley wag, Sam-i-vel Clem-ens Ekswire, the handsomest man in the Territory."

friends.[2] He was born in Ohio in 1829, moved to Iowa with his family in 1847, and ten years later migrated to California. He prospected in California and Nevada, and contributed articles to the San Francisco *Golden Era*. From May 1862, when he joined the *Enterprise* as the local editor,[3] until 1893, when the newspaper suspended publication, Dan was a mainstay of the *Enterprise* staff. By the time of this "eulogy" he was already one of the best-known and best-liked journalists in the West, and his reputation would continue to prosper. In addition to voluminous newspaper correspondence, including humorous sketches as well as straight reporting (especially about mining), he wrote portions of Myron Angel's *History of Nevada* (1881) and a small guidebook called *A History of the Comstock Silver Lode & Mines* (1889). His major work, encouraged by Clemens, was *The History of the Big Bonanza* (1876), issued by the American Publishing Company. He died at the home of his daughter in West Liberty, Iowa, on 16 March 1898.[4]

---

[2]See the headnote to "Frightful Accident to Dan De Quille" (no. 73).

[3]"For the East," clipping from the Virginia City *Territorial Enterprise*, 27 December 1862, carton 1, folder 120, William Wright Papers, Bancroft. The writer says that Dan "for the past eight months has been connected with the ENTERPRISE in the capacity of local editor."

[4]C. A. V. Putnam, "Dan De Quille and Mark Twain," Salt Lake City *Tribune*, 25 April 1898, p. 3.

The Illustrious Departed

OLD DAN IS GONE, that good old soul, we ne'er shall see him more—
for some time. He left for Carson yesterday, to be duly stamped and
shipped to America, by way of the United States Overland Mail. As
the stage was on the point of weighing anchor, the senior editor
dashed wildly into Wasserman's and captured a national flag, which
he cast about Dan's person to the tune of three rousing cheers from
the bystanders. So, with the gorgeous drapery floating behind him, our
kind and genial hero passed from our sight; and if fervent prayers
from us, who seldom pray, can avail, his journey will be as safe and
happy as though ministering angels watched over him. Dan has gone
to the States for his health, and his family. He worked himself down
in creating big strikes in the mines and keeping all the mills in this
district going, whether their owners were willing or not. These
herculean labors gradually undermined his health, but he went
bravely on, and we are proud to say that as far as these things were
concerned, he never gave up—the miners never did, and never could
have conquered him. He fell under a scarcity of pack-trains and hay-
wagons. These had been the bulwark of the local column; his confidence in them was like unto that which men have in four aces;
murders, robberies, fires, distinguished arrivals, were creatures of
chance, which might or might not occur at any moment; but the
pack-trains and the hay-wagons were certain, predestined, immutable!
When these failed last week, he said *"Et tu Brute,"* and gave us his
pen. His constitution suddenly warped, split and went under, and

Daniel succumbed. We have a saving hope, though, that his trip across the Plains, through eighteen hundred miles of cheerful hay-stacks, will so restore our loved and lost to his ancient health and energy, that when he returns next fall he will be able to run our five hundred mills as easily as he used to keep five-score moving. Dan is gone, but he departed in a blaze of glory, the like of which hath hardly been seen upon this earth since the blameless Elijah went up in his fiery chariot.

33. *Our Stock Remarks*

30–31 December 1862

"Our Stock Remarks" is preserved in a clipping from the Virginia City *Territorial Enterprise* in one of the scrapbooks Orion kept for his brother. The spoof is the first item in a column of nine routine local items. Although the column is of course unsigned, Clemens identified himself in the piece as "Sam," some four weeks before he adopted the name "Mark Twain" (see "Letter from Carson City," no. 40).

The scrapbook clipping is undated, but it must have appeared on Tuesday or Wednedsay, 30 or 31 December 1862. Two other items in the column announce forthcoming events (an election and a school reopening) that are to take place "next Monday." A second *Enterprise* column, which must have appeared on Sunday, 4 January 1863, is preserved in another scrapbook, and it mentions the same events and says they will take place "to-morrow" (Monday, January 5).[1] "Our Stock Remarks" could therefore have appeared anytime in the week prior to January 4. Still another item in the column containing the sketch says that the "Virginia Cadets . . . will appear in public on New Year's Day," which allows us to rule out January 1–3. Since the *Enterprise* did not publish on Mondays, we can also exclude December 29. And since Clemens says "New Year's Day" rather than "to-morrow," it seems likely that he wrote on December 30 rather than 31, although either date is possible.

Like other newspapers on the Comstock Lode, the *Enterprise* closely followed mining activity and the stock exchange. Its daily column "Stock Remarks" (to which Clemens' title alludes) combined news of stock quotations, market trends, mining litigation, and endorsements of specific mines or mining districts.

---

[1]Scrapbook 1, p. 66, MTP.

Our Stock Remarks

OWING TO THE FACT that our stock reporter attended a wedding last evening, our report of transactions in that branch of robbery and speculation is not quite as complete and satisfactory as usual this morning. About eleven o'clock last night the aforesaid remarker pulled himself up stairs by the banisters, and stumbling over the stove, deposited the following notes on our table, with the remark: "S(hic)am, just 'laberate this, w(hic)ill, yer?" We said we would, but we couldn't. If any of our readers think they can, we shall be pleased to see the translation. Here are the notes: "Stocks brisk, and Ophir has taken this woman for your wedded wife. Some few transactions have occurred in rings and lace veils, and at figures tall, graceful and charming. There was some inquiry late in the day for parties who would take them for better or for worse, but there were few offers. There seems to be some depression in this stock. We mentioned yesterday that our Father which art in heaven. Quotations of lost reference, and now I lay me down to sleep," &c., &c., &c.

34. More Ghosts

1 January 1863

"More Ghosts" is preserved in a clipping from the Virginia City *Territorial Enterprise* in one of the scrapbooks Orion kept for his brother. Orion wrote "Sams Column" at the top of the clipping and thus identified it as part of the new local editor's daily contribution.[1] The clipping is undated, but Orion pasted a second item from the local column, "New Year's Day" (no. 35), immediately below it. Since it seems likely that both pieces are from the same column, and since "New Year's Day" must have appeared on 1 January 1863, "More Ghosts" has been assigned that date as well.

Clemens' allusion in this sketch to "the haunted house humbug" implies that "More Ghosts" was occasioned by "A Ghost Story," an article that had appeared in the *Enterprise* probably on 25 or 26 December 1862 and that is preserved in the same scrapbook.[2] "A Ghost Story" relates in about fifteen hundred words a tale of apparitions, ominous footsteps and groans, and the miraculous materialization of "large gouts of fresh blood" in "a real, old-fashioned haunted house" on E Street in Virginia City.

The shooting gallery with its sidewalk effigy described in "More Ghosts" has not been identified. But the nearby Winn's International Hotel was the finest in the city, a newly built three-story brick building on Union and C streets.[3]

---

[1] The local column heading, "Daily Territorial Enterprise," appears at the top of the clipping.

[2] Scrapbook 4, p. 13, MTP. The article is undated, but the reverse side of the clipping carries an account of "Ordinance No. 43.—Passed December 24th A.D. 1862" by the Virginia City board of aldermen.

[3] Advertisement, Virginia City *Territorial Enterprise*, 10 January 1863, p. 2, PH in MTP.

More Ghosts

ARE WE TO BE scared to death every time we venture into the street? May we be allowed to go quietly about our business, or are we to be assailed at every corner by fearful apparitions? As we were plodding home at the ghostly hour last night, thinking about the haunted house humbug, we were suddenly riveted to the pavement in a paroxysm of terror by that blue and yellow phantom who watches over the destinies of the shooting gallery, this side of the International. Seen in daylight, placidly reclining against his board in the doorway, with his blue coat, and his yellow pants, and his high boots, and his fancy hat, just lifted from his head, he is rather an engaging youth than otherwise; but at dead of night, when he pops out his pallid face at you by candle light, and stares vacantly upon you with his uplifted hat and the eternal civility of his changeless brow, and the ghostliness of his general appearance heightened by that grave-stone inscription over his stomach, "to-day shooting for chickens here," you are apt to think of spectres starting up from behind tomb-stones, and you weaken accordingly—the cold chills creep over you—your hair stands on end—you reverse your front, and with all possible alacrity, you change your base.

35. New Year's Day

1 January 1863

"New Year's Day" is preserved in a clipping from the Virginia City *Territorial Enterprise*, pasted immediately below "More Ghosts" (no. 34). For evidence of Clemens' authorship, see the headnote to that piece.

"New Year's Day" must have appeared on 1 January 1863. Three days later the *Enterprise* local items column carried a very brief follow-up squib, almost certainly by Clemens as well, elaborating on the custom of "friendly calls":

NEW YEARS EXTENSION.—Yesterday was New Years Day for the ladies. We kept open house, and were called upon by seventy-two ladies—all young and handsome. This stunning popularity is pleasant to reflect upon, but we are afraid some people will think it prevented us from scouting for local matters with our usual avidity. This is a mistake; if anything had happened within the county limits yesterday, those ladies would have mentioned it.[1]

---

[1]Virginia City *Territorial Enterprise*, 4 January 1863, Scrapbook 1, p. 66, MTP.

New Year's Day

Now is the accepted time to make your regular annual good resolutions. Next week you can begin paving hell with them as usual. Yesterday, everybody smoked his last cigar, took his last drink, and swore his last oath. To-day, we are a pious and exemplary community. Thirty days from now, we shall have cast our reformation to the winds and gone to cutting our ancient shortcomings considerably shorter than ever. We shall also reflect pleasantly upon how we did the same old thing last year about this time. However, go in, community. New Year's is a harmless annual institution, of no particular use to anybody save as a scapegoat for promiscuous drunks, and friendly calls, and humbug resolutions, and we wish you to enjoy it with a looseness suited to the greatness of the occasion.

36. Unfortunate Thief

8 January 1863

Clemens' hat was stolen while he attended the Odd Fellows' Ball in Gold Hill on 7 January 1863.[1] This brief sketch—the victim's announcement that inevitable retribution would be visited upon the thief—appeared in the local items column of the Virginia City *Territorial Enterprise*, probably the following morning. The *Enterprise* for that day is not extant, but the sketch is preserved in the Stockton (Calif.) *Independent* for January 14. The *Independent* editor explained: "At a ball in Gold Hill, on the eve of the 8th instant, some fellow stole the hat of the 'local' of the *Enterprise*, whereat that indignant individual sympathises with the thief in the following strain."[2] When Clemens' hat was again stolen some twenty months later in San Francisco, he called down a similar plague upon the head of the culprit; see "Due Warning" (no. 89).

---

[1]*MTVC*, p. 28. That Clemens did attend this event is confirmed by a brief squib in his column for 10 January 1863, following his sketch "The Sanitary Ball" (no. 37): "Millington & McCluskey's band furnished the music for the Sanitary Ball on Thursday night, and also for the Odd Fellows' Ball the other evening in Gold Hill, and the excellence of the article was only equalled by the industry and perseverance of the performers. We consider that the man who can fiddle all through one of those Virginia Reels without losing his grip, may be depended upon in any kind of musical emergency" ("The Music," Virginia City *Territorial Enterprise*, 10 January 1863, p. 3, PH in MTP).

[2]Stockton (Calif.) *Independent*, 14 January 1863, p. 1.

Unfortunate Thief

We HAVE BEEN suffering from the seven years' itch for many months. It is probably the most aggravating disease in the world. It is contagious. That man has commenced a career of suffering which is frightful to contemplate; there is no cure for the distemper—it must run its course; there is no respite for its victim, and but little alleviation of its torments to be hoped for; the unfortunate's only resource is to bathe in sulphur and molasses and let his finger nails grow. Further advice is unnecessary—instinct will prompt him to scratch.

37. The Sanitary Ball

10 January 1863

"The Sanitary Ball" filled two-thirds of Clemens' local items column in the Virginia City *Territorial Enterprise* for Saturday, 10 January 1863. A complete copy of that day's paper is preserved in the library of the Nevada Historical Society at Reno.[1]

The United States Sanitary Commission was founded in 1861 and was headed by Henry W. Bellows, whom Clemens came to know and admire in San Francisco in 1864. Its objective during the Civil War years was to help sick and wounded Union soldiers, and for this purpose local branches of the organization held auctions, promoted fairs, and gave balls to raise money.[2] The commission held a Virginia City ball on Thursday, January 8; Clemens had publicized the event in his local column as early as Sunday, January 4. His methods seem somewhat unorthodox, for although he was obviously trying to boost attendance, he did so by ironically predicting failure:

To be present and see such a phenomenon, would be well worth the price of the ticket—six dollars, supper included. Wherefore, we advise every citizen of Storey to go to the ball—early—and stand ready to enjoy the joke. The fun to be acquired in this way, for a trifling sum of money, cannot be computed by any system of mathematics known to the present generation. And the more the merrier. We all know that a thousand people can enjoy that failure more extensively than a smaller number.[3]

It is unclear what kind of failure Clemens had in mind. But he was apparently alluding to his own mock prediction when he wrote the first sentence and the last paragraph of "The Sanitary Ball."

---

[1] The sketch was first identified as Clemens' work by William C. Miller, "Mark Twain at the Sanitary Ball—and Elsewhere?" *California Historical Society Quarterly* 36 (1957): 35–40.

[2] *MTVC*, pp. 186–187, 194.

[3] Virginia City *Territorial Enterprise*, 4 January 1863, Scrapbook 1, p. 66, MTP.

The six-dollar ticket for the ball included late supper at the What Cheer House on South B Street as well as dancing at the spacious La Plata Hall across the way. Mr. Unger, proprietor of the What Cheer House, had contributed tableware and waiters' services for the event, and Clemens concluded his January 4 notice of the forthcoming ball with an appeal for matching contributions:

This generosity—this liberality in a noble cause—calls for a second from somebody. Get your contributions ready—money, wines, cakes, and knick-nacks and substantials of all kinds—and when the ladies call for them, deliver your offerings with a grace and dignity graduated by the market value of the same, the condition of your pecuniary affairs, and the sympathy you feel for maimed and suffering humanity. The ladies may be looked for to-morrow.[4]

---

[4]Virginia City *Territorial Enterprise*, 4 January 1863, Scrapbook 1, p. 66, MTP.

The Sanitary Ball

THE SANITARY BALL at La Plata Hall on Thursday night was a very marked success, and proved beyond the shadow of a doubt, the correctness of our theory, that ladies never fail in undertakings of this kind. If there had been about two dozen more people there, the house would have been crowded—as it was, there was room enough on the floor for the dancers, without trespassing on their neighbors' corns. Several of those long, trailing dresses, even, were under fire in the thickest of the fight for six hours, and came out as free from rips and rents as they were when they went in. Not all of them, though. We recollect a circumstance in point. We had just finished executing one of those inscrutable figures of the plain quadrille; we were feeling unusually comfortable, because we had gone through the performance as well as anybody could have done it, except that we had wandered a little toward the last; in fact, we had wandered out of our own and into somebody else's set—but that was a matter of small consequence, as the new locality was as good as the old one, and we were used to that sort of thing anyhow. We were feeling comfortable, and we had assumed an attitude—we have a sort of talent for posturing—a pensive attitude, copied from the Colossus of Rhodes—when the ladies were ordered to the centre. Two of them got there, and the other two moved off gallantly, but they failed to make the connection. They suddenly broached to under full headway, and there was a sound of parting canvas. Their dresses were anchored under our boots, you know. It was unfortunate, but it could not be helped. Those two beautiful pink dresses let go amidships, and remained in a ripped and damaged condition to the end of the ball. We did not apologize, because our presence of mind happened to be absent at the very moment that we had the greatest need of it. But we beg permission to do so now.

An excellent supper was served in the large dining-room of the new What Cheer House, on B street. We missed it there, somewhat. We were not accompanied by a lady, and consequently we were not eligible to a seat at the first table. We found out all about that at the Gold Hill ball, and we had intended to be prepared for this one. We engaged a good many young ladies last Tuesday to go with us, thinking that out of the lot we should certainly be able to secure one, at the appointed time, but they all seemed to have got a little angry about something—nobody knows what, for the ways of women are past finding out. They told us we had better go and invite a thousand girls to go to the ball. A thousand. Why, it was absurd. We had no use for a thousand girls. A thou—but those girls were as crazy as loons. In every instance, after they had uttered that pointless suggestion, they marched magnificently out of their parlors—and if you will believe us, not one of them ever recollected to come back again. Why, it was the most unaccountable circumstance we ever heard of. We never enjoyed so much solitude in so many different places, in one evening, before. But patience has its limits; we finally got tired of that arrangement—and at the risk of offending some of those girls, we stalked off to the Sanitary Ball alone—without a virgin, out of that whole litter. We may have done wrong—we probably did do wrong to disappoint those fellows in that kind of style—but how could we help it? We couldn't stand the temperature of those parlors more than an hour at a time: it was cold enough to freeze out the heaviest stockholder on the Gould & Curry's books.

However, as we remarked before, everybody spoke highly of the supper, and we believe they meant what they said. We are unable to say anything in the matter from personal knowledge, except that the tables were arranged with excellent taste, and more than abundantly supplied, and everything looked very beautiful, and very inviting, also; but then we had absorbed so much cold weather in those parlors, and had had so much trouble with those girls, that we had no appetite left. We only eat a boiled ham and some pies, and went back to the ball room. There were some very handsome cakes on the tables, manufactured by Mr. Slade, and decorated with patriotic mottoes, done in fancy icing. All those who were happy that evening, agree that the supper was superb.

After supper the dancing was jolly. They kept it up till four in the morning, and the guests enjoyed themselves excessively. All the dances were performed, and the bill of fare wound up with a new style of plain quadrille called a medley, which involved the whole list. It involved us also. But we got out again—and we staid out, with great sagacity. But speaking of plain quadrilles reminds us of another new one—the Virginia reel. We found it a very easy matter to dance it, as long as we had thirty or forty lookers-on to prompt us. The dancers are formed in two long ranks, facing each other, and the battle opens with some light skirmishing between the pickets, which is gradually resolved into a general engagement along the whole line; after that, you have nothing to do but stand by and grab every lady that drifts within reach of you, and swing her. It is very entertaining, and elaborately scientific also; but we observed that with a partner who had danced it before, we were able to perform it rather better than the balance of the guests.

Altogether, the Sanitary ball was a remarkably pleasant party, and we are glad that such was the case—for it is a very uncomfortable task to be obliged to say harsh things about entertainments of this kind. At the present writing we cannot say what the net proceeds of the ball will amount to, but they will doubtless reach quite a respectable figure—say $400.

38. *Due Notice*

10 January 1863

This slight sketch appeared in the same Virginia City *Territorial Enterprise* column that contained the ambitious "Sanitary Ball" (no. 37). Clemens' allusion to Czar Nicholas' interest in the "minarets of Byzantium"—which had resulted in the 1853 Crimean War—contains a nearly harmless pun. The *Enterprise* offices, from which the "local" gazed upon "that old gobbler," were at this time located on A Street. Almack's Oyster and Liquor Saloon at Taylor and C streets was a favorite meeting place for the city's journalists.[1]

Clemens would return to the subject of "raising poultry" on 4 June 1870, when he published "More Distinction" (no. 307) in the Buffalo *Express*.

---

[1]J. Wells Kelly, *First Directory of Nevada Territory* (San Francisco: Valentine and Co., 1862), pp. 138, 150.

Due Notice

MORALISTS AND philosophers have adjudged those who throw temptation in the way of the erring, equally guilty with those who are thereby led into evil; and we therefore hold the man who suffers that turkey to run at large just back of our office as culpable as ourself, if some day that fowl is no longer perceptible to human vision. The Czar of Russia never cast his eye on the minarets of Byzantium half as longingly as we gaze on that old gobbler. Turkey stuffed with oysters is our weakness—our mouth waters at the recollection of sundry repasts of that character—and this bird aforementioned appears to us to have an astonishing capacity for oyster-stuffing. Wonder if those fresh oysters at Almack's are all gone? We grow ravenous—pangs of hunger gnaw our vitals—if to-morrow's setting sun gleams on the living form of that turkey, we yield our reputation for strategy.

39. Territorial Sweets

22-28 January 1863

On 31 January 1863 the Santa Cruz (Calif.) *Sentinel* reprinted this item from the now lost Virginia City *Territorial Enterprise* under the title "Territorial Sweets." The *Sentinel* editor supplied a brief explanatory preface: "The local of the *Enterprise* dropped early one morning upon a loose missive which he thus publicly notices." Clemens was, of course, the *Enterprise* local at this time. On Wednesday, January 28, he sat up all night to take the stage to Carson City, where he would spend the first week of February. Therefore the piece probably appeared sometime between January 22 and 28.

The love-stricken Madeline in this sketch seems to have been born of the same impulse that, in two weeks' time, would produce "Ye Sentimental Law Student" (no. 44). She also bears some resemblance to "A Lady at the Lick House" in "Mark Twain—More of Him" (no. 64), as well as to Arabella in "A Notable Conundrum" (no. 91).

Territorial Sweets

THE FOLLOWING, which will do to sweeten some bachelor's coffee with, was picked up in front of the International:

"DARLING: I have not had time to write you to-day—I have worked hard entertaining company. *Do* come and see your little pet. I yearn for the silvery cadence of your voice—I thirst for the bubbling stream of your affection.

YOUR MADELINE."

We feel for that girl. The water privilege which she pines for so lovingly has probably dried up and departed, else her sweet note would not have been floating around the streets without a claimant. We feel for her deeply—and if it will afford her any relief, if it will conduce to her comfort, if it will satisfy her yearning even in the smallest degree, we will cheerfully call around and "bubble" awhile for her ourself, if she will send us her address.

40. *Letter from Carson City*

3 February 1863

In all probability this letter was completed on Saturday evening, 31 January 1863, mailed to Virginia City the next day, and published in the *Territorial Enterprise* on Tuesday, February 3. (The paper did not publish on Mondays.) The text is preserved in a clipping in one of Clemens' scrapbooks.[1] It is likely that this letter was the first piece to which Clemens signed the name "Mark Twain," in which case his remark "I feel very much as if I had just awakened out of a long sleep" seems deeply appropriate. The appearance of the taciturn Joseph T. Goodman in Clemens' account of the trip to Carson City is also significant. As proprietor and senior editor of the *Enterprise*, Goodman shared responsibility for hiring Clemens and for establishing the journalistic policy that fostered his development as a reporter and humorist in Nevada. In fact, this early example of an out-of-town newspaper letter is a sign of Goodman's willingness to give Clemens great freedom. Clemens had served as local editor for only a month, but had already managed to persuade his boss to give him a vacation: "They let me go, about the first of the month, to stay twenty-four hours in Carson," he reported to his family, "and I staid a week."[2] It was a productive week: in that time he wrote and sent three letters signed "Mark Twain."

In 1863 the newspaper letter from distant points was a standard, often a rather personal, way of reporting the news. Clemens learned to use the form more inventively than most other reporters did. At his best, he could float bits of hard news in a strong current of personal narrative and imaginative comedy, and he soon achieved an appealing informality and a flexible medium which commanded a large audience. In 1865 Goodman would

---

[1]The dating is fully discussed in *MTEnt*, pp. 47–48.
[2]Clemens to Jane Clemens and Pamela Moffett, 16 February 1863, *CL1*, letter 65.

agree to pay him $100 a month for a daily letter from San Francisc
in 1866 the Sacramento *Union* and the San Francisco *Alta California* would
commission him to write two long series of travel letters.[3]

To sustain the comedy and provide an element of continuity in such a
letter, Clemens often employed a stooge who was sometimes purely imaginary, sometimes based on a real acquaintance. In reporting the proceedings
of the Territorial Legislature in November and December 1862 Clemens had
adopted a character called the Unreliable—in reality Clement T. Rice, his
friend of at least a year's standing and a respected reporter for the Virginia
City *Union*.[4] On 23 December 1862, for instance, Clemens sent his paper an
account of the postadjournment celebration held in Washoe City, and he
said in part:

The supper and the champagne were excellent and abundant, and I offer no
word of blame against anybody for eating and drinking pretty freely. If I
were to blame anybody, I would commence with the Unreliable—for he
drank until he lost all sense of etiquette. I actually found myself in bed with
him with my boots on. However, as I said before, I cannot blame the cuss;
it was a convivial occasion, and his little shortcomings ought to be overlooked.[5]

Rice, who was probably also the original of the character Boggs in *Roughing
It*, was an especially good straight man because he was cheerfully willing to
keep the game going—making the Reliable, or Mark Twain, *his* stooge in the
columns of the *Union*. Rice was a thoroughly reputable figure in Nevada
society: he was the registrar of the United States Land Office in Carson City
from 1862 to 1864, and like Clemens he had prospected and staked out
Nevada mining claims. In 1863 he was secretary of the Watson Consolidated
Gold and Silver Mining Company. Reputed to have made a sizable fortune
in Nevada, Rice later went into business in New York City. Clemens reported
his presence there in March 1867.[6]

---

[3]That is, the letters from the Sandwich Islands and the Holy Land.

[4]The Unreliable appears in nine other pieces in the present collection: nos. 41, 42,
44, 46, 47, 50, 51, 53, and 57.

[5]"A Big Thing in Washoe City," reprinted from the *Enterprise* by the Placer County
(Calif.) *Courier*, 17 January 1863, p. 3, quoted in *MTNev*, p. 227. The letter is sched-
uled to appear in the collection of social and political writings in The Works of Mark
Twain.

[6]"Resignation and Appointment," Lyon County *Sentinel*, 16 July 1864, p. 2; Virginia
City *Territorial Enterprise*, 3 April 1863, p. 3; "Old Washoeites," ibid., 15 May 1869,
p. 3; " 'Mark Twain' in New York," San Francisco *Alta California*, 28 March 1867, p. 1.

Letter from Carson City

EDS. ENTERPRISE: I feel very much as if I had just awakened out of a long sleep. I attribute it to the fact that I have slept the greater part of the time for the last two days and nights. On Wednesday, I sat up all night, in Virginia, in order to be up early enough to take the five o'clock stage on Thursday morning. I was on time. It was a great success. I had a cheerful trip down to Carson, in company with that incessant talker, Joseph T. Goodman. I never saw him flooded with such a flow of spirits before. He restrained his conversation, though, until we had traveled three or four miles, and were just crossing the divide between Silver City and Spring Valley, when he thrust his head out of the dark stage, and allowed a pallid light from the coach lamp to illuminate his features for a moment, after which he returned to darkness again, and sighed and said, "Damn it!" with some asperity. I asked him who he meant it for, and he said, "The weather out there." As we approached Carson, at about half past seven o'clock, he thrust his head out again, and gazed earnestly in the direction of that city—after which he took it in again, with his nose very much frosted. He propped the end of that organ upon the end of his finger, and looked down pensively upon it—which had the effect of making him appear cross-eyed—and remarked, "O, damn it!" with great bitterness. I asked him what he was up to this time, and he said, "The cold, damp fog—it is worse than the weather." This was his last. He never spoke again in my hearing. He went on over the mountains, with a lady fellow-passenger from here. That will stop his clatter, you know, for he seldom speaks in the presence of ladies.

In the evening I felt a mighty inclination to go to a party somewhere. There was to be one at Governor J. Neely Johnson's, and I went there and asked permission to stand around awhile. This was granted in the most hospitable manner, and visions of plain quadrilles soothed my weary soul. I felt particularly comfortable, for if there is one thing more grateful to my feelings than another, it is a new house—a large house, with its ceilings embellished with snowy mouldings; its floors glowing with warm-tinted carpets; with cushioned chairs and sofas to sit on, and a piano to listen to; with fires so arranged that you can see them, and know that there is no humbug about it; with walls garnished with pictures, and above all, mirrors, wherein you may gaze, and always find something to admire, you know. I have a great regard for a good house, and a girlish passion for mirrors. Horace Smith, Esq., is also very fond of mirrors. He came and looked in the glass for an hour, with me. Finally, it cracked—the night was pretty cold—and Horace Smith's reflection was split right down the centre. But where his face had been, the damage was greatest—a hundred cracks converged from his reflected nose, like spokes from the hub of a wagon wheel. It was the strangest freak the weather has done this Winter. And yet the parlor seemed very warm and comfortable, too.

About nine o'clock the Unreliable came and asked Gov. Johnson to let him stand on the porch. That creature has got more impudence than any person I ever saw in my life. Well, he stood and flattened his nose against the parlor window, and looked hungry and vicious —he always looks that way—until Col. Musser arrived with some ladies, when he actually fell in their wake and came swaggering in, looking as if he thought he had been anxiously expected. He had on my fine kid boots, and my plug hat and my white kid gloves, (with slices of his prodigious hands grinning through the bursted seams), and my heavy gold repeater, which I had been offered thousands and thousands of dollars for, many and many a time. He took these articles out of my trunk, at Washoe City, about a month ago, when we went out there to report the proceedings of the Convention. The Unreliable intruded himself upon me in his cordial way, and said, "How are you, Mark, old boy? when d'you come down? It's brilliant,

ain't it? Appear to enjoy themselves, don't they? Lend a fellow two
bits, can't you?" He always winds up his remarks that way. He appears
to have an insatiable craving for two bits.

The music struck up just then, and saved me. The next moment
I was far, far at sea in a plain quadrille. We carried it through with
distinguished success; that is, we got as far as "balance around," and
"half-a-man-left," when I smelled hot whisky punch, or something
of that nature. I tracked the scent through several rooms, and finally
discovered the large bowl from whence it emanated. I found the
omnipresent Unreliable there, also. He set down an empty goblet, and
remarked that he was diligently seeking the gentlemen's dressing
room. I would have shown him where it was, but it occurred to him
that the supper table and the punch-bowl ought not to be left un-
protected; wherefore, we staid there and watched them until the
punch entirely evaporated. A servant came in then to replenish the
bowl, and we left the refreshments in his charge. We probably did
wrong, but we were anxious to join the hazy dance. The dance was
hazier than usual, after that. Sixteen couples on the floor at once,
with a few dozen spectators scattered around, is calculated to have
that effect in a brilliantly lighted parlor, I believe. Everything seemed
to buzz, at any rate. After all the modern dances had been danced
several times, the people adjourned to the supper-room. I found my
wardrobe out there, as usual, with the Unreliable in it. His old distemper was upon him: he was desperately hungry. I never saw a man
eat as much as he did in my life. I have the various items of his supper
here in my note-book. First, he ate a plate of sandwiches; then he ate
a handsomely iced poundcake; then he gobbled a dish of chicken
salad; after which he ate a roast pig; after that, a quantity of blanc-
mange; then he threw in several glasses of punch to fortify his appetite, and finished his monstrous repast with a roast turkey. Dishes
of brandy-grapes, and jellies, and such things, and pyramids of fruits,
melted away before him as shadows fly at the sun's approach. I am
of the opinion that none of his ancestors were present when the five
thousand were miraculously fed in the old Scriptural times. I base my
opinion upon the twelve baskets of scraps and the little fishes that
remained over after that feast. If the Unreliable himself had been
there, the provisions would just about have held out, I think.

After supper, the dancing was resumed, and after awhile, the guests indulged in music to a considerable extent. Mrs. J. sang a beautiful Spanish song; Miss R., Miss T., Miss P., and Miss S., sang a lovely duett; Horace Smith, Esq., sang "I'm sitting on the stile, Mary," with a sweetness and tenderness of expression which I have never heard surpassed; Col. Musser sang "From Greenland's Icy Mountains" so fervently that every heart in that assemblage was purified and made better by it; Mrs. T. and Miss C., and Mrs. T. and Mrs. G. sang "Meet me by moonlight alone" charmingly; Judge Dixson sang "O, Charming May" with great vivacity and artistic effect; Joe Winters and Hal Clayton sang the Marseilles Hymn in French, and did it well; Mr. Wasson sang "Call me pet names" with his usual excellence—(Wasson has a cultivated voice, and a refined musical taste, but like Judge Brumfield, he throws so much operatic affectation into his singing that the beauty of his performance is sometimes marred by it—I could not help noticing this fault when Judge Brumfield sang "Rock me to sleep, mother;") Wm. M. Gillespie sang "Thou hast wounded the spirit that loved thee," gracefully and beautifully, and wept at the recollection of the circumstance which he was singing about. Up to this time I had carefully kept the Unreliable in the back ground, fearful that, under the circumstances, his insanity would take a musical turn; and my prophetic soul was right; he eluded me and planted himself at the piano; when he opened his cavernous mouth and displayed his slanting and scattered teeth, the effect upon that convivial audience was as if the gates of a graveyard, with its crumbling tombstones, had been thrown open in their midst; then he shouted some thing about he "would not live alway"—and if I ever heard anything absurd in my life, that was it. He must have made up that song as he went along. Why, there was no more sense in it, and no more music, than there is in his ordinary conversation. The only thing in the whole wretched performance that redeemed it for a moment, was something about "the few lucid moments that dawn on us here." That was all right; because the "lucid moments" that dawn on that Unreliable are almighty few, I can tell you. I wish one of them would strike him while I am here, and prompt him to return my valuables to me. I doubt if he ever gets lucid enough for that, though. After the Unreliable had finished squawking, I sat down to the piano and sang—however, what I sang is of no consequence to anybody. It was only a graceful little gem from the horse opera.

At about two o'clock in the morning the pleasant party broke up and the crowd of guests distributed themselves around town to their respective homes; and after thinking the fun all over again, I went to bed at four o'clock. So, having been awake forty-eight hours, I slept forty-eight, in order to get even again, which explains the proposition I began this letter with.

Yours, dreamily,
MARK TWAIN.

41. *Letter from Carson*

5 February 1863

"Letter from Carson" survives in one of Mark Twain's scrapbooks in an undated clipping from the Virginia City *Territorial Enterprise*. Clemens' dateline ("CARSON, Tuesday Night") and his opening reference to the morning he arrived in Carson City ("Thursday Morning") establish the date of writing as 3 February 1863 and the probable date of publication as February 5.

The letter falls into three parts: an opening section describing the fantastic adventures of Mark Twain and the Unreliable; a second section containing the chatty and relatively straightforward description of the wedding festivities; and finally, two factual paragraphs, omitted in the present text, about a court case and several recent mine incorporations.

The section on the Unreliable clearly continues the feud over the articles stolen from Mark Twain's trunk in Washoe City—a matter described in the previous sketch, "Letter from Carson City" (no. 40), which was published on Tuesday, February 3. However, in the present piece the dateline of the Unreliable's challenge letter is January 29, five days before sketch no. 40 was published. The Unreliable's letter may therefore allude to an earlier *Enterprise* article (now lost) which also described the stolen articles. Certainly these became a fairly constant theme of raillery between Clemens and Rice, and they may easily have done so before the February 3 letter.

On the other hand, it seems somewhat more likely that when writing the present letter, two days after the first one appeared in the *Enterprise* and while he was still in Carson City, Mark Twain simply got his fictional chronology confused. The "atrocious document" from the Unreliable was inadvertently dated before the publication of the letter to which it refers; the Unreliable's sarcastic allusion to "those *valuables*" and his challenge are both answers to Mark Twain's request in sketch no. 40 that his adversary "return my valuables."

The Unreliable's response to Mark Twain's counterchallenge to engage in "mortal combat with boot-jacks" employs a typical burlesque device: a brilliant concoction of the conventional rhetoric used by the stricken, desperate romantic, eager to embrace his tragic fate.

Letter from Carson

CARSON, Tuesday Night.

EDS. ENTERPRISE:—I received the following atrocious document the morning I arrived here. It is from that abandoned profligate, the Unreliable, and I think it speaks for itself:

CARSON CITY, Thursday Morning.

TO THE UNRELIABLE—SIR:—Observing the driver of the Virginia stage hunting after you this morning, in order to collect his fare, I infer you are in town.

In the paper which you represent, I noticed an article which I took to be an effusion of your muddled brain, stating that I had "cabbaged" a number of valuable articles from you the night I took you out of the streets in Washoe City and permitted you to occupy my bed.

I take this opportunity to inform you that I will compensate you at the rate of $20 *per head* for every one of those *valuables* that I received from you, providing you will relieve me of their presence. This offer can either be accepted or rejected on your part; but, providing you don't see proper to accept it, you had better procure enough lumber to make a box 4x8, and have it made as early as possible. Judge Dixson will arrange the preliminaries, if you don't accede. An early reply is expected by

RELIABLE.

Not satisfied with wounding my feelings by making the most extraordinary references to allusions in the above note, he even sent me a challenge to fight, in the same envelop with it, hoping to work upon my fears and drive me from the country by intimidation. But I was not to be frightened; I shall remain in the Territory. I guessed his

object at once, and determined to accept his challenge, choose weapons and things, and scare him, instead of being scared myself. I wrote
a stern reply to him, and offered him mortal combat with boot-jacks
at a hundred yards. The effect was more agreeable than I could have
hoped for. His hair turned black in a single night, from excess of fear;
then he went into a fit of melancholy, and while it lasted he did
nothing but sigh, and sob, and snuffle, and slobber, and blow his nose
on his coat-tail, and say "he wished he was in the quiet tomb;" finally,
he said he would commit suicide—he would say farewell to the cold,
cold world, with its cares and troubles, and go and sleep with his
fathers, in perdition. Then rose up this young man, and threw his
demijohn out of the window, and took a glass of pure water, and
drained it to the very, very dregs. And then he fell on the floor in
spasms. Dr. Tjader was called in, and as soon as he found that the cuss
was poisoned, he rushed down to the Magnolia Saloon and got the
antidote, and poured it down him. As he was drawing his last breath,
he scented the brandy and lingered yet a while upon the earth, to
take a drink with the boys. But for this, he would have been no more
—and possibly a good deal less—in another moment. So he survived;
but he has been in a mighty precarious condition ever since. I have
been up to see how he was getting along two or three times a day. He
is very low; he lies there in silence, and hour after hour he appears to
be absorbed in tracing out the figures in the wall paper. He is not
changed in the least, though; his face looks just as natural as anything
could be—there is no more expression in it than a turnip. But he is
a very sick man; I was up there a while ago, and I could see that his
friends had begun to entertain hopes that he would not get over it.
As soon as I saw that, all my enmity vanished; I even felt like doing
the poor Unreliable a kindness, and showing him, too, how my feelings towards him had changed. So I went and bought him a beautiful
coffin, and carried it up and set it down on his bed, and told him to
climb in when his time was up. Well, sir, you never saw a man so
affected by a little act of kindness as he was by that. He let off a sort
of war-whoop, and went to kicking things around like a crazy man;
and he foamed at the mouth, and went out of one fit and into another
faster than I could take them down in my note-book. I have got thirteen down, though, and I know he must have had two or three before
I could find my pencil. I actually believe he would have had a thou-

sand, if that old fool who nurses him hadn't thrown the coffin out of the window, and threatened to serve me in the same way if I didn't leave. I left, of course, under the circumstances, and I learn that although the patient was getting better a moment before this circumstance, he got a good deal worse immediately afterward. They say he lies in a sort of a stupor now, and if they cannot rally him, he is gone in, as it were. They may take their own course now, though, and use their own judgment. I shall not go near them again, although I think *I* could rally him with another coffin.

I did not return to Virginia yesterday, on account of the wedding. The parties were Hon. James H. Sturtevant, one of the first Pi-Utes of Nevada, and Miss Emma Curry, daughter of Hon. A. Curry, who also claims that his is a Pi-Ute family of high antiquity. Curry conducted the wedding arrangements himself, and invited none but Pi-Utes. This interfered with me a good deal. However, as I had heard it reported that a marriage was threatened, I felt it my duty to go down there and find out the facts in the case. They said I might stay, as it was me; the permission was unnecessary, though—I calculated to do that anyhow. I promised not to say anything about the wedding, and I regard that promise as sacred—my word is as good as my bond. At three o'clock in the afternoon, all the Pi-Utes went up stairs to the old Hall of Representatives in Curry's house, preceded by the bride and groom, and the bridesmaids and groomsmen (Miss Jo. Perkins and Miss Mettie Curry, and Hon. John H. Mills and Wm. M. Gillespie,) and followed by myself and the fiddlers. The fiddles were tuned up, three quadrille sets were formed on the floor. Father Bennett advanced and touched off the high contracting parties with the hymeneal torch (married them, you know), and at the word of command from Curry, the fiddle-bows were set in motion, and the plain quadrilles turned loose. Thereupon, some of the most responsible dancing ensued that you ever saw in your life. The dance that Tam O'Shanter witnessed was slow in comparison to it. They kept it up for six hours, and then they carried out the exhausted musicians on a shutter, and went down to supper. I know they had a fine supper, and plenty of it, but I do not know much else. They drank so much shampain around me that I got confused, and lost the hang of things, as it were. Mills, and Musser, and Sturtevant, and Curry, got to making speeches, and I got to looking at the bride and bridesmaids—they looked uncommonly handsome—and finally I fell into a sort of trance. When I recovered from it the brave musicians were all right again, and the dance was ready to commence. They went to slinging plain quadrilles around as lively as ever, and never rested again until nearly midnight, when the dancers all broke down and the party broke up. It was all mighty pleasant, and jolly, and sociable, and I wish to thunder I was married myself. I took a large slab of the bridal cake home with me to dream on, and dreampt that I was still a single man, and likely to remain so, if I live and nothing happens—which has given me a greater confidence in dreams than I ever felt before. I cordially wish my newly-married couple all kinds of happiness and posterity, though.

MARK TWAIN.

42. *Letter from Carson*

8 February 1863

This sketch survives in an undated clipping from the Virginia City *Territorial Enterprise* in one of Mark Twain's scrapbooks. It is the last of three letters that Mark Twain sent from Carson City before returning to his post as the *Enterprise* local editor. Clemens headed his letter "Thursday Morning" (5 February 1863) and said that the Wayman-Ormsby wedding took place "last night." There is a good possibility that Clemens mistook the day of the week. A contemporary account said that the wedding took place on Thursday evening (not Wednesday, as Clemens had it). If this report is accurate, then Clemens probably wrote his letter on Friday morning and published it slightly later, say on February 7 or 8.[1] The latter date seems somewhat more plausible, for on February 9 one "Isreal Putnam" wrote Clemens from Virginia City that John Nugent, an intimate friend of the late John Phoenix (George H. Derby), had inquired of him "who Mark Twain was, and added that he had not seen so amusing a thing in newspaper literature in a long while as your letter in the Enterprise this morning."[2] This must refer to "Letter from Carson," but since "Putnam" wrote on a Monday, the day the *Enterprise* did not publish, the piece must have appeared the previous day, Sunday, February 8, instead of "this morning."

The activities of the Unreliable described in this sketch dovetail with those of his last appearance in the previous piece, and this time Clemens uses them as a vehicle for reporting the wedding festivities: a small but significant advance in technique.

---

[1]*MTEnt*, p. 57, cites a letter from Charles Lewis Anderson to his wife, dated Friday, 6 February 1863, now in Bancroft (P–G 266, vol. 4, p. 93). The letter says in part: "I forgot to say that another one of our Drs. committed matrimony Thursday evening."

[2]"Isreal Putnam" to Clemens, 9 February 1863, MTP. The writer has not been further identified.

The second half of the letter—a long, half-facetious argument about calling the Territorial Legislature into special session—is not reprinted here,[3] nor is a perfunctory list of recent certificates of incorporation issued by the secretary of the territory, Orion Clemens.

---

[3]This section of the letter is scheduled to appear in the collection of social and political writings in The Works of Mark Twain. It is reprinted in *MTEnt*, pp. 60–61.

Letter from Carson

CARSON, Thursday Morning.

EDS. ENTERPRISE:—The community were taken by surprise last night, by the marriage of Dr. J. H. Wayman and Mrs. M. A. Ormsby. Strategy did it. John K. Trumbo lured the people to a party at his house, and corraled them, and in the meantime Acting Governor Clemens proceeded to the bride's dwelling and consolidated the happy couple under the name and style of Mr. and Mrs. Wayman, with a life charter, perpetual succession, unlimited marital privileges, principal place of business at ho—blast those gold and silver mining incorporations! I have compiled a long list of them from the Territorial Secretary's books this morning, and their infernal technicalities keep slipping from my pen when I ought to be writing graceful poetical things. After the marriage, the high contracting parties and the witnesses there assembled, adjourned to Mr. Trumbo's house. The ways of the Unreliable are past finding out. His instincts always prompt him to go where he is not wanted, particularly if anything of an unusual nature is on foot. Therefore, he was present and saw those wedding ceremonies through the parlor windows. He climbed up behind Dr. Wayman's coach and rode up to Trumbo's—this shows that his faculties were not affected by his recent illness. When the bride and groom entered the parlor he went in with them, bowing and scraping and smiling in his imbecile way, and attempting to pass himself off for the principal groomsman. I never saw such an awkward, ungainly lout in my life. He had on a pair of Jack Wilde's pantaloons, and a swallow-tail coat belonging to Lytle ("Schemerhorn's Boy"), and they fitted him as neatly as an elephant's hide would fit a poodle dog. I would be ashamed to appear in any parlor in such a costume. It never enters his head to be ashamed of anything, though. It would have killed me with mortification to parade around there as he did, and have people stepping on my coat tail every moment. As soon as the guests found out who he was, they kept out of his way as well as they could, but there were so many gentlemen and ladies present that he was never at a loss for somebody to pester with his disgusting familiarity. He worried them from the parlor to the sitting-room, and from thence to the dancing-hall, and then proceeded up stairs to see if he could find any more people to stampede. He found Fred. Turner, and stayed with him until he was informed that he could have nothing more to eat or drink in that part of the house. He went back to the dancing-hall then, but he carried away a codfish under one arm, and Mr. Curry's plug hat full of sour-krout under the other. He posted himself right where he could be most in the way, and fell to eating as comfortably as if he were boarding with Trumbo by the week. They bothered him some, though, because every time the order came to "all promenade," the dancers would sweep past him and knock his codfish out of his hands and spill his sour-krout. He was the most loathsome sight I ever saw; he turned everybody's stomach but his own. It makes no difference to him, either, what he eats when hungry. I believe he would have eaten a corpse last night, if he had one. Finally, Curry came and took his hat away from him and tore one of his coat tails off and threatened to thresh him with it, and that checked his appetite for a moment. Instead of sneaking out of the house, then, as anybody would have done who had any self-respect, he shoved his codfish into the pocket of his solitary coat tail (leaving at least eight inches of it sticking out), and crowded himself into a double quadrille. He had it all to himself pretty soon; because the order "gentlemen to the right" came, and he passed from one lady to another, around the room, and wilted each and every one of them with the horrible fragrance of his breath. Even Trumbo, himself, fainted. Then the Unreliable, with a placid expression of satisfaction upon his countenance, marched forth and swept the parlors like a pestilence. When the guests had been persecuted as long as they could stand it, though, they got him to drink some kerosene oil, which neutralized the sour-krout and codfish, and restored his breath to about its usual state, or even improved it, perhaps, for it generally smells like a hospital.

The Unreliable interfered with Col. Musser when he was singing the pea-nut song; he bothered William Patterson, Esq., when that baritone was singing, "Ever of thee I'm fondly dreaming;" he interrupted Epstein when he was playing on the piano; he followed the bride and bridegroom from place to place, like an evil spirit, and he managed to keep himself and his coat-tail eternally in the way. I did hope that he would stay away from the supper-table, but I hoped against an impossibility. He was the first one there, and had choice of seats also, because he told Mr. Trumbo he was a groomsman; and not only that, but he made him believe, also, that Dr. Wayman was his uncle. Then he sailed into the ice cream and champagne, and cakes and things, at his usual starvation gait, and he would infallibly have created a famine, if Trumbo had not been particularly well fortified with provisions. There is one circumstance connected with the Unreliable's career last night which it pains me to mention, but I feel that it is my duty to do it. I shall cut the melancholy fact as short as possible, however: seventeen silver spoons, a New Testament and a gridiron were missed after supper. They were found upon the Unreliable's person when he was in the act of going out at the back door.

Singing and dancing commenced at seven o'clock in the evening, and were kept up with unabated fury until half-past one in the morning, when the jolly company put on each other's hats and bonnets and wandered home, mighty well satisfied with Trumbo's "corn shucking," as he called it.

MARK TWAIN.

43. *Silver Bars—How Assayed*

17–22 February 1863

"Silver Bars—How Assayed" was first published in the Virginia City *Territorial Enterprise* but survives only in the Stockton (Calif.) *Independent*, which reprinted the *Enterprise* on 26 February 1863. The *Independent* attributed the article to "the local editor of the Territorial *Enterprise*," but gave no publication date. The date assigned here is therefore a conjecture: the piece might easily have appeared somewhat earlier or even a little later.

Had Dan De Quille been in town, he probably would have covered this assignment with skill and clarity. But his account would have lacked Clemens' humor, the enlivening shock of his similes, his cocky stance, and his casual but stubborn refusal to permit impersonal technology to be taken more seriously than human traits—even such imperfections as a porous memory and an inordinate love of lager beer. The sketch is a good example of Clemens' capacity to assimilate technical information to his humorous vision, transforming it yet also presenting the basic facts in a reasonably intelligible way. It frankly records the fascination he always felt for eye-opening statistics and scientific marvels, while it simultaneously reveals his constitutional disposition to see even the most materialistic subject within a saving humanistic context—his plug hats, salamanders, assayed Hebrew children, and lost sinners.

Silver Bars—How Assayed

W<small>E PROPOSE</small> to speak of some silver bars which we have been look-ing at, and to talk science a little, also, in this article, if we find that what we learned in the latter line yesterday has not escaped our memory. The bars we allude to were at the banking house of Paxton & Thornburgh, and were five in number; they were the concentrated result of portions of two eight-day runs of the Hoosier State Mill, on Potosi rock. The first of the bricks bore the following inscription, which is poetry stripped of flowers and flummery, and reduced to plain common sense: "No. 857; Potosi Gold and Silver Mining Com-pany; Theall & Co., assayers; 688.48 ounces, gold, 020 fine, silver, 962 fine; gold $572.13, silver $1,229.47." Bars No. 836 and No. 858 bore about the same inscription, save that their values differed, of course, the one being worth $1,800, and the other a fraction under $1,300. The two largest bars were still in the workshop, and had not yet been assayed; one of them weighed nearly a hundred pounds and was worth about $3,000, and the other, which contained over 900 ounces, was worth in the neighborhood of $2,000. The weight of the whole five bars may be set down in round numbers at 300 pounds, and their value, at say, $10,000. Those are about the correct figures. We are very well pleased with the Hoosier State mill and the Potosi mine—we think of buying them. From the contemplation of this result of two weeks' mill and mining labor, we walked through the assaying rooms, in the rear of the banking house, with Mr. Theall, and examined the scientific operations there, with a critical eye. We

absorbed much obtuse learning, and we propose to give to the ignorant the benefit of it. After the amalgam has been retorted at the
mill, it is brought here and broken up and put into a crucible (along
with a little borax,) of the capacity of an ordinary plug hat; this vessel
is composed of some kind of pottery which stands heat like a sala-
mander; the crucible is placed in a brick furnace; in the midst of
a charcoal fire as hot as the one which the three Scriptural Hebrew
children were assayed in; when the mass becomes melted, it is well
stirred, in order to get the metals thoroughly mixed, after which it is
poured into an iron brick mould; such of the base metals as were not
burned up, remain in the crucible in the form of a "sing." The next
operation is the assaying of the brick. A small chip is cut from each
end of it and weighed; each of these is enveloped in lead and placed
in a little shallow cup made of bone ashes, called a cupel, and put in
a small stone-ware oven, enclosed in a sort of parlor stove furnace,
where it is cooked like a lost sinner; the lead becomes oxydized and
is entirely absorbed by the pores of the cupel—any other base metals
that may still linger in the precious stew, meet the same fate, or go up
the chimney. The gold and silver come from the cupel in the shape of
a little button, and in a state of perfect purity; this is weighed once
more, and what it has lost by the cooking process, determines the
amount of base metal that was in it, and shows exactly what proportion of it the bar contains—the lost weight was base metal you understand, and was burned up or absorbed by the cupel. The scales used
in this service are of such extremely delicate construction that they
have to be shut up in a glass case, since a breath of air is sufficient
to throw them off their balance—so sensitive are they, indeed, that
they are even affected by the particles of dust which find their way
through the joinings of the case and settle on them. They will figure
the weight of a piece of metal down to the thousandth part of a grain,
with stunning accuracy. You might weigh a musquito here, and then
pull one of his legs off, and weigh him again, and the scales would
detect the difference. The smallest weight used—the one which
represents the thousandth part of a grain—is composed of aluminum,
which is the metallic base of common clay, and is the lightest metal
known to science. It looks like an imperceptible atom clipped from
the invisible corner of a piece of paper whittled down to an impossible degree of sharpness—as it were—and they handle it with pincers

like a hair pin. But with an excuse for this interesting digression, we will return to the silver button again. After the weighing, melting and re-weighing of it has shown the amount of base metal contained in the brick, the next thing to be done is to separate the silver and gold in it, in order to find out the exact proportions of these in the bar. The button is placed in a mattrass filled with nitric acid, (an elongated glass bottle or tube, shaped something like a bell clapper) which is half buried in a box of hot sand—they called it a sand bath—on top of the little cupel furnace, where all the silver is boiled out of said button and held in solution, (when in this condition it is chemically termed "nitrate of silver.") This process leaves a small pinch of gold dust in the bottom of the mattrass which is perfectly pure; its weight will show the proportion of pure gold in the bar, of course. The silver in solution is then precipitated with muriatic acid (or something of that kind—we are not able to swear that this was the drug mentioned to us, although we feel very certain that it was,) and restored to metal again. Its weight, by the musquito scales, will show the proportion of silver contained in the brick, you know. Now just here, our memory is altogether at fault. We cannot recollect what in the world it is they do with the "dry cups." We asked a good many questions about them—asking questions is our regular business—but we have forgotten the answers. It is all owing to lager beer. We are inclined to think, though, that after the silver has been precipitated, they cook it a while in those little chalky-looking "dry cups," in order to turn it from fine silver dust to a solid button again for the sake of convenient handling—but we cannot begin to recollect anything about it. We said they made a separate assay of the chips cut from each end of a bar; now if these chips do not agree—if they make different statements as to the proportions of the various metals contained in the bar, it is pretty good proof that the mixing was not thorough, and the brick has to be melted over again; this occurrence is rare, however. This is all the science we know. What we do not know is reserved for private conversation, and will be liberally inflicted upon any body who will come here to the office and submit to it. After the bar has been assayed, it is stamped as described in the beginning of this dissertation, and then it is ready for the mint. Science is a very pleasant subject to dilate upon, and we consider that we are as able to dilate upon it as any man that walks—but if we have been guilty of carelessness in any part of this article, so that our method of assaying as set forth herein may chance to differ from Mr. Theall's, we would advise that gentleman to stick to his own plan nevertheless, and not go to following ours—his is as good as any known to science. If we have struck anything new in our method, however, we shall be happy to hear of it, so that we can take steps to secure to ourself the benefits accruing therefrom.

44. *Ye Sentimental Law Student*

19 February 1863

"Ye Sentimental Law Student" is of particular interest for Mark Twain's early career. According to Joseph T. Goodman, it was the "first special article" to which the author signed the name "Mark Twain," and it appeared in the *Enterprise* on 19 February 1863. Goodman remembered the title only as "The Sugar Loaf," and some scholars have therefore presumed that the text was lost.[1] But this inexact title clearly refers to Sugar-Loaf Peak, where the Unreliable composed (and lost) his valentine in praise of the view. Our text is taken from Kate Milnor Rabb's *The Wit and Humor of America*, which reprinted the sketch in 1907; but the reliability of Rabb's text is in doubt. For instance, Mark Twain's allusion in the first sentence to an unidentified summit suggests that at least one previous sentence has been omitted. And despite Goodman's explicit testimony that the sketch was signed, Mark Twain's signature does not appear in Rabb.[2]

In this sketch Clemens draws heavily on the humor of scrambled vocabularies. He fastens upon the Unreliable a Babel of tongues: "the beautiful language of love and the infernal phraseology of the law," intermixed throughout with the platitudes of romantic landscape description and echoes of pious church rhetoric and the Bible. Clemens undoubtedly had in mind that genre of romantic and preromantic poetry in which a solitary observer climbs a hill and meditates on the view, thinks elevated thoughts, and then tries to render the sublime landscape in a painterly description. Solon Lycurgus observes the basic conventions of this kind of poetry: writing in solitude, imaginatively identifying with a beloved absent one, moving

---

[1]Goodman to Albert Bigelow Paine, ca. 1907, quoted in *MTEnt*, p. 48. Goodman's source of information was a "memorandum-book" containing, as he said, "two exact dates."

[2]For a critique of the reliability of Rabb's texts, see the textual commentary.

from sorrow and despair to delight and hope, and then absentmindedly leaving his composition lying about to be discovered by the next passerby. Gazing around him in "holy delight," he is a comic replica of such figures as the speaker in Coleridge's "This Lime-Tree Bower My Prison," who stands thinking of his absent friend and

> Silent with swimming sense; yea, gazing round
>   On the wide landscape, gaze till all doth seem
> Less gross than bodily; and of such hues
>   As veil the Almighty Spirit, when yet he makes
> Spirits perceive his presence.[3]

One can find similar romantic figures in the novels of Scott. For instance, Reuben Butler in *The Heart of Midlothian* has (like Solon Lycurgus) a penchant for picturesque scenery, and at one point he retreats to Arthur's Seat, a mountain just outside Edinburgh, to watch the sunrise. And in *Redgauntlet* the young lawyer Alan Fairford, like Solon, prefers wandering the countryside to his legal studies.

Mark Twain's audience would have recognized Solon's attitudinizing about the landscape as patently absurd. The conical Sugar-Loaf Peak, in Six Mile Cañon just east of Virginia City, is dwarfed by Mount Davidson to the west and by other peaks in the vicinity. From that modest height Solon describes what cannot be seen: the vast extent of the "softly tinted" Carson River valley, from the river's source in the Sierra Nevada southwest of Virginia City to the valley's northeastern extremity near the Carson Sink—"the loveliest picture," mantled in "purple glory," with which "the hand of the Creator has adorned the earth." In October 1863 the unidentified local of the *Enterprise* reported that only barren mountainous wastes were visible in any direction from even the top of Mount Davidson. Yet, he remarked, "a great deal has been said and written eulogistic of the view from the summit. . . . In the name of truth and reason, let us have no more of it."[4] Solon's letter is a travesty of such excursions into unreality, a mock paean to God's creation. Clemens may even have been recalling a passage from Genesis: "And the Lord God planted a garden eastward in Eden. . . . And a river went out of Eden to water the garden."[5]

---

[3]Lines 40–44.
[4]"Mount Davidson," reprinted from the *Enterprise* by the Gold Hill *News*, 16 October 1863, p. 3.
[5]Gen. 2:8, 10.

Ye Sentimental Law Student

EDS. ENTERPRISE—I found the following letter, or Valentine, or whatever it is, lying on the summit, where it had been dropped unintentionally, I think. It was written on a sheet of legal cap, and each line was duly commenced within the red mark which traversed the sheet from top to bottom. Solon appeared to have had some trouble getting his effusion started to suit him. He had begun it, "Know all men by these presents," and scratched it out again; he had substituted, "Now at this day comes the plaintiff, by his attorney," and scratched that out also; he had tried other sentences of like character, and gone on obliterating them, until, through much sorrow and tribulation, he achieved the dedication which stands at the head of his letter, and to his entire satisfaction, I do cheerfully hope. But what a villain a man must be to blend together the beautiful language of love and the infernal phraseology of the law in one and the same sentence! I know but one of God's creatures who would be guilty of such depravity as this: I refer to the Unreliable. I believe the Unreliable to be the very lawyer's-cub who sat upon the solitary peak, all soaked in beer and sentiment, and concocted the insipid literary hash I am talking about. The handwriting closely resembles his semi-Chinese tarantula tracks.

SUGAR LOAF PEAK, February 14, 1863.
To the loveliness to whom these presents shall come, greeting:—
This is a lovely day, my own Mary; its unencumbered sunshine reminds me of your happy face, and in the imagination the same doth

217

now appear before me. Such sights and scenes as this ever remind me, the party of the second part, of you, my Mary, the peerless party of the first part. The view from the lonely and segregated mountain peak, of this portion of what is called and known as Creation, with all and singular the hereditaments and appurtenances thereunto appertaining and belonging, is inexpressively grand and inspiring; and I gaze, and gaze, while my soul is filled with holy delight, and my heart expands to receive thy spirit-presence, as aforesaid. Above me is the glory of the sun; around him float the messenger clouds, ready alike to bless the earth with gentle rain, or visit it with lightning, and thunder, and destruction; far below the said sun and the messenger clouds aforesaid, lying prone upon the earth in the verge of the distant horizon, like the burnished shield of a giant, mine eyes behold a lake, which is described and set forth in maps as the Sink of Carson; nearer, in the great plain, I see the Desert, spread abroad like the mantle of a Colossus, glowing by turns, with the warm light of the sun, hereinbefore mentioned, or darkly shaded by the messenger clouds aforesaid; flowing at right angles with said Desert, and adjacent thereto, I see the silver and sinuous thread of the river, commonly called Carson, which winds its tortuous course through the softly tinted valley, and disappears amid the gorges of the bleak and snowy mountains—a simile of man!—leaving the pleasant valley of Peace and Virtue to wander among the dark defiles of Sin, beyond the jurisdiction of the kindly beaming sun aforesaid! And about said sun, and the said clouds, and around the said mountains, and over the plain and the river aforesaid, there floats a purple glory—a yellow mist—as airy and beautiful as the bridal veil of a princess, about to be wedded according to the rites and ceremonies pertaining to, and established by, the laws or edicts of the kingdom or principality wherein she doth reside, and whereof she hath been and doth continue to be, a lawful sovereign or subject. Ah! my Mary, it is sublime! it is lovely! I have declared and made known, and by these presents do declare and make known unto you, that the view from Sugar Loaf Peak, as hereinbefore described and set forth, is the loveliest picture with which the hand of the Creator has adorned the earth, according to the best of my knowledge and belief, so help me God.

Given under my hand, and in the spirit-presence of the bright being whose love has restored the light of hope to a soul once groping in the darkness of despair, on the day and year first above written.

(Signed)   SOLON LYCURGUS.

Law Student, and Notary Public in and for the said County of Storey, and Territory of Nevada.

To Miss Mary Links, Virginia (and may the laws have her in their holy keeping).

45. *A Sunday in Carson*

24 February–31 March 1863

This sketch was part of a letter that Mark Twain sent to the Virginia City *Territorial Enterprise* from Carson City. The text survives only in Kate Milnor Rabb's *The Wit and Humor of America*. It was written on an undetermined Sunday, the day Clemens arrived in Carson for a brief visit, probably in late February or March 1863.

Internal evidence establishes that Clemens could not have written the letter in January. On 23 January 1863, H. F. Swayze, whom Clemens pictured busily writing in jail, was arrested for murdering George W. Derickson, the editor of the Washoe City *Times*, who had criticized him in print.[1] Clemens was not in Carson on the Sunday after Swayze's arrest (January 25, the last Sunday in the month). And although he did visit Carson for the week from January 29 to February 6, he could not have written "A Sunday in Carson" on that visit because he arrived on a Thursday, not a Sunday.[2] In a letter to his mother and sister dated February 16, Clemens referred to his Carson visit in early February and made it clear that he had been nowhere since then. He also indicated that he was eager for a change: "I am not in a very good humor, to-night. I wanted to rush down and take some comfort for a few days, in San Francisco, but there is no one here now, to take my place."[3]

It seems likely that Clemens' frustration on Wednesday, February 16, was relieved on the following Sunday, February 22, and that "A Sunday in Carson" was written then. Since the *Enterprise* did not publish on Mondays, he had

---

[1]Myron Angel, ed., *History of Nevada* (Oakland: Thompson and West, 1881), p. 328; Richard G. Lillard, *Desert Challenge: An Interpretation of Nevada* (New York: Alfred A. Knopf, 1942), pp. 201–202.

[2]See "Letter from Carson City" (no. 40).

[3]Clemens to Jane Clemens and Pamela Moffett, 16 February 1863, *CL1*, letter 65.

Sunday and part of Monday to "take some comfort" before he had to be back in Virginia City. Moreover, in "Reportorial" (no. 47), published later that week on Thursday or Friday (February 26 or 27), Clemens said that "last Saturday" (presumably February 21) the Unreliable had abused him in the Virginia City *Union,* and that he had also recently published "a list of Langton's stage passengers" wherein Clemens' name appeared "between those of 'Sam Chung' and 'Sam Lee.' " Clemens did in fact take "Langton's express" to Carson, as he wrote in the first sentence of "A Sunday in Carson," and the list in the *Union* may have recorded his departure on Sunday, February 22. If the sketch was written on that day, it could not have appeared in the *Enterprise* before Tuesday, February 24.

On the other hand, we cannot exclude the possibility that Clemens took a stagecoach to Carson and wrote the letter on some Sunday in March, although no trip of his to Carson in that month can now be documented. A still later date, say in April, seems unlikely: the allusion to Swayze, who was arrested on January 23, implies that his crime was a fairly recent event.

A Sunday in Carson

I ARRIVED IN this noisy and bustling town of Carson at noon to-day, per Langton's express. We made pretty good time from Virginia, and might have made much better, but for Horace Smith, Esq., who rode on the box seat and kept the stage so much by the head she wouldn't steer. I went to church, of course,—I always go to church when I— when I go to church—as it were. I got there just in time to hear the closing hymn, and also to hear the Rev. Mr. White give out a long-metre doxology, which the choir tried to sing to a short-metre tune. But there wasn't music enough to go around: consequently, the effect was rather singular, than otherwise. They sang the most interesting parts of each line, though, and charged the balance to "profit and loss;" this rendered the general intent and meaning of the doxology considerably mixed, as far as the congregation were concerned, but inasmuch as it was not addressed to them, anyhow, I thought it made no particular difference.

By an easy and pleasant transition, I went from church to jail. It was only just down stairs—for they save men eternally in the second story of the new court house, and damn them for life in the first. Sheriff Gasherie has a handsome double office fronting on the street, and its walls are gorgeously decorated with iron convict-jewelry. In the rear are two rows of cells, built of bomb-proof masonry and furnished with strong iron doors and resistless locks and bolts. There was but one prisoner—Swayze, the murderer of Derickson—and he was writing; I do not know what his subject was, but he appeared to be handling it in a way which gave him great satisfaction. . . .

46. *The Unreliable*

25 February 1863

This sketch appeared in the local items column of the Virginia City *Territorial Enterprise* for 25 February 1863[1] and clearly belongs to Mark Twain's continuing comic feud with Clement T. Rice. The immediate occasion of the Unreliable's antics was the Firemen's Ball, held on February 23 at Topliffe's Theater on North C Street, Virginia City, as part of the annual fund raising for Virginia Engine Company No. 1. Clemens reported the ball straightforwardly in an adjacent column in the same paper. He said that the decoration of the hall and the dancers, who were "thoroughly fuddled with plain quadrilles," were actually "charming to the last degree."

We have not one particle of fault to find with the ball; the managers kept perfect order and decorum, and did everything in their power to make it pass pleasantly to all the guests. They succeeded. But of all the failures we have been called upon to chronicle, the supper was the grandest. It was bitterly denounced by nearly everybody who sat down to it—officers, firemen, men, women and children. Now, the supposition is, that somebody will come out in a card and deny this, and attribute base motives to us: but we are not to be caught asleep, or even napping, this time—we have got all our proofs at hand, and shall explode at anybody who tries to show that we cannot tell the truth without being actuated by unworthy motives. Chief Engineer Peas[le]y and officer Birdsall said that the supper contract was for a table supplied with everything the market could afford, and in such profusion that the last who came might fare as well as the first (the contractor to receive a stipulated sum for each supper furnished)—and they also say that no part or portion of that contract was entirely fulfilled. The entertainment broke up about four o'clock in the morning, and the guests returned to their homes well satisfied with the ball itself, but not with the supper.[2]

---

[1]PH in MTP.

[2]"The Firemen's Ball," Virginia City *Territorial Enterprise*, 25 February 1863, p. 3, PH in MTP.

In "The Unreliable" Clemens undertook to give still further "proofs" for this accusation, but in a somewhat less strident fashion: the voracious and vindictive appetite of the Unreliable accounted for "the scarcity of provisions at the Firemen's supper."

The Unreliable

THIS POOR MISERABLE outcast crowded himself into the Firemen's Ball, night before last, and glared upon the happy scene with his evil eye for a few minutes. He had his coat buttoned up to his chin, which is the way he always does when he has no shirt on. As soon as the managers found out he was there, they put him out, of course. They had better have allowed him to stay, though, for he walked straight across the street, with all his vicious soul aroused, and climbed in at the back window of the supper room and gobbled up the last crumb of the repast provided for the guests, before he was discovered. This accounts for the scarcity of provisions at the Firemen's supper that night. Then he went home and wrote a particular description of our ball costume, with his usual meanness, as if such information could be of any consequence to the public. He never vouchsafed a single compliment to our dress, either, after all the care and taste we had bestowed upon it. We despise that man.

47. *Reportorial*

26 February 1863

Clemens published an obituary of the Unreliable in the Virginia City *Territorial Enterprise* sometime in late February 1863. The original printing is not extant, but the Marysville (Calif.) *Appeal* for 28 February 1863 reprinted the concluding paragraphs of the piece, and it is the source of the present text. The *Appeal* editor noted: "The reporters for the Virginia *Union* and the Virginia *Enterprise*, over the mountains, have a lovely time 'sparring' at each other. The *Enterprise* reporter publishes an obituary notice of his cotem. winding up as follows."

The sketch was not one of Clemens' local items, for it was signed "Mark Twain." It was probably the second special article that he contributed to the *Enterprise*. (The first such article was "Ye Sentimental Law Student," no. 44, published on 19 February 1863.) The *Appeal* did not give the date of the *Enterprise* printing. However, Mark Twain refers within the piece to the Unreliable's "abuse of me in the Virginia *Union* of last Saturday." Since the obituary must have appeared after February 19 (the date of "Ye Sentimental Law Student") and before February 28, "last Saturday" must refer to February 21. The obituary might therefore have been published anytime between Tuesday, February 24, and Friday, February 27. Since "The Unreliable" (no. 46) appeared on February 25 and made no allusion to that character's recent extraordinary demise and resurrection, our best conjecture is that the obituary appeared on Thursday, February 26, one week after Mark Twain's first special article. Presumably the *Enterprise* of February 26 left Virginia City at 8:00 that morning and arrived in Marysville by noon of the following day, in time to be reprinted by the *Appeal* on the morning of February 28.[1]

---

[1] Advertisement for the California Stage Company, Virginia City *Territorial Enterprise*, 10 January 1863, p. 4, PH in MTP.

Reportorial

HE BECAME a newspaper reporter, and crushed Truth to earth and kept her there; he bought and sold his own notes, and never paid his board; he pretended great friendship for Gillespie, in order to get to sleep with him; then he took advantage of his bed fellow and robbed him of his glass eye and his false teeth; of course he sold the articles, and Gillespie was obliged to issue more county scrip than the law allowed, in order to get them back again; the Unreliable broke into my trunk at Washoe City, and took jewelry and fine clothes and things, worth thousands and thousands of dollars; he was present, without invitation, at every party and ball and wedding which transpired in Carson during thirteen years. But the last act of his life was the crowning meanness of it: I refer to the abuse of me in the Virginia *Union* of last Saturday, and also to a list of Langton's stage passengers sent to the same paper by him, wherein my name appears between those of "Sam Chung" and "Sam Lee." This is his treatment of me, his benefactor. That malicious joke was his dying atrocity. During thirteen years he played himself for a white man: he fitly closed his vile career by trying to play me for a Chinaman.

He is dead and buried now, though: let him rest, let him rot. Let his vices be forgotten, but let his virtues be remembered: it will not infringe much upon any man's time.

MARK TWAIN.

P. S.—By private letters from Carson, since the above was in type, I am pained to learn that the Unreliable, true to his unnatural instincts, came to life again in the midst of his funeral sermon, and remains so to this moment. He was always unreliable in life—he could not even be depended upon in death. The shrouded corpse shoved the coffin lid to one side, rose to a sitting posture, cocked his eye at the minister and smilingly said, "O let up, Dominie, this is played out, you know—loan me two bits!" The frightened congregation rushed from the house, and the Unreliable followed them, with his coffin on his shoulder. He sold it for two dollars and a half, and got drunk at a "bit house" on the proceeds. He is still drunk.

                                                                M. T.

48. Examination of Teachers

March–April 1863

"Examination of Teachers" is extant only in an undated clipping from the Virginia City *Territorial Enterprise*, preserved in a scrapbook in the Morse Collection at Yale. The piece probably appeared in that newspaper's local column sometime in March or April 1863, but a more precise date cannot now be determined, and even this conjecture must remain very tentative.

The examination in question probably took place sometime in 1863: the names mentioned in Clemens' text are found, for the most part, in the Nevada Territory directories of that year. Moreover, it was not until December 1862 that the second Territorial Legislature acted to "provide for a Board of Education in Storey county."[1] That board was first elected on 5 January 1863, and probably held its first meeting one week later. It was empowered, as Clemens wrote at the time, to "issue bonds for a sum sufficient to defray the expenses of the respective schools of the county, from the beginning of the present month [January] until the first of November" and to "establish schools of all grades, engage and examine teachers, etc."[2]

The first sign of activity based upon this mandate was reported by Clemens in the *Enterprise* on February 25:

SCHOOL-HOUSE.—An addition is being built to the public school-house, and will be completed and put in order for occupation as soon as possible. Mr. Mellvile's school has increased to such an extent that the old premises were found insufficient to accommodate all the pupils. As soon as the new building is completed, the school will be divided into three departments—advanced, intermediate and infant—and one of these will occupy it.[3]

---

[1]Andrew J. Marsh, *Letters from Nevada Territory: 1861–1862*, ed. William C. Miller, Russell W. McDonald, and Ann Rollins (Nevada: Legislative Counsel Bureau, 1972), p. 631.

[2]"Election," Virginia City *Territorial Enterprise*, 4 January 1863, Scrapbook 1, p. 66, MTP.

[3]Virginia City *Territorial Enterprise*, 25 February 1863, p. 3.

230 EARLY TALES & SKETCHES

It is not known when the new building was completed, but it was probably not before the end of the month. The earliest possible date for "Examination of Teachers" seems, therefore, to be March, for Clemens clearly refers to the new building when he reports that the "grand examination" was held "in one of the rooms of the Public School of this city." Moreover, it seems plausible that the board of education would take steps to staff the new school building at about the same time it undertook construction. We know that by October 1863 the number of school-age children had, in fact, grown to 420, at least 400 more than the year before:[4] this in itself would suggest the urgent need for an additional twelve teachers, who, as Clemens says here, were to be chosen by examination. The most likely time for such an examination, therefore, seems to be in March or possibly April 1863. It could not have taken place in May or June, because Clemens was in San Francisco for the whole of both months and so could not have reported it. On the other hand, it is conceivable that teacher recruitment was delayed until July or August, or even later. No record of such an examination has, however, been found in the file of the Virginia City *Evening Bulletin* (6 July 1863–December 1864).

Clemens' sketch bears a resemblance to "Silver Bars—How Assayed" (no. 43), for it, too, humanizes an inherently dry subject by comically injecting the author's own feelings of inadequacy and anxiety. His account throws light on the surprisingly rigorous standards for teacher selection in Storey County: the newly elected board of education seems to have established a formidable range of subjects on which to examine candidates. But Clemens' admiration for such standards is balanced by his set of mock questions especially designed for teachers of "little Washoeites": a small tour de force aimed at needling "the Board" for its overweening thoroughness.

---

[4]"School Children," Gold Hill *News*, 27 October 1863, p. 3.

Examination of Teachers

A GRAND EXAMINATION of candidates for positions as teachers in our public schools was had yesterday in one of the rooms of the Public School in this city. Some twenty-eight candidates were present —twenty-three of whom were ladies and five gentlemen. We do the candidates but simple justice when we say that we have never seen more intelligent faces in a crowd of the size. The following gentlemen constituted the Board of Examiners: Dr. Geiger, Mr. J. W. Whicher and John A. Collins. We observed that Messrs. Feusier, Adkison and Robinson of the Board of Trustees were also present yesterday. Printed questions are given to each of the candidates, the answers to which are written out and handed in with the signature of the applicant appended. These are all examined in private by the Board, and those who have best acquitted themselves are selected as teachers. In all, we believe, about twelve teachers are to be chosen. Upon each of the following subjects a great number of questions are to be answered: General questions, methods of teaching, object teaching; spelling, reading, writing, defining, arithmetic, grammar, geography, natural philosophy, history of the United States, physiology and hygiene, chemistry, algebra, geometry, natural history, astronomy—in all, eighteen subjects, with about as many questions upon each. Yesterday they had got as far as the ninth subject, grammar, at the time of our visit, and we presume have got but little further. To-day the examination will be resumed. If there is anything that terrifies us it is an examination. We don't even like an examination in a Police Court.

In vain we looked from face to face yesterday through the whole list of candidates for signs of fright or trepidation. All appeared perfectly at ease, though quite in earnest. We took a look at some of the questions and were made very miserable by barely glancing them over. We became much afraid that some member of the Board would suddenly turn upon us and require us on pain of death or a long imprisonment, to answer some of the questions. Under the head of "Object Teaching," we found some ten questions—some of them, like a wheel within a wheel, containing ten questions in one. We barely glanced at the list, reading here and there a question, when we felt great beads of perspiration starting out upon our brow—our massive intellect oozing out. Happening to read a question like this, "Name four of the faculties of children that are earliest developed," we at once became anxious to get out of the room. We expected each moment that one of the Board would seize us by the collar and ask, "Why is it?" or something of the kind, and we wanted to leave— thought we would feel better in the open air. When the answers of all the candidates are opened and read we will try to be on hand; we are anxious for information on those "four faculties." We think the above a good deal like the conundrum about the young man who "went to the Sandwich Islands; learned the language of the Kanakas, came home, got married, got drunk, went crazy, was sent to Stockton —Why is it?" Then under the same head we noticed ten questions about mining for silver ores and ten more about the reduction of silver ores. Why these twenty-three "school marms" are expected to be posted on amalgamating processes, is more than we can guess. As this is a mining country, we presume it is necessary for a lady to give satisfactory answers to such questions as the following, before being entrusted with the education of our little Washoeites: "What is your opinion of the one-ledge theory? Have you seen the Ophir horse? Have you conscientious scruples as to black dyke? Are you committed to the sage-brush process? Give your opinion on vein matter, and state your reasons for thinking so; and tell wherein you differ with those who do not agree with you."

49. City Marshal Perry

4 March 1863

John Van Buren (Jack) Perry, the subject of this burlesque biography, was reelected city marshal of Virginia City on 2 March 1863.[1] Since Clemens tells us in the piece that Perry was reelected "day before yesterday," we conjecture that it appeared in the *Territorial Enterprise* on March 4. The *Enterprise* printing is not extant; our text is taken from Kate Milnor Rabb's *The Wit and Humor of America.*

In early May 1863, when Clemens temporarily relinquished his post as editor of the *Enterprise* local column in order to spend two months in San Francisco, an *Enterprise* writer—almost certainly Joseph T. Goodman— published a good-natured farewell in the form of a mock eulogy of Mark Twain, in which he dubbed him "Monarch of Mining Items, Detailer of Events, Prince of Platitudes, Chief of Biographers."[2] Although Goodman may have been thinking especially of "City Marshal Perry," it seems likely that Clemens had in fact contributed his share of more serious work as well, since it was not unusual for the *Enterprise* staff to write brief biographies of candidates for public office.[3]

In mid-August 1863 the *Enterprise* published a straightforward biography of Perry (not now extant), perhaps on the occasion of his campaign for reelection as city constable.[4] Clemens, who was then at Steamboat Springs, wrote the *Enterprise* in mock dismay on August 18:

---

[1]San Francisco *Evening Bulletin*, 3 March 1863, p. 2; J. Wells Kelly, *Second Directory of Nevada Territory* (San Francisco: Valentine and Co., 1863), p. 270.

[2]"Mark Twain," Virginia City *Territorial Enterprise*, 3 May 1863, Scrapbook 2, p. 43, MTP.

[3]See, for example, "Biographical Sketches of the Union Nominees," Virginia City *Territorial Enterprise*, August 1863, Scrapbook 2, pp. 62–63, MTP.

[4]On September 2 Perry was elected constable of Virginia City on the Union ticket ("Election Returns," Virginia City *Evening Bulletin*, 3 September 1863, p. 3).

I notice in this morning's ENTERPRISE, a lame, impotent abortion of a biography of Marshal Perry. . . . You either want to impose upon the public with an incorrect account of that monster's career . . . or else you wish to bring into disrepute my own biography of him, which is the only correct and impartial one ever published. Which is it? If you really desired that the people should know the man they were expected to vote for, why did you not republish that history?

The real Jack Perry, he insisted, "was born in New Jersey; . . . is by occupation a shoemaker,—by nature a poet, and by instinct a great moral humbug."[5]

"City Marshal Perry," by relentlessly piling up outlandish genealogies and "facts," became an elaborate joke on a well-known town character. But this technique also ridiculed by implication the usual pompous tone and deferential rhetoric of real newspaper campaign biographies, some of which Clemens himself must certainly have written, and which used similar means to extol the candidates' accomplishments.

Far from being a shoemaker, as Clemens asserted, Perry was trained as a pressman. Politically he was known as a fierce Unionist. He figured prominently in anecdotes about Virginia City life in the 1860s, which characterized him as a large, aggressive, emotional man equally capable of weeping at *East Lynne* and of smashing the face of a "Secesh." He was president of the Virginia Fire Department in 1862, foreman of Hook and Ladder Company No. 1, twice city marshal (1862 and 1863), and a habitual practical joker.[6]

---

[5]Virginia City *Territorial Enterprise*, 19 August 1863, Scrapbook 2, p. 62, MTP, reprinted in *MTEnt*, p. 68.

[6]*MTEnt*, pp. 66–67; Kelly, *Second Directory*, pp. 270, 299; Margaret G. Watson, *Silver Theatre* (Glendale, Calif.: Arthur H. Clark Co., 1964), p. 149. Perry is also mentioned in chapter 49 of *Roughing It*.

City Marshal Perry

JOHN VAN BUREN PERRY, recently re-elected City Marshal of Virginia City, was born a long time ago, in County Kerry, Ireland, of poor but honest parents, who were descendants, beyond question, of a house of high antiquity. The founder of it was distinguished for his eloquence; he was the property of one Baalam, and received honorable mention in the Bible.

John Van Buren Perry removed to the United States in 1792—after having achieved a high gastronomical reputation by creating the first famine in his native land—and established himself at Kinderhook, New Jersey, as a teacher of vocal and instrumental music. His eldest son, Martin Van Buren, was educated there, and was afterwards elected President of the United States; his grandson, of the same name, is now a prominent New York politician, and is known in the East as "Prince John;" he keeps up a constant and affectionate correspondence with his worthy grandfather, who sells him feet in some of his richest wildcat claims from time to time.

While residing at Kinderhook, Jack Perry was appointed Commodore of the United States Navy, and he forthwith proceeded to Lake Erie and fought the mighty marine conflict, which blazes upon the pages of history as "Perry's Victory." In consequence of this exploit, he narrowly escaped the Presidency.

Several years ago Commodore Perry was appointed Commissioner Extraordinary to the Imperial Court of Japan, with unlimited power to treat. It is hardly worth while to mention that he never exercised that power; he never treated anybody in that country, although he patiently submitted to a vast amount of that sort of thing when the opportunity was afforded him at the expense of the Japanese officials. He returned from his mission full of honors and foreign whisky, and was welcomed home again by the plaudits of a grateful nation.

After the war was ended, Mr. Perry removed to Providence, Rhode Island, where he produced a complete revolution in medical science by inventing the celebrated "Pain Killer" which bears his name. He manufactured this liniment by the ship-load, and spread it far and wide over the suffering world; not a bottle left his establishment without his beneficent portrait upon the label, whereby, in time, his features became as well known unto burned and mutilated children as Jack the Giant Killer's.

When pain had ceased throughout the universe Mr. Perry fell to writing for a livelihood, and for years and years he poured out his soul in pleasing and effeminate poetry. . . . His very first effort, commencing:

> "How doth the little busy bee
> Improve each shining hour," etc.—

gained him a splendid literary reputation, and from that time forward no Sunday-school library was complete without a full edition of his plaintive and sentimental "Perry-Gorics." After great research and profound study of his subject, he produced that wonderful gem which is known in every land as "The Young Mother's Apostrophe to Her Infant," beginning:

> "Fie! fie! oo itty bitty pooty sing!
> To poke oo footsy-tootsys into momma's eye!"

This inspired poem had a tremendous run, and carried Perry's fame into every nursery in the civilized world. But he was not destined to wear his laurels undisturbed: England, with monstrous perfidy, at once claimed the "Apostrophe" for her favorite son, Martin Farquhar Tupper, and sent up a howl of vindictive abuse from her polluted press against our beloved Perry. With one accord, the American people rose up in his defense, and a devastating war was only averted by a public denial of the paternity of the poem by the great Proverbial over his own signature. This noble act of Mr. Tupper gained him a high place in the affection of this people, and his sweet platitudes have been read here with an ever augmented spirit of tolerance since that day.

The conduct of England toward Mr. Perry told upon his constitution to such an extent that at one time it was feared the gentle bard would fade and flicker out altogether; wherefore, the solicitude of influential officials was aroused in his behalf, and through their generosity he was provided with an asylum in Sing Sing prison, a quiet retreat in the state of New York. Here he wrote his last great poem, beginning:

> "Let dogs delight to bark and bite,
>   For God hath made them so—
> Your little hands were never made
>   To tear out each other's eyes with—"

and then proceeded to learn the shoemaker's trade in his new home, under the distinguished masters employed by the commonwealth.

Ever since Mr. Perry arrived at man's estate his prodigious feet have been a subject of complaint and annoyance to those communities which have known the honor of his presence. In 1835, during a great leather famine, many people were obliged to wear wooden shoes, and Mr. Perry, for the sake of economy, transferred his boot-making patronage from the tan-yard which had before enjoyed his custom, to an undertaker's establishment—that is to say, he wore coffins. At that time he was a member of Congress from New Jersey, and occupied a seat in front of the Speaker's throne. He had the uncouth habit of propping his feet upon his desk during prayer by the chaplain, and thus completely hiding that officer from every eye save that of Omnipotence alone. So long as the Hon. Mr. Perry wore orthodox leather boots the clergyman submitted to this infliction and prayed behind them in singular solitude, under mild protest; but when he arose one morning to offer up his regular petition, and beheld the cheerful apparition of Jack Perry's coffins confronting him, "The jolly old bum went under the table like a sick porpus" (as Mr. P. feelingly remarks), "and never shot off his mouth in that shanty again."

Mr. Perry's first appearance on the Pacific Coast was upon the boards of the San Francisco theaters in the character of "Old Pete" in

Dion Boucicault's "Octoroon." So excellent was his delineation of that celebrated character that "Perry's Pete" was for a long time regarded as the climax of histrionic perfection.

Since John Van Buren Perry has resided in Nevada Territory, he has employed his talents in acting as City Marshal of Virginia, and in abusing me because I am an orphan and a long way from home, and can therefore be persecuted with impunity. He was re-elected day before yesterday, and his first official act was an attempt to get me drunk on champagne furnished to the Board of Aldermen by other successful candidates, so that he might achieve the honor and glory of getting me in the station-house for once in his life. Although he failed in his object, he followed me down C street and handcuffed me in front of Tom Peasley's, but officers Birdsall and Larkin and Brokaw rebelled against this unwarranted assumption of authority, and released me—whereupon I was about to punish Jack Perry severely, when he offered me six bits to hand him down to posterity through the medium of this Biography, and I closed the contract. But after all, I never expect to get the money.

50. [Champagne with the Board of Brokers]

7 March 1863

Myron Angel's *History of Nevada* is the only extant source of this account of the champagne supper at Almack's Oyster and Liquor Saloon following the organization of the Washoe Stock and Exchange Board in Virginia City on Friday, 6 March 1863. Because Mark Twain "adjourned to make this report," we can be fairly certain that the item appeared in the *Territorial Enterprise* the next day.

The president of the new board was A. C. Wightman, who with his partner, John A. Mitchell, headed an important firm of stockbrokers in the city. The vice-president was Jackson McKenty.[1] Presumably Rollin M. Daggett was present not only in his role as good fellow, but also as the vice-president of the Virginia Stock and Exchange Board—an already established group—and as a leading stockbroker. Daggett, who came to the Pacific Coast from Ohio in 1849, began the *Golden Era* in San Francisco in 1852. He came to Nevada in 1862, and two years later became an editor on the *Enterprise*.[2]

---

[1]Virginia City *Territorial Enterprise*, 10 January 1863, p. 2, PH in MTP; ibid., 3 April 1863, p. 1.

[2]See *MTEnt*, p. 227, and Francis P. Weisenburger, *Idol of the West: The Fabulous Career of Rollin Mallory Daggett* (Syracuse: Syracuse University Press, 1965).

[Champagne with the Board of Brokers]

B$_Y$ A SORT OF instinct we happened in at Almack's just at the moment that the corks were about to pop, and discovering that we had intruded we were retreating when Daggett, the soulless, insisted upon our getting —— with the Board of Brokers, and we very naturally did so. The President had already been toasted, the Vice-President had likewise been complimented in the same manner. Mr. Mitchell had delivered an address through his unsolicited mouth-piece, Mr. Daggett, whom he likened unto Baalam's ass—and very aptly too— and the press had been toasted, and he had attempted to respond and got overcome by something—feelings perhaps—when that ever-lasting, omnipresent, irrepressible, "Unreliable" crowded himself into the festive apartment, where he shed a gloom upon the Board of Brokers, and emptied their glasses while they made speeches. The imperturbable impudence of that iceberg surpasses anything we ever saw. By a concerted movement the young man was partially put down at length, however, and the Board launched out into speech-making again, but finally somebody put up five feet of "Texas," which changed hands at eight dollars a foot, and from that they branched off into a wholesale bartering of "wildcat"—for their natures were aroused by the first smell of blood of course—and we adjourned to make this report. The Board will begin its regular meetings Monday next.

51. Advice to the Unreliable
on Church-Going

12 April 1863

Kate Milnor Rabb's *The Wit and Humor of America* supplies us with the text of "Advice to the Unreliable on Church-Going." The satire was probably published in the Virginia City *Territorial Enterprise* on 12 April 1863, for on April 11 Clemens wrote to his mother and his sister, "I have just finished writing up my report for the morning paper, and giving the Unreliable a column of advice about how to conduct himself in church."[1] Since Rabb's text is scarcely "a column" long, and since it ends with ellipsis points, the original piece may well have been somewhat longer.

---

[1]Clemens to Jane Clemens and Pamela Moffett, 11–12 April 1863, *CL1*, letter 67.

Advice to the Unreliable
on Church-Going

I<small>N THE FIRST</small> place, I must impress upon you that when you are dressing for church, as a general thing, you mix your perfumes too much; your fragrance is sometimes oppressive; you saturate yourself with cologne and bergamot, until you make a sort of Hamlet's Ghost of yourself, and no man can decide, with the first whiff, whether you bring with you air from Heaven or from hell. Now, rectify this matter as soon as possible; last Sunday you smelled like a secretary to a consolidated drug store and barber shop. And you came and sat in the same pew with me; now don't do that again.

In the next place when you design coming to church, don't lie in bed until half past ten o'clock and then come in looking all swelled and torpid, like a doughnut. Do reflect upon it, and show some respect for your personal appearance hereafter.

There is another matter, also, which I wish to remonstrate with you about. Generally, when the contribution box of the missionary department is passing around, you begin to look anxious, and fumble in your vest pockets, as if you felt a mighty desire to put all your worldly wealth into it—yet when it reaches your pew, you are sure to be absorbed in your prayer-book, or gazing pensively out of the window at far-off mountains, or buried in meditation, with your sinful head supported by the back of the pew before you. And after the box is gone again, you usually start suddenly and gaze after it with a yearning look, mingled with an expression of bitter disappointment (fumbling your cash again meantime), as if you felt you had missed the

242

one grand opportunity for which you had been longing all your life. Now, to do this when you have money in your pockets is mean. But I have seen you do a meaner thing. I refer to your conduct last Sunday, when the contribution box arrived at our pew—and the angry blood rises to my cheek when I remember with what gravity and sweet serenity of countenance you put in fifty cents and took out two dollars and a half. . . .

52. Horrible Affair

16–18 April 1863

"Horrible Affair" was first published in the Virginia City *Territorial Enterprise* but is extant only in the Oroville (Calif.) *Butte Record*, from which our text is taken. The double murder by John Campbell to which the piece alludes occurred in the early morning hours of 12 April 1863, and Campbell was captured by April 13. Since Clemens says that the events following this murder had been rumored "for a day or two," he probably wrote the item between April 14 and 16, and published it between April 16 and 18.

The *Butte Record* gave no indication which *Enterprise* staff member wrote "Horrible Affair," but such a story normally fell to the local editor—at that time Samuel Clemens. Clemens, indeed, is linked to the piece by several bits of convincing evidence. In a letter of April 11 he wrote to his mother and sister, "P. S. I have just heard five pistol shots down street—as such things are in my line, I will go and see about it." At 5 A.M. on the twelfth he added a second postscript to his letter: "The pistol did its work well—one man—a Jackson County Missourian, shot two of my friends, (police officers,) through the heart—both died within three minutes. Murderer's name is John Campbell."[1]

According to a contemporary newspaper account dated April 13, the two murdered policemen were Dennis McMahon and Thomas Reed; Campbell, who was twenty-six years old, was arrested after the momentary escape alluded to in the sketch.[2] All these events would of course have interested Clemens, as would the rumor of the five suffocated Indians—the "horrible affair" supposedly resulting from the effort to apprehend Campbell.

---

[1]Clemens to Jane Clemens and Pamela Moffett, 11–12 April 1863, *CL1*, letter 67.
[2]"Murders at Virginia City," San Francisco *Evening Bulletin*, 14 April 1863, p. 2.

Some five years later in a letter to the *Enterprise* Clemens recalled this story of the dead Indians:

To find a petrified man, or break a stranger's leg, or cave an imaginary mine, or discover some dead Indians in a Gold Hill tunnel, or massacre a family at Dutch Nick's, were feats and calamities that *we* never hesitated about devising when the public needed matters of thrilling interest for breakfast. The seemingly tranquil ENTERPRISE office was a ghastly factory of slaughter, mutilation and general destruction in those days.[3]

It is of some interest that Clemens here grouped the tale of the Indians with his two most famous Nevada hoaxes and with other newspaper "sensation" stories, which were not unknown to sacrifice truth to their readers' appetite for gory detail. "Horrible Affair" takes on verisimilitude by being linked with the Campbell murders, but its content is based entirely on rumor. Despite Clemens' concluding protestation that he believed the Indian story, the possibility remains that it was in reality "a sensation hoax" that he acquiesced in publicizing or perhaps even invented. This was, at any rate, the opinion of the San Francisco *Herald and Mirror*, which concluded its brief paraphrase of the story with the following observation: "The *Enterprise* is given to 'sells,' and we shouldn't wonder if the above is one of them. We don't forget the story about [the] stony natured toll-keeper, from the same source, which went the rounds."[4]

---

[3]"Mark Twain's Letters from Washington. Number IX," Virginia City *Territorial Enterprise*, 7 March 1868, p. 1.

[4]"Horrible Affair," San Francisco *Herald and Mirror*, 25 April 1863, p. 3.

Horrible Affair

For a day or two a rumor has been floating around, that five Indians had been smothered to death in a tunnel back of Gold Hill, but no one seemed to regard it in any other light than as a sensation hoax gotten up for the edification of strangers sojourning within our gates. However, we asked a Gold Hill man about it yesterday, and he said there was no shadow of a jest in it—that it was a dark and terrible reality. He gave us the following story as being the version generally accepted in Gold Hill:—That town was electrified on Sunday morning with the intelligence that a noted desperado had just murdered two Virginia policemen, and had fled in the general direction of Gold Hill. Shortly afterward, some one arrived with the exciting news that a man had been seen to run and hide in a tunnel a mile or a mile and a half west of Gold Hill. Of course it was Campbell—who else would do such a thing, on that particular morning, of all others? So a party of citizens repaired to this spot, but each felt a natural delicacy about approaching an armed and desperate man in the dark, and especially in such confined quarters; wherefore they stopped up the mouth of the tunnel, calculating to hold on to their prisoner until some one could be found whose duty would oblige him to undertake the disagreeable task of bringing forth the captive. The next day a strong posse went up, rolled away the stones from the mouth of the sepulchre, went in and found five dead Indians!—three men, one squaw and one child, who had gone in there to sleep, perhaps, and been smothered by the foul atmosphere after the tunnel had been closed up. We still hope the story may prove a fabrication, notwithstanding the positive assurances we have received that it is entirely true. The intention of the citizens was good, but the result was most unfortunate. To shut up a murderer in a tunnel was well enough, but to leave him there all night was calculated to impair his chances for a fair trial—the principle was good, but the application was unnecessarily "hefty." We have given the above story for truth—we shall continue to regard it as such until it is disproven.

53. Letter from Mark Twain

19–21 May 1863

A clipping of this San Francisco letter to the Virginia City *Territorial Enterprise* is preserved in one of Mark Twain's scrapbooks. Since Mark Twain dated his letter 16 May 1863, a Saturday, it probably appeared in the *Enterprise* sometime between May 19 and 21. It is the first example of Clemens' writing known to use "Mark Twain" in the heading, a change that signifies his growing reputation in Nevada.

On May 2 Clemens stepped down temporarily from his post as local editor of the *Enterprise* and, along with Clement T. Rice, set off for a two-month visit to San Francisco.[1] The next day the *Enterprise* announced his departure and speculated facetiously about his reasons for leaving:

As he assigned no adequate reason for this sudden step, we thought him the pitiable victim of self-conceit and the stock mania. He possessed some wildcat, and had lectured the Unreliable on manners till he fancied himself a Chesterfield. Yes, the poor fellow actually thought he possessed some breeding—that Virginia was too narrow a field for his graces and accomplishments; and in this delusion he has gone to display his ugly person and disgusting manners and wildcat on Montgomery street. In all of which he will be assisted by his protegee, the Unreliable. It is to be regretted that such scrubs are ever permitted to visit the Bay, as the inevitable effect will be to destroy that exalted opinion of the manners and morality of our people which was inspired by the conduct of our senior editor. We comfort ourselves, however, with the reflection that they will not be likely to shock the sensibilities of San Francisco long. The ordinances against nuisances are stringently enforced in that city.[2]

---

[1] See " 'Mark Twain's' Letter" (no. 54).

[2] "Mark Twain," Virginia City *Territorial Enterprise*, 3 May 1863, Scrapbook 2, p. 43, MTP. The author was probably Joseph T. Goodman, the "senior editor" himself.

The present sketch—Clemens' earliest extant letter written during his visit to San Francisco—clearly plays upon the expectations thus aroused. Its chief focus is on that "species of villainy" spawned by the Unreliable's "fertile brain," but in several respects the sketch anticipates the fictional "Mr. Brown" and "Mr. Twain" which Clemens would exploit in his 1866 letters from the Sandwich Islands. The Unreliable is presented as a deadbeat, characterized by his uncivilized use of current slang, as well as mining and legal jargon, which types him as a "scrub" and superficially distinguishes him from the more genteel "Mr. Mark Twain," one of the *invited* guests at the wedding. But the Unreliable is also less fatuous than this genteel character—interrupting, for instance, his "glowing and poetical" thoughts about the "weather": "You make a fool of yourself that way; everybody gets disgusted with you; stuff! be a man or a mouse, can't you?" Likewise, in Mark Twain's fourth letter from the Sandwich Islands Mr. Brown interrupts a similar "reverie" with hard facts: "Oh, fill me up about this lovely country! You can go on writing that slop about balmy breezes and fragrant flowers, and all that sort of truck, but you're not going to leave out them santipedes and things for want of being reminded of it, you know."[3]

---

[3]Sacramento *Union*, 19 April 1866, p. 2, reprinted in *MTH*, p. 278.

Letter from Mark Twain

SAN FRANCISCO, May 16, 1863.
EDS. ENTERPRISE:—The Unreliable, since he has been here, has conducted himself in such a reckless and unprincipled manner that he
has brought the whole Territory into disrepute and made its name a
reproach, and its visiting citizens objects of suspicion. He has been a
perfect nightmare to the officers of the Occidental Hotel. They give
him an excellent room, but if, in prowling about the house, he finds
another that suits him better, he "locates" it (that is his slang way of
expressing it). Judging by his appearance what manner of man he was,
the hotel clerk at first gave him a room immediately under the shingles—but it was found impossible to keep him there. He said he could
not stand it, because spinning round and round, up that spiral staircase, caused his beer to ferment, and made him foam at the mouth
like a soda fountain; wherefore, he descended at the dead of night
and "jumped" a room on the second floor (the very language he used
in boasting of the exploit). He said they served an injunction on him
there, "and," says he, "if Bill Stewart had been down here, Mark, I'd
have sued to quiet title, and I'd have held that ground, don't you
know it?" And he sighed; and after ruminating a moment, he added,
in a tone of withering contempt: "But these lawyers won't touch a
case unless a man has some rights; humph! they haven't any more
strategy into 'em than a clam. But Bill Stewart—thunder! Now, you
just take that Ophir suit that's coming off in Virginia, for instance—
why, God bless you, Bill Stewart'll worry the witnesses, and bullyrag

the Judge, and buy up the jury and pay for 'em; and he'll prove things that never existed—hell! what won't he prove! that's the idea—what won't he prove, you know? Why, Mark, I'll tell you what he done when—"

The Unreliable was interrupted here by a messenger from the hotel office, who handed him several sheets of legal cap, very neatly folded. He took them and motioned the young man to retire. "Now," said he, confidentially, "do you know what that is, Sweetness?" I said I thought it was a wash bill, or a hotel bill, or something of that kind. His countenance beamed with admiration: "You've struck it, by the Lord; yes, sir, that's just what it is—it's another of them d—d assessments; they levied one on me last week, and I meant to go and see a lawyer about it, but"—The Unreliable simmered down into a profound reverie, and I waited in silence to see what species of villainy his fertile brain would bring forth. At last he started up exultingly, with a devilish light in his eye: "I've got them in the door, Mark! They've been trying all they knew how to freeze me out, but they can't win. This hotel ain't incorporated under the laws of the Territory, and they can't collect—they are only a lot of blasted tenants in common! O, certainly" (with bitter scorn), "they'll get rich playing me for a Chinaman, you know." I forbear to describe how he reveled in the prospect of swindling the Occidental out of his hotel bill—it is too much humiliation even to think of it.

This young man insisted upon taking me to a concert last night, and I refused to go at first, because I am naturally suspicious of him, but he assured me that the Bella Union Melodeon was such a chaste and high-toned establishment that he would not hesitate to take any lady there who would go with him. This remark banished my fears, of course, and we proceeded to the house of amusement. We were the first arrivals there. He purchased two pit tickets for twenty-five cents apiece; I demurred at this kind of hospitality, and reminded him that orchestra seats were only fifty cents, and private boxes two dollars and a half. He bent on me a look of compassion, and muttered to himself that some people have no more sense than a boiled carrot—that some people's intellects were as dark as the inside of a cow. He walked into the pit, and then climbed over into the orchestra seats as coolly as if he had chartered the theatre. I followed, of course. Then he said, "Now, Mark, keep your eye skinned on that doorkeeper, and do as I do." I did as he did, and I am ashamed to say that he climbed a station and took possession of a private box. In due course several gentlemen performers came on the stage, and with them half a dozen lovely and blooming damsels, with the largest ankles you ever saw. In fact, they were dressed like so many parasols—as it were. Their songs, and jokes, and conundrums were received with rapturous applause. The Unreliable said these things were all copyrighted; it is probably true— I never heard them anywhere else. He was well pleased with the performance, and every time one of the ladies sang, he testified his approbation by knocking some of her teeth out with a bouquet. The Bella Union, I am told, is supported entirely by Washoe patronage. There are forty-two single gentlemen here from Washoe, and twenty-six married ones; they were all at the concert last night except two —both unmarried. But if the Unreliable had not told me it was a moral, high-toned establishment, I would not have observed it.

Hon. Wm. H. Davenport, of Virginia, and Miss Mollie Spangler, of Cincinnati, Ohio, were married here on the 10th instant, at the residence of Colonel John A. Collins. Among the invited guests were Judge Noyes and lady, Messrs. Beecher and Franz, of Virginia, and Mr. Mark Twain; among the uninvited I noticed only the Unreliable. It will probably never be known what became of the spoons. The bridal party left yesterday for Sacramento, and may be expected in Virginia shortly. Old, fat, jolly B. C. Howard, a Lyon county Commissioner, is here, at the Russ House, where he will linger a while and then depart for his old home in Vermont, to return again in the Fall. Col. Raymond, of the Zephyr-Flat mill, is in the city, also, and taking up a good deal of room in Montgomery street and the Bank Exchange; he has invested in some fast horses, and I shall probably take them over to Washoe shortly. There are multitudes of people from the Territory here at the three principal hotels—consequently, provisions are scarce. If you will send a few more citizens down we can carry this election, and fill all these city offices with Carson and Virginia men.

There is not much doing in stocks just now, especially in the Boards. But I suspect it is the case here as it is in Virginia, that the Boards do precious little of the business. Many private sales of Union (Gold Hill) and Yellow Jacket have transpired here during the past week at much higher prices than you quote those stocks at. Three hundred feet of Golden Gate changed hands at $100 per foot, and fifty feet at $110; but a telegram from Virginia yesterday, announcing that they had "struck it"—and moderately rich—in the San Francisco, raised both stocks several figures, as also the Golden Eagle (first south extension of the Golden Gate), which had been offered the day before at $30 a foot. Two hundred feet of Oriental were sold at private sale to-day at $7 a foot. Now, you hear no talk in Virginia but the extraordinary dullness of the San Francisco market. Humbug! It may be dull in the Boards, but it is lively enough on the street. If you doubt it, say so, and I will move around a little and furnish you with all the statistics you want.

I meant to say something glowing and poetical about the weather, but the Unreliable has come in and driven away refined emotion from my breast. He says: "Say it's bully, you tallow-brained idiot! that's enough; anybody can understand that; don't write any of those infernal, sick platitudes about sweet flowers, and joyous butterflies, and worms and things, for people to read before breakfast. You make a fool of yourself that way; everybody gets disgusted with you; stuff! be a man or a mouse, can't you?"

I must go out, now, with this conceited ass—there is no other way to get rid of him.

MARK TWAIN.

54. "Mark Twain's" Letter

9 July 1863

After spending May and June of 1863 in San Francisco, Clemens arrived by stagecoach in Virginia City on July 2, ready to resume work as the local editor on the *Territorial Enterprise*. He had made arrangements while away to correspond with the San Francisco *Morning Call*, and the following letter, dated July 5, was the first of a series of ten that he published there. Newsy, relaxed, and personal, it is a happy example of his style of newspaper correspondence, having an ample and completely disarming mixture of narrative and descriptive material.

Clemens played up his return trip to Nevada, made by way of the Henness Pass route, and the bustling activity and the violence which he found in Virginia City. During his absence Thomas Maguire, the "Napoleon" of the San Francisco stage,[1] had completed his new Virginia City Opera House in good time to accommodate the traditional Fourth of July festivities described by Clemens. The letter also recorded a glimpse of Thomas Fitch in action before he and Clemens became acquainted.[2] Seven years later Clemens still held a high opinion of Fitch's oratorical capacities. He wrote: "I know him to be an orator by birth, education, and instinct. He is a fascinating speaker. I pledge my word that he will hold any audience willing prisoners for two hours. . . . And no matter what subject he chooses, whether it be worn or fresh, old or new, he will make his audience think they never listened to any thing so delightful before."[3]

---

[1] See the headnote to "A Rich Epigram" (no. 142).
[2] See the headnote to "A Duel Prevented" (no. 56).
[3] Clemens to James Redpath, July 1870, *CL2*, letter 209.

"Mark Twain's" Letter

VIRGINIA CITY, N. T., July 5, 1863.

HOME AGAIN.

EDITORS CALL:—After an absence of two months, I stand in the midst of my native sage-brush once more; and in the midst of bustle and activity, and turmoil and confusion, to which lunch-time in the Tower of Babel was foolishness. B and C streets swarm with men, and horses, and wagons, and pack-trains, and dry-goods, and quartz, and bricks, and stone, and lumber, to such a degree that it is almost impossible to navigate them. And then the infernal racket—O, for the solitude of Montgomery street again! Everybody is building, apparently. The boundaries of the city of Virginia have not been extended during the past two months, but the number of houses has been fearfully increased—doubled, I may say. Some portions of the town have grown clear out of my recollection since I have been away. Maguire has erected a spacious and beautiful theatre on D street, exactly after the pattern of the Opera House in San Francisco, and it is nightly crowded with admirers of Mr. Mayo, Mrs. Hayne, and other "theatricides," whose names are familiar to Californians.

THE HENNESS PASS.

I came by the Henness Pass route. I don't like it. I brought my other shirt along, and they charged me extra baggage. Besides, Uncle John Atchison, Mr. Harris and Mr. Chapelle were in the party, and they created a famine at every station we stopped at. They fell upon the

Barnum Restaurant in Sacramento, and ate the proprietor out of house and home; then they attacked the first station this side of Lincoln, and brought ruin and desolation upon it. I am a mighty responsible artist at a dinner-table myself, when I get a chance—but I never got one until we arrived at Lake City, on Wednesday evening. We met the down stage there, with five or six men in it who were considerably battered and bruised by a recent upset. They were unable to eat. But the landlord lost nothing by it—I disposed of those extra rations. The only man among the wounded who was seriously hurt was a Mr. Tomlinson, from Humboldt Bay—shoulder dislocated. We seventeen passengers, however, traveled without fear of accident on this part of the route—from Nevada to Tracy's—as our driver was the best in the world except Woodruff (they call him Wood), who drives on the Placerville route from Genoa or Carson to Strawberry. They gave us a fish breakfast at Hunter's, on the Truckee—trout, Uncle John said, but it was hardly tender enough for that—I expect it was whale. We dashed by the Ophir on Thursday morning at half-past eleven o'clock, twenty-nine hours out from Sacramento—which reminds me of an anecdote, one of Mr. Merritt's, President of the Imperial Gold and Silver Mining Company.

WHAT OUR FUTURE PROSPERITY DEPENDS UPON.

Thus. Mr. Nathaniel Page, of San Francisco, was coming into Virginia one morning, in one of the Pioneer coaches, and enjoying the conversation of a sociable old sot, who decorated the middle seat. The sociable man pointed to the hill-side, and remarked:

"When I first come here, two years ago, that Savage, there, 'n' the Hale, 'n' the Norcrus, 'n' the Potosi, could be had for the askin'—any of 'em. Now look at 'em! (hic) Bilin', ain't they? H—ll! thousands couldn't touch 'em this very minute!"

Mr. Page said, "Well, those claims have increased in value very rapidly—but do you think they will continue to do so?"

To which the sociable man replied, "Blessed if I know—'n' no other man don't know, either. It's all owin' (hic) to how many more d—d fools comes here f'm Sanfercisco!"

THE FOURTH IN VIRGINIA.

Yesterday was the greatest day Virginia ever saw. From morning till night her streets were crowded to suffocation with processions of citizens, and soldiers, and fire companies, and the air was filled with the music of brass bands and the booming of cannon. I traversed the city in company with Billy Welch, of the California mine, in his "Washoe carriage," (being favored with the vacant seat aft the middle gangway, on that gentleman's little mule,) and had a notable opportunity of wondering where such multitudes of people could have come from, and of never arriving at any satisfactory conclusion about it. The reading of the poem, and the Farewell Address, and the President's Message and accompanying documents, and so forth, came off in the afternoon, at the theatre. Of course, the house could only contain a very small fraction of the public, but that fraction was well satisfied with the exercises. Mr. Frank Mayo read the poem (written by Joseph T. Goodman, Esq.,) which was a masterly production, as was amply attested by the tremendous applause with which it was received. Had I dreamed of such an enthusiastic reception as that, I would have dashed off a dusty old poem myself for the occasion. Thomas Fitch, Esq., delivered the oration. I don't know Mr. Fitch personally, but by reputation I don't like him. He is a "born" orator, though. If he always swings the English language as grandly as he did yesterday, I shall always be happy to hear him. He is a regular masked battery. He lulls you into a treacherous repose, with a few mild and graceful sentences, and then suddenly explodes in your midst with a bombshell of eloquence which shakes you to your very foundations. Yesterday evening, a grand display of fireworks on Virginia Hill finished the Fourth of July festivities in this metropolis. Our wonderfully clear atmosphere vouchsafed to the pyrotechnics a splendor and brilliancy never attained at lower altitudes. Various figures and mottoes were represented, and the beauty of the designs and the excellence of the execution did infinite credit to Virginia.

MAN SHOT.

The good order and freedom from disturbance which prevailed yesterday, were the subject of general remark. I hardly think old citizens were fooled by it though. If they did not speak of it openly, many of them must have been speculating inwardly as to what man we were likely to have for breakfast. The fearful question was solved —or almost solved—just before midnight. Two Irishmen got to fighting in the San Francisco Saloon, and the proprietor of the establishment, Mike Millenovich, attempted to separate them. Two policemen

—McGee and Scott—came in, attracted by the noise, and a general row ensued, in the course of which nine pistol shots were fired, one of which broke Millenovich's arm, and another entered his side, inflicting an ugly and probably fatal wound. I get this meagre and unsatisfactory statement from an eye-witness, who says "they made it so warm for him in there that he don't rightly know much about it." I entertain a similar opinion myself. Another witness tells me several outsiders were wounded by chance shots, but I have been unable to stumble upon any such.

THE MINES.

I cannot say anything about the mines this time, because I have not had time to visit them since I got home. That villainous trip over the mountains has relaxed my tremendous energies to some extent, also. From the increasing richness of the developments being made in the Hale & Norcross mine, however, I think you may count on a great advance in the price of that stock within the next few days.

FALSE REPORT.

There was a report about town, last night, that Charles Strong, Esq., Superintendent of the Gould & Curry, had been shot and very effectually killed. I asked him about it at church this morning. He said there was no truth in the rumor. And speaking of the church, I am at this moment suffering with an itching to do up the fashions there, but I expect it might not be an altogether safe speculation.

MARK TWAIN.

55. "Mark Twain's" Letter

30 July 1863

This installment of Clemens' correspondence to the San Francisco *Morning Call* was cut short for reasons he has graphically explained. The fire that burned down the White House, where he roomed in Virginia City, transformed him into "a bankrupt community": he had to abandon his trunk of wildcat stocks when he jumped out the window. Furthermore, the fire lost to us a treatise on crime in Nevada that may have been a feint to mask an even sharper jab at those "most moral, honest, virtuous, upright, high-toned, Christian" inhabitants of California mentioned in the initial sentence of the second section.

"Mark Twain's" Letter

THE JUDICIAL WAR ENDED.

THE WAR between Judges Jones and Mott, about the Judgeship of this District, has come to an end, it grieves me to say, without bloodshed. Not that I cared a straw, either way, but then the people expected blood, and the sovereign people should never be baulked in their desires. Yes, Judge Mott returned from the East, and marched up and reinstalled D. M. Hanson in the District Clerk's office, without a show of resistance from anybody. This manner of ending a war which promised so much destruction and desolation, is what the late William Shakspeare would have called a "lame and impotent conclusion," and I concur.

TRIBUTE TO CALIFORNIA.

I have every reason to believe that at this moment California contains the most moral, honest, virtuous, upright, high-toned, Christian population that exists upon the earth. God be praised for his mercy! O, happy, happy Commonwealth, within whose boundaries thieves and assassins abide not! Because all those fellows are over here, you know. Numerous? Why, about two-thirds of us are professional thieves, according to my estimate. Nothing that can be stolen is neglected. Watches that never would go in California, generally go fast enough before they have been in the Territory twenty-four hours; horses that—[but this house being on fire at the present moment, and it being no time to be choice in the matter of language, I expect I had better "get up and dust," as it were.]

APOLOGY FOR A LETTER.

I just send this to show that I had commenced my regular letter, though I was never permitted to finish it, because of that fire at the White House, yesterday. I discovered that the room under mine was on fire, gave the alarm, and went down to see how extensive it was likely to be. I thought I had plenty of time, then, and went back and changed my boots. The correctness of my judgment is apparent in this instance; for, so far from having a week to fool around in, I came near not escaping from the house at all. I started to the door with my trunk, but I couldn't stand the smoke, wherefore I abandoned that valuable piece of furniture in the hall, and returned and jumped out at the window. But I gathered up my San Francisco letter and shoved it into my pocket. Now do you know that trunk was utterly consumed, together with its contents, consisting of a pair of socks, a package of love-letters, and $300,000 worth of "wildcat" stocks? Yes, Sir, it was; and I am a bankrupt community. Plug hat, numerous sets of complete harness—all broadcloth—lost—eternally lost. However, the articles were borrowed, as a general thing. I don't mind losing them. But I had notes burned up there, from which I meant to elaborate a letter which all San Francisco would have read and been the better for it—been redeemed by it—so to speak. I had gossip in abundance, concerning San Francisco people sojourning among us. What I lost by the fire don't amount to a great deal, but what they have lost in the non-completion of that letter, it is impossible to estimate. I started out with an apology—if I have done so, well; if I have not, I'm d—d if I read this note again to find it out.

MARK TWAIN.

56. A Duel Prevented

2 August 1863

"A Duel Prevented" was published in the Virginia City *Territorial Enterprise* on 2 August 1863. The *Enterprise* printing is not extant, but the sketch survives in the Sacramento *Union* of August 4, which attributed it to the *Enterprise* of August 2. In his *History of Nevada* Myron Angel also reprinted the latter third of the piece in a somewhat garbled form, and he attributed it to Clemens, who in August 1863 was still handling the local news for the *Enterprise* in Dan De Quille's continued absence.

Clemens' authorship is established by a brief telegram about the duel which he sent the San Francisco *Morning Call* on August 2, as well as by the straightforward news story he included in his signed *Call* letter, written on the same day:

A DUEL RUINED.

The Virginia Union and the Territorial Enterprise have been sparring at each other for some time, and I watched the contest with great satisfaction, because I felt within me a presentiment that somebody was going to get into trouble. On the 30th of July, the thing culminated in an article in the Enterprise, headed "The Virginia Union—not the Federal," which was extremely personal towards Thomas Fitch, Esq., editor of the Union. Mr. Fitch immediately challenged Mr. Goodman, the author of it, naming John Church, Esq., as his "friend." Mr. Goodman accepted, and appointed Thomas Peasley, Esq., to act with Mr. Church in arranging the preliminaries and bossing the funerals. Yesterday morning, I followed the parties to the foot of the cañon below the Gould & Curry mill, to see them destroy each other with navy revolvers at fifteen paces, but the officers of the law arrived in time to spoil the sport. They arrested the principals, and brought them back to town, where they were placed under bonds in the sum of five thousand dollars each, to keep the peace.[1]

The quarrel between Joseph T. Goodman and the fiery Thomas Fitch presumably grew out of factional differences within the Union party in Nevada, but its precise origin and nature are not known. As Clemens said in his letter to the *Call*, the papers had been "sparring at each other for some time," but the implication is that Goodman's July 30 editorial, "The Virginia Union—not the Federal" (not extant), struck a more personal tone than usual. The Virginia City *Evening Bulletin* of July 30 also noted the change: "The *Enterprise* this morning smelt of blood. In fact it was red all over. . . . While perusing the leading article we imagined we saw pistols, bowieknives, blunderbusses, and bludgeons issue from the face of every type."[2]

Fitch's powerful command of the English language may have contributed to the heat of this quarrel. A month earlier Clemens had described Fitch's technique in his Fourth of July oration at Virginia City in glowing, albeit humorous, terms: "He lulls you into a treacherous repose, with a few mild and graceful sentences, and then suddenly explodes in your midst with a bomb-shell of eloquence which shakes you to your very foundations." A native of New York State, Fitch came to California from Wisconsin. He worked as a journalist in San Francisco and Placerville, was admitted to the bar, and in 1862 won a seat in the California Legislature. He migrated to Virginia City in 1863 and that same year founded the *Occidental*, the literary weekly described in chapter 51 of *Roughing It*. He continued to be active in Nevada politics and journalism and was elected to Congress in 1868. On at least two occasions in the 1860s Clemens expressed a dislike for Fitch, but in later years the two men occasionally corresponded in a friendly way.[3]

Although Fitch's challenge on July 30 did not end in a duel the next day, two months later, on September 28, the men did fight in California, and Fitch was wounded in the right leg below the knee. Clemens may have written the September 29 report of this event in the *Enterprise*—a perfectly straightforward news account—since forty-five years later he recalled the

---

[1] "'Mark Twain's' Letter," San Francisco *Morning Call*, 6 August 1863, p. 1. The telegram, "Tom Fitch in a Duel—Officer Interposes," appeared in the *Call* on 2 August 1863, p. 1, and is reprinted in *CofC*, p. 286.

[2] "Belligerent Controversy," Virginia City *Evening Bulletin*, 30 July 1863, p. 3.

[3] "'Mark Twain's' Letter" (no. 54); *CofC*, pp. 306–307 n. 107. Some eight letters from Fitch to Clemens, written between 1881 and 1890, are in MTP.

event with great clarity and some embellishment in his autobiographical dictation.[4] By contrast, "A Duel Prevented" is an instructive example of Clemens' capacity for elaborating on a nearly insignificant news item, for inflating the circumstances surrounding a nonevent: "a duel that did not come off," as the Sacramento *Union* said in introducing the *Enterprise* story. Less a news report than a story with ironic and burlesque overtones, "A Duel Prevented" is a personal account of much ado about nothing, a tale of comic frustration. The newsmen fail to get their bloody item and the "two desperadoes" tamely submit to "miserable meddling" lawmen, who return to a city left at "the mercy of thieves and incendiaries." Especially in contrast with the factual report in the *Call*, "A Duel Prevented" reveals the incipient writer of fiction in the guise of the reporter.

---

[4]The *Enterprise* story is extant in two California papers: "The Fitch and Goodman Duel," Sacramento *Union*, 1 October 1863, p. 2; and "The Washoe Editorial Duel," San Francisco *Alta California*, 1 October 1863, p. 1. Clemens' recollection in 1906 appears in *MTA*, 1:350–354.

A Duel Prevented

W<small>HEREAS</small>, Thomas Fitch, editor of the *Union*, having taken umbrage at an article headed "The Virginia Union—not the Federal," written by Joseph T. Goodman, our chief editor, and published in these columns; and whereas said Fitch having challenged said Goodman to mortal combat, naming John Church as his "friend;" and whereas the said Goodman having accepted said challenge, and chosen Thos. Peasley to appoint the means of death—

Therefore, on Friday afternoon it was agreed between the two seconds that the battle should transpire at nine o'clock yesterday morning (which would have been late in the day for most duelists, but it was fearfully early for newspaper men to have to get up)—place, the foot of the cañon below the Gould & Curry mill; weapons, navy six-shooters; distance, fifteen paces; conditions, the first fire to be delivered at the word, the others to follow at the pleasure of the targets, as long as a chamber in their pistols remained loaded. To say that we felt a little proud to think that in our official capacity we were about to rise above the recording of ordinary street broils and the monotonous transactions of the Police Court to delineate the ghastly details of a real duel, would be to use the mildest of language. Much as we deplored the state of things which was about to invest us with a new dignity, we could not help taking much comfort in the reflection that it was out of our power, and also antagonistic to the principles of our class, to prevent the state of things above mentioned. All conscientious scruples—all generous feelings must give way to our inexorable duty—which is to keep the public mind in a healthy state of excitement, and experience has taught us that blood alone can do this. At midnight, in company with young Wilson, we took a room at the International, to the end that through the vigilance of the watchman we might not be suffered to sleep until past nine o'clock. The policy was good—our strategy was faultless. At six o'clock in the morning we were on the street, feeling as uncomfortable in the gray dawn as many another early bird that founded its faith upon the inevitable worm and beheld too late that that worm had failed to come to time, for the friends of the proposed deceased were interfering to stop the duel, and the officers of the law were seconding their efforts. But the two desperadoes finally gave these meddlers the slip, and drove off with their seconds to the dark and bloody ground. Whereupon young Wilson and ourself at once mounted a couple of Olin's fast horses and followed in their wake at the rate of a mile a minute.

Since then we enjoy more real comfort in standing up than sitting down, being neither iron-clad nor even half-soled. But we lost our bloody item at last—for Marshal Perry arrived early with a detachment of constables, and also Deputy Sheriff Blodgett came with a lot of blasted Sheriffs, and the battle ground lying and being in Storey county, these miserable, meddling whelps arrested the whole party and marched them back to town. And at the very moment that we were suffering for a duel. The whole force went off down there and left the city at the mercy of thieves and incendiaries. Now, that is about all the strategy those fellows know. We have only to add that Goodman and Fitch were obliged to give bonds in the sum of $5,000 each to keep the peace, and if anything were lacking to make this robbery of the reporters complete, that last circumstance furnished the necessary material. In interfering with our legitimate business, Mr. Perry and Mr. Blodgett probably think they are almighty smart, but we calculate to get even with them.

57. [An Apology Repudiated]

4 August 1863

This brief sketch probably appeared in the Virginia City *Territorial Enterprise* for 4 August 1863, which is not extant. Only a portion of it has been preserved in Myron Angel's *History of Nevada*, the source of the present text.[1]

According to Angel, Clement T. Rice agreed to write Clemens' local items while Clemens was laid up with a cold, but took advantage of Clemens' absence to play a practical joke on him. Rice wrote and published the following in the *Enterprise*, probably on Sunday, August 2.

AUGUST 1, 1863.

APOLOGETIC.—It is said, "an open confession is good for the soul." We have been on the stool of repentance for a long time, but have not before had the moral courage to acknowledge our manifold sins and wickedness. We confess to this weakness. We have commenced this article under the head of 'Apologetic'—we mean it, if we ever meant anything in our life. To Mayor Arick, Hon. Wm. M. Stewart, Marshal Perry, Hon. J. B. Winters, Mr. Olin, and Samuel Witherel, besides a host of others whom we have ridiculed from behind the shelter of our reportorial position, we say to these gentlemen, we acknowledge our faults, and in all weakness and simplicity—upon our bended marrow-bones—we ask their forgiveness, promising that in future we will give them no cause for anything but the best of feeling toward us. To "Young Wilson," and the "Unreliable", (as we have wickedly termed them), we feel that no apology we can make begins to atone for the many insults we have given them. Towards these gentlemen we have been as mean as a man could be—and we have always prided ourself on this base quality. We feel that we are the least of all humanity, as it were. We will now go in sack-cloth and ashes for the next forty days. What more can we do? The latter-named gentleman has saved us several

---

[1]Albert Bigelow Paine also reprinted the text in *MTB*, 1:235, probably from Angel.

times from receiving a sound threshing for our impudence and assurance. He has sheltered and clothed us. We have had a hankering, "my boy," to redeem our character—or what little we have. To-morrow we may get in the same old way again. If we do, we want it now understood that this confession stands. Gentlem[e]n do you accept our good intentions?[2]

Mark Twain's rebuttal refers to this item in "yesterday's paper" and was probably written on Monday; but it could not appear until the paper's next issue, on Tuesday, August 4.

---

[2]Myron Angel, ed., *History of Nevada* (Oakland: Thompson and West, 1881), p. 293.

[An Apology Repudiated]

WE ARE TO blame for giving "the Unreliable" an opportunity to misrepresent us, and therefore refrain from repining to any great extent at the result. We simply claim the right to *deny the truth* of every statement made by him in yesterday's paper, to annul all apologies he coined as coming from us, and to hold him up to public commiseration as a reptile endowed with no more intellect, no more cultivation, no more Christian principle than animates and adorns the sportive jackass rabbit of the Sierras. We have done.

58. Letter from Mark Twain

25 August 1863

This letter is preserved in clippings in two of Mark Twain's scrapbooks. It originally appeared in the Virginia City *Territorial Enterprise* on 25 August 1863: an *Enterprise* banner headline for that date has been pasted at the top of one of the clippings.

Clemens caught a severe cold after July 26, when a fire in the White House, where he roomed in Virginia City, consumed most of his belongings (see "'Mark Twain's' Letter," no. 55). The cold kept him away from work until the Unreliable published his "Apologetic" (see the previous sketch), but after that Clemens spent two weeks "recuperating" on a visit to Lake Tahoe with his friend Adair Wilson. Evidently the social life was so exciting at Tahoe that he "failed to cure" his cold, and so he headed for Steamboat Springs in Washoe County, near the junction of the Marysville–Virginia City road and the road to Washoe City and Carson.[1] He arrived at dusk on August 17 to stay six days, writing this letter to the *Enterprise* on Sunday, August 23, the day he left for Virginia City; the letter was published on Tuesday.

Evidently Clemens felt no real compunction about his casual schedule, for he remarked in his first sentence, "I have overstepped my furlough a full week." He was confident after his first year on the *Enterprise* staff: five days before this letter he had told his family that he was "prone to boast of having the widest reputation as a local editor, of any man on the Pacific coast."[2]

---

[1]Clemens to Jane Clemens and Pamela Moffett, 19 August 1863, *CL1*, letter 75; advertisement, Washoe City *Times*, 28 February 1863, p. 4. See also "'Mark Twain's' Letter" (no. 59).

[2]Clemens to Jane Clemens and Pamela Moffett, 19 August 1863, *CL1*, letter 75.

At Steamboat Springs (discovered in 1860) customers frequented a hotel with a reputation for good food, a hospital with accommodations for thirty-four patients, and a bath house, as Clemens noted, with room for twelve. A. W. Stowe was the hospitable hotel owner, and Dr. Joseph I. Ellis owned most of the land, as well as the bath house and hospital, which burned to the ground in 1867.[3] Clemens told his family, "You get baths, board & lodging, all for $25 a week—cheaper than living in Virginia without baths."[4] Perhaps the obvious puff he gave the resort in this letter helped to pay for part of the cost of his week-long "furlough."

---

[3] "A Trip to Steamboat Springs," reprinted from the *Enterprise* by the San Francisco *Alta California*, 2 September 1864, p. 1; Myron Angel, ed., *History of Nevada* (Oakland: Thompson and West, 1881), pp. 644–645.

[4] Clemens to Jane Clemens and Pamela Moffett, 19 August 1863, *CL1*, letter 75.

Letter from Mark Twain

STEAMBOAT SPRINGS HOTEL, ⎱
August 23, 1863. ⎰

THE SPRINGS.

EDS. ENTERPRISE: I have overstepped my furlough a full week—but then this is a pleasant place to pass one's time. These springs are ten miles from Virginia, six or seven from Washoe City and twenty from Carson. They are natural—the devil boils the water, and the white steam puffs up out of crevices in the earth, along the summits of a series of low mounds extending in an irregular semi-circle for more than a mile. The water is impregnated with a dozen different minerals, each one of which smells viler than its fellow, and the sides of the springs are embellished with very pretty parti-colored incrustations deposited by the water. From one spring the boiling water is ejected a foot or more by the infernal force at work below, and in the vicinity of all of them one can hear a constant rumbling and surging, somewhat resembling the noises peculiar to a steamboat in motion—hence the name.

THE HOTEL.

The Steamboat Springs Hotel is very pleasantly situated on a grassy flat, a stone's throw from the hospital and the bath houses. It is capable of accommodating a great many guests. The rooms are large, "hard-finished" and handsomely furnished; there is an abundant supply of pure water, which can be carried to every part of the house, in case of

272

fire, by means of hose; the table is furnished with fresh vegetables and meats from the numerous fine ranches in the valley, and lastly, Mr. Stowe is a pleasant and accommodating landlord, and is ably seconded by Messrs. Haines, Ellsworth and Bingham. These gentlemen will never allow you to get ill-humored for want of polite attention—as I gratefully remember, now, when I recall the stormy hours of Friday, when that accursed "Wake-up Jake" was in me. But I haven't got to that, yet. God bless us! it is a world of trouble, and we are born to sorrow and tribulation—yet, am I chiefest among sinners, that I should be prematurely damned with "Wake-up Jake," while others not of the elect go free? I am trying to go on with my letter, but this thing bothers me; verily, from having "Wake-up Jake" on the stomach for three days, I have finally got it on the brain. I am grateful for the change. But I digress.

THE HOSPITAL.

Dr. Ellis, the proprietor of the Springs, has erected a large, tastefully designed, and comfortable and well ventilated hospital, close to the bath-houses, and it is constantly filled with patients afflicted with all manner of diseases. It would be a very profitable institution, but a great many who come to it half dead, and leave it again restored to robust health, forget to pay for the benefits they have received. Others, when they arrive, confess at once that they are penniless, yet few men could look upon the sunken cheeks of these, and upon their attenuated forms and their pleading, faded eyes, and refuse them the shelter and assistance we all may need some day. Without expectation of reward, Dr. Ellis gives back life, hope and health to many a despairing, poverty-stricken devil; and when I think of this, it seems so strange that he could have had the meanness to give me that "Wake-up-Jake." However, I am wandering away from the subject again. All diseases (except confirmed consumption,) are treated successfully here. A multitude of invalids have attended these baths during the past three years, yet only an insignificant number of deaths have occurred among them. I want to impress one thing upon you: it is a mistaken notion that these Springs were created solely for the salvation of persons suffering venereal diseases. True, the fame of the baths rests chiefly upon the miracles performed upon such patients, and upon others afflicted with rheumatism, erysipelas, etc., but then all ordinary ailments can be quickly and pleasantly cured here without a resort to deadly physic. More than two-thirds of the people who come here are afflicted with venereal diseases—fellows who know that if "Steamboat" fails with them they may as well go to trading feet with the undertaker for a box—yet all here agree that these baths are none the less potent where other diseases are concerned. I know lots of poor, feeble wretches in Virginia who could get a new lease of life by soaking their shadows in Steamboat Springs for a week or two. However, I must pass on to

THE BATHS.

My friend Jim Miller has charge of these. Within a few days the new bath-house will be finished, and then twelve persons may bathe at once, or if they be sociable and choose to go on the double-bed principle, four times as many can enjoy the luxury at the same time. Persons afflicted with loathsome diseases use bath-rooms which are never entered by the other patients. You get up here about six o'clock in the morning and walk over to the bath-house; you undress in an ante-room and take a cold shower-bath—or let it alone, if you choose; then you step into a sort of little dark closet floored with a wooden grating, up through which come puffs and volumes of the hottest steam you ever performed to, (because the awkwardest of us feel a hankering to waltz a little under such circumstances, you know), and then if you are alone, you resolve to have company thenceforward, since to swap comments upon your sensations with a friend, must render the dire heat less binding upon the human constitution. I had company always, and it was the pleasantest thing in the world to see a thin-skinned invalid cavorting around in the vapory obscurity, marveling at the rivers of sweat that coursed down his body, cursing the villainous smell of the steam and its bitter, salty taste—groping around meanwhile, for a cold corner, and backing finally, into the hottest one, and darting out again in a second, only remarking "Outch!"—and repeating it when he sits down, and springs up the same moment off the hot bench. This was fun of the most comfortable character; but nothing could be more agreeable than to put your eye to the little square hole in the door, and see your boiled and smoking comrade writhing under the cold shower-bath, to see him shrink till his shoulders are level with the top of his head, and then shut his eyes and gasp and catch his breath, while the cruel rain pattered down on his back and sent a ghastly shiver through every fibre of his body. It will always be a comfort to me to recall these little incidents. After the shower-bath, you return to the ante-room and scrub yourself all over with coarse towels until your hide glows like a parlor carpet—after which, you feel as elastic and vigorous as an acrobat. Then if you are sensible, you take no exercise, but just eat your breakfast and go to bed—you will find that an hour's nap will not hurt you any.

THE "WAKE-UP-JAKE."

A few days ago I fell a victim to my natural curiosity and my solicitude for the public weal. Everybody had something to say about "wake-up-Jake." If a man was low-spirited; if his appetite failed him; if he did not sleep well at night; if he were costive; if he were bilious; or in love; or in any other kind of trouble; or if he doubted the fidelity of his friends or the efficacy of his religion, there was always some one at his elbow to whisper, "Take a 'wake-up,' my boy." I sought to fathom the mystery, but all I could make out of it was that the "Wake-up Jake" was a medicine as powerful as "the servants of the lamp," the secret of whose decoction was hidden away in Dr. Ellis' breast. I was not aware that I had any use for the wonderful "wake-up," but then I felt it to be my duty to try it, in order that a suffering public might profit by my experience—and I would cheerfully see that public suffer perdition before I would try it again. I called upon Dr. Ellis with the air of a man who would create the impression that he is not so much of an ass as he looks, and demanded a "Wake-up-Jake" as unostentatiously as if that species of refreshment were not at all new to me. The Doctor hesitated a moment, and then fixed up as repulsive a mixture as ever was stirred together in a table-spoon. I swallowed the nauseous mess, and that one meal sufficed me for the space of forty-eight hours. And during all that time, I could not have enjoyed a viler taste in my mouth if I had swallowed a slaughter-house. I lay down with all my clothes on, and with an utter indifference to my fate here or hereafter, and slept like a statue from six o'clock until noon. I got up, then, the sickest man that ever yearned to vomit and couldn't. All the dead and decaying matter in nature seemed buried in my stomach, and I "heaved, and retched, and heaved again," but I could not compass a resurrection—my dead would not come forth. Finally, after rumbling, and growling, and producing agony and chaos within me for many hours, the dreadful dose began its work, and for the space of twelve hours it vomited me, and purged me, and likewise caused me to bleed at the nose.

I came out of that siege as weak as an infant, and went to the bath with Palmer, of Wells, Fargo & Co., and it was well I had company, for it was about all he could do to keep me from boiling the remnant of my life out in the hot steam. I had reached that stage wherein a man experiences a solemn indifference as to whether school keeps or not. Since then, I have gradually regained my strength and my appetite, and am now animated by a higher degree of vigor than I have felt for many a day. 'Tis well. This result seduces many a man into taking a second, and even a third "wake-up-Jake," but I think I can worry along without any more of them. I am about as thoroughly waked up now as I care to be. My stomach never had such a scouring out since I was born. I feel like a jug. If I could get young Wilson or the Unreliable to take a "wake-up-Jake," I would do it, of course, but I shall never swallow another myself—I would sooner have a locomotive travel through me. And besides, I never intend to experiment in physic any more, just out of idle curiosity. A "wake-up-Jake" will furbish a man's machinery up and give him a fresh start in the world—but I feel I shall never need anything of that sort any more. It would put robust health, and life and vim into young Wilson and the Unreliable—but then they always look with suspicion upon any suggestion that I make.

GOOD-BYE.

Well, I am going home to Virginia to-day, though I dislike to part from the jolly boys (not to mention iced milk for breakfast, with eggs laid to order, and spiced oysters after midnight with the Reverend Jack Holmes and Bingham) at the Steamboat Springs Hotel. In conclusion, let me recommend to such of my fellow citizens as are in feeble health, or are wearied out with the cares of business, to come down and try the hotel, and the steam baths, and the facetious "wake-up-Jake." These will give them rest, and moving recreation—as it were.

MARK TWAIN.

59. "Mark Twain's" Letter

30 August 1863

This installment of Clemens' correspondence with the San Francisco *Morning Call* was actually written from the Steamboat Springs Hotel three days before the previous letter, but it was not published until ten days later, on 30 August 1863. It is a triumphant example of the kind of newspaper letter that Clemens learned to write: its artful opening, its personal, colloquial tone, its intrinsic narrative interest, and its casually controlled progression from topic to topic are all the work of a craftsman. Moreover, within the framework story of his efforts to cure his cold, Clemens told a tale ("A Rich Decision") which was his first version of a story he afterward made famous in "The Facts in the Great Land-Slide Case" (no. 286), and then later in chapter 34 of *Roughing It*.[1] It is difficult to think of this letter to the *Call* as newspaper reporting at all: it clearly anticipates the narrative and fictional techniques of Mark Twain's mature fiction.

"A Rich Decision" is certainly the high point of the letter: like most of Clemens' best stories it is based squarely on real events. The landslide—or, more accurately, the heavy wash—that covered Dick Sides's farm with detritus from the mountain slopes occurred in Washoe Valley, Nevada, sometime in late January 1862. The mock trial pitting the hapless United States attorney Benjamin B. Bunker against the former territorial governor Isaac Roop must have occurred in the first half of February 1862.

The institution of the mock trial was a thriving form of community entertainment in Nevada during the 1860s. According to Dan De Quille, Clemens himself was once the judge of such a trial in Virginia City. Dan described the episode, which probably occurred during the first six months

---

[1] "The Facts in the Great Land-Slide Case" appeared in the Buffalo *Express* on 2 April 1870, p. 2.

of 1864, in a reminiscence written for the *Territorial Enterprise* several years later. While Clemens and a fellow reporter were drinking beer across the street from the courtroom of Judge William H. Davenport, they were arrested by the city marshal, Jack Perry, for "high treason," which the judge defined as "guzzling beer in plain sight of the Court, without inviting it over to take a glass." A crowd gathered, and before the argument was over, Clemens ascended the bench himself, found Judge Davenport guilty of "malicious prosecution," and imposed a fine of "beer for the crowd." "Finding himself fairly caught," said Dan, the judge "marched all hands over to the brewery, and treated everybody to the beer."[2] Moreover, on 29 November 1865, the *Enterprise* reported another mock trial in which Tom Peasley was the resplendently robed "judge" and Hal Clayton the counsel for the prisoner, a prominent journalist disguised as a woman of the town.[3]

---

[2]"A Treasonable Conspiracy," undated clipping in carton 1, folder 145, William Wright Papers, Bancroft.

[3]"Making Light of Justice in Virginia City," reprinted from the *Enterprise* by the San Francisco *Morning Call*, 2 December 1865, p. 1. The events leading up to the mock landslide trial are fully documented in *The Great Landslide Case*, ed. Frederick Anderson and Edgar M. Branch (Berkeley: Friends of the Bancroft Library, University of California, 1972).

"Mark Twain's" Letter

STEAMBOAT SPRINGS HOTEL, August 20, 1863.

"MARK" GETS INVALIDED AND GOES TO TAHOE.

EDITORS MORNING CALL:—Some things are inevitable. If you tell a girl she is pretty, she will "let on" that she is offended; if seventeen men travel by stage-coach, they will grumble because they cannot all have outside seats; if you leave your room vacant all the forenoon to give the chambermaid a chance to put it in order, you will find that urbane but inflexible officer ready to begin her labors there at the exact moment of your return. These are patent—but I am able to add another to the list of inevitable things: if you get a week's leave of absence for a visit to Lake Bigler, or to Steamboat Springs, you will transcend the limits of your furlough. I speak from personal knowledge. I carried over to the lake a heavy cold, and acted so imprudently during a week, that it constantly grew heavier and heavier—until at last it came near outweighing me. Lake Bigler is a paradise to a healthy person, but there is too much sailing, and fishing, and other dissipation of a similar nature going on there to allow a man with a cold time to nurse it properly.

FROM THENCE TO STEAMBOAT SPRINGS.

I was exceedingly sorry to leave the place, but I knew if I staid there, and nothing interfered with my luck, I should die before my time—wherefore I journeyed back over the mountains last Monday, and have since been an interesting invalid at Steamboat Springs. These are boiling hot, and emit steam enough to run all the mills in the Territory. Learned men say the water is heated by a combination of combustible chemicals—the unlearned say it is done by a combination of combustible devils. However, like Governor Roop, I consider that it is no business of mine to inquire into the means which the Creator has seen fit to make use of in the consummation of his will regarding this or any other portion of his handiwork.

A RICH DECISION.

And possibly it may be interesting to you to know how Governor Roop came to deliver himself of that burst of inspiration. Two years ago, during the season of avalanches, Tom Rust's ranch slid down from the mountain side and pretty nearly covered up a ranch belonging to Dick Sides. Some of the boys in Carson thought the circumstance offered a fair opportunity for playing a hoax on our former simple-minded Attorney-General, old Mr. Bunker, and they got Sides to employ him to bring suit in a Referee's Court for the recovery of his ranch; which Mr. S. did, alleging that Rust now claimed the surface of the ground as his own, although he freely admitted that the ranch underneath it belonged to Sides, who, it grieved him to reflect, would probably never see his property again. Mr. Bunker was naturally stunned at so preposterous a proposition, and bade his client be of good cheer, and count without fear upon the restoration of his rights. The Court-room was crowded; Roop, as Judge Referee, presided with a grave dignity in keeping with his lofty position; the Sheriff guarded the sacred precincts of the Court from disturbance and indecorum with exaggerated vigilance. The witnesses were examined, and all the evidence of any value went in favor of General Bunker's client. The General appeared, with eleven solemn law-books under his arm, and with the light of triumph beaming in his eye, and made a ponderous speech of two hours in length. The opposing counsel replied feebly, by design, and the case went to the Judge. All who heard Judge Roop's inspired decision, and noted the holy serenity of his countenance when he gave it, will cherish the memory of it while they continue to live in a world where meteors of joy flash only at intervals athwart a sky darkened with clouds of sorrow always. He said: "Gentlemen, I have listened with profound interest to the arguments of counsel in this important case, and while

I admit that the reasoning of the distinguished gentleman who appeared for the plaintiff was almost resistless, and that all the law and
evidence adduced are in favor of his client, yet considerations of a
far more sacred and exalted nature than these compel me to decide
for the defendant, and to decree that the property remain in his
possession. The Almighty created the earth and all that is in it, and
who shall presume to dictate to Him the disposition of His handiwork?
If He saw that defendant's ranch was too high up the hill, and chose,
in His infinite wisdom, to move it down to a more eligible location,
albeit to the detriment of the plaintiff and *his* ranch, it is meet that we
bow in humble submission to His will, without inquiring into His
motives or questioning His authority. My verdict, therefore, is,
gentlemen, that the plaintiff, Sides, has lost his ranch by the dispensation of God!" The monstrous verdict paralyzed Mr. Bunker
where he stood. The crowd of spectators, defying the Sheriffs, shook
the house with laughter. But after the Court adjourned, poor Bunker,
oblivious of the joke, hunted up Governor Roop, and asked to appeal
the case. The great Judge frowned upon him, with severe dignity,
for a moment, and then replied solemnly, that there was no appeal
from the decision of the Lord! Cursing Roop's imbecility, the General
told me afterwards that the only recourse ever offered his client was
the privilege, if the defendant would give his consent, of either removing Rust's ranch, or digging his own out from under it! That hoax
finally drove Mr. Bunker back to New Hampshire, and lost to us the
densest intellect the President ever conferred upon the Territory.

THE HOTEL AND ITS OCCUPANTS.

But I digress. Being in the vicinity of Dick Sides' ranch, overcame
me with the memories of other days. As I was saying, these Springs
are situated in Steamboat Valley, something over twenty miles from
Carson, and about half that distance from Gold Hill and Virginia,
and are visited daily by stage-coaches from those places. There is a
hospital, kept by Dr. Ellis, the proprietor of the Springs, which is neat,
roomy and well-ventilated. The Steamboat Springs Hotel, kept by Mr.
Stowe and Mr. Holmes, formerly of Sacramento, is capable of accommodating a great many guests, and has constantly a large number
within its walls; the table is not as good as that at the Occidental, but
the sleeping apartments are unexceptionable. In the bath houses near
the hospital, twelve persons may bathe at once, or four times that

number if they be individuals who like company. There are about thirty-five patients, suffering under all kinds and degrees of affliction, in the hospital at present; there are also several at the hotel. Some walk with canes, some with crutches, some limp about without artificial assistance, and some do not pretend to walk at all, and look dejected and baggy; they mope about languidly and slowly; there is no eagerness in their eyes, and in their faces only sad indifference; the features of some are marred by old sores, and—but if it is all the same to you, I will speak of pleasanter things. The steam baths here restore to health, or at least afford relief, to all classes of patients but consumptives. These must seek assistance elsewhere. Erysipelas, rheumatism, and most other human distempers, have been successfully treated here for three years. Scarcely a case has been lost; the majority are sent home entirely cured, and none go away without having derived some benefit.

THE EFFECT OF A BATH.

The boiling, steaming Springs send their jets of white vapor up out of fissures in the earth, extending in an irregular semi-circle for more than a mile; the water has a sulphurous smell, and a crust, composed of sulphur and other villanous drugs, is deposited by it in the beds of the little streams that flow from the Springs. The Indians (who don't mind an offensive smell, you know,) boil their meat, when they have any, poor devils! in this sickening water. When you are shut up in the little dark bath rooms, with a dense cloud of scalding steam rising up around you and compelling you to schottische whether you want to or not, you are obliged to keep your mouth open or smother, and this enables you to taste copper, and sulphur, and ipecac, and turpentine, and blood, hair and corruption—not to mention the multitude of other ghastly tastes in the steam which you cannot recollect the names of. And when you come out, and before you get to the cold shower-bath, you notice that you smell like a buzzard's breath, and are disgusted with your own company; but after your clothes are on again, you feel as brisk and vigorous as an acrobat, and your disrespect for the fragrant bath lingers with you no longer.

HAS A QUARREL WITH "JOHN HALIFAX."

Hark! methinks that sound—ah, no, it cannot be—and yet, it is! it is! Now, all those exclamations are original with me, but they were superinduced by reading that high-flown batch of contradictions and inconsistencies, "John Halifax, Gentleman." The "sound" referred to was simply a call to our regular "hash," and I only wanted to see how such silly language would fit so sensible a subject, under the circumstances; though, I cannot stop now to discuss it.

MARK TWAIN.

60. Unfortunate Blunder

3 September 1863

This sketch comprises the final part of "'Mark Twain's' Letter" to the San Francisco *Morning Call* written on 30 August 1863 and published on September 3. Two sections of the letter, which report political activity and a riot and fire in Virginia City, are not reprinted here.

Virginia City's Union League was probably organized soon after the outbreak of the Civil War when Union clubs were springing up in many communities of California and Nevada. The stated purpose of these clubs was in general to support the federal government and the Union war effort, and in particular to rally both Democrats and Republicans in support of Union candidates.

On 14 February 1863, for instance, the Democratic Central Committee of Storey County issued a statement of principles, which was answered a few days later by a call from Rollin M. Daggett for the formation of "a Union party, embracing loyal Democrats and Republicans."[1] On February 27 the Union men of Virginia City met to nominate candidates for the coming local elections and to pledge their support. Their statement affirmed that they would "ignore all former party associations, alliance or name, and unite as a party for the Union, and the whole Union."[2]

Colonel John A. Collins, who is addressed by the drunken Irishman in "Unfortunate Blunder," was a principal speaker at this meeting. A vigorous orator and writer, Collins was a strong supporter of Lincoln and a veteran of the antislavery movement who had come to San Francisco in 1849. After

---

[1] "To the Democracy of Nevada Territory," unidentified clipping in Scrapbook 2, pp. 13–14, MTP; "To the Loyal of Nevada Territory," ibid., p. 19.

[2] "Union Convention," Virginia City *Union*, 28 February 1863, Scrapbook 2, p. 19, MTP.

experiencing variable business success, he became wealthy through quartz milling at Grass Valley. Twice, running as a Whig, he was defeated for public office. He became an editor on the Sacramento *Union*, and he eventually migrated to Virginia City early in 1860, where he owned a lumber-yard and mining interests. He was superintendent of the city's first public school and later county school superintendent, and he represented Storey County in the first and second constitutional conventions (1863 and 1864). He was an unsuccessful candidate for United States senator in 1864, but nevertheless retained a strong position in the Republican party.[3] Clemens' references to Collins were invariably favorable: see the explanatory notes to "Examination of Teachers" (no. 48).

---

[3]"John A. Collins," Virginia City *Territorial Enterprise*, ca. August 1863, Scrapbook 2, p. 63, MTP; Myron Angel, ed., *History of Nevada* (Oakland: Thompson and West, 1881), pp. 81, 85, 86, 571, 607; J. Wells Kelly, *First Directory of Nevada Territory* (San Francisco: Valentine and Co., 1862), p. 121; *MTEnt*, pp. 88, 113–114.

Unfortunate Blunder

W<small>E SHIPPED</small> ten thousand dollars in silver bars to the Sanitary Fund yesterday. But I cannot write to-day; I have no more animation than a sick puppy. However, I suppose I ought to inform the public about a circumstance which happened in the Court House this morning, and which was a most

UNFORTUNATE BLUNDER.

The Union League holds its meetings in the District Court Room on certain nights during the week; on Sundays the services of the First Presbyterian Church are held in the same apartment. This morning an Irish member of the League, who had been drinking a good deal, came reeling down the street, and as he passed the Court House, he chanced to look in; he saw the Rev. Mr. White (who had just sat down after the first prayer,) occupying the pulpit—the place of the President of his society; he also saw familiar faces among the congregation, and he concluded at once that the Union League was in session. With drunken promptness, he marched in at once, as soon as his mind was made up. He reached the centre of the room in safety, and supported himself in an unstable manner by resting one hand upon the railing; with the other he removed from his mouth a cigar, one-half of which was chewed to mush; he spat,—partly on the floor, and principally on his chin—then hiccoughed, with such startling emphasis as to jerk his hat to the back part of his head; after which he gave the sign of salutation, and said: "Misrer Pres'zent: They been imposing on me at the mine, but d—n my thiev'n *soul* but I'll get

even wid 'em, you know! [Sensation.] The fo'man o' Th' Pride o' the
West has dis—dis—ch—(hic!)—*airged* me, bekase I'm a bloody
d——d Blaick Republikin!" Seeing a familiar face in the congregation,
he addressed his remarks to the owner of it, pointing there with his
dilapidated cigar: "D'ye know me, Kuhrnel, an'"——[Voice: "But
my good friend"——] "Be d——d to yer good friend! an' can't ye see
it's meself that has the flewr? Ah! now, there's ould John A. Collins,
an' h—(hic!)—e's wan o' the principal bretherin. I'll tell ye the whole
of the dhirty thievin' saircumstance, ye see." By this time, men,
women, children and parson were smothering with suppressed
laughter, as the dancing eyes that looked out over white handkerchiefs plainly testified. Col. Collins rose to his feet, blushing like a
lobster, and succeeded in making the persecuted Irishman understand
that he was not telling his troubles to the Union League, but to the
First Presbyterian Church. The information stunned him. He stood
a moment gathering again the ideas which had been scattered by
this bombshell, and then backed himself out of the house, bowing
repeatedly, and ejaculating: "Ladies and gintlemen, I beg yer pairdon.
I thought 'twas the Union Laig. I did, upon my sowl; but I beg yer
pairdon, ladies and gintlemen—I *beg* yer pairdon!" They used to go
to Goldsmith's church to laugh, and remain to pray; but the Presby-
terians here reversed the thing this morning.

61. Bigler vs. Tahoe

4–5 September 1863

On 13 September 1863 the San Francisco *Golden Era* reprinted this spirited sketch from the Virginia City *Territorial Enterprise* of unknown date. In a brief prefatory remark the *Era* noted: "In the *Territorial Enterprise* appears a 'Letter from Lake Bigler,' signed 'Grub' and addressed personally to 'Mr. Twain'—and that rough and ready writer last named, who does the humorous local columns of the aforesaid journal, discourses his friend 'Grub,' thus wise." Clemens' remark in the last sentence ("I mean to start to Lake Bigler myself, Monday morning, or somebody shall come to grief") may indicate that the piece appeared as early as August 10 or 11, just before he did in fact go there to try to cure his cold (see "Letter from Mark Twain," no. 58). Yet it seems unlikely that the *Era* waited for more than a month to reprint such an item, and in fact Mark Twain's cold persisted into early September. Although he may have been contemplating another trip to Tahoe, he evidently decided to go to San Francisco instead, leaving Virginia City on September 5 (see the headnote to "Letter from Mark Twain," no. 62). This suggests that the piece probably appeared sometime late in the first week of September, while he was still writing the local columns for the *Enterprise*.

Clemens' enduring admiration for Lake Tahoe's beauty dated from his first visit to the lake in the late summer of 1861.[1] The lake was discovered in 1844 by John Frémont and Charles Preuss. It was named Bigler in 1852 after Democrat John Bigler, California's third governor (1852–1858). Bigler's southern sympathies led Union supporters in 1861 to question the propriety

---

[1]See *Roughing It*, chapter 22.

of naming the lake after him. The name "Tahoe" was suggested in 1862 and gradually won public acceptance.[2]

In chapter 20 of *The Innocents Abroad* Clemens asserted that "Tahoe" meant "grasshopper soup, the favorite dish of the Digger tribe—and of the Pi-utes as well." The word actually comes from the Washoe Indian dialect and is usually translated "big water" or "lake water."[3]

---

[2]Edward B. Scott, *The Saga of Lake Tahoe* (Crystal Bay, Nevada: Sierra-Tahoe Publishing Company, 1957), pp. 461–463.

[3]Erwin G. Gudde, *California Place Names*, 2d ed. (Berkeley: University of California Press, 1960), p. 312.

Bigler vs. Tahoe

Hope some early bird will catch this Grub the next time he calls Lake Bigler by so disgustingly sick and silly a name as "Lake Tahoe." I have removed the offensive word from his letter and substituted the old one, which at least has a Christian English twang about it whether it is pretty or not. Of course Indian names are more fitting than any others for our beautiful lakes and rivers, which knew their race ages ago, perhaps, in the morning of creation, but let us have none so repulsive to the ear as "Tahoe" for the beautiful relic of fairy-land forgotten and left asleep in the snowy Sierras when the little elves fled from their ancient haunts and quitted the earth. They say it means "Fallen Leaf"—well suppose it meant fallen devil or fallen angel, would that render its hideous, discordant syllables more endurable? Not if I know myself. I yearn for the scalp of the soft-shell crab—be he injun or white man—who conceived of that spoony, slobbering, summer-complaint of a name. Why, if I had a grudge against a half-price nigger, I wouldn't be mean enough to call him by such an epithet as that; then, how am I to hear it applied to the enchanted mirror that the viewless spirits of the air make their toilets by, and hold my peace? "Tahoe"—it sounds as weak as soup for a sick infant. "Tahoe" be—forgotten! I just saved my reputation that time. In conclusion, "Grub," I mean to start to Lake Bigler myself, Monday morning, or somebody shall come to grief.

Mark Twain.

62. Letter from Mark Twain

17 September 1863

The text of this letter is preserved in a clipping from the Virginia City *Territorial Enterprise* in one of Mark Twain's scrapbooks. Written in San Francisco on Sunday, 13 September 1863, the letter probably appeared in the *Enterprise* on the following Thursday, September 17: a dated banner headline from the *Enterprise* of that date is pasted above the immediately preceding article in the scrapbook, and probably applies to this letter as well.

Apparently a visit to San Francisco was the new cure Clemens thought he needed for his persistent cold—a solution made possible, in part, by Dan De Quille's return to Virginia City from the Midwest.[1] On September 5 the Virginia City *Evening Bulletin* announced Clemens' impending departure: "MARK TWAIN.—This gentleman leaves Virginia for San Francisco today, and we are sorry to say on account of ill health. Mark has made his mark in a remarkable manner upon the good will of the people of Virginia, among whom he has hosts of warm friends."[2] Clemens evidently took the Carpenter and Hoog stagecoach to Carson City, probably leaving there on the Pioneer stagecoach the following day. Since his traveling companion, R. W. Billet, checked in at the Russ House on September 8, Clemens was no doubt happily installed that same evening at the Lick House.[3] He attended the Anniversary Ball of the Society of California Pioneers the next night, and before long saw Adah Isaacs Menken in *Mazeppa*.

The first two parts of this letter comprise a sketch of Clemens' stagecoach trip, unified more by his interest in character and anecdote than by any

---

[1]*MTNev*, pp. 242–243.

[2]Virginia City *Evening Bulletin*, 5 September 1863, p. 2.

[3]"Arrivals at the Russ House, September 8th," San Francisco *Evening Bulletin*, 9 September 1863, p. 2.

desire to describe the journey itself. The third part, a sassy review of
Mazeppa, is here omitted.[4]

---

[4]The review of *Mazeppa* is scheduled to appear in the collection of criticism in The
Works of Mark Twain. It is reprinted in *MTEnt*, pp. 78–80.

Letter from Mark Twain

SAN FRANCISCO, September 13.

OVER THE MOUNTAINS.

EDITORS ENTERPRISE:—The trip from Virginia to Carson by Messrs. Carpenter & Hoog's stage is a pleasant one, and from thence over the mountains by the Pioneer would be another, if there were less of it. But you naturally want an outside seat in the day time, and you feel a good deal like riding inside when the cold night winds begin to blow; yet if you commence your journey on the outside, you will find that you will be allowed to enjoy the desire I speak of unmolested from twilight to sunrise. An outside seat is preferable, though, day or night. All you want to do is to prepare for it thoroughly. You should sleep forty-eight hours in succession before starting, so that you may not have to do anything of that kind on the box. You should also take a heavy overcoat with you. I did neither. I left Carson feeling very miserable for want of sleep, and the voyage from there to Sacramento did not refresh me perceptibly. I took no overcoat, and I almost shivered the shirt off myself during that long night ride from Strawberry Valley to Folsom. Our driver was a very companionable man, though, and this was a happy circumstance for me, because, being drowsy and worn out, I would have gone to sleep and fallen overboard if he had not enlivened the dreary hours with his conversation. Whenever I stopped coughing, and went to nodding, he always watched me out of the corner of his eye until I got to pitching in his direction, and then he would stir me up and inquire if I were

293

asleep. If I said "No," (and I was apt to do that,) he always said "it was a bully good thing for me that I warn't, you know," and then went on to relate cheerful anecdotes of people who had got to nodding by his side when he wasn't noticing, and had fallen off and broken their necks. He said he could see those fellows before him now, all jammed and bloody and quivering in death's agony—"G'lang! d—n that horse, he knows there's a parson and an old maid inside, and that's what makes him cut up so; I've saw him act jes' so more'n a thousand times!" The driver always lent an additional charm to his conversa-tion by mixing his horrors and his general information together in this way. "Now," said he, after urging his team at a furious speed down the grade for awhile, plunging into deep bends in the road brimming with a thick darkness almost palpable to the touch, and darting out again and again on the verge of what instinct told me was a precipice, "Now, I seen a poor cuss—but you're asleep again, you know, and you've rammed your head agin' my side-pocket and busted a bottle of nasty rotten medicine that I'm taking to the folks at the Thirty-five Mile House; do you notice that flavor? ain't it a ghastly old stench? The man that takes it down there don't live on anything else—it's vittles and drink to him; anybody that ain't used to him can't go a-near him; he'd stun 'em—he'd suffocate 'em; his breath smells like a graveyard after an earthquake—you Bob! I allow to skelp that ornery horse, yet, if he keeps on this way; you see he's been on the overland till about two weeks ago, and every stump he sees he cal'lates it's an Injun." I was awake by this time, holding on with both hands and bouncing up and down just as I do when I ride a horseback. The driver took up the thread of his discourse and proceeded to soothe me again: "As I was a saying, I see a poor cuss tumble off along here one night—he was monstrous drowsy, and went to sleep when I'd took my eye off of him for a moment—and he fetched up agin a boulder, and in a second there wasn't anything left of him but a promiscus pile of hash! It was moonlight, and when I got down and looked at him he was quivering like jelly, and sorter moaning to himself, like, and the bones of his legs was sticking out through his pantaloons every which way, like that." (Here the driver mixed his fingers up after the manner of a stack of muskets, and illuminated them with the ghostly light of his cigar.) "He warn't in misery long though. In a minute and a half he was deader'n a smelt—Bob! I say

I'll cut that horse's throat if he stays on this route another week." In this way the genial driver caused the long hours to pass sleeplessly away, and if he drew upon his imagination for his fearful histories, I shall be the last to blame him for it, because if they had taken a milder form I might have yielded to the dullness that oppressed me, and got my own bones smashed out of my hide in such a way as to render me useless for ever after—unless, perhaps, some one chose to turn me to account as an uncommon sort of hat-rack.

MR. BILLET IS COMPLIMENTED BY A STRANGER.

Not a face in either stage was washed from the time we left Carson until we arrived in Sacramento; this will give you an idea of how deep the dust lay on those faces when we entered the latter town at eight o'clock on Monday morning. Mr. Billet, of Virginia, came in our coach, and brought his family with him—Mr. R. W. Billet of the great Washoe Stock and Exchange Board of Highwaymen—and instead of turning his complexion to a dirty cream color, as it generally serves white folks, the dust changed it to the meanest possible shade of black: however, Billet isn't particularly white, anyhow, even under the most favorable circumstances. He stepped into an office near the railroad depot, to write a note, and while he was at it, several lank, gawky, indolent immigrants, fresh from the plains, gathered around him. Missourians—Pikes—I can tell my brethren as far as I can see them. They seemed to admire Billet very much, and the faster he wrote the higher their admiration rose in their faces, until it finally boiled over in words, and one of my countrymen ejaculated in his neighbor's ear,—"Dang it, but he writes mighty well for a nigger!"

MARK TWAIN.

63. How to Cure a Cold

20 September 1863

"How to Cure a Cold" was written during the first week or ten days after Clemens arrived in San Francisco on 8 September 1863 and was published in the San Francisco *Golden Era* on September 20. The sketch is the first of three feature articles that Clemens composed specifically for the *Era* in September and early October 1863, and one of four he published there during that period.[1] This San Francisco weekly had close ties with the Virginia City *Territorial Enterprise*. Both Joseph T. Goodman and Denis McCarthy of the *Enterprise* had worked on the *Era*, and Dan De Quille was its Virginia City correspondent. Clemens also knew others on its staff: his comment in 1864 about having visited "some of their haunts with those dissipated Golden Era fellows"[2] probably goes back to memories of May and June 1863, his first long visit to San Francisco. Certainly by September the Washoe reporter fully recognized the literary opportunity which the *Era* provided, and was energetically trying to exploit it.

At the time Clemens wrote "How to Cure a Cold" he had been troubled with a severe head cold and bronchitis for more than a month. Indeed, the sketch repeatedly alludes to his quite real difficulties in trying to cure himself, many of which he had already mentioned publicly in newspaper letters to the *Enterprise* and the San Francisco *Call* (see nos. 58–62 of this collection). Even the angry digression toward the end of the sketch about the "lady acquaintance" who snubbed him seems to reflect the facts.

---

[1] The other three are "Mark Twain—More of Him" (no. 64), reprinted with a new preface from the *Enterprise*; "The Lick House Ball" (no. 65); and "The Great Prize Fight," *Golden Era* 11 (11 October 1863): 8, reprinted in *WG*, pp. 25–31. This last piece is scheduled to appear in the collection of social and political writings in The Works of Mark Twain.

[2] "Those Blasted Children" (no. 72).

Some readers have regarded the sketch as a burlesque of home remedies per se—like those frequently advertised in eastern newspapers, for instance. Clemens' account of the decoction mixed by the "lady who had just arrived from over the plains" does in fact seem quite outlandish. However, most of the remedies that the author tried were standard prescriptions of folk medicine: unexamined rituals and superstitions inflicted on the sufferer and only occasionally—as with the gin and whisky—enjoyed by him. Of course, all are discredited here because none of them works; in that sense Mark Twain does ridicule the singleminded credulity of those who offer and those who rely on remedies for the irremediable.

The structure of "How to Cure a Cold" approaches incoherence, and its humor is occasionally more heavy-handed than the author's work in Nevada; he may well have been overreacting to his new San Francisco audience. Yet for all its frothy turmoil, the sketch does express, through Mark Twain's pose of innocence, a rather sardonic view of the world which seems to hold the incongruent elements together. Ineffective folk remedies imposed upon the suffering author are only part of the trouble: the girl who intrudes on his thoughts does not act as a pretty girl should, and even the power of friendship fails him when "young Wilson" eats the mustard plaster, the sick man's last, best hope.

Whatever modern readers may think of "How to Cure a Cold," Clemens himself seems to have regarded it with favor, for he revised and reprinted it in his *Jumping Frog* book in 1867, and he continued to revise and reprint it—removing topical allusions, digressions, and "coarseness"—until it was finally reprinted in *Sketches, New and Old* in 1875.[3] It is the earliest example of his apprentice work to be thus preserved for a larger audience.

---

[3]See the textual commentary.

How to Cure a Cold

It is a good thing, perhaps, to write for the amusement of the public, but it is a far higher and nobler thing to write for their instruction—their profit—their actual and tangible benefit.

The latter is the sole object of this article.

If it prove the means of restoring to health one solitary sufferer among my race—of lighting up once more the fire of hope and joy in his faded eyes—of bringing back to his dead heart again the quick, generous impulses of other days—I shall be amply rewarded for my labor; my soul will be permeated with the sacred delight a Christian feels when he has done a good, unselfish deed.

Having led a pure and blameless life, I am justified in believing that no man who knows me will reject the suggestions I am about to make, out of fear that I am trying to deceive him.

Let the public do itself the honor to read my experience in doctoring a cold, as herein set forth, and then follow in my footsteps.

When the White House was burned in Virginia, I lost my home, my happiness, my constitution and my trunk.

The loss of the two first named articles was a matter of no great consequence, since a home without a mother or a sister, or a distant young female relative in it, to remind you by putting your soiled linen out of sight and taking your boots down off the mantle-piece, that there are those who think about you and care for you, is easily obtained.

And I cared nothing for the loss of my happiness, because, not being a poet, it could not be possible that melancholy would abide with me long.

But to lose a good constitution and a better trunk were serious misfortunes.

I had my Gould and Curry in the latter, you recollect; I may get it back again, though—I came down here this time partly to bully-rag the Company into restoring my stock to me.

On the day of the fire, my constitution succumbed to a severe cold caused by undue exertion in getting ready to do something.

I suffered to no purpose, too, because the plan I was figuring at for the extinguishing of the fire was so elaborate that I never got it completed until the middle of the following week.

The first time I began to sneeze, a friend told me to go and bathe my feet in hot water and go to bed.

I did so.

Shortly afterward, another friend advised me to get up and take a cold shower-bath.

I did that also.

Within the hour, another friend assured me that it was policy to "feed a cold and starve a fever."

I had both.

I thought it best to fill myself up for the cold, and then keep dark and let the fever starve a while.

In a case of this kind, I seldom do things by halves; I ate pretty heartily; I conferred my custom upon a stranger who had just opened his restaurant that morning; he waited near me in respectful silence until I had finished feeding my cold, when he inquired if the people about Virginia were much afflicted with colds?

I told him I thought they were.

He then went out and took in his sign.

I started down toward the office, and on the way encountered another bosom friend, who told me that a quart of salt water, taken warm, would come as near curing a cold as anything in the world.

I hardly thought I had room for it, but I tried it anyhow.

The result was surprising; I must have vomited three-quarters of an hour; I believe I threw up my immortal soul.

Now, as I am giving my experience only for the benefit of those who are troubled with the distemper I am writing about, I feel that they will see the propriety of my cautioning them against following such portions of it as proved inefficient with me—and acting upon this conviction, I warn them against warm salt water.

It may be a good enough remedy, but I think it is too severe. If I had another cold in the head, and there was no course left me but to take either an earthquake or a quart of warm salt water, I would cheerfully take my chances on the earthquake.

After the storm which had been raging in my stomach had subsided, and no more good Samaritans happening along, I went on borrowing handkerchiefs again and blowing them to atoms, as had been my custom in the early stages of my cold, until I came across a lady who had just arrived from over the plains, and who said she had lived in a part of the country where doctors were scarce, and had from necessity acquired considerable skill in the treatment of simple "family complaints."

I knew she must have had much experience, for she appeared to be a hundred and fifty years old.

She mixed a decoction composed of molasses, aquafortis, turpentine, and various other drugs, and instructed me to take a wine-glass full of it every fifteen minutes.

I never took but one dose; that was enough; it robbed me of all moral principle, and awoke every unworthy impulse of my nature.

Under its malign influence, my brain conceived miracles of meanness, but my hands were too feeble to execute them; at that time had it not been that my strength had surrendered to a succession of assaults from infallible remedies for my cold, I am satisfied that I would have tried to rob the graveyard.

Like most other people, I often feel mean, and act accordingly, but until I took that medicine I had never reveled in such supernatural depravity and felt proud of it.

At the end of two days, I was ready to go to doctoring again. I took a few more unfailing remedies, and finally drove my cold from my head to my lungs.

I got to coughing incessantly, and my voice fell below Zero; I conversed in a thundering bass two octaves below my natural tone; I could only compass my regular nightly repose by coughing myself down to a state of utter exhaustion, and then the moment I began to talk in my sleep, my discordant voice woke me up again.

My case grew more and more serious every day.

Plain gin was recommended; I took it.

Then gin and molasses; I took that also.

Then gin and onions; I added the onions and took all three.

I detected no particular result, however, except that I had acquired a breath like a buzzard's.

I found I had to travel for my health.

I went to Lake Bigler with my reportorial comrade, Adair Wilson. It is gratifying to me to reflect that we traveled in considerable style; we went in the Pioneer coach, and my friend took all his baggage with him, consisting of two excellent silk handkerchiefs and a daguerreotype of his grandmother.

I had my regular gin and onions along.

Virginia, San Francisco and Sacramento were well represented at the Lake House, and we had a very healthy time of it for a while. We sailed and hunted and fished and danced all day, and I doctored my cough all night.

By managing in this way, I made out to improve every hour in the twenty-four.

But my disease continued to grow worse.

A sheet-bath was recommended. I had never refused a remedy yet, and it seemed poor policy to commence then; therefore I determined to take a sheet-bath, notwithstanding I had no idea what sort of arrangement it was.

It was administered at midnight, and the weather was very frosty. My breast and back were bared, and a sheet (there appeared to be a thousand yards of it) soaked in ice-water, was wound around me until I resembled a swab for a Columbiad.

It is a cruel expedient. When the chilly rag touches one's warm flesh, it makes him start with sudden violence and gasp for breath just as men do in the death agony. It froze the marrow in my bones and stopped the beating of my heart.

I thought my time had come.

Young Wilson said the circumstance reminded him of an anecdote about a negro who was being baptised, and who slipped from the Parson's grasp and came near being drowned; he floundered around, though, and finally rose up out of the water considerably strangled and furiously angry, and started ashore at once, spouting water like a whale, and remarking with great asperity that "One o' dese days, some gen'lman's nigger gwyne to git killed wid jes' sich dam foolishness as dis!"

Then young Wilson laughed at his silly, pointless anecdote, as if he had thought he had done something very smart. I suppose I am not to be affronted every day, though, without resenting it—I coughed my bed-fellow clear out of the house before morning.

Never take a sheet-bath—never. Next to meeting a lady acquaintance, who, for reasons best known to herself, don't see you when she looks at you and don't know you when she does see you, it is the most uncomfortable thing in the world.

It is singular that such a simile as that, happened to occur to me; I haven't thought of that circumstance a dozen times to-day. I used to think she was so pretty, and gentle, and graceful, and considerate, and all that sort of thing.

But I suspect it was all a mistake.

In reality, she is as ugly as a crab; and there is no expression in her countenance, either; she reminds me of one of those dummies in the milliner shops. I know she has got false teeth, and I think one of her eyes is glass. She can never fool me with that French she talks, either; that's Cherokee—I have been among that tribe myself. She has already driven two or three Frenchmen to the verge of suicide with that unchristian gibberish. And that complexion of her's is the dingiest that ever a white woman bore—it is pretty nearly Cherokee itself. It shows out strongest when it is contrasted with her monstrous white sugar-shoveled bonnet; when she gets that on, she looks like a sorrel calf under a new shed. I despise that woman, and I'll never speak to her again. Not unless she speaks to me, anyhow.

But as I was saying, when the sheet-bath failed to cure my cough, a lady friend recommended the application of a mustard plaster to my breast.

I believe that would have cured me effectually, if it had not been for young Wilson.

When I went to bed I put my mustard plaster—which was a very gorgeous one, eighteen inches square—where I could reach it when I was ready for it.

But young Wilson got hungry in the night, and ate it up.

I never saw anybody have such an appetite; I am confident that lunatic would have eaten me if I had been healthy.

After sojourning a week at Lake Bigler, I went to Steamboat Springs, and besides the steam baths, I took a lot of the vilest medicines that were ever concocted. They would have cured me, but I had to go back to Virginia, where, notwithstanding the variety of new remedies I absorbed every day, I managed to aggravate my disease by carelessness and undue exposure.

I finally concluded to visit San Francisco, and the first day I got here a lady at the Lick House told me to drink a quart of whisky every twenty-four hours, and a friend at the Occidental recommended precisely the same course.

Each advised me to take a quart—that makes half a gallon.

I calculate to do it or perish in the attempt.

Now, with the kindest motives in the world, I offer for the consideration of consumptive patients the variegated course of treatment I have lately gone through. Let them try it—if it don't cure them, it can't more than kill them.

64. Mark Twain—More of Him

27 September 1863

The main body of this sketch—Mark Twain's letter headed "All about the Fashions"—is a double-barreled burlesque ridiculing society columns in general and reviews of current fashions in particular. It was written on 19 June 1863 while Mark Twain was still in San Francisco, and it was probably first published sometime between June 21 and 24 in the Virginia City *Territorial Enterprise*.[1] Three months later, when Clemens returned to San Francisco, he republished it in the *Golden Era* in the form presented here. The author evidently made no revisions in the text of his letter, but he did supply a prefatory note from "A Lady at the Lick House" (manifestly by Mark Twain himself) that purported to explain why his description of the toilettes at a June ball at the Lick House was appearing in the September *Era*. The *Enterprise* sketch thus belongs to late June and would ordinarily have appeared in this collection following "Letter from Mark Twain" (no. 53), also written from San Francisco. But since the author revised the piece by adding the preface (if not by changing his words), it has seemed best to place it according to the date of its republication in the *Era*. The whole item was headed "Mark Twain—More of Him," the title adopted here.

It seems likely that the editors of the *Era* wanted to capitalize on Mark Twain's rising popularity and on the widespread interest in San Francisco's unusually active social season. Mark Twain's "How to Cure a Cold" (no. 63) had appeared there one week before and made a hit. "The Lick House Ball" (no. 65), a second and more elaborate burlesque of the fashionable world, appeared in the same issue that carried "Mark Twain—More of Him." Presumably the editors felt that their readers would not be jaded by an

---

[1]The *Enterprise* piece is actually subtitled "All about the Latest Fashions."

extra helping of Mark Twain's mock society columns and his burlesque of the recherché vocabulary promoted by the fashion industry.

The Lick House was at this time Clemens' preferred San Francisco hotel, and it was a favorite site for the periodic "re-unions" mentioned by the "Lady at the Lick House." This year the fall social season had begun with a "fête" given by the Hungarian Baron Castro d'Estrala at the new Clarendon Hotel on September 3. This was followed by an even more lavish event, the talk of the town for weeks, William E. Barron's ball on September 17 at his Stockton Street "palace." Then on September 24, three days before the present sketch appeared, the Lick House gave a second ball. By that time the ladies were already planning for the following month's Spanish Ball, honoring Admiral Pinzon of the Spanish Squadron of the Pacific. And in mid-November Admiral Popoff and the officers of the Russian Pacific Fleet would provide the occasion for a great Russian Ball, which received ecstatic notices in the press.[2]

Mark Twain's description of the ladies' June toilettes bears a relation to reality about like that of his description of the massacre near Dutch Nick's (see "A Bloody Massacre near Carson," no. 66). Just as his massacre hoax caught the breathless tell-it-all quality of the latest "sensation" item, so the present sketch mimics the tritely effusive descriptions that were standard fare with society reporters. For example, in describing Barron's ball one week before, "Sarah Smith" wrote in the *Era:* "The toilette of the beautiful and *distingue* Mrs. H——, of corn-colored tulle puffed over silk of the same color, and adorned with *groseille* flowers with silver leaves, was a miracle of good taste and elegance."[3] And on September 27, also in the *Era,* "Peregrine" wrote: "Mrs. Hon. F. F. L— wore a dark pink silk beautifully and tastefully trimmed with black lace; the arrangement of her hair was faultless, and the ornaments neat and apropos. She was beautiful and captivating—the 'fairest of the fair.'"[4] Part of Clemens' satirical point, here and in "The Lick House Ball," was to demonstrate that male reporters lacked an aptitude for describing or appreciating feminine fashions—an observation that may be a clue to the sex of Sarah Smith and Peregrine.

The current bible of the fashion industry was *Madame Demorest's Quarterly Mirror of Fashions and Journal du Grand Monde,* issued from the Emporium of Fashion in New York City. The fall 1863 number was

---

[2]See the *Golden Era*—11 (6 September 1863): 4; 11 (20 September 1863): 4; 11 (22 November 1863): 5; 11 (27 September 1863): 8; San Francisco *Evening Bulletin,* 15 October 1863, p. 3; and "The Lick House Ball" (no. 65).

[3]"Letter from a Lady. Mr. Barron's Ball," *Golden Era* 11 (20 September 1863): 5.

[4]"Peregrine at the Lick House Hop," *Golden Era* 11 (27 September 1863): 4.

embellished (typically) with a steel engraving of the Empress Eugénie and her maids of honor, several steel fashion plates, and five full-size patterns. Although this journal was distributed in the West, San Francisco had several fashion magazines of its own. The *California Magazine and Mountaineer* (mentioned by the "Lady at the Lick House") specialized in "splendidly executed and high colored Fashion Plates . . . direct from the fashionable headquarters of the world, Paris,"[5] and like the *Era*, it regularly reviewed the outstanding social events and reported the ladies' toilettes. San Francisco's *Hesperian* also published dress patterns, accompanied by full-page illustrations and descriptions as well as by reviews of the latest styles. For instance, one of *Hesperian's* editors, Mrs. F. H. Day, knew the fashion jargon, like many of her colleagues, down to the last gimp and bugle. In a "Summary of Fashion Direct from Paris," published in January 1863, she wrote:

The foulards of plain colors seem this season to be preferred; cream color, Solferino, strawberry, violet, etc. The Pekins are of maroon and black. . . . For gauze de Chambery, flounces and bands put on alternately, are used, the bands having ruches, the body square with cannezous. White muslins are made with very wide insertions of colored ribbon. . . . The camails, or round cloaks, are ornamented with gimps. One of white cachemire was with bands of guipure, and macarons of black gimp, terminating with chenille fringe; others are with bugles and chenille. But the burnous and the saute-en-barque are almost the only outdoor toilette worn at this moment.[6]

Mark Twain had an excellent ear for this imposing vocabulary and managed to make it even more outlandish, superbly reproducing its tendency to degenerate (at least for the average male reader) into a meaningless mush. The comic effect he achieves with his own rendition of the jargon is only occasionally heightened by knowing how completely he has misused it: the explanatory notes accordingly confine themselves to identifying a mere handful of such terms, even though one might easily be more exhaustive.

While Mark Twain's main target in this sketch remains the society column and fashion review, his account of his own "appearance" at the party belongs to the role he played vis-à-vis the Unreliable. When Clemens attended the First Annual Fair of the Washoe Agricultural, Mining and Mechanical Society, which was climaxed with a ball, the Virginia City *Union* gave an account of his costume. The *Union* reporter, in all likelihood Clement T. Rice, wrote in the "Gentlemen's Department": "S. C—, we did not catch the full name—was present, and the Misses declared

---

[5]*California Magazine and Mountaineer* 7 (May 1863): 758.
[6]*Hesperian* 9 (January 1863): 503–504.

(quotation) he did look sweet. His costume consisted chiefly of an exquisitely tinted vest of the age of Louis XIV. His hair was entirely without ornament, and his finger nails were clean and well trimmed, making an unusual effect in an assemblage where everything depends upon contrasts."[7]

[7]"First Annual Fair of the Washoe Agricultural, Mining and Mechanical Society," Virginia City *Union*, 18 October 1863, Scrapbook 2, p. 97, MTP.

Mark Twain—More of Him

"A LADY AT THE LICK HOUSE" WRITES:

"EDRS. GOLDEN ERA—We are all delighted with the 'Letter,' describing the brilliant Ball at Mr. Barron's. I am a Washoe widow, was among the favored few, and went. Sarah Smith skipped me in the toilettes. I suppose I wasn't very stunning, although Brigham & Co. said I looked 'swell,' and that 'Robergh' couldn't get up anything better. Some months ago, when my spouse, now at Reese River, first brought me down from Virginia City to stop in San Francisco, I arrived in the nick of time to attend one of those charming re-unions which are all the rage in the Pacific Metropolis. We have had several soirees since that, but nobody gave any account of them to the papers. It's too bad. Now we are eagerly looking forward to the next soiree, expecting the GOLDEN ERA to tell all about it. One of our boarders says she knows Florence Fane, and means to invite her; but I can't for the life of me get her to tell me the real name of your charming feuilletonist. I hope she'll come. And may-be Mark Twain will stay in town, to be there too. There is some talk of getting up a special gathering in compliment to him. He's such a favorite—stops here for his health—hoping to find out how to cure a cold. I am going to wear a new dress, made precisely after the pattern of one of those sweet Paris Fashion Plates in the *California Magazine*. That Ball Dress in the May number—I think it was—I've kept it in my boudoir ever since. Then if Mark Twain is only there to see; how happy, how happy, I shall be. (I don't mean that for poetry—Like what you put in the GOLDEN ERA.) (To take that license

I am free—I write with such facility.) But I have not told you what I wanted. Mark Twain was at our party, last June, and sent the *Territorial Enterprise* an account of the affair. My husband enclosed me the paper in which it appeared. I cut it out and you can copy it. Please do. I've been bothered to death to let everybody see it, and it's dreadfully tattered and torn."

Here it is!

LETTER FROM MARK TWAIN.

ALL ABOUT THE FASHIONS.

SAN FRANCISCO, June 19.

EDS. ENTERPRISE:—I have just received, per Wells-Fargo, the following sweet scented little note, written in a microscopic hand in the center of a delicate sheet of paper—like a wedding invitation or a funeral notice—and I feel it my duty to answer it:

"VIRGINIA, June 16.

"MR. MARK TWAIN:—*Do* tell us something about the fashions. I am dying to know what the ladies of San Francisco are wearing. Do, now, tell us all you know about it, won't you? Pray excuse brevity, for I am in *such* a hurry.

BETTIE.

"P. S.—Please burn this as soon as you have read it."

"*Do* tell us"—and she is in "*such* a hurry." Well, I never knew a girl in my life who could write three consecutive sentences without italicising a word. They can't do it, you know. Now, if I had a wife, and she—however, I don't think I shall have one this week, and it is hardly worth while to borrow trouble.

Bettie, my love, you do me proud. In thus requesting me to fix up the fashions for you in an intelligent manner, you pay a compliment to my critical and observant eye and my varied and extensive information, which a mind less perfectly balanced than mine could scarcely contemplate without excess of vanity. Will I tell you something about the fashions? I will, Bettie—you better bet you bet, Betsey, my darling. I learned those expressions from the Unreliable; like all the phrases which fall from his lips, they are frightfully vulgar—but then they sound rather musical than otherwise.

A happy circumstance has put it in my power to furnish you the fashions from headquarters—as it were, Bettie: I refer to the assemblage of fashion, elegance and loveliness called together in the parlor of the Lick House last night—[a party given by the proprietors on the occasion of my paying up that little balance due on my board bill.] I will give a brief and lucid description of the dresses worn by several of the ladies of my acquaintance who were present. Mrs. B. was arrayed in a superb speckled foulard, with the stripes running fore and aft, and with collets and camails to match; also, a rotonde of Chantilly lace, embroidered with blue and yellow dogs, and birds and things, done in cruel, and edged with a Solferino fringe four inches deep— lovely. Mrs. B. is tall, and graceful and beautiful, and the general effect of her costume was to render her appearance extremely lively.

Miss J. W. wore a charming robe polonais of scarlet ruche a la vieille, with yellow fluted flounces of rich bombazine, fourteen inches wide; low neck and short sleeves; also a Figaro veste of bleached domestic—selvedge edge turned down with a back-stitch, and trimmed with festoons of blue chicoree taffetas—gay?—I reckon not. Her head-dress was the sweetest thing you ever saw: a bunch of stately ostrich plumes—red and white—springing like fountains above each ear, with a crown between, consisting of a single *fleur de soliel*, fresh from the garden—Ah, me! Miss W. looked enchantingly pretty; however, there was nothing unusual about that—I have seen her look so, even in a milder costume.

Mrs. J. B. W. wore a heavy rat-colored brocade silk, studded with large silver stars, and trimmed with organdy; balloon sleeves of nankeen pique, gathered at the wrist, cut bias and hollowed out some at the elbow; also, a bournous of black Honiton lace, scolloped, and embroidered in violent colors with a battle piece representing the taking of Holland by the Dutch; low neck and high-heeled shoes; gloves; palm-leaf fan; hoops; her head-dress consisted of a simple maroon-colored Sontag, with festoons of blue illusion depending from it; upon her bosom reposed a gorgeous bouquet of real sage brush, imported from Washoe. Mrs. W. looked regally handsome. If every article of dress worn by her on this occasion had been multiplied seven times, I do not believe it would have improved her appearance any.

Miss C. wore an elegant *Cheveux de la Reine* (with ruffles and furbelows trimmed with bands of guipre round the bottom), and a mohair Garibaldi shirt; her unique head-dress was crowned with a graceful *pomme de terre* (Limerick French), and she had her hair done up in papers—greenbacks. The effect was very rich, partly owing to the market value of the material, and partly to the general loveliness of the lady herself.

Miss A. H. wore a splendid Lucia de Lammermoor, trimmed with green baize: also, a cream-colored mantilla-shaped *pardessus*, with a deep gore in the neck, and embellished with a wide greque of taffetas ribbon, and otherwise garnished with ruches, and radishes and things. Her *coiffure* was a simple wreath of sardines on a string. She was lovely to a fault.

Now, what do you think of that effort, Bettie (I wish I knew your other name) for an unsanctified newspaper reporter, devoid of a milliner's education? Doesn't it strike you that there are more brains and fewer oysters in my head than a casual acquaintance with me would lead one to suppose? Ah, well—what I don't know, Bet, is hardly worth the finding out, I can tell you. I could have described the dresses of all the ladies in that party, but I was afraid to meddle with those of strangers, because I might unwittingly get something wrong, and give offense. You see strangers never exercise any charity in matters of this kind—they always get mad at the least inaccuracies of description concerning their apparel, and make themselves disagreeable. But if you will just rig yourself up according to the models I have furnished you, Bets, you'll do, you know—you can weather the circus.

You will naturally wish to be informed as to the most fashionable style of male attire, and I may as well give you an idea of my own personal appearance at the party. I wore one of Mr. Lawlor's shirts, and Mr. Ridgway's vest, and Dr. Wayman's coat, and Mr. Camp's hat, and Mr. Paxton's boots, and Jerry Long's white kids, and Judge Gilchrist's cravat, and the Unreliable's brass seal-ring, and Mr. Toll-road McDonald's pantaloons—and if you have an idea that they are anyways short in the legs, do you just climb into them once, sweetness. The balance of my outfit I gathered up indiscriminately from various individuals whose names I have forgotten and have now no means of ascertaining, as I thoughtlessly erased the marks from the different garments this morning. But I looked salubrious, B., if ever a man did.

Messrs Editors, I never wrote such a personal article as this before. I expect I had better go home, now. Well, I have been here long enough, anyhow. I didn't come down to stay always, in the first place. I don't know of anything more here that I want to see. I might just as well go home now, as not. I have been wanting to go home for a good while. I don't see why I haven't gone before this. They all say it is healthier up there than it is here. I believe it. I have not been very well for a week. I don't eat enough, I expect. But I would stay here just as long as I pleased though, if I wanted to. But I don't. Well, I don't care—I am going home—that is the amount of it—and very soon, too—maybe sooner.

MARK TWAIN.

65. The Lick House Ball

27 September 1863

"The Lick House Ball" appeared in the same number of the *Golden Era* which carried the previous sketch, "Mark Twain—More of Him" (no. 64). Two other writers, "Peregrine" and "Pandora," also gave their impressions of the event in the same issue. "It was on Thursday evening, the 24th inst.," wrote Peregrine, "when the boarders of that highly popular hotel, the Lick House, gave another of those social and fashionable re-unions which have formed so marked a feature of this establishment."[1] Pandora noted the presence of Governor-elect Low and his wife, as well as "a live Baron" (probably Castro d'Estrala, the lion of the social season), and the officers of the U.S.S. *Lancaster*, the flagship of Admiral Ball, commander in chief of the United States naval forces in the Pacific. After the company "Quadrilled, Polked, Lanced, Waltzed, Galloped and Tuckered," she wrote, supper was served about twelve, followed by more dancing until morning.[2]

The party was an important event, for the *Lancaster* had arrived in port only recently, on September 15, and scarcely two weeks earlier, on September 2, Frederick Low had soundly defeated John G. Downey in the race for governor.[3] As though to do the occasion justice, Clemens dipped more deeply into the pool of fashion terms, expended more effort on individual descriptions, and singled out more wives of well-known men than he had done in "Mark Twain—More of Him."

---

[1]"Peregrine at the Lick House Hop," *Golden Era* 11 (27 September 1863): 4.

[2]"Pandora at the Party," *Golden Era* 11 (27 September 1863): 5.

[3]San Francisco *Alta California*, 16 September 1863, p. 1; San Francisco *Evening Bulletin*, 2 September 1863, p. 2; *Golden Era* 11 (4 October 1863): 4.

The Lick House Ball

EDS. ERA: I have received a letter from the land of eternal summer—Washoe, you understand—requesting a short synopsis of the San Francisco fashions for reference. There are ten note paper pages of it. I read it all. For two hours I worked along through it—spelling a word laboriously here and there—figuring out sentences by main strength—getting three or four of them corraled, all ragged and disjointed, and then skirmishing around after the connection—two hours of unflagging labor, determination and blasphemy, unrewarded by one solitary shadow of a suspicion of what the writer was trying to get through her head or what she could possibly be up to—until I bore down upon the three lines at the bottom of the last page, marked "P.S.," which contained the request about the fashions, and was the only paragraph in the document wherein the light of reason glimmered. All that went before it was driveling stupidity—all that the girl really wished to say was in the postscript. It was not strange that I experienced a warm fellow-feeling for the dog that drank sixty gallons of water to get at a spoonful of mush in the bottom of the tank.

The young lady signs herself "Œnone." I am not acquainted with her, but the respect, the deference which, as a white man and a Christian, I naturally feel for members of her sex, impels me to take no less pains in obliging her than were the circumstances different.

A fortunate occurrence has placed it in my power to furnish Œnone with the very latest fashions: I refer to the great ball given me at the Lick House last Thursday night by a portion of the guests of that hotel,

314

on the occasion of my promising to "let up" on Messrs. Jerome Rice, John B. Winters, Brooks, Mason, Charley Creed, Capt. Pease, and the other "billiard sharps" of the establishment.

It was a graceful acknowledgment of my proficiency in the beautiful science of billiards, as well as of the liberality I have shown in paying for about every game I ever played in the house.

I expect I have been rather hard upon those gentlemen, but it was no fault of mine—they courted their own destruction. As one of them expressed it, they "could not resist the temptation to tackle me;" and if they baited their hooks for a sardine and caught a whale, who is to blame? Possibly it will be a comfort to Capt. Pease to know that I don't blame him, anyhow; that there is no animosity whatever, and that I feel the same filial affection, the same kindly regard, etc., etc., just as if nothing had happened.

Œnone, (or Unknown, if it is all the same to you,) the ball was a grand success. The army was present and also the navy. The nobility were represented by his Grace the Duke of Benicia, the Countess of San Jose, Lord Blessyou, Lord Geeminy, and many others whose titles and whose faces have passed from my memory. Owing to a press of imperial business, the Emperor Norton was unable to come.

The parlors were royally decorated, and the floors covered with a rich white carpet of mauve domestique, forty dollars a yard, imported from Massachusetts or the kingdom of New Jersey, I have forgotten which. The moment I entered I saw at a glance that this was the most extraordinary party ever given in San Francisco. I mentioned it to Benish, (the very friendly, not to say familiar, relations existing between myself and his Grace the Duke of Benicia, permit of my addressing him in this way without impropriety,) and he said he had never seen anything like it where he came from. He said there were more diamonds here than were displayed at the very creditable effort of the Messrs. Barron, recently. This remark revived in his breast a reminiscence of that ball. He observed that the evening before it came off, he visited all the jewelry shops in town for the purpose of leasing some diamonds for his wife, who had been invited; but others had gone before him and "cleaned out," (as the facetious nobleman expressed it,) every establishment. There was but one shop where a diamond remained on hand; and even there, the proprietor was obliged to tell him—though it cost him pain to do it—

that he only had a quart left, and they had already been engaged by the Duchess of Goat Island, who was going to the ball and could not do without them.

The memory of the incident affected the noble Benish almost to tears, and we pursued the theme no further. After this, we relapsed into a desultory conversation in French, in which I rather had the best of him; he appeared to have an idea that he could cypher out what I was driving at, whereas I had never expected to understand him in the first place.

But you are suffering for the fashions, Œnone. I have written such things before, but only by way of burlesquing the newspaper descriptions of balls and dresses launched at the public every now and then by individuals who do not seem to know that writing fashion articles, like wet nursing, can only be done properly by women. A rightly constituted man ought to be above filching from the prerogatives of the other sex. As I have said, the fashion synopses heretofore written by myself, have been uncouth burlesques—extravagant paraphrases of the eloquence of female costume, as incomprehensible and as conflicting as Billy Birch's testimony in the case of the atrocious assassination of Erickson's bull by "Jonesy," with his infamous "stuffed club." But this time, since a lady requests it, I will choke down my distaste for such feminine employment, and write a faithful description of the queenly dresses worn at the Lick House party by several ladies whose tempers I think I can depend on. Thus:

Mrs. F. F. L. wore a superb *toilette habillee* of Chambery gauze; over this a charming Figaro jacket, made of mohair, or horse-hair, or something of that kind; over this again, a Raphael blouse of *cheveux de la reine*, trimmed round the bottom with lozenges formed of insertions, and around the top with bronchial troches; nothing could be more graceful than the contrast between the lozenges and the troches; over the blouse she wore a *robe de chambre* of regal magnificence, made of *Faille* silk and ornamented with maccaroon (usually spelled "maccaroni,") buttons set in black guipre. On the roof of her bonnet was a menagerie of rare and beautiful bugs and reptiles, and under the eaves thereof a counterfeit of the "early bird" whose specialty it hath been to work destruction upon such things since time began. To say that Mrs. L. was never more elaborately dressed in her life, would be to express an opinion within the range of possibility, at least—to say that she did or could look otherwise than charming, would be a deliberate departure from the truth.

Mrs. Wm. M. S. wore a gorgeous dress of silk bias, trimmed with tufts of ponceau feathers in the *Frondeur* style; elbowed sleeves made of chicories; plaited Swiss habit-shirt, composed of Valenciennes, *a la vieille*, embellished with a delicate nansook insertion scolloped at the edge; Lonjumeau jacket of maize-colored *Geralda*, set off with *bagnettes*, bayonets, clarinets, and one thing or other—beautiful. Rice-straw bonnet of Mechlin tulle, trimmed with devices cut out of sole-leather, representing aigrettes and arastras—or asters, whichever it is. Leather ornaments are becoming very fashionable in high society. I am told the Empress Eugenie dresses in buckskin now, altogether; so does Her Majesty the Queen of the Shoshones. It will be seen at a glance that Mrs. S.'s costume upon this occasion was peculiarly suited to the serene dignity of her bearing.

Mrs. A. W. B. was arrayed in a sorrel organdy, trimmed with fustians and figaros, and canzou fichus, so disposed as to give a splendid effect without disturbing the general harmony of the dress. The body of the robe was of zero velvet, goffered, with a square pelerine of solferino *poil de chevre* amidships. The fan used by Mrs. B. was of real palm-leaf and cost four thousand dollars—the handle alone cost six bits. Her head dress was composed of a graceful cataract of white chantilly lace, surmounted by a few artificial worms, and butterflies and things, and a tasteful tarantula done in jet. It is impossible to conceive of anything more enchanting than this toilet—or the lady who wore it, either, for that matter.

Mrs. J. B. W. was dressed in a rich white satin, with a body composed of a gorgeously figured Mackinaw blanket, with five rows of ornamental brass buttons down the back. The dress was looped up at the side with several bows of No. 3 ribbon—yellow—displaying a skirt of cream-colored Valenciennes crocheted with pink cruel. The coiffure was simply a tall cone of brilliant field-flowers, upon the summit of which stood a glittering 'golden beetle'—or, as we call him at home, a "straddle-bug." All who saw the beautiful Mrs. W. upon this occasion will agree that there was nothing wanting about her dress to make it attract attention in any community.

Mrs. F. was attired in an elegant Irish foulard of figured aqua marine, or aqua fortis, or something of that kind with thirty-two perpendicular rows of tulle puffings formed of black zero velvets (Fahrenheit.) Over this she wore a rich balmoral skirt—Pekin stripe—looped up at the sides with clusters of field flowers, showing the handsome dress beneath. She also wore a white Figaro postillion pea-jacket, ornamented with a profusion of Gabriel bows of crimson silk. From her head depended tasteful garlands of fresh radishes. It being natural to look charming upon all occasions, she did so upon this, of course.

Miss B. wore an elegant goffered flounce, trimmed with a grenadine of *bouillonnee*, with a crinoline waistcoat to match; pardessus open behind, embroidered with paramattas of passementerie, and further ornamented at the shoulders with epaulettes of wheat-ears and string-beans; tule hat, embellished with blue-bells, hare-bells, hash-bells, etc., with a frontispiece formed of a single magnificent cauliflower imbedded in mashed potatoes. Thus attired Miss B. looked good enough to eat. I admit that the expression is not very refined, but when a man is hungry the similes he uses are apt to be suggested by his stomach.

It is hardly worth while to describe the costumes of the gentlemen, since, with the exception of a handsome uniform here and there, (there were six naval Brigadier Generals present from the frigate *Lancaster*) they were all alike, and as usual, there was nothing worthy of particular notice in what they wore.

Œnone, I could furnish you with an accurate description of the costume of every lady who attended that party if it were safe to do it, but it isn't, you know. Over in Washoe I generally say what I please about anybody and everybody, because my obliging fellow citizens have learned to put up with it; but here, common prudence teaches me to speak of those only who are slow to anger, when writing about ladies. I had rather lose my scalp, anyhow, than wound a lady's feelings.

But there is one thing you can rest assured of, Œnone: The pleasantest parties in the world are those given at the Lick House every now and then, and to which scarcely any save the guests of the establishment are invited; and the ladies are handsomer, and dress with more taste and greater magnificence—but there come the children again. When that last invoice of fifteen hundred infants come around and get to romping about my door with the others, and hurrahing for their several favorite candidates for Governor, (unaware that the election is over, poor little miscreants,) I cannot write with such serene comfort as I do when they are asleep. Yet there is nothing I love so dearly as a clean, fat, healthy infant. I calculate to eat that whole tribe before I leave the Lick House.

Now, do you know, Œnone—however, I hear the stately tread of that inveterate chambermaid. She always finds this room in a state of chaos, and she always leaves it as trim as a parlor. But her instincts infallibly impel her to march in here just when I feel least like marching out. I do not know that I have ever begged permission to write "only a few moments longer"—never with my tongue, at any rate, although I may have *looked* it with my expressive glass eye. But she cares nothing for such spooney prayers. She is a soldier in the army of the household; she knows her duty, and she allows nothing to interfere with its rigid performance. She reminds me of U. S. Grant; she marches in her grand military way to the centre of the room, and comes to an "order arms" with her broom and her slop-bucket; then she bends on me a look of uncompromising determination, and I reluctantly haul down my flag. I abandon my position—I evacuate the premises—I retire in good order—I vamose the ranch. Because that look of hers says in plain, crisp language, "I don't want you here. If you are not gone in two minutes, I propose to move upon your works!" But I bear the chambermaid no animosity.

MARK TWAIN.

66. *A Bloody Massacre near Carson*

28 October 1863

This famous hoax was published on 28 October 1863 in the Virginia City *Territorial Enterprise*, probably under the title adopted here, "A Bloody Massacre near Carson." Although the *Enterprise* printing is not extant, three contemporary reprintings from that paper permit a full recovery of the text: on the afternoon of October 28 the Gold Hill *News* reprinted the item, partly verbatim and partly in paraphrase; the Sacramento *Union* reprinted it verbatim on October 30; and the San Francisco *Evening Bulletin* did likewise on October 31. Other western papers picked up the story as well and provide additional textual evidence.[1]

Judging by these newspapers it seems that the almost universal reaction to the unsigned item was credulous horror, swiftly followed by anger and outrage when the hoax was discovered. The day after it appeared, in fact, Mark Twain himself published a retraction:

I TAKE IT ALL BACK.

The story published in the Enterprise reciting the slaughter of a family near Empire was all a fiction. It was understood to be such by all acquainted with the locality in which the alleged affair occurred. In the first place, Empire City and Dutch Nick's are one, and in the next there is no "great pine forest" nearer than the Sierra Nevada mountains. But it was necessary to publish the story in order to get the fact into the San Francisco papers that the Spring Valley Water company was "cooking" dividends by borrowing money to declare them on for its stockholders. The only way you

---

[1]The title has been recovered from "A Canard," Reese River *Reveille* supplement, 7 November 1863, p. 1. See the textual commentary.

can get a fact into a San Francisco journal is to smuggle it in through some great tragedy.[2]

This jocular explanation failed to impress Mark Twain's critics. The Virginia City *Evening Bulletin* characterized it as "even worse than that published yesterday," and together with the Gold Hill *News*, the Sacramento *Union*, and other newspapers condemned the author for sickening his readers, blackening the name of the territory, and betraying journalistic responsibility for truthful reporting.[3] For more than a year negative comments continued to appear in the local press, and Mark Twain often alluded somewhat defensively to his infamous item.

The origin of the hoax is of interest to students of Mark Twain's apprenticeship at least in part because of this adverse and (to the author) surprising reaction. Paul Fatout has suggested that a "bottle imp" was responsible for Mark Twain's misjudging his audience,[4] but there seems no need to invoke such extenuating circumstances. In fact, it is likely that the hoax originated very much as Mark Twain said in his retraction—as a fiction designed to hoodwink San Francisco papers into publishing a criticism of the Spring Valley Water Company. To be sure, it used the kind of gory detail that was standard fare in Nevada newspapers, drawing specifically on the real ax murders committed by William Cornwell at Reese River the previous July.[5] But as the author pointed out, the deliberate errors in his "fiction" were designed to alert any reader "acquainted with the locality"— that is, Nevada residents but not San Franciscans.

In June 1870, seven years after the hoax appeared, Clemens recalled that he had in fact written it as a "scathing satire" exposing the "dividend-cooking system" of California and Nevada corporations, and he indicated that to his chagrin readers *"never got down* to where the satire part of it began." Virtually all readers greedily devoured the "horrible details" which he had made "so carefully and conscientiously interesting" that they never

[2]Quoted in C. A. V. Putnam's "Dan De Quille and Mark Twain," Salt Lake City *Tribune*, 25 April 1898, p. 3. Putnam's version of the retraction was probably set down from memory, and so may well be impressionistic or incomplete. The San Francisco *Evening Bulletin*, however, confirmed at least one sentence: *"I take it all back"* (31 October 1863, p. 5). The *Enterprise* printing is not extant.

[3]The Virginia City *Evening Bulletin* is quoted by Richard G. Lillard in "Contemporary Reaction to 'The Empire City Massacre,' " *American Literature* 16 (November 1944): 200. Lillard's article ably documents the reaction to Mark Twain's hoax.

[4]*MTVC*, p. 100.

[5]William C. Miller, "Mark Twain's Source for 'The Latest Sensation' Hoax?" *American Literature* 32 (March 1960): 75–78. See also Myron Angel, ed., *History of Nevada* (Oakland: Thompson and West, 1881), pp. 470–471.

noticed the contradictions, and never understood the "satire part" which came at the end of the piece. There Mark Twain blamed Hopkins' derangement on financial losses from such "dividend cooking," a practice he defined in 1870 as "increasing the value" of stock so that the trustees could "sell out at a comfortable figure and then scramble from under the tumbling concern."[6] Clemens also recalled that the occasion for his interest in the matter stemmed from the severe criticism heaped upon the Daney Gold and Silver Mining Company by the San Francisco papers for just this practice.

Clemens' memory is corroborated by the files of the San Francisco *Evening Bulletin* and by C. A. V. Putnam, a colleague of the author on the *Enterprise*. Putnam recalled in 1898 that C. L. Low, an old friend and San Francisco businessman in 1863, told him that two editors of the *Bulletin* (George K. Fitch and Lorin Pickering) "had been roped in . . . to the amount of $65,000" on bogusly inflated Daney mine stock. In retaliation the editors had published spiteful slurs on Comstock mines in general, including the irreproachable Gould and Curry. Low suggested that Putnam defend the honor of the local mines in the *Enterprise*, and that he urge the *Bulletin* to "confine its criticism to corporations whose property was nearer at home which resorted to 'cooking dividends.'" Low had a particular San Francisco company in mind: the Spring Valley Water Company, which he said "had hired the money to pay its last three dividends," thereby inflating its stock, a fact for which he could vouch. Putnam, however, was at a loss how to dramatize the facts in a way that would be copied by the "thick-skinned San Francisco journals," and so turned to Clemens for help. A few hours later Clemens told him "he had solved the problem," but that he had had "to manufacture a diabolical murder in order to work out his plot." Putnam's response was to say "all right; go ahead," and "A Bloody Massacre near Carson" was the result.[7]

Clemens also recalled in 1870 that the San Francisco press "while abusing the Daney . . . did not forget to urge the public to get rid of all their silver stocks and invest in sound and safe San Francisco stocks, such as the Spring Valley Water Company."[8] This is an exaggeration, however, probably deriving from the fiction of his own hoax: one of the editors of the San Francisco *Bulletin* "who had suffered pecuniarily by the dividend-cooking system as applied to the Daney Mining Company" was allegedly responsible for advising Hopkins to trade his silver stocks for those of the water company. The *Bulletin* had, in fact, severely criticized the situation with the Daney mine,

---

[6]"A Couple of Sad Experiences" (no. 299), first published in the *Galaxy* 9 (June 1870): 860–861.

[7]"Dan De Quille and Mark Twain," Salt Lake City *Tribune*, 25 April 1898, p. 3.

[8]"A Couple of Sad Experiences," *Galaxy*, p. 860.

and had even cast aspersions on the Gould and Curry, but nowhere advised a general transfer of investment funds. At least one *Bulletin* article suggested that the editors knew personally what it felt like to be victimized: "To hook a big fat fish is very fine," they wrote, "but it isn't very pleasant to be pulled in, taken down, and gobbled up." And still another article emphasized the cardinal sin of mining-company trustees: inflating stock values in a poor mine before selling out at great profit to themselves.[9]

Mark Twain's hoax also exaggerated the financial difficulties of the Spring Valley Water Company. While he asserted that the newspapers of San Francisco had neglected their watchdog role, the fact was that the *Bulletin* had itself criticized the company for failing to supply adequate water to the southern districts of the city. The company's policy of turning off the water overnight, it was alleged, created a danger in case of fire, was the cause of coffeeless breakfasts, and, ironically, improved the purity of locally marketed milk.[10] This policy may reflect financial difficulty not otherwise documented: after the *Bulletin* published its criticism the company's stock fell from eighty points to forty. But some recovery was made, and the stock never "went down to nothing" as Clemens asserted in the hoax.[11]

---

[9]The quotation is from "Selling Short," San Francisco *Evening Bulletin*, 24 September 1863, p. 3. The *Bulletin's* critique of the Daney mine appeared in "How Dividends Are Cooked—Trustees of a Mining Company Taken to Task," 8 September 1863, p. 3, and "How to Prevent the Cooking of Dividends," 10 September 1863, p. 3. The Gould and Curry was criticized in "Stock Review," 22 October 1863, p. 1. The article on trustees, "For the Careful Consideration of Mining Trustees and the Stockholders," appeared on 29 September 1863, p. 2.

[10]"Shortness of Water—Peril of the City South of Mission Street," San Francisco *Evening Bulletin*, 16 October 1863, p. 3; "Milk and Water Troubles," ibid., 19 October 1863, p. 5; "Water Stocks Beware," *Golden Era* 11 (18 October 1863): 4.

[11]San Francisco *Evening Bulletin*, 19 October 1863, p. 5, and 2 November 1863, p. 5. By late December the stock had risen to fifty points (ibid., 26 December 1863, p. 5).

A Bloody Massacre
near Carson

FROM ABRAM CURRY, who arrived here yesterday afternoon from Carson, we have learned the following particulars concerning a bloody massacre which was committed in Ormsby county night before last. It seems that during the past six months a man named P. Hopkins, or Philip Hopkins, has been residing with his family in the old log house just at the edge of the great pine forest which lies between Empire City and Dutch Nick's. The family consisted of nine children—five girls and four boys—the oldest of the group, Mary, being nineteen years old, and the youngest, Tommy, about a year and a half. Twice in the past two months Mrs. Hopkins, while visiting in Carson, expressed fears concerning the sanity of her husband, remarking that of late he had been subject to fits of violence, and that during the prevalence of one of these he had threatened to take her life. It was Mrs. Hopkins' misfortune to be given to exaggeration, however, and but little attention was paid to what she said. About ten o'clock on Monday evening Hopkins dashed into Carson on horseback, with his throat cut from ear to ear, and bearing in his hand a reeking scalp from which the warm, smoking blood was still dripping, and fell in a dying condition in front of the Magnolia saloon. Hopkins expired in the course of five minutes, without speaking. The long red hair of the scalp he bore marked it as that of Mrs. Hopkins. A number of citizens, headed by Sheriff Gasherie, mounted at once and rode down to Hopkins' house, where a ghastly scene met their gaze. The scalpless corpse of Mrs.

Hopkins lay across the threshold, with her head split open and her right hand almost severed from the wrist. Near her lay the ax with which the murderous deed had been committed. In one of the bedrooms six of the children were found, one in bed and the others scattered about the floor. They were all dead. Their brains had evidently been dashed out with a club, and every mark about them seemed to have been made with a blunt instrument. The children must have struggled hard for their lives, as articles of clothing and broken furniture were strewn about the room in the utmost confusion. Julia and Emma, aged respectively fourteen and seventeen, were found in the kitchen, bruised and insensible, but it is thought their recovery is possible. The eldest girl, Mary, must have taken refuge, in her terror, in the garret, as her body was found there, frightfully mutilated, and the knife with which her wounds had been inflicted still sticking in her side. The two girls, Julia and Emma, who had recovered sufficiently to be able to talk yesterday morning, state that their father knocked them down with a billet of wood and stamped on them. They think they were the first attacked. They further state that Hopkins had shown evidence of derangement all day, but had exhibited no violence. He flew into a passion and attempted to murder them because they advised him to go to bed and compose his mind. Curry says Hopkins was about forty-two years of age, and a native of Western Pennsylvania; he was always affable and polite, and until very recently we had never heard of his ill treating his family. He had been a heavy owner in the best mines of Virginia and Gold Hill, but when the San Francisco papers exposed the game of cooking dividends in order to bolster up our stocks he grew afraid and sold out, and invested to an immense amount in the Spring Valley Water Company of San Francisco. He was advised to do this by a relative of his, one of the editors of the San Francisco *Bulletin,* who had suffered pecuniarily by the dividend-cooking system as applied to the Daney Mining Company recently. Hopkins had not long ceased to own in the various claims on the Comstock lead, however, when several dividends were cooked on his newly acquired property, their water totally dried up, and Spring Valley stock went down to nothing. It is presumed that this misfortune drove him mad and resulted in his killing himself and the greater portion of his family. The newspapers of San Francisco permitted this water company to go on borrowing money and cooking dividends, under cover of which cunning financiers crept out of the tottering concern, leaving the crash to come upon poor and unsuspecting stockholders, without offering to expose the villainy at work. We hope the fearful massacre detailed above may prove the saddest result of their silence.

67. *Letter from Mark Twain*

17 November 1863

This letter was written in Carson City on Sunday, 15 November 1863, and probably appeared on Tuesday, November 17, in the Virginia City *Territorial Enterprise*. The text is taken from an *Enterprise* clipping in one of Mark Twain's scrapbooks.

The elaborately casual tone of this sequel to "A Bloody Massacre near Carson" (no. 66) cannot disguise its painfully contrived nature—a failing which may betray Clemens' concern over some of the blistering newspaper criticism of his original hoax. His allusion in the postscript to the editor of the San Francisco *Evening Journal* is probably explained by A. C. Benham's assertion in that paper of November 2: "We are not fond of hoaxing our readers, and hereby give the *Enterprise* notice that as long as they keep the author of that hoax in their employ we shall not trouble their columns for news matter."[1]

---

[1]Quoted in *MTVC*, p. 103.

Letter from Mark Twain

CARSON, November 15, 1863.

EDITORS ENTERPRISE:—"Compiled by our own Reporter!" Thus the Virginia Union of this morning gobbles up the labors of another man. That "Homographic Record of the Constitutional Convention" was compiled by Mr. Gillespie, Secretary of the Convention, at odd moments snatched from the incessant duties of his position, and unassisted by "our own reporter" or anybody else. Now this isn't fair, you know. Give the devil his due—by which metaphor I refer to Gillespie, but in an entirely inoffensive manner, I trust; and do not go and give the credit of this work to one who is not entitled to it. I copied that chart myself, and sent it to you yesterday, and I don't see why you couldn't have come out and done the complimentary thing, by claiming its paternity for me. In that case, I should not have mentioned this matter at all. But the main object of the present letter is to furnish you with the revolting details of—

ANOTHER BLOODY MASSACRE!

A massacre, in which no less than a thousand human beings were deprived of life without a moment's warning of the terrible fate that was in store for them. This ghastly tragedy was the work of a single individual—a man whose character was gifted with many strong points, among which were great benevolence and generosity, and a kindness of heart which rendered him susceptible of being persuaded to do things which were really, at times, injurious to himself, and which noble trait in his nature made him a very slave to those whom he loved—a man whose disposition was a model of mildness until a fancied wrong drove him mad and impelled him to the commission of this monstrous crime—this wholesale offering of blood to the angry spirit of revenge which rankled in his bosom. It is said that some of his victims were so gashed, and torn, and mutilated, that they scarcely retained a semblance of human shape. As nearly as I can get at the facts in the case—and I have taken unusual pains in collecting them —the dire misfortune occurred about as follows: It seems that certain enemies ill-treated this man, and in revenge he burned a large amount of property belonging to them. They arrested him, and bound him hand and foot and brought him down to Lehi, the county seat, for trial. And the Spirit of the Lord came mightily upon him, and the cords that were upon his arms became as flax that was burnt with fire, and his bands loosed from off his hands. And he found a new jaw-bone of an ass, and put forth his hand and took it, and slew a thousand men therewith. When he had finished his terrible tragedy, the desperado, criminal (whose name is Samson), deliberately wiped his bloody weapon upon the leg of his pantaloons, and then tried its edge upon his thumb, as a barber would a razor, simply remarking, "With the jaw-bone of an ass, heaps upon heaps, with the jaw of an ass have I slain a thousand men." He even seemed to reflect with satisfaction upon what he had done, and to derive great comfort from it—as if he would say, "ONLY a mere thousand—Oh, no I ain't on it, I reckon."

I am sorry that it was necessary for me to furnish you with a narrative of this nature, because my efforts in this line have lately been received with some degree of suspicion; yet it is my inexorable duty to keep your readers posted, and I will not be recreant to the trust, even though the very people whom I try to serve, upbraid me.

MARK TWAIN.

P. S.—Now keep dark, will you? I am hatching a deep plot. I am "laying," as it were, for the editor of that San Francisco Evening Journal. The massacre I have related above is all true, but it occurred a good while ago. Do you see my drift? I shall catch that fool. He will look carefully through his Gold Hill and Virginia exchanges, and when he finds nothing in them about Samson killing a thousand men, he will think it is another hoax, and come out on me again, in his feeble way, as he did before. I shall have him foul, then, and I will never let up on him in the world, (as we say in Virginia.) I expect it will worry him some, to find out at last, that one Samson actually did kill a thousand men with the jawbone of one of his ancestors, and he never heard of it before.

MARK.

68. A Tide of Eloquence

1–3 December 1863

On 6 December 1863 the San Francisco *Golden Era* published this brief excerpt from what must have been Mark Twain's much longer account in the Virginia City *Territorial Enterprise*, which is not extant. In their preface the editors of the *Golden Era* commented that "'Mark Twain' . . . lately attended a presentation affair at Virginia City, and distinguished himself— in his own words." Very probably this "affair" was the ball and supper given on November 30 at Sutliffe's Hall by the Virginia City Eagle Engine Company No. 3, which five hundred people attended. Such balls were often the occasion for presenting garlands, wreaths, and other tokens, and the presumption must be that Mark Twain was asked to speak. He already had a reputation as an after-dinner speaker, and in this case we know that he returned to Virginia City that weekend from Carson City, where he had been reporting the first Constitutional Convention.[1] Since the Virginia City *Evening Bulletin* published its account of the ball on December 1, Mark Twain's account must have appeared in the *Enterprise* on the same day or shortly thereafter.

---

[1]Virginia City *Evening Bulletin:* "Arrivals Yesterday and To-day," 28 November 1863, p. 2; "Sutliffe's Hall," 30 November 1863, p. 3; "The Ball Last Night," 1 December 1863, p. 3.

A Tide of Eloquence

AFTERWARDS, Mr. Mark Twain being enthusiastically called upon, arose, and without previous preparation, burst forth in a tide of eloquence so grand, so luminous, so beautiful and so resplendent with the gorgeous fires of genius, that the audience were spell-bound by the magic of his words, and gazed in silent wonder in each other's faces as men who felt that they were listening to one gifted with inspiration [Applause.] The proceedings did not end here, but at this point we deemed it best to stop reporting and go to dissipating, as the dread solitude of our position as a sober, rational Christian, in the midst of the driveling and besotted multitude around us, had begun to shroud our spirits with a solemn sadness tinged with fear. At ten o'clock the curtain fell.

69. Letter from Mark Twain

19–20 January 1864

Like "Examination of Teachers" (no. 48) and "An Excellent School" (no. 71), the present sketch contains a vivid testimony to Clemens' interest and pleasure in observing children at work in the classroom. As he admits in the letter itself, the subject literally absorbed him beyond his expectations, and he wrote "a dozen pages" that ultimately left out all other matters of "current news of the day." The immediate object of this letter, and of his later piece ("An Excellent School"), was to encourage the passage of a school appropriation bill soon to come before the third Territorial Legislature. Miss Hannah K. Clapp and Mrs. E. G. Cutler together ran one of two private schools in Carson City;[1] the other was run by William B. Lawlor. But this letter makes it apparent that Clemens was far more taken with the "absorbing delight in educational gossip" than his immediate task demanded: his interest was indeed literary, and as Henry Nash Smith pointed out, "every reader will recognize in the description of Miss Clapp's school . . . material which ten years later would go into the 'Examination Evening' scene in chapter xxi of *Tom Sawyer*."[2]

---

[1]Myron Angel, *History of Nevada* (Oakland: Thompson and West, 1881), p. 220.
[2]*MTEnt*, p. 22.

Letter from Mark Twain

MISS CLAPP'S SCHOOL.

BY AUTHORITY OF an invitation from Hon. Wm. M. Gillespie, member of the House Committee on Colleges and Common Schools, I accompanied that statesman on an unofficial visit to the excellent school of Miss Clapp and Mrs. Cutler, this afternoon. The air was soft and balmy—the sky was cloudless and serene—the odor of flowers floated upon the idle breeze—the glory of the sun descended like a benediction upon mountain and meadow and plain—the wind blew like the very devil, and the day was generally disagreeable.

The school—however, I will mention, first that a charter for an educational institution to be called the Sierra Seminary, was granted to Miss Clapp during the Legislative session of 1861, and a bill will be introduced while the present Assembly is in session, asking an appropriation of $20,000 to aid the enterprise. Such a sum of money could not be more judiciously expended, and I doubt not the bill will pass.

The present school is a credit both to the teachers and the town. It now numbers about forty pupils, I should think, and is well and systematically conducted. The exercises this afternoon were of a character not likely to be unfamiliar to the free American citizen who has a fair recollection of how he used to pass his Friday afternoons in the days of his youth. The tactics have undergone some changes, but these variations are not important. In former times a fellow took

his place in the luminous spelling class in the full consciousness that
if he spelled cat with a "k," or indulged in any other little orthograph-
ical eccentricities of a similar nature, he would be degraded to the
foot or sent to his seat; whereas, he keeps his place in the ranks now,
in such cases, and his punishment is simply to "'bout face." Johnny
Eaves stuck to his first position, to-day, long after the balance of the
class had rounded to, but he subsequently succumbed to the word
"nape," which he persisted in ravishing of its final vowel. There was
nothing irregular about that. Your rightly-constructed schoolboy will
spell a multitude of hard words without hesitating once, and then
lose his grip and miss fire on the easiest one in the book.

The fashion of reading selections of prose and poetry remains the
same; and so does the youthful manner of doing that sort of thing.
Some pupils read poetry with graceful ease and correct expression,
and others place the rising and falling inflection at measured intervals, as if they had learned the lesson on a "see-saw;" but then they
go undulating through a stanza with such an air of unctuous satisfaction, that it is a comfort to be around when they are at it.

> "The boy—stoo-dawn—the bur—ning deck—
> When-sawl—but *him* had fled—
> The flames—that shook—the battle—zreck—
> Shone round—him *o'er*—the dead."

That is the old-fashioned *impressive* style—stately, slow-moving
and solemn. It is in vogue yet among scholars of tender age. It always
will be. Ever since Mrs. Hemans wrote that verse, it has suited the
pleasure of juveniles to emphasize the word "him," and lay atrocious
stress upon that other word "o'er," whether she liked it or not; and
I am prepared to believe that they will continue this practice unto the
end of time, and with the same indifference to Mrs. Hemans' opinions
about it, or any body's else.

They sing in school, now-a-days, which is an improvement upon
the ancient regime; and they don't catch flies and throw spit-balls
at the teacher, as they used to do in my time—which is another improvement, in a general way. Neither do the boys and girls keep a
sharp look-out on each other's shortcomings and report the same at
headquarters, as was a custom of by-gone centuries. And this reminds

me of Gov. Nye's last anecdote, fulminated since the delivery of his message, and consequently not to be found in that document. The company were swapping old school reminiscences, and in due season they got to talking about that extinct species of tell-tales that were once to be found in all minor educational establishments, and who never failed to detect and impartially denounce every infraction of the rules that occurred among their mates. The Governor said that he threw a casual glance at a pretty girl on the next bench one day, and she complained to the teacher—which was entirely characteristic, you know. Says she, "Mister Jones, Warren Nye's looking at me." Whereupon, without a suggestion from anybody, up jumped an infamous, lisping, tow-headed young miscreant, and says he, "Yeth, thir, I *thee* him do it!" I doubt if the old original boy got off that ejaculation with more gusto than the Governor throws into it.

The "compositions" read to-day were as exactly like the compositions I used to hear read in our school as one baby's nose is exactly like all other babies' noses. I mean the old principal ear-marks were all there: the cutting to the bone of the subject with the very first gash, without any preliminary foolishness in the way of a gorgeous introductory; the inevitable and persevering tautology; the brief, monosyllabic sentences (beginning, as a very general thing, with the pronoun "I"); the penchant for presenting rigid, uncompromising facts for the consideration of the hearer, rather than ornamental fancies; the depending for the success of the composition upon its general merits, without tacking artificial aids to the end of it, in the shape of deductions, or conclusions, or clap-trap climaxes, albeit their absence sometimes imparts to these essays the semblance of having come to an end before they were finished—of arriving at full speed at a jumping-off place and going suddenly overboard, as it were, leaving a sensation such as one feels when he stumbles without previous warning upon that infernal "To be Continued" in the midst of a thrilling magazine story. I know there are other styles of school compositions, but these are the characteristics of the style which I have in my eye at present. I do not know why this one has particularly suggested itself to my mind, unless the literary effort of one of the boys there to-day left with me an unusually vivid impression. It ran something in this wise:

COMPOSITION.

"I like horses. Where we lived before we came here, we used to have a cutter and horses. We used to ride in it. I like winter. I like snow. I used to have a pony all to myself, where I used to live before I came here. Once it drifted a good deal—very deep—and when it stopped I went out and got in it."

That was all. There was no climax to it, except the spasmodic bow which the tautological little student jerked at the school as he closed his labors.

Two remarkably good compositions were read. Miss P.'s was much the best of these—but aside from its marked literary excellence, it possessed another merit which was peculiarly gratifying to my feelings just at that time. Because it took the conceit out of young Gillespie as completely as perspiration takes the starch out of a shirt-collar. In his insufferable vanity, that feeble member of the House of Representatives had been assuming imposing attitudes, and beaming upon the pupils with an expression of benignant imbecility which was calculated to inspire them with the conviction that there was only one guest of any consequence in the house. Therefore, it was an unspeakable relief to me to see him forced to shed his dignity. Concerning the composition, however. After detailing the countless pleasures which had fallen to her lot during the holidays, the authoress finished with a proviso, in substance as follows—I have forgotten the precise language: "But I have no cheerful reminiscences of Christmas. It was dreary, monotonous and insipid to the last degree. Mr. Gillespie called early, and remained the greater part of the day!" You should have seen the blooming Gillespie wilt when that literary bombshell fell in his camp! The charm of the thing lay in the fact that that last naive sentence was the only suggestion offered in the way of accounting for the dismal character of the occasion. However, to my mind it was sufficient—entirely sufficient.

Since writing the above, I have seen the architectural plans and specifications for Miss Clapp and Mrs. Cutler's proposed "Sierra Seminary" building. It will be a handsome two-story edifice, one hundred feet square, and will accommodate forty "boarders" and any number of pupils beside, who may board elsewhere. Constructed of wood, it will cost $12,000; or of stone, $18,000. Miss Clapp has devoted ten acres of ground to the use and benefit of the institution.

I sat down intending to write a dozen pages of variegated news. I have about accomplished the task—all except the "variegated." I have economised in the matter of current news of the day, considerably more than I purposed to do, for every item of that nature remains stored away in my mind in a very unwritten state, and will afford unnecessarily ample material for another letter. It is useless material, though, I suspect, because, inasmuch as I have failed to incorporate it into this, I fear me I shall not feel industrious enough to weave out of it another letter until it has become too stale to be interesting. Well, never mind—we must learn to take an absorbing delight in educational gossip; nine-tenths of the revenues of the Territory go into the bottomless gullet of that ravenous school fund, you must bear in mind.

MARK TWAIN.

70. *Winters' New House*

12 February 1864

This sketch of Theodore Winters' new house in Washoe Valley forms the first section of a "Letter from Mark Twain" written on Friday, 5 February 1864, from Carson City.[1] It survives in a clipping in one of Mark Twain's scrapbooks; a banner headline for the Virginia City *Territorial Enterprise* of February 12 has been pasted above it. Presumably Clemens was a little slow in mailing his dispatch from Carson City.

Clemens knew Winters well. In October 1863 he had reported Winters' connection with the First Annual Fair of the Washoe Agricultural, Mining and Mechanical Society. And shortly before Clemens visited Winters' home and described it in this sketch, his host and A. W. (Sandy) Baldwin had presented him with a handsome gold watch inscribed "To Gov. Mark Twain" of the Third House of the 1863 Nevada Constitutional Convention.[2] In 1905, the year before Winters died, Clemens remembered him as one of the "unforgettable antiques" of his Nevada days.[3]

Winters migrated from Illinois to Forest City, California, in 1849. There he joined his father and his two brothers, Joseph and John D., in cattle raising, placer mining, and freighting to the California mining camps and to settlements in Carson Valley. At the time of the Mormon exodus from Nevada in 1857, he acquired a mile-square tract of land in Washoe Valley southwest of Washoe City and north of Washoe Lake. Two years later he struck it rich when a mining stake that his brother Joseph had bought turned out to be on the Ophir vein. Winters became a principal stockholder in the Spanish mine and for a time managed its Virginia City mill. He was

---

[1] The second section is "An Excellent School" (no. 71).

[2] *MTEnt*, pp. 85, 145.

[3] Clemens to Robert Fulton, 24 May 1905, *MTL*, 2:773.

a member of the Nevada Territorial Legislature of 1862 but thereafter remained politically inactive until 1890, when he ran (unsuccessfully) as the Democratic candidate for governor of Nevada.

The party Clemens attended at Winters' house was given by Theodore's brother Joseph and by Pete Hopkins, two men who, like Theodore, were leading figures in western horseracing circles—a sport which also interested Clemens.[4] Winters' three-story mansion, no less than Sandy Bowers' house a few miles away, was a Washoe Valley showplace comparable in elegance and conspicuous consumption to the Hartford house that Clemens erected a decade later. Aided by John A. Steele, a Washoe City architect and contractor, Winters had planned his house in 1860 and completed its construction in 1863. The solidly built, luxuriously furnished structure was amply proportioned for Winters' large family. It was set among well-tended gardens, and nearby were a pool and a quarter-mile racecourse where Winters trained and raced his famous thoroughbreds. Eventually Winters' Rancho del Sierra stretched over four thousand acres of land, and there he outlived the nineteenth century raising hay and grain for his cattle, operating a dairy, and cultivating large orchards.[5]

---

[4]See "How I Went to the Great Race between Lodi and Norfolk" (no. 103) and Edgar M. Branch, "Mark Twain Reports the Races in Sacramento," *Huntington Library Quarterly* 32 (February 1969): 179–186.

[5]Myra Sauer Ratay, *Pioneers of the Ponderosa* (Sparks, Nevada: Western Printing and Publishing Co., 1973), pp. 293–328; Thomas Wren, ed., *A History of the State of Nevada: Its Resources and People* (New York: Lewis Publishing Co., 1904), pp. 479–481. A photograph of Winters' house is reproduced in *MTEnt*, illustration no. 16.

Winters' New House

THEODORE WINTERS' handsome dwelling in Washoe Valley, is an eloquent witness in behalf of Mr. Steele's architectural skill. The basement story is built of brick, and the spacious court which surrounds it, and whose columns support the verandah above, is paved with large, old-fashioned tiles. On this floor is the kitchen, dining-room, bath-room, bed chambers for servants, and a commodious store-room, with shelves laden with all manner of substantials and luxuries for the table. All these apartments are arranged in the most convenient manner, and are fitted and furnished handsomely and plainly, but expensively. Water pipes are numerous in this part of the house, and the fluid they carry is very pure, and cold and clear. On the next floor above, are two unusually large drawing-rooms, richly furnished, and gotten up in every respect with faultless taste—which is a remark one is seldom enabled to apply to parlors and drawing-rooms on this coast. The colors in the carpets, curtains, etc., are of a warm and cheerful nature, but there is nothing gaudy about them. The ceilings are decorated with pure, white mouldings of graceful pattern. Two large bed-chambers adjoin the parlors, and are supplied with elaborately carved black walnut four-hundred-dollar bedsteads, similar to those used by Dan and myself in Virginia; the remainder of the furniture of these chambers is correspondingly sumptuous and expensive. On the floor above are half a dozen comfortable bed-rooms for the accommodation of visitors; also a spacious billiard-room which will shortly be graced by a table of superb workmanship.

341

The windows of the house are of the "Gothic" style, and set with stained glass; the chandeliers are of bronze; the stair railings of polished black walnut, and the principal doors of some kind of dark-colored wood—mahogany, I suppose. There are two peculiarly pleasant features about this house—the ceilings are high, and the halls of unusual width. The building—above the basement story—is of wood, and strongly and compactly put together. It stands upon tolerably high ground, and from its handsome verandah, Mr. Winters can see every portion of his vast farm. From the stables to the parlors, the house and its belongings is a model of comfort, convenience and substantial elegance; everything is of the best that could be had, and there is no circus flummery visible about the establishment.

I went out there to a party a short time ago, in the night, behind a pair of Cormack's fast horses, with John James. On account of losing the trail of the telegraph poles, we wandered out among the shingle machines in the Sierras, and were delayed several hours. We arrived in time, however, to take a large share in the festivities which were being indulged in by the Governor and the Supreme Court and some twenty other guests. The party was given by Messrs. Joe Winters and Pete Hopkins, (at Theodore Winters' expense,) as a slight testimonial of their regard for the friends they invited to be present. There was nothing to detract from the pleasure of the occasion, except Lovejoy, who detracted most of the wines and liquors from it.

71. *An Excellent School*

12 February 1864

This sketch forms the second section of a "Letter from Mark Twain" written from Carson City on Friday, 5 February 1864, and published in the Virginia City *Territorial Enterprise* on February 12.[1]

The school described in this sketch, conducted by William B. Lawlor, was one of two private schools in Carson City. (See the headnote to "Letter from Mark Twain," no. 69, for Clemens' practical reasons for writing about the schools at this time.)

---

[1]The first section is "Winters' New House" (no. 70). A final section, "Concerning Undertakers," is scheduled to appear in the collection of social and political writings in The Works of Mark Twain. It is reprinted in *MTEnt*, pp. 151–152.

An Excellent School

I EXPECT Mr. Lawlor keeps the best private school in the Territory—or the best school of any kind, for that matter. I attended one of his monthly examinations a week ago, or such a matter, with Mr. Clagett, and we arrived at the conclusion that one might acquire a good college education there within the space of six months. Mr. Lawlor's is a little crib of a school-house, papered from floor to ceiling with black-boards adorned with impossible mathematical propositions done in white chalk. The effect is bewildering, to the stranger, but otherwise he will find the place comfortable enough. When we arrived, the teacher was talking in a rambling way upon a great many subjects, like a member of the House speaking to a point of order, and three boys were making verbatim reports of his remarks in Graham's phonographic short-hand on the walls of the school-room. These pupils had devoted half an hour to the study and practice of this accomplishment every day for the past four or five months, and the result was a proficiency usually attained only after eighteen months of application. It was amazing. Mr. Lawlor has so simplified the art of teaching in every department of instruction, that I am confident he could impart a thorough education in a short time to any individual who has as much as a spoonful of brains to work upon. It is in no spirit of extravagance that I set it down here as my serious conviction that Mr. Lawlor could even take one of our Miss Nancy "Meriden" Prosecuting Attorneys and post him up so in a month or two that he could tell his own witnesses from those of the defense in nine cases out of ten. Mind, I do not give this as an absolute certainty, but merely as an opinion of mine—and one which is open to grave doubts, too, I am willing to confess, now, when I come to think calmly and dispassionately about it. No—the truth is, the more I think of it, the more I weaken. I expect I spoke too soon—went off before I was primed, as it were. With your permission, I will take it all back. I know two or three prosecuting attorneys, and I am satisfied the foul density of their intellects would put out any intellectual candle that Mr. Lawlor could lower into them. I do not say that a Higher Power could not miraculously illuminate them. No, I only say I would rather see it first. A man always has more confidence in a thing after he has seen it, you know: at least that is the way with me. But to proceed with that school. Mr. Clagett invited one of those phonographic boys—Master Barry Ashim—to come and practice his short-hand in the House of Representatives. He accepted the invitation, and in accordance with resolutions offered by Messrs. Clagett and Stewart, he was tendered the compliment of a seat on the floor of the House during the session, and the Sergeant-at-Arms instructed to furnish him with a desk and such stationery as he might require. He has already become a reporter of no small pretensions. There is a class in Mr. Lawlor's school composed of children three months old and upwards, who know the spelling-book by heart. If you ask them what the first word is, in any given lesson, they will tell you in a moment, and then go on and spell every word (thirty-five) in the lesson, without once referring to the book or making a mistake. Again, you may mention a word and they will tell you which particular lesson it is in, and what words precede it and follow it. Then, again, you may propound an abstruse grammatical enigma, and the school will solve it in chorus—will tell you what language is correct, and what isn't; and why and wherefore; and quote rules and illustrations until you wish you hadn't said anything. Two or three doses of this kind will convince a man that there are youngsters in this school who know everything about grammar that can be learned, and what is just as important, can explain what they know so that other people can understand it. But when those fellows get to figuring, let second-rate mathematicians stand from under! For behold, it is their strong suit. They work miracles on a black-board with a piece of chalk. Witchcraft and sleight-of-hand, and all that sort of thing is foolishness to the facility with which they can figure a moral impossibility down to an infallible result. They only require about a dozen figures to do a sum which by all ordinary methods would consume a hundred and fifty. These fellows could cypher a week on a sheet of foolscap. They can find out anything they want to with figures, and they are very quick about it, too. You tell them, for instance, that you were born in such and such a place, on such and such a day of the month, in such and such a year, and they will tell you in an instant how old your grandmother is. I have never seen any banker's clerks who could begin to cypher with those boys. It has been Virginia's unchristian policy to grab everything that was of any account that ever came into the Territory—Virginia could do many a worse thing than to grab this school and move it into the shadow of Mount Davidson, teacher and all.

72. Those Blasted Children

21 February 1864

In mid-December 1863 Artemus Ward visited Virginia City, where he lectured successfully and, in company with Mark Twain, Dan De Quille, and other members of the *Territorial Enterprise* staff, participated in what Albert Bigelow Paine called "a period of continuous celebration."[1] Mark Twain and Ward became good friends and remained so until his untimely death in March 1867. In fact, Ward was soon so impressed by Mark Twain's talents that he volunteered an endorsement of his work to the New York *Sunday Mercury*, a well-known eastern weekly. Moreover, Clemens told his mother, when Ward realized that Mark Twain's "gorgeous talents" were being publicly acknowledged in San Francisco, he urged the author to appreciate them himself, and even to "leave sage-brush obscurity, & journey to New York with him." Clemens added, with mock arrogance, "I preferred not to burst upon the New York public too suddenly & brilliantly, & so I concluded to remain here."[2]

But the new audience represented by the *Mercury* was not to be so casually dismissed. Ward wrote Mark Twain from Austin, Nevada, on 1 January 1864, reiterating his recent promise: "I shall write soon, a powerfully convincing note to my friends of 'The Mercury.' "[3] The letter did not reach Clemens in Carson City until January 9 or 10, and by then he had already written and presumably mailed his first contribution to the eastern press since the Philadelphia *American Courier* had published his youthful

---

[1]*MTL*, 1:93.

[2]Clemens to Jane Clemens, 1–9 January 1864, *CL1*, letter 76. Internal evidence shows that this letter must have been written after Ward left Virginia City on December 31, but before Clemens wrote his family on January 10; he probably wrote it on January 8 or 9.

[3]Ward to Clemens, 1 January 1864, *MTL*, 1:94.

"Hannibal, Missouri" (no. 3) in 1852. The sketch, called "Doings in Nevada," a lively, satirical account of efforts to draft a constitution for the emerging state of Nevada, was written on January 4 and appeared in the *Mercury* on February 7.[4] "Doings in Nevada" is very much in Mark Twain's best manner, and it surmounts the difficulty of addressing an eastern audience about western subjects with great inventiveness and humor. Mark Twain must have recognized this, for shortly after writing it he advised his family that at Ward's suggestion he intended to "write semi-occasionally for the New York Sunday Mercury," although he did not have the time to do so regularly. "But I sometimes throw a pearl before these swine here (there's no self-conceit about that, I beg you to observe,) which ought, for the eternal welfare of my race, to have a more extended circulation than is afforded by a local daily paper."[5]

"Those Blasted Children" appeared in the *Mercury* only two weeks after this first effort: it was introduced by a preface entitled "Important to Parents," in which Clemens was billed as "our unique correspondent, 'Mark Twain.'" Clemens completed the sketch during a long night session lasting until 7 A.M. of January 10—only six days after writing "Doings in Nevada" and about the time he actually received Ward's encouraging letter from Austin. Clemens told his family that he spent the early part of the evening of January 9 socializing, but that he "wrote the balance of the night—an article for the New York Sunday Mercury. If I send it at all, it will be in a few days, & consequently it may appear the first Sunday or so after you get this."[6] It was published on February 21.

The subject and many of the details of "Those Blasted Children" suggest that Mark Twain had begun it the previous year, during or following his spring and fall visits to San Francisco. It is dated, for instance, "Lick House, San Francisco, Wednesday, 1863," even though it was manifestly completed in January 1864 in Carson City. It is a rather heavy-handed, imperfectly executed comic sketch, more self-conscious and less controlled than "Doings in Nevada." Mark Twain's delay in finishing the piece, as well as his hesitation about sending it, both suggest that he was aware of its limitations.

To his family he emphasized his desire to needle his old friend Zeb Leavenworth, the steamboat pilot to whom he had given a ridiculous role in

---

[4]Mark Twain published extracts from Ward's letter in a letter to the *Enterprise* dated 10 January 1864, and he explained, "I received a letter from Artemus Ward, to-day, dated 'Austin, January 1'" (*MTEnt*, p. 129). "Doings in Nevada" is scheduled to appear in the collection of social and political writings in The Works of Mark Twain. It is reprinted in *MTEnt*, pp. 121–126.

[5]Clemens to Jane Clemens, 1–9 January 1864, *CL1*, letter 76.

[6]Clemens to Jane Clemens and Pamela Moffett, 10 January 1864, *CL1*, letter 77.

the sketch: "You tell Beck Jolly to get a lot of those papers & stick them around everywhere there is anyone acquainted with Zeb Leavenworth, & drive the old fool into the river. The article contains an absurd certificate for a patent medicine, purporting to come from 'Mr. Zeb. Leavenworth, of St. Louis, Mo.' I wrote it especially for Beck Jolly's use—so he could pester Zeb."[7] This alludes, of course, to a testimonial supporting Mark Twain's alleged remedy for stammering ("remove the under-jaw"). The comic device of suggesting lethal remedies for minor complaints may have been borrowed from George H. Derby (John Phoenix). Derby's "Antidote for Fleas" had advocated coating the body with tar or dipping the bitten part into boiling water.[8] To Derby's medical mayhem Mark Twain added his own pose of savage child destroyer. And in the instance of Zeb Leavenworth's letter, he devised a burlesque of the extravagant advertisements and testimonials for patent medicines that could be found in most newspapers. In San Francisco, for example, Dr. J. C. Ayer touted his "Cathartic Pills," good for almost anything, including erysipelas, dropsy, worms, and gout. Dr. J. F. Gibbon's "Female Pills" were "a sovereign remedy . . . in all Hypochondriac, Hysteric or Vaporish disorders" of both sexes. Dr. Czapkay featured a half column of fulsome testimonials like that of his patient M. Michels, who, having suffered from "headache, fearfulness, want of confidence, dizziness, restlessness, weakness in the limbs, loss of memory, confusion of ideas" and many other symptoms, poured out the gratitude of a cured man: "My existence had become a burthen to me, and nothing afforded me the least gratification, whilst now, I feel perfectly well and can enjoy life to my entire satisfaction."[9] The writers of such testimonials, like Zeb Leavenworth in the sketch, invariably concluded by granting the doctor permission to make their letters public for the good of mankind.

Mark Twain's list of remedies seems to have been grafted onto the first half of the sketch, his account of the raucous children who besiege him in his room at the Lick House—a story which he may have had some difficulty resolving to his satisfaction. The first portion of the sketch is noteworthy, however, because it is an early instance of Mark Twain's interest in children's psychology and his use of colloquial speech as a means of satirizing adult pretensions. Although the children are not well differentiated as characters, their function is really to serve as an effective chorus opposing the solitary, reflective, romantically inclined character of Mark Twain,

---

[7]Clemens to Jane Clemens and Pamela Moffett, 10 January 1864, *CL1*, letter 77.

[8]John Phoenix [George H. Derby], *Phoenixiana; or, Sketches and Burlesques* (New York: D. Appleton and Co., 1856), pp. 71–72.

[9]San Francisco *Evening Bulletin*, 26 December 1863, p. 4; San Francisco *Evening Journal*, 8 January 1863, p. 4.

who, as he tries to write, luxuriates in memories of the pleasant past. It is of interest as well that Mark Twain probably used the names of real offspring of prominent San Francisco citizens—a kind of private joke that may suggest he originally planned to publish the sketch in a paper like the San Francisco *Golden Era*, which indeed reprinted it from the *Mercury* on 27 March 1864. Ada Clare, writing in that paper early in April, declared that Mark Twain had misunderstood "God's little people."[10]

"Those Blasted Children" was the last sketch Mark Twain contributed to the *Mercury* until he resumed writing for it in 1867, although on 18 March 1864 he told his sister, Pamela, that he planned "in a day or two" to address his mother "through the columns of the N. Y. Sunday Mercury."[11] The sketch he alluded to may never have been written, or it may have been an early version of "An Open Letter to the American People" (no. 181), which teases his mother about her style of letter writing; it was not published in the *Mercury* but in the New York *Weekly Review*, almost two years later, on 17 February 1866.[12] In brief, Mark Twain did not carry out his plan to "write semi-occasionally" for the *Mercury*—perhaps because the editors were not satisfied with "Those Blasted Children," or perhaps because he was still too diffident about pursuing his eastern audience with much tenacity.

---

[10]*Golden Era* 12 (3 April 1864): 4.

[11]Clemens to Pamela Moffett, 18 March 1864, *CL1*, letter 80.

[12]"An Open Letter to the American People" was reprinted in the 1867 *Jumping Frog* book, where it was retitled "A Complaint about Correspondents"; see the textual commentary to no. 181.

Those Blasted Children

LICK HOUSE, SAN FRANCISCO, Wednesday, 1863.

EDITORS T.T.:—No. 165 is a pleasant room. It is situated at the head of a long hall, down which, on either side, are similar rooms occupied by sociable bachelors, and here and there one tenanted by an unsociable nurse or so. Charley Creed sleeps in No. 157. He is my time-piece —or, at least, his boots are. If I look down the hall and see Charley's boots still before his door, I know it is early yet, and I may hie me sweetly to bed again. But if those unerring boots are gone, I know it is after eleven o'clock, and time for me to be rising with the lark. This reminds me of the lark of yesterday and last night, which was altogether a different sort of bird from the one I am talking about now. Ah me! Summer girls and summer dresses, and summer scenes at the "Willows", Seal Rock Point, and the grim sea-lions wallowing in the angry surf; glimpses through the haze of stately ships far away at sea; a dash along the smooth beach, and the exhilaration of watching the white waves come surging ashore, and break into seething foam about the startled horse's feet; reveries beside the old wreck, half buried in sand, and compassion for the good ship's fate; home again in a soft twilight, oppressed with the odor of flowers—home again to San Francisco, drunk, perhaps, but not disorderly. Dinner at six, with ladies and gentlemen, dressed with faultless taste and elegance, and all drunk, apparently, but very quiet and well-bred—unaccountably so, under the circumstances, it seemed to my cloudy brain. Many things happened after that, I remember—such as visiting some of their haunts with those dissipated Golden Era fellows, and—

Here come those young savages again—those noisy and inevitable children. God be with them!—or they with him, rather, if it be not asking too much. They are another time-piece of mine. It is two o'clock now; they are invested with their regular lunch, and have come up here to settle it. I will soothe my troubled spirit with a short season of blasphemy, after which I will expose their infamous proceedings with a relentless pen. They have driven me from labor many and many a time; but behold! the hour of retribution is at hand.

That is young Washington Billings, now—a little dog in long flaxen curls and Highland costume.

"Hi, Johnny! look through the keyhole! here's that feller with a long nose, writing again—less stir him up!" [A double kick against the door—a grand infant war-hoop in full chorus—and then a clatter of scampering feet down the echoing corridors.] Ah—one of them has fallen, and hurt himself. I hear the intelligent foreign nurse boxing his ears for it (the parents, Mr. and Mrs. Kerosene, having gone up to Sacramento on the evening boat, and left their offspring properly cared for.)

Here they come again, as soldiers—infantry. I know there are not more than thirty or forty of them, yet they are under no sort of discipline, and they make noise enough for a thousand. Young Oliver Higgins is in command. They assault my works—they try to carry my position by storm—they finally draw off with boistrous cheers, to harrass a handful of skirmishers thrown out by the enemy—a bevy of chambermaids.

Once more they come trooping down the hall. This time as cavalry. They must have captured and disarmed the skirmishers, for half my young ruffians are mounted on broomsticks. They make a reconnoissance in force. They attack my premises in a body, but they achieve nothing approaching a success. I am too strongly intrenched for them.

They invest my stronghold, and lay siege to it—that is to say, they sit down before my camp, and betake themselves to the pastimes of youth. All talking at once, as they do, their conversation is amusing, but not instructive to me.

"Ginn me some o' that you're eat'n." "I won't—you wouldn't lemme play with that dead rat, the peanut-boy give you yesterday." "Well! I don't care; I reckon I know summun't you don't; Oho, Mr. Smarty, 'n' I ain't a goin' to tell you, neither; now, see what you got by

it; it's summun't my ma said about your ma, too. I'll tell you, if you'll
gimme ever so little o' that, will you? Well." (I imagine from the break
in this conversation, while the other besiegers go on talking noisily,
that a compromise is being effected.) "There, don't take so much.
Now, what'd she say?" "Why, ma told my pa 't if your ma is so mighty
rich now she wasn't nobody till she come to Sanf'cisco. That's what
she said." "Your ma's a big story-teller, 'n' I'm goin' jes' as straight as
I can walk, 'n' tell my ma. You'll see what she'll do." (I foresee a
diversion in one or two family circles.) "Flora Low, you quit pulling
that doll's legs out, it's mine." "Well, take your old doll, then. I'd thank
you to know, Miss Florence Hillyer, 't my pa's Governor, 'n' I can have
a thousan' dolls if I want to, 'n' gold ones, too, or silver, or anything."
(More trouble brewing.) "What do I care for that. I guess my pa could
be Governor, too, if he wanted to; but he don't. He owns two hundred
feet in the Chollar, 'n' he's got lots more silver mines in Washoe
besides. He could fill this house full of silver, clear up to that chan-
delier, so he could, now, Miss." "You, Bob Miller, you leg go that
string—I'll smack you in the eye." "You will, will you? I'd like to see
you try it. You jes' hit me if you dare!" "You lay your hands on me, 'n'
I will hit you." "Now I've laid my hand on you, why don't you hit?"
"Well, I mean, if you lay 'em on me so's to hurt." "Ah-h! you're afraid,
that's the reason." "No I ain't, neither, you big fool." (Ah, now they're
at it. Discord shall invade the ranks of my foes, and they shall fall by
their own hands. It appears from the sound without that two nurses
have made a descent upon the combatants, and are bearing them from
the field. The nurses are abusing each other. One boy proclaims that
the other struck him when he wasn't doin' nothin'; and the other boy
says he was called a big fool. Both are going right straight, and tell their
pa's. Verily, things are going along as comfortably as I could wish,
now.) "Sandy Baker, I know what makes your pa's hair kink so; it's
'cause he's a mulatter; I heard my ma say so." "It's a lie!" (Another
row, and more skirmishing with the nurses. Truly, happiness flows in
upon me most bountifully this day.) "Hi, boys! here comes a Chinaman!" (God pity any Chinaman who chances to come in the way of
the boys hereabout, for the eye of the law regardeth him not, and the
youth of California in their generation are down upon him.) "Now,
boys! grab his clothes basket—take him by the tail!" (There they go,
now, like a pack of young demons; they have confiscated the basket,

and the dismayed Chinaman is towing half the tribe down the hall by his cue. Rejoice, O my soul, for behold, all things are lovely, etc.—to speak after the manner of the vulgar.) "Oho, Miss Susy Badger, my uncle Tom's goin' across the bay to Oakland, 'n' down to Santa Clara, 'n' Alamedy, 'n' San Leandro, 'n' everywheres—all over the world, 'n' he's goin' to take me with him—he said so." "Humph! that ain't noth'n—I been there. My aunt Mary'd take me to any place I wanted to go, if I wanted her to, but I don't; she's got horses 'n' things—O, ever so many!—millions of 'em; but my ma says it don't look well for little girls to be always gadd'n about. That's why you don't ever see me goin' to places like some girls do. I despise to—" (The end is at hand; the nurses have massed themselves on the left; they move in serried phalanx on my besiegers; they surround them, and capture the last miscreant—horse, foot, and dragoons, munitions of war, and camp equipage. The victory is complete. They are gone—my castle is no longer menaced, and the rover is free. I am here, staunch and true!)

It is a living wonder to me that I haven't scalped some of those children before now. I expect I would have done it, but then I hardly felt well enough acquainted with them. I scarcely ever show them any attention anyhow, unless it is to throw a boot-jack at them or some little nonsense of that kind when I happen to feel playful. I am confident I would have destroyed several of them though, only it might appear as if I were making most too free.

I observe that that young officer of the Pacific Squadron—the one with his nostrils turned up like port-holes—has become a great favorite with half the mothers in the house, by imparting to them much useful information concerning the manner of doctoring children among the South American savages. His brother is brigadier in the Navy. The drab-complexioned youth with the Solferino mustache has corraled the other half with the Japanese treatment. The more I think of it the more I admire it. Now, I am no peanut. I have an idea that I could invent some little remedies that would stir up a commotion among these women, if I chose to try. I always had a good general notion of physic, I believe. It is one of my natural gifts, too, for I have never studied a single day under a regular physician. I will jot down a few items here, just to see how likely I am to succeed.

In the matter of measles, the idea is, to bring it out—bring it to the surface. Take the child and fill it up with saffron tea. Add something to make the patient sleep—say a table-spoonful of arsenic. Don't rock it—it will sleep anyhow.

As far as brain fever is concerned: This is a very dangerous disease, and must be treated with decision and dispatch. In every case where it has proved fatal, the sufferer invariably perished. You must strike at the root of the distemper. Remove the brains; and then— Well, that will be sufficient—that will answer—just remove the brains. This remedy has never been known to fail. It was originated by the lamented J. W. Macbeth, Thane of Cawdor, Scotland, who refers to it thus: "Time was, that when the brains were out, the man would die; but, under different circumstances, I think not; and, all things being equal, I believe you, my boy." Those were his last words.

Concerning worms: Administer a catfish three times a week. Keep the room very quiet; the fish won't bite if there is the least noise.

When you come to fits, take no chances on fits. If the child has them bad, soak it in a barrel of rain-water over night, or a good article of vinegar. If this does not put an end to its troubles, soak it a week. You can't soak a child too much when it has fits.

In cases wherein an infant stammers, remove the under-jaw. In proof of the efficacy of this treatment, I append the following certificate, voluntarily forwarded to me by Mr. Zeb. Leavenworth, of St. Louis, Mo.:

"ST. LOUIS, May 26, 1863.

"MR. MARK TWAIN—DEAR SIR:—Under Providence, I am beholden to you for the salvation of my Johnny. For a matter of three years, that suffering child stuttered to that degree that it was a pain and a sorrow to me to hear him stagger over the sacred name of 'p-p-p-pap'. It troubled me so that I neglected my business; I refused food; I took no pride in my dress, and my hair actually began to fall off. I could not rest; I could not sleep. Morning, noon, and night, I did nothing but moan pitifully, and murmur to myself: 'Hell's fire! what am I going to do about my Johnny?' But in a blessed hour you appeared unto me like an angel from the skies; and without hope of reward, revealed your sovereign remedy—and that very day, I sawed off my Johnny's under-jaw. May Heaven bless you, noble Sir. It afforded instant relief; and my Johnny has never stammered since. I honestly believe he never will again. As to disfigurement, he does seem to look sorter ornery and hog-mouthed, but I am too grateful in having got him effectually saved from that dreadful stuttering, to make much account of small matters. Heaven speed you in your holy work of healing the afflictions of humanity. And if my poor testimony can be of any service to you, do with it as you think will result in the greatest good to our fellow-creatures. Once more, Heaven bless you.

"Zeb. Leavenworth."

Now, that has such a plausible ring about it, that I can hardly keep from believing it myself. I consider it a very fair success.

Regarding Cramps. Take your offspring—let the same be warm and dry at the time—and immerse it in a commodious soup-tureen filled with the best quality of camphene. Place it over a slow fire, and add reasonable quantities of pepper, mustard, horse-radish, saltpetre, strychnine, blue vitriol, aqua fortis, a quart of flour, and eight or ten fresh eggs, stirring it from time to time, to keep up a healthy reaction. Let it simmer fifteen minutes. When your child is done, set the tureen off, and allow the infallible remedy to cool. If this does not confer an entire insensibility to cramps, you must lose no time, for the case is desperate. Take your offspring, and parboil it. The most vindictive cramps cannot survive this treatment; neither can the subject, unless it is endowed with an iron constitution. It is an extreme measure, and I always dislike to resort to it. I never parboil a child until everything else has failed to bring about the desired end.

Well, I think those will do to commence with. I can branch out, you know, when I get more confidence in myself.

O infancy! thou art beautiful, thou art charming, thou art lovely to contemplate! But thoughts like these recall sad memories of the past, of the halcyon days of my childhood, when I was a sweet, prattling innocent, the pet of a dear home-circle, and the pride of the village.

Enough, enough! I must weep, or this bursting heart will break.

—MARK TWAIN.

73. Frightful Accident to Dan De Quille

20 April 1864

Although the original printing of this sketch in the Virginia City *Territorial Enterprise* is not extant, both the text and the probable date of publication can be retrieved from three contemporary reprintings: the Nevada (Calif.) *Gazette* of 26 April 1864, the San Francisco *Golden Era* of May 1, and the Unionville (Nev.) *Humboldt Register* of May 14. The *Gazette* reprinting establishes that the *Enterprise* must have appeared shortly before April 26, and the *Era* reprinting allows us to conjecture that the date was actually Wednesday, April 20. Along with Mark Twain's sketch the *Era* also reprinted two sequels from the *Enterprise*, both written by Dan De Quille, which must have appeared about the same time. The first of these was Dan's humorous response to Mark Twain's exaggerated account of his accident, titled "An Infamous Proceeding." The second was "Mark Twain Takes a Lesson in the Manly Art," which was Dan's elaborate revenge for the ridicule of "Frightful Accident."

"An Infamous Proceeding" must have appeared within two or three days of Mark Twain's sketch. Dan wrote in part:

Some three days since, in returning to this city from American Flat, we had the misfortune to be thrown from a fiery untamed steed of Spanish extraction—a very strong extract, too. Our knee was sprained by our fall and we were for a day or two confined to our room—of course knowing little of what was going on in the great world outside. Mark Twain, our *confrere* and room-mate, a man in whom we trusted, was our only visitor during our seclusion. We saw some actions of his that almost caused us to suspect him of contemplating treachery towards us, but it was not until we regained in some degree the use of our maimed limb that we discovered the full extent— the infamousness of this wretch's treasonable and inhuman plottings. He wrote such an account of our accident as would lead the public to believe that we were injured beyond all hope of recovery.

Dan went on to allege that Mark Twain subsequently stole his toothbrush, clothes, stocks, and indeed most of his belongings, and he closed his sketch with a mock threat to have Mark Twain arrested if he failed to "shell out our tooth-brush and take off our socks and best shirt."[1]

Dan's second sketch, "Mark Twain Takes a Lesson in the Manly Art," clearly alluded to what he had said in "An Infamous Proceeding" and so must have followed it within a few days. In the second piece Dan apologized for having "said some harsh things of Mark Twain" and reported that "yesterday" his friend had "brought back all our things and promised us that he intended hereafter to lead a virtuous life." Dan went on, however, to describe how Mark Twain had suffered a bloody and swollen nose while taking his "first lesson in boxing," an elaborate tall tale which, like "Frightful Accident," was nevertheless based on the facts.[2]

The *Era* said only that all three items it reprinted were taken from "recent issues of the *Territorial Enterprise*." But it is apparent from other evidence that Mark Twain's boxing accident and Dan's description of its consequences must have occurred shortly before Monday, April 25: in 1893 Dan recalled that Mark Twain had been so sensitive about his swollen nose that he volunteered for an assignment that would take him to Silver Mountain (in Alpine County, Calif.) away from the kidding he was getting in Virginia City.[3] We know from a letter that Mark Twain wrote the *Enterprise* on Monday, April 25, that he must have left Virginia City no later than Sunday or Monday, April 24 or 25, and that he went first to Carson City, from which he intended to "depart for Silver Mountain" the next day.[4] Since "Mark Twain Takes a Lesson" must have appeared no later than Sunday, April 24, and since all three pieces appeared within days of each other, "Frightful Accident" must have been published in the early part of the week preceding April 24. Monday can be excluded because the *Enterprise* did not publish on that day. In the first sentence of the *Era* text of the sketch Dan is alleged to have met with his accident on "Tuesday," but in the *Gazette* and *Humboldt Register* texts his accident is said to have happened "yesterday." In all probability the *Enterprise* actually read "yesterday"—certainly this was the normal style of such local items— which suggests that the *Era* editor or compositor supplied "Tuesday" because his source, the *Enterprise*, had appeared on a Wednesday. We have

---

[1]*Golden Era* 12 (1 May 1864): 5. The Nevada (Calif.) *Gazette* also reprinted the piece on 28 April 1864, p. 1, two days after it reprinted Mark Twain's sketch. All three items are reprinted in *WG*, pp. 50–53.

[2]*Golden Era* 12 (1 May 1864): 5.

[3]"Salad Days of Mark Twain," San Francisco *Examiner*, 19 March 1893, p. 14.

[4]*MTEnt*, p. 182.

therefore conjectured that Mark Twain's sketch was first published in the
Enterprise for Wednesday, April 20.

"Frightful Accident" is in Mark Twain's best vein—a typical product of
the mutual raillery that he carried on with Dan De Quille, resembling his
earlier "feuds" with the Unreliable. It will be recalled that Dan had begun
reporting for the *Enterprise* in May 1862, several months before Clemens
joined the staff. By December 1862, when Dan left Nevada for his long visit
to Iowa, the two men had already become friends.[5] But only after his return
in September 1863 and after Clemens' return from a visit to San Francisco
did the friendship ripen. Probably in late October they began rooming
together in a second-floor apartment in the Daggett and Meyers brick building on B Street. They got along well and their relationship provided ample
material for good-natured mutual ridicule. In December 1863, while Clemens
was in Carson City reporting the first Constitutional Convention, Dan
raised the curtain on their housekeeping arrangements in an article for the
Era.[6] And between December 1863 and April 1864 there were probably other
such items in the *Enterprise*, by both men, that are now lost. As we have
seen, Dan's "An Infamous Proceeding" and "Mark Twain Takes a Lesson"
were typical specimens of this mock feuding—and within days of Clemens'
departure for Silver Mountain Dan had published a further installment
(see the next sketch, "Dan Reassembled," no. 74).

---

[5]See the headnote to "The Illustrious Departed" (no. 32).
[6]"No Head nor Tail," *Golden Era* 12 (6 December 1863): 5.

Frightful Accident
to Dan De Quille

O UR TIME-HONORED confrere, Dan, met with a disastrous accident, yesterday, while returning from American City on a vicious Spanish horse, the result of which accident is that at the present writing he is confined to his bed and suffering great bodily pain. He was coming down the road at the rate of a hundred miles an hour (as stated in his will, which he made shortly after the accident,) and on turning a sharp corner, he suddenly hove in sight of a horse standing square across the channel; he signaled for the starboard, and put his helm down instantly, but too late, after all; he was swinging to port, and before he could straighten down, he swept like an avalanche against the transom of the strange craft; his larboard knee coming in contact with the rudder-post of the adversary, Dan was wrenched from his saddle and thrown some three hundred yards (according to his own statement, made in his will, above mentioned,) alighting upon solid ground, and bursting himself open from the chin to the pit of the stomach. His head was also caved in out of sight, and his hat was afterwards extracted in a bloody and damaged condition from between his lungs; he must have bounced end-for-end after he struck first, because it is evident he received a concussion from the rear that broke his heart; one of his legs was jammed up in his body nearly to his throat, and the other so torn and mutilated that it pulled out when they attempted to lift him into the hearse which we had sent to the scene of the disaster, under the general impression that he might need it; both arms were indiscriminately broken up until they were jointed like a bamboo; the back was considerably fractured and bent into the shape of a rail fence. Aside from these injuries, however, he sustained no other damage. They brought some of him home in the hearse and the balance on a dray. His first remark showed that the powers of his great mind had not been impaired by the accident, nor his profound judgment destroyed—he said he wouldn't have cared a d—n if it had been anybody but himself. He then made his will, after which he set to work with that earnestness and singleness of purpose which have always distinguished him, to abuse the assemblage of anxious hash-house proprietors who had called on business, and to repudiate their bills with his customary promptness and impartiality. Dan may have exaggerated the above details in some respects, but he charged us to report them thus, and it is a source of genuine pleasure to us to have the opportunity of doing it. Our noble old friend is recovering fast, and what is left of him will be around the Brewery again to-day, just as usual.

74. [Dan Reassembled]

28–30 April 1864

This brief scrap appears to be Mark Twain's further comment on Dan De Quille's accident (see "Frightful Accident to Dan De Quille," no. 73). The sketch, of which this is presumably only a fragment, was published in the Virginia City *Territorial Enterprise* in late April after Mark Twain returned from his assignment in Silver Mountain. The text is preserved only in Albert Bigelow Paine's *Mark Twain: A Biography*, where he mistakenly identified it as the author's initial response to Dan's accident. Indeed, since Paine's source is not known, and since the fragment bears some similarity to the previous sketch, there is a remote possibility that Paine printed Mark Twain's recollection of what he had written there.

However, on balance, it seems somewhat more likely that Mark Twain did write a second piece on the accident for the *Enterprise*. The very much more sarcastic tone suggests that he was responding to what transpired after he left Virginia City with his swollen nose. In 1893 Dan recalled:

No sooner was Mark away than I wrote for the *Enterprise* a description of his arrival at Silver Mountain. In this it was said that as the stage was entering the town Mark placed himself at the window of the vehicle. The alert suburban inhabitants caught sight of his nose and raised the cry that a "freak" show was coming. . . . This was a mild and innocent squib for a Comstock paper in those days, but Mark said "it wasn't a d—— bit smart." He was hot about it when he got back to Virginia City. He said I had caused him to be annoyed by all the bums in Carson when he got back to that town, as he was obliged to stand treat to shut their mouths.

Dan further recalled—mistakenly, however—that Clemens' response was to publish "Frightful Accident." Since that sketch clearly appeared before Mark Twain's departure for Silver Mountain, it seems more likely that

"Dan Reassembled" was Mark Twain's response. Dan, at any rate, remembered that when he discovered the piece his friend chuckled and said: "Now, blast you, may be you'll hereafter let my nose alone!"[1]

---

[1]"Salad Days of Mark Twain," San Francisco *Examiner*, 19 March 1893, p. 14.

[Dan Reassembled]

THE IDEA OF a plebeian like Dan supposing he could ever ride a horse! He! why, even the cats and the chickens laughed when they saw him go by. Of course, he would be thrown off. Of course, any well-bred horse wouldn't let a common, underbred person like Dan stay on his back! When they gathered him up he was just a bag of scraps, but they put him together, and you'll find him at his old place in the *Enterprise* office next week, still laboring under the delusion that he's a newspaper man.

75. Washoe.—"Information Wanted"

1–15 May 1864

The original printing of "Washoe.—'Information Wanted'" in the Virginia City *Territorial Enterprise* is not extant, but the sketch was reprinted in the San Francisco *Golden Era* on 22 May 1864. It had probably appeared in the *Enterprise* shortly before May 15, when Clemens became involved in raising money for the Sanitary Fund.[1] Although it seems likely that the *Era* would republish such an item fairly promptly, the sketch could in fact have appeared in the *Enterprise* any time in the first two weeks of May. The *Era* editors added a brief explanatory preface before reprinting it: "A citizen of Virginia, Washoe's world-famed metropolis, lately received a letter from a friend in Missouri who 'Wanted Information' concerning Silver-Land. This letter was handed over to Mark Twain. In the *Territorial Enterprise* we find the whole correspondence."[2]

On 29 May 1864, less than a month after composing "Washoe.—'Information Wanted,'" Mark Twain left Nevada for San Francisco. His growing disenchantment with "Silver-Land" is evident in this sketch, which is a kind of travesty of hyperbolic land-promotion literature. Mark Twain's disenchantment had been brought to a head by his two-pronged controversy—with the ladies of Carson City and with the editors of the Virginia City *Union*—revolving around contributions to the Sanitary Fund.[3] His sardonic praise of the country reflects an attitude evident in his earlier Nevada writing, but its prominence and severity here help transform his reply to "William" into an appropriate farewell to the territory.

---

[1]See *MTEnt*, pp. 186–189.
[2]*Golden Era* 12 (22 May 1864): 5.
[3]*MTEnt*, pp. 27–30, 189–205.

"Washoe.—'Information Wanted'" was reprinted in the 1867 *Jumping Frog* book under the title "Information for the Million." But in 1873 when Mark Twain revised the *Choice Humorous Works* for Andrew Chatto he decided to omit it, writing simply "Leave out this puerile hogwash."[4]

---

[4]See the textual commentary.

Washoe.—"Information Wanted"

"SPRINGFIELD, MO., April 12.

"DEAR SIR:—My object in writing to you is to have you give me a full history of Nevada: What is the character of its climate? What are the productions of the earth? Is it healthy? What diseases do they die of mostly? Do you think it would be advisable for a man who can make a living in Missouri to emigrate to that part of the country? There are several of us who would emigrate there in the spring if we could ascertain to a certainty that it is a much better country than this. I suppose you know Joel H. Smith? He used to live here; he lives in Nevada now; they say he owns considerable in a mine there. Hoping to hear from you soon, etc., I remain yours, truly,

WILLIAM ——."

DEAREST WILLIAM:—Pardon my familiarity—but that name touchingly reminds me of the loved and lost, whose name was similar. I have taken the contract to answer your letter, and although we are now strangers, I feel we shall cease to be so if we ever become acquainted with each other. The thought is worthy of attention, William. I will now respond to your several propositions in the order in which you have fulminated them.

Your object in writing is to have me give you a full history of Nevada. The flattering confidence you repose in me, William, is only equalled by the modesty of your request. I could detail the history of Nevada in five hundred pages octavo, but as you have never done me any harm, I will spare you, though it will be apparent to everybody that I would be justified in taking advantage of you if I were a mind to do it.

However, I will condense. Nevada was discovered many years ago by
the Mormons, and was called Carson county. It only became Nevada
in 1861, by act of Congress. There is a popular tradition that God
Almighty created it; but when you come to see it, William, you will
think differently. Do not let that discourage you, though. The country
looks something like a singed cat, owing to the scarcity of shrubbery,
and also resembles that animal in the respect that it has more merits
than its personal appearance would seem to indicate. The Grosch
brothers found the first silver lead here in 1857. They also founded
Silver City, I believe. (Observe the subtle joke, William.) But the "history" of Nevada which you demand, properly begins with the discovery of the Comstock lead, which event happened nearly five years ago.
The opinion now prevailing in the East that the Comstock is on the
Gould & Curry is erroneous; on the contrary, the Gould & Curry is
on the Comstock. Please make the correction, William. Signify to your
friends, also, that all the mines here do not pay dividends as yet; you
may make this statement with the utmost unyielding inflexibility—it
will not be contradicted from this quarter. The population of this
Territory is about 35,000, one-half of which number reside in the
united cities of Virginia and Gold Hill. However, I will discontinue
this history for the present, lest I get you too deeply interested in this
distant land and cause you to neglect your family or your religion. But
I will address you again upon the subject next year. In the meantime,
allow me to answer your inquiry as to the character of our climate.

It has no character to speak of, William, and alas! in this respect it
resembles many, ah, too many chambermaids in this wretched,
wretched world. Sometimes we have the seasons in their regular order,
and then again we have winter all the summer and summer all winter.
Consequently, we have never yet come across an almanac that would
just exactly fit this latitude. It is mighty regular about not raining,
though, William. It will start in here in November and rain about four,
and sometimes as much as seven days on a stretch; after that, you may
loan out your umbrella for twelve months, with the serene confidence
which a Christian feels in four aces. Sometimes the winter begins in
November and winds up in June; and sometimes there is a bare
suspicion of winter in March and April, and summer all the balance of
the year. But as a general thing, William, the climate is good, what
there is of it.

What are the productions of the earth? You mean in Nevada, of course. On our ranches here, anything can be raised that can be produced on the fertile fields of Missouri. But ranches are very scattering—as scattering, perhaps, as lawyers in heaven. Nevada, for the most part, is a barren waste of sand, embellished with melancholy sage-brush, and fenced in with snow clad mountains. But these ghastly features were the salvation of the land, William, for no rightly constituted American would have ever come here if the place had been easy of access, and none of our pioneers would have staid after they got here if they had not felt satisfied that they could not find a smaller chance for making a living anywhere else. Such is man, William, as he crops out in America.

"Is it healthy?" Yes, I think it is as healthy here as it is in any part of the West. But never permit a question of that kind to vegetate in your brain, William, because as long as providence has an eye on you, you will not be likely to die until your time comes.

"What diseases do they die of mostly?" Well, they used to die of conical balls and cold steel, mostly, but here lately erysipelas and the intoxicating bowl have got the bulge on those things, as was very justly remarked by Mr. Rising last Sunday. I will observe, for your information, William, that Mr. Rising is our Episcopal minister, and has done as much as any man among us to redeem this community from its pristine state of semi-barbarism. We are afflicted with all the diseases incident to the same latitude in the States, I believe, with one or two added and half a dozen subtracted on account of our superior altitude. However, the doctors are about as successful here, both in killing and curing, as they are anywhere.

Now, as to whether it would be advisable for a man who can make a living in Missouri to emigrate to Nevada, I confess I am somewhat mixed. If you are not content in your present condition, it naturally follows that you would be entirely satisfied if you could make either more or less than a living. You would exult in the cheerful exhilaration always produced by a change. Well, you can find your opportunity here, where, if you retain your health, and are sober and industrious, you will inevitably make more than a living, and if you don't you won't. You can rely upon this statement, William. It contemplates any line of business except the selling of tracts. You cannot sell tracts here, William; the people take no interest in tracts; the very best efforts in

the tract line—even with pictures on them—have met with no encouragement here. Besides, the newspapers have been interfering; a
man gets his regular text or so from the Scriptures in his paper, along
with the stock sales and the war news, every day, now. If you are in
the tract business, William, take no chances on Washoe; but you can
succeed at anything else here.

"I suppose you know Joel H. Smith?" Well—the fact is—I believe I
don't. Now isn't that singular? Isn't it very singular? And he owns
"considerable" in a mine here, too. Happy man. Actually owns in a
mine here in Nevada Territory, and I never even heard of him. Strange
—strange—do you know, William, it is the strangest thing that ever
happened to me? And then he not only owns in a mine, but owns
"considerable;" that is the strangest part about it—how a man could
own considerable in a mine in Washoe and I not know anything about
it. He is a lucky dog, though. But I strongly suspect that you have made
a mistake in the name; I am confident you have; you mean John
Smith—I know you do; I know it from the fact that he owns considerable in a mine here, because I sold him the property at a ruinous
sacrifice on the very day he arrived here from over the plains. That
man will be rich one of these days. I am just as well satisfied of it as I am
of any precisely similar instance of the kind that has come under my
notice. I said as much to him yesterday, and he said he was satisfied of
it, also. But he did not say it with that air of triumphant exultation
which a heart like mine so delights to behold in one to whom I have
endeavored to be a benefactor in a small way. He looked pensive a
while, but, finally, says he, "Do you know, I think I'd a been a rich man
long ago if they'd ever found the d—d ledge?" That was my idea about
it. I always thought, and I still think, that if they ever do find that ledge,
his chances will be better than they are now. I guess Smith will be all
right one of these centuries, if he keeps up his assessments—he is a
young man yet. Now, William, I have taken a liking to you, and I
would like to sell you "considerable" in a mine in Washoe. I think I
could get you a commanding interest in the "Union," Gold Hill, on
easy terms. It is just the same as the "Yellow Jacket," which is one of
the richest mines in the Territory. The title was in dispute between the
two companies some two years ago, but that is all settled now. Let me
hear from you on the subject. Greenbacks at par is as good a thing as I
want. But seriously, William, don't you ever invest in a mining stock

which you don't know anything about; beware of John Smith's experience.

You hope to hear from me soon? Very good. I shall also hope to hear from you soon, about that little matter above referred to. Now, William, ponder this epistle well; never mind the sarcasm, here and there, and the nonsense, but reflect upon the plain facts set forth, because they *are* facts, and are meant to be so understood and believed.

Remember me affectionately to your friends and relations, and especially to your venerable grand-mother, with whom I have not the pleasure to be acquainted—but that is of no consequence, you know. I have been in your town many a time, and all the towns of the neighboring counties—the hotel keepers will recollect me vividly. Remember me to them—I bear them no animosity.

Yours, affectionately,

MARK TWAIN.

APPENDIXES

APPENDIX A

CIRCUMSTANTIAL AND STYLISTIC evidence suggests that Clemens may have written the three pieces reproduced below. On the other hand, we have rejected as nonauthorial the following items that have been attributed to him in the past: "All Right!"—published in the Boston *Carpet-Bag* on 14 June 1851, ten months before "The Dandy Frightening the Squatter" (no. 2);[1] comic doggerel in Joseph P. Ament's *Missouri Courier* of 6 December 1848 and in Orion Clemens' Hannibal *Journal* of 1 and 16 April 1852 and 7 May 1853;[2] and "The ———— Troupe," published in the Hannibal *Journal and Union* on 18 March 1852, a piece that tells of the appearance in town of a "celebrated" theatrical troupe made up of two men and a "danseuse" whose amateurish performances may suggest the king and the duke of *Huckleberry Finn*. Although the details of Clemens' biography are compatible with his writing these items, we are not convinced he did so.

Each item reprinted below is furnished with a textual commentary which attends to the matters of copy-text, emendation, and problems in establishing the text.

---

[1]Norman Bassett, "Did Mark Twain Write 'All Right!'" *Demcourier* 4 (November 1935): 22–28; "'All Right!' from 'The Carpet-Bag'—Possibly Twain?" *Twainian* 26 (November–December 1967): 1–2.

[2]Edgar M. Branch, "A Chronological Bibliography of the Writings of Samuel Clemens to June 8, 1867," *American Literature* 18 (May 1946): 113, 115; *SCH*, pp. 245–246.

A1. Sunday Amusements

10 May 1853

A subheading in the Hannibal *Daily Journal* indicates that this sketch was written "For the Journal"; it was signed "J." Since it was published in the paper (and republished in the *Weekly Journal* two days later) at a time when Clemens was responsible for managing the newspaper in Orion's absence, he may well have written it.

SINCE THE ENACTMENT, by our City Council, of the ordinance prohibiting the sale of liquor, on Sunday, several of the b'hoys, old and young, have been in the habit, in the place of attending church, of taking a pleasure trip on the ferry boat, to the head of the Sny, and making themselves generally useful, in helping to wood, &c., in consideration of the privilege of taking a jug of the *creeter* along. On last Sunday, some person added a little tartar to the contents of the jug, and the way it produced symptoms of cholera, cramp cholic, &c., was a caution. The first feelings were a little grumbling at the stomach, and the boys would take a little more to settle it, and soon it would need still a little more to settle, until, finally, the Captain, finding he was about to lose crew and passengers, as a means of saving them, threw the jug overboard; but the consequence did not cease here—they presented a picture of a vessel going to sea with a crowd of landsmen on board, all laboring with sea-sickness at once, and between the groans of the suffering could be heard threatenings loud and deep against their self-appointed doctor, could they find him. One of the party thought it was all up with him; declared he never had such an attack of cramp cholic before in his life; sent for two physicians, and finally prepared to give up the ghost. Another made an onslaught on a pile of raw potatoes, as a means of settling his stomach, but he could not get over one potatoe down before 'twould come roaring back again, with a sound like some one hallooing "New York!" "New York!"

Now, we think that if this is the effect of stringent temperance laws; if the health, comfort and happiness of free people are to be obstructed, and their rights trampled upon in this manner, then I say, for one, that this is no longer a free country; and that our constitution is abused, and we had best not have any at all!

$A2.$ The Great Fair at St. Louis

21 October 1856

This sketch was signed "SAM" and appeared in the Keokuk (Iowa) *Post* on 21 October 1856, and then in the *Saturday Post* on October 25. In both cases it was preceded by an unsigned note:

Messrs. Editors:
    The following, which I have received in a letter, I turn over to you for publication, provided, you think it will interest your readers.

If Clemens was the author of the sketch, he may have submitted it to Orion, then living in Keokuk, for publication in the *Post*.
    The first fair of the St. Louis Agricultural and Mechanical Association was held from Monday, 13 October 1856, through Saturday, October 18. The rainy weather mentioned in the sketch, and allusions to topics in the day's news, indicate that the author attended the fair on opening day. It is also apparent that he was from Keokuk and, like Clemens, was familiar with the Keokuk Guards.[1] Since mid-1855 Clemens had been employed at Orion's Ben Franklin Book and Job Office in Keokuk. Having determined in August 1856 to go to South America, Clemens first briefly visited his mother in St. Louis in the fall of the year. His visit occurred while the fair was in progress, for his first Thomas Jefferson Snodgrass letter, published in the Keokuk *Saturday Post* on 1 November 1856, was dated October 18 from St. Louis.

IT COMMENCED RAINING about sunrise this morning—cold, drizzly, uncomfortable rain. People in the slashy streets looked sour, drew their over-coats tightly about them, and stubbornly refused to move their umbrellas a single inch out of the way of the heads of passers-by. This did not promise well for the Fair. However, my friend and I ventured down to Fourth street, when we were caught up by the 9 o'clock tide of humanity, and borne to the Planters' House, where we smoked a cigar, read the morning papers, and heard the people "d—n the weather." Having gained a large amount of useful knowledge from the two sole topics discussed in said morning papers, viz: the corre-spondence between Botts and Pryor, and the fact that the Messrs. Arnot had generously fitted up a portion of their fine new building in

---
[1]Clemens to Henry Clemens, 5 August 1856, *CL1*, letter 15.

Chestnut street, for the accommodation of five hundred strangers, we waded up to Olive street, where several huge omnibuses arrived five minutes later, with "For the Fair," displayed in great capitals on the sides thereof. It was one thing to see the omnibuses, but an entirely separate and distinct thing to get in one. About a hundred men stormed vehicle No. 1. A big man with a blue cotton umbrella, led the attack. The assault was successful. A good many got in, and of course a good many didn't. I formed a part of the latter respectable majority. I think if I had got in, I would have carried about twenty with me, for I am certain there were that many hanging to my coat tail. Amid cries of "Form a line!" "One at a time!" "Put that man out!" &c., omnibus No. 2 was attacked, and this time myself and friend were successful, and away we flew down Franklin Avenue, at the rate of fourteen miles in fifteen hours.

Arrived at the Fair grounds. Saw an immense number of knick-knack stalls lining Grand Avenue for a quarter of a mile or more.

But we went there to see the Fair, and were not to be seduced by such luxuries as hump-backed horses and Georgia Bays, so we paid our quarters and marched in at the grand entrance. Here was a sight. Fifty acres of grass, with ten acres of men and women—pants rolled up and dresses elevated—going with a hop, step and jump over it, and sprinkled by fifty acres of fourth-quality rain every half-second. The second story of this plat was formed of umbrellas, and the third was the great amphitheatre. On the left was the pretty cottage for the ladies, with fountains near it; on the right was the repository of the fine arts. Still further to the right was the building for furniture, stoves, &c.; in the rear a steam bakery. Still further to the right was Wm. M. Plant's ware-house of agricultural implements. Behind the amphitheatre was the building containing steam machinery, driven by a locomotive engine; near it were others, devoted to sewing machines, carriages, &c.; and all around the vast inclosure were stalls for the various kinds of stock.

Surrounding the base of the amphitheatre are eighty-six eating and drinking stalls. In the centre of the huge building was a clear, open arena, of perhaps 250 feet in diameter, with tall Pagoda for judges and musicians in the middle—the stars and stripes waving from the summit. All around the arena, and slanting up from it, were the fifteen tiers of seats, with a promenade at the top. The National Guards, with their red coats and immense muff-like hats, entered the arena and went through various military evolutions, which were exceedingly 'small potatoes,' compared with what I have seen the Keokuk Guards do. They were joined by the Washington Guards—a fine looking set of men, and well drilled—and finally, by the St. Louis Grays, who have always been the pets of St. Louis. The military proceedings wound up with a grand review, on a small scale, of the united companies. It seemed to me that the Washington Guards showed the most complete drilling, and deserved far more credit than the other soldiers, though they received the least applause. For the sake of their reputation, the Grays should have stayed at home—for they were very ungraceful, and went through with their manœuvres very awkwardly. The military did not come into the amphitheatre.

Next was the exhibition of match horses, I think. There were about six or eight buggies—two horses hitched to each buggy. They came in one by one, and followed each other slowly around the circle. One young fellow, in a jockey cap, behind two noble iron greys, attracted particular attention, by his excellent driving. Soon the horses broke into a gentle trot—faster, faster,—and the beautiful cavalcade sailed around the circle—the iron grays turned out and passed the big sorrels under headway, with a cheer from the multitude—the sorrel man whips up his team—faster, faster, good!—look to your laurel, iron gray,—he nears him—half the buggies turn now, and start around in the opposite direction, and in a moment they were meeting each other at lightning speed, in every quarter—in the melee, 'sorrel' gets ahead—another cheer—'iron gray' whips up—hurrah! he gains on his opponent—'go it iron gray!' and the lash falls keen and fast—the multitude rise to their feet—good! good! hurrah for 'iron gray!'—another furious lash—he's even with him—and a yell burst from those fifteen thousand throats, that shook the building to its foundations. But stop! The noise has frightened the horses out of their senses, and woe to the man that stands before them now—they dart in wild dismay in every direction, and the swaying, speechless crowd stands appalled. At the moment of victory, 'iron gray' comes in collision with a passing buggy, a crash ensues, and one hind wheel goes spinning to the middle of the circle, and the balance of the vehicle drags the ground. But 'iron gray' is pluck, he sticks to the remnant of the seat, ten yards further—another collision—and 'iron gray's' buggy is ground to pieces beneath hoofs and wheels, and himself trodden under foot—a groan went up from the crowd who stood there, bent forward and straining their eyes to catch a glimpse of the dead man —one moment of suspense, and then, full of life, but his clothes torn to shreds, the man stood before them uninjured, and his ears were greeted with a deafening shout. Order was finally restored, and trial commenced again. 'Iron gray' hitched his horses to another buggy, and soon joined the competitors, welcomed to the ring with another storm of applause. There were no more accidents, and fun was now the order of the day. A negro driving one of the buggies did not keep up very well. Somebody yelled out, 'Hello, Fremont, you're behind time!' The people took it up, and the poor devil was assailed with 'go it Fremont!' from every side—and it was easy to see that he didn't think it much of a compliment. I think the iron grays took the first premium, the big sorrels, the second, and the negro's horses the third.

We now left the amphitheatre, and wandered over the grounds in the rain, and finally started home. Finding no chance in the omnibuses at the gate, we went down the road to meet one coming from town. The first one that came along, we crowded into. We had twenty-one men and women inside, and certainly spent a jolly time on the way home. We were safely landed at Olive and Fourth, at half-past six in the evening, after a happily spent day.

SAM.

A3. [Cincinnati Boarding House Sketch]

18 November 1856

This untitled sketch, signed "L," was published in the Keokuk (Iowa) *Post* on 18 November 1856, and it was dated November 8 from Cincinnati. After his return from St. Louis to Keokuk in late October 1856, Clemens went to Cincinnati, where he was employed as a typesetter until he embarked on the steamer *Paul Jones* in April 1857. "L's" sketch is contemporaneous with Clemens' second Thomas Jefferson Snodgrass letter, dated 14 November 1856 from Cincinnati and published in the Keokuk *Post* on November 29.

In his autobiography Clemens recalled his conversations with the amateur philosopher Macfarlane in their Cincinnati boarding house. He described Macfarlane as "six feet high and rather lank, a serious and sincere man" and a "diligent talker."[1] Albert Bigelow Paine termed him "a long, lank, unsmiling Scotchman."[2] It is therefore interesting that Mr. Blathers in the present sketch is called "a long, lank Irishman" and, together with Mr. Luculus ("Sir Oracle") Cabbage, is the character most given to speculating about man's capacity for achieving knowledge and about the relative importance of heredity and training in human development.

CINCINNATI, O., Nov. 8th, 1856.

MESSRS. EDITORS:—I propose now to show you the inside of our boarding house, remarking at the outset, that our boarding house is like all other boarding houses. The scene is the front parlor, this frosty Sunday morning, the 8th day of November, and a number of chairs are drawn up in a semi-circle round a coal fire, snapping and sputtering, in the grate. Breakfast is just over. During the few minutes silence which follows, and which time is employed by these gentlemen in picking their teeth, I'll point out the principal characters.

In the chair next the stove, sits an "old residenter," entirely bald, with the exception of a fringe of hair commencing at the top of his forehead and running clear round the head, giving that otherwise bare but shining organ something of the appearance of the moon in a dim

---

[1] *MTA*, 1:144. See William Baker, "Mark Twain in Cincinnati: A Mystery Most Compelling," forthcoming in *American Literary Realism*.
[2] *MTB*, 1:114.

halo. This is Mr. Luculus (or, as he is sometimes called, "Sir Oracle") Cabbage, and his remarks and decisions are always received with the utmost reverence.

Not far from him sits his first born Mr. Jonas Cabbage, whose name has gone through several modifications, commencing with Jones; then Jone; then Jack, and finally Jack-*ass*. (The latter probably the most appropriate.) He, too, has lost the hair from the top of his youthful head—which has the soft appearance of mush done up in a cotton rag, with a dent here and there—but he has an abundance of red whiskers and moustachios to make amends for the bereavement. He knows when the laugh comes in after an anecdote, by watching the faces of his neighbors.

Mr. Blathers sits next to him. He is rashly fond of an argument, and his eternal misfortune is to get the whole house arrayed against him. He is a long, lank Irishman.

The other gentlemen of importance are Mr. Pottery, Mr. Doodle and Mr. Toploftical. Discussion opens.

Doodle. Have you heard of the homicide in Philadelphia the other day, where a clerk killed his employer, on account of improper intimacy between the latter and the former's wife?

Pottery. Is that so! Served him right.

Toploftical. Be not too hasty. Killing is a terrible thing.

Blathers. Did serve him right. A man who would treat a dependant in such a manner, has no more soul than a horse.

D. Hold on. I spose you think a horse has got no soul.

B. I *know* it hasn't.

T. Wait a moment, Mr. B. Human beings, poor worms, can't *know* of the existence of anything which they cannot *see*, and you cannot see the soul.

B. Tut, tut. I'm *not* obliged to see a thing in order to know it. Now there's that bloody murder sometime ago. I knew that deed was done, but I didn't see it, and I know the man that done it richly deserved hanging, but was cleared, and left the country, but I didn't see him.

Cabbage Senior. Ah, Mr. Blathers, you shouldn't say the man deserved hanging till you know something more about the matter. Some men are born to be murderers and they ain't responsible for their natures.

B. It's no difference, though, Mr. Cabbage, you know, how a man is born—if he's brought up right he won't be a murderer. However yours is a knotty proposition, I must admit.

C. No. 1. Well, but I tell you bringin' up has got nothing to do with it. Individuals and even nations are born murderers.

C. No. 2. That's so, dad! Look at the Injins, darn 'em. Don't they kill people from June till January, and who teaches *them?* Some of 'em, too, is as intelligent as *we* are.

(Voice.) Amen!

B. Bah! Their fathers taught them. (Silence of two minutes.)

C. No. 2. The devil they did! Who taught their fathers! He! he! he!

(Voice.) D——d fool. (Aside.)

B. *Their* fathers—and so on, from generation to generation back to the days when idiots kept their mouths closed.

(No. 2. who thinks B. "soaked it" to T. that time, enjoys the joke exceedingly; but not seeing any good opening to begin his argument again, goes partially asleep.)

P. What was that about the intelligence of this assemblage?

No. 2. I didn't say anything about the intelligence of this assemblage. I meant the—ah,—the—country. Yes, the country—United States. I meant to say that we—that is,—the United States—as a people—ah— is more intellectually developed—in developed in—an intellectual extent of capacity than—that is to say—the intellectual powers is more strong in the development of—of the United States as a people— that is, the intellectuality of the whole country. (Dern this argerin.)

B. Well, well, well. If I've a soul to be saved—

T. Soul, again? How do you know you've got a soul?

B. How do I know I've got a soul? Why, how do I know there is a God?

C. No. 1. Well, how *do* you know there is a God? You can't see him, you can't feel him, you can't hear him. Come—don't hesitate.

Everybody. Out with it! Out with it!

B. Well, upon my soul. Now you are confounding finite matters with the infinite. Listen, gentlemen. I know that there is a God, by the works of his hands—the gorgeous sun—the gentle moon—the twinkling stars that bespangle the blue dome above our heads. Yea, the vast rivers and the trackless—

No. 1. Oh! dam nonsense. That is nothing but the belief, the faith imparted by imagination. There is a great difference between knowledge and belief.

No. 2. The old man let him have it that time. That cabbage is a knowin' old vegetable. Why, of course the twinkling sun, and gorgeous stars, and the—the vast area—and the—rivers—vastly spangled with—with—water—why *that* ain't no evidence—*that* don't prove—prove—don't prove—pap, what the devil *was* he tryin to prove?

No. 1. The existence of a Deity, my son. Don't exert yourself.

B. Nonsense, yourself. Faith and belief *is* knowledge. If a man isn't to know anything but what comes under his personal observation, what's the use of having courts of law, where men are sworn?

T. Why, in that case, a man believes a witness—but his belief won't amount to knowledge—absolute knowledge, my dear sir.

B. There you are, confounding the finite with the infinite, again. Now, *don't* I know that James Buchanan is elected President of these United States?

Several voices. No Sir! You don't know any such thing. If you think so, you'll be about as badly fooled as that old man Doodle tells about.

Others. Tell it, Doodle. Hurrah for the yarn.

D. Well, it was about this way. An old farmer had a big buck ram which would invariably chase him out of one of his fields every time he went into it; and one day, as he stood on the stile, bowing and smirking with excessive politeness to some ladies passing by, the ram took a stand about twenty yards behind him, and then measuring his distance and his target with a knowing eye, he darted forward, planted his head with tremendous force just beneath the old man's short coat tail, and sent him heels over head into a hog-wallow on the other side. The old gentleman swore vengeance; and after thinking over divers plans, he at last hit upon this one: He got an old wooden chair seat and filled one side of it with sharp-pointed nails, allowing them to project about half an inch. Went to the meadow—knelt down near the stile, and placed the board against his wounded seat of honor, but through some mistake, turned the nail side next himself.

No. 2. Oh! ha! ha! ha!—that was a good one!—tell us another.

Others. Dry up—dry up—the yarn ain't finished.

Doodle. In about three seconds the old enemy sent his head against that board like a battering ram, driving the nails home so effectually that the old man says he felt like a sieve for three weeks afterwards.

Everybody. Ha! ha! Served him right.

No. 2. Yes, served him right, but then what the devil did he turn the nails *in* for?

T. Well, that reminds me of an old ram that once got into a man's cellar one dark night. The servant maid went down and come up frightened to death at the *devil* she had seen. Then the old man went down, and finally the oldest son, all seeing the devil. Then they sent for the parson, and he went down, wrapped in his cloak, and kneeling on the ground, began to pray. The ram came up behind and butted him clear across the cellar. "Save yourselves, brethren;" said he, "for the devil's got my cloak."

Doodle looks vacantly at Pottery; Pottery looks at the elder Cabbage, and the younger vegetable gazes into everybody's faces. There's a damper on that conversation! No man knowing whether the anecdote was intended to be funny or serious; they are afraid to risk a laugh, so the company assumes a grave air, and one by one they leave, until finally the room is deserted—a conversation murdered by a pointless anecdote.

Yours.

L.

APPENDIX B

ATTRIBUTED ITEMS: NEVADA TERRITORY
(1862–1864)

A NUMBER OF ITEMS which Clemens almost certainly wrote for the Virginia City *Territorial Enterprise,* but which lack sufficient corroboration or are too slight to be included in the body of this collection, are reprinted in this appendix.

In January 1878, when Mark Twain had already published *The Innocents Abroad, Roughing It, The Gilded Age, Tom Sawyer,* and many shorter works, a former colleague of his on the *Enterprise* observed that "the brightest paragraphs 'Mark' ever penned were written for the local columns of this journal, while he was part of the dreamy, reckless and adventurous throng whose tents were pitched almost a generation ago along the Comstock." And when Henry Nash Smith published *Mark Twain of the "Enterprise"* in 1957, he wrote that "because examples of Mark Twain's routine reporting are scarce," he had "included whatever scraps of such material" he could find.[1] We share the interest implied by both writers in Mark Twain's routine journalism, precisely because this kind of work eventually gave rise to his tales and sketches.

Since 1957 some progress has been made both in finding local items and in fixing their dates of publication and even their authenticity. The following selections are, we believe, by Mark Twain—a conjecture supported by stylistic features, and by the chronology for Clemens' and Dan De Quille's whereabouts in Nevada and California for these years.

We exclude from this appendix several brief items that stylistic and other evidence suggests were probably written by Dan De Quille: "The Poor Fellow!" or "The Washoe Canary," "Mount Davidson," and

---

[1]"In the Harness Again," Virginia City *Territorial Enterprise,* 15 January 1878, Scrapbook 8, p. 36, MTP; *MTEnt,* p. 8.

"Time for Her to Come Home."[2] We exclude several items reprinted in the San Francisco press and attributed to the *Enterprise*, but which lack the author's stylistic signature.[3] We also exclude two items probably by Mark Twain, attributed to the *Enterprise* by Paul Fatout, but which we have been unable to find as cited, or otherwise.[4] Finally, we exclude several unsigned *Enterprise* articles and editorials that are preserved in Mark Twain's scrapbooks: "A Ghost Story" does not suggest his manner, and was probably written by another hand, prior to Clemens' return to Virginia City from Carson in late December 1862; "The Lager Beer Club," two sketches published on 10 and 24 May 1863, were probably not written by Mark Twain because he was then in San Francisco; and two editorials, "Salaries" and "Nevada's Bounty," might have been written by him, but fail to show his stylistic signature.[5]

Items that are probably not by Mark Twain, but that were published in one of the local columns to which he contributed, are here omitted, as are several items of such routine character that they have no literary interest (bills passed at a meeting of the board of aldermen, for instance). Items appearing in the main body of the collection are also omitted. Whenever an item from a column has been skipped over, ellipsis points appear to show the omission. Individual textual commentaries attend to the matters of copy-text, emendation, and problems in establishing the text.

---

[2]These appeared in the Downieville (Calif.) *Mountain Messenger*, 4 October 1862, p. 4; San Francisco *Alta California*, 20 October 1862, p. 1; Gold Hill *News*, 16 October 1863, p. 3; Jackson (Calif.) *Amador Weekly Ledger*, 14 November 1863, p. 1; and the Cedar Falls (Iowa) *Gazette*, 20 November 1863, clipping in Bancroft. The first two titles reprint the same item from the *Enterprise*; the last title is reprinted in both the *Ledger* and the *Gazette*.

[3]For instance, "Richest Yet," San Francisco *Herald and Mirror*, 5 January 1863, p. 3; and "A Brisk Business in the Shooting and Slashing Way at Washoe," San Francisco *Evening Bulletin*, 10 March 1864, p. 3.

[4]*MTVC*, pp. 42, 137.

[5]These are preserved in Scrapbook 4, pp. 13, 15, and Scrapbook 2, pp. 44, 129–130, MTP.

B1. Local Column

1 October 1862

The following three items appeared in the *Enterprise* on 1 October 1862. They are the earliest extant articles that Clemens wrote for the newspaper. The *Enterprise* printing is not extant, but the text for the first item is preserved in a contemporary reprinting in the Oroville (Calif.) *Butte Record* for 11 October 1862, which introduced it as follows: "They have had windy times of late in Washoe. The Virginia City Enterprise graphically describes the consequent movement in real estate, and says." The texts for the second and third items survive in the Marysville (Calif.) *Appeal* for 5 October 1862, which attributed them to the *Enterprise* "of Oct. 1st." The authenticity of the first is attested chiefly by its comic style (see the introduction, pp. 20–21), while the authenticity of the second and third is attested by Mark Twain's own memory of his initial days on the *Enterprise*, particularly his memory of how he filled "two nonpareil columns" without benefit of hard news. In chapter 42 of *Roughing It* he said:

Next I discovered some emigrant wagons going into camp on the plaza and found that they had lately come through the hostile Indian country and had fared rather roughly. I made the best of the item that the circumstances permitted, and felt that if I were not confined within rigid limits by the presence of the reporters of the other papers I could add particulars that would make the article much more interesting. However, I found one wagon that was going on to California, and made some judicious inquiries of the proprietor. When I learned, through his short and surly answers to my cross-questioning, that he was certainly going on and would not be in the city next day to make trouble, I got ahead of the other papers, for I took down his list of names and added his party to the killed and wounded. Having more scope here, I put this wagon through an Indian fight that to this day has no parallel in history.

A GALE.—About 7 o'clock Tuesday evening (Sept. 30th) a sudden blast of wind picked up a shooting gallery, two lodging houses and a drug store from their tall wooden stilts and set them down again some ten or twelve feet back of their original location, with such a degree of roughness as to jostle their insides into a sort of chaos. There were many guests in the lodging houses at the time of the accident, but it is pleasant to reflect that they seized their carpet sacks and vacated the premises with an alacrity suited to the occasion. No one hurt.

THE INDIAN TROUBLES ON THE OVERLAND ROUTE.—Twelve or fifteen emigrant wagons arrived here on Monday evening, and all but five
moved on towards California yesterday. One of the five wagons which
will remain in the city is in charge of a man from Story county, Iowa,
who started across the plains on the 5th of May last, in company with
a large train composed principally of emigrants from his own section.
From him we learn the following particulars: When in the vicinity of
Raft river, this side of Fort Hall, the train was attacked, in broad
daylight by a large body of Snake Indians. The emigrants, taken entirely by surprise—for they had apprehended no trouble—made but a
feeble resistance, and retreated, with a loss of six men and one woman
of their party. The Indians also captured the teams belonging to thirteen wagons, together with a large number of loose cattle and horses.
The names of those killed in the affray are as follows: Charles Bul-
winkle, from New York; William Moats, Geo. Adams and Elizabeth
Adams, and three others whose names our informant had forgotten.
The survivors were overtaken on the afternoon by a train numbering
111 wagons, which brought them through to Humboldt. They occasionally discovered the dead bodies of emigrants by the roadside; at
one time twelve corpses were found, at another four, and at another
two—all minus their scalps. They also saw the wrecks of many wagons
destroyed by the Indians. Shortly after the sufferers by the fight
recorded above had joined the large train, it was also fired into in the
night by a party of Snake Indians, but the latter, finding themselves
pretty warmly received, drew off without taking a scalp. About a week
before these events transpired, a party of emigrants numbering 40
persons was attacked near City Rocks by the same tribe of uncivilized
pirates. Five young ladies were carried off, and, it is thought, women
and children in all to the number of fifteen. All the men were killed
except one, who made his escape and arrived at Humboldt about the
20th of September. This train was called the "Methodist Train," which
was not altogether inappropriate, since the whole party knelt down
and began to pray as soon as the attack was commenced. Every train
which has passed over that portion of the route in the vicinity of City
Rocks since the 1st of August has had trouble with the Indians. When
our informant left Humboldt several wagons had just arrived whose
sides and covers had been transformed into magnified nutmeg-graters
by Indian bullets. The Snakes corralled the train, when a fight ensued,

which lasted forty-eight hours. The whites cut their way out, finally, and escaped. We could not learn the number of killed and wounded at this battle.

[MORE INDIAN TROUBLES.—] Mr. L. F. Yates, who arrived in this city a few days since from Pike's Peak, has given us the following particulars of a fight his train had on the 8th of last August, about one and a-half miles this side of the junction of the Lander's Cut-off and Fort Bridger roads. Their train consisted of 15 wagons and 40 men, with a number of women and children. The train was attacked while passing along a ravine by a party of Indians being concealed in among a thick growth of poplar bushes. When the attack commenced, most of the front wagons were some 80 rods in advance. They formed in corral, and intrenched behind their wagons, refused the slightest aid to those who were struggling with the savages in the rear. The party thus left to fight their way through the ambushed Indians numbered but nine men, and there were but four guns with which to maintain the battle. Five of the nine were killed and one wounded. The names of the killed are as follows: Parmelee, James Steele, James A. Hart, Rufus C. Mitchell, from Central City, Colorado Territory, and McMahan, residence unknown; the name of the man wounded is Frank Lyman. He was shot through the lungs—recovered. The thirty-one men who were hidden snugly behind their wagons, with a single honorable exception, refused to render the slightest assistance to those who were fighting for their lives and the lives of their families so near them. Although they had 27 guns they refused to lend a single gun, when at one time four men went to ask assistance. The cowards all clung to their arms, and lay trembling behind their wagons. A man named Perry, or Berry, was the only one who had sufficient courage to attempt to render his struggling friends any assistance. He was shot in the face before reaching the rear wagons, and was carried back to the corral. The fight lasted nearly two hours, and some seven or eight Indians were killed, as at various times they charged out of the bushes on their ponies. Several Indian horses were killed, and at length the few left alive fought through to where their thirty heroic friends (?) were corraled, leaving the killed and two wagons in possession of the Indians. Thirty bigger cowards and meaner men than those above mentioned never crossed the plains; we are certain that every man of them left the States for fear of being drafted into the army.

B2. Local Column

1–10 November 1862

The following item appeared in the *Enterprise* sometime in early November 1862, before Mark Twain took up his duties in the Territorial Legislature on November 11. The *Enterprise* printing is not extant, but the text is preserved in a contemporary reprinting in the Oroville (Calif.) *Butte Record* for 15 November 1862, which attributed it to the *Enterprise*.

THE PETRIFIED MAN.—Mr. Herr Weisnicht has just arrived in Virginia City from the Humboldt mines and regions beyond. He brings with him the head and one foot of the petrified man, lately found in the mountains near Gravelly Ford. A skillful assayer has analyzed a small portion of dirt found under the nail of the great toe and pronounces the man to have been a native of the Kingdom of New Jersey. As a trace of "speculation" is still discernible in the left eye, it is thought the man was on his way to what is now the Washoe mining region for the purpose of locating the Comstock. The remains brought in are to be seen in a neat glass case in the third story of the Library Building, where they have been temporarily placed by Mr. Weisnicht for the inspection of the curious, and where they may be examined by any one who will take the trouble to visit them.

B3. Local Column

30–31 December 1862

The following eight items appeared in the same *Enterprise* local column that began with "Our Stock Remarks" (no. 33). The rationale for attributing the column to Clemens, and for the date assigned, may be found in the headnote to that piece (p. 175). The column itself is preserved in a clipping in one of the scrapbooks Orion Clemens kept for his brother. This column was among the first Clemens wrote on his own, after Dan De Quille left for the East (see "The Illustrious Departed," no. 32).

. . . .

BOARD OF EDUCATION.—In accordance with a law passed at the late session of the legislature, a Board of Education is to be organized in each of the several counties. The Storey county Board will be composed of seven members, apportioned as follows: Four from Virginia, two from Gold Hill, and one from Flowery. The Chairman of the Board will be County School Superintendent. These officers will have power to issue bonds sufficient to defray the expenses of the schools, from the 1st of January until the 1st of November; to establish schools of all grades, engage and examine teachers, etc. The election for the Board of Education will be held next Monday, at the Court House, in Virginia; at the Postoffice, in Gold Hill, and at the house of I. W. Knox, in Flowery, the polls to be open from 8 o'clock in the morning until 6 in the evening. The Board will meet and organize on the Monday following their election.

BLOWN DOWN.—At sunset yesterday, the wind commenced blowing after a fashion to which a typhoon is mere nonsense, and in a short time the face of heaven was obscured by vast clouds of dust all spangled over with lumber, and shingles, and dogs and things. There was no particular harm in that, but the breeze soon began to work damage of a serious nature. Thomas Moore's new frame house on the east side of C street, above the Court House, was blown down, and the fire-wall front of a one story brick building higher up the street was also thrown to the ground. The latter house was occupied as a store by Mr. Heldman, and owned by Mr. Felton. The storm was very severe for a while, and we shall not be surprised to hear of further destruction having been caused by it. The damage resulting to Mr. Heldman's grocery store, amounts to $2,200.

AT HOME.—Judge Brumfield's nightmare—the Storey county delegation—have straggled in, one at a time, until they are all at home once more. Messrs. Mills, Mitchell, Meagher and Minneer returned several days ago, and we had the pleasure of meeting Mr. Davenport, also, yesterday. We do not know how long the latter gentleman has been here, but we offer him the unlimited freedom of the city, anyhow. Justice to a good representative is justice, you know, whether it be tardy or otherwise.

THE SCHOOL.—Mr. Mellvile's school will open again next Monday, and in the meantime the new furniture is being put up in the school house. The Virginia Cadets (a company composed of Mr. Mellvile's larger pupils,) will appear in public on New Year's Day, the weather permitting, armed and equipped as the law directs. The boys were pretty proficient in their military exercises when we saw them last, and they have probably not deteriorated since then.

SAD ACCIDENT.—We learn from Messrs. Hatch & Bro., who do a heavy business in the way of supplying this market with vegetables, that the rigorous weather accompanying the late storm was so severe on the mountains as to cause a loss of life in several instances. Two sacks of sweet potatoes were frozen to death on the summit, this side of Strawberry. The verdict rendered by the coroner's jury was strictly in accordance with the facts.

THRILLING ROMANCE.—On our first page, to-day, will be found the opening chapters of a thrilling tale, entitled "An Act to amend and supplemental to an Act to provide for Assessing and Collecting County and Territorial Revenue." This admirable story was written especially for the columns of this paper by several distinguished authors. We have secured a few more productions of the same kind, at great expense, and we design publishing them in their regular order. Our readers will agree with us that it will redound considerably to their advantage to read and preserve these documents.

FIRE, ALMOST.—The roof of the New York Restaurant took fire from the stovepipe, yesterday morning, and but for the timely discovery of the fact, a serious conflagration would have ensued, as the restaurant is situated in a nest of frame houses, which would have burned like tinder. As it was, nothing but a few shingles were damaged.

PRIVATE PARTY.—The members of Engine Co. No. 2, with a number of invited guests, are to have a little social dance at La Plata Hall, this evening. They have made every arrangement for having a pleasant time of it, and we hope they may succeed to the very fullest extent of their wishes.

B4. *Local Column*

4 January 1863

The following nine items appeared in the local column of the *Enterprise* on 4 January 1863. The rationale for assigning this date to the column is discussed in the headnote to "Our Stock Remarks" (p. 175). The column itself is preserved in a clipping in one of Mark Twain's scrapbooks, but the clipping does not contain the beginning lines of the first item about the forthcoming Sanitary Ball.

. . . benevolent enterprise, and to be present and see such a phenomenon, would be well worth the price of the ticket—six dollars, supper included. Wherefore, we advise every citizen of Storey to go to the ball—early—and stand ready to enjoy the joke. The fun to be acquired in this way, for a trifling sum of money, cannot be computed by any system of mathematics known to the present generation. And the more the merrier. We all know that a thousand people can enjoy that failure more extensively than a smaller number. Mr. Unger has tendered the use of the large dining hall of the What Cheer House (nearly opposite the La Plata Hall) with all the necessary table ware, and the waiters employed in the hotel, free of charge. This generosity—this liberality in a noble cause—calls for a second from somebody. Get your contributions ready—money, wines, cakes, and knicknacks and substantials of all kinds—and when the ladies call for them, deliver your offerings with a grace and dignity graduated by the market value of the same, the condition of your pecuniary affairs, and the sympathy you feel for maimed and suffering humanity. The ladies may be looked for to-morrow.

ELECTION.—To-morrow morning, at eight o'clock, the polls will be opened at the Court House, on C street, for the election of the four members of the County Board of Education to which Virginia is entitled. Gold Hill is entitled to two members, and Flowery to one. In the former place, the polls will be at the Post Office, and in the latter at the house of Mr. I. W. Knox. The Board will meet and organize on the Monday following their election. They will have power to issue bonds for a sum sufficient to defray the expenses of the respective schools of the county, from the beginning of the present month until the first of November. They will also have power to establish schools of all grades, engage and examine teachers, etc. The Chairman of the Board will be County School Superintendent. Let those who feel interested in school matters go and deposit their opinions in the ballot-box to-morrow.

PUBLIC SCHOOL.—The juveniles are hereby notified to put away their sleds and doll-babies and go into the traces again, at Mr. Mellvile's school-house, corner of E and Washington streets, to-morrow morning, at 10 o'clock. The pupils used to learn fast under the old regime of puritanical straight-back benches. We shall expect the new chairs and desks to impart a telegraphic celerity to their improvement henceforward.

NEW YEARS EXTENSION.—Yesterday was New Years Day for the ladies. We kept open house, and were called upon by seventy-two ladies—all young and handsome. This stunning popularity is pleasant to reflect upon, but we are afraid some people will think it prevented us from scouting for local matters with our usual avidity. This is a mistake; if anything had happened within the county limits yester-day, those ladies would have mentioned it.

SUPREME COURT.—Gen. Williams finished his long and able ar-gument in the Chollar and Potosi case, at a late hour last night. This was the closing speech. It is said that the Supreme Court cannot reasonably be expected to render a decision in this important case before the end of the present month.

BALL IN CARSON.—Just as we are going to press, we learn that Mrs. Williamson is to give a ball at the White House in Carson City, next Thursday evening. We have no particulars, but we suppose that one of those pleasant, sociable affairs, which are Mrs. Williamson's speciality, is in contemplation.

MASS.—Rev. Father Manogue notifies the Roman Catholics of Car-son City that Mass will be celebrated there this forenoon at 11 o'clock. We presume that this service will take place at Miss Clapp's school-house, as it has been used by that denomination for some time past as a chapel.

FIREMEN'S MEETING.—The Virginia Engine Company will hold a meeting at the engine house, A street, on Tuesday evening, January 6th, for the purpose of electing officers to serve during the present year.

RECORDER'S COURT.—Business in this institution is still feeble. Only one case yesterday—a scion of the noble house of Howard— Christian name, John Doe, d. d., fined ten dollars and costs—paid the same and was discharged.

B5. *Local Column*

6 January 1863

The following five items appeared in the *Enterprise* for 6 January 1863, which is not extant. The text is preserved in a contemporary reprinting in the Marysville (Calif.) *Appeal* for 9 January 1863, which attributed it to the *Enterprise* of January 6. The authenticity of the first item is discussed in the introduction (pp. 20–21).

[FREE FIGHT.—] A beautiful and ably conducted free fight came off in C street yesterday afternoon, but as nobody was killed or mortally wounded in a manner sufficiently fatal to cause death, no particular interest attaches to the matter, and we shall not publish the details. We pine for murder—these fist fights are of no consequence to anybody.

Humboldt stocks are plenty in the market, at figures which we have no doubt are low for the claims. The want of buyers is probably attributable to the indefinite knowledge of these claims. There are unquestionably many valuable ledges in the district offered at exceedingly low prices.

The old friends and acquaintances of Jno. D. Kinney (who came to Nevada Territory with Chief Justice Turner, and who returned to the States last March,) will be gratified to learn that that sterling patriot is now a captain in the Seventh Ohio Cavalry.

Milstead, who murdered a man named Varney, some time ago, near Ragtown, in Humboldt county, will be hung in Dayton next Friday.

James Leconey, W. H. Barstow, Jas. Phelan and John A. Collins were elected members of the Board of Education at Virginia.

B6. *Local Column*

10 January 1863

The following two items were included in the same *Enterprise* local column that contained Mark Twain's "The Sanitary Ball" (no. 37) and "Due Notice" (no. 38). His undoubted authorship of these sketches makes it more than likely that he wrote the entire column.

. . . .

THE NEW COURT HOUSE.—Messrs. Unger & Denninger's new brick house, on B street, has been leased by the County Commissioners for court rooms and offices. The first floor, we believe, is to be used for a United States District Court room, and the second story will be partitioned into offices and a Probate Court room. It would probably have been better to have reversed this order of things, on account of the superior light and the freedom from dust and noise afforded by the upper story; yet it is possible that these advantages may be as necessary in one case as the other—we do not care about dictating much in the matter so long as no one will be likely to pay us for it. But nevertheless, since the first story is to be used for the District Court, we wish to suggest that that box, that partition, be removed, and the whole of it set apart for that purpose. It would then be a large, handsome and well-lighted hall, whereas, in its present shape, it is not very greatly superior to the present court room on C street. A gentleman informed us yesterday that he thought the intention was to remove the partition, but he could not be positive about it.

. . . .

THE MUSIC.—Millington & McCluskey's band furnished the music for the Sanitary Ball on Thursday night, and also for the Odd Fellows' Ball the other evening in Gold Hill, and the excellence of the article was only equalled by the industry and perseverance of the performers. We consider that the man who can fiddle all through one of those Virginia Reels without losing his grip, may be depended upon in any kind of musical emergency.

B7. *Local Column*

11–21 January 1863

The following item appeared in the *Enterprise* sometime in mid-January 1863. The *Enterprise* printing is not extant, but the text is preserved in a contemporary reprinting in the San Francisco *Herald and Mirror* for 23 January 1863, which introduced the article as follows: "The Virginia City *Territorial Enterprise* has the following account of a pork speculation in that region."

HIGH PRICE OF PORK.—In our record of probate proceedings to-day, will be found the case of John Hill vs. John Doe Wentworth. As a matter of principle, it may be well enough to stand by your rights until the lake of fire and brimstone is no longer in a state of liquification, but whether it be good policy to do so at all times is a question which admits of argument. This case is an instance in point. The property involved is about twenty or thirty dollars' worth of pork in a crude state—we mean, two living hogs, probably worth but little more than ten dollars each; yet this suit to determine their ownership has already cost the parties to it some six or seven hundred dollars, and the defeated but plucky plaintiff has given notice that he will apply for a new trial! The new trial will double the bill of expenses, in all human probability.

We learn from gentlemen who were present at the trial to-day, that there were about thirty witnesses on the stand, and one of them a woman. The hog dispute afforded those concerned and the lookers-on a good deal of fun, but it was very costly. Those two distinguished pigs ought to be taken care of and exhibited at the first agricultural fair of Nevada Territory. At any rate, we shall officially spread the proceedings of this trial upon the records of the Washoe Agricultural, Mining and Mechanical Society, as evidence of the high value placed upon the hog in Nevada Territory.

B8. *Local Column*

19 February 1863

The following three items, two of which are incomplete, are preserved in a photograph of the *Enterprise* for 19 February 1863 (MTP), the same issue that carried "Ye Sentimental Law Student" (no. 44). The paper has been torn, obscuring most of the first article; only the portions that form intelligible sentences are reproduced here. The photograph cuts off the last article in mid-sentence.

[LA PLATA ORE COMPANY.—] . . . The company was organized under a deed of trust, and has been steadily at work, with scarce any inter- mission, since the 1st of May, 1861—under the general superin- tendence of the President, Col. W. H. Howard. The claim is believed to comprise some of the finest ledges in the Virginia and Gold Hill range, and from present appearances it looks as if the company were about to commence realizing the reward of their long and well-bestowed labor, as in addition to the ledges already noticed, the top of a fine ledge has already been uncovered on the west side of the claim, where the chimney ranging with the Butler's Peak and Mount Davidson ledges crops out.

. . . .

THE CHINA TRIAL.—We were there, yesterday, not because we were obliged to go, but just because we wanted to. The more we see of this aggravated trial, the more profound does our admiration for it become. It has more phases than the moon has in a chapter of the almanac. It commenced as an assassination; the assassinated man neglected to die, and they turned it into assault and battery; after this the victim *did* die, whereupon his murderers were arrested and tried yesterday for perjury; they convicted one Chinaman, but when they found out it was the wrong one, they let him go—and why they should have been so almighty particular is beyond our comprehension; then, in the afternoon, the officers went down and arrested Chinatown again for the same old offense, and put it in jail—but what shape the charge will take this time, no man can foresee: the chances are that it will be about a stand-off between arson and robbing the mail. Capt. White hopes to get the murderers of the Chinaman hung one of these days, and so do we, for that matter, but we do not expect anything of the kind. You see, these Chinamen are all alike, and they cannot identify each other. They mean well enough, and they really show a disinterested anxiety to get some of their friends and relatives hung, but the same misfortune overtakes them every time: they make mistakes and get the wrong man, with unvarying accuracy. With a zeal in behalf of justice which cannot be too highly praised, the whole Chinese population have accused each other of this murder, each in his regular turn, but fate is against them. They cannot tell each other apart. There is only one way to manage this thing with strict equity: hang the gentle Chinamen promiscuously, until justice is satisfied.

THE CONCERT.—We shall always guard against insinuating that the citizens of Virginia are not filled with a fondness for music, after what we saw at Mr. Griswold's Concert last night. The house was filled, from dome to cellar (we speak figuratively, since there was neither dome nor cellar to the house,) with people who entirely appreciated the performance, and testified pleasure by frequent and hearty applause. The Concert was a notable credit to the talent of Virginia, and we think we speak the public desire when we ask for another like it. Mr. James Gilmore, a very youthful looking poet, recited a martial poem whereof himself was the author. It was received with great applause. We only heard five of the songs set . . .

B9. *Local Column*

25 February 1863

The following eight items are preserved in a photograph of the *Enterprise* for 25 February 1863 (MTP), the same issue that carried "The Unreliable" (no. 46).

"MANY CITIZENS."—In another column of this paper will be found a card signed by "Many Citizens of Carson," stating that the County Commissioners of Ormsby county have removed the Sheriff from office and appointed some one else in his stead. They also ask whether the Commissioners really possess the power to remove the Sheriff, or the Governor of the Territory, or the President of the United States, at pleasure. This is all well enough, except that in the face of our well known ability in the treatment of ponderous questions of unwritten law, these citizens have addressed their inquiries to the chief editor of this paper—a man who knows no more about legal questions than he does about religion—and so saturated with self-conceit is he, that he has even attempted, in his feeble way, to answer the propositions set forth in that note. We ignore his reply entirely, and notwithstanding the disrespect which has been shown us, we shall sink private pique for the good of our fellow men, and proceed to set their minds at rest on this question of power. We declare that the County Commissioners do possess the power to remove the officers mentioned in that note, at pleasure. The Organic Act says so in so many words. We invite special attention to the first clause of section 2 of that document, where this language is used, if we recollect rightly: "The executive power and authority in and over said Territory of Nevada shall be vested in a Governor and other officers, who shall hold their offices for four years, and until their successors shall be appointed and qualified, unless sooner removed by the County Commissioners." That is explicit enough, we take it. "Other officers" means any or *all* other officers, of course, else such dignitaries as it was intended to refer to would have been specifically mentioned; consequently, the President of the United States, and the Governor and Sheriff being "officers," come within the provisions of the law, and may be shoved out of the way by the Commissioners as quietly as they would abate a nuisance. We might enlarge upon this subject until Solomon himself couldn't understand it—but we have settled the question, and we despise to go on scattering pearls before swine who have not asked us for them. In thus proving by the Organic Act, and beyond the shadow of a doubt, that the County Commissioners are invested with power to remove the Sheriff or the Governor or the President, whenever they see fit to do so, we have been actuated solely by a love of the godlike principles of right and justice, and a desire to show the public what an unmitigated ass the chief editor of this paper is. Having succeeded to our entire satisfaction, we transfer our pen to matters of local interest, although we could prove, if we wanted to, that the County Commissioners not only possess the power to depose the officers above referred to but to hang them also, if they feel like it. When people want a legal opinion in detail, they must address their communications to us, individually, and not to irresponsible smatterers, like the chief editor.

THE FIREMEN'S BALL.—About seventy couples assembled at Topliffe's Theatre night before last, upon the occasion of the annual ball of Virginia Engine Company No. 1. The hall was ablaze, from one end to the other, with flags, mirrors, pictures, etc.; and when the crowd of dancers had got into violent motion, and thoroughly fuddled with plain quadrilles, the looking-glasses multiplied them into a distracted and countless throng. Verily, the effect was charming to the last degree. The decoration of the theatre occupied several days, and was done under the management of a committee composed of Messrs. Brokaw, Robinson, Champney, Claresy, Garvey and Sands, and they certainly acquitted themselves with marked ability. The floor was covered with heavy canvass, and we rather liked the arrangement— but the wind got under it and made it fill and sag like a circus tent, insomuch that it impeded the Varsovienne practice, and caused the ladies to complain occasionally. Benham's "People's Band" made excellent music; however, they always do that. We have not one particle of fault to find with the ball; the managers kept perfect order and decorum, and did everything in their power to make it pass pleasantly to all the guests. They succeeded. But of all the failures we have been called upon to chronicle, the supper was the grandest. It was bitterly denounced by nearly everybody who sat down to it—officers, firemen,

men, women and children. Now, the supposition is, that somebody will come out in a card and deny this, and attribute base motives to us: but we are not to be caught asleep, or even napping, this time—we have got all our proofs at hand, and shall explode at anybody who tries to show that we cannot tell the truth without being actuated by unworthy motives. Chief Engineer Peasley and officer Birdsall said that the supper contract was for a table supplied with everything the market could afford, and in such profusion that the last who came might fare as well as the first (the contractor to receive a stipulated sum for each supper furnished)—and they also say that no part or portion of that contract was entirely fulfilled. The entertainment broke up about four o'clock in the morning, and the guests returned to their homes well satisfied with the ball itself, but not with the supper.

. . . .

SMALL POX.—From Carson we learn, officially, that Dr. Munckton has been sent down to Pine Nut Springs to look after some cases of small pox, reported as existing among the Washoe Indians there. It is said that three men and a mahala are afflicted with it; the doctor intends vaccinating their attendants and warning the other Indians to keep away. Capt. Jo says one of the Indians caught the disease from a shirt given him by a white man. We do not believe any man would do such a thing as that maliciously, but at the same time, any man is censurable who is so careless as to leave infected clothing lying about where these poor devils can get hold of it. The commonest prudence ought to suggest the destruction of such dangerous articles.

SCHOOL-HOUSE.—An addition is being built to the public school-house, and will be completed and put in order for occupation as soon as possible. Mr. Mellvile's school has increased to such an extent that the old premises were found insufficient to accommodate all the pupils. As soon as the new building is completed, the school will be divided into three departments—advanced, intermediate and infant —and one of these will occupy it.

TRIAL TO-DAY.—Sam Ingalls, who attempted the life of Pease the other day with a bowie knife, will be up before Judge Atwill to-day on a charge of drawing a deadly weapon. A case of this kind should never be allowed to pass without a severe rebuke, and if the evidence finds the prisoner guilty, he will probably catch it to-day; if it does not, why, no one wants him rebuked, of course.

DISTRICT COURT.—The testimony for both sides in the case of the Burning Moscow vs. Madison Company was completed yesterday, and the lawyers will begin to throw hot shot at each other this morning—which is our military way of saying that the arguments of counsel herein will be commenced to-day. A great deal of interest is manifested in this suit, and the lobbies will be crowded during its trial.

SUICIDE.—We learn by a note received last night per Langton's Express, that a German named John Meyer, a wood dealer in Downieville, committed suicide there on the night of the 19th inst., by blowing his brains out with a pistol. The cause is supposed to have been insanity.

TELEGRAPHIC.—A message for S. S. Harman remains uncalled for at the Telegraph office.

B10. Local Column

17–26 February 1863

The following item appeared in the *Enterprise* sometime in late February 1863. The *Enterprise* printing is not extant, but the text is preserved in a contemporary reprinting in the Oroville (Calif.) *Butte Record* for 28 February 1863, which introduced the article as follows: "Local of the Virginia Enterprise, who is continually blundering in his items—making misstatements one day, and correcting them the day following—gives one of his victims satisfaction after this style." The item is an early example of one of Mark Twain's favorite forms, the apology which only makes matters worse: see "Explanation of a Mysterious Sentence" (no. 173).

APOLOGETIC.—We are always happy to apologize to a man when we do him an injury. We have wounded William Smiley's feelings, and we will heal them up again or bust. We said in yesterday's police record that Bill (excuse the familiarity, William,) was drunk. We lied. It is our opinion that Sam Wetherill did, too, for he gave us the statement. We have gleaned the facts in the case, though, from William himself, and at his request we hasten to apologize. His offense was mildness itself. He only had a pitched battle with another man, and resisted an officer. That was all. Come up, William, and take a drink.

B11. Local Column

1–12 March 1863

The following item appeared in the *Enterprise* sometime in early March 1863. The *Enterprise* printing is not extant, but the text is preserved in a contemporary reprinting in the Oroville (Calif.) *Butte Record* for 14 March 1863, which attributed it to the *Enterprise*.

CALICO SKIRMISH.—Five Spanish women, of unquestionable character, were arraigned before Judge Atwill yesterday, some as principals and some as accessories to a feminine fight of a bloodthirsty description in A street. It was proved that one of them drew a navy revolver and a bowie-knife and attempted to use them upon another of the party, but being prevented, she fired three shots through the floor, for the purpose of easing her mind, no doubt. She was bound over to keep the peace, and the whole party dismissed.

B12. Local Column

3 April 1863

The following five items are preserved in a copy of the *Enterprise* for 3 April 1863. We have omitted the extracts mentioned in the first article. The column is more than usually factual, but most items bear Mark Twain's stylistic signature.

A DISTINGUISHED VISITOR.—Madame Clara Kopka arrived in Virginia a few days since, and is still sojourning in the city. To many of our citizens the name will be unfamiliar, yet such is by no means the case in the hospitals and upon the battle-fields of the East, where she has devoted nearly twelve months to arduous labor in tending the sick and wounded soldiers. In this service she has endured all the hardships and privations of camp life, without hope or desire of reward, and to the serious detriment of her health. She comes among us partly to satisfy a taste for travel, and partly to gather renewed vigor by a change of climate. She asked Mayor Arick for a homestead, supposing, in the simplicity of her heart, that the barren but beautiful landscape which surrounds Virginia was free to any who thought they could make use of it. Unfortunately, this is not the case; but the Silver Terrace Company could give Madame the homestead she covets without inconveniencing themselves in the least, and we have an idea that they will consider it a pleasure to do so. Madame Kopka brings with her a bundle of letters from military officers, from brigade and subordinate surgeons in the army, from Secretary Stanton, and letters of recommendation to General Halleck, all of which speak of her in the highest terms of praise. We cannot spare room for these letters, but we publish two newspaper extracts which will answer every purpose, perhaps. The first is from a long article, written by an army surgeon, in the N. Y. Home Journal of September 13th, and the other from the N. Y. Tribune of July 5th. . . .

THE LOIS ANN.—This claim is situated in a ravine which runs up in a northwesterly direction out of American Flat, and is on the Ophir Grade, about two miles and a half from Gold Hill. The ledge did not crop out, but was uncovered by a small slide in the hillside, and found by Mr. Lightford, the present Superintendent, and located some four or five weeks ago. A well timbered incline has since been sunk upon it to the depth of twenty-five feet, and work in it is still going on day and night, although a stream of water from the vein materially interferes with the operations of the men. In the bottom of the incline the ledge is about ten feet wide, has a casing of blue clay, and is well defined; a great quantity of quartz has been taken from it, which looks exactly like third or fourth-class Ophir, but it won't pay to crush yet awhile, although choice specimens of it have assayed as high as ninety-two dollars to the ton. We visited the mine in company with Mr. H. C. Brown and Mr. Lightford, the Superintendent, and we share their opinion, that there is big pay rock in it somewhere, and it is only necessary to sink a reasonable depth to find it. Such promising indications as have been found in this claim are not often discovered so near the surface. Three north extensions have been located on the Lois Ann, and shafts sunk, and the lead struck on the first and third, the character and appearance of the rock in both instances proving identical with that of the original—coarse crystalized quartz, of a porous nature, and of a dark blue color like Comstock rock. There are fourteen hundred feet in the discovery claim, and the property is owned principally by mill men of Gold Hill. One of the best indications about the Lois Ann is at present much the most troublesome—we refer to the stream of water which pours from the ledge; work in the incline will have to be suspended on account of it and a tunnel commenced from the ravine—this will be about a hundred and fifty feet long, and will tap the lead at a depth of seventy-five feet. A mill-site has been taken up in the vicinity with the intention of turning the water to useful account in case the ledge proves as excellent as it is expected it will. Another good-looking ledge lies back of the Lois Ann, and parallel with it, which belongs to the same company. There is a claim of a thousand feet in the vicinity of these leads which is called the Zanesville, and the rock from it pays in gold from the very surface; every pound of it is saved, and mill men who have tested it say it will yield about a hundred dollars to the ton; there is only a mere trace of silver in it. The ledge is only about two feet wide, in the bottom of a shaft twelve feet deep, but is increasing in width slowly; possibly the Zanesville may peter out and go to thunder, but there is no prospect of such a result at present. It is rich, but as it is only a gold ledge, and is so small, we have less confidence in it than in the Lois Ann.

ISLAND MILL.—The Island Mill, built on Carson river by Mr. Hite, of Gold Hill, is about completed now, and the machinery was set in motion yesterday to see if there was anything wrong about it. The result was satisfactory, and the Island Mill will go to work formally and forever next Tuesday.

. . . .

GOULD & CURRY.—They struck it marvelously rich in a new shaft in the Gould & Curry mine last Saturday night. We saw half a ton of native silver at the mouth of the tunnel, on Tuesday, with a particle of quartz in it here and there, which could be readily distinguished without the aid of a glass. That particular half ton will yield somewhere in the neighborhood of ten thousand dollars. We have long waited patiently for the Gould & Curry to flicker out, but we cannot discover much encouragement about this last flicker. However, it is of no consequence—it was a mere matter of curiosity anyhow; we only wanted to see if she would, you know.

. . . .

THE MINSTRELS.—We were present at La Plata Hall about two minutes last night, and heard Sam. Pride's banjo make a very excellent speech in English to the audience. The house was crowded to suffocation.

B13. Local Column

19–30 April 1863

The following item must have appeared in the *Enterprise* toward the end of April 1863, before Mark Twain left for San Francisco. The *Enterprise* printing is not extant, but the text is preserved in a contemporary reprinting in the Oroville (Calif.) *Butte Record* for 2 May 1863.

ELECTRICAL MILL MACHINERY.—Mr. Wm. L. Card, of Silver City, has invented a sort of infernal machine, which is to turn quartz mills by electricity. It consists of wheels and things, and—however, we could not describe it without getting tangled. Mr. Card assures us that he can apply his invention to all the mills in Silver City, and work the whole lot with one powerful Grove battery. We believe—and if we had galvanic sense enough to explain the arrangement properly, others would also. A patent has already been applied for.

B14. Local Column

27 August 1863

The following item appeared in the *Enterprise* on 27 August 1863. It is preserved in a clipping in one of Mark Twain's scrapbooks. Mark Twain was reacting to an editorial, probably written by Charles A. Parker (the "Obese"), for the Virginia City *Evening Bulletin* of August 26:

Yesterday we gave a small item in which was set down the annual production of the precious metals in this Territory, in the gross, at $730,000,000. We also gave the data on which the calculation was made. These data may vary slightly from those given, upon an exact and actual investigation of the facts. Some probably will be found too high, but others again will exceed the numbers estimated upon. For instance, we have set down the number of quartz mills at one hundred; there are probably, however, nearer one hundred and fifty than one hundred, as this calculation was based upon statistics collected more than three months since. On the other hand, we may be a little too high in estimating the average yield per ton at $1,000. Upon the whole, however, we believe that the errors or miscalculations will be found nearly to counterbalance each other, and thus make the general result about the same.[1]

The "small item" referred to in the first sentence appeared in the *Bulletin* on August 25 (p. 3):

A SMALL CALCULATION.—There are one hundred Quartz Mills in this Territory, which crush upon an average twenty tons of mineral rock per day. This rock yields all the way from $100 to $4,000 per ton; and may be averaged at about $1,000 per ton. Giving a total turn out of 2,000,000 per day; and an annual production of $730,000,000—more than one half our present national debt according to official accounts.[2]

Mark Twain's fascination with calculations of this kind is well known. In this case, he was so pleased with his own arguments that he eventually incorporated part of "Ye Bulletin Cyphereth" in chapter 52 of *Roughing It*, adding in a bracketed comment, however, that his figuring was "a considerable over estimate."

---

[1]"What Nevada Contributes," Virginia City *Evening Bulletin*, 26 August 1863, p. 2.

[2]The Virginia City *Union* local editor, Adair Wilson (the "Unimportant"), published a brief squib in comment on this item on August 26: "If the capacity of the 'Obese' can be estimated by his ability for making calculations, it must require about three restaurants to supply him" (reprinted in the Virginia City *Evening Bulletin*, 26 August 1863, p. 3).

YE BULLETIN CYPHERETH.—The Bulletin folks have gone and swallowed an arithmetic; that arithmetic has worked them like a "wake-up-Jake," and they have spewed up a multitude of figures. We cypher up the importance of the Territory sometimes so recklessly that our self-respect lies torpid within us for weeks afterwards—but we see now that our most preposterous calculations have been as mild as boarding-house milk; we perceive that we haven't the nerve to do up this sort of thing with the Bulletin. It estimates the annual yield of the precious metals at $730,000,000! Bully! They say figures don't lie—but we doubt it. We are distanced—that must be confessed; yet, appalled as we are, we will venture upon the Bulletin's "boundless waste" of figures, and take the chances. A Gould & Curry bar with $2,000 in it weighs nearly 100 pounds; $100,000 worth of their bullion would weigh between two and two and a half tons; it would take two of Wells Fargo's stages to carry that $100,000 without discommoding the passengers; it would take 100 stages to carry $5,000,000, 2,000 stages to carry $100,000,000, and 14,600 stages to carry the Bulletin's annual yield of $730,000,000! Wells, Fargo & Co. transport all the bullion out of the Territory in their coaches, and to attend to this little job, they would have to send forty stages over the mountains daily throughout the year, Sundays not excepted, and make each of the forty carry considerably more than a ton of bullion!—yet they generally send only two stages, and the greatest number in one day, during the heaviest rush, was six coaches; they didn't each carry a ton of bullion, though, old smarty from Hongkong. The Bulletin also estimates the average yield of ore from our mines at $1,000 a ton! Bless your visionary soul, sixty dollars—where they get it "regular like"—is considered good enough in Gold Hill, and it is a matter of some trouble to pick out many tons that will pay $400. From sixty to two hundred is good rock in the Ophir, and when that company, or the Gould & Curry, or the Spanish, or any other of our big companies get into a chamber that pays over $500, they ship it to the Bay, my boy. But they don't ship thousands of tons at a time, you know. In Esmeralda and Humboldt, ordinary "rich rock" yields $100 to $200, and when better is found, it is shipped also. Reese River appears to be very rich, but you can't make an "average" there yet awhile; let her mines be developed first. We place the average yield of the ore of our Territory at $100 a ton— that is high enough; we couldn't starve, easily, on forty-dollar rock.

Lastly, the Bulletin puts the number of our mills at 150. That is another mistake; the number will not go over a hundred, and we would not be greatly amazed if it even fell one or two under that. While we are on the subject, though, we might as well estimate the "annual yield" of the precious metals, also; we did not intend to do it at first. Mr. Valentine, Wells Fargo's handsome and accomplished agent, has handled all the bullion shipped through the Virginia office for many a month. To his memory—which is excellent—we are indebted for the following exhibit of the company's business in the Virginia office since the first of January, 1862: From January 1st to April 1st, about $270,000 worth of bullion passed through that office; during the next quarter, $570,000; next quarter, $800,000; next quarter, $956,000; next quarter, $1,275,000; and for the quarter ending on the 30th of last June, about $1,600,000. Thus in a year and a half, the Virginia office only shipped $5,330,000 in bullion. During the year 1862 they shipped $2,615,000, so we perceive the average shipments have more than doubled in the last six months. This gives us room to promise for the Virginia office $500,000 a month for the year 1863, and now, perhaps, judging by the steady increase in the business, we too, like the Bulletin, are "underestimating," somewhat. This gives us $6,000,000 for the year. Gold Hill and Silver City together can beat us—we will give them eight, no, to be liberal, $10,000,000. To Dayton, Empire City, Ophir and Carson City, we will allow an aggregate of $8,000,000, which is not over the mark, perhaps, and may possibly be a little under it. To Esmeralda we give $4,000,000. To Reese River and Humboldt $2,000,000, which is liberal now, but may not be before the year is out. So we prognosticate that the yield of bullion this year will be about $30,000,000. Placing the number of mills in the Territory at 100, this gives to each the labor of $300,000 in bullion during the twelve months. Allowing them to run 300 days in the year, (which none of them more than do) this makes their work average $1,000 a day—one ton of the Bulletin's rock, or ten of ours. Say the mills average 20 tons of rock a day and this rock worth $50 as a general thing, and you have got the actual work of our 100 mills figured down just about "to a spot"—$1,000 a day each, and $30,000,000 a year in the aggregate. Oh no!—we have never been to school—we don't know how to cypher. Certainly not—we are probably a natural fool, but we don't know it.

Anyhow, we have mashed the Bulletin's estimate all out of shape and cut the first left-hand figure off its $730,000,000 as neatly as a regular banker's clerk could have done it.

B15. Letter from Dayton

November 1863–February 1864

The following is not a local item, but an extract from one of Mark Twain's out-of-town letters. The *Enterprise* printing is not extant, but the text is preserved in Carl Burgess Glasscock's *The Big Bonanza*. Glasscock indicates that the letter appeared "a little later" than Mark Twain's famous hoax "A Bloody Massacre near Carson" (no. 66), and that another article ("A Brisk Business in the Shooting and Slashing Way in Washoe"), not by Clemens, appeared "not long after" the letter. "A Bloody Massacre" was published on 28 October 1863; "A Brisk Business" on 10 March 1864. We have therefore conjectured a date of publication sometime between November 1863 and the end of February 1864.

[TRAVELING WITH ADOLPH SUTRO.—] Eight left Virginia yesterday and came down to Dayton with Mr. Sutro. Time 30 minutes—distance 8 or 9 miles. There is nothing very slow about that kind of travel. We found Dayton the same old place but taking up a good deal more room than it did the last time I saw it, and looking more brisk and lively with its increase of business, and more handsome on account of the beautiful dressed stone buildings with which it is being embellished of late.

Just as we got fairly under way, and were approaching Ball Robert's bridge, Sutro's dog, "Carlo," got to skirmishing around in the extravagant exuberance of his breakfast, and shipped up a fight with six or seven other dogs whom he was entirely unacquainted with, had never met before and probably has no desire to meet again. He waltzed into them right gallantly and right gallantly waltzed out again.

We also left at about this time and trotted briskly across Ball Robert's bridge. I remarked that Ball Robert's bridge was a good one and a credit to that bald gentleman. I said it in a fine burst of humor and more on account of the joke than anything else, but Sutro is insensible to the more delicate touches of American wit, and the effort was entirely lost on him. I don't think Sutro minds a joke of mild character any more than a dead man would. However, I repeated it once or twice without producing any visible effect, and finally derived what comfort I could by laughing at it myself.

Mr. Sutro being a confirmed business man, replied in a practical and businesslike way. He said the bridge was a good one, and so were all public blessings of a similar nature when entrusted to the hands of private individuals. He said if the county had built the bridge it would have cost an extravagant sum of money, and would have been eternally out of repair. He also said the only way to get public work well and properly done was to let it out by contract.

"For instance," says he, "they have fooled away two or three years trying to capture Richmond, whereas if they had let the job by contract to some sensible business man, the thing would have been accomplished and forgotten long ago." It was a novel and original idea and I forgot my joke for the next half hour in speculating upon its feasibility. . . .

B16. *Local Column*

25–27 December 1863

The following item appeared in the *Enterprise*, possibly as early as Christmas, but probably on 26 or 27 December 1863. The *Enterprise* printing is not extant, but the text is preserved in a contemporary reprinting in the Marysville (Calif.) *Appeal* for 30 December 1863, which introduced the article as follows: "Mark Twain, local of the *Territorial Enterprise*, received a Christmas present, which he acknowledges as follows."

A CHRISTMAS GIFT.—"Mr. Twain—compliments of Miss Chase—Christmas, 1863." This handwriting disposed us to suspect treachery, and to regard the box as a deadly infernal machine. It was on this account that we got a stranger to open it. This precaution was unnecessary. The diabolical box had nothing in it but a ghastly, naked, porcelain doll baby. However, we are much obliged—we always had a hankering to have a baby, and now we are satisfied—the mythical "Miss Chase" helped us to the business, and she has our cordial thanks for her share in it.

B17. *Local Column*

29 December 1863

The following item appeared in the *Enterprise* on 29 December 1863. It is preserved in a clipping in one of Mark Twain's scrapbooks. The printed date, "Tuesday, ... December 29, 1863," is pasted immediately above the clipping.

CHRISTMAS PRESENTS.—We received from Carson, Saturday, a long yellow box, of suspicious appearance, with the following inscription upon it: "Mark Twain, ENTERPRISE Office, Virginia—Free—Politeness Langton's Pioneer Express—*Be-hi-me-soi-vin.*" That last phrase is Greek, and means "Bully for you!" We are not sure that it was written by Mrs. H. F. R., of Carson, and there was no evidence accompanying the box to show that it was. This is what makes us so obstinate in the opinion that it might have been written by somebody else. The box contained a toy rabbit, of the jackass persuasion, gifted with ears of aggravated dimensions, and swathed in sage-brush; an Indian chief—a mere human creation—made of raisins, strung on a skeleton formed of a single knitting-needle, with a solitary fig for a body, and a chicken feather driven into the head of the effigy, to denote its high official character. One more present remained—the same being a toy watchman's rattle, made of pine and tastefully painted. We are glad to have that rattle now, but when we asked for such a thing at a certain convivial party in Carson, it will be remembered that we meant to bestow it upon another young man who was present, and whose absent mind, we imagined, might be collected together and concentrated by means of such an instrument. We have presented the rabbit to Artemus Ward, to be preserved as a specimen of our resources; the other presents we shall always wear near our heart. The following report of the committee, accompanying the box, has been received, accepted, adopted, and the same referred to the Committee of the Whole—people:

CARSON CITY, December 25, 1863.

Mr. MARK TWAIN—*Sir:* The undersigned has the honor to be selected by the gay company of ladies and gentlemen and boys and girls and Santa Claus, who came in person with Judge Dixson's wolf-skin cap, coat, pants and a mask, and sleigh bells around his waist, and dashed in the room just after Mrs. Cutler and two long rows of children had sung a pretty piece, and read a letter from Santa Claus, when that individual immediately dashed into the room to the terror of some of the children, thirty-six in all, and climbed the Christmas tree, all covered with presents, and little lighted candles, and handed down things for everybody, and afterwards danced with the now reconciled children, and then dashed out; after which there was supper and dancing by the ladies and gentlemen; and the school which was thus made to enjoy themselves last night till midnight, was Miss H. K. Clapp and Mrs. Cutler's Seminary, which is one of the best there is, and instructed me to send you these things, which I do by Langton's Express, handed down from the Christmas tree by Santa Claus, marked "Mark Twain," to wit: One rabbit under a sage brush, to represent your design for a seal in the Constitutional Convention; one rattle, presented by a lady of whom you begged for one when you were here last, and a Pi-Ute to be eaten, being a chief with a chicken feather in his hat, composed of a fig for his body and otherwise raisins, sent to you by request of a lady of the medical profession, all of which is submitted by

WILLIAM A. TRINITY, Committee.

B18. Letter from Carson City

12–13 January 1864

The following is not a local item, but an extract from one of Mark Twain's letters from Carson City. The *Enterprise* printing is not extant, but the text is preserved in a contemporary reprinting in the Gold Hill *News* for 13 January 1864, which attributed it to "Mark Twain, writing from Carson," and probably reprinted it on the day of its appearance or very shortly thereafter. Since the *Enterprise* did not appear on Mondays, the letter probably appeared on January 12 or 13.

THE MINT.—Speaking of the mint, I have an item of news relating to that subject. Mr. Lockhart, the Indian Agent, has just received a letter from Commissioner Bennet, in which he says he has been informed by Secretary Chase that no further steps will be taken toward building a mint in this region until our *State Representatives* arrive in Washington! This is in consequence of efforts now being made by Mr. Conness to have the mint located at Virginia. The authorities want advice from representatives direct from the people. As I said before, the people of Ormsby will oppose the Constitution. O, certainly they will! They will if they are sick—or sentimental—or consumptive—or don't know their own interests—or can't see when God Almighty smiles upon them, and don't care anyhow. Now if Ormsby votes against the Constitution, let us clothe ourselves in sack-cloth and put ashes on our heads; for in that hour religious liberty will be at an end here—her next step will be to vote against her eternal salvation. However the anti-Constitutional sentiment here is growing weak in the knees.

B19. Local Column

17–24 April 1864

The following item appeared in the *Enterprise* probably sometime between 17 and 24 April 1864. The *Enterprise* printing is not extant, but the text is preserved in a contemporary reprinting in the Jackson (Calif.) *Amador Weekly Ledger* for 30 April 1864. Since Mark Twain left town for Silver Mountain on or about April 24, he could have written it any time in the week before his departure (see the headnote to "Frightful Accident to Dan De Quille," no. 73). The *Ledger* introduced the item as follows: "Missionaries are greatly needed in Virginia City, as witness the following from the Territorial Enterprise."

MISSIONARIES WANTED.—Yesterday morning Gashwiler and Charley Funk, citizens of Virginia City and of the Territory of Nevada, and officers of the great Virginia and Gold Hill Water Company, came rushing into our office in a state of excitement bordering on lunacy, and pointed out to us the following advertisement in the Evening Bulletin, with a fierce demand upon us to read it and render unto them our opinion concerning it:

"In the last day, that great day of the feast, Jesus stood and cried, saying: If any man thirst, let him come unto me and drink.—St. John, vii, 27.

"Whosoever drinketh of the water that I shall give him shall never thirst; but the water that I shall give him shall be in him a well of water springing up into everlasting life.—St. John, iv, 14.

"The lamb, which is in the midst of the throne, shall feed them, and shall lead them unto living fountains of waters, and God shall wipe away all tears from their eyes.—Rev. vii, 17."

We ask, now, in all candor, if there is a man in all Virginia who is competent by reason of his extraordinary natural or acquired stupidity, to guess what these gentlemen found in the above extracts to fill their souls with rage? As we hope for mercy past and present, they thought it was an attempt to ring in an opposition water company on the people! We call that infernal ignorance—and if we could think of a stronger term Gashwiler and Charley Funk should have the benefit of it. When men get so far gone that they do not know the Sermon on the Mount from a bid for a water franchise, it is time for them to begin to reform and stop taking desperate chances on the hereafter.

APPENDIX C

WE HAVE REPRINTED here a variety of collateral documents—contracts, advertisements, and prefaces—which bear upon Mark Twain's sketchbooks and plans for sketchbooks. They are arranged by title, and the titles are ordered chronologically. The mnemonic abbreviations are those used in the textual introduction and defined in the description of texts. Canceled words are enclosed in angle brackets.

C1. Collateral Documents for JF1

*The Celebrated Jumping Frog of Calaveras County,
And other Sketches.*
By Mark Twain. Edited by John Paul.
New York: C. H. Webb, 1867.

Mark Twain's dedication in JF1.

TO

JOHN SMITH,

WHOM I HAVE KNOWN IN DIVERS AND SUNDRY PLACES ABOUT THE WORLD, AND
WHOSE MANY AND MANIFOLD VIRTUES DID ALWAYS COMMAND
MY ESTEEM, I

Dedicate this Book.

It is said that the man to whom a volume is dedicated, always buys a
copy. If this prove true in the present instance, a princely affluence is about
to burst upon

THE AUTHOR.

C. H. Webb's "Advertisement" in JF1.

"MARK TWAIN" is too well known to the public to require a formal introduction at my hands. By his story of the Frog, he scaled the heights of popularity at a single jump, and won for himself the *sobriquet* of The Wild Humorist of the Pacific Slope. He is also known to fame as The Moralist of the Main; and it is not unlikely that as such he will go down to posterity. It is in his secondary character, as humorist, however, rather than in the primal one of moralist, that I aim to present him in the present volume. And here a ready explanation will be found for the somewhat fragmentary character of many of these sketches; for it was necessary to snatch threads of humor wherever they could be found—very often detaching them from serious articles and moral essays with which they were woven and entangled. Originally written for newspaper publication, many of the articles referred to events of the day, the interest of which has now passed away, and contained local allusions, which the general reader would fail to understand; in such cases excision became imperative. Further than this, remark or comment is unnecessary. Mark Twain never resorts to tricks of spelling nor rhetorical buffoonery for the purpose of provoking a laugh; the vein of his humor runs too rich and deep to make surface-gilding necessary. But there are few who can resist the quaint similes, keen satire, and hard good sense which form the staple of his writings.

J. P.

C2. Collateral Documents for BA1

Mark Twain's (Burlesque)
Autobiography and First Romance.
New York: Sheldon and Company, [1871].

First letter of agreement for BA1 (MTP). Mark Twain wrote on the back:
"Sheldon | Brochure contract." See the next item.

New York, December 9th 1870

Dear Sir

Your dispatch has just been received and we have answered by
telegraph that we will publish it, and of course do our very best as to
getting it out in time &c &c; and give you half of all the book can be
made to pay. This is much better for you than any copyright we could
name, if the book proves a success.

It is now of course late in the season to get out a book and there are
always delays we can never calculate on, as each step in the process of
manufacturing is made, but we can get it out as soon as anyone, and
should not lose a moment.

We are Very Truly Yours

Sheldon & Co [per] W.G.

P.S. Should you prefer a copyright we would give 15 per cent on the
retail price.

S&Co [per] W.G.

To S. S. Clemens Esq.
Editor Buffalo Express

Contract for BA1 (MTP). On 4 April 1871 Isaac E. Sheldon wrote Clemens: "Your favor of Apl 3rd is at hand. I rec'd also a few days since yours of Mar 22nd. Inclosed find a contract as you desire. It is just like the one you sent except that settlements are made 1st of Aug. & Feb each year. At these times we make up a/cs of copyright in all our books" (MTP). Clemens' copy of the contract and both of his letters have been lost; Sheldon's contract is reproduced here.

New York, April 4th 1871.

This memorandum certifies that before publishing Mark Twains pamphlet "Autobiography and First Romance" we agreed to pay him a royalty of *six cents* on every copy sold. Said agreement is still in force—and we further agree to make a full statement to him of sales every first of August and first of February and accompany the same with the amount of money due him.

Signed.
Sheldon & Co

C3. Collateral Documents for MTSk

Mark Twain's Sketches.
Selected and Revised by the Author.
Copyright Edition. London:
George Routledge and Sons, 1872.

"Author's Advertisement" for MTSk, which appeared in various newspaper advertisements as well as on p. [iii] of the book. Copies vary slightly: the one reproduced here appeared in the London *Spectator* for 25 May 1872 (p. 670); it is this copy that the Routledges referred to in their letter to the editor of the *Spectator*, dated 21 May 1872 (quoted in the textual introduction, p. 592). The copy in the book was dated "HARTFORD, 1872."

Messrs. George Routledge and Sons are *the only English Publishers* who pay me any Copyright on my books. That is something, but a courtesy which I prize even more is the opportunity which they have given me to edit and revise the matter for publication myself. This enables me to leave out a good deal of literature which has appeared in England over my name, *but which I never wrote.* And, as far as this particular volume is concerned, it also enables me to add a number of sketches which I *did* write, but which have not heretofore been published abroad.

This book contains all of my sketches which I feel at all willing to father.

MARK TWAIN.

Mark Twain's "Prefatory" for MTSk, which appeared on p. [v] of the book. Mark Twain probably composed it shortly before sending the printer's copy for MTSk to England, that is, in late March 1872.

IF I were to sell the reader a barrel of molasses, and he, instead of sweetening his substantial dinner with the same at judicious intervals, should eat the entire barrel at one sitting, and then abuse me for making him sick, I would say that he deserved to be made sick for not knowing any better how to utilize the blessings this world affords. And if I sell to the reader this volume of nonsense, and he, instead of seasoning his graver reading with a chapter of it now and then, when his mind demands such relaxation, unwisely overdoses himself with several chapters of it at a single sitting, he will well deserve to be nauseated, and he will have nobody to blame but himself if he *is*. There is no more sin in publishing an entire volume of nonsense than there is in keeping a candy store with no hardware in it. It lies wholly with the customer whether he will injure himself by means of either, or will derive from them the benefits which they will afford him if he uses their possibilities judiciously.

Respectfully submitted,

THE AUTHOR.

C4. Collateral Documents for Sk#1

Mark Twain's Sketches. Number One.
Authorised Edition. With Illustrations by R. T. Sperry.
New York: American News Company, [1874].

Prefatory note for Mark Twain's planned but never published pamphlet about the Shah of Persia (*MTLP*, pp. 79–80), a precursor of Sk#1. The location of the original manuscript is not now known; it was written on 7 July 1873.

To the Reader

It is not my desire to republish these New York Herald letters in this form; I only do it to forestall some small pirate or other in the book trade.

If I do not publish some such person may, and I then become tacitly accessory to a theft. I have had a recent unpleasant experience of this kind. I have copyrighted the letters here in London simply to prevent their republication in Great Britain in pamphlet form. My objection to such republication, either in America or England, is, that I think everybody has already had enough of the Shah of Persia. I am sure I have. To the letters I have added certain sketches of mine which are little known or not known at all in America, to the end that the purchaser of the pamphlet may get back a portion of his money and skip the chapters that refer to the Shah altogether.

With this brief apology, I am

Respectfully
Mark Twain

London, July 7

C5. Collateral Documents for SkNO

Mark Twain's Sketches, New and Old.
Now First Published in Complete Form.
Hartford and Chicago: American Publishing Company, 1875.

Contract for SkNO (Yale Za/Clemens/22). Mark Twain's contract was drawn up on 29 December 1870 and sent to him; it was presumably signed shortly thereafter. Elisha Bliss and Clemens revised it on 12 February 1875. The document is all in Bliss's hand, except for a sentence following the codicil: "It is satisfactory to me, Bliss." This appears to be Mark Twain's answer to a note written at the bottom by Bliss: "If all right sign & send back & I will send copy signed." Bliss also noted on the back: "The matter for book contracted for by within contract by S. L. Clemens has been delivered to us, & called 'M. T.'s Sketches.' | Am Pub Co | per E Bliss Jr." Mark Twain's copy of the contract itself has not been found, but his copy of the codicil is in MTP. His copy varies slightly from Bliss's, and it is attached to another statement by Bliss. Both are reproduced here. On the codicil Mark Twain has written: "Addition to Sketch Book copyright of '70." (Bliss corrected "copyright" to "contract.") Mark Twain also wrote: "Please file this away, Mr. Perkins. S. L. C.," addressing his lawyer at this time, Thomas C. Perkins of Hartford.

This memorandum made this Twenty ninth day December 1870 between Sam¹ L Clemens of Buffalo N.Y. & American Publishing Co. of Hartford State of Connecticut—witnesseth that the said Clemens is to prepare for the said Co. <a> matter for a book to be published by them in addition to the two already arranged for. Sd book to be got ready as soon as practicable by sd Clemens & so that it can be published in the early spring of /71 if possible. Sd matter to be made up in part of old articles written by sd Clemens & published heretofore, but to be altered if possible to do so in such a manner that a new copyright will hold upon them—Other parts of the book to be of new matter— The sd Company agrees to pay to sd Clemens the copyright of Seven & one half (7½) per cent—statements & settlements—free copies to editors & others to be the same as in contract for Innocents Abroad— & for the two other books arranged for.

> Saml L. Clemens.
> E Bliss Jr Secty
> Am Pub Co.

Hartford Feby. 12. 1875

It is agreed in consideration of the great increase of Mr Clemens fame that if the book above proposed sells <50,000> not to exceed 50,000 the copyright is to remain as above, but if it exceeds 50,000 it shall be 10% on all sold. Settlements to be made at rate of $7\frac{1}{2}$% until sale exceeds 50^{000} when the other $2\frac{1}{2}$ shall be paid.

Saml. L. Clemens.

E Bliss Jr prest

The following addition is to be made to the contract now existing between Sam[l] L Clemens & the American Publishing Co. dated Dec 29 1870, to wit.

Hartford Feby. 12. 1875

It is agreed that in consideration of the great increase of Mr. Clemens' fame, that if the book proposed, sells not to exceed 50,000 copies, the copyright is to remain as above, viz $7\frac{1}{2}$%, but if <that> it exceeds 50,000 it shall be 10% on all sold. Settlements to be made at rate of $7\frac{1}{2}$% until sale exceeds 50,000 copies, when the other $2\frac{1}{2}$% shall be paid.

Signed.

Saml. L. Clemens.

E Bliss Jr. prest

We have received from S. L. Clemens the Ms. for book contracted for in contract dated Dec. 29, 1870, & also recd from S L Clemens & C Dudley Warner, the Ms for book contracted for in contract dated May 8, 1873—& we have endorsed the receipt by us of same on the respective contracts.

There is no contract existing between S. L. Clemens & the Am. Pub Co., for a book or books, made prior to the latest above mentioned dates, on which the ms. contracted for has not been delivered to us.

Am Pub Co

pr E Bliss Jr prest

Mark Twain's "Preface" to SkNO as it appeared in the salesmen's prospectus. The manuscript for this preface survives in the Rare Book Room of the Cornell University Library, and it is reproduced here without emendation.

PREFACE.

I have scattered through this volume a mass of matter which has never been in print before, (such as "Those Annual Bills," the Jumping Frog restored to the English tongue after martyrdom in the French, the "Membranous Croup" sketch, & many others which I need not specify): not doing this in order to make an advertisement of it, but because these things seemed <worthy to my partial mind.> instructive.

Mark Twain.

Hartford, March, 1875.

Mark Twain's "Preface" for SkNO as it appeared in revised form in the book itself.

I have scattered through this volume a mass of matter which has never been in print before, (such as "Learned Fables for Good Old Boys and Girls," the "Jumping Frog restored to the English tongue after martyrdom in the French," the "Membranous Croup" sketch, and many others which I need not specify): not doing this in order to make an advertisement of it, but because these things seemed instructive.

MARK TWAIN.

HARTFORD, 1875.

FACING PAGE. Advertising copy from the American Publishing Company prospectus. Very rough working notes on the verso of unused advertising copy written by Mark Twain (quoted on p. 645 below) show that Bliss wrote what follows here.

MARK TWAIN'S SKETCHES,

NEW AND OLD.

NOW FIRST PUBLISHED IN COMPLETE FORM.

WE are happy to announce another volume by that incomparable humorist, MARK TWAIN, which we are sure will be welcomed by the public most enthusiastically. Unlike its predecessors this is not a connected story, yet has all the peculiar features which have so characterized his former works; and is made up of the very best of all that has emanated from the pen of its popular author. Nowhere does his ready wit and keen satire more forcibly display itself than in his sketch writings; in fact, his richest vein of humor seems to empty itself into *these*. Sharp, pithy, and always to the point, they stir up the subject discussed and the reader's *risibles* at the same time.

Many of his sketches have a world wide renown, and a constant and increasing demand exists for copies of them, bound in a shape for preservation. Such have been selected and find a place in this volume and are now offered for the first time complete in book form. Among them will be found the story of

THE FAMOUS "JUMPING FROG,"

as originally written; to which is added a new version with many exceedingly interesting variations.

HIS ESSAYS ON " POLITICAL ECONOMY," " CANNIBALISM," ETC., ETC., ARE ALSO RETAINED.

New sketches occupy large space in the volume and bear upon their faces abundant evidence of their authorship; being " *Twainish* " in every sense of the word.

Artist has vied with Author in the preparation of this book, and the result is a volume of rare beauty;

THE MOST ARTISTIC ILLUSTRATIONS

are profusely scattered over its pages, and the reader will often hesitate which first to enjoy—the sparkling humor of the Pen or of the Pencil.

Printed on the finest of super-calendered, delicate tinted paper, in the most perfect manner,—with its large, open, honest pages, its dainty blue cover so tastefully adorned with fanciful designs in black, and pure gold, its profusion of *Superb Illustrations* and the almost inexhaustible wealth of its text,—this book is without doubt a model one, unequalled in its combinations by any in print.

Mark Twain's readers and admirers are " Legion," and to them we say—this volume will in no wise disappoint you. It is " *The Big Bonanza* " of the Literary world; a perfect store-house of good things.

That the pen of our author is not a useless one is proven by the fact that his readers are largely men and women of a highly cultivated class. Scarcely a greater favorite of the Clergy can be named, and Lawyers, Scholars, Merchants, Mechanics and Farmers all read him with undisguised pleasure. While graver men are making war upon the vices or weaknesses of a community with heavy guns and by slow approaches, our author by a bold sally and sudden onslaught, under cover of some ridiculous, laughable story, overwhelms the enemy and ends his career; or what is oftener the case, his ready pen by some sharp and cutting satire arouses the public to a sense of wrong existing in their midst, heretofore undiscerned. His most extravagant tales have an application and a moral.

The specimen pages shown in this PROSPECTUS are taken from the sheets as printed for the book itself, consequently, are precisely what will be given to the subscriber in regard to quality of paper, printing, engravings, etc. A close scrutiny of them is solicited that their many superior points may be seen.

The volume will contain between 300 and 400 Quarto pages, with about 150 illustrations and will be

SOLD ONLY BY SUBSCRIPTION.

Price in Elegant Blue English Cloth, with Chaste Designs in Black and Gold, $3.00;
Gilt Edge, do. do. $3.50; Leather, (Library Style) $3.50;
In Half Turkey, Elegantly Bound, $4.50.

AMERICAN PUBLISHING CO., Publishers,

284 Asylum St., Hartford, Conn.

EXPLANATORY
NOTES

SECTION 1
HANNIBAL AND THE RIVER: 1851–1861

The following works are cited in section 1 by a shortened title. (For the list of abbreviations used, such as *SCH*, see pp. xix–xxii.)

Bates, Allan. "Sam Clemens, Pilot-Humorist of a Tramp Steamboat." *American Literature* 39 (March 1967): 102–109.

Conclin, George. *Conclin's New River Guide*. Cincinnati: George Conclin, 1848.

Cummings, Samuel. *The Western Pilot*. Cincinnati: J. A. and U. P. James, 1854.

Hunter, Louis C. *Steamboats on the Western Rivers*. Cambridge: Harvard University Press, 1949.

James, Uriah Pierson. *James' River Guide*. Cincinnati: U. P. James, 1857.

Weaver, George Sumner. *Lectures on Mental Science According to the Philosophy of Phrenology*. New York: Fowlers and Wells, 1854.

1. *A GALLANT FIREMAN*

No notes.

2. *THE DANDY FRIGHTENING THE SQUATTER*

64.2   "wood-yard,"] A small riverside community that supplied steamboats with seasoned cordwood for fuel (Hunter, *Steamboats*, p. 265).

64.18   guards] "One of the most important and distinctive features of the western steamboat were the 'guards,' the extensions of the main deck beyond the line of the hull at the sides" (Hunter, *Steamboats*, p. 91).

3. *HANNIBAL, MISSOURI*

67.13   railroad] The Hannibal and St. Joseph Railroad, completed in 1859, linked the Mississippi and Missouri rivers. John Marshall Clemens, Clemens' father, was one of the early advocates of the line (Return Ira Holcombe, *History of Marion County, Missouri* [St. Louis: E. F. Perkins, 1884], pp. 942–948; *SCH*, p. 110;

MTSM, p. 91). In a letter of 20 January 1886 to J. W. Atterbury, Clemens professed ignorance of his father's interest in the railroad (*SCH*, p. 110).

67.22   plank-road] The Missouri State Legislature passed a law in 1850 or 1851 encouraging the construction of plank roads; the first one was probably built in 1852. After 1856, existing plank roads were repaired with gravel and no new ones were built (Howard L. Conard, ed., *Encyclopedia of the History of Missouri*, 6 vols. [New York: The Southern History Company, 1901], 5:367). Both John and Orion Clemens promoted construction of roads leading out of Hannibal to various points (*SCH*, pp. 110–111).

4. *A FAMILY MUSS*

70.1   "Holliday's Hill"] Called Cardiff Hill in *Tom Sawyer*, this hill lay to the north of Hannibal and was part of a long elevation overlooking the Mississippi River (*SCH*, p. 58).

70.6   "brick" carefully in his hat] The phrase alludes to the top-heavy unsteadiness of a drunken man.

70.22   Marshal Hawkins] Benjamin M. Hawkins was marshal of Hannibal in 1852, 1853, and 1855, and he was elected county sheriff in 1856. Clemens listed him in "Villagers of 1840–3" (Walter Blair, ed., *Hannibal, Huck & Tom* [Berkeley and Los Angeles: University of California Press, 1969], pp. 30, 353).

[THE DOG CONTROVERSY]

§5. *"LOCAL" RESOLVES TO COMMIT SUICIDE*

75.5   Bear Creek] This tributary to the Mississippi River flowed through the southern part of Hannibal (see *SCH*, p. 170). Clemens nostalgically recalled it as a favorite swimming hole in chapter 55 of *Life on the Mississippi*.

§6. *"PICTUR' " DEPARTMENT*

76.1   "LOCAL" discovers something interesting in the *Journal*] That is, he discovers the attack in the previous week's issue, " 'Local' Resolves to Commit Suicide" (no. 5).

77.5   hit the man] The cannon, of course, backfires upon "Local."

7. *HISTORICAL EXHIBITION—A NO. 1 RUSE*

79.11   "saw the elephant,"] Saw the world, or gained knowledge by
         new experience: "the cost is oftentimes understood to be more
         than the thing is worth" (John S. Farmer, *Americanisms—Old
         & New: A Dictionary of Words, Phrases and Colloquialisms*
         [London: Thomas Poulter & Sons, 1889], p. 224).

81.34–35 "seeker after knowledge under difficulties."] In chapter 33 of
         Dickens' *The Posthumous Papers of the Pickwick Club*, Tony
         Weller sees his son Sam writing a valentine at the Blue Boar
         pub and asks: "But wot's that, you're a-doin' of—pursuit of
         knowledge under difficulties—eh Sammy?"

8. *[BLAB'S TOUR]*

9. *"CONNUBIAL BLISS"*

10. *THE HEART'S LAMENT*

§11–16. *[THE "KATIE OF H————L" CONTROVERSY]*

17. *SEPARATION*

No notes.

18. *"OH, SHE HAS A RED HEAD!"*

104.1   red heads] In his 1855 journal Clemens copied passages from
         George Sumner Weaver's *Lectures on Mental Sciencè Accord-
         ing to the Philosophy of Phrenology* which suggest a connec-
         tion between the color red and the sanguine temperament. For
         example, this temperament "is the burning, flaming, flashing
         temperament. Hence, it hangs out its signs of fire in its red,
         blazing hair and countenance, its florid or sandy skin" (*N&J1*,
         pp. 21–22; Alan Gribben, "Mark Twain, Phrenology and the
         'Temperaments': A Study of Pseudoscientific Influence," *Amer-
         ican Quarterly* 24 [March 1972]: 45–68). "Oh, She Has a Red
         Head!" precedes Clemens' interest in the phrenological theory
         of temperaments by two years, but the 1855 notebook entry
         makes it clear that he was consistent in favoring the sanguine
         temperament over the other three.

105.4   "The chief among ten thousand, and altogether lovely,"] Song
             of Sol. 5:10, 16. The fraudulent "Letter of Lentulus," supposedly
             written in Christ's lifetime, described his hair as "the colour of
             ripe chestnuts" (Charles Guignebert, *Jesus*, trans. S. H. Hooke
             [New York: Alfred A. Knopf, 1935], p. 166).

105.6–7   Adam's hair was red—for he was made of "red earth"] Nine-
             teenth-century biblical glosses and dictionaries, with which
             Clemens was evidently familiar, commonly derived the name
             "Adam" from the ancient Hebrew root signifying redness, or
             red earth, from which the first man was made.

                    19. *THE BURIAL OF SIR ABNER GILSTRAP,*
             EDITOR OF THE BLOOMINGTON "REPUBLICAN"

                              No notes.

                          20. *"JUL'US CAESAR"*

112.30–32   Approbativeness ... Self-Conceit] According to standard
             phrenological doctrine, "Approbativeness" and "Self-Esteem"
             (here called "Self-Conceit") were contiguous, closely related
             organs at the crown of the head. They were the seat of the
             "selfish sentiments" which, as George Sumner Weaver wrote,
             "are ever consulting the dignity, the importance, and nobility of
             this wonderful child of God I; ... First is Self-Esteem, the
             preacher of human dignity; the second is Approbativeness, the
             lover of glory, or the applause of men; the inspirer of ambition."
             The character dominated by Self-Esteem "is wonderfully
             satisfied with himself. He is a genius, and he knows it. His
             judgment is superior to every body's else, and he is sure of
             it. ... He places an exalted value, not only upon himself, but
             upon every thing that issues from himself" (Weaver, *Lectures*,
             pp. 89–90, 136–138). Clemens consistently preferred the term
             "Self-Conceit" to "Self-Esteem" when describing the selfish
             propensities.

112.35–36   "Flag of our Union," and "Boston True Flag,"] These leading
             Sunday papers, both published in Boston, carried sketches and
             stories by such authors as Poe, Mrs. Osgood, Mrs. Sigourney,
             Park Benjamin, and Horatio Alger (Frank Luther Mott, *A His-
             tory of American Magazines*, 4 vols. [Cambridge, Mass.: Har-
             vard University Press, 1957], 2:35–36). But Clemens' allusion to

literary "gems" suggests that he had lesser figures in mind. The *Flag of Our Union*, for instance, regularly printed poems like "Winter" by T. A. Selden:

> Stern winter is coming—
> O, winter is here!
> And no more the humming
> Of hives do we hear;
> The cold winds are wailing—
> Their loud blasts draw near;
> And winter comes trailing
> The past summer's bier.
> (*Flag of Our Union* 11 [12 January 1856]: 14)

112.37   "The Black Avenger of the Spanish Main," "Jack Sheppard,"] Ned Buntline's (Edward Z. C. Judson's) *The Black Avenger of the Spanish Main*, published serially by the *Flag of Our Union* in 1847, was a lurid adventure story that would capture Tom Sawyer's imagination. John Sheppard, an English thief and highwayman, was ultimately hanged after many imprisonments and escapes. He became the subject of numerous ballads, tracts (including Defoe's), and novels. William Harrison Ainsworth's *Jack Sheppard, A Romance*, which appeared serially in *Bentley's Miscellany* (1839–1840), spawned several nineteenth-century imitations (S. M. Ellis, "Bibliography of Jack Sheppard," in Horace Bleackley, *Jack Sheppard* [Edinburgh and London: William Hodge and Co., 1933], pp. 127–136).

117.1–2   "No further . . . dread abode,"] A close approximation of two lines from the last stanza of Thomas Gray's "Elegy Written in a Country Churchyard."

21. *TO MOLLIE*

22. *"LINES SUGGESTED BY A REMINISCENCE"*

23. *TO JENNIE*

No notes.

24. [*RIVER INTELLIGENCE*]

131.2   Railroad Line] A highly successful steamboat line between St. Louis and New Orleans which connected with the Ohio and

Mississippi Railroad and the Illinois Central Railroad (Hunter, *Steamboats*, p. 631).

131.2   Trombone] A fictitious steamboat, perhaps suggesting Sellers' windiness (*MTMR*, p. 219).

131.9   'close,'] That is, "skilful in coming near, but not too near, to the shore or other obstructions" (Robert L. Ramsay and Frances G. Emberson, *A Mark Twain Lexicon* [Columbia: University of Missouri, 1938], p. 46).

131.14–15   Glasscock's Island] Almost certainly not the obscure island of this name near Hannibal, but a well-known one below Natchez. The river landmarks characterized in the sketch as difficult to navigate were known to pose no difficulty. The channel at Glasscock's Island lay well to the west in a broad section of the river; to go "up to the right" of Old Hen Island was to follow the safe channel. Albert Bigelow Paine noted, probably on Clemens' authority, that both islands were "phenomenally safe places." Likewise, the channels at Hickman, Kentucky, and Island 8 five miles below were apparently safe and unproblematic (*MTMR*, p. 217 n. 1; *MTB*, 3:1594 n. 1; Cummings, *Western Pilot*, pp. 88, 89, 95, 96, 114, 116).

131.16   scarcely more than bank full] A river in that condition "would give all channels more than enough water to float a steamboat safely without, as in a flood, obscuring landmarks along the banks" (*MTMR*, p. 217).

132.12   "Kiho"] Clemens used the name of this unidentified landmark twice in his 1857 river notebook in passages that record steering data for approaching and departing from St. Louis (*N&J1*, p. 43).

132.12   Kamschatka] Kamchatka Peninsula in northeastern Russia.

132.17   since the niggers . . . fall of 1813] A serious slave revolt near New Orleans in 1811 and a conspiracy between slaves and whites the following year led to executions in that city (Herbert Aptheker, *American Negro Slave Revolts* [New York: International Publishers, 1963], pp. 249–250, 254). The accompanying allusion in the text to high waters also suggests that Clemens was thinking of 1811, a year of severe river flooding.

132.19   *St. Charles Hotel*] The principal hotel in New Orleans (*MTMR*, p. 220).

132.33–34   old first "Jubilee."] Sellers piloted the *Jubilee* early in his career, but here Clemens dates the event almost half a century before the first Mississippi River steamboat (*MTMR*, p. 220).

132.36   jackstaff] A pole that served as a steering device: seen against the background of the river bank, it enabled a pilot to gauge his position (Hunter, *Steamboats*, p. 70).

132.39   Selma] Clemens recalled the bluff at Selma, Missouri, in chapter
            58 of *The Innocents Abroad*.

132.41   "seven up"] This card game was popular with pilots, and
            Clemens mentioned it frequently in his writings. In "Pilot's
            Memoranda" (no. 26), for example, the name is used in a joke
            with sexual overtones (Bates, "Pilot-Humorist," p. 107); and in
            chapter 40 of *The Innocents Abroad* it is used for a pun in "The
            Legend of the Seven Sleepers." "Science *vs.* Luck" (no. 328) is a
            sketch about seven-up as a game of science.

133.7   Gayoso House] A Memphis hotel (*MTMR*, p. 222).

133.22–24   Bolivar Landing . . . Donaldsonville] The river was exception-
            ally wide at Bolivar Landing, Mississippi, as well as at Donald-
            sonville, Louisiana, where the channel was also quite deep
            (James, *River Guide*, pp. 38, 41; Cummings, *Western Pilot*,
            pp. 122, 123).

25. [*THE MYSTERIOUS MURDERS IN RISSE*]

No notes.

26. *PILOT'S MEMORANDA*

144.3   Arago] A new transient, or roving, steamer of only 268 tons
            which Clemens piloted from 28 July until 9 September 1860,
            when it sank near Goose Island. The *Arago* was notably less
            prestigious than the *City of Memphis* or the *Alonzo Child*, the
            boats which Clemens piloted before and after he piloted the
            Arago (*MTMR*, p. 147; Bates, "Pilot-Humorist," pp. 102–103).

144.5   Sovereign] The first of twenty-one real steamboats mentioned
            in the memoranda. The others are the *Great Western, Min-
            nehaha, William M. Morrison, John Walsh, Skylark, Twilight,
            Daniel G. Taylor, Planet, South Wester, J. C. Swon, D. A. Jan-
            uary, Emma, Tycoon, City of Memphis, John H. Dickey, John
            D. Perry, Edward J. Gay, Gladiator, Choctaw,* and *Edward
            Walsh* (William M. Lytle, *Merchant Steam Vessels of the
            United States: 1807–1868* [Mystic, Conn.: The Steamship His-
            torical Society of America, 1952]). Bates reports that a real
            memoranda from the *Alonzo Child*, which made the same trip
            on the same days, mentioned all these boats (Bates, "Pilot-
            Humorist," pp. 105–106).

144.5   Port Hudson] Clemens mentioned this small town at the end of
                 chapter 39 in *Life on the Mississippi* as the scene of two impor-
                 tant Civil War battles. The following actual landmarks are
                 mentioned in the sketch in the order in which they would have
                 been· encountered on a trip up river: Port Hudson (La.), Pal-
                 metto Point (Miss.), Rodney (Miss.), Lake Providence (La.),
                 Island 76 at Bolivar Landing (Miss.), Napoleon (Ark.), Old
                 Town (Ark.), Friar's Point (Ark.), Greenock (Ark.), Island 36 at
                 the Third Chickasaw Bluff (Tenn.), Ashport (Tenn.), Forked
                 Deer River (Tenn.), and New Madrid (Mo.). See James' *River
                 Guide*, Conclin's *New River Guide*, and Cummings' *Western
                 Pilot* for more detailed identifications.

144.6–7   Tommy-whack at Dead Mare] Both the name of the steamboat
                 and the place name are invented. Eight other fictitious steamers
                 are named in the sketch, always in conjunction with fictitious
                 place names: the *Yahoo* at Cotton Gin, the *Skylight* and *Day-
                 light* (in conjunction with the real *Twilight*) at Mud Bar, the
                 Saltpetre and *North Wester* at Seven-Up, the *Don Cæsar de
                 Bazan* at Wood Pile, the *Grand Duke of Kiho* at John Battese's,
                 and the *Kangaroo Belle* at Blackjack. One real steamboat, the
                 Tycoon, is sighted at an imaginary place, Boomerang.

144.11   Lake Providence] In chapter 34 of *Life on the Mississippi*
                 Clemens characterized Lake Providence as "the first distinctly
                 Southern-looking town you come to, downward-bound."

144.12   Napoleon] In *Life on the Mississippi* Clemens mentioned
                 Napoleon as the site of the buried treasure in Karl Ritter's
                 narrative (chapter 31); later he discovered that it had been
                 inundated by the river and completely destroyed (chapter 32).
                 The last sentence of chapter 32 suggests the personal
                 significance of Napoleon to Clemens: it was a "town where I
                 had used to know the prettiest girl, and the most accomplished
                 in the whole Mississippi Valley; town where we were handed
                 the first printed news of the 'Pennsylvania's' mournful disaster a
                 quarter of a century ago; a town no more—swallowed up, van-
                 ished." Toward the end of chapter 2 Clemens also mentioned
                 the town's historical significance when discussing the explora-
                 tions of Marquette, Joliet, and De Soto.

144.13   Don Cæsar de Bazan] Clemens was familiar with this character
                 in Victor Hugo's play *Ruy Blas* by at least 1856, when he men-
                 tioned him in his first Thomas Jefferson Snodgrass letter (*TJS*,
                 p. 14).

144.13–14   Wood Pile] The name is fictitious, or at least facetious.

144.15   Boomerang] The name is fictitious. Mark Twain would use
                 "Boomerang" as the name of the mining camp in the unpub-

lished draft "The Only Reliable Account of the Celebrated
Jumping Frog . . . together with some reference to the decaying
city of Boomerang" (no. 117) and in the subsequent completed
tale, "Jim Smiley and His Jumping Frog" (no. 119), both written
in October 1865. He used "Boomerang" again for the name of
the schooner *Emeline* in his eighteenth letter from the Sandwich Islands (Sacramento *Daily Union*, 18 August 1866, p. 1,
reprinted in *MTH*, p. 365).

144.16   lighting her off] Clemens' readers would have recognized the
            absurdity of attempting to lighten a boat by removing the cargo
            from the main deck to the hurricane deck above it (Bates,
            "Pilot-Humorist," p. 109).

144.17   Capt. Bladders] The brief characterization of Captain Bladders
            suggests that he, like Sergeant Fathom in "River Intelligence"
            (no. 24), is a satirical portrait of Captain Isaiah Sellers (Bates,
            "Pilot-Humorist," pp. 108–109).

144.21   Grand Duke of Kiho] A fictional steamboat, bathetically
            named. *Grand Duke* was a real steamboat. Kiho was a river
            landmark—an island or point near St. Louis—so obscure that
            contemporary river guides do not identify it (see the explana-
            tory note to "River Intelligence," no. 24). *Grand Duke of Kiho*
            can therefore be compared with more prestigious steamboats
            named for their home ports, like the *City of Memphis*, men-
            tioned next in the text.

144.23–24   New Madrid] Clemens found this town little changed in 1882
            (see the end of chapter 26, *Life on the Mississippi*).

144.24   "pilot factory" in full operation] An allusion to "a pilot or boat
            that (in the eyes of the young pilot-author) was creating exces-
            sive professional competition by training too many apprentice
            pilots" (Bates, "Pilot-Humorist," p. 107).

145.2–3   they considered . . . well established] A statement of the ob-
            vious, facetiously offered as news (Bates, "Pilot-Humorist,"
            p. 107).

145.7   Helena] Clemens revisited this Arkansas town in 1882 (see the
            end of chapter 30, *Life on the Mississippi*). One river guide gives
            unusually explicit directions for the crossing below Helena, as
            though it presented difficulties (Cummings, *Western Pilot*,
            p. 99).

145.8   Island 34] Extremely careful navigation was mandatory from
            the head of this large island along its right side (descending)
            until Randolph, Tennessee, was reached (Cummings, *Western
            Pilot*, p. 94).

145.15   all the boats we passed] Of the eight boats "passed" seven were fictitious, and as Clemens notes, he only took " 'cognizance' of the fast ones." The tall tale is aimed at ridiculing the usual practice in memoranda of listing competitors that were "passed" but never remarking on *being* passed (Bates, "Pilot-Humorist," p. 106).

145.18–19   Major General Sobeisky Jolly, on his way to Japan] For four months in the fall of 1857 Clemens had served as cub pilot on the *John J. Roe* under Sobeisky (or Sobieski) Jolly, an impressive man and a prominent pilot (*MTB*, 1:128; *MTMR*, pp. 48, 50). Clemens' references to "Beck" Jolly in other writings always imply a close and friendly relationship between the two men. The facetious remark here about Jolly's visit to Japan and a later reference to him as "the distinguished traveler, the mighty hunter of lions, the brilliant Chinese linguist & the dreaded scourge of the nations of the Orient" (Clemens to William Bowen, 25 August 1866, *CL1*, letter 109) probably had a basis in fact which remains obscure. For a discussion of Clemens' relationship with Jolly, see *MTMR*, pp. 51–52.

145.19–20   Col. Joseph Bryant . . . other members of Congress] Bryant has not been identified, but he was probably a fellow pilot; no member of Congress bore that name. Pilots had frequent occasion to "look at the river," as Clemens explained in chapter 7 of *Life on the Mississippi*, because it changed its channel "so constantly that the pilots used to always find it necessary to run down to Cairo to take a fresh look, when their boats were to lie in port a week." Moreover, "a deal of this 'looking at the river' was done by poor fellows who seldom had a berth. . . . And a good many of them constantly ran up and down inspecting the river, not because they ever really hoped to get a berth, but because (they being guests of the boat) it was cheaper to 'look at the river' than stay ashore and pay board." Bates suggests that Clemens called these pilots "members of Congress" because "looking at the river" resembled congressional junketing (Bates, "Pilot-Humorist," p. 107).

27. GHOST LIFE ON THE MISSISSIPPI

147.8   Joseph Millard] It has not been possible to connect the names of any characters in this tale with persons Clemens knew. He did indeed use "fictitious names . . . throughout the narrative."

147.16   "Boreas,"] Three steamers of this name were on the river in the 1840s, but none at the time Clemens wrote. He clearly wished to avoid using real names, and chose one appropriate to the time of the events in his tale. The *Boreas* also appears in chapters 4 and 5 of *The Gilded Age*.

147.19   Dog Tooth Bend] This very sharp bend about ten miles below Goose Island had a number of small islands in it (*MTMR*, p. 239; Cummings, *Western Pilot*, p. 86).

147.20   "Texas,"] An enclosed structure on a steamboat just below the pilot house and above the hurricane deck; it provided cabins for the officers and for some passengers. On early steamboats it was added behind the pilot house, and "it became known as the 'texas,' according to a contemporary explanation, 'probably because it was annexed' " (Hunter, *Steamboats*, p. 90).

147.21   Goose Island] About thirty miles above Cairo. In September 1860 Clemens' boat *Arago* sank at Goose Island, but was soon on the river again (*MTMR*, p. 147). And in chapter 25 of *Life on the Mississippi* Clemens recalled how he used to navigate "slowly and gingerly" through the "numberless wrecks" in the perilous "grave-yard."

147.24   Buffalo Island] About five miles below Goose Island, twenty-five miles up river from Cairo (*MTMR*, p. 239).

148.22–23   Egyptian darkness] Compare Exodus 10:21–22. Clemens often qualified darkness as "Egyptian."

149.3   "Shingle Pile,"] Perhaps a channel near Goose Island (*MTMR*, p. 241).

149.6   gained the foot of the bend] This seems to imply that Millard was approaching Goose Island going up river, as William Jones had done. But other details show that Clemens' overall intention was to represent the ship approaching the passage from St. Louis, going down river. See the following note.

150.25   rounded to under Philadelphia Point] This point was two miles *down* river from Goose Island (*MTMR*, p. 241). Moreover, as Bates points out, the term "rounded to" means that the steamboat was going down river and turned around into the current in order to land gently against the shore (*MTMR*, p. 236). Clemens may not have clearly decided whether or not Millard's passage of the "grave-yard" was to be in the same direction as Jones's original extraordinary one.

SECTION 2
NEVADA TERRITORY: 1862–1864

The following works are cited in section 2 by a shortened title. (For the list of abbreviations used, such as *MTEnt,* see pp. xix–xxii.)

Angel, Myron, ed. *History of Nevada.* Oakland: Thompson and West, 1881.

Bancroft, Hubert Howe. *History of Nevada, Colorado, and Wyoming: 1540–1888.* The Works of Hubert Howe Bancroft, vol. 25. San Francisco: The History Company, 1890.

Collins, Charles, comp. *Mercantile Guide & Directory for Virginia City, Gold Hill, Silver City and American City.* Virginia City: Agnew and Deffebach, 1864–1865.

Estavan, Lawrence, ed. *San Francisco Theatre Research.* 18 vols. San Francisco: Work Projects Administration, 1938–1942.

Gudde, Erwin G. *California Place Names.* 2d ed. Berkeley: University of California Press, 1960.

Kelly, J. Wells. *First Directory of Nevada Territory.* San Francisco: Valentine and Co., 1862.

————. *Second Directory of Nevada Territory.* San Francisco: Valentine and Co., 1863.

Langley, Henry G., comp. *The San Francisco Directory for the Year Commencing October, 1863.* San Francisco: Towne and Bacon, 1863.

————. *The San Francisco Directory for the Year Commencing October, 1864.* San Francisco: Towne and Bacon, 1864.

————. *The San Francisco Directory for the Year Commencing December, 1865.* San Francisco: Towne and Bacon, 1865.

Lord, Eliot. *Comstock Mining and Miners.* Berkeley: Howell-North, 1959.

Mack, Effie Mona. *Nevada: A History of the State from the Earliest Times through the Civil War.* Glendale, California: Arthur H. Clark Company, 1935.

Marsh, Andrew J.; Clemens, Samuel L.; and Bowman, Amos. *Reports of the 1863 Constitutional Convention of the Territory of Nevada.* Edited by William C. Miller and Eleanore Bushnell. Nevada: Legislative Counsel Bureau, 1972.

Phelps, Alonzo. *Contemporary Biography of California's Leading Men.* 2 vols. San Francisco: A. L. Bancroft and Co., 1882.

Rabb, Kate Milnor, ed. *The Wit and Humor of America.* 5 vols. Indianapolis: Bobbs-Merrill Company, 1907.

Ratay, Myra Sauer. *Pioneers of the Ponderosa*. Sparks, Nevada: Western Printing and Publishing Company, 1973.

Scott, Edward B. *The Saga of Lake Tahoe*. Crystal Bay, Nevada: Sierra-Tahoe Publishing Company, 1957.

28. *PETRIFIED MAN*

159.1–2   mountains south of Gravelly Ford] Gravelly Ford was a well-known emigrant crossing on the Humboldt River a few miles west of present-day Palisade, Nevada. The Cortez mountain range lay to the south (Francis C. Lincoln, *Mining Districts and Mineral Resources of Nevada* [Reno: Nevada Newsletter Publishing Co., 1923], p. 96).

159.8–11   right thumb ... spread apart] Compare the following description of a figurehead on a clipper ship: "a female carved figure, with one thumb resting on the extreme tip of her nose, fingers extended in the act of gyrating; the first finger of the left hand in the act of drawing down the lower lid of the eye" (George H. Derby, "On Clipper Ships," *The Squibob Papers* [New York: Carleton, 1865], p. 239. George R. Stewart and Derby's contemporary, Ferdinand C. Ewer, believed that this sketch was actually written by Podgers [Richard L. Ogden]; see *John Phoenix, Esq., the Veritable Squibob: a Life of Captain George H. Derby, U.S.A.* [New York: Da Capo Press, 1969], p. 211, and *The Pioneer* 4 [September 1855]: 180).

159.13   Humboldt City] Situated on the northern end and western slope of the Humboldt mountain range, Humboldt City in 1862 was a flourishing mining camp of several hundred people. It was more than one hundred miles west of Gravelly Ford and approximately ten miles northwest of Unionville, Clemens' headquarters during his visit to the Humboldt area (Harrison Wheelock, *Guide and Map of Reese River and Humboldt* [San Francisco: Towne and Bacon, 1864], frontispiece map).

[TWO DESCENTS INTO THE SPANISH MINE]

§29. *THE SPANISH MINE*

No notes.

§30. *THE SPANISH*

167.8–9   general Superintendent, Mr. J. P. Corrigan] John P. Corrigan was
              also the secretary of the Spanish mine company (Kelly, *First
              Directory*, p. 121).

168.14   hoisting apparatus is about perfect] The new steam-hoisting
              apparatus, which Clemens said was "in the process of erection"
              in October (see "The Spanish Mine," no. 29), fed ore into
              wagons that went to the brand-new Silver State Reduction
              Works, usually known as the Mexican mill, located near Empire
              City, an important milling town on the west bank of the Carson
              River about two and one-half miles east of Carson City. The
              Mexican mill had forty-four stamps (not forty, as Clemens says
              in the sketch) capable of crushing up to seventy-five tons of rock
              daily, the largest capacity of any mill then operating in Nevada
              (Kelly, *Second Directory*, p. 88).

168.21   Mr. Dorsey] Edward B. Dorsey, the mill superintendent, lived
              in Empire City. He was a member of the 1863 Constitutional
              Convention from Empire City, Ormsby County (Kelly, *Second
              Directory*, p. 91; Marsh, Clemens, and Bowman, *Reports*, p. 464
              n. 12).

168.21   Mr. Janin] Louis Janin, Jr., also a resident of Empire City, was
              the assayer of the Silver State Reduction Works (Kelly, *Second
              Directory*, p. 120).

31. *THE PAH-UTES*

No notes.

32. *THE ILLUSTRIOUS DEPARTED*

173.4   senior editor] Joseph T. Goodman, also a proprietor of the
              Enterprise.

173.5   Wasserman's] The store of S. Wasserman and Company, deal-
              ers in tobacco and cigars, was on the first floor of the Inter-
              national Hotel building at Union and C streets. All stagecoaches
              left from the International Hotel (Kelly, *First Directory*,
              pp. 137, 143).

173.17–18   pack-trains and hay-wagons] A standing joke among Comstock
              journalists was the alleged frequency with which newspapers
              printed items on hay wagons and pack trains, as Clemens sug-

gests in chapter 42 of *Roughing It* when describing his first day's activities as a reporter; there Goodman advises him: "Dan used to make a good thing out of the hay wagons in a dry time when there were no fires or inquests." An unidentified journalist, writing of Dan's trip East, commented: "During his absence his position will be filled by that inveterate Carson Valley wag, Sam-i-vel Clem-ens Ekswire, the handsomest man in the Territory. We wish 'Dan' an agreeable journey and a speedy return, and Sam as many hay items as he imagines the public appetite will appreciate" ("Gone Home," unidentified clipping reprinting a notice in the San Francisco *Police Gazette*, carton 1, folder 120, William Wright Papers, Bancroft).

173.23   "*Et tu Brute*,"] *Julius Caesar*, act 3, scene 1, line 77.

174.7–8   Elijah went up in his fiery chariot] Compare 2 Kings 2:11.

33. OUR STOCK REMARKS

176.1   our stock reporter] If Clemens had a real reporter in mind, he must have been Stephen E. Gillis, with whom he shared a room at the time. According to Dan De Quille, both Gillis and C. A. V. Putnam were long engaged by the *Enterprise* to do much of the writing other than editorials and local items (Dan De Quille, "The Passing of a Pioneer," San Francisco *Examiner*, 22 January 1893, p. 15). The reference cannot be to Putnam, for he did not join the paper until May 1863 (C. A. V. Putnam, "Dan De Quille and Mark Twain," Salt Lake City *Tribune*, 25 April 1898, p. 3). Nor could Clemens refer to Dan, who ordinarily reported on mining news, for he had left Virginia City on 27 December 1862 (see "The Illustrious Departed," no. 32).

176.9   Ophir] The Ophir was an exceptionally wealthy mining company on the Comstock Lode. In a letter to his family Clemens related his experience of descending deep into the "Ophir perpendicular" and touring the famous mine (Clemens to Jane Clemens et al., February 1862, *CL1*, letter 42).

34. MORE GHOSTS

35. NEW YEAR'S DAY

36. UNFORTUNATE THIEF

No notes.

37. THE SANITARY BALL

185.14–15   we had wandered out of our own and into somebody else's set]
            According to Calvin Higbie, this was indeed Clemens' danc-
            ing style:

> In changing partners, whenever he saw a hand raised he would
> grasp it with great pleasure and sail off into another set. His
> partner would have a hard time to hunt him up and herd him
> back to his rightful place. . . . Sometimes he would act as though
> there was no use in trying to go right or in trying to dance like
> other people and would rush off into another set with his eyes
> half closed, declaring to everybody that he never dreamed there
> was so much pleasure to be had at a ball.

> (Quoted in Michael J. Phillips, "Mark Twain's Partner," *Satur-
> day Evening Post* 193 [11 September 1920]: 73)

186.10   Gold Hill ball] Gold Hill was an important mining town on the
            Comstock Lode at the head of Gold Canyon and immediately
            south of Virginia City (Angel, *History*, pp. 55–56, 572). Clemens
            may have meant the Odd Fellows' Ball which he attended in
            Gold Hill on Wednesday, January 7. But if so, he misremem-
            bered the day, for he goes on to say that he started looking for
            female partners on Tuesday.

186.29–30   to freeze out the heaviest stockholder on the Gould & Curry's
            books] By the beginning of 1863 the famous Gould and Curry
            Silver Mining Company on the Comstock Lode had replaced the
            Ophir as the richest incorporated mining company in the West,
            and by July its stock had soared to $6,300 a share (San Francisco
            Evening Bulletin, 2 July 1863, p. 1).

38. DUE NOTICE

39. TERRITORIAL SWEETS

No notes.

40. LETTER FROM CARSON CITY

194.8   Joseph T. Goodman] Proprietor and senior editor of the *Enter-
            prise*. Goodman came to California in 1854. With Denis
            McCarthy he purchased the *Enterprise* in 1861 and remained
            with the paper until 1874. He became a stockbroker in San

Francisco and later a farmer in Fresno County (Goodman to A. B. Nye, 6 November 1905, A. B. Nye Collection, Bancroft). In 1897 Goodman published *The Archaic Maya Inscriptions*, the outcome of a long-standing interest in Central American archaeology.

194.11   Silver City] A mining town in Gold Canyon just below Devil's Gate and south of Gold Hill, about halfway between Virginia City and Dayton (Angel, *History*, p. 502; Collins, *Mercantile Guide*, p. 313).

194.11   Spring Valley] An area within the Devil's Gate mining district that lay to the south of Silver City not far from Empire City ("Our Washoe Correspondence, Letter from Dan De Quille," *Golden Era* 11 [27 September 1863]: 8; "A Slight Mistake," Virginia City *Evening Bulletin*, 31 October 1863, p. 3).

195.4   Governor J. Neely Johnson's] Johnson served as California's fourth governor from 1856 to 1858. He moved to Nevada in 1860, practiced law in Carson City, represented Ormsby County in the Nevada constitutional conventions of 1863 and 1864, and served as a justice of the state supreme court from 1867 to 1871. Clemens gave him a prominent place in his burlesque address to the Third House of the 1863 Nevada Constitutional Convention, delivered on December 11. And in 1905 Clemens included him among the "unforgettable antiques" of his Nevada days (*MTEnt*, pp. 105, 228; Clemens to Robert Fulton, 24 May 1905, *MTL*, 2:773).

195.16   Horace Smith] A former mayor of Sacramento, Smith was a well-liked and successful Carson City lawyer. In December 1863 he died of gunshot wounds received during a quarrel over payment he claimed for the sale of his shares in the Yellow Jacket mine (Angel, *History*, p. 345; "The Shooting of Horace Smith," Sacramento *Union*, 31 October 1863, p. 2).

195.28   Col. Musser] John J. Musser was an original settler of Carson City in 1858. He was president of the convention that met in July 1859 in Genoa, Utah Territory, to frame a constitution for the proposed Territory of Nevada. Later that year, having been selected delegate to Washington, D.C., he unsuccessfully urged Congress to establish the new territory. In May 1863 he became prosecuting attorney for the Second Judicial District of Nevada. Clemens satirized him in the burlesque Third House address (Kelly, *First Directory*, p. 31; Angel, *History*, p. 335; Mack, *History*, pp. 181, 183–184; *MTEnt*, p. 108).

195.35   Washoe City] Laid out in 1860 on the shores of Little Washoe Lake, this settlement quickly became the largest town in Washoe Valley and remained the Washoe County seat until

1871. During the 1860s the city was the major supplier of timber for the Comstock mines, as well as of fuel, food, and water for the people of Virginia City and other nearby mining towns. Washoe City was also the site of several large ore-reduction mills ("The Water Power at Washoe City," Washoe City *Times*, 28 February 1863, p. 4; Angel, *History*, p. 646; Ratay, *Pioneers*, pp. 347–413).

195.35–36   when we went out there to report the proceedings of the Convention] After the 1862 Territorial Legislature adjourned in Carson City on December 20, Clemens and Rice—who had reported it for their respective papers—took the stage to Washoe City to help celebrate the adjournment. In a letter to the *Enterprise* dated December 23, Clemens termed the festivities "a Grand Bull Drivers' Convention" that had assembled the day before to greet the returning Washoe County legislators ("A Big Thing in Washoe City," reprinted from the *Enterprise* by the Placer County [Calif.] *Courier*, 17 January 1863, p. 3; quoted in *MTNev*, pp. 224–227). The notion of conventions held by Nevada bull drivers was apparently a public joke which Clemens drew upon (see "Wo-Haw!" Placer County [Calif.] *Courier*, 13 September 1862, p. 3).

196.7   "half-a-man-left,"] That is, "allemande left," a common step in the quadrille in which the man turns his partner on the left.

196.33–36   the five thousand ... that feast] Compare Mark 6:42–44.

197.3   "I'm sitting on the stile, Mary,"] The first line of "Irish Emigrant's Lament," music by William R. Dempster and words by Helen S. Sheridan. A humorous song entitled "Yankee Sarahnade" by "Samuel Slocum of Goslin Run," which begins with the same line, is pasted in Scrapbook 1 (p. 76, MTP). Other songs mentioned in this paragraph are "From Greenland's Icy Mountains," music by Lowell Mason and words by Reginald Heber; "Meet Me by Moonlight Alone," music and words by Joseph Augustine Wade; "The Marseilles Hymn," by Claude Joseph Rouget de Lisle; "Call Me Pet Names," music by Charles Jarvis and words by Frances Mary Osgood; "Rock Me to Sleep, Mother," music by J. Max Mueller and words by Elizabeth Akers Allen (Clemens parodied it in "An Important Question Settled," Cincinnati *Evening Chronicle*, 9 March 1868, p. 3); "Thou Hast Wounded the Spirit That Loved Thee," words and music by Mrs. Porter; "I Would Not Live Always," music by George Kingsley and words by William A. Muhlenberg. The correct reading of the penultimate line in this last song, which Clemens distorts to "the few lucid moments that dawn on us here," is "the few lurid mornings that dawn on us here." "O,

Charming May" could be an English translation of Mendels-
sohn's "Maienlied," op. 8, no. 7, or of Mozart's "Komm' Lieber
Mai," or of Schumann's "Im Wunderschönen Monat Mai."
Clemens' own "little gem from the horse opera" was almost
certainly "I Had an Old Horse Whose Name Was Methusalem,"
the routine at the piano he sometimes used to enliven private
gatherings and eventually to introduce his lectures (see *MTEnt*,
pp. 49, 219 section 4 n. 5). On 25 August 1866 Clemens wrote
his "oldest friend," William Bowen: "Do you recollect the old
hoss that died in the wilderness? I have made that famous in
Washoe" (*CL1*, letter 109).

197.8   Judge Dixson] E. C. Dixson was justice of the peace in Carson
            City (1861) and later (1861–1863) probate judge, and then
            commissioner, of Ormsby County. He represented Lander
            County in the third Territorial Legislature, January to February
            1864. Clemens occasionally satirized him in his legislative
            reports (Carson City *Silver Age*, 13 July 1861, p. 1; Angel,
            History, p. 529; *MTEnt*, p. 168).

197.9   Joe Winters] Clemens' acquaintance Joseph Winters of Carson
            City migrated from Illinois to California in 1848 and engaged
            in placer mining and freighting with his brothers John D. and
            Theodore Winters. He made a fortune from his early Comstock
            stake, which became part of the Ophir claim. Later he was an
            owner of the Aurora mill near Dayton, and like his brother
            Theodore he became prominent, for a time, in the racing
            circles of Nevada and California ("Lucky," Reese River
            Reveille, supplement, 21 November 1863, p. 1; " 'Mark Twain's'
            Letter," San Francisco *Morning Call*, 15 July 1863, p. 1; Angel,
            History, pp. 56, 57, 67, 503; Bancroft, *Works*, 25:101–102;
            Ratay, *Pioneers*, pp. 293, 296, 299, 300, 325 n. 14).

197.9–10   Hal Clayton] P. H. Clayton was an early settler in Carson City
            who became prosecuting attorney there in 1860. Early in 1863
            he helped organize the Democratic party in Nevada and was
            arrested the following July for making disloyal statements,
            an episode that evidently did not detract from his professional
            success or personal popularity: repeatedly during the 1860s
            he presided over the convivial Third House. Clemens remem-
            bered him with fondness in 1905 when recalling the good old
            days in Nevada (Angel, *History*, pp. 73, 265, 551; *MTEnt*,
            pp. 100–101, 226; *MTL*, 2:773).

197.10–11   Mr. Wasson] A native of New York State, Warren H. Wasson
            first crossed the plains in his early teens in 1849; he came to
            Nevada in 1857. He was a man of unusual versatility: miner,
            rancher, organizer of the provisional territorial government

of Nevada (1859), United States marshal of Nevada Territory, an effective and intelligent Indian agent for many years, assessor of internal revenue for Nevada (1862–1869), holder of military commissions, and Ormsby County delegate to the November 1863 Nevada Constitutional Convention. Clemens first knew Wasson in the spring of 1862 while prospecting in Esmeralda County (Clemens to Orion Clemens, 13 April 1862, *CL1*, letter 47; Clemens to Orion Clemens, [24 April 1862], *CL1*, letter 49; Angel, *History*, pp. 81, 166–168, 533–534).

197.12–13   Judge Brumfield] W. H. Brumfield, a prominent attorney in Carson City, was also assemblyman from Ormsby County in the second and third territorial legislatures (1862 and 1864). In February 1864 Clemens praised him as an "intelligent, industrious and upright" representative (*MTEnt*, p. 165; Angel, *History*, pp. 334, 529).

197.16   Wm. M. Gillespie] Clemens' good friend William Martin Gillespie came to Virginia City in 1861 from New York State. As clerk of the first Territorial Legislature and secretary of the Nevada constitutional conventions of 1863 and 1864, Gillespie worked closely with Clemens and other legislative reporters. He was dubbed "Jefferson's Manual" by Clemens because of his knowledge of parliamentary rules ("Legislative Proceedings. House—Thirty-first Day," dated Carson, 11 February 1864, Scrapbook 3, p. 106, MTP). The two men also worked together when Clemens reported the First Annual Fair of the Washoe Agricultural, Mining and Mechanical Society, held in October 1863 in Carson City. Gillespie was deputy clerk of Storey County in 1863. He represented his county as delegate to the third Territorial Legislature and to the constitutional conventions of 1863 and 1864. Throughout Clemens' legislative reports, Gillespie is the object of good-natured chaffing (Kelly, *Second Directory*, p. 215; Angel, *History*, pp. 81, 86; *MTEnt*, pp. 81, 228).

197.21   my prophetic soul] *Hamlet*, act 1, scene 5, line 40.

41. *LETTER FROM CARSON*

202.8–10   he wished ... cares and troubles] The distant Shakespearian echoes in this passage suggest the burlesques of Shakespeare commonly presented in minstrel shows, or the mode of mock grief expressed by some of Artemus Ward's mountebank characters, who burst into tears or complain of the "cold world" upon slight provocation (Charles F. Browne, *Artemus Ward: His Book* [New York: Carleton, 1865], pp. 51, 57, 88).

202.10–11   sleep with his fathers] Compare Deut. 31:16, 2 Sam. 7:12, and 1 Kings 1:21.

202.13   drained it to the very, very dregs] Compare Thomas Hood, "The Last Man," lines 219–220.

202.14   Dr. Tjader] Dr. Anton W. Tjader was an early settler and a leading physician and surgeon in Carson City. He was on the governor's staff as official surgeon to the Nevada militia (Carson City *Silver Age*, 13 July 1861, p. 1; Kelly, *Second Directory*, p. 10). In Clemens' burlesque Third House address, Dr. Tjader prescribes gin and molasses for the reporter's cold (*MTEnt*, p. 109).

202.15   Magnolia Saloon] Peter Hopkins' billiard saloon in the Great Basin Hotel building, Carson City—a favorite rendezvous for journalists and politicians (Kelly, *First Directory*, p. 80; *MTNev*, p. 194).

203.11   James H. Sturtevant] A native of New York State, Sturtevant came to San Diego in 1850 and soon moved to San Francisco, where he engaged in business and mining activities. In 1857 he settled on a farm in Washoe Valley near Franktown and became a leading citizen of the valley, serving Washoe County first as road commissioner and later as county commissioner. He represented the county as assemblyman and then as councilman in the territorial legislatures of 1861 and 1862, and he was a forceful member of the Constitutional Convention of 1864. Sturtevant and his family left Nevada in 1871 to manage a sheep ranch in California (Ratay, *Pioneers*, pp. 39, 59, 205–209; *MTEnt*, p. 231; Virginia City *Territorial Enterprise*, 10 January 1863, p. 1, PH in MTP; Kelly, *Second Directory*, p. 149; Angel, *History*, pp. 86, 624, 629, 680).

203.11–12   Pi-Utes of Nevada] A term used to indicate the white settlers of Nevada who had arrived before May 1860 (*MTEnt*, pp. 35, 99).

203.12   Miss Emma Curry, daughter of Hon. A. Curry] Abram V. Z. Curry was the main founder of Carson City, who, from the city's beginnings in 1858, intended to make it the capital of the territory. For many years he remained a leading merchant and a public-spirited citizen of the community, and was so recognized by Clemens in *Roughing It* (chapters 24 and 25). Curry, his wife, and five daughters lived in his hotel at Warm Springs, about two miles from Carson City. The bridesmaid, sister to the seventeen-year-old Emma, was Metta Curry, familiarly known as Mettie (*MTNev*, p. 84; Angel, *History*, pp. 532, 550, 556;

Bancroft, *Works*, 25:159; Myra S. Ratay to Edgar M. Branch, 28 August 1974).

203.21–22   Hall of Representatives in Curry's house] In the absence of other suitable quarters, the first Territorial Legislature of Nevada convened on 1 October 1861 on the second floor of Curry's Warm Springs Hotel (Bancroft, *Works*, 25:159; *MTNev*, pp. 84, 89). Compare Clemens' account in chapter 25 of *Roughing It*.

203.24   John H. Mills] Mills, who was in the mining and milling business, represented Gold Hill and vicinity in the first and second territorial legislatures. In 1865 he was appointed one of three commissioners to establish a United States mint at Carson City (Angel, *History*, pp. 68, 79, 556; Kelly, *First Directory*, p. 187; Bancroft, *Works*, 25:158–159 n. 35; *MTEnt*, p. 43).

203.26   Father Bennett] The Reverend Jesse L. Bennett was the pioneer minister of the Methodist Episcopal church in the Eagle, Carson, and Washoe valleys, and on the Comstock. In 1863 he lived near Washoe City (Angel, *History*, pp. 207–210; Kelly, *Second Directory*, p. 134).

203.31   dance that Tam O'Shanter witnessed] See Robert Burns, "Tam O'Shanter: A Tale," lines 115ff.

42. *LETTER FROM CARSON*

207.3   Dr. J. H. Wayman] Dr. John Hudson Wayman, a Carson physician associated with Dr. Anton Tjader (see "Letter from Carson City," no. 40; Kelly, *First Directory*, p. 91).

207.3   Mrs. M. A. Ormsby] The widow of Major William M. Ormsby, who, with Abram Curry, was a principal founder of Carson City. Ormsby was killed in Indian warfare in 1860 (Mack, *History*, pp. 179, 241). Late in 1863 Clemens noted her effort to claim the "land upon which the large town of Dayton, Lyon county, stands, by authority of a deed made to Major Ormsby" ("'Mark Twain's' Letter," San Francisco *Morning Call*, 19 November 1863, p. 1).

207.4   John K. Trumbo] Trumbo, formerly of Salt Lake City, Sacramento, and Genoa, took part in early efforts to organize the Territory of Nevada. After periods of mining and of selling lumber, he became a real-estate dealer in Carson City (Angel, *History*, pp. 43–45, 374, 553–554).

207.5   Acting Governor Clemens] During Governor Nye's absence, Orion Clemens was acting governor of the Nevada Territory from 27 December 1862 until 24 July 1863 ("Secretary Clemens Defends Himself," Scrapbook 3, p. 96, MTP).

207.9–11   incorporations . . . Territorial Secretary's books] Corporations were required by law to register with the territorial secretary (Orion Clemens), who received a fee for each registration (see *MTEnt*, p. 14, for Clemens' account of the procedure). Clemens appended the list of incorporations to this letter, but it is not reprinted here.

207.24   Jack Wilde's] Co-proprietor of the Mint Saloon in Carson City (Kelly, *Second Directory*, p. 112).

208.1   Lytle ("Schemerhorn's Boy")] Proprietor of the Stage Saloon and perhaps of the adjoining Johnny Moore Theater in Carson City (Kelly, *First Directory*, p. 89). The reason for the appellation "Schemerhorn's Boy," which was also the name of a popular minstrel farce, remains unclear (George R. MacMinn, *The Theater of the Golden Era in California* [Caldwell, Idaho: Caxton Printers, 1941], p. 423). Edward P. Hingston, Artemus Ward's manager, stated that the Johnny Moore Theater (where Ward first appeared in Nevada) was owned by one "Dr. Schemmerhorn," whom he described as "a tall, gaunt, large-limbed man." Hingston claimed that "Schemmerhorn" obtained his actors locally, wrote his own pieces, and produced ultra-realistic stage effects (*The Genial Showman* [London: John Camden Hotten, 1871], pp. 409–410). Don C. Seitz, however, maintained that " 'Schermerhorn' was a local celebrity who made the theater and its annex his lounging-place" and that "his real name was Charles S. Lightle and he enjoyed a local reputation as a wit" (*Artemus Ward: A Biography and Bibliography* [New York and London: Harper and Brothers, 1919], p. 141).

209.4   the pea-nut song] An anonymous student song, driving home the moral contained in its first stanza:

> The man who has plenty of good peanuts,
> And giveth his neighbor none,
> He shan't have any of my peanuts,
> When his peanuts are gone.

(Albert E. Wier, ed., *The Book of a Thousand Songs* [New York: World Syndicate Company, 1918], p. 383)

209.4   William Patterson] William H. Patterson, a veteran of the Mexican War, was a Carson City lawyer who was elected district attorney of Ormsby County three times during the 1870s (Angel, *History*, pp. 271, 338, 529; Kelly, *Second Directory*, p. 108). In the Third House address of December 1863

Clemens called him "Uncle Billy Patterson" and appointed him "First Assistant Page" (*MTEnt*, p. 102).

209.5   "Ever of thee I'm fondly dreaming;"] A song, music by Foley Hall and words by George Linley.

209.6   Epstein] Either Henry Epstein, a rancher near Genoa and a Douglas County assemblyman at the first Nevada State Legislature (1864), or Louis Epstein, a well-known hotel keeper and restaurateur of Washoe City (Angel, *History*, pp. 275, 376; Ratay, *Pioneers*, p. 381).

43. *SILVER BARS—HOW ASSAYED*

211.4–5   Paxton & Thornburgh] The Virginia City banking firm of John A. Paxton and W. B. Thornburgh, located at South C and Taylor streets, was established early in 1863 (Collins, *Mercantile Guide*, pp. 40, 179, 204; Phelps, *Contemporary Biography*, 2:359).

211.6   Hoosier State Mill] Erected in 1862 on Silver Street in Virginia City, the Hoosier State mill had eight stamps and was owned by Jacob Clark and George Hurst (Collins, *Mercantile Guide*, p. 45).

211.7   Potosi] The Potosi Gold and Silver Mining Company, whose holdings were on the Comstock Lode in the Virginia mining district, was incorporated in January 1861 for $1.4 million. It and the Chollar Gold and Silver Mining Company would soon become parties in a notorious lawsuit (Kelly, *First Directory*, pp. 15, 107).

211.10   Theall & Co.] The assaying office of H. W. Theall was located under Paxton and Thornburgh's bank (Collins, *Mercantile Guide*, pp. 40, 203).

44. *YE SENTIMENTAL LAW STUDENT*

217.15–16   language of love and the infernal phraseology of the law] Clemens may have adapted this particular device from John B. Lamar's "Polly Peablossom's Wedding," in which a magistrate begins the marriage ceremony with the words "Know all men by these presents" (Thomas A. Burke, ed., *Polly Peablossom's Wedding; and Other Tales* [Philadelphia: T. B. Peterson and Brothers, 1851], p. 22).

45. *A SUNDAY IN CARSON*

222.7   Rev. Mr. White] The Reverend A. F. White was minister of the First Presbyterian Church of Carson City from 1861 to 1868. He was well known to both Sam and Orion Clemens; Orion was on the church board of trustees (Angel, *History*, p. 215). Writing to William H. Clagett on 8 March 1862, Clemens derided the pastor as a "whining, nasal, Whangdoodle preacher" (*CL1*, letter 43), and later he comically portrayed him in his Carson City journalism (*MTEnt*, pp. 125, 133). The Reverend White was also the first superintendent of public instruction for both the Territory and the State of Nevada. Only upon completion of the church building in 1864 could he abandon such temporary quarters as the second floor rooms of the courthouse at Carson and Musser streets (Angel, *History*, pp. 77, 87, 215, 543).

222.19   Sheriff Gasherie] D. J. Gasherie was Ormsby County sheriff from 1862 to 1864 (Angel, *History*, p. 530). He was the same man whom Clemens vainly petitioned in 1862 for a commission as deputy sheriff (Clemens to Orion Clemens, [24 April] 1862, *CL1*, letter 49). Gasherie later figured in Clemens' Dutch Nick massacre hoax (see "A Bloody Massacre near Carson," no. 66).

46. *THE UNRELIABLE*

No notes.

47. *REPORTORIAL*

227.1   crushed Truth to earth] William Cullen Bryant's line in "The Battle-field"—"Truth, crushed to earth, shall rise again"—was a slogan frequently used on newspaper mastheads.

227.6   to issue more county scrip] As deputy clerk for Storey County, Gillespie undoubtedly issued licenses and other papers at prescribed fees (Kelly, *Second Directory*, p. 215).

227.7–8   broke into my trunk] Compare Clemens' original charge in "Letter from Carson City" (no. 40).

227.13   a list of Langton's stage passengers] Langton's Express ran daily stagecoaches between Virginia and Carson cities, as well as between Virginia City and various points in California and mining camps in the Humboldt and Reese River mining areas

(Kelly, *First Directory*, p. 73). The newspapers customarily printed lists of daily arrivals on the various stagecoach lines; however, no copies of the Virginia City *Union* for this period have survived.

228.8   "bit house"] In a bit house beer sold for twelve and one-half cents, or one bit, twice the cost of beer in ordinary saloons and bars (Ratay, *Pioneers*, p. 259 n. 1).

48. *EXAMINATION OF TEACHERS*

231.7   Dr. Geiger] Dr. D. M. Geiger of Virginia City was the proprietor of the Geiger toll road and lived at the head of Cedar Ravine (Kelly, *Second Directory*, p. 214).

231.7   Mr. J. W. Whicher] Not listed in the Nevada Territory directories from 1862 to 1864. Whicher was, however, eventually appointed superintendent of Storey County schools on 22 July 1867, succeeding John A. Collins, who resigned. Whicher was elected to that post on 3 November 1868, and again on 8 November 1870 (Angel, *History*, p. 607).

231.8   John A. Collins] A Vermont native with a strong interest in numerous social causes, Collins had moved to San Francisco in 1849. In 1863 he was a lumber dealer in Virginia City, known for his active promotion of the public schools. He became superintendent of the first public school in Virginia City in 1862 (when only seventeen pupils were enrolled), and he was elected to the board of school trustees of Storey County in 1863, serving as president of the board and superintendent of schools. On 29 May 1865 he was appointed county superintendent of schools and was elected to that office in November 1866, resigning in favor of J. W. Whicher in July 1867. Collins eventually returned to San Francisco, where he practiced law (Kelly, *Second Directory*, p. 167; Angel, *History*, pp. 571, 607; "School Children," Gold Hill *News*, 27 October 1863, p. 3; Marsh, Clemens, and Bowman, *Reports*, p. 464 n. 11). In November 1863 Clemens wrote: "Mr. Collins stands at the head of the educational interests of the Territory, and in fact at the head of every other department of progress of a purely public nature" ("'Mark Twain's' Letter," San Francisco *Morning Call*, 19 November 1863, p. 1). See the headnote to "Unfortunate Blunder" (no. 60).

231.8   Feusier] Louis Feusier, an original trustee of Virginia City upon its incorporation in 1861, owned a grocery and provision store at South C and Taylor streets (Kelly, *Second Directory*, p. 210).

231.8   Adkison] D. O. Adkison of Virginia City is listed in Collins'
             1864–1865 *Mercantile Guide* (p. 49) as superintendent of the
             Fairview Mining Company.

231.9   Robinson] S. H. Robinson of Gold Hill was treasurer of the
             Storey County board of education in 1863. Later he became the
             police judge and a city trustee of Gold Hill (Kelly, *Second
             Directory*, p. 347; Collins, *Mercantile Guide*, p. 291).

232.30   one-ledge theory] See the explanatory note for "Letter from
             Mark Twain" (no. 53).

232.30   Ophir horse] The expression was proverbial. It reflects the rela-
             tively low prices or low-value property which the original loca-
             tors of the Ophir and other valuable Comstock claims accepted
             in trade for their interests. Clemens wrote of the Ophir horse in
             his "Around the World. Letter Number 6" (no. 268), first pub-
             lished in the Buffalo *Express* on 8 January 1870 (p. 2) and
             reprinted (with revisions) in chapter 46 of *Roughing It*:

             An individual who owned 20 feet in the Ophir mine before its
             great riches were revealed to men, traded it for a horse, and a
             very sorry looking brute he was too. A year or so afterward,
             when Ophir stock went up to $3000 a foot, this man, who hadn't
             a cent, used to say he was the most startling example of
             magnificence and misery the world had ever seen—because he
             was able to ride a 60,000-dollar horse and yet had to ride him
             bareback because he couldn't scare up cash enough to buy a
             saddle. He said if fortune were to give him another 60,000-
             dollar horse it would ruin him.

             The individual in Clemens' anecdote has not been identified,
             but other "Ophir horse" stories abound in histories of the
             Comstock Lode. John D. Winters and Joseph A. Osborn, for
             example, acquired a two-sixths interest in the Ophir from Peter
             O'Riley and Patrick McLaughlin for two arrastras and two horses
             or mules, and both O'Riley and McLaughlin eventually lost
             everything. Another commonly told story was that Alva Gould
             sold his claim to a California buyer for $450 and drunkenly rode
             his horse down Gold Canyon shouting "Oh, I've fooled the
             Californian" (Lord, *Comstock Mining*, pp. 54, 60).

232.31   black dyke] A dyke, or dike, is an intrusive rock forced into a
             fissure or fault in a stratum of other mineral substance. By
             "black dyke" Clemens may have meant the famous vein of
             black silver sulphurets that Peter O'Riley and Patrick McLaugh-
             lin are said to have uncovered in June 1859 while looking for
             gold on top of the as yet undiscovered Ophir bonanza. The
             black mineral was at first discarded as a curiosity of no value.
             When an assay made in Grass Valley in July revealed its rich-
             ness, the word quickly spread, and the silver rush to Washoe

began (Francis Church Lincoln, *Mining Districts and Mineral Resources of Nevada* [Reno: Nevada Newsletter Publishing Company, 1923], p. 223).

232.32   sage-brush process] According to Dan De Quille, before the reduction of silver ore was well understood, almost any and every substance was tried out in the amalgamating pans to "physic" the silver out of the ore. Men known as "process-peddlers" went from mill to mill, selling their secret concoctions out of closely guarded vials. "The native sagebrush," he recalled in 1874, "which everywhere covered the hills, being the bitterest, most unsavory, and nauseating shrub to be found in any part of the world, it was not long before a genius in charge of a mill conceived the idea of making a tea of this and putting it into his pans. Soon the wonders performed by the 'sagebrush process,' as it was called, were being heralded through the land" (Dan De Quille, *The History of the Big Bonanza* [New York: Alfred A. Knopf, 1947], pp. 92–93).

49. *CITY MARSHAL PERRY*

235.9-10   Kinderhook, New Jersey] Kinderhook, New York, was the birthplace and home of Martin Van Buren, eighth president of the United States. New Jersey often had comic associations in Clemens' early writings.

235.12   grandson, of the same name] John Van Buren, son of Martin Van Buren.

235.14   "Prince John;"] In 1832, while serving as attaché to the American legation in London, John Van Buren attended a court dinner, and the list of guests published in the British court journal included his name in the roster of princes. American Whig publications consequently dubbed him "Prince John." For more than two decades he was very active in New York State politics; in 1844 he headed the Barnburners faction at the Democratic national convention, and for a period in the mid-1840s he stumped for the Free Soil faction.

235.17-20   Commodore . . . "Perry's Victory."] Oliver Hazard Perry, the American naval commander on Lake Erie, defeated the British naval forces for control of the lake on 10 September 1813. His famous announcement was: "We have met the enemy and they are ours."

235.22-23   Commissioner Extraordinary to the Imperial Court of Japan] In 1852 Matthew Calbraith Perry, brother to Oliver Hazard Perry, led the American trade delegation to Japan.

236.8   "Pain Killer" which bears his name] In 1840 Perry Davis of

Massachusetts (after 1843 a resident of Providence, Rhode Island) invented "Perry Davis's Celebrated Painkiller," which became an enormously popular cure-all on several continents. (For example, Hannibal newspapers advertised it in 1849, and Virginia City newspapers in 1863). The label on each bottle bore his name and picture (Stewart H. Holbrook, *The Golden Age of Quackery* [New York: Macmillan Co., 1959], pp. 149–156). Aunt Polly prescribed it for Tom Sawyer, who in turn dosed Peter the cat with it. Its main component was alcohol, with an admixture of gum myrrh, gum opium, and a few other minor ingredients: "simply fire in a liquid form" (*Tom Sawyer*, chapter 12).

236.12–13   unto burned . . . Jack the Giant Killer's] While Davis was making a batch of Painkiller in March 1844, the alcohol he was using exploded, severely burning his face and arms. After curing his burns by applying his own medicine, he employed an artist to depict him prostrate and engulfed with flames. The drawing was widely publicized (Holbrook, *Golden Age*, pp. 152–153). The English folktale hero Jack the Giant Killer, known to generations of children, saved many tortured victims from Blunderbore, Rebecks, and other giants.

236.18–19   "How doth . . . shining hour,"] The first two lines of Song 20, "Against Idleness and Mischief," in Isaac Watts, *Divine and Moral Songs for the Use of Children* (London: John Van Voorst, 1848), p. 49. About 4 October 1887 Clemens wrote in his notebook:

> How doth the little busy bee
> Improve each shining hour b'gosh,
> Gathering honey all the day
> From many a lovely flower b'gosh.
>
> (*N&J3*, p. 334)

Watts's popular hymn "Alas! and Did My Saviour Bleed!" may have been a source of Emmeline Grangerford's "Ode to Stephen Dowling Bots, Dec'd" in *Huckleberry Finn* (John R. Byers, Jr., "Miss Emmeline Grangerford's Hymn Book," *American Literature* 43 [May 1971]: 259–263). Watts's hymns and moral songs were ideal targets for Clemens' satirical thrusts at the false conception of life promoted by the literature of church and Sunday school.

236.22   "Perry-Gorics."] A multiple pun.

236.31–32   Martin Farquhar Tupper] An English poet and moralist (1810–1889), best known for *Proverbial Philosophy* (1838), a work whose didactic intention was to provide the reading public with moral reflections on scores of subjects such as Humility, Self-acquaintance, Flattery, Faith, and Estimating Character.

Tupper's poetry was uninspired and often fatuously sentimental, reaching extremes of banality in his poems to and about
children. Thus some of the lines in "A Family Picture" ("The
last, an infant toothless one, now prattling on my knee, / Whose
bland, benevolent, soft face is shining upon me") approach a
male equivalent to "The Young Mother's Apostrophe to Her
Infant" in Clemens' text (*Tupper's Complete Poetical Works*
[Boston: Phillips, Sampson, and Co., 1857], pp. 332–334). Tupper toured America, reading from his works, in 1851 and again
in 1876. Clemens said in chapter 38 of *Life on the Mississippi*
that among the books on the parlor table of the "best dwelling"
in every river town was "Tupper, much penciled."

237.11–14   "Let dogs ... eyes with—"] Isaac Watts's Song 16, "Against
Quarrelling and Fighting," verses one and two, reads:

> Let dogs delight to bark and bite,
>   For God hath made them so:
> Let bears and lions growl and fight,
>   For 'tis their nature, too.
>
> But children, you should never let
>   Such angry passions rise:
> Your little hands were never made
>   To tear each other's eyes.
>   (*Divine and Moral Songs*, p. 39)

237.17   his prodigious feet] According to C. A. V. Putnam, who also
wrote for the *Enterprise*, "if there was any one thing that particularly distinguished Jack Perry at that time, it was the faultless style of his footwear. Boots that any dandy might envy were
constantly worn by him, and were always well polished." Putnam recalled that Clemens published the following local item as
a way to needle Perry about this dandyism:

> Found—Yesterday the local reporter of this paper found a
> gigantic horse or muleshoe. On showing it around at the
> different blacksmith shops the reporter was informed that it was
> of a size larger by a good deal than any of the shoes made by
> machinery in any of the Eastern factories and that to replace it
> on the animal's foot a new shoe will have to be made expressly
> to fill the bill. Therefore, if this should meet the eye of the
> teamster losing the shoe from one of his animals, he is hereby
> informed that he can have it by calling at this office.
> P. S.—Since the foregoing was in type we have learned that it
> was no horse or muleshoe at all. It was simply a plate from Jack
> Perry's bootheel.

("Dan De Quille and Mark Twain," Salt Lake City *Tribune*,
25 April 1898, p. 3)

237.24   member of Congress from New Jersey] Nehemiah Perry was a New Jersey member of the House of Representatives from 1861 to 1865.

237.26   propping his feet ... the chaplain] Compare *Roughing It*, chapter 25.

237.37–238.1 "Old Pete" in Dion Boucicault's "Octoroon."] Dion Boucicault (1820–1890), a prolific Irish-American playwright and actor, first produced *The Octoroon; or, Life in Louisiana*, his play on slavery and miscegenation, in 1859. The following year the play ran successfully in San Francisco, and during the Civil War years it became a fairly standard drama on the San Francisco and Virginia City repertory stage (Margaret G. Watson, *Silver Theatre* [Glendale, Calif.: Arthur H. Clark Co., 1964], pp. 186, 279, 293). The character Pete, originally played by George Jamieson, was perhaps the most famous Negro stage character of the day. He was the type of kindly, authoritative, paternal, respected plantation slave later developed by Joel Chandler Harris and others (Townsend Walsh, *The Career of Dion Boucicault* [New York: The Dunlap Society, 1915], p. 68). The actor Harry A. Perry was particularly praised as early as June 1861 for his representation of Pete at Maguire's Opera House in San Francisco ("Maguire's—The Octoroon," San Francisco *Evening Journal*, 11 June 1861, p. 2; advertisement, San Francisco *Evening Bulletin*, 11 June 1861, p. 1). Perry's wife, Agnes Land Perry, starred in the role of Zoe, the octoroon, about the time Clemens wrote his burlesque.

238.9   Board of Aldermen] As of July, the board consisted of R. J. Mitchell, Charles Jones, G. H. Shaw, James Bolan, S. A. Chapin, and Alexander Coryell, with Mayor Rufus E. Arick presiding ("Municipal Officers of the City of Virginia," Virginia City *Evening Bulletin*, 16 July 1863, p. 3).

238.12   handcuffed me] "A Treasonable Conspiracy" by Dan De Quille, an account that appeared in the *Enterprise*, relates the arrest and handcuffing of Clemens by Jack Perry and Deputy Marshal George Birdsall, who is mentioned in chapter 49 of *Roughing It*, at a popular saloon in Virginia City. The incident was an elaborate practical joke that led to a mock trial in which Clemens, according to Dan, participated as judge rather than as defendant (undated clipping in carton 1, folder 145, William Wright Papers, Bancroft).

238.13   Tom Peasley's] Thomas Peasley of New York State, who came to Virginia City in 1860 from Mokelumne Hill, California, owned the Sazerac Saloon on South C Street. He was foreman of Virginia Engine Company No. 1 and later chief engineer of the Virginia Fire Department. He exerted great political influence upon the police and fire departments and among the "sports" and "roughs" of the city. In 1865 he became manager of Maguire's Virginia City Opera House. At the time of his death from gunshot wounds in February 1866 he was sergeant-at-arms of the Nevada State Legislature ("Two Men Killed, in Carson," San Francisco *Morning Call*, 3 February 1866, p. 3; "The Recent Tragedy in Carson, Nevada," San Francisco *Evening Bulletin*, 6 February 1866, p. 2; Angel, *History*, pp. 599–600; Sam P. Davis, ed., *The History of Nevada*, 2 vols. [Reno and Los Angeles: Elms Publishing Co., 1913], 1:249–251, 256–258).

238.13   Larkin and Brokaw] Peter Larkin and Isaac Brokaw were prominent Virginia City police officers and members of the Virginia Fire Department (Kelly, *Second Directory*, pp. 147, 167, 177, 299).

50. [*CHAMPAGNE WITH THE BOARD OF BROKERS*]

240.8   Baalam's ass] An early appearance of one of Mark Twain's favorite comic similes. Compare 2 Pet. 2:15–16 and Num. 22:27–31. Mark Twain alludes indirectly to Baalam's ass in "City Marshal Perry" (no. 49) when he says that the founder of the house of Perry "was the property of one Baalam."

240.17   "Texas,"] The mine of the Texas Mining Company was on Cedar Hill near Virginia City (Kelly, *Second Directory*, p. 155).

51. *ADVICE TO THE UNRELIABLE ON CHURCH-GOING*

52. *HORRIBLE AFFAIR*

No notes.

53. *LETTER FROM MARK TWAIN*

250.6   Occidental Hotel] Formally opened on 1 January 1863, the lavishly furnished Occidental Hotel (Lewis Leland and Company, proprietors) was at Bush and Montgomery streets (San Francisco *Morning Call*, 3 January 1863, p. 1). The Occidental would supplant the Lick House as Clemens' favorite place to room and board in San Francisco—when he could afford it.

250.17   Bill Stewart] William M. Stewart, a New Yorker of unusual
            native force, came to California in 1850. He began practicing
            law in 1852 and became attorney general of California in 1854.
            In 1860 he migrated to Nevada, where he became a member of
            the council of the Territorial Legislature in 1861 and a domi-
            nating presence in the Constitutional Convention of 1863.
            His success and influence as a lawyer for major mining inter-
            ests was enormous. He served Nevada as United States senator
            from 1864 to 1875, and again from 1887 to 1905. For approxi-
            mately two months beginning in November 1867, Clemens was
            Stewart's secretary in Washington, D.C., an arrangement that
            ended with hard feelings on both sides (*MTEnt*, p. 230;
            MTB, 1:346–347).

250.18   sued to quiet title] A "proceeding to establish the plaintiff's
            title to land by bringing into court an adverse claimant and
            there compelling him either to establish his claim or be forever
            after estopped from asserting it" (Henry Campbell Black,
            Black's Law Dictionary, rev. 4th ed. [St. Paul: West Publishing
            Company, 1968], p. 1416).

250.23   Ophir suit that's coming off in Virginia] The general reference
            of Clemens' remark is to the four years of contention and
            complex litigation between the Ophir Silver Mining Company
            and the Burning Moscow Company. The mines of the two
            companies were adjacent, and title to 800 feet was in dispute.
            Before a final compromise was effected in October 1864, more
            than $1 million had been expended in the Ophir-Moscow
            trials, according to the estimate of S. H. Marlette, surveyor
            general of Nevada (*Annual Report of the Surveyor-General
            of the State of Nevada, for the Year 1865*, p. 28). Stewart, the
            highly paid chief counsel for Ophir, vigorously propounded
            the "one-ledge" theory to sustain his client's claim to the
            contested ground, whereas the Burning Moscow lawyers
            supported the "many-ledge" theory to prove that the Moscow
            ledge was distinct from that of the Ophir and not a spur or
            offshoot of it. (See "A Card. Burning Moscow Company vs.
            Madison Company," 9 March 1863, a letter from D. W. Perley
            in "Bancroft Scraps, Nevada Mining" [set W, vol. 94:1], p. 54,
            Bancroft, and a reply from Leonard W. Ferris, 16 March 1863,
            ibid., p. 58; Lord, *Comstock Mining*, pp. 137–144, 173–177;
            Charles Howard Shinn, *The Story of the Mine* [New York:
            D. Appleton and Co., 1901], pp. 131–133.)
               Clemens appears to have favored the "many-ledge" theory.
            With the Ophir-Moscow contention in mind, he complained
            to his brother about the "preposterous wrong" of the jury's
            decision in another famous legal battle, the Chollar-Potosi suit:

"If that decision stands," he wrote, "the Ophir will open its mighty jaws and swallow Mount Davidson" (Clemens to Orion [and Mollie] Clemens, 21 October 1862, *CL1*, letter 64).

In particular, however, Clemens refers to the suit brought by Ophir against Burning Moscow on 16 March 1863 in the First District Court, Virginia City. On 14 May 1863, while the suit was in progress and two days before Clemens' letter, Ophir miners, who were working in the westward extension of the tunnel into the middle lead, cut into the Burning Moscow works and were physically repulsed. Ophir successfully applied for a temporary injunction restraining the Burning Moscow Company from extracting ore from the contested ground but permitting Ophir to do so ("The Ophir Monopoly," letter from "A Subscriber," Virginia City *Union*, 1 September 1863, clipping in "Bancroft Scraps, Nevada Mining" [set W, vol. 94:1], pp. 117–118, Bancroft).

251.1   the Judge] On 8 April 1863 Acting Governor Orion Clemens temporarily assigned Associate Justice Horatio N. Jones of the Third Judicial District to the bench of absent Judge Gordon N. Mott of the First Judicial District (Virginia City) for the May term. Judge Jones granted the restraining order to the Ophir Company. On September 14 Judge John W. North, Judge Mott's successor, opened court in Virginia City. During the first week of November he enjoined the Ophir from further operations in the Burning Moscow works, and late in December he upheld the injunction ("Settled at Last," Virginia City *Union*, 9 April 1863, clipping in Scrapbook 2, p. 38, MTP; "The Question Settled," Virginia City *Territorial Enterprise*, 9 April 1863, ibid., p. 43; "An Important Decision," Virginia City *Evening Bulletin*, 29 December 1863, p. 3).

251.26   Bella Union Melodeon] Originally a notorious gambling saloon at Washington Street opposite Portsmouth Square, the Bella Union had since 1856 been a music hall specializing in variety acts not invariably "chaste and high-toned" (Estavan, *Theatre Research*, 15:3, 5–6).

252.16   Wm. H. Davenport] William H. Davenport was a prominent attorney in the Nevada Territory. He was elected assemblyman from Storey County on 3 September 1862 and attended the Territorial Legislature that year. In December 1863 he was elected one of the secretaries of the "bolters' convention." By early April 1864 he had become judge of the police court in Virginia City, and on 2 November 1880 he would be elected district attorney of Eureka County (Angel, *History*, pp. 338, 427, 606; *MTEnt*, pp. 42–43, 113; Collins, *Mercantile Guide*, p. 73).

252.18   Colonel John A. Collins] Collins was formally a resident of
          Virginia City (see the explanatory note to "Examination of
          Teachers," no. 51). But he evidently maintained a house on
          North Street in San Francisco (Langley, *Directory for 1863*,
          p. 104).

252.19   Judge Noyes] J. W. Noyes had evidently been justice of the
          peace in Virginia City before Joseph F. Atwill replaced him in
          1862. Noyes was a member, like Davenport, of the "bolters'
          convention" in December 1863 ("Constable's Sale," Virginia
          City *Territorial Enterprise*, 10 January 1863, p. 4, PH in MTP;
          Kelly, *First Directory*, pp. 108, 144; *MTEnt*, p. 114).

252.19   Messrs. Beecher and Franz, of Virginia] Beecher has not been
          identified. Franz may be Bernhard Franz, who sold books,
          stationery, and music in Virginia City and was an agent for
          H. H. Bancroft and Company's Law Publications in San Fran-
          cisco (advertisement, Virginia City *Territorial Enterprise*,
          10 January 1863, p. 4, PH in MTP).

252.23   B. C. Howard] Howard was elected Lyon County commissioner
          on 14 January 1862 and reelected on September 3 of that year.
          He resigned on 5 May 1866 (Angel, *History*, p. 495).

252.26   Col. Raymond, of the Zephyr-Flat mill] In 1863 H. H. Raymond
          was one of two owners of the Zephyr Flat mill, which was
          situated about three and a half miles from Empire City and
          was powered by water from the Carson River (Angel, *History*,
          p. 541).

252.32   this election] The local elections in San Francisco (for mayor,
          county clerk, sheriff, supervisors, and many other officers)
          were held on 19 May 1863 (Langley, *Directory for 1863*, p. 13).

54. "MARK TWAIN'S" LETTER

255.17   Mr. Mayo] Frank Mayo, who migrated from Boston to San
          Francisco in 1853, began his stage career in 1856 and by 1863
          was taking leading roles at Maguire's San Francisco Opera
          House. Returning to the East in 1865, Mayo made his New
          York debut in 1869. He excelled in Shakespearian parts
          and in such popular plays as *The Streets of New York* and
          Davy Crockett. Late in his career he adapted Clemens'
          Pudd'nhead Wilson for the stage and opened in it at Hartford
          on 8 April 1895.

255.17   Mrs. Hayne] Julia Dean Hayne played leading roles on the
          western stage from 1856 to 1865 and was well known to
          Clemens for her performances in *East Lynne* and many other

plays (T. Allston Brown, *History of the American Stage* [New York: Dick and Fitzgerald, 1870], p. 97; "'Mark Twain's' Letter," San Francisco *Morning Call*, 15 July 1863, p. 1).

255.21-22   Uncle John Atchison] John H. (Uncle John) Atchison migrated in 1849 from Iowa to California, where he successfully mined near Sacramento. In 1860 he became an incorporator of the Ophir Silver Mining Company and of the Washoe Mining and Manufacturing Company, which was instrumental in developing Washoe City. With his brothers, Silas and Sam, he built mills at Washoe and Empire cities, and he was an early promoter of the Virginia and Truckee Railroad (Ratay, *Pioneers*, pp. 264, 283 n. 10, 347, 409 n. 3). In "Letter from Mark Twain," published in the Chicago *Republican* on 31 May 1868 (p. 2), Clemens mentioned Atchison's purchase of Genessee mining stock.

255.22   Mr. Harris] Possibly H. Harris, assayer in the Gold Hill banking house of Almarin B. Paul (Collins, *Mercantile Guide*, p. 269).

255.22   Mr. Chapelle] R. C. Chappell was a Virginia City lumber dealer in 1862, and in 1863 he was a partner in the Virginia City firm of Wightman and Chappell, "commission and stock brokers" (Kelly, *First Directory*, p. 120, and *Second Directory*, p. 182).

256.3   Lincoln] In the remainder of the paragraph Clemens alludes to several cities and stagecoach stops along the Henness Pass route between Sacramento and Virginia City. Lincoln, Nevada City, and Lake City are well-known California locations today. Hunter's, in 1863 the site of a hotel and bridge over the Truckee River, was about midway between Reno and Verdi (Angel, *History*, p. 643).

256.19-20   Mr. Merritt's, President of the Imperial Gold and Silver Mining Company] The office of the Imperial Company was in Gold Hill, and its mine was on the Comstock just north of the Yellow Jacket claim (Langley, *Directory for 1863*, p. 197; Lord, *Comstock Mining*, p. 79). The records of incorporation for the company name Merritt as a member of the board of directors.

256.22   Nathaniel Page] San Francisco directories list Nathaniel Page as a lumber dealer (Langley, *Directory for 1863*, p. 284, and *Directory for 1864*, p. 314).

257.3   Billy Welch] William Welch was foreman of the California mine, Virginia district (Kelly, *Second Directory*, p. 292).

257.38-258.1   Mike Millenovich ... McGee and Scott] Joseph McGee shot and killed the proprietor of the San Francisco Saloon in Virginia City on 4 July 1863 (Angel, *History*, p. 344). The proprietor is variously identified as "Mark Milinovick" and

"M. Milanovich" in Kelly's 1862 and 1863 directories of Nevada Territory (p. 154 and p. 278, respectively). A "Joe McGhee" is named as a special policeman in 1863, but there is no Scott listed (Kelly, *Second Directory*, p. 167).

258.15   Hale & Norcross mine] Sam and Orion Clemens later acquired stock in this important Comstock mine but soon disposed of it at a loss (*Autobiography of Mark Twain*, ed. Charles Neider [New York: Harper and Brothers, 1959], p. 218).

258.18   Charles Strong] For several years, commencing in 1860, Strong was the wealthy and influential superintendent of the Gould and Curry Company. In about 1864 he became its president and moved to San Francisco (Angel, *History*, p. 68; Kelly, *Second Directory*, p. 200).

55. "MARK TWAIN'S" LETTER

260.11–12   "lame and impotent conclusion,"] *Othello*, act 2, scene 1, line 162.

56. A DUEL PREVENTED

265.5   John Church] In November 1862 John Church and his partners moved their newspaper, the Carson City *Silver Age*, to Virginia City and renamed it the *Union*. Church acted as business manager for the paper. In mid-1862, while mining in Esmeralda shortly before he joined the *Enterprise* staff, Clemens considered corresponding for the *Silver Age*. Church continued as a proprietor of the *Union* until May 1865 (Angel, *History*, pp. 312, 323; Clemens to Orion Clemens, 9 July 1862, *CL1*, letter 58; Kelly, *First Directory*, p. 69).

266.3   young Wilson] Clemens' friend, twenty-two-year-old Adair Wilson from Missouri, was the junior local editor of the Virginia City *Union*. He was admitted to the bar in 1860 and practiced law in San Francisco from 1861 to 1863. He left the *Union* in October 1863 to become editor of the Reese River *Reveille*, and then local reporter on the San Francisco *American Flag* in 1865. Eventually he became a Colorado state senator (1887–1890), president of the Colorado Legislature, an associate judge of the Colorado Court of Appeals, and a member of the Democratic National Committee (Angel, *History*, p. 304; Langley, *Directory for 1865*, n.p.; Frank Hall,

History of the State of Colorado, 4 vols. [Chicago: Blakely Printing Co., 1895], 4:610; *Portrait and Biographical Record of the State of Colorado* [Chicago: Chapman Publishing Co., 1899], pp. 321–325).

266.15 Olin's fast horses] Ansel S. Olin owned the Pioneer Stables on B Street near Taylor in Virginia City (Kelly, *First Directory*, p. 156).

266.20 Deputy Sheriff Blodgett] Deputy Sheriff Henry L. Blodgett had his office on South B Street. When Clemens was commissioned a notary public in the spring of 1864, he and Blodgett set up as "Blodgett and Clemens, Notaries Public" in the Virginia City post office building. The firm's advertisement last appeared in the Virginia City *Evening Bulletin* on April 16. By April 22 Clemens had resigned his commission (Kelly, *Second Directory*, p. 175; daily advertisements in the Virginia City *Evening Bulletin*, 1–16 April 1864; "Still Another," ibid., 22 April 1864, p. 3).

57. [*AN APOLOGY REPUDIATED*]

No notes.

58. *LETTER FROM MARK TWAIN*

273.7 "Wake-up Jake"] A real, not fictional, but quite mysterious potion. The journalist William Brief was also impressed by it, calling it "a certain medicine employed by the Doctor, known as Wake up Jake" ("San Francisco Letter," Carson City *Appeal*, 31 May 1865, p. 1).

275.17 "the servants of the lamp,"] The allusion is to Florence Nightingale (Longfellow's "lady with a lamp" in his poem "Santa Filomena") and her corps of nurses, who were said to have performed miracles while caring for wounded soldiers during the Crimean War. Miss Nightingale worked at the Scutari military hospital under the most trying conditions, making her rounds at night carrying a lamp.

276.4 Palmer] W. A. Palmer was a Wells Fargo agent in Folsom, California, in 1862 and 1863 (Noel Loomis, *Wells Fargo* [New York: Clarkson N. Potter, 1968], p. 166).

276.26–27 Reverend Jack Holmes] Kelly's *Second Directory* (p. 141) lists John Holmes as the proprietor of the Steamboat Springs Hotel; Clemens' other references to him imply that he and A. W. Stowe were co-managers ("'Mark Twain's' Letter," no. 59; "Letter from Mark Twain," Virginia City *Territorial Enterprise*, 19 August 1863, reprinted in *MTEnt*, p. 69).

59. "MARK TWAIN'S" LETTER

279.11   Lake Bigler] See "Bigler vs. Tahoe" (no. 61).

280.12   season of avalanches] Washoe Valley, northwest of Carson City, was subject to both avalanches (as attested by the scars on Slide Mountain) and heavy washes from the mountain slopes to the west. Devastating floods during the winter of 1861–1862 caused landslides of both kinds in many areas of California and Nevada (see, for example, "The Great California Flood," San Francisco *Evening Bulletin*, 30 January 1862, p. 2, and "Sublimity of Land Slides on the Sierra Nevada," ibid., 4 February 1865, p. 2). Dick Sides's farm was on the arable land of Washoe Valley, part of which was covered by a wash of sand and gravel in January 1862 ("Nevada Territory," San Francisco *Alta California*, 4 February 1862, p. 1).

280.12   Tom Rust's ranch] No mention of Rust has been found in the memoirs of early Nevada settlers, in land records, or in printed sources. Nevertheless, Clemens' repetition of the name in his 1865 notebook supports the conjecture that someone named Rust was in fact the defendant in the trial (see *N&J1*, p. 79).

280.14   Dick Sides] Richard D. (Ole Dick) Sides of North Carolina was one of the earliest pioneers of western Carson County, Utah Territory, having purchased land there in the middle 1850s. He became a leading citizen of Franktown, in Washoe Valley, where he farmed and for a time operated a sawmill. He was elected treasurer of Carson County in 1855. With Isaac Roop and others he tried to organize a new territory from portions of Utah, California, and New Mexico during the late 1850s. He was a member of the R. D. Sides Company, whose early claim on the Comstock Lode eventually became part of the Consolidated Virginia mine. An ardent Unionist and a large, vigorous man of violent temper, he was known throughout the region (Angel, *History*, pp. 37–38, 40–43, 49; Virginia City *Territorial Enterprise*, 10 January 1863, p. 1, PH in MTP; Lord, *Comstock Mining*, p. 48; Ratay, *Pioneers*, pp. 149–153).

280.16   Mr. Bunker] Benjamin B. Bunker of New Hampshire was appointed United States attorney for Nevada Territory on 27 March 1861, and he returned to the East on 1 May 1862. While in Nevada, he was senior partner in the Carson City law firm of Bunker, Corson, and White (Carson City *Silver Age*, 20 July 1861, p. 2; Angel, *History*, pp. 77, 679). He and Clemens were well acquainted, and a number of Bunker's activities are recorded in Clemens' letters of the period. In 1865 at age fifty Bunker enlisted briefly in the Union army. Apparently he spent most of the rest of his long life practicing law in New Hampshire.

Bunker related two apocryphal tales, "Mark Twain's First Story" and "Mark Twain's Reckless Gambling," in an unpublished 1900 interview. Clemens wrote to Arthur Lumley on 16 October 1900: "Gen. Bunker means well, & so I'll not criticise his history, though I give you my word there isn't a single molecule of truth in it anywhere" (Berg). A letter of 2 August 1906 from Julia A. Bunker to Arthur Lumley reveals that Bunker, ninety-one, was still alive but paralyzed and "mixed up in his mind" (Berg).

280.23   be of good cheer] Compare Matt. 14:27.

280.24   Roop] Isaac Roop of Maryland came to Shasta, California, in 1850. In 1853 he became the first settler in the Honey Lake Valley region of northeastern California, where he founded the town of Susanville. He took a leading part in the attempts to form a territorial government in 1857 and 1859, and he was elected governor of the provisional territory the latter year. In 1861 he was a member of the council of the first Territorial Legislature of Nevada. Later he served on a commission to negotiate Nevada's western boundary with California. Before his death in 1869 he was twice elected district attorney for Lassen County, California. Roop, who was known for his sense of humor, was present in Carson City at the conjectured time of the mock trial, early February 1862 (Angel, *History*, pp. 42–43, 563; Mack, *History*, pp. 181, 395, 398; James Thomas Butler, "Isaac Roop, Pioneer and Political Leader of Northeastern California" [M.A. thesis, University of California, Berkeley, 1958], pp. 6, 23, 52–68, 79–91, 111, 113, 115).

280.26   Sheriff] Possibly William L. Marley, appointed Ormsby County sheriff late in 1861 (Angel, *History*, p. 530).

281.24   drove Mr. Bunker back to New Hampshire] Bunker may have gone East to help his family move to Nevada. The illness of his wife and daughter, however, seemingly prevented his return to Nevada up to the time in mid-1863 when President Lincoln removed him from office (Abraham Lincoln, *The Collected*

Works of Abraham Lincoln, ed. Roy P. Basler, 9 vols. [New Brunswick, N.J.: Rutgers University Press, 1953–1955], 6:255).

282.35   "JOHN HALIFAX."] A novel by the prolific Dinah Maria Mulock (later Mrs. George L. Craik), published in 1857. The style of this "high-flown batch of contradictions and inconsistencies" gives point to the opening sentence in Clemens' final paragraph: it is excessively staccato, repetitive, and exclamatory. The dialogue is stilted and includes numerous words from "the Friends' mode of phraseology" in the speech of such characters as Phineas Fletcher, as well as a host of expletives like "Verily!" "Courage!" "Bravo!" "Alas!" and "Hush!" Lady Caroline Brithwood offers some typical dialogue when she learns that her lover has left her: "Gone away! the only living soul that loves me. Gone away! I must follow him—quick—quick" (*John Halifax, Gentleman* [New York: Thomas Y. Crowell, 1897], pp. 30, 298).

60. *UNFORTUNATE BLUNDER*

286.2–3   no more animation than a sick puppy] Clemens was still sick with the cold he had caught at the end of July.

286.4   Court House] In January 1863 the Storey County commissioners leased a new brick building at 14 South B Street to be used for courtrooms and offices ("The New Court House," Virginia City *Territorial Enterprise*, 10 January 1863, p. 3, PH in MTP).

286.9   First Presbyterian Church] This church was organized on 21 September 1862 in Virginia City by the Reverend W. W. Bryan (Collins, *Mercantile Guide*, p. 27).

287.1–2   Th' Pride o' the West] A prominent mine in the Devil's Gate district (Angel, *History*, p. 498; Collins, *Mercantile Guide*, p. 368).

287.20–21   go to Goldsmith's church to laugh, and remain to pray] Compare Oliver Goldsmith's "The Deserted Village": "And fools, who came to scoff, remained to pray" (line 180).

61. *BIGLER* vs. *TAHOE*

290.18   viewless spirits of the air] An ingenious conflation of "the sightless couriers of the air" (*Macbeth*, act 1, scene 7, line 23), "the viewless wings of Poesy" (Keats, "Ode to a Nightingale," line 33), and "the viewless spirit of the tempest" (Scott, *The Pirate* [Edinburgh: Adam and Charles Black, 1863], chapter 6, p. 44).

62. *LETTER FROM MARK TWAIN*

293.4   Carpenter & Hoog's stage] According to contemporary newspapers, from late July through September 1863 the stagecoach line between Carson and Virginia cities bore this name (see, for example, the Virginia City *Evening Bulletin*, 30 July 1863, p. 3, and 14 September 1863, p. 3). In a letter of 5 August 1891 the hospitalized William H. Hoog recalled the old stagecoach days and begged Clemens for financial aid. He also identified his partner, Carpenter, as Thomas Fitch's brother-in-law (MTP).

293.5   Pioneer] The Pioneer Stage Company, established in 1857, ran daily stagecoaches from Virginia City to Sacramento by way of Gold Hill, Carson City, Genoa, and Placerville (Angel, *History*, p. 588). The company carried Wells Fargo express and United States mail as well as passengers (Collins, *Mercantile Guide*, p. 35).

293.18   Strawberry Valley] A station in California on the stagecoach route between Carson City and Sacramento, south and a little west of Lake Tahoe, and about fifty miles east of Placerville.

293.18   Folsom] The terminus of the Sacramento Valley Railroad, approximately twenty-two miles northeast of Sacramento.

294.18   Thirty-five Mile House] A stagecoach station a few miles west of Strawberry Valley.

294.24   overland] The Overland Stage Company ran daily stagecoaches between Sacramento and the Missouri River, by way of Austin, Reese River, and Salt Lake City (Collins, *Mercantile Guide*, p. 36). Sam and Orion Clemens came to Nevada on the Overland.

295.9   MR. BILLET] R. W. Billet was a Virginia City stockbroker, the owner of the Empire State mill near Sugar Loaf Peak, and secretary to several mining companies. In December 1863 he was elected vice-president of the Washoe Stock and Exchange Board. He was a leader in the Nevada Democratic party (Kelly, *First Directory*, pp. 113, 117, and *Second Directory*, p. 230; advertisement, Virginia City *Territorial Enterprise*, 3 April 1865, p. 2; Angel, *History*, p. 265; "The Broker's Election," Virginia City *Evening Bulletin*, 5 December 1863, p. 2).

63. HOW TO CURE A COLD

298.2   it is a far higher and nobler thing] Compare Sydney Carton's last
            reflection, the closing lines of Dickens' *A Tale of Two Cities.*

299.5   Gould and Curry] Clemens lost stock certificates in the fire,
            but almost certainly none of these were valuable Gould and
            Curry stock.

301.15   Lake House] Captain Augustus W. Pray's Lake Shore House at
            Glenbrook on Lake Tahoe was completed in 1863 (Scott, *Lake
            Tahoe*, p. 265).

302.9   don't see you] This passage and the following three paragraphs
            may derive from Clemens' experience with Jennie Woodruff
            in San Francisco the preceding May. To his confusion, Jennie,
            "a pretty girl," alternately smiled at him and ignored him in
            successive meetings (Clemens to Jane Clemens and Pamela
            Moffett, 4 June 1863, *CL1*, letter 71).

64. MARK TWAIN—MORE OF HIM

308.1   LICK HOUSE] A new hotel of three and one-half stories on
            Montgomery Street between Post and Sutter streets noted for
            its fine furnishings, many comforts, and active social life
            (Julia Cooley Altrocchi, *The Spectacular San Franciscans*
            [New York: E. P. Dutton and Co., 1949], p. 117). Clemens
            stayed there in 1863 during his summer and fall visits to
            the city.

308.3   brilliant Ball at Mr. Barron's] William E. Barron was a wealthy
            stockholder in the Gould and Curry mine, an organizer of the
            Bank of California in June 1864, and a principal stockholder
            in the New Almaden Company. In 1868 he became an incor-
            porator and trustee of the Union Mill and Mining Company,
            created by William C. Ralston as a holding company to control
            operations in the Comstock mines (Leonard Ascher, "Lincoln's
            Administration and the New Almaden Scandal," *Pacific His-
            torical Review* 5 [March 1936]: 49; Cecil G. Tilton, *William
            Chapman Ralston: Courageous Builder* [Boston: Christopher
            Publishing House, 1935], pp. 97, 145). A writer in the *Era*
            gave as one reason for the ball Barron's relief at the settlement
            of eleven-year-old litigation over ownership of the Almaden
            quicksilver mine ("The Ball of Mr. Wm. Barron," *Golden Era*
            11 [20 September 1863]: 4).

308.3   Washoe widow] In her weekly columns for the *Era*, Florence

Fane (Frances Fuller Victor) had invented the imaginary
Washoe and Reese River Widows' Association "to provide for
the entertainment of widows during desertion" ("Florence
Fane in San Francisco," *Golden Era* 11 [13 September 1863]: 5).
See the note below on Florence Fane.

308.4–5   Sarah Smith skipped me in the toilettes] That is, did not
describe her appearance at Barron's ball. Sarah Smith also wrote
for the *California Magazine and Mountaineer*, published by
Brooks and Lawrence, proprietors of the *Era*. One week before
it published Mark Twain's burlesques, the *Era* printed her
"Letter" describing Barron's ball. The name "Sarah Smith"
was supposedly the pseudonym of an innocent filly recently
arrived in San Francisco, but it seems more likely that it was
that of an experienced stallion from the *Era's* stable of writers.
After describing *"the* Ball *par excellence* . . . of all seasons in
San Francisco" and reviewing the ladies' costumes in the
customary flattering manner, Miss Smith noted that Barron,
a bachelor, gave his splendid ball to honor the bride of a friend.
She commented: "I heard many ladies wondering why a man
who knew so well what was due to a bride, did not have one of
his own to give balls to" ("Letter from a Lady. Mr. Barron's
Ball," *Golden Era* 11 [20 September 1863]: 5). Clemens himself
would never have used such a bold *double entendre* in print,
but in November 1865 he did venture a slightly risqué fashion
description, noting that "Mrs. C. N. was superbly arrayed in
white kid gloves. Her modest and engaging manner accorded
well with the unpretending simplicity of her costume, and
caused her to be regarded with absorbing interest by every one"
("The Pioneers' Ball," no. 137).

308.5–6   Brigham & Co. said I looked 'swell,'] S. O. Brigham and Company of 111 Montgomery Street sold silverware and sewing
machines, but also housed a branch office of Madame
Demorest's Emporium of Fashion in New York City (Langley,
Directory for 1863, p. 78).

308.6   'Robergh'] The name of a fashionable but otherwise unidentified couturier ("Beauty at the Ball," *Golden Era* 11 [20 September 1863]: 4).

308.7   Reese River] The Reese River mining district of Lander
County, Nevada, was about one hundred and fifty miles east
of Virginia City. Organized in mid-1862 following the discovery
of rich veins of ore, it was the site of a mining rush of major
proportions (Bancroft, *Works*, pp. 264–265).

308.14   Florence Fane] The pseudonym of Frances Fuller Victor. In
1863 Mrs. Victor was an editorial writer for the San Francisco

Evening Herald and a columnist for the *Era*. She wrote poems, stories, portions of Hubert Howe Bancroft's histories, and books of social history focusing on pioneer Oregon and Washington (Franklin Walker, *San Francisco's Literary Frontier* [New York: Alfred A. Knopf, 1939], pp. 137–138).

308.17–18   special gathering in compliment to him] In an untitled item the *Era* quoted the *Enterprise* early in October: "Mark Twain— our old Mark—is quite a lion down at the Bay. We understand that the ladies of the Lick House gave him, or were to give him a complimentary ball last Thursday night. Bully for him!" (*Golden Era* 11 [4 October 1863]: 4). The reference is to the Lick House Ball, described in sketch no. 65.

310.25   Mrs. J. B. W.] Mrs. John B. Winters, for whom Clemens had "a special friendship ... because she is the very image of Pamela" (Clemens to Jane Clemens and Pamela Moffett, 4 June 1863, *CL1*, letter 71). Clemens also liked her husband: see the explanatory note on John B. Winters in "The Lick House Ball" (no. 65).

310.32   Sontag] A cape or jacket, usually knitted or crocheted, with ends crossing in back.

311.4   greenbacks] These United States Treasury notes, first issued in 1862, were legal tender, but on the market they were worth considerably less than face value.

311.28   Mr. Lawlor's] William B. Lawlor was a prominent Carson City schoolteacher whose classroom Clemens once visited (see "An Excellent School," no. 71). In September 1864 Lawlor was elected Ormsby County superintendent of schools (*MTEnt*, pp. 149–151; Angel, *History*, p. 530). The men mentioned in this paragraph are presumably all Nevada residents, although one of them, Mr. Ridgway, has not been identified.

311.29   Mr. Camp's] In an 1865 notebook Clemens wrote: "Herman Camp has sold some Washoe Stock in New York for $270,000" (*N&J1*, p. 73). Later that same year Clemens called him an old friend and described him as a successful businessman with New York connections: "Camp offered me half, 2 years ago, if I would go with him to New York & help him sell some mining claims, & I, like a fool, refused. He went, & made $270,000 in two months" (Clemens to Orion Clemens, 13 December 1865, *CL1*, letter 96). Camp, who arrived in Nevada Territory in 1859, is said to have purchased Comstock's interest in the Ophir mine for a trivial sum, but he was subsequently forced to relinquish his claim. Later he owned stock in the Gould and Curry mine ("Comstock Papers. No. 8," *Mining and Scientific Press* 33 [4 November 1876]: 305).

311.30   Mr. Paxton's] John A. Paxton came to San Francisco in 1849,
              prospered in business, and in 1853 became a Marysville banker.
              In 1863 he established his banking firm, Paxton and Thorn-
              burgh, in Virginia City (Phelps, *Contemporary Biography*,
              2:358–360).

311.30   Jerry Long's] An early Nevada settler, Long surveyed the site
              of Carson City in 1858 and became the Carson County sur-
              veyor in 1859 (Angel, *History*, pp. 59, 64).

311.30–31   Judge Gilchrist's] Probably S. F. Gilchrist, a Carson attorney.
              Clemens reported on his journey to Reese River in August 1863
              ("'Mark Twain's' Letter," San Francisco *Morning Call*, 13 Aug-
              ust 1863, p. 1).

311.31–32   Mr. Toll-road McDonald's] In 1862 Mark L. McDonald con-
              structed a profitable road from Carson City to a point near
              Empire City. It was used by teams going between Carson and
              Virginia cities (Kelly, *Second Directory*, p. 85).

65. THE LICK HOUSE BALL

315.1   Jerome Rice] Rice, who lived at the Lick House, was a San
              Francisco real-estate dealer and auctioneer; he and Clemens
              were good friends. On 7 September 1864 Rice's carriage went
              over an embankment near Vallejo Mills and he suffered
              injuries that soon caused his death. Clemens, who was then
              reporting for the San Francisco *Morning Call*, wrote a long and
              emotional account of the incident for his newspaper (*CofC*,
              pp. 122–124).

315.2   John B. Winters] Winters, a Nevada businessman active in
              mining and milling after 1859, became president and super-
              intendent of the Yellow Jacket Mining Company in April 1864.
              He was an assemblyman in the second Nevada Territorial
              Legislature and a candidate for congressman under the first
              (defeated) state constitution (Como [Nev.] *Sentinel*, 16 April
              1864, p. 2; Angel, *History*, pp. 375, 495; *MTEnt*, pp. 124–125).
              Clemens indicated his liking and respect for Winters several
              times in his Nevada and California journalism, mentioning
              him good-humoredly in "The Great Prize Fight," "Concerning
              Notaries," and "Doings in Nevada" (*Golden Era* 11 [11 Octo-
              ber 1863]: 8, reprinted in *WG*, pp. 25–31; Virginia City *Terri-
              torial Enterprise*, 9 February 1864, p. 2, reprinted in *WG*,
              pp. 67–70; New York *Sunday Mercury*, 7 February 1864, p. 3,
              reprinted in *MTEnt*, pp. 122–126). All three sketches are
              scheduled to appear in the collection of social and political

writings in The Works of Mark Twain. (Winters also figures in appendix C of *Roughing It.*)

315.2   Brooks] Probably Thaddeus R. Brooks, a resident of the Lick House and secretary to the San Francisco board of engineers (Langley, *Directory for 1863*, p. 79).

315.2   Mason] Probably Frederick Mason, a resident of the Lick House and a San Francisco real-estate agent (Langley, *Directory for 1863*, p. 241).

315.2   Charley Creed] Neither the San Francisco directories nor other sources mention Creed, but he appears again in "Those Blasted Children" (no. 72) along with Flora Low. That association and the mention of Governor Low's wife (Mollie Creed Low) in the present sketch suggest that he may have been related to Mrs. Low.

315.2   Capt. Pease] Probably E. T. Pease, a resident of the Lick House and a San Francisco broker of stock and real estate (Langley, *Directory for 1863*, p. 288).

315.17   his Grace the Duke of Benicia] Benicia, a small settlement on the northern shore of Carquinez Strait, had been the capital of California in 1853–1854. Clemens' fictional "nobility" may have been suggested by Charles Henry Webb's Duke de Cariboo and Fitzhugh Ludlow's Duke de Virginia City—characters in their respective *Era* columns which appeared shortly before Clemens' fashion burlesques were published ("Things," *Golden Era* 11 [13 September 1863]: 5; "On Marrying Men," *Golden Era* 11 [20 September 1863]: 4).

315.20   Emperor Norton] Joshua A. Norton came to San Francisco in 1849 and soon became wealthy, but he lost his money in 1853, an event which affected his sanity. He became a likable lunatic who believed he was emperor of the United States, and for almost three decades lived in San Francisco supported by the townspeople. Clemens was quite familiar with him. (See Clemens to William Dean Howells, 3 September 1880, *MTHL*, 1:326, and Robert Ernest Cowen, Anne Bancroft, and Addie L. Ballou, *The Forgotten Characters of Old San Francisco* [Los Angeles: Ward Ritchie Press, 1964], pp. 30–59.)

315.31   Messrs. Barron] According to one anonymous writer in the *Era*, William E. Barron gave his ball of September 17 in part to provide Eustace Barron (probably a nephew) with the opportunity to take leave of friends before going to Paris ("The Ball of Mr. Wm. Barron," *Golden Era* 11 [20 September 1863]: 4).

316.2   Goat Island] "Goat Island" was then the name for Yerba Buena Island in San Francisco Bay (Gudde, *California Names*, p. 115).

316.19   Billy Birch's] William Birch (Brudder Bones) was one of
              Clemens' favorite minstrels. He frequently appeared in Nevada
              and California theaters, having first played in San Francisco
              in 1851. With Charley Backus, Dave Wambold, and William H.
              Bernard he formed the famous San Francisco Minstrel Troupe,
              which later included Tommy Peel and Lew Rattler. The skit
              that Clemens alludes to here has not been identified. (See
              MTE, pp. 110–118, and Edward Le Roy Rice, *Monarchs of
              Minstrelsy, from "Daddy" Rice to Date* [New York: Kenny
              Publishing Co., 1911], p. 68.)

316.25   Mrs. F. F. L.] Most probably Mrs. Frederick Ferdinand Low,
              who with her husband, Governor-elect Low, opened the Lick
              House Ball.

316.28–29   lozenges ... troches] Lace or embroidery inserted into fabric
              to form a lozenge, a diamond-shaped embellishment, would
              indeed contrast with a troche, a button set with three or more
              jewels: all of which permits Clemens a mild pharmaceu-
              tical pun.

317.3   Mrs. Wm. M. S.] Probably Mrs. William M. Stewart. See
              "Letter from Mark Twain" (no. 53).

317.10   arastras] The arrastra was a mechanism for reducing ore by
              grinding the quartz between stones in a circular hole. It is
              comically appropriate for a mining term to stray into this
              paragraph in view of Stewart's importance as an attorney for
              major mining companies.

317.11   Leather ornaments] "Bonneval," who wrote for the *Era* and
              the *California Magazine and Mountaineer*, had recently
              pointed out that "leathern ornaments" had become fashion-
              able in Paris ("Our Paris Correspondence," *Golden Era* 11
              [20 September 1863]: 2).

317.12   Empress Eugenie] The wife of Emperor Napoleon III frequently
              set fashion, and her picture was often featured in women's
              magazines.

317.13   Shoshones] This tribe of Indians, inhabiting northeast Nevada,
              were still remembered for their part in the 1860 uprisings near
              Pyramid Lake (Mack, *History*, pp. 301–307).

317.16   Mrs. A. W. B.] Probably Mrs. Alexander W. Baldwin. Her
              husband, Sandy Baldwin, whom Clemens knew well in Nevada
              and remembered warmly in old age, was a leading Virginia City
              attorney and William Stewart's law partner. During the 1864
              Territorial Legislature Baldwin represented Storey County,
              and he was appointed United States district judge when Nevada
              became a state in October 1864. Clemens often mentioned him
              in his Nevada political reporting (Mack, *History*, p. 252;

MTEnt, pp. 3, 225; *MTNev,* p. 283). "A Fair Career Closed" (no. 273) is Clemens' warm tribute to Baldwin following his death in a railroad accident in 1869.

317.23   butterflies and things] Artificial butterflies and grasshoppers, as well as flowers and foliage of all kinds, were indeed fashionable ornaments for the hair ("A Feast of Fashion," *Golden Era* 11 [15 November 1863]: 3).

317.27   Mrs. J. B. W.] Probably Mrs. John B. Winters.

317.37   Mrs. F.] Effie Mona Mack suggested that Clemens was alluding to Anna M. Fitch, whose husband, Thomas Fitch, was a Virginia City lawyer, editor, and politician of unusual oratorical ability. Clemens knew the Fitches well in Virginia City (*MTNev,* pp. 239, 385; *MTEnt,* pp. 227–228).

318.12   tule hat] A pun on "tulle." Tule is a common bulrush that grows in swampy or marshy land in California and parts of the southern United States; since it was often used for thatching, it makes an appropriate hat, very much in keeping with the botanical idiom of Miss B.'s outfit.

66. *A BLOODY MASSACRE NEAR CARSON*

324.1   ABRAM CURRY] Attributing the story to Curry was calculated to increase its plausibility. The Gold Hill *News,* which reprinted the story the same day, said: "Were it not for the respectable source from which our cotemporary [Mark Twain] received it, we should refuse it any credence" ("Horrible," Gold Hill *News,* 28 October 1863, p. 3).

324.4–5   P. Hopkins, or Philip Hopkins] By leaving the name indefinite, and then by having the character die in front of the Magnolia Billiard Saloon, Clemens intentionally suggested that the insane man was its owner, Pete Hopkins, whom he liked to banter. Hopkins was also proprietor of the Carson racecourse (Kelly, *First Directory,* p. 80; "Personal," Gold Hill *News,* 19 September 1865, p. 2; *MTEnt,* p. 89). Unlike the insane man, however, Pete Hopkins was a bachelor ("A Couple of Sad Experiences," no. 299, first published in the *Galaxy* 9 [June 1870]: 860).

324.7   Dutch Nick's] Nicholas Ambrose (Ambrosia), an early settler known as Dutch Nick, established a trading post on the Carson River three and one-half miles northeast of Carson. In March 1860 the mill town of Empire City was laid out on the site of this post. Ambrose opened the new Dutch Nick's Hotel in Empire City on 15 August 1861 (Angel, *History*, p. 562; Mack, *Nevada*, p. 205; Carson City *Silver Age*, 20 August 1861, p. 2; Kelly, *First Directory*, p. 92).

325.28   Spring Valley Water Company] San Francisco's main supplier of water. When the company was incorporated in April 1858, it was capitalized at $3 million. Its main reservoir was Lake Honda, from which water was first brought to the city on 2 July 1863 (Langley, *Directory for 1863*, pp. xl, 14).

325.29-30   one of the editors of the San Francisco *Bulletin*] The *Evening Bulletin* had long been a major San Francisco daily. Its editors were George K. Fitch, Lorin Pickering, and John W. Simonton (E. T. H. Bunje et al., *Journals of the Golden Gate: 1846-1936* [Berkeley: University of California, 1936], p. 38).

325.31-32   Daney Mining Company] A flourishing gold and silver mine incorporated on 23 November 1861 at $480,000 capital and located on the Comstock Lode in the Devil's Gate district (Kelly, *First Directory*, pp. 16, 194). For details of its troubles with "dividend cooking" see the headnote.

67. LETTER FROM MARK TWAIN

328.3   Virginia Union] The Virginia City *Union* was the main competitor of the *Enterprise*. Begun on 4 November 1862, it was published by S. A. Glessner, James L. Laird, and John Church (Angel, *History*, p. 323).

328.4   "Homographic Record of the Constitutional Convention"] This item was reprinted in Angel's *History* (p. 81). It gives biographical information about the convention delegates.

329.8-16   It seems that ... men therewith] Compare Judg. 15:1-15. Clemens' last two sentences are a quotation from verses 14 and 15.

329.19-21   "With the jaw-bone ... thousand men."] A quotation from Judg. 15:16.

68. A TIDE OF ELOQUENCE

No notes.

69. *LETTER FROM MARK TWAIN*

335.19–22   "The boy ... the dead."] With slight variations, this is the first stanza of Felicia Dorothea Hemans' poem "Casabianca," a favorite satirical target of Mark Twain's. See, for example, his 5 December 1863 dispatch from Carson City parodying L. O. Sterns's oratorical style (*MTEnt*, p. 94) and Mr. Dobbins' "examination day" program in chapter 21 of *Tom Sawyer*.

336.1   Gov. Nye's] James W. Nye of New York was governor of the Nevada Territory from 1861 to 1864 and United States senator from Nevada from 1864 to 1873.

70. *WINTERS' NEW HOUSE*

342.14   Cormack's fast horses] J. B. Cormack ran a livery stable in Carson City (Kelly, *Second Directory*, p. 97). In January 1862 he had run for tax collector of Ormsby County (Angel, *History*, p. 528).

342.14   John James] John C. James was elected to represent Carson County at the Utah Legislature in 1860, when he was one of the leading businessmen of Carson City. By 1863 he had moved to Austin, a growing town in recently formed Lander County, and established a practice as an attorney and notary public (Angel, *History*, pp. 73, 555; Kelly, *Second Directory*, p. 460).

342.22   Lovejoy] John K. Lovejoy, known as the "Old Piute," was an outspoken, flamboyant journalist noted for his extravagant dress. Lisle Lester described him as a kindhearted man of "large liberality," a "witty, genial, manner," and "a sparkling intellect and lively address that invariably pleases and grows upon long acquaintance" ("The 'Old Piute,'" *Pacific Monthly* 11 [June 1864]: 679–680). In December 1863 Lovejoy purchased the Washoe City *Times* and changed its title to the *Old Pah-Utah*. The following April he sold his interest, moved to Virginia City, and established the daily *Old Piute*. Clemens reported assemblyman Lovejoy's activities at the second Territorial Legislature of 1862 and also favorably noticed the first issue of the *Old Pah-Utah* (*MTEnt*, p. 99). When Clemens left Nevada for California in May 1864 Lovejoy wrote: "The world is blank—the universe worth but 57½, and we are childless. We shall miss Mark ... to know was to love him. ... We can't dwell on this subject; we can only say—God bless you, Mark! be virtuous and happy" (Unionville [Nev.] *Humboldt Register*, 11 June 1864, p. 3).

71. *AN EXCELLENT SCHOOL*

344.3   Mr. Clagett] William H. (Billy) Clagett, an attorney whom
             Clemens first knew as a law student in Keokuk, Iowa, accom-
             panied Clemens in 1861 to the Humboldt mining area. Clagett
             remained in that area and eventually represented Humboldt
             County in the territorial legislatures of 1862 and 1864, as well
             as in the state House of Representatives in 1864. Later he
             moved to Montana Territory, where he was elected delegate
             to the United States Congress in 1871 (*MTEnt*, p. 226).

344.23   "Meriden"] An unknown person using the pseudonym "Mer-
             iden" had recently attacked Clemens in print for using coarse
             humor and scandalous, contemptible expressions ("'The
             Third House' and Other Burlesques," Virginia City *Union*,
             30 January 1864, p. 2). The Storey County district attorney
             between September 1863 and November 1866 was Dighton
             Corson (Angel, *History*, p. 607). No evidence has been found
             to link Meriden or Clemens with Corson.

72. *THOSE BLASTED CHILDREN*

351.2   EDITORS T. T.] The editors of "Sunday Table-Talk," the depart-
             ment of the *Mercury* where Mark Twain's letter appeared.

351.13   "Willows"] This popular resort at Mission and Eighteenth
             streets was badly damaged by fire five weeks before Clemens'
             sketch appeared, but was in operation again by July 1864. It
             offered a hotel and restaurant, gardens, outdoor tables, an
             aquarium and zoo, a merry-go-round, facilities for bowling
             and dancing, and a minstrel and variety theater among its
             attractions (Estavan, *Theatre Research*, 16:23–29; advertise-
             ment, San Francisco *Morning Call*, 4 August 1864, p. 1).

351.13   Seal Rock Point] Going to see the Seal Rocks from Ocean
             Beach near the Cliff House was a favorite excursion for
             San Franciscans.

351.25   those dissipated Golden Era fellows] Clemens alludes to such
             convivial *Era* contributors as Prentice Mulford, Ralph Keeler,
             and Fitzhugh Ludlow.

352.9   Washington Billings] In most instances it has proved impos-
             sible to learn whether Clemens invented the children's names
             or used real ones. But two names, "Flora Low" and "Florence
             Hillyer" (see below), allude unmistakably to children of well-
             known San Franciscans, and so suggest that the author may
             have followed this practice throughout the sketch. Unfor-

tunately, surviving biographical records of prominent citizens rarely yield the names of their offspring. Washington Billings might have been the son of Frederick Billings, a pioneer San Francisco lawyer and a wealthy stock manipulator who became president of the Northern Pacific Railroad (Hubert Howe Bancroft, *Chronicles of the Builders of the Commonwealth*, 7 vols. [San Francisco: The History Co., 1891], 1:108–147; Oscar T. Shuck, ed., *History of the Bench and Bar of California* [Los Angeles: Commercial Printing House, 1901], pp. 467–468). Inexplicably, one of the witnesses in "The Evidence in the Case of Smith *vs.* Jones" (no. 78) is also named Washington Billings.

352.21–22   Oliver Higgins] Perhaps the son of William L. Higgins, a leading San Francisco real-estate dealer and stockbroker (Langley, *Directory for 1865*, p. 226).

353.9   Flora Low] The only child of Frederick F. Low, who was elected governor of California on 2 September 1863 (*The San Francisco Blue Book* [San Francisco: Bancroft Co., 1888], p. 54). A group photograph in the California Historical Society shows ex-Governor Low and Flora, who never married.

353.11   Florence Hillyer] Probably the daughter of Mitchell C. Hillyer of Virginia City, president of the Chollar Gold and Silver Mining Company. In August 1863 he was accused of bribery in connection with a notorious lawsuit between the Chollar and the Potosi mining companies. Later he became a trustee and the vice-president of the Chollar-Potosi Mining Company. He maintained a house in San Francisco ("How Legal Decisions Are Obtained in Mining Cases in Nevada," Bancroft Scraps: Nevada Mining [set W, vol. 94:1], p. 114, Bancroft; Collins, *Mercantile Guide*, p. 99; Angel, *History*, p. 279; *Annual Report of the Chollar-Potosi Mining Co., June 10, 1867* [San Francisco: Turnbull and Smith, 1867]). Clemens mentioned Hillyer in his mid-1863 newspaper correspondence as one of several mining experts who inspected the North Ophir mining claim (" 'Mark Twain's' Letter," San Francisco *Morning Call*, 23 July 1863, p. 1).

354.3   Susy Badger] Perhaps the daughter of William G. Badger, an important San Francisco importer and jobber who was active in civic affairs. The name "Badger" also appears in "Daniel in the Lion's Den—and out Again All Right" (no. 96) in a list of fictitious names of San Francisco stockbrokers. Furthermore, there is a Bayham Badger in Dickens' *Bleak House*, a novel Clemens knew.

354.4–5   Santa Clara, 'n' Alamedy, 'n' San Leandro] Communities in the San Francisco Bay Area.

354.16   rover is free] Possibly an allusion to James Fenimore Cooper's
            character the Rover, a conquering sea captain who wages his
            own war of independence against England during colonial
            days and scorns "to be the subject of a subject" (*The Red
            Rover* [New York: Stringer and Townsend, 1856], p. 363).

354.29   Solferino] A purplish-red color that came into favor in 1859,
            the year of the French victory over the Austrians at the Italian
            village of Solferino.

355.10–11   "Time was ... think not] Compare *Macbeth*, act 3, scene 4,
            lines 78–82.

355.21   Zeb. Leavenworth] During August and September 1857
            Clemens was cub pilot on the *Jonathan J. Roe*, piloted by
            Zebulon Leavenworth, who remained a special friend of his
            (*MTB*, 1:128; *MTMR*, pp. 47–53).

356.28   pride of the village] Washington Irving's story with this title
            in *The Sketch Book* concerns a sweet and innocent heroine
            who is also the pet of her home circle.

73. FRIGHTFUL ACCIDENT TO DAN DE QUILLE

360.2   American City] A rapidly growing mining town laid out on
            the flatlands about one and one-half miles southwest of Gold
            Hill, Nevada (Collins, *Mercantile Guide*, p. 339).

361.15   Brewery] A subtle dig: according to Lucius Beebe, the *Enter-
            prise* printers and compositors frequented the Philadelphia
            Brewery opposite Maguire's Opera House on South D Street,
            whereas the owners and editorial staff preferred the Magnolia
            Saloon (*Comstock Commotion* [Stanford, Calif.: Stanford
            University Press, 1954], p. 27; Collins, *Mercantile Guide*, p. 40).

74. [DAN REASSEMBLED]

No notes.

75. WASHOE.—"INFORMATION WANTED"

368.2   Mormons, and was called Carson county] Mormon settlers
            first came to Carson Valley in June 1849 and were followed in

succeeding years by many others. On 17 January 1854 the
Utah Legislature created Carson County to provide the settlers
of western Utah with a local government (Mack, *History*,
pp. 143–155).

368.2–3   became Nevada in 1861, by act of Congress] President Buchanan signed the organic act creating the Territory of Nevada
on 2 March 1861 (Mack, *History*, p. 218).

368.8–9   Grosch brothers] Hosea and Ethan Grosch are commonly
credited with having discovered the first rich silver vein on the
Comstock Lode. As early as 1853 they prospected in Gold
Canyon, and in 1857 they are said to have staked claims that
later passed into the hands of Henry Comstock and others
(Angel, *History*, p. 52; Mack, *History*, pp. 200–205).

368.9–10   founded Silver City] The Grosch brothers' cabin was near the
future site of Silver City, where Hosea Grosch was buried
(Mack, *History*, p. 203 n. 358).

368.18–19   population of this Territory is about 35,000] Clemens' figure
is moderate compared with a contemporary estimate which
gave Nevada 60,000 inhabitants by the end of 1863 ("State
of Nevada," Bancroft Scraps: Nevada Mining [set W, vol. 94:1],
p. 190, Bancroft). But according to United States census figures
Nevada's population was 16,374 in 1861 and 42,491 in 1870.

369.18   erysipelas] In 1863 erysipelas, called "the scourge of the
mountains," was by far the most common reason for hospital-
ization in the Storey County Hospital, a mile southeast of
Virginia City ("Erysipelas," Virginia City *Evening Bulletin*,
10 July 1863, p. 3; "Storey County Hospital," ibid., 1 August
1863, p. 3).

369.20   Mr. Rising] The Reverend Franklin S. Rising was rector of
St. Paul's Protestant Episcopal Church, formally dedicated in
Virginia City in February 1863 (Angel, *History*, p. 199).
Clemens' references to him were uniformly friendly.

370.3   regular text or so from the Scriptures in his paper] Both the
Gold Hill *News* and the Virginia City *Evening Bulletin* ran a
daily text from the Bible, courtesy of the San Francisco Scripture Text Society ("An Explanation," Virginia City *Evening
Bulletin*, 19 April 1864, p. 3).

370.33–36   "Union," . . . all settled now] Clemens here refers to a law
suit between the Union and the Yellow Jacket mining companies which was decided in favor of the latter on 23 October
1863. These Comstock Lode mines were located near Gold Hill
in 1859, the Union on the slope directly below and parallel
to the Yellow Jacket. When the Union discovered rich ore,
the Yellow Jacket extended its claim 300 feet downhill over

the Union claim. The subsequent law suit was notorious for suborned witnesses and efforts to bribe jurors. The price per share of Union stock fell from $80 to $5 within twenty-four hours after the jury's verdict, while by May 1866 Yellow Jacket stock sold for $800 a foot (Grant H. Smith, *The History of the Comstock Lode: 1850–1920* [Reno: Nevada State Bureau of Mines and Mackay School of Mines, 1943], p. 69; Virginia City *Evening Bulletin:* "Washoe Stock and Exchange Board," 23 October 1863, p. 3; "The Great Mining Decision," 24 October 1863, p. 2; "Washoe Stock and Exchange Board," 24 October 1863, p. 3).

TEXTUAL APPARATUS

TEXTUAL INTRODUCTION

Fʀᴏᴍ ᴛʜᴇ ʙᴇɢɪɴɴɪɴɢ of his career as a professional journalist Mark Twain took steps to gather and preserve clippings of his work, intending to republish them. "Put all of Josh's letters in my scrap book," he told Orion Clemens when his first contributions to the Virginia City *Territorial Enterprise* began to appear in 1862, "I may have use for them some day." The request was typical, and, indeed, the files were maintained so carefully that four years later, in June 1866, Mark Twain said he was able to lend Anson Burlingame "pretty much everything I ever wrote."[1]

But Mark Twain's early impulse to preserve and republish his newspaper and magazine work was often accompanied by a counter-current of procrastination—a pretense of laziness or of indifference toward his literary future. As early as September 1864 we find him making excuses to Orion: "I *would* commence on my book, but . . . Steve [Gillis] & I are getting things ready for his wedding." He promised, however, "As soon as this wedding business is over, I believe I will send to you for the files, & begin on my book."[2] What became of this project, or when "the files" were sent to San Francisco, is not known—but it would probably be at least another year before Orion's brotherly prompting took effect.

It was not until October 1865 that Mark Twain privately resolved to "drop all trifling, & sighing after vain impossibilities," and determined to strive for fame as a humorist—"unworthy & evanescent though it must of necessity be."[3] This resolution immediately produced "Jim Smiley and His Jumping Frog" (no. 119), published in the

---

[1]Clemens to Orion Clemens, 22 June 1862, *CL1*, letter 56; Clemens to Jane Clemens and Pamela Moffett, 21 June 1866, *CL1*, letter 105. Insignificant cancellations in letters have been silently dropped from quotations throughout. When cancellations are included, they appear within angle brackets.

[2]Clemens to Orion and Mollie Clemens, 28 September 1864, *CL1*, letter 92.

[3]Clemens to Orion and Mollie Clemens, 19 October 1865, *CL1*, letter 95.

eastern press that November,[4] but it also returned Mark Twain's
attention to the problem of how to make use of his newspaper clippings. The success of his "Jumping Frog" tale brought him at least one
offer to reprint the journal pieces, for on 20 January 1866 he told his
family that Bret Harte, "late editor of the 'Californian,'" wanted him
to "club a lot of old sketches together with a lot of his, & publish a
book together." He explained his interest in the collaboration in some
detail, emphasizing his own laziness and indifference to fame by
placing the focus of interest on the money he would make:

I wouldn't do it, only he agrees to take all the trouble. But I want to
know whether we are going to make anything out of it, first, however.
He has written to a New York publisher, & if we are offered a bargain
that will pay for a month's labor, we will go to work & prepare the
volume for the press. My labor will not occupy more than 24 hours,
because I will only have to take the scissors & slash my old sketches
out of the Enterprise & the Californian—I burned up a small cart-load
of them lately—so *they* are forever ruled out of any book—but they
were not worth republishing.[5]

Either the "New York publisher" declined to offer the requisite terms
or the would-be collaborators changed their minds; no collection of
sketches by the two men was ever published, although Mark Twain
may have begun to prepare his material "for the press" in January
and February 1866. The air of indifference and the pretense of hard
bargaining seem to mask tenderer feelings commonly associated with
literary ambition. Certainly the weeding out of sketches "not worth
republishing" indicates that Mark Twain was not wholly indifferent
to his literary reputation. Ultimately, however, this early emphasis
on easy money—the "scissors & slash" method—came to dominate
Mark Twain's attitude toward republishing his short works and to
influence the way in which he collected and reprinted them long
after he had achieved a measure of renown.

Mark Twain's early diffidence about his literary ambition has
important consequences for the textual critic, affecting not only how
the author collected and revised his sketches, but also how we assess
the evidence of his revision. He talked expansively about burning up
cartloads of his old sketches and about ruling them forever "out of

---

[4]Edgar M. Branch, " 'My Voice Is Still for Setchell': A Background Study of 'Jim
Smiley and His Jumping Frog,' " *PMLA* 82 (December 1967): 591–601. See also the
historical introduction, pp. 29–30, 32–33.
[5]Clemens to Jane Clemens and Pamela Moffett, 20 January 1866, *CL1*, letter 97.

any book"; but he also claimed he was willing to republish this work only if someone else took "all the trouble." Was he in fact so self-critical or so indifferent? These are questions that bear directly on the preparation of his first collection of sketches, issued in the spring of 1867.

The textual introduction that follows here undertakes to give more than an account of purely textual matters. The long history of Mark Twain's revision and republication of his apprentice writing begins in 1867, when he published his first sketchbook, and ends in 1875, when he collected fifty early pieces in *Sketches, New and Old*. It is a history complicated by the sheer quantity of sketches; by the large number of sketchbooks Mark Twain published, or planned but never produced; by the variety and instability of his publishing arrangements in the early phase of his career; by the multiple reprintings of the early pieces in numerous collections; and by the participation of his publishers and editors—Charles Henry Webb, John Camden Hotten, and Elisha Bliss—in revising the sketches. But the rewards that this long and complex history yields are surprisingly rich and various. As we shall see, the story not only provides a precise record of what and how Mark Twain revised, it also sheds light on other matters of general interest: the author's habitual practice of self-censorship for varying audiences, the differing attitudes of various editors in this country and in England, the conditions of the publishing trade in both countries, and the reactions of critics and readers to Mark Twain's early work—reactions that can now be documented not only by reviews, but by English sales figures. In short, the textual introduction is necessarily long and detailed, but should nevertheless be of interest to anyone concerned with the early period of Mark Twain's professional development.

1. *The Celebrated Jumping Frog of Calaveras County, And other Sketches (1867): JF1*

Twenty-seven sketches from Mark Twain's early newspaper and magazine work were reprinted in his first book, *The Celebrated Jumping Frog* (JF1).[6] These sketches had first appeared in six western and two eastern journals between September 1863 and December 1866:

---

[6]Textually significant editions discussed in this introduction have been assigned a mnemonic abbreviation that is fully defined in the description of texts.

one each in the San Francisco *Dramatic Chronicle, Golden Era,* and
California Youths' Companion; two in the New York *Saturday Press;*
three in the New York *Weekly Review;* three in the Sacramento
Union; six in the Virginia City *Territorial Enterprise;* and ten in the
Californian. Collation shows, however, that some of the JF1 texts
contained errors because they derived from unauthorized, edited
texts instead of the original printing. Eighteen sketches were demonstrably set from the *Californian,* for example, while only ten of these
had first appeared there. In addition, collation indicates that almost
every sketch in JF1 had been revised in some small way, and a handful had been quite radically altered. These facts alone pose the most
fundamental textual questions: What kind of document served as
printer's copy? Who selected and who revised that copy? Were variants
introduced only in the printer's copy, or were there changes in proof
as well?[7]

Our most detailed firsthand account of how JF1 was produced
comes from Mark Twain himself in a recollection dictated in 1906,
thirty-nine years after the event:

My experiences as an author began early in 1867. I came to New York
from San Francisco in the first month of that year and presently
Charles H. Webb, whom I had known in San Francisco as a reporter
on *The Bulletin* and afterward editor of *The Californian,* suggested
that I publish a volume of sketches. I had but a slender reputation to
publish it on, but I was charmed and excited by the suggestion and
quite willing to venture it if some industrious person would save me
the trouble of gathering the sketches together.

In fact, Mark Twain asserted, "Webb undertook to collate the
sketches. He performed this office, then handed the result to me, and
I went to [George W.] Carleton's establishment with it." Mark Twain
also recalled—with undiminished bitterness—that Carleton rudely
declined to publish it:

He began to swell, and went on swelling and swelling and swelling
until he had reached the dimensions of a god of about the second or

---

[7]Although the original journal printings for every sketch in JF1 save one ("Advice for
Good Little Girls," no. 114) have been identified, some of them are not extant. It is
therefore not always possible to say unequivocally what served as printer's copy for JF1.
An annotated table of contents for this and all other textually significant editions
discussed in this introduction will appear in an appendix to the final volume of this
edition.

third degree. . . . Finally he made an imposing sweep with his right hand which comprehended the whole room and said, "Books—look at those shelves. Every one of them is loaded with books that are waiting for publication. Do I want any more? Excuse me, I don't. Good morning."

When Mark Twain reported this "adventure," Webb "bravely said that not all the Carletons in the universe should defeat that book, he would publish it himself on a ten per cent royalty. And so he did. . . . He made the plates and printed and bound the book through a job printing house and published it through the American News Company."[8]

This is a circumstantial and generally accurate account—so far as it goes—and its central implication is clear: Webb alone was responsible for assembling and editing, as well as for publishing, the volume of sketches. Moreover, Webb's 1867 prefatory "Advertisement" to JF1 appears to corroborate Mark Twain's recollection. By way of offering an "explanation . . . for the somewhat fragmentary character of many of these sketches," Webb wrote that

it was necessary to snatch threads of humor wherever they could be found—very often detaching them from serious articles and moral essays with which they were woven and entangled. Originally written for newspaper publication, many of the articles referred to events of the day, the interest of which has now passed away, and contained local allusions, which the general reader would fail to understand; in such cases excision became imperative.[9]

Despite its facetious allusion to "serious articles and moral essays," the advertisement accurately describes how the JF1 sketches were edited. Certainly Webb seems to suggest that, as the editor, he performed these operations for Mark Twain. In addition, shortly before publication Mark Twain himself wrote the San Francisco *Alta California* in a way that tends to confirm both Webb's version and his own 1906 recollection:

Webb ("Inigo") has fixed up a volume of my sketches, and he and

---

[8]AD, 21 May 1906, *MTE*, pp. 143–146. Carleton himself evidently said that he declined the manuscript "because the author looked so disreputable" (William Webster Ellsworth, *A Golden Age of Authors* [Boston and New York: Houghton Mifflin Company, 1919], p. 222).

[9]The "Advertisement" was signed "J.P."—John Paul, one of Webb's pseudonyms. It is reproduced in full in Appendix C1, volume 1.

the American News Company will publish it on Thursday, the 25th
of the present month. He has gotten it up in elegant style, and has
done everything to suit his own taste, which is excellent. I have made
no suggestions. He calls it "THE CELEBRATED JUMPING FROG, AND
OTHER SKETCHES, by 'Mark Twain.' Edited by C. H. Webb."[10]

Publicly and privately, in 1867 and 1906, Mark Twain said that his
first book was edited and produced by Charles Henry Webb.

Yet despite Mark Twain's claim that he "made no suggestions,"
and his assertion that Webb alone "undertook to collate the sketches,"
some evidence has survived to show that the author himself played
a large and important role in shaping JF1 for the press. Although Webb
must have performed the editorial chores to which he alludes—
extracting threads of humor from longer articles and removing local
references—it is apparent that Mark Twain helped to collect, to select,
and to revise the sketches used in his book. The evidence for this
conclusion has not been recognized before. It is contained in one
of the scrapbooks kept by Mark Twain and now preserved in the
Beinecke Rare Book and Manuscript Library at Yale.

The Yale Scrapbook (1863–1867): YSMT

The Yale Scrapbook now contains part or all of forty-eight newspaper
and journal articles by Mark Twain: twenty from the *Californian*,
twenty-one from the *Territorial Enterprise*, six from papers such as
the *Golden Era* and *Dramatic Chronicle* reprinting the *Enterprise*,
and one from the Sacramento *Union* reprinting the New York
Weekly Review. Their dates of publication range from mid-December
1863 to late October 1866. Mark Twain assembled the clippings into
roughly two groups: those from the *Californian* (October 1864–
December 1865) occupy the first half of the scrapbook, while those
from the *Enterprise* and its reprints (December 1863–March 1866)
occupy the second half, with the solitary clipping from the Sacramento *Union* (23 October 1866) coming last of all.[11] The two groups
of clippings are not arranged chronologically within themselves,
which suggests that Mark Twain did not assemble the clippings as

---

[10]Clemens to San Francisco *Alta California*, written 19 April 1867, *MTTB*,
pp. 157–158.
[11]An annotated table of contents for the Yale Scrapbook will appear in an appendix
to the final volume of this edition.

they were published, but reviewed his files of the two journals some-time in February or March 1866, shortly after he told his family, "I will only have to take the scissors & slash my old sketches out of the Enterprise & the Californian." The Yale Scrapbook is almost certainly the result of that plan.

It has long been known that this collection of clippings "shows many revisions and explanatory footnotes in Mark Twain's hand-writing, as if he were preparing copy for a printer."[12] In fact, these revisions and footnotes often suggest that he had a book, and an eastern audience, in mind. For example, Mark Twain added a note to an *Enterprise* clipping of his speech before the Nevada Third House, justifying his impulse to reprint it: "Conventions & legislatures are a good deal alike, all America over—which fact may excuse the inser-tion of this burlesque."[13] At another point he wrote, "It is hardly worth while to explain that gold & silver coin form the circulating medium on the Pacific coast." Still other changes removed or modi-fied his slang and obscure topical references, and deleted or softened allusions to sex, damnation, and drink.

Yet most of the revisions preserved in the scrapbook were never used in a collection of Mark Twain's sketches. And perhaps for this reason it has generally been supposed that JF1 must have been "com-piled from scrapbooks which have since disappeared."[14] Close exami-nation of the Yale Scrapbook, however, shows conclusively that it provided at least half of the printer's copy for JF1. The evidence is clear, but somewhat elusive, because so much of what survives in the scrapbook was *not* used in the published work: we are usually left not the actual printer's copy, but the eloquent testimony of gaps and holes created by the compilers of that copy.

The scrapbook shows that Mark Twain revised—or crossed out—every clipping in it, thereby making a tentative selection from a limited sample of his early work. Subsequent to that revision, some-one removed clippings from the scrapbook using two distinct meth-ods. Where clippings occupied only one side of a leaf (usually in the front of the scrapbook), the leaf was scissored out, preserving the

---

[12]*MTEnt*, p. 8.

[13]Yale Scrapbook, p. 38. The speech is scheduled to appear in the collection of social and political writings in The Works of Mark Twain.

[14]*MTEnt*, p. 8.

clipping intact with the author's revisions in the margin. But where clippings filled both sides of a scrapbook leaf, the requisite article or part of an article was *peeled away*, leaving Mark Twain's revisions behind in the margin. This double method had a number of interesting consequences, but the simplest of these can be easily stated: what was demonstrably removed from the scrapbook, by either method, was almost always reprinted in JF1.

For instance, page stubs in the scrapbook show that eleven full leaves and two half-leaves have been scissored out. Ten of the eleven missing leaves were taken from the front part of the scrapbook where Mark Twain had pasted his *Californian* clippings. Since fully eighteen sketches in JF1 were demonstrably set from the *Californian*, and since collation indicates that some of these were revised by the author, it seems possible that the missing leaves were used as printer's copy, or at least as a source for such copy. Two cases, fortunately, are more conclusive. Only the last half of "An Unbiased Criticism" (no. 100) survives in the scrapbook, where it is preceded by three page stubs from missing leaves. And only the last half of "The Facts" (no. 116) survives in the scrapbook, where it too is preceded by three page stubs. In both cases Mark Twain's penciled revisions appear on the part of the clipping which remains intact—and in both cases, the *missing portion* was reprinted, slightly revised, in JF1. This is persuasive evidence that the Yale Scrapbook supplied printer's copy for at least these two sketches. Of course, it also implies that some of the JF1 variants are Mark Twain's revisions, while at the same time it raises the question of who decided—subsequent to the author's revision of these two sketches—to reprint only part of each in JF1.

In addition to these missing leaves, sixteen scrapbook pages have had part or all of their clippings peeled away—a process that often left the pages blank except for Mark Twain's holograph revisions, which now float mysteriously in the margin. For instance, Mark Twain revised a portion in each of two separate *Enterprise* letters before these two portions were peeled away from the scrapbook page. In both cases, the missing portions can be identified from what remains, and in both cases the missing portions were reprinted in JF1: see the discussion of "Voyage of the Ajax" (no. 182) below, and the textual commentary for "The Spiritual Séance" (no. 202). Printer's copy must have been made by removing and then remounting the clippings on separate sheets, to which Mark Twain's revisions and corrections could then be transferred. This second method probably encouraged further revision, and it clearly resulted in several small errors, since a number of authorial corrections in the Yale Scrapbook were simply lost in the process of preparing the printer's copy.

The gaps and holes in the scrapbook can, in these two ways, be precisely matched with half a dozen sketches reprinted in JF1, and this evidence firmly establishes that the scrapbook was a major source of printer's copy. Once given this tangible link, moreover, we are sometimes afforded a deeper glimpse into the processes that lay behind the preparation of JF1. This is especially true whenever clippings have been peeled away from the scrapbook page, for in almost every case it has proved feasible to reconstruct the page as Mark Twain originally revised it—that is, to reconstruct the first stage of a printer's copy that has itself been lost. From such reconstructions we can learn many things, simple and complex. For instance, we can show that the printer's copy for "A New Biography of Washington" (no. 183) was not its original printing in the *Enterprise*, nor a reprinting of the *Enterprise* in the *Californian*, but a 4 March 1866 reprinting in the San Francisco *Golden Era*, a clipping of which once occupied a page in the scrapbook (see figures 1 and 2). This relatively simple case also shows that Mark Twain corrected the clipping and in that sense authorized its use as printer's copy.

On the other hand, our reconstructions sometimes show that Mark Twain's revisions in the scrapbook were further altered, quietly ignored, or simply lost in the shuffle. The Yale Scrapbook thereby refutes Mark Twain's overmodest claim to have made "no suggestions," while it supports Webb's claim to have edited the JF1 sketches. In fact, the one recurrent textual problem for JF1 is to decide, in each separate sketch, just how fully Mark Twain joined in its preparation and revision, and ultimately to distinguish between the author's revisions and those of his editor. The mix of editorial and authorial variants is different from sketch to sketch, and the scrapbook itself provides much less evidence for some sketches than for others. As it turns out, deciding which of the two humorists was responsible for any given variant is a lively problem that renews itself with every sketch in JF1.

To illustrate the range of evidence we may look closely at the longest sketch in JF1, "Burlesque 'Answers to Correspondents' " (no. 201).

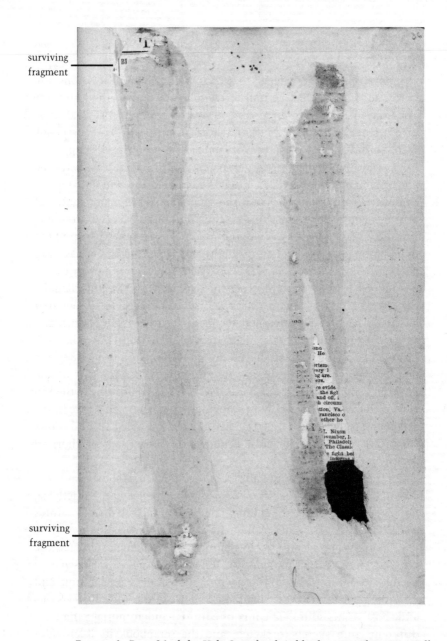

surviving
fragment

surviving
fragment

FIGURE 1. Page 36 of the Yale Scrapbook is blank except for two small fragments of clipping, one near the top and one near the bottom of the page. (A clipping on the verso can be seen through a hole torn in the page when the original clipping was removed.) Mark Twain made one marginal revision: the deletion mark near the bottom of the page.

FIGURE 2. Reconstruction of page 36 of the Yale Scrapbook after Mark Twain corrected the clipping but before it was peeled away. This shows that the missing clipping came from the *Golden Era* of 4 March

The Golden [Era]

BIOGRAPHICAL SKETCH OF GEORGE WASHINGTON, BY MARK TWAIN.

This day, many years ago precisely, George Washington was born. How full of significance the thought! Especially to those among us who have had a similar experience, though subsequently; and still more especially to the young, who should take him for a model and faithfully try to be like him, undeterred by the frequency with which the same thing has been attempted by American youths before them and not satisfactorily accomplished. George Washington was the youngest of nine children, eight of whom were the offspring of his uncle and his aunt. As a boy he gave no promise of the greatness he was one day to achieve. He was ignorant of the commonest accomplishments of youth. He could not even lie. But then he never had any of those precious advantages which are within the reach of the humblest of the boys of the present day. Any boy can lie, now. I could lie before I could stand—yet this sort of sprightliness was so common in our family that little notice was taken of it. Young George appears to have had no sagacity whatever. It is related of him that he once chopped down his father's favorite cherry tree, and then didn't know enough to keep dark about it. He came near going to sea, once, as a midshipman; but when his mother represented to him that he must necessarily be absent when he was away from home, and that this must continue to be the case until he got back, the sad truth struck him so forcibly that he ordered his trunk ashore, and quietly but firmly refused to serve in the navy and fight the battles of his king so long as the effect of it would be to discommode his mother. The great rule of his life was, that procrastination was the thief of time, and that we should always do unto others. This is the golden rule. Therefore, he would never discommode his mother.

Young George Washington was actuated in all things, by the highest and purest principles of morality, justice and right. He was a model in every way worthy of the emulation of youth. Young George was always prompt and faithful in the discharge of every duty. It has been said of him, by the historian, that he was always on hand, like a thousand of brick. And well deserved with this compliment. The aggregate of the building material specified might have been largely increased—might have been doubled—even without doing full justice to these high qualities in the subject of this sketch. Indeed, it would hardly be possible to express in bricks the exceeding promptness and fidelity of young George Washington. His was a soul whose manifold excellencies were beyond the ken and computation of mathematics, and bricks are, at the least, but an inadequate vehicle for the conveyance of a comprehension of the moral sublimity of a nature so pure as his.

Young George W. was a surveyor in early life—a surveyor of an inland port—a sort of county surveyor; and under a commission from Gov. Dinwiddie, he set out to survey his way four hundred miles through a trackless forest, infested with Indians, to procure the liberation of some English prisoners. The historian says the Indians were the most depraved of their species, and did nothing but lay for white men, whom they killed for the sake of robbing them. Considering that white men only traveled through the country at the rate of one a year, they were probably unable to do what might be termed a land-office business in their line. They did not rob young G. W.; one savage made the attempt, but failed; he fired at the subject of this sketch from behind a tree, but the subject of this sketch immediately snaked him out from behind a tree and took him prisoner.

The long journey failed of success; the French would not give up the prisoners, and Wash went sadly back home again. A regiment was raised to go and make a rescue, and he took command of it. He caught the French out in the rain and tackled them with great intrepidity. He defeated them in ten minutes, and their commander handed in his checks. This was the battle of Great Meadows.

After this, a good while, George Washington became Commander in Chief of the American armies, and had an exceedingly dusty time of it all through the Revolution. But every now and then he turned a jack from the bottom and surprised the enemy. He kept up his lick for seven long years, and hazed the British from Harrisburg to Halifax—and America was free! He served two terms as President, and would have been President yet if he had lived—even so did the people honor the Father of his Country. Let the youth of America take his incomparable character for a model and try it one jolt, anyhow. Success is possible—let them remember that—success is possible, though there are chances against it.

I could continue this biography, with profit to the rising generation, but I shall have to drop the subject at present, because of other matters which must be attended to.

SEVERAL FELLOWS near the Vir...

1866, which was reprinting the *Enterprise* of 25–28 February 1866. The clipping, like others now in the scrapbook, probably extended below the page and was folded to keep it within the covers. Mark Twain's deletion mark probably removed the r from "country," a correction that was followed in JF1.

Collation establishes that the JF1 text of this sketch was created by revising, selecting, and then rearranging parts of four long articles that first appeared in the *Californian*.[15] It can be further shown that ten pages in the scrapbook once held complete copies of these same four *Californian* articles. Yet those ten pages are now almost completely blank, preserving only a few sections of clipping that were struck through and presumably rejected, some that were revised but not ultimately removed, a number of floating marginal revisions, and a few telltale scraps of clipping containing only two or three characters. From this evidence it can be demonstrated that when Mark Twain wrote in the scrapbook margin "Make paragraph in 5th line of 'Arithmeticus,' after 'Conchology,'" his change was followed in JF1. And when he inserted the phrase "and soaked in a spittoon" at another point, his change was likewise followed. Roughly speaking, about half of Mark Twain's marginal changes in the scrapbook were reproduced verbatim in the JF1 text for this sketch.

For example, figure 3 shows a page of the Yale Scrapbook from which part of a clipping has been peeled away. It is possible to identify the missing portion from the small surviving fragment, to determine how that clipping was mounted on the scrapbook page, and, by comparing the reconstruction with the corresponding passage in JF1, to demonstrate Mark Twain's insertion of "would" and his deletion of "you" (see figures 4 and 5). Indeed, once the compilers had removed the clipping, remounted it, and transferred the author's changes, this portion of the JF1 printer's copy must have looked very much like the top half of figure 4.

In other cases our reconstruction shows that additional revision was undertaken after the clipping was removed from the scrapbook. In figures 6, 7, and 8 (another portion from the same sketch) we see that three changes entered by Mark Twain were incorporated in the JF1 text, but that his footnote was omitted. And in figures 9, 10, and 11 we find a complete discrepancy between Mark Twain's scrapbook revisions and the JF1 text: none of his scrapbook changes was included in the book, and, moreover, the JF1 text included further revisions not

---

[15]Four of the six columns of "Answers to Correspondents" which Mark Twain published in 1865. The original versions appear in this collection as nos. 105–110; the new version made from nos. 105–108 appears as a separate sketch, no. 201.

entered in the scrapbook. The phrase "with your eyes buried in the cushion" replaced "always pay your debts in greenbacks," thereby obviating Mark Twain's explanatory footnote in the scrapbook.

These examples show that while it is easy to reconstruct what Mark Twain did to his sketches in the scrapbook, it is by no means easy to discover what occurred after the copy was removed from it.[16] In this particular case, however, we are left several clues about what happened and who was responsible. It seems that Mark Twain played an unusually active role in preparing printer's copy: he clearly selected which elements in the original articles he wanted to reprint, and he even supplied a new title ("Burlesque 'Answers to Correspondents' ") in the scrapbook. Moreover, he seems to have made further changes on the culled printer's copy: the substituted phrase "with your eyes buried in the cushion" is very characteristic, and, in another passage, JF1 "sprawling" instead of "vast gloved" as in the scrapbook may also be authorial. On the other hand, it is significant that Mark Twain's new title was not adopted in JF1, and that two of the three changes illustrated in figure 10 and not made in JF1 ("wretched" and "any") were almost identically reproduced by the author when he revised and reprinted the text in 1872.[17] Both these omissions suggest that Webb was an active editorial presence, sifting and judging the changes supplied by Mark Twain in the scrapbook.

One particular discrepancy between the scrapbook and JF1 indicates that Webb indeed exerted significant editorial power. The scrapbook shows that Mark Twain drafted a footnote to explain the original circumstances of the sly hoax in the "Melton Mowbray" section of the sketch: "This absurd squib was received in perfect good faith by

---

[16]Even when we can match the revisions in the scrapbook with those in JF1 we cannot always be certain that the clipping from the scrapbook actually served as printer's copy, for it was always possible to use a duplicate. Indeed, in a few cases, it seems likely that a duplicate clipping or handwritten copy was prepared for the printer—but prepared from the scrapbook copy. The precise correlation between the gaps and holes in the scrapbook and the material reprinted in JF1 excludes the more general possibility that the scrapbook was merely a discarded stage of revision that Mark Twain managed to repeat on a wholly different set of clippings.

[17]In the Yale Scrapbook Mark Twain appears to have replaced "ceaseless and villainous" with "wretched," and "a particle of" with "any." MTSk (1872), a volume he is known to have prepared, replaced "ceaseless and villainous" with "tiresome" and again substituted "any" for "a particle of." MTSk derived from JF1.

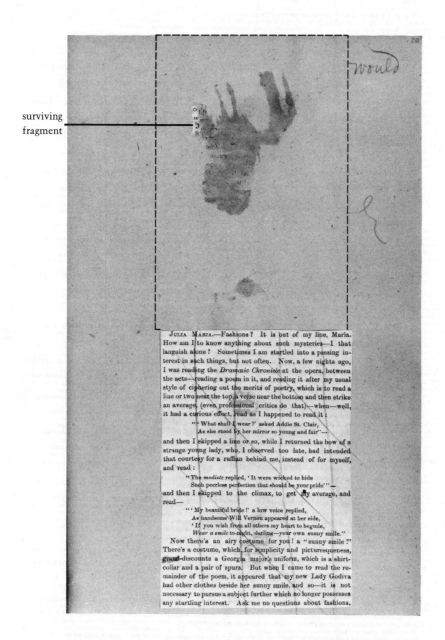

FIGURE 3. Page 20 of the Yale Scrapbook now contains only part of a clipping from the *Californian* of 10 June 1865. Two authorial revisions are visible in the right margin. The dotted line shows the outline of the original clipping. Mark Twain canceled the bottom half of the clipping, which was not reprinted in JF1, but before he canceled the section he deleted "grand" from "grand-discounts."

surviving
fragment

creatures. Tenthly, don't go serenading at all—it is a wicked, unhappy and seditious practice, and a calamity to all souls that are weary and desire to slumber and be at rest. **would** Eleventhly and lastly, the father of the young lady in the next block says that if you come prowling around his neighborhood again with your infamous scraping and tooting and yelling, he will sally forth and deliver you into the hands of the police. As far as I am concerned myself, I would like to have you come, and come often, but as long as the old man is so prejudiced perhaps you had better serenade mostly in Oakland, or San José, or around there somewhere.

ST. CLAIR HIGGINS, *Los Angeles.*—" My life is a failure; I have adored, wildly, madly, and she whom I love has turned coldly from me and shed her affections upon another; what would you advise me to do?" You should shed your affections on another, also—or on several, if there are enough to go round. Also, do everything you can to make your former flame unhappy. There is an absurd idea disseminated in novels, that the happier a girl is with another man, the happier it makes the old lover she has blighted. Don't you allow yourself to believe any such nonsense as that. The more cause that girl finds to regret that she did not marry you, the more comfortable you will feel over it. It isn't poetical, but it is mighty sound doctrine.

ARITHMETICUS, *Virginia, Nevada.*—" If it would take a cannon-ball 3¼ seconds to travel four miles, and 3⅜ seconds to travel the next four, and 3⅝ seconds to travel the next four, and if its rate of progress continued to diminish in the same ratio, how long would it take it to go fifteen hundred millions of miles?" I don't know.

AMBITIOUS LEARNER, *Oakland.*—Yes, you are right—America was not discovered by Alexander Selkirk.

JULIA MARIA.—Fashions? It is out of my line, Maria. How am I to know anything about such mysteries—I that languish alone? Sometimes I am startled into a passing interest in such things, but not often. Now, a few nights ago, I was reading the *Dramatic Chronicle* at the opera, between the acts—reading a poem in it, and reading it after my usual style of ciphering out the merits of poetry, which is to read a line or two near the top, a verse near the bottom and then strike an average, (even professional critics do that)—when—well, it had a curious effect, read as I happened to read it:

" ' What shall I wear?' asked Addie St. Clair,
As she stood by her mirror so young and fair'

and then I skipped a line or so, while I returned the bow of a strange young lady, who, I observed too late, had intended that courtesy for a ruffian behind me, instead of for myself, and read:

The *modiste* replied, ' It were wicked to hide
Such peerless perfection that should be your pride ' "—

and then I skipped to the climax, to get my average, and read—

" ' My beautiful pride !' a low voice replied,
As handsome Will Vernon appeared at her side,
' If you wish from all others my heart to beguile,
Wear a smile to-night, darling—your own sunny smile."

Now there's an airy costume for you ! a "sunny smile !" There's a costume, which, for simplicity and picturesqueness, grand-discounts a Georgia major's uniform, which is a shirt-collar and a pair of spurs. But when I came to read the remainder of the poem, it appeared that my new Lady Godiva had other clothes beside her sunny smile, and so—it is not necessary to pursue a subject further which no longer possesses any startling interest. Ask me no questions about fashions,

FIGURE 4. Reconstruction of page 20 of the Yale Scrapbook after Mark Twain revised the *Californian* clipping but before it was peeled away. Mark Twain's revisions have been redrawn, and the surviving fragment has been circled.

a frenzy of crowing, and cackling, and yawling, and caterwauling, put up your dreadful instruments and go home. Eighthly, as soon as you start, gag your tenor—otherwise he will be letting off a screech every now and then, to let the people know he is around. Your amateur tenor is notoriously the most self-conceited of all God's creatures. Tenthly, don't go serenading at all; it is a wicked, unhappy, and seditious practice, and a calamity to all souls that are weary and desire to slumber and would be at rest. Eleventhly and lastly, the father of the young lady in the next block says that if you come prowling around his neighborhood again, with your infamous scraping and tooting and yelling, he will sally forth and deliver you into the hands of the police. As far as I am concerned myself, I would like to have you come, and come often; but as long as the old man is so prejudiced, perhaps you had better serenade mostly in Oakland, or San José, or around there somewhere.

"ST. CLAIR HIGGINS," *Los Angeles.*—"My life is a failure; I have adored, wildly, madly, and she whom I love has turned coldly from me and shed her affections upon another. What would you advise me to do?"

You should shed your affections on another, also—or on several, if there are enough to go round. Also, do every thing you can to make your former flame unhappy. There is an absurd idea disseminated in novels, that the happier a girl is with another man, the happier it makes the old lover she has blighted. Don't allow yourself to believe any such nonsense as that. The more cause that girl finds to regret that she did not marry you, the more comfortable you will feel over it. It isn't poetical, but it is mighty sound doctrine.

"ARITHMETICUS," *Virginia, Nevada.*—"If it would take a cannon ball 3⅓ seconds to travel four miles, and 3⅜ seconds to travel the next four, and 3⅝ seconds to travel the next four, and if its rate of progress continued to diminish in the same ratio, how long would it take it to go fifteen hundred millions of miles?"

I don't know.

"AMBITIOUS LEARNER," *Oakland.*—Yes, you are right—America was not discovered by Alexander Selkirk.

"DISCARDED LOVER."—"I loved, and still love, the beautiful Edwitha Howard, and intended to marry her. Yet, during my temporary absence at Benicia, last week, alas! she married Jones. Is my happiness to be thus blasted for life? Have I no redress?"

FIGURE 5. Pages 44 and 45 of JF1, reprinting the clipping from the *Californian* which originally occupied page 20 of the Yale Scrapbook. The marginal arrows indicate Mark Twain's revisions inscribed in the scrapbook.

several editors on the Pacific Coast, & they rated the author unsparingly for not knowing that the 'Destruction of the Sennacherib['] was not originally composed in Dutch Flat!" Like several other footnotes inscribed in the scrapbook, this one never appeared in print. In JF1 the footnote reads as follows: "This piece of pleasantry, published in a San Francisco paper, was mistaken by the country journals for seriousness, and many and loud were their denunciations of the ignorance of author and editor in not knowing that the lines in question were 'written by Byron.' " It seems unlikely that Mark Twain wrote this flat-footed revision of his original note. The style of the JF1 version, along with its pointed allusion to the alleged "ignorance of author and editor," both suggest that the revised version was supplied by Webb: he was the editor of the *Californian*, where the sketch first appeared.

Webb's editing can be detected in other cases where it runs counter to or otherwise modifies what Mark Twain wrote in the scrapbook. For instance, JF1 reprinted "Bearding the Fenian in His Lair" (no. 170), retitling it "Among the Fenians." This sketch first appeared as part of Mark Twain's letter to the *Enterprise* of 30–31 January 1866, and in the scrapbook Mark Twain canceled the entire letter, indicating that he found nothing in it worth republishing. Moreover, the JF1 text begins with a revised introductory sentence that does not seem to be Mark Twain's work: "Wishing to post myself on one of the most current topics of the day, I, Mark, hunted up an old friend, Dennis McCarthy, who is editor of the new Fenian journal in San Francisco, *The Irish People*." The awkward locution "most current" is not typical of the author, nor is the superfluous "Mark," which Mark Twain deleted in a subsequent revision of this sketch.[18] Although such evidence is not conclusive, it does suggest that Webb independently decided to include the sketch in JF1, that he copied out the relevant section from the canceled *Enterprise* letter, and that he added a new introductory sentence.

In other cases we seem to detect Webb's altering further what Mark Twain had begun to revise in the scrapbook—a tendency illustrated by "Voyage of the Ajax" (no. 182), part of an *Enterprise* letter that was reprinted in JF1 as "Remarkable Instances of Presence of Mind." The

---

[18] The author deleted "Mark" in 1873 on HWa**MT**. For further details, see the textual commentary to "Bearding the Fenian in His Lair."

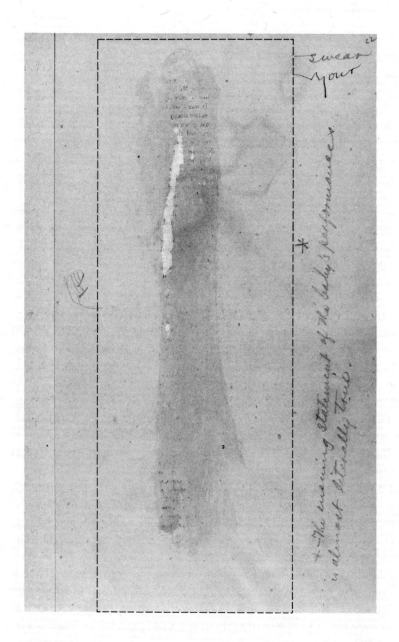

FIGURE 6. Page 22 of the Yale Scrapbook now contains only Mark Twain's four marginal revisions of a clipping no longer present. The dotted line shows the outline of the original clipping.

rid of my cold. I feel the bitterest animosity toward you at this moment—bothering me in this way, when I can do ~~noth~~ing but sneeze and ~~quote poetry~~ and snort pocket-handkerchiefs to atoms. If I had you in range of my nose, now, I would blow/brains out. *swear your*

YOUNG MOTHER.—And so you think a baby is a thing of beauty and a joy forever? Well, the idea is pleasing, but not original—every cow thinks the same of its own calf. Perhaps the cow may not think it so elegantly, 'but still she thinks it, nevertheless. I honor the cow for it. We all honor this touching maternal instinct wherever we find it, be it in the home of luxury or in the humble cow-shed. But really, madam, when I come to examine the matter in all its bearings, I find that the correctness of your assertion does not manifest itself in all cases. A sore-faced baby with a neglected nose cannot be conscientiously regarded as a thing of beauty, and inasmuch as babyhood spans but three short years, no baby is competent to be a joy "forever." It pains me thus to demolish two-thirds of your pretty sentiment in a single sentence, but the position I hold in this chair requires that I shall not permit you to deceive and mislead the public with your plausible figures of speech. I know a female baby aged eighteen months, in this city, which cannot hold out as a "joy" twenty-four hours on a stretch, let alone "forever." And it possesses some of the most remarkable eccentricities of character and appetite that have ever fallen under my notice. I will set down here a statement of this infant's operations, (conceived, planned and carried out by itself, and without suggestion or assistance from its mother or any one else,) ~~during a single day~~—and what I shall say can be substantiated by the sworn testimony of witnesses.) It commenced by eating one dozen large blue-mass pills, box and all; then it fell down a flight of stairs, and arose with a bruised and purple knot on its forehead, after which it proceeded in quest of further refreshment and amusement. It found a glass trinket ornamented with brasswork—mashed up and ate the glass, and then swallowed the brass. Then it drank about twenty or thirty drops of laudanum, and more than a dozen table-spoonful of strong spirits of camphor. The reason why it took no more laudanum was, because there was no more to take. After this it lay down on its back, and shoved five or six inches of a silver-headed whalebone cane down its throat; got it fast there, and it was all its mother could do to pull the cane out again, without pulling out some of the child with it. Then, being hungry for glass again, it broke up several wine glasses, and fell to eating and swallowing the fragments, not minding a cut or two. Then it ate a quantity of butter, pepper, salt and California matches, actually taking a spoonful of butter, a spoonful of salt, a spoonful of pepper, and three or four lucifer matches, at each mouthful. (I will remark here that this thing of beauty likes painted German lucifers, and eats all she can get of them; but she infinitely prefers California matches—which I regard as a compliment to our home manufactures of more than ordinary value, coming, as it does, from one who is too young to flatter.) Then she washed her head with soap and water, and afterwards ate what soap was left, and drank as much of the suds as she had room for, after which she sallied forth and took the cow familiarly by the tail, and got kicked heels over head. At odd times during the day, when this joy forever happened to

The ensuing statement of the baby's performances is almost literally true.

FIGURE 7. Reconstruction of page 22 of the Yale Scrapbook after Mark Twain revised the clipping but before it was peeled away. This shows that the missing clipping came from the *Californian* of 24 June 1865. Mark Twain's marginal revisions have been redrawn.

will be answered. But don't torture me with any more of your ghastly arithmetical horrors (for I do detest figures any how) until you know I am rid of my cold. I feel the bitterest animosity toward you at this moment—bothering me in this way, when I can do nothing but sneeze and swear and snort pocket-handker- ◄───── chiefs to atoms. If I had you in range of my nose, now, I would blow your brains out. ◄─────

"S.

─────────────────────────────── ,.... of speech. I know a female baby, aged eighteen months, in this city, which can not hold out as a "joy" twenty-four hours on a stretch, let alone "forever." ◄───── And it possesses some of the most remarkable eccentricities of character and appetite that have ever fallen under my notice. I will set down here a statement of this infant's operations, (conceived, planned, and carried out by itself, and without suggestion or assistance from its mother or any one else,) during a single day ; and what I shall say can be substantiated by the sworn testimony of witnesses.

It commenced by eating one dozen large blue- ◄───── mass pills, box and all ; then it fell down a flight of stairs, and arose with a bruised and purple knot on its forehead, after which it proceeded

FIGURE 8. Portions of pages 55 (top) and 51 (bottom) of JF1, reprinting the clipping from the *Californian* which originally occupied page 22 of the Yale Scrapbook. The marginal arrows indicate Mark Twain's revisions inscribed in the scrapbook, one of which (the footnote) was ignored.

scrapbook shows that Mark Twain revised a section of the letter, which was then peeled away, presumably remounted, and reinscribed with his marginal revisions (see figure 12). He corrected the punctuation by inserting a needed dash, changed "sung" to "sang" and "God!" to "Heaven," and altered the personal reference to "Leland" to the anonymous initial "L." or "L——."[19] Collation with the JF1 text shows, however, that at some point further changes were introduced. JF1 followed Mark Twain's correction of the punctuation, his change from "sung" to "sang," and his shortening of "Leland," but it also extended the modification of local allusions, very much in accord with the policy Webb articulated in his "Advertisement" to JF1. The book changed "Fretz, of the Bank of California" to "F——, of a great banking-house in San Francisco"; it changed "Lewis Leland, of the Occidental" to "Lewis L——, of a great hotel in San Francisco." Moreover, it failed to make Mark Twain's reverent substitution of "Heaven" for "God!" and made one long deletion not indicated in the scrapbook. Of course, it is not impossible that Mark Twain made some or all of these later alterations on the culled printer's copy, but the mundane style of revision and the careless omission of one change both hint that Webb was the person responsible. Indeed, when Mark Twain revised this sketch again in 1874–1875, he deleted the phrases "a great banking-house in" and "of a great hotel in San Francisco," and he again canceled "God!"—substituting for it the milder expletive "Pooh."[20]

Webb's editing is perhaps most clearly evident in two sketches which, unlike the others, were not removed from the scrapbook after Mark Twain had revised and corrected them. These interesting anomalies are "Whereas" (no. 94) and all but the opening paragraphs of "Jim Smiley and His Jumping Frog" (no. 119)—as it happens, the first two sketches reprinted in JF1. In both cases what appears to be printer's copy has survived intact in the scrapbook, and in both cases most of Mark Twain's revisions and corrections (some of them quite minute alterations of his text) were incorporated in JF1, but collation shows

---

[19]Identifying Mark Twain's scrapbook revisions of this sketch (and others like it) is more challenging than usual because there is no extant copy of the *Enterprise* from which to reconstruct the clipping as Mark Twain revised it. The missing text here has, in fact, been reconstructed from contemporary reprintings in the *Californian* and the Eureka (Calif.) *Humboldt Times*, as well as the JF1 reprinting.

[20]He made these revisions and corrections on HWb**MT** sometime in 1874 or 1875. For further details, see the textual commentary to "Voyage of the Ajax."

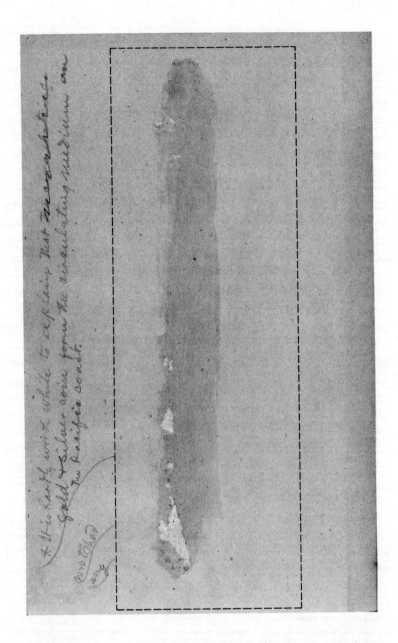

FIGURE 9. Page 22A of the Yale Scrapbook now contains only Mark Twain's three marginal revisions of a clipping no longer present. The dotted line shows the outline of the original clipping.

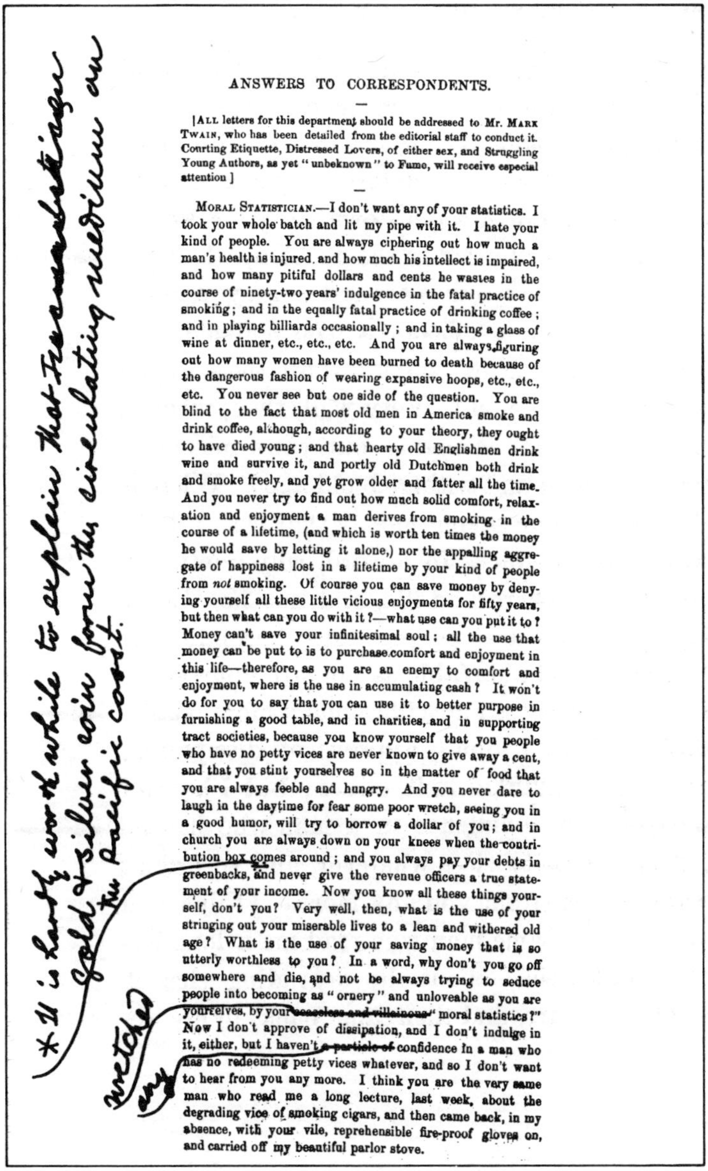

ANSWERS TO CORRESPONDENTS.

[ALL letters for this department should be addressed to Mr. MARK TWAIN, who has been detailed from the editorial staff to conduct it. Courting Etiquette, Distressed Lovers, of either sex, and Struggling Young Authors, as yet "unbeknown" to Fame, will receive especial attention]

MORAL STATISTICIAN.—I don't want any of your statistics. I took your whole batch and lit my pipe with it. I hate your kind of people. You are always ciphering out how much a man's health is injured, and how much his intellect is impaired, and how many pitiful dollars and cents he wastes in the course of ninety-two years' indulgence in the fatal practice of smoking; and in the equally fatal practice of drinking coffee; and in playing billiards occasionally; and in taking a glass of wine at dinner, etc., etc., etc. And you are always figuring out how many women have been burned to death because of the dangerous fashion of wearing expansive hoops, etc., etc., etc. You never see but one side of the question. You are blind to the fact that most old men in America smoke and drink coffee, although, according to your theory, they ought to have died young; and that hearty old Englishmen drink wine and survive it, and portly old Dutchmen both drink and smoke freely, and yet grow older and fatter all the time. And you never try to find out how much solid comfort, relaxation and enjoyment a man derives from smoking in the course of a lifetime, (and which is worth ten times the money he would save by letting it alone,) nor the appalling aggregate of happiness lost in a lifetime by your kind of people from *not* smoking. Of course you can save money by denying yourself all these little vicious enjoyments for fifty years, but then what can you do with it?—what use can you put it to? Money can't save your infinitesimal soul; all the use that money can be put to is to purchase comfort and enjoyment in this life—therefore, as you are an enemy to comfort and enjoyment, where is the use in accumulating cash? It won't do for you to say that you can use it to better purpose in furnishing a good table, and in charities, and in supporting tract societies, because you know yourself that you people who have no petty vices are never known to give away a cent, and that you stint yourselves so in the matter of food that you are always feeble and hungry. And you never dare to laugh in the daytime for fear some poor wretch, seeing you in a good humor, will try to borrow a dollar of you; and in church you are always down on your knees when the contribution box comes around; and you always pay your debts in greenbacks, and never give the revenue officers a true statement of your income. Now you know all these things yourself, don't you? Very well, then, what is the use of your stringing out your miserable lives to a lean and withered old age? What is the use of your saving money that is so utterly worthless to you? In a word, why don't you go off somewhere and die, and not be always trying to seduce people into becoming as "ornery" and unloveable as you are yourselves, by your ~~ceaseless and villainous~~ moral statistics?" Now I don't approve of dissipation, and I don't indulge in it, either, but I haven't ~~a particle of~~ confidence in a man who has no redeeming petty vices whatever, and so I don't want to hear from you any more. I think you are the very same man who read me a long lecture, last week, about the degrading vice of smoking cigars, and then came back, in my absence, with your vile, reprehensible fire-proof gloves on, and carried off my beautiful parlor stove.

*It is hardly worth while to explain that Greenbacks & gold & silver coin form the circulating medium on the Pacific coast.

FIGURE 10. Reconstruction of page 22A of the Yale Scrapbook after Mark Twain revised the clipping but before it was peeled away. This shows that the missing clipping came from the *Californian* of 17 June 1865. Mark Twain's marginal revisions have been redrawn.

that you are always feeble and hungry. And you never dare to laugh in the daytime for fear some poor wretch, seeing you in a good humor, will try to borrow a dollar of you ; and in church you are always down on your knees, with your eyes buried in the cushion, when the contribution-box comes around ; and you never give the revenue officers a true statement of your income. Now you know all these things yourself, don't you ? Very well, then, what is the use of your stringing out your miserable lives to a lean and withered old age ? What is the use of your saving money that is so utterly worthless to you ? In a word, why don't you go off somewhere and die, and not be always trying to seduce people into becoming as "ornery" and unlovable as you are yourselves, by your ceaseless and villainous " moral statistics" ? Now, I don't approve of dissipation, and I don't indulge in it, either ; but I haven't a particle of confidence in a man who has no redeeming petty vices whatever, and so I don't want to hear from you any more. I think you are the very same man who read me a long lecture, last week, about the degrading vice of smoking cigars, and then came back, in my ab-

FIGURE 11. Page 36 of JF1, reprinting the clipping from the *Californian* which originally occupied page 22A of the Yale Scrapbook. None of the revisions inscribed there was adopted. The marginal arrows indicate where these revisions would have appeared, and where a further revision was made.

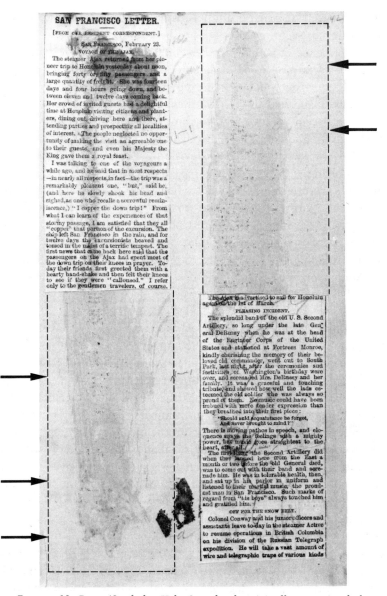

FIGURE 12. Page 42 of the Yale Scrapbook originally contained the whole of an *Enterprise* letter of 25–28 February 1866. Mark Twain revised a portion of it, reprinted in this collection as "Voyage of the Ajax," before it was peeled away; the marginal arrows indicate his revisions. The dotted line shows the outline of the original clipping. Reconstruction is impossible because no copy of the *Enterprise* is extant.

that there were also significant departures from the marked clippings which do not seem, by and large, to be authorial.

The presence of actual printer's copy in the scrapbook is itself a problem warranting some explanation: if, as we have conjectured, printer's copy was generally removed after it had been revised, what must have happened to preserve these two sketches alone? Two explanations seem possible: (1) Webb or Mark Twain may have used duplicate clippings, now lost, to which they transferred some (but not all) of Mark Twain's scrapbook revisions, and to which they added further changes; or (2) they may have handed the scrapbook itself to the "job printing house" and introduced the additional changes in proof. The alternatives are of some interest because it seems unlikely, as we shall see, that Mark Twain read proof. So if a duplicate set of clippings was used, the author cannot be excluded as the agent of some of the later changes. But if it seems more likely that the clippings in the scrapbook were actual printer's copy, then we must attribute quite bold and major changes to Webb.

"Whereas" is the simpler of the two cases. The complete text of the sketch, revised and corrected by Mark Twain, survives in the Yale Scrapbook. On the first part of the clipping Mark Twain made two substantive revisions and also supplied a new title: "LOVE'S BAKERY. *To which is added the Singular History of Aurelia Maria.*" On the second part he made six meticulous changes in the paragraphing and inserted one substantive revision. Although the JF1 printing carefully followed each of the seven changes in the second part, it omitted the first part entirely: the long digression about "Love's Bakery" was not reprinted, and the remaining material was of course not given the new scrapbook title, but was called instead "Aurelia's Unfortunate Young Man." Since this radical deletion is in no way indicated on the scrapbook clipping, the question arises, How was the change given to the compositor? Webb or Mark Twain might have copied his minute changes onto a duplicate clipping or a transcription of this one, now lost. But if either did so, his motive remains unclear, for the scrapbook clipping was completely legible and could easily have been extracted with the scissors, as others manifestly were. It therefore seems slightly more likely that the scrapbook clipping itself was printer's copy, and that Webb either told the compositor where to start with the clipping or else deleted the first section in proof. Such a procedure is consistent with his stated policy of extracting threads of humor from "moral essays."

"Jim Smiley and His Jumping Frog" presents the more complex as well as the more interesting case. The scrapbook pages show that Mark Twain fully revised and corrected a clipping from the *Californian* of 16 December 1865, which reprinted his sketch from the New York *Saturday Press.* Not counting his correction of "Greeley" to "Smiley" throughout, he made eleven substantive revisions or corrections on this clipping, ranging all the way from an explanatory footnote to minute adjustments in the dialect spelling ("setting" instead of "sitting," for instance). At some point the first three paragraphs were peeled away from the scrapbook page, presumably remounted, and then further revised to remove all allusions to Artemus Ward (see figures 13, 14, and 15). It is by no means certain that Mark Twain authorized these changes, and the omission of one of his corrections (the deletion of "me" in the third paragraph) may suggest that the new version was prepared by Webb. At any rate, only the first page of the clipping was removed from the scrapbook, presumably because it required more extensive editing than the scrapbook margin permitted. The other sections of the clipping remain in place, except for the last one: at some point it too was peeled away from a page that had been scissored out. The clipping itself was remounted, out of order, in the scrapbook—and two corrections that Mark Twain had originally inscribed on it (the word "lively" and the deletion of *n* from "an") were both lost (see figures 16, 17, and 18).[21]

Collation shows that the JF1 text of the "Jumping Frog" story was indeed set from the *Californian* reprinting, and that it followed six of the eleven changes Mark Twain had inscribed in the scrapbook. Of the five changes not made, one was the footnote about Artemus Ward (now superfluous because of the revisions in the early paragraphs); the second was the phrase written almost vertically in the left scrapbook margin, "it took him to make the trip" (omitted in favor of the original reading, clearly legible beneath the canceling pencil marks); and three were the corrections ("me," "lively," and "a" for "an") that had probably been inadvertently lost in preparation of the scrapbook

---

[21]Mark Twain's revisions in figure 18 are visible in the original only as faint pencil lines leading to the left and right margins. We have conjectured that he tried to restore the original reading of the *Saturday Press.*

FIGURE 13. Page 23A of the Yale Scrapbook originally contained a clipping from the *Californian* of 16 December 1865. Mark Twain revised the clipping before it was peeled away and further revised. The dotted line shows the outline of the original clipping.

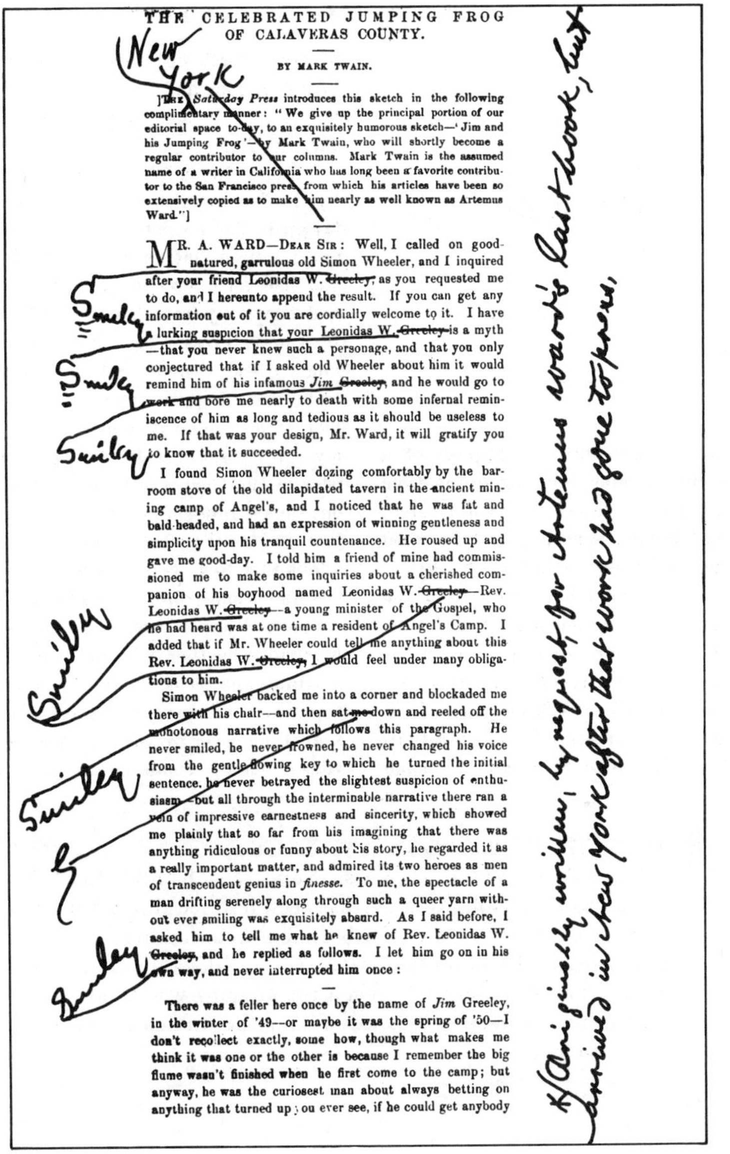

THE CELEBRATED JUMPING FROG
OF CALAVERAS COUNTY.

BY MARK TWAIN.

[The *Saturday Press* introduces this sketch in the following complimentary manner: " We give up the principal portion of our editorial space to-day, to an exquisitely humorous sketch—' Jim and his Jumping Frog'—by Mark Twain, who will shortly become a regular contributor to our columns. Mark Twain is the assumed name of a writer in California who has long been a favorite contributor to the San Francisco press from which his articles have been so extensively copied as to make him nearly as well known as Artemus Ward."]

MR. A. WARD—DEAR SIR: Well, I called on good-natured, garrulous old Simon Wheeler, and I inquired after your friend Leonidas W. Greeley, as you requested me to do, and I hereunto append the result. If you can get any information out of it you are cordially welcome to it. I have a lurking suspicion that your Leonidas W. Greeley is a myth—that you never knew such a personage, and that you only conjectured that if I asked old Wheeler about him it would remind him of his infamous Jim Greeley, and he would go to work and bore me nearly to death with some infernal reminiscence of him as long and tedious as it should be useless to me. If that was your design, Mr. Ward, it will gratify you to know that it succeeded.

I found Simon Wheeler dozing comfortably by the bar-room stove of the old dilapidated tavern in the ancient mining camp of Angel's, and I noticed that he was fat and bald-headed, and had an expression of winning gentleness and simplicity upon his tranquil countenance. He roused up and gave me good-day. I told him a friend of mine had commissioned me to make some inquiries about a cherished companion of his boyhood named Leonidas W. Greeley—Rev. Leonidas W. Greeley—a young minister of the Gospel, who he had heard was at one time a resident of Angel's Camp. I added that if Mr. Wheeler could tell me anything about this Rev. Leonidas W. Greeley, I would feel under many obligations to him.

Simon Wheeler backed me into a corner and blockaded me there with his chair—and then sat me down and reeled off the monotonous narrative which follows this paragraph. He never smiled, he never frowned, he never changed his voice from the gentle-flowing key to which he turned the initial sentence, he never betrayed the slightest suspicion of enthusiasm—but all through the interminable narrative there ran a vein of impressive earnestness and sincerity, which showed me plainly that so far from his imagining that there was anything ridiculous or funny about his story, he regarded it as a really important matter, and admired its two heroes as men of transcendent genius in *finesse*. To me, the spectacle of a man drifting serenely along through such a queer yarn without ever smiling was exquisitely absurd. As I said before, I asked him to tell me what he knew of Rev. Leonidas W. Greeley, and he replied as follows. I let him go on in his own way, and never interrupted him once:

There was a feller here once by the name of *Jim* Greeley, in the winter of '49—or maybe it was the spring of '50—I don't recollect exactly, some how, though what makes me think it was one or the other is because I remember the big flume wasn't finished when he first come to the camp; but anyway, he was the curiosest man about always betting on anything that turned up; ou ever see, if he could get anybody

Smiley
Smiley
Smiley
Smiley
Smiley
Smiley

Originally written, by request, for Artemus Ward's last book, but arrived in New York after that work had gone to press.

FIGURE 14. Reconstruction of page 23A of the Yale Scrapbook after Mark Twain revised the *Californian* clipping but before it was peeled away. Note the correction of the error "me" in the third paragraph.

THE CELEBRATED JUMPING FROG

or

ʃALAVERAS ʃOUNTY.

———◆◆◆———

IN compliance with the request of a friend of mine, who wrote me from the East, I called on good-natured, garrulous old Simon Wheeler, and inquired after my friend's friend, *Leonidas W.* Smiley, as requested to do, and I hereunto append the result. I have a lurking suspicion that *Leonidas W.* Smiley is a myth; that my friend never knew such a personage; and that he only conjectured that, if I asked old Wheeler about him, it would remind him of his infamous *Jim* Smiley, and he would go to work and bore me

nearly to death with some infernal reminiscence of him as long and tedious as it should be useless to me. If that was the design, it certainly succeeded.

I found Simon Wheeler dozing comfortably by the bar-room stove of the old, dilapidated tavern in the ancient mining camp of Angel's, and I noticed that he was fat and bald-headed, and had an expression of winning gentleness and simplicity upon his tranquil countenance. He roused up and gave me good-day. I told him a friend of mine had commissioned me to make some inquiries about a cherished companion of his boyhood named *Leonidas W.* Smiley—*Rev. Leonidas W.* Smiley—a young minister of the Gospel, who he had heard was at one time a resident of Angel's Camp. I added that, if Mr. Wheeler could tell me any thing about this Rev. Leonidas W. Smiley, I would feel under many obligations to him.

Simon Wheeler backed me into a corner and blockaded me there with his chair, and then sat me down and reeled off the monotonous narrative which follows this paragraph. He never smiled, he never frowned, he never changed his voice from the gentle-flowing key to which he

FIGURE 15. The JF1 text shows that the *Californian* clipping which probably served as printer's copy was extensively changed after being revised in the scrapbook. "Smiley" has been restored throughout, but all allusions to Artemus Ward have been removed, and the footnote in the scrapbook has been omitted. Moreover, the deletion of "me" has not been followed. Presumably when the clipping was removed and remounted, this correction was lost among the numerous marks removing "Greeley."

to bet on the other side, and if he couldn't he'd change sides
—any way that suited the other man would suit *him*—any
way just so's he got a bet, *he* was satisfied. But still, he was
lucky—uncommon lucky; he most always come out winner
He was always ready and laying for a chance; there couldn't
be no solitry thing mentioned but that feller'd offer to bet on
it—and take any side you please, as I was just telling you:
if there was a horse race. you'd find him flush or you find him
busted at the end of it; it there was a dog-fight, he'd bet on
it; if there was a cat fight, he'd bet on it; if there was a
chicken-fight, he'd bet on it; why if there was two birds
sitting on a fence, he would bet you which one would fly first
—or if there was a camp-meeting he would be there reglar
to bet on Parson Walker, which he judged to be the best
exhorter about here, and so he was, too, and agood man; if
he even see a straddle-bug start to go any wheres, he would
bet you how long it would take him to get wherever he was
going to, and if you took him up he would foller that straddle-
bug to Mexico but what he would find out where he was
bound for and how long he was on the road. Lots of the
boys here has seen that Greeley and can tell you about him.
Why, it never made no difference to *him*—he would bet on
anything—the dangdest feller. Parson Walker's wife laid
very sick, once, for a good while, and it seemed as if they
warn't going to save her; but one morning he come in and
Greeley asked how she was, and he said she was considerable
better—thank the Lord for his inf'nit mercy—and coming on
so smart that with the blessing of Providence she'd get well
yet—and Greeley before he thought, says: "Well, I'll resk
two-and-a-half that she don't, anyway."

Thish-yer Greeley had a mare—the boys called her the
fifteen-minute nag, but that was only in fun, you know, because, of course, she was faster than that—and he used to
win money on that horse, for all she was so slow and always
had the asthma, or the distemper, or the consumption, or
something of that kind. They used to give her two or three
hundred yard's start, and then pass her under way; b
always at the fag-end of the race she'd get excited and de
perate like. and come cavorting and spraddling up, and scat
tering her legs around limber, sometimes in the air, and some
times out to one side amongst the fences, and kicking up
m-o-r-e dust, and raising m-o-r-e racket with her coughing and
sneezing and blowing her nose—and always fetch up at the
stand just about a neck ahead, as near as you could cipher it
down.

And he had a little small bull pup, that to look at him you'd
think he warn't worth a cent, but to set around and look
ouery, and lay for a chance to steal something. But as soon
as money was up on him he was a different dog—his under-
jaw'd begin to stick out like the fo'castle of a steamboat, and
his teeth would uncover, and shine savage like the furnaces.
And a dog might tackle him, and bully-rag him, and bite him,
and throw him over his shoulder two or three times, and
Andrew Jackson—which was the name of the pup—Andrew
Jackson would never let on but what he was satisfied, and
hadn't expected nothing else—and the bets being doubled and
doubled on the other side all the time, till the money was all
up—and then all of a sudden he would grab that other dog
just by the joint of his hind leg and freeze to it—not chaw,
you understand, but only just grip and hang on till they
throwed up the sponge, if it was a year. Greeley always came
out winner on that pup till he harnessed a dog once that
didn't have no hind legs, because they'd been sawed off in a

FIGURE 16. Page 24 of the Yale Scrapbook, containing about one-fourth
of the *Californian* reprint of the "Jumping Frog" story. In addition to
four restorations of "Smiley," there are six substantive revisions. Only
the longest of these was not adopted in the JF1 text.

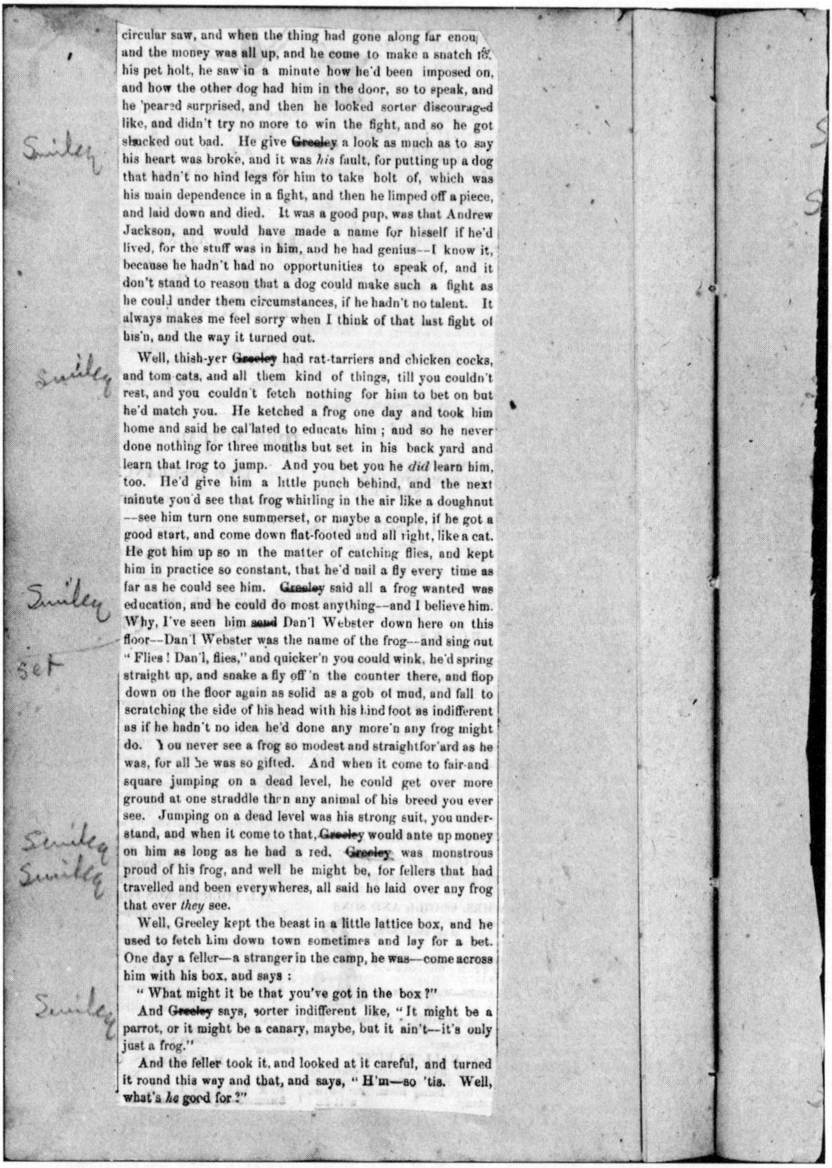

circular saw, and when the thing had gone along far enou;
and the money was all up, and he come to make a snatch to
his pet holt, he saw in a minute how he'd been imposed on,
and how the other dog had him in the door, so to speak, and
he 'peared surprised, and then he looked sorter discouraged
like, and didn't try no more to win the fight, and so he got
shucked out bad. He give Greeley a look as much as to say
his heart was broke, and it was *his* fault, for putting up a dog
that hadn't no hind legs for him to take holt of, which was
his main dependence in a fight, and then he limped off a piece,
and laid down and died. It was a good pup, was that Andrew
Jackson, and would have made a name for hisself if he'd
lived, for the stuff was in him, and he had genius--I know it,
because he hadn't had no opportunities to speak of, and it
don't stand to reason that a dog could make such a fight as
he could under them circumstances, if he hadn't no talent. It
always makes me feel sorry when I think of that last fight of
his'n, and the way it turned out.

Well, thish-yer Greeley had rat-tarriers and chicken cocks,
and tom-cats, and all them kind of things, till you couldn't
rest, and you couldn't fetch nothing for him to bet on but
he'd match you. He ketched a frog one day and took him
home and said he cal'lated to educate him ; and so he never
done nothing for three months but set in his back yard and
learn that frog to jump. And you bet you he *did* learn him,
too. He'd give him a little punch behind, and the next
minute you'd see that frog whirling in the air like a doughnut
--see him turn one summerset, or maybe a couple, if he got a
good start, and come down flat-footed and all right, like a cat.
He got him up so in the matter of catching flies, and kept
him in practice so constant, that he'd nail a fly every time as
far as he could see him. Greeley said all a frog wanted was
education, and he could do most anything--and I believe him.
Why, I've seen him send Dan'l Webster down here on this
floor--Dan'l Webster was the name of the frog--and sing out
"Flies! Dan'l, flies," and quicker'n you could wink, he'd spring
straight up, and snake a fly off 'n the counter there, and flop
down on the floor again as solid as a gob of mud, and fall to
scratching the side of his head with his hind foot as indifferent
as if he hadn't no idea he'd done any more'n any frog might
do. You never see a frog so modest and straightfor'ard as he
was, for all he was so gifted. And when it come to fair-and-
square jumping on a dead level, he could get over more
ground at one straddle than any animal of his breed you ever
see. Jumping on a dead level was his strong suit, you understand, and when it come to that, Greeley would ante up money
on him as long as he had a red. Greeley was monstrous
proud of his frog, and well he might be, for fellers that had
travelled and been everywheres, all said he laid over any frog
that ever *they* see.

Well, Greeley kept the beast in a little lattice box, and he
used to fetch him down town sometimes and lay for a bet.
One day a feller--a stranger in the camp, he was--come across
him with his box, and says :

"What might it be that you've got in the box?"

And Greeley says, sorter indifferent like, "It might be a
parrot, or it might be a canary, maybe, but it ain't--it's only
just a frog."

And the feller took it, and looked at it careful, and turned
it round this way and that, and says, "H'm--so 'tis. Well,
what's *he* good for?"

Smiley

Smiley

Smiley
set

Smiley
Smiley

Smiley

FIGURE 17. Page 25A of the Yale Scrapbook, containing another portion of the *Californian* reprint. Aside from the restoration of "Smiley"
throughout, only one correction ("set" for "send") was made. A page
stub is visible to the right; it now contains four *S*'s and originally held
the clipping in figure 18: the *S*'s come from Mark Twain's restoration
of "Smiley."

Smiley *Smiley*

"Well," Greeley says, easy and careless, "He's good enough for *one* thing I should judge—he can out-jump ary frog in Calaveras county."

The feller took the box again, and took another long, particlar look, and give it back to Greeley and says, very deliberate, "Well—I don't see no points about that frog that's any better'n any other frog."

"Maybe you don't," Greeley says. "Maybe you understand frogs, and maybe you don't understand 'em; maybe you've had experience, and maybe you ain't only a amatuer, as it were. Anyways, I've got *my* opinion, and I'll resk forty dollars that he can outjump ary frog in Calaveras county."

And the feller studied a minute, and then says, kinder sad, like, "Well—I'm only a stranger here, and I ain't got no frog—but if I had a frog I'd bet you."

And then Greeley says, "That's all right—that's all right—if you'll hold my box a minute I'll go and get you a frog;" and so the feller took the box, and put up his forty dollars along with Greeley's, and set down to wait.

Smiley

So he set there a good while thinking and thinking to himself, and then he got the frog out and prized his mouth open and took a teaspoon and filled him full of quail-shot—filled him pretty near up to his chin—and set him on the floor. Greeley he went to the swamp and slopped around in the mud for a long time, and finally he ketched a frog and fetched him in and give him to this feller and says:

"Now if you're ready, set him alongside of Dan'l, with his fore-paws just even with Dan'l's, and I'll give the word." Then he says, 'one—two—three—jump!' and him and the feller touched up the frogs from behind, and the new frog *lively—* hopped off, but Dan'l give a heave, and hysted up his shoulders—so—like a Frenchman, but it wa'n't no use—he *ℓ* couldn't budge; he was planted as solid as an anvil, and he couldn't no more stir than if he was anchored out. Greeley was a good deal surprised, and he was disgusted too, but he didn't have no idea what the matter was, of course.

The feller took the money and started away, and when he was going out at the door he sorter jerked his thumb over his shoulders—this way—at Dan'l, and says again, very deliberate: "Well—*I* don't see no points about that frog that's any better'n any other frog."

Greeley he stood scratching his head and looking down at Dan'l a long time, and at last he says, "I do wonder what in the nation that frog throw'd off for—I wonder if there ain't something the matter with him—he 'pears to look mighty baggy, somehow," and he ketched Dan'l by the nap of the neck, and lifted him up and says, "Why blame my cats if he don't weigh five pounds," and turned him upside down, and he belched out about a double-handful of shot. And then he see how it was, and he was the maddest man—he set the frog down and took out after that feller, but he never ketched him. And——

[Here Simon Wheeler heard his name called from the front-yard, and got up to see what was wanted.] And turning to me as he moved away, he said: "Just set where you are, stranger, and rest easy—I ain't going to be gone a second."

But by your leave, I did not think that a continuation of the history of the enterprising vagabond Jim Greeley would be likely to afford me much information concerning the Rev. Leonidas W. Greeley, and so I started away.

At the door I met the sociable Wheeler returning, and he buttonholed me and recommenced:

"Well, thish yer Greeley had a yaller one-eyed cow that didn't have no tail only just a short stump like a bannanner, and——"

Smiley

"O, curse Greeley and his afflicted cow!" I muttered, good-naturedly, and bidding the old gentleman good-day, I departed.

Your, truly. MARK TWAIN.

FIGURE 18. Page 25 of the Yale Scrapbook, containing the last portion of the *Californian* reprint. This portion originally occupied a page facing 25A, as shown in figure 17. Mark Twain's restoration of "lively" and his deletion of the *n* from "an" were lost when the clipping was peeled away and remounted on the present scrapbook page. Mark Twain's marginal revisions have been redrawn to reconstruct how the original page looked before the clipping was peeled away and remounted.

clipping. The loss of these three changes in JF1 is strong evidence that the clipping now in the scrapbook was the ultimate source of, if not the actual, printer's copy. Nothing less will account for the coincidence of the lost corrections.

However, in addition to rejecting the revision "it took him to make the trip," JF1 introduced numerous small substantive changes that did not appear in the scrapbook clipping—many of them in dialect spellings, some of them suspiciously like authorial revisions elsewhere in the scrapbook. JF1 substituted "hang" for "curse," for example, and "been doin' " for "done"—both revisions that Mark Twain could have made. If he was responsible for any of these later changes, however, he must have made them on a duplicate clipping—for he did not read or revise proof.

In spite of this puzzling situation, it seems unlikely that a duplicate clipping or transcription was prepared or, therefore, that Mark Twain made any revision of his sketch which is not preserved in the scrapbook. As in the case of "Whereas," the scrapbook clipping could provide legible printer's copy without the chore of transcribing minute changes from one clipping to another. Nevertheless, the use of a duplicate cannot be positively excluded: the omission of one change, and the very characteristic substitution of "hang" for "curse" and "being doin'" for "done," may indicate that Mark Twain or Webb did the inexplicable—transferred some but not all of the author's changes to a second clipping, which was then further revised.

It is of some interest, however, that even if a duplicate was used, none of the variants between the marked scrapbook clipping and JF1 may be safely attributed to Mark Twain. For Webb was entirely capable of making changes like this, and clearly did so elsewhere. Moreover, we know that Mark Twain was particularly dissatisfied with the JF1 text of his most famous sketch. When he revised a copy of JF1 in 1869 he restored sixteen substantive readings that had been present in the original marked clipping in the scrapbook—including many correct dialect spellings and the three lost changes.[22] Mark Twain's

---

[22] He made the revisions on JF1**MT**, an 1869 copy now in the Doheny collection. For example he again deleted "me," inserted "lively," and changed "an anvil" to "a church." For further details, see the textual commentary to "Jim Smiley and His Jumping Frog."

restoration of so many scrapbook readings argues not that he wavered in his judgment, but rather that he failed to control the JF1 printing of this sketch beyond the scrapbook stage—for he would surely have made the corrections then that he later made, presumably from memory, in 1869. If the clipping in the scrapbook was indeed printer's copy, then we must suppose that Webb was a sufficiently adept editor to simulate authorial changes ("hang" for "curse") on the proof, and that either he or an overzealous and somewhat careless compositor was responsible for tinkering with Mark Twain's dialect spellings. While it remains possible that Mark Twain further revised a duplicate clipping, making a few changes and failing to see the errors he corrected two years later, it seems somewhat more likely that no duplicate was used, that the omissions and errors were compositorial or editorial, and that we have a rather striking example of the way Mark Twain could abandon even his best early work to the arbitrary judgment of others.

These examples and others like them confirm that the Yale Scrapbook was mined for the JF1 printer's copy. They show that Mark Twain certainly initiated some variants in JF1, but that these are everywhere intermingled with variants probably introduced by his editor, Webb, who also took it upon himself to select material for the book, and to reject or modify revisions that the author had supplied in the scrapbook. These facts alter the description that Mark Twain and Webb gave of the production of JF1 in 1867. Using the new information, we can revise Mark Twain's 1906 recollection to accord with the facts, and to provide some general constraints for interpreting the textual variants we find in JF1.

As we have already indicated, Mark Twain must have begun by revising—or rejecting—every clipping in the scrapbook. We cannot say with certainty when he began this revision, but if we assume that the scrapbook was first compiled and then revised, he could not have begun before March 1866, for the scrapbook contains articles that did not appear until then. Mark Twain sailed for the Sandwich Islands on 7 March 1866 and spent the rest of the year writing travel letters for the Sacramento *Union*, preparing a book composed from those

letters, and making his first lecture tour. He sailed again from San
Francisco on December 15, this time as the official traveling correspondent for the *Alta California*, intending to go around the world
in that capacity, and he did not arrive in New York City until 12
January 1867.[23]

Mark Twain's first preoccupation on arrival was completing and
publishing his Sandwich Islands travel book, but Webb must soon
have tempted him with the easier "scissors & slash" project of a book
of sketches.[24] Many years later, in a letter to Webb, Mark Twain
fondly recalled "that January day in your rooms in Broadway"—
presumably an early meeting in New York, and very possibly the
occasion of Webb's proposal.[25] Webb had himself just published
Liffith Lank, or Lunacy with George W. Carleton, and may have
suggested that Mark Twain too would find him a willing publisher
of western humor.[26] Since Mark Twain encountered Webb in January
and did not meet with Carleton's painful indifference until sometime
in February, there was certainly time to select and revise the clippings
in his scrapbook.[27]

Contrary to Mark Twain's recollection in 1906, there is no reason
to suppose that Webb collected the clippings that the author presented to Carleton: the scrapbook is manifestly a document that was
most readily compiled in San Francisco. And it likewise seems im-

---

[23]*N&J1*, pp. 103, 111, 176; Clemens to San Francisco *Alta California*, written 12
January 1867, *MTTB*, p. 73.

[24]On 15 January 1867 Mark Twain told Edward P. Hingston that he planned to
lecture "as soon as I get my illustrated book on the Sandwich Islands in the hands of
the printers" (*CL1*, letter 120). Mark Twain did complete this book in the spring of
1867, and he submitted it to the prospective publishers, Dick and Fitzgerald, but withdrew it in May (*N&J1*, p. 177 n. 166).

[25]Clemens to Webb, 16 February 1896, Yale.

[26]Bindery records show that *Liffith Lank* had been issued on 3 January 1867 in a first
printing of 1,200 copies (MTP).

[27]"Carleton insulted me in Feb, 1867" (Clemens to William Dean Howells, 26 April
1876, *MTHL*, 1:132). The provenance of the scrapbook indicates that Mark Twain
could not have revised it later than June 1867, when he sailed in the *Quaker City*.
Albert Bigelow Paine made the following notation in the scrapbook: "This Scrapbook
was presented to me by Gov. Frank Fuller—1912." Fuller had acted as Mark Twain's
informal business agent in the spring of 1867, arranging his first New York lecture,
collecting reviews of it for him, and later trying to collect royalties of *JF1* while the
author was away (Clemens to Fuller, 7 June 1867, *CL1*, letter 138). It seems likely that
Fuller was also charged with some of the author's personal belongings, including this
scrapbook, and that he did not relinquish it until Mark Twain's official biographer
came to him looking for information.

plausible that Mark Twain removed some of the clippings from the scrapbook instead of carrying it intact to Carleton: he would have removed both the "Jumping Frog" and "Whereas" if he removed anything, and both of these are preserved in the scrapbook. When Carleton declined to publish the contents of the scrapbook, Mark Twain returned with it to Webb, who said "he would publish it himself." One contemporary source, evidently close to Webb, said that Mark Twain's " 'book' in the form in which he had prepared it, was refused on all sides," implying that the author had taken the scrapbook to Carleton (and perhaps to other publishers, like Dick and Fitzgerald) before Webb undertook to edit it. The same source also said that the author was "very much indebted to 'John Paul' for his skill displayed in editing," and wondered "what the book would have been without judicious excision." Webb himself recalled, in an autobiographical letter written to Edmund Clarence Stedman about 1889: "While publishing some skits of his own to demonstrate his conviction that publishers did not know what they discarded, Mr. Webb also edited and published the first book of Mark Twain, which the regular publishers to whom it was offered one and all refused."[28] As we have seen, the scrapbook itself shows that Webb's editorial work must have followed Mark Twain's initial revision of the contents. It was in this sense, then, that Webb "undertook to collate the sketches" (as Mark Twain recalled in 1906), and he must have done so by selecting and removing clippings from the scrapbook and probably from other sources as well.

Mark Twain's cancellation of many sketches (and parts of sketches) in the Yale Scrapbook was probably a preliminary stage in the selection of contents for JF1. The revised scrapbook as Carleton presumably saw it still contained more material than was ultimately desired: the author probably anticipated that the publisher or Webb would make the final choice after some agreement had been reached. When Webb took over the editing he seems to have been given a relatively

---

[28]New York *Citizen*, 20 July 1867, quoted in "A Fair Hit," *Californian*, 24 August 1867, p. 8; Webb to Stedman, ca. 1889, quoted in the catalog of the American Art Association, sale of 17 February 1926, item 71. Mark Twain had the last word on this matter. When someone asked him, "Did John Paul discover you or did you know you were a good thing yourself?" the author responded: "John Paul never discovered anything nor anybody. He was not even a very good liar" (marginalia in a copy of JF1, MTP).

free hand, but Mark Twain continued to be actively involved in
selecting which pieces to reprint. On the last page of the scrapbook
he made two lists that seem to name sketches which are now, or once
were, in the scrapbook. The first reads:

> Petrified Man.
>
> Children's Christmas Stories.
>
> Volcano Kileaua.
>
> Accidental Insurance.
>
> Wandering Jew.

The second, written toward the bottom of the page and at right angles
to the first, gives seven seemingly more doubtful selections, as follows:

> ?—Sacramento Letter.
>
> Portion after Hawks
>
> Dream of Stars
>
> Badlam Sharks.
>
> Séances—2
>
> Geewhillikens
>
> Graceful Compliment[29]

On the facing endpaper Mark Twain drew a line pointing to the
second list of seven and added "(Don't run average)," meaning that

[29]"Petrified Man" is piece no. 28, the *Enterprise* hoax of 4 October 1862. "Children's
Christmas Stories" alludes to "The Christmas Fireside" (no. 148), a *Californian* sketch
of 23 December 1865, reprinted in JF1 as "The Story of the Bad Little Boy Who Didn't
Come to Grief." "Volcano Kileaua" (Mark Twain meant "Kilauea") is probably "A
Strange Dream" (no. 189), reprinted in JF1 from a *Californian* reprinting of 7 July 1866;
"Volcano Kileaua" might refer instead to a Sacramento *Union* letter (16 November
1866, *MTH*, pp. 416–419) describing the volcano: the letter was not reprinted in JF1.
"Accidental Insurance" is "How, for Instance?" (no. 192), reprinted in JF1 from a
Californian reprinting of 27 October 1866 as "An Inquiry about Insurances." "Wander-
ing Jew" has not been identified, but it was certainly not reprinted in JF1.
"Sacramento Letter" is "Letter from Mark Twain" (no. 184), published in the
Enterprise sometime between 27 February and 5 March 1866. "Portion after Hawks"
is part of "Further of Mr. Mark Twain's Important Correspondence" (no..102), a
Californian sketch of 13 May 1865. "Dream of Stars" is "A Full and Reliable Account
of the Extraordinary Meteoric Shower of Last Saturday Night" (no. 98), a *Californian*
sketch of 19 November 1864. "Badlam Sharks" is part of an *Enterprise* letter published
ca. 11 January 1866, reprinted in this collection as " 'White Man Mighty Onsartain' "
(no. 160). "Séances—2" alludes to "Among the Spiritualists" and " 'Mark Twain'
among the Spirits" (nos. 165 and 166), which were joined together in JF1 as "Among
the Spirits"; the composite sketch is reprinted in this collection with the new title
Mark Twain inscribed in the scrapbook, "The Spiritual Séance" (no. 202). "Gee-
whillikens" is part of a *Californian* "Answers to Correspondents" column of 1 July 1865
(no. 109). "Graceful Compliment" is part of an *Enterprise* letter published sometime
between 10 and 31 December 1865, reprinted in this collection as "A Graceful Compliment" (no. 143).

they were either much shorter or much longer than the other sketches already chosen for JF1.[30]

The lists now seem cryptic, but they are clearly linked with the production of JF1 and were probably intended to supply some guidance to Webb in compiling the book. Only one sketch in the first list of five survives in the scrapbook: "How, for Instance?" (no. 192), in a clipping from the Sacramento *Union*. Three of these five sketches —including "How, for Instance?"—were in fact reprinted in JF1, all of them set from printings or reprintings in the *Californian*. This suggests that copies of all five were removed from the front part of the scrapbook to serve, at least tentatively, as printer's copy. (The *Union* clipping survives only because the same sketch was reprinted in the *Californian* as well; in other words, there were duplicate clippings of at least this one sketch.) On the other hand, the reverse situation holds with the seven sketches that didn't "run average": all but one of these remains completely intact in the scrapbook, where Mark Twain revised them, and only that single exception (designated "Séances—2") was reprinted in JF1.[31]

The lists cannot be preliminary selections for the book, because they omit such obvious choices as the "Jumping Frog" story. They appear to be additional choices to fill out a volume for which the main selections have already been made: of the twelve sketches named only four were reprinted in JF1, which contained twenty-seven sketches in all. This last conjecture indicates that the lists and the scrapbook revisions to which they refer were probably not completed until sometime in February 1867, when Webb began to act as Mark Twain's editor and publisher.

Although the scrapbook clearly contained more than enough revised material for a modest collection of sketches, several pieces in

---

[30]In fact, they are not conspicuously longer or shorter than the sketches in JF1. Perhaps Webb was tending to shorten the average length of the sketches he reprinted, and Mark Twain therefore really had no idea what was "average." As we have noted, Mark Twain fully revised "An Unbiased Criticism" (no. 100) and "The Facts" (no. 116), both of which were long *Californian* sketches, but only short portions of them were reprinted in JF1.

[31]"The Spiritual Séance" was set from alternating sections of the *Enterprise* and the *Californian*, but in fact only the *Enterprise* clipping was demonstrably removed from the scrapbook. The printer's copy was probably made from the *Enterprise* clipping combined with a duplicate, or handwritten copy, of the *Californian*, the original clipping of which remained in the scrapbook.

JF1 were typeset from other sources. When Webb began to "collate the sketches" he undoubtedly mined the 1866 *Californian*, in which he, Bret Harte, and James F. Bowman had loyally reprinted a number of selections from Mark Twain's Sandwich Islands letters to the Sacramento *Union*, as well as everything that the author published in the eastern press. Collation establishes that all of the *Union* sketches reprinted in JF1, as well as several other pieces, were set from *Californian* reprints. Since Webb undoubtedly had access to his personal file of the journal, he may have used it to supply copy for the printer: altogether six sketches, not much altered by Mark Twain, were reprinted in JF1 from the 1866 *Californian*.[32]

Having revised and helped select the sketches for JF1, could Mark Twain also have edited the printer's copy further? Conclusive evidence of such activity is hard to find. As we have already suggested, he probably helped to piece together composite sketches like "Burlesque 'Answers to Correspondents'" and "The Spiritual Séance" (nos. 201 and 202), and it seems likely that he made some additional changes on the culled printer's copy: both sketches contain revisions in JF1 which are characteristic of the author but do not appear in the scrapbook margins.[33] Nevertheless, Webb was clearly responsible for a number of other revisions (and mistakes), and could conceivably have introduced these as well.

Although it is possible that Mark Twain made minor revisions in the culled printer's copy, he almost certainly did not read proof for JF1 at all. After making preliminary arrangements to sail on the *Quaker City* in early June, he left New York on 3 March 1867 to spend six weeks in St. Louis with his family. On March 19 he wrote to ask Webb "what date" he expected to publish, and he promised

---

[32]Webb's bound volumes of the *Californian* are also (coincidentally) at Yale. The absence of a few issues indicates that they might have provided printer's copy. Webb made several notations about Mark Twain's sketches on the endpapers, and a few in the texts themselves. But it seems likely that most of these notations were made when he contemplated reissuing JF1 in late 1870, or even as late as 1875. For example the sections he lists for "Burlesque 'Answers to Correspondents'" do not correspond with those in the JF1 printing, but with those in the much revised and shortened version ultimately included in SkNO (1875). Still, some of the notations may be contemporary with JF1.

[33]For instance, in "The Spiritual Séance" Mark Twain's "seized" in the scrapbook margin was replaced in JF1 by "boarded," a change so characteristic that it is almost certainly authorial.

to lecture in New York if the book were to be issued "before March is out." We must regard this as a measure of Mark Twain's lack of participation in the later stages of production. He did return to the city by April 15, two weeks before publication was accomplished, but he probably could not have made any changes during the final days of binding and distribution. Moreover, he wrote Bret Harte when the book appeared: "It is full of damnable errors of grammar & deadly inconsistencies of spelling in the Frog sketch because I was away & did not read the proofs."[34] Although Mark Twain was elsewhere less than candid about his role in producing JF1, there is good reason to suppose that he spoke the truth to Harte. As we have already noted, when he subsequently revised a copy of JF1 in 1869, he corrected sixteen substantive errors in that sketch alone. This fact is persuasive evidence that Mark Twain did not read proof for JF1, for he would surely have done so on the title sketch if at all.

To sum up: we conjecture that Mark Twain participated in the preparation of JF1 printer's copy first by revising and selecting sketches in his scrapbook and then by assisting Webb in removing that copy from the scrapbook and tinkering it into final shape. Many of his revisions in the scrapbook appear in the texts of JF1. While Mark Twain seems to have left the final selection of sketches to Webb, he did make preliminary choices in the scrapbook and even provided a list of alternates. But he probably confined his work on the culled printer's copy to a few sketches, and he almost certainly did not read or revise the work in proof. Webb, on the other hand, assumed the main responsibility for extracting and preparing printer's copy from Mark Twain's scrapbook. He decided which of the author's revisions to reproduce and even rewrote some of these revisions; and he decided which sketches to include, sometimes contradicting Mark Twain's original judgment. And he alone saw the book through the press while Mark Twain was in St. Louis.

These conjectures provide a set of constraints for interpreting the variants in JF1. We are able to identify some variants as merely the result of using an unauthorized reprinting for printer's copy—a choice that both author and editor unthinkingly endorsed. Variants that can

---

[34]Clemens to San Francisco *Alta California*, written 15 March 1867, *MTTB*, p. 122; Clemens to Webb, 19 March 1867, *CL1*, letter 122; Clemens to Jane Clemens et al., 15 April 1867, *CL1*, letter 124; Clemens to Bret Harte, 1 May 1867, *CL1*, letter 130.

be matched with holograph revisions in the scrapbook are of course clearly authorial. But when JF1 differs from the scrapbook revision we must consider at least three possibilities: further revision by the author, further revision by the editor, or mistakes of the author or the editor. The generous sampling of Mark Twain's revisions preserved in the scrapbook helps us to characterize variants in JF1 for which no holograph evidence survives. But Webb's skill as an editor, his capacity for imitating what Mark Twain had begun to do in the scrapbook, poses the constant possibility that variants undocumented by holograph evidence are in fact the editor's. Therefore where Mark Twain's active presence cannot be demonstrated, we must always suspect that Webb was the responsible agent.

JF1 presents an unusual situation in Mark Twain's works, for all of the sketches that it reproduces are in some degree the product of an intermingling of authorial and editorial decisions about what sketches to reprint, which portions to select, and even what words to use. The editorial process was carried out in such a way that confident distinctions between the literary contributions of Webb and Mark Twain are now no longer possible. We know that Mark Twain entrusted Webb with the editing of his sketches, and that for at least a while he accepted what Webb had done. It was only in retrospect that Mark Twain came to regret the amount of autonomy he had given his first editor and publisher. Early in 1869 he told Elisha Bliss of the American Publishing Company, when Bliss wanted to intervene in the same way with *The Innocents Abroad* manuscript, "I don't much like to entrust even slight alterations to other hands. It is n't a judicious thing to do, exactly."[35]

JF1 was at last published late in April 1867. Webb's advertisements announced, too optimistically, that it would be ready "on Wednesday, April 24,"[36] but it was evidently delayed until April 30. On April 15 Mark Twain was back in New York, predicting that his book would "probably be in the booksellers' hands in about two weeks." By April

---

[35]Clemens to Bliss, 14 February 1869, *CL2*, letter 8.
[36]*Nation* 4 (25 April 1867): 342. JF1 was listed under "Books of the Day" (p. 341), but since it was also mentioned there on May 2, we can infer nothing from this about the actual publication date.

19 he may have seen an early copy, for he told the San Francisco *Alta California* that it would have a "truly gorgeous gold frog on the back of it, and that frog alone will be worth the money." Webb filed for copyright on April 15, but a copy of the book was not deposited until May 14. The bindery records indicate that the first impression was bound on April 30.[37] On that day Mark Twain also wrote the *Alta*:

Webb has gotten up my "Jumping Frog" book in excellent style, and it is selling rapidly. A lot of copies will go to San Francisco per this steamer. I hope my friends will all buy a few copies each, and more especially am I anxious to see the book in all the Sunday School Libraries in the land. I don't know that it would instruct youth much, but it would make them laugh anyway, and therefore no Sunday School Library can be complete without the "Jumping Frog." But candidly, now, joking aside, it is really a very handsome book, and you know yourself that it is a very readable one.[38]

The uneasy, almost apologetic tone of this newspaper letter suggests that Mark Twain was not wholly sanguine about the prospective sale of his first book. Webb, who had invested his own money in the project, was worried about the same problem, and wrote to John Russell Young of the New York *Tribune* to complain that the paper had not given his new publishing venture sufficient publicity.[39] The advertising material directed at the trade shows a similar concern for JF1: "This is the first published book of this celebrated and rising humorist. Abounding with the quaintest and rarest wit, which never degenerates into coarseness, it cannot fail to have an extensive sale."[40]

Nevertheless, JF1 did fail in this respect. Mark Twain and his editor had both tried to delete offensive words and allusions from his

[37]Clemens to Jane Clemens et al., 15 April 1867, *CL1*, letter 124; Clemens to San Francisco *Alta California*, written 19 April 1867, *MTTB*, p. 158. The copyright notice listed Webb as proprietor and gave the title as "The Jumping Frog of Calaveras County | By Mark Twain | Edited by John Paul" (Copyright Records for New York, Southern District, vol. 88, 4 March–6 May 1867, Rare Books Division, Library of Congress). For the bindery records, see note 43 below. Publication was not later than May 1, for on that day the author inscribed a copy, "To My Mother—The dearest Friend I ever had, & the truest. Mark Twain | New York, May 1, 1867" (PH in MTP).
[38]Clemens to San Francisco *Alta California*, written 30 April 1867, *MTTB*, p. 165.
[39]Webb to Young, 24 April 1867, Library of Congress.
[40]From the advertisement in the *Nation*, p. 342. The phrase recurred in other advertising copy.

newspaper pieces—thus saving the book from "coarseness"[41]—but economic conditions and Webb's limited capacity for advertising probably combined against the merit of its humor to prevent a large sale. The book was favorably but briefly noticed by such papers as the Boston *Evening Transcript*, the Chicago *Times*, the *Nation*, and the New York *Tribune* and *Times*. The *Transcript* noted that Mark Twain had "acquired a wide newspaper reputation, not only for his drollery, but for his sagacity of observation, his keen perception of character, and the individuality of his style and tone of thinking," and it singled out the "Jumping Frog" story as "the best representation of one phase of California life and character that we have seen." The *Times* thought the title sketch "a fair specimen of the whimsical fancies in which the book abounds," but asserted that there were "other sketches nearly equal to it in merit." Mark Twain was different from "other recent writers of his class in not resorting to the adventitious aid of bad spelling to make his jokes seem more absurd, and this is, of course, decidedly in his favor. There is a great deal of quaint humor and much pithy wisdom in his writings, and their own merit, as well as the attractive style in which they are produced, must secure them a popularity which will buy its own profit." The *Nation* said only that JF1 was "a volume not unworthy of a place beside the works of John Phœnix, A. Ward's books, and the two volumes of the Rev. Mr. Nasby." In the West, JF1 was favorably reviewed by the *Enterprise* and by the *Californian*—but like the eastern reviews, these were to little avail. According to one contemporary source the sale in California was "only two hundred copies."[42] The records of the printer and binder, John A. Gray and Green, show that 1,000 copies were bound by April 30 and another 552 followed shortly on May 20; these

---

[41]The criterion was an important one, at least in the author's eyes. When he briefly reviewed George Washington Harris' *Sut Lovingood: Yarns* three weeks after JF1 appeared, he said in part: "It contains all his early sketches, that used to be so popular in the West. . . . The book abounds in humor, and is said to represent the Tennessee dialect correctly. It will sell well in the West, but the Eastern people will call it coarse and possibly taboo it" (Clemens to San Francisco *Alta Californian*, written 23 May 1867, *MTTB*, p. 221).

[42]New York *Times*, 1 May 1867, p. 2; New York *Tribune*, 4 May 1867, p. 6; Boston *Evening Transcript*, 4 May 1867, p. 1; Chicago *Times*, 5 May 1867, p. 2; *Nation* 4 (9 May 1867): 369; *American Literary Gazette & Publishers' Circular* 9 (15 May 1867): 46; Virginia City *Territorial Enterprise*, 1 June 1867, p. 1; *Californian*, 1 June 1867, p. 9. The report of the California sales appeared in the New York *Citizen*, 20 July 1867, but is here quoted from a reprinting in the *Californian*, 24 August 1867, p. 8. We are indebted to Kenneth M. Sanderson for his help in locating reviews of JF1.

were supplemented by 150 and 182 on September 6 and October 3, and 101 on 3 February 1868. By the end of the year only about 2,200 copies had been sold—a disappointing record.[43]

Although before publication Mark Twain had followed Webb's progress from St. Louis, he now seemed to lose interest in his book. When he wrote to his family on May 20, he was discouraged and pretended to be indifferent: "Don't know how my book is coming on—shall leave instructions here to send such money as may accrue from it to Ma every few weeks," he wrote, but added sardonically, "It may make her rich, or it may reduce her to abject poverty, possibly." On June 1, only a week before sailing to Europe and the Holy Land, he asked Frank Fuller to collect the "ten cents a copy due me on all sales of my book . . . from my publisher, C. H. Webb, from time to time, & remit all such moneys to my mother."[44] By June 7 he had quite given up hope for it: "As for the Frog book, I don't believe that

---

[43]The record that survives is not an official ledger book, but what appears to be a copy of the bindery records made from the company records for Webb and Mark Twain on 10 December 1870, when they were negotiating Mark Twain's acquisition of the copyright and plates. The record is in MTP. It reads in full:

1867		1868		1869		1870	
30 Apl	1000	3 Feb.	101	25 Feb	200	Feb 16	250
20 May	552	14 Mch	221	16 Aug	159	May 13	311
6 Sept	150	17 Sept	250	9 Dec	200	Oct 21	250
3 Oct	182					& 250 left in sheets	

The total number of copies printed, including those left in sheets, was 4,076. By contrast, the other books that Webb published in 1867 did somewhat better: 4,670 copies of *Liffith Lank* were produced by 19 March 1867, and 4,902 copies of *St. Twel'mo* (published on 9 May 1867) were produced by 9 October 1869. Presumably they continued to sell into 1870, but no figures are available.

[44]Clemens to Jane Clemens et al., 20 May 1867, *CL1*, letter 132; Clemens to Fuller, 1 June 1867, *CL1*, letter 139. The payment due Mark Twain remains in doubt, but it was probably 10 percent (about $600) rather than 10¢ per copy ($400). In this 1867 letter he himself seemed uncertain, for he first wrote "per cent" and then "cents."

If Webb did make payments to Jane Clemens, Mark Twain nowhere recorded the fact. In 1906 he recalled that Webb had been unable to pay him royalties when he returned from the *Quaker City* voyage in November 1867. And when he came to settle with Webb in late 1870, he told Elisha Bliss that in addition to paying Webb $800, he had forgiven him "what he owed me ($600⁰⁰)," a figure that probably reflects a 10 percent royalty on 4,076 books at $1.50 each (Clemens to Bliss, 22 December 1870, *CL2*, letter 267). The problem cannot be resolved because the contract was oral. In April 1875 Mark Twain (quoting *Twelfth Night*) made a note to himself on a letter from Webb: "*Mem*—'The whirligig of time brings round its revenges.' He swindled me on a verbal publishing contract on my first book (Sketches), (8 years ago) and now he has got caught himself and appealed to me for help. I have advised him to do as I did—make the best of a bad bargain and be wiser next time" (*MTLP*, p. 87 n. 1). Mark Twain's account of this "swindle" may be found in AD, 23 May 1906, *MTE*, pp. 148–150.

will ever pay anything worth a cent. I published it simply to advertise myself & not with the hope of making anything out of it." Yet this was clearly a rationalization, for in December 1870, when *The Innocents Abroad* had salved the wound of his first book by selling 80,000 copies in sixteen months, Mark Twain admitted that in 1867 he had "fully expected the 'Jumping Frog' to sell 50,000 copies & it only sold 4,000."[45]

2. English Piracies of JF1:
George Routledge (1867, 1870, and 1872): JF2, JF4a, and JF4b
John Camden Hotten (1870): JF3

Despite its relatively modest sale in the United States, JF1 was well received in England, even by sophisticated literary journals like the *Saturday Review*:

The Celebrated Jumping Frog and its companions may be heartily recommended to any one who is capable of appreciating humour, or enjoying a good laugh. There are not many of these sketches which could be read by the most confirmed of hypochondriacs with an unmoved countenance; and not one of them which might not be read aloud, without missing a word, by the most fastidious mother to a family circle.[46]

Nevertheless, probably only a few copies of JF1 were sold in England, for it was soon pirated by George Routledge and Sons, who thereby drove Webb's edition out of the market. The Routledges' JF2 reprinted the whole of JF1, sold for at most one-sixth the price, and was enthusiastically reviewed in the press. The *London Review* said on 21 September 1867:

This is a dry, clever book, with a vein of originality running throughout it, which imparts an unusual and an agreeable flavour to the contents. . . . We have been so heartily amused by Mr. Twain and his frog that we sincerely wish his book may be purchased by the typical gentleman to whom he dedicates it and by others. It is not often

---

[45]Clemens to Jane Clemens et al., 7 June 1867, *CL1*, letter 137; Clemens to F. S. Drake, 26 December 1870, *CL2*, letter 272.

[46]*Saturday Review* 24 (24 August 1867): 268. The book was distributed by Sampson Low, Son, and Marston, an active importer of American books. The Routledges reprinted the *Saturday Review* notice on the back cover of JF2.

that we meet a genuine collection of harmless drollery and mirth, unforced, natural, and exhilarating like "The Jumping Frog."[47]

And in October, Tom Hood lavishly praised the book in *Fun:*

We hereby present our thanks to Messrs. Routledge for giving to the British public one of the funniest books that we have met with for a long time. . . . There are no misspellings, no contortions of words in Mark [T]wain; his fun is entirely dependent upon the inherent humour in his writings. And although many jokers have sent us *brochures* like the present from the other side of the Atlantic, we have had no book fuller of more genuine or more genial fun than the "Celebrated Jumping Frog." Our advice to our readers, therefore, is immediately to invest a shilling in it.[48]

Needless to say, this kind of support was helpful: according to the Routledge records, the first impression of JF2, ordered on 1 August 1867, consisted of 6,000 copies, and a second impression ordered less than a year later, on 1 April 1868, was for an additional 2,000 copies.[49]

The Routledges' chief competitor, especially when it came to reprinting American authors, was John Camden Hotten. By late 1867 he was publishing a veritable library of American humor that included what he termed "the authorized and only complete editions" of Artemus Ward's books, "the only Complete and Correct Edition published in this country" of Lowell's *Biglow Papers*, an edition of Josh Billings' *His Book of Sayings*, and one of the *Orpheus C. Kerr Papers* (the last two edited by Edward P. Hingston).[50] Mark Twain's *Jumping Frog*, however, was conspicuously absent from this list. Hotten seems to have respected the Routledges' prior claim—at least at first—for he

---

[47]*London Review of Politics, Society, Literature, Art, & Science* 15 (21 September 1867): 330–331.

[48]*Fun* 6 (19 October 1867): 65.

[49]Routledge Ledger Book 4, p. 261, Routledge and Kegan Paul, London. JF2 was deposited in the British Museum on 12 September 1867, and publication was announced in the biweekly *Publishers' Circular and General Record* on September 16 (*BAL* 3586).

[50]Hotten listed these titles in an advertisement in the *Athenaeum*, 14 December 1867, p. 819. It is of some interest that he here claimed the exclusive right to republish Artemus Ward in England by virtue of the author's request: "*It is my wish that with Mr. Hotten alone the right of publishing my books in England should rest.* CHAS. F. BROWNE (Artemus Ward)." This was a moral and, to some extent, a sentimental claim: Artemus Ward was, of course, recently dead and widely mourned, but most of his books were not legally protected by British copyright law and were not Hotten's property any more than they were the Routledges', who also reprinted them.

did not begin to republish Mark Twain's books until early 1870, when it became apparent that *The Innocents Abroad* was selling extraordinarily well in the United States. Although *Innocents* was probably his primary incentive, Hotten began by publishing his own edition of the *Jumping Frog* book, JF3, sometime in late March or early April 1870. Hotten's edition, coming as it did some two and a half years after JF2, was initially less successful, selling only about 5,700 copies (in two formats) by July 1871.[51] Yet despite this late start, within another two years Hotten had sold more than 18,900 copies of JF3—a very respectable showing that must have had an adverse effect on the sales of his competitor. By the same time (July 1873) the Routledges had printed only 24,000 copies of their piracy—certainly an excellent sale, but only about half what it might have been without Hotten's interference.[52]

Collation shows that JF3 was not set "from the original edition," as Hotten's title page proclaimed, but from a copy of the Routledges' JF2. The initial textual differences between JF2 and JF3 were few, but they were perpetuated (and increased) in later printings of these sketches because each house subsequently used its own text for printer's copy. Collation also demonstrates that Mark Twain had nothing whatever to

---

[51]The precise time of publication in 1870 remains in doubt, but it was earlier than the date given by Jacob Blanck (*BAL* 3587). Hotten's records show that he began JF3 on 9 February 1870, but no record of binding appears until April 25. The books probably issued before April, however: the first two impressions, also imperfectly recorded, probably totaled about 2,000 copies, for Hotten ordered that many covers on March 18. A third impression of 2,000 copies was ordered on April 12, but these were not all bound and sold until early July 1871, when a fourth impression was called for. To these 4,000 copies we must add 1,700 copies of *A 3rd Supply of Yankee Drolleries: The Most Recent Works of the Best American Humourists* (*BAL,* p. 246), which contained (among other things) the entire text of JF3 printed from the same or duplicate plates. Although Hotten ordered 2,500 copies of *Yankee Drolleries* on 20 September 1870, by 20 June 1871 only 1,700 had been bound, and a second impression of 1,000 copies was not made until 19 September 1872 (Chatto and Windus Ledger Book 1, pp. 438, 89, Chatto and Windus, London).

[52]Hotten's firm had bound 16,000 copies of JF3 and 2,900 copies of *Yankee Drolleries* by July 1873, for a combined total of 18,900. The Routledges, as we shall see, reset the book once and added material twice in that period, but still bound a total of only 24,000 copies between mid-1867 and mid-1873. This is not to say that the Routledges or Hotten lost money, except to each other: Routledge spent a total of about £320 on manufacturing and, at a shilling a book (discounted by 30 percent to the bookseller), grossed some £840 ($4,200). Binding, advertising, and storage certainly reduced this profit, but the Routledges found it lucrative to keep the *Jumping Frog* book in print until 1902. The manufacturing costs are taken from Routledge Ledger Book 4, p. 261. Hotten's costs are not recorded, but because he used tighter leading and less paper, they were probably less than the Routledges': the records show that paper and binding far exceeded typesetting as an expense in book production.

do with either piracy—all their variants are errors or sophistications—but he was scarcely unaware of their combined effect on his
reputation. In January 1888 he recalled in his notebook: "It may be a
good thing sometimes for an author to have *one* book pirated & a
scramble made—I think it true. Look at my first book."[53] Indeed, the
double piracy of JF1 yielded double benefits for Mark Twain: it introduced him to thousands of English readers who had never seen any
of his work, even his most famous sketch, and it produced a "scramble" between the Routledges and Hotten (and Hotten's successors) to
secure his cooperation on future books—a scramble that did not end
until August 1881, when Mark Twain agreed to an arrangement that
was to provide a steady, lifelong income from British and Continental
publication of his works.[54]

But in 1867 no copyright was possible, and no British firm could
guarantee its own profits, much less payments to the author, for an
American book. British piracies of American publications were, of
course, commonplace: the United States had balked repeatedly at
making any provision for international copyright, and British law
recognized such a copyright only where the other nation had a recip-
rocating regulation. All of the American humorists could be republished in England without the author's permission and without any
payment to the author—a situation that undoubtedly contributed to
their international popularity. There were methods for "copyrighting"
American books, but they all depended on the moral restraint of other
English publishers. An American author could sell early sheets for a
flat fee to an English publisher, who might then be permitted to issue
the works without interference simply because he had preceded his
competitors. Another method was to have the author publicly desig-
nate an "official" publisher, as Artemus Ward did with Hotten. But
Hotten was unpopular with his fellow London publishers in part

---

[53]N&J3, p. 364.

[54]The agreement was with Chatto and Windus. The Routledges, however, were
actively bidding on Mark Twain's work as late as 1881, when they made an offer to
issue the British edition of *The Prince and the Pauper*. In late August of that year Mark
Twain decided to remain with the English publishers who had actively marketed his
books in England and had returned him profits of several thousand pounds per book
(Clemens to Chatto and Windus, 25 August 1881, Chatto and Windus Letter Book 13,
p. 386). This decision effectively ended the competition, even though the Routledges
continued to publish some books by Mark Twain until 1902.

because he did not always respect their prior claims or claims of exclusivity.[55]

An important change in this situation came about on 29 May 1868, when the Routledges lost their appeal in the well-known case of *Routledge* v. *Low*. The American author Maria Susanna Cummins had taken up brief residence in Canada while Sampson Low published and copyrighted her *Haunted Hearts* in London. The Routledges had nevertheless reprinted the book. Sampson Low sued and won, and the case was appealed to the House of Lords. That body ruled unanimously in favor of Sampson Low, saying that "a foreign author, residing in any part of this empire and publishing his work for the first time in London, is entitled to copyright in the same way as an English writer." Moreover, one justice, Lord Cairns, "went far beyond this point in his 'liberal interpretation of a liberal Act.' He expressed an unusually strong conviction that the Act of Parliament gives a real copyright to every author who first publishes his book in England, no matter where he lives. . . . Lord Cranworth objected to this view, and Lord Chelmsford doubted whether it was good in law."[56]

Thus in late May 1868 the highest British court ruled that an American could obtain a valid British copyright by publishing first in London while residing or "sojourning" in Canada or indeed any other part of the British Empire. And some support was held for the proposition that an author might even be able to obtain such a copyright without British residency. Since the Routledges had lost this case, we may be sure that they were alert to the significance of the new ruling: it meant that if they could secure an American author's cooperation, they could hold a legal copyright to his works and foil the kind of interference that Hotten or another publisher might offer.

By June or July 1868 the Routledges had already approached Mark

---

[55]In 1869, for instance, Hotten had angered an American humorist, Charles Leland, and Leland's official English publisher, Nicholas Trübner, by pirating the 1868 American edition of the complete *Hans Breitmann Ballads* (*Athenaeum*, 24 April 1869, pp. 570–571). In the columns of the *Athenaeum* Leland, Hotten, and then Trübner argued the moral and legal issues. Hotten said, "I have always held the view that an alien author, in the absence of any copyright convention, has no claim in good morals —as he certainly has none in law—to anything more than the right to stamp with his approval a particular edition" (*Athenaeum*, 1 May 1869, p. 606). For Trübner's response, see the *Athenaeum*, 8 May 1869, p. 637.

[56]*Athenaeum*, 6 June 1868, p. 799. The court ruling was fully reported in the London *Times*, 1 June 1868, p. 11.

Twain. In an early August advertisement for their house journal, *The Broadway: A London Magazine,* they announced, "The friendly relations we continue to preserve with American writers have enabled us to secure from Mr. Mark Twain, the author of 'The Celebrated Jumping Frog,'—one of the raciest and dryest works of humour,—a number of articles of a similar character, which it is anticipated will even distance the celebrated frog in their capacity for 'jumping' for the public approbation."[57] These articles were probably solicited by Joseph L. Blamire, the Routledges' New York agent, at a time when Mark Twain was just completing his first draft of *The Innocents Abroad.*[58] There is no record that Blamire made any offer for the British rights to *Innocents,* but he did finally secure one original sketch: "Cannibalism in the Cars" (no. 232), which was published in the November 1868 issue of the *Broadway.* The Routledges paid Mark Twain generously for this work—ten or fifteen pounds (fifty or seventy-five dollars)— and they doubtless held a valid British copyright on the sketch. Mark Twain remembered the occasion many years later, for the Routledges had succeeded in flattering him at a time when his national and international reputation were not yet established.[59]

Mark Twain spent the rest of 1868 and much of 1869 preparing his *Innocents* manuscript for the press, courting Olivia Langdon, lecturing throughout the eastern states, and then proofreading and further revising his book. He first expected to publish in the winter of 1868,

---

[57]*Athenaeum,* 8 August 1868, p. 165.

[58]Mark Twain completed the first draft in San Francisco on 23 June 1868: "The book is finished, & I think it will do" (Clemens to Elisha Bliss, *CL1,* letter 208). He left San Francisco early in July, arriving in New York on July 29. Since he spent several busy days in the city before going to Hartford on August 4, Blamire could have solicited the work then and cabled the agreement to London in time for the August 8 issue of the *Athenaeum.* It is unlikely, but possible, that he solicited a contribution by mail, when Mark Twain was still in San Francisco.

[59]Although Mark Twain could command as much as fifty dollars for one of his New York *Tribune* or *Herald* travel letters, he was deeply impressed by the Routledges' generosity. Many years later, on 7 May 1898, Clemens told Richard Watson Gilder that he had been offered a magazine's top price only three or four times in his career, and that he still remembered "the first two instances without any difficulty—they set no strain upon my memory. One was 31 years ago, when a now forgotten London magazine went down into its treasury & paid me $12.50 per mag. page for a 4-page article; the other was 22 years ago when the Atlantic paid me $18 per mag. page for a series of articles" (Yale). Mark Twain mistook a few details: the year was 1868, not 1867; the article was six, not four, pages long. But the occasion must certainly have made an impression on him if he ranked it with William Dean Howells' agreement for the "Old Times on the Mississippi" series in the *Atlantic Monthly* (*MTHL,* 1:68).

then in the spring of 1869, but publication was not finally accomplished until late summer of that year. Either because he was still naive about British copyright law, or because he was distracted by his wedding plans and a second lecture tour, Mark Twain delayed seven months—until February 1870—before contacting Blamire about British copyright for his book. On March 3 he asked his publisher, Elisha Bliss, to send a copy of *Innocents* to "*George Routledge & Sons, 416 Broome street, N. Y.*" He explained, "I wrote them to know if it would pay me to go over the Niagara river & get a British copyright, & you see what he says."[60] Blamire's letter, evidently enclosed to Bliss, has been lost—but his answer must certainly have been discouraging: first publication in England was a requirement for valid copyright there. *The Innocents Abroad* was, at least in Great Britain, exactly like a book whose copyright had expired and could not be renewed.

Nevertheless, at this time no British piracy of *Innocents* had yet appeared, and Mark Twain still naively hoped to forestall one. On March 11 he mentioned his wish to visit England and asked Bliss: "Have you heard yet what the possibilities are in the matter of selling our book there?"[61] Just what plan they were considering is not known, but it is clear that Mark Twain was trying to protect himself—albeit belatedly. The Routledges stoically refrained from republishing the book because of their desire to develop and maintain good relations with the author, not because of the hazards of competition, which they were well prepared to meet. Perhaps to reassert their moral claim to the humorist's work, they ordered a new edition of JF2, which they received on April 1. This edition, JF4a, contained a "New Copyright Chapter"—the sketch first published in their November 1868 *Broadway*, "Cannibalism in the Cars" (no. 232).[62] Collation shows that JF4a was set from a copy of JF2 and perpetuated most of its few errors while adding several more: Mark Twain did not revise the "copyright chapter" or any other sketch in the book. Although there is no evidence that he authorized the new edition, we can assume that he

---

[60]Clemens to Bliss, 3 March 1870, *CL2*, letter 168.

[61]Clemens to Bliss, 11 March 1870, *CL2*, letter 172.

[62]*Athenaeum*, 9 April 1870, p. 474; see *BAL* 3319. The Routledge records indicate that they paid £22 12s. for "Comp & Casting" on 1 April 1870, and that the initial impression of JF4a was of 2,000 copies. By 24 October 1871 they had printed 8,000 copies of JF4a (Routledge Ledger Book 4, p. 261).

endorsed it; in fact the Routledges probably sent him a complimentary copy.

It is not clear whether the Routledges issued JF4a in response to, or in anticipation of, Hotten's piracy, JF3. The records show that Hotten began his edition in February 1870, and did not issue it until sometime in late March or early April. We know that the Routledges first advertised JF4a on April 9, and that they asserted their claim of priority and authenticity by calling it "the only Complete Edition," which of course implicitly acknowledged competition.[63] If their decision to publish a new edition anticipated Hotten, they may have hoped to trap him with the "copyright chapter"; but they were, as we have noted, too late. Hotten's JF3 was set from JF2 and ran no risk of infringement of the Routledges' copyright.

JF3 was only the beginning for Hotten. In March 1870 he had also started work on his edition of *The Innocents Abroad*. In May he began to advertise it: "A delightfully fresh and amusing Volume of Travel. . . . There has been no work like it issued here for years."[64] And in August and October he finally published his two-volume edition—more than a year after first publication in the United States —and soon made a large sale.[65] Despite the obvious financial sacrifice, the Routledges still refrained from publishing a competing edition; they continued instead to work slowly toward an effective sanction from Mark Twain whereby they would secure British copyright and become the "official" English publishers of his future works.

In early March 1871 Mark Twain published a little pamphlet called *Mark Twain's (Burlesque) Autobiography*. Probably because of complications in its production, he failed to notify the Routledges ahead of time, and both they and Hotten yielded to temptation, pirating the

---

[63]*Athenaeum*, 9 April 1870, p. 474.

[64]*Athenaeum*, 7 May 1870, p. 602.

[65]Hotten's edition appeared in two separate volumes, *The Innocents Abroad* in August (*BAL* 3590) and *The New Pilgrim's Progress* in October (*BAL* 3591). By mid-1873 Hotten's firm had printed 49,000 copies of the first volume and 42,700 copies of the second. Moreover, in June 1871 Hotten issued *Mark Twain's Pleasure Trip on the Continent* (*BAL* 3597), which contained both volumes in one, printed from the same (or duplicate) plates but on smaller pages; by mid-1873 he had printed 5,000 of these. In addition, *A 3rd Supply of Yankee Drolleries* contained *The Innocents Abroad* (volume 1), likewise printed from the same (or duplicate) plates. By July 1873 about 2,900 of these had been sold. Total sale: 56,900 of *Innocents* and 47,700 of *New Pilgrim's Progress* (Chatto and Windus Ledger Book 1, pp. 89, 447, 448, 450).

little book in London. By June, however, Mark Twain seemed more alert to the same danger confronting his next book, *Roughing It*, and began negotiations well ahead of time. "Have you heard anything from Routledge?" he asked Bliss. "Considering the large English sale he made of one of my other books (Jumping Frog,) I thought maybe we might make something if I could give him a secure copyright."[66] His concern was stimulated not only by Hotten's piracy of *Innocents*, a copy of which he had certainly seen by February 1871, but also by the appearance of a Canadian piracy of the same book.[67]

By late 1871 Mark Twain had reached an agreement with the Routledges to "simultane" *Roughing It* in London. Meanwhile Hotten had industriously exploited the numerous sketches that Mark Twain was publishing in the Buffalo *Express*, the *Galaxy*, and other papers. Late in November 1870 Hotten had published 10,000 copies of *The Piccadilly Annual of Entertaining Literature*, which contained (among other things) five Mark Twain sketches from the *Galaxy*.[68] Then late in 1871 Hotten published *Eye Openers* and *Screamers*, two little volumes that collected many more of Mark Twain's *Galaxy* pieces and a few from the *Express*. Moreover, early in 1872 Hotten announced plans to publish *Practical Jokes with Artemus Ward*, which turned out to include seventeen more Mark Twain pieces. And in August 1872 he began plans for *The Choice Humorous Works of Mark Twain*, an immense single-volume collection of all the material he had previously published under separate titles—and then some.

As we shall see, all this furious activity did not ingratiate Hotten with Mark Twain, who earned nothing from such books. Indeed, Hotten's growing catalog of Mark Twain's books soon prompted the author and the Routledges to cooperate on several more "authorized" or "copyright" editions after *Roughing It*, including a new issue of

[66]Clemens to Bliss, [21] June 1871, *CL3*, letter 60.

[67]Mark Twain was aware of Hotten's edition as early as 24 October 1870, when the Buffalo *Express* reprinted the *Saturday Review's* notice of it (see "An Entertaining Article," no. 334). Hotten also sent him a copy, which arrived in Hartford in January 1871 (Orion Clemens to Clemens, 25 January 1871, MTP). A Canadian piracy of *Innocents* set from the American edition appeared sometime in 1870; a Canadian piracy of JF4a also appeared sometime after April 1870 (Gordon Roper, "Mark Twain and His Canadian Publishers: A Second Look," *Papers of the Bibliographical Society of Canada* 5 [1966]: 32). Mark Twain noted in his letter to Bliss: "There seems to be no convenient way to beat those Canadian re-publishers anyway" ([21] June 1871, *CL3*, letter 60).

[68]Chatto and Windus Ledger Book 1, p. 7; see *BAL* 3323.

JF4a. On 16 May 1872, some 4,000 copies of JF4b were received by the Routledges; they had been printed from the unaltered plates of JF4a, but the two sketches from the *Burlesque Autobiography* pamphlet were reset and added at the end.[69] On JF4b the author finally acknowledged the Routledges in the same way Artemus Ward had acknowledged Hotten: "'*Messrs. George Routledge & Sons are my only authorized London publishers.*'—MARK TWAIN."[70] This position was one they were to hold, as it turned out, only very briefly during 1872 and 1873.

3. *Early Plans for* "Mark Twain's Sketches" *(1868–1870)*

The enormous success of the English piracies of JF1 had very little effect on Mark Twain's basic dissatisfaction with the book—a dissatisfaction that arose early and lasted long. When his new friend Mrs. Fairbanks wrote to praise the book as "authentic" in February 1868, he responded with bitter sarcasm:

You just smother me with compliments about that book! There is nothing that makes me prouder than to be regarded by intelligent people as "authentic." A name I have coveted so long—& secured at last! *I* don't care anything about being humorous, or poetical, or eloquent, or anything of that kind—the end & aim of my ambition is to be authentic—is to be considered authentic. But don't italicise it—don't do that—there isn't any need of it—*such* a compliment as

---

[69]Routledge Ledger Book 4, p. 261. JF4b (*BAL* 3338) is textually identical with JF4a except in the new sketches, both of which were set in slightly smaller type from a copy of BA2 (see section 4 below). JF4b was not the last edition published by the Routledges. Hotten's plates for JF3 were sold by Chatto and Windus in July 1874 to Ward, Lock and Co., who reissued them with slight alterations and a new title page; these plates eventually found their way into the Routledges' hands. A book printed from the JF3 plates but bearing the Routledges' title page was deposited with the British Museum on 21 April 1882 (call number 12316.d.34), but it is not apparent from the Routledge records how many copies of this reissue were sold. The records do show that the plates of JF4b continued in use until 1902, and that between the first impression (16 May 1872) and the last (28 May 1902) the Routledges printed 60,845 copies of it. Added to 8,000 copies each of JF2 and JF4a, that yields a grand total of 76,845 copies between 1867 and 1902 (Routledge Ledger Book 4, p. 261; Book 5, p. 305; Book 6, p. 341). Chatto and Windus sold 2,000 copies of JF3 in 1874 before selling the plates, bringing the sale of JF3 to 21,000 copies overall. Not counting copies issued from these plates after 1874, the total number of copies of Mark Twain's first book sold in England by Hotten, Chatto and Windus, and the Routledges comes to nearly 98,000.

[70]Title page, JF4b. The phrase recurs throughout the Routledges' advertising copy.

that, wouldn't have escaped my notice, even without the underscore.[71]

By late December his bitterness had grown still more emphatic. When
Olivia wrote that she had been reading his work, he responded with
violent emphasis: *"Don't* read a word in that Jumping Frog book,
Livy—*don't.* I hate to hear that infamous volume mentioned. I would
be glad to know that every copy of it was burned, & gone forever." And
he resolved that he would "never write another like it."[72] The
vehemence of this rejection is so remarkable that it is tempting to
regard it as merely the result of damaged pride. But there were objective grounds for his unhappiness: he was manifestly dissatisfied with
the accuracy of the texts and even with the choice of sketches for a
book which, as we have conjectured, was largely the work of his editor,
Webb.

The immense task of writing and revising *The Innocents Abroad*
effectively forestalled any plans Mark Twain had to supersede Webb's
collection of sketches, but in May 1869, even as he was reading the
revised proofs of *Innocents* in Hartford, his interest in a new sketchbook was rekindling: "Livy dear, please send me that mutilated copy
of the Jumping Frog of mine, if it is there—send by express, not mail. It
has writing in it & would require letter postage—& it is considered
improper to break the law."[73] Apparently Mark Twain had already
begun to revise the texts of his twenty-seven JF1 sketches.

The Doheny *Jumping Frog* (1869): JF1**MT**

Mark Twain's earliest known revisions of JF1 are preserved in a copy of
the book now in the Estelle Doheny Collection, St. John's Seminary,
Camarillo, California. Like a number of other books in the Doheny
collection, this copy of JF1 (here designated JF1**MT**) was preserved in
the author's library at the time of his death:[74] the inside front cover is
signed "Mark Twain," and his revisions, in pencil and ink, appear
throughout. The date of the revisions cannot be certainly fixed, but he
could not have made them before 1869, the date of the title page.

---

[71]Clemens to Mary Mason Fairbanks, 20 February 1868, *CL1*, letter 193.

[72]Clemens to Olivia Langdon, 31 December 1868, *CL1*, letter 258.

[73]Clemens to Olivia Langdon, 13 May 1869, *CL2*, letter 53.

[74]Alan Gribben, "The Library and Reading of Samuel L. Clemens" (Ph.D. diss.,
University of California, Berkeley, 1974), pp. 252–253.

Moreover, the revisions, in their striving for even greater propriety and restraint, seem to accord with Mark Twain's conciliatory attitude in that year—the year of his courtship. Indeed, JF1**MT** is almost certainly the "mutilated copy" that he asked Olivia to send in May 1869.

Mark Twain singled out eight sketches in the table of contents, using a dash or a plus sign, and he revised four of these in the book itself. Three additional sketches not so marked in the table of contents were also revised, making a total of seven. The revisions vary from the extensive alterations and corrections in "Jim Smiley and His Jumping Frog" to the deletion of merely two sentences in "Depart, Ye Accursed!": "I have cursed them in behalf of outraged bachelordom. They deserve it" (presumably a sentiment not worthy of a man about to become a husband). Among other changes, he canceled "tearful" and "infernal" in "Whereas" and changed "get up and snort" to "just rair & charge" in "The Christmas Fireside."[75]

Despite these meticulous (though uneven) changes, JF1**MT** was never used as printer's copy for a later edition of Mark Twain's sketches. Its interest lies in the fact that Mark Twain would eventually make many identical or similar changes in collections that appeared in 1872 and 1873. When we do not have his marked printer's copy for these later editions, characteristic changes detected by collation must remain only conjecturally authorial in the absence of corroborating evidence. But when these changes coincide with the autograph evidence in JF1**MT**, we may be almost certain that they were instituted by Mark Twain. For instance, when in JF1**MT** he canceled "nearly" and "certainly" in "Jim Smiley and His Jumping Frog," he provided strong evidence that the same changes in the Routledges' 1872 *Mark Twain's Sketches* were his work.

When *The Innocents Abroad* was published in August 1869, it soon demonstrated Mark Twain's enormous popularity, selling nearly

---

[75]The seven sketches revised in JF1**MT** are "Whereas" (no. 94), "A Touching Story of George Washington's Boyhood" (no. 95), "The Facts" (no. 116), "Jim Smiley and His Jumping Frog" (no. 119), "The Christmas Fireside" (no. 148), "Voyage of the Ajax" (no. 182), and "Depart, Ye Accursed!" (no. 199). Of these only nos. 94, 119, 148, and 199 were marked in the table of contents, all with a dash. The four additional sketches indicated there but not revised are "How to Cure a Cold" (no. 63), " 'Mark Twain' on the Launch of the Steamer 'Capital' " (no. 136), "The Pioneers' Ball" (no. 137), and "Origin of Illustrious Men" (no. 193). Both nos. 63 and 193 were designated by plus signs, nos. 136 and 137 by dashes.

40,000 copies by the end of January 1870. It was on the strength of this showing that Mark Twain decided not only to move ahead with plans for another book like the first one—*Roughing It*[76]—but also to clear the ground for a new book of sketches. "I am prosecuting Webb in the N. Y. Courts," he wrote Bliss, "—think the result will be that he will yield up the copyright & plates of the Jumping Frog, if I let him off from paying me money. Then I shall break up those plates, & prepare a new Vol. of Sketches, but on a different & more 'taking' model."[77]

The issue of the JF1 copyright was not resolved until the end of the year—but it was a year that the author filled with ambitious literary plans and a great deal of bargaining with Bliss. Mark Twain's wedding in early February, his obligations to the Buffalo *Express*, and a series of illnesses in the family were all major distractions. But early in March the author engaged to write short sketches on a monthly basis for the *Galaxy* magazine, and his agreement with the editors specified that he was to retain the copyright of all his material. On March 11 he told Bliss, "They want a publishing house there to <issue> have the privilege of issuing the matter in book form at the end of the year in a $1.50 book (250 pp. 12mo,) & pay me a royalty of 20 <per> cents on each copy sold"—that is, about 14 percent, more than double his percentage on *Innocents*. Of course, he said, Bliss would "have to have a bid" in the project as well, but he added, "I *own* the matter after use in the magazine & have the privilege of doing just what I please with it." Such veiled threats were not, of course, lost on "one of the smartest business men in America" (as Mark Twain described him in November):[78] Bliss spent most of the year bargaining with Mark Twain for his exclusive devotion to the American Publishing Company.

Mark Twain clearly understood his position, and his correspondence with Bliss shows that he also knew how to bargain. On March 11 he told Bliss that he had "a sort of vague half-notion of spending the

---

[76]"I mean to write another book during the summer. This one has proven such a surprising success that I féel encouraged" (Clemens to Mary Mason Fairbanks, 6 January 1870, *CL2*, letter 141).

[77]Clemens to Bliss, 22 January 1870, *CL2*, letter 153.

[78]Clemens to Bliss, 11 March 1870, *CL2*, letter 172; Clemens to Orion Clemens, 5 November 1870, *CL2*, letter 239.

summer in England.—I could write a telling book." By April 1 Bliss had taken this bait, for the author reported that his publisher was *"very anxious that I should go abroad during the summer & get a book written for next spring."* But on April 23 Mark Twain indicated that he was not quite ready to pursue the English book: "When you come," he wrote Bliss from Buffalo, "we'll talk books & business. I wish my wife wanted to spend the summer in England, but I'm afraid she don't." This was tantalizing indeed. In fact, Mark Twain went on to tease Bliss with vague allusions to a variety of projects: "I have a bid for a book from a Philada subscription house offering unlimitedly," he wrote on May 5, deliberately withholding details. And on May 20 he reported, "Appleton wants me to furnish a few lines of letter press for a humorous picture-book—that is, two lines of remarks under each picture. I have intimated that if the pictures & the pay are both good, I will do it. What do you think of it?" Bliss must have grumbled, for on July 4 Mark Twain backed away from both projects: "I fancy the book you speak of must be the Appleton book," he wrote, forgetting the offer from the Philadelphia subscription house. "I cannot think of any other, & have no knowledge of any other. But I shall probably never have to do the Appleton book." The company disliked his terms: "Therefore it is *far from likely* that any 'humorous book' will issue from my pen shortly."[79]

Just a few days later, on July 15, this strategy bore its first fruit: Bliss traveled to Elmira, where he and Mark Twain signed a contract for *Roughing It* which set the author's royalty at $7\frac{1}{2}$ percent—an unprecedented figure for subscription publishing. Mark Twain agreed, overoptimistically, to submit the printer's copy within six months.[80] But even now that he had formally assumed the burden of writing a second long book, his appetite for other projects was unappeased. He certainly knew, as he told Orion in November, that Bliss was still trying to keep him "from 'whoring after strange gods,' which is Scripture for deserting to other publishers," and his persistent interest in

---

[79]Clemens to Bliss, 11 March 1870, *CL2*, letter 172; Clemens to Mr. and Mrs. Jervis Langdon, 1 April 1870, *CL2*, letter 180; Clemens to Bliss: 23 April 1870, *CL2*, letter 187; 5 May 1870, *CL2*, letter 191; 20 May 1870, *CL2*, letter 195; 4 July 1870, *CL2*, letter 210.

[80]Mark Twain's contract specified that he was to deliver the manuscript "as soon as practicable, but as early as 1st of January next if said Company shall desire it" (Yale).

such projects was in part a means of covert bargaining. By late November, for instance, he had put his "greedy hands on the best man in America," J. H. Riley, with whom he planned to collaborate on a book about the South African diamond mines. He wrote Bliss demanding not only an advance of $1,500, but a royalty of 10 percent —settling in the end for $8\frac{1}{2}$ percent. But bargaining with Bliss was only part of Mark Twain's drive toward other projects: he was fascinated by the prospect of fast, easy money and by the wide publicity he hoped to achieve with "a humorous picture-book"—the kind of publicity he did achieve, for example, with the graphic comedy of his "Fortifications of Paris" (no. 323) in the September 17 Buffalo *Express*. In fact, as his clippings from the *Express* and the *Galaxy* gradually accumulated, he was strongly tempted to reprint them in some spectacular way. On October 13 he wrote Bliss that he had a "notion to let the Galaxy publishers have a volume of old sketches for a 'Mark Twain's Annual—1871'—provided they will pay me about 25 per cent. That is what they offered once, I believe." His initial thought was to excuse this project as an ephemeral one: "My idea is to use in this, among other things, some few sketches which will not 'keep.' " But he considered more carefully, canceled the sentence, and put the matter squarely in business terms: "I believe a Christmas volume will out-pay Josh Billings' Allminax. What do you think? Write me at once—& don't discourage me."[81]

Evidently Bliss did discourage him, probably by reminding him that the *Roughing It* contract stipulated that he was "not to write or furnish manuscript for any other book unless for said company during the preparation & sale of said manuscript & book."[82] *Roughing It* was far from done, and would not be done until October of the following year. So when Webb proposed a revised edition of JF1 in late November 1870, Mark Twain diplomatically declined: "I could not consent to a new edition of the J. F. any time within two or three years without vitiating my contracts with my present publishers & creating dissatisfaction." And he explained that he would have issued his "Galaxy . . . & other sketches, in a couple of volumes, before this, but

---

[81]Clemens to Orion Clemens, 5 November 1870, *CL2*, letter 239; Clemens to Bliss: 28 November 1870, *CL2*, letter 258; 13 October 1870, *CL2*, letter 233.

[82]So sweeping a prohibition ("during the preparation & sale") may seem merely the result of Bliss's sloppy legal writing, but as later developments show, Bliss knew perfectly well what the contract meant (see section 4 below).

for the reason abovementioned." This response shows admirable restraint; indeed, on November 14 Mark Twain had told another correspondent that he could not "meddle with the Almanac business with a clear conscience—have had heaps of offers, but that belongs to Josh & I won't touch it."[83] Nevertheless, within a few weeks the temptation had become irresistible, and while he put Webb off with polite excuses, Mark Twain quietly forged ahead with two plans to reprint his sketches: a comprehensive collection with Bliss, and the kind of cheap illustrated pamphlet that had been tempting him all year, with Sheldon and Company of New York.

4. *Mark Twain's (Burlesque) Autobiography and First Romance (1870–1871): BA1, BA2, and BA3*

The production of *Mark Twain's (Burlesque) Autobiography* (BA1), a fifty-page pamphlet, was an experimental interlude in the evolution of Mark Twain's plans to issue an American edition of his sketches. As it turned out, the complications of production with an unfamiliar publisher, the friction created with Bliss, and finally the disappointing sales and hostile reactions of the press were at least momentarily discouraging, and they influenced Mark Twain's attitude toward similar projects in the future. BA1 was not to be the last of such cheap sketchbooks, but as a publishing venture it proved an instructive mistake.

On 8 December 1870 Mark Twain wired a proposal for the pamphlet to Sheldon and Company, his *Galaxy* publishers, who had been urging him to collect his magazine sketches. Although his telegram is not extant, it seems likely that he proposed essentially what BA1 now contains: one new sketch, "A Burlesque Autobiography" (no. 355); a slightly revised version of "An Awful—Terrible Medieval Romance" (no. 276);[84] and a series of cartoons for which he devised the captions, "The House That Jack Built."[85] The audience Mark Twain aimed for

---

[83]Clemens to Webb, 26 November 1870, *CL2*, letter 257; Clemens to Mr. Haney, 14 November 1870, *CL2*, letter 249.

[84]First published in the Buffalo *Express*, 1 January 1870, p. 6.

[85]Mark Twain adapted this nursery rhyme to ridicule the principals in the Erie Railroad scandal: he must therefore have made some plan for the illustrator to follow. The piece is scheduled to appear in the collection of social and political writings in The Works of Mark Twain.

was the holiday crowd—the same that made Josh Billings' *Allminax* a best seller at Christmas and New Year's.

On December 9 Isaac E. Sheldon agreed to undertake the pamphlet: "We will publish it, and of course do our very best as to getting it out in time &c &c; and give you half of all the book can be made to pay. This is much better for you than any copyright we could name, if the book proves a success." In a postscript Sheldon added, "Should you prefer a copyright we would give 15 per cent on the retail price." Although Mark Twain himself may have suggested the half-profit arrangement (it was a favorite scheme of his), he ultimately decided instead to take the latter offer, which was the safer if the less profitable of the two. At any rate, Sheldon went on to warn in the same letter that it was "of course late in the season to get out a book and there are always delays we can never calculate on, as each step in the process of manufacturing is made."[86] The author evidently dismissed this caution, for he set out for New York the next day "to issue a pamphlet," as he told Mrs. Fairbanks. He stayed a week before returning home to Buffalo on December 17, well before the little book was ready to "issue." Two days later Sheldon assured him that he would "see that the book is copyrighted before it is issued," and that he would also send "a complete proof . . . before we attempt to print the book."[87] The implication of this letter is that Mark Twain thought, and Sheldon tacitly agreed, that proofs of the book would soon be ready. In reality, however, Mark Twain would see no proofs of the text until sometime in mid-January 1871.

The delay was caused by just those incalculable problems that Sheldon had mentioned on December 9. The drawings for "The House That Jack Built" were to be done by Henry Louis Stephens and engraved by D. B. Gulick, but the drawings were not ready for the engraver until December 22. On that day Sheldon assured Mark Twain that he would send him "proofs as soon as they are engraved, which they promise shall be the end of next week." And he himself promised, "As soon as the engravings are done I will get the book into type &

---

[86]Sheldon and Company to Clemens, 9 December 1870, MTP. Sheldon later wrote that his company had "agreed to pay [Mark Twain] a royalty of *six cents* on every copy sold" (Appendix C2, volume 1). Since the paper-covered pamphlet sold for forty cents, Mark Twain's royalty amounted to 15 percent.

[87]Clemens to Mary Mason Fairbanks, 17 December 1870, *CL2*, letter 263; Sheldon to Clemens, 19 December 1870, MTP.

have you see the whole before it is printed. You will probably see some changes which can be made to advantage."[88]

Mark Twain must have recognized at this point that the little pamphlet could not possibly appear before New Year's, and perhaps not even in January. On December 29 Sheldon reassured him that the unexpected delay would have no effect on overall sales: "I think the book will do quite as well 6 or 8 weeks from this time as it could now. During the month of Jan almost every bookseller is engaged on his inventory." Sheldon agreed, however, that "it is best to get the book ready just as fast as possible; even if we hold them for a time after they are all made." And he repeated that "the engrav[ings] are promised for the end of this week." Sheldon managed to send Mark Twain "proofs of all the cuts" (that is, engravings) on December 31 as promised, and he asked the author to approve and return them: "Please also send in 'The House that Jack built' just as you want it set up. I understood that you were to make some changes in it to make it fit this case better. Please also indicate where each cut is to go. . . . As soon as I hear from you, the whole book will go into type."[89]

On 4 January 1871 Bliss wrote to inquire after Mark Twain's health. "Have looked for advt. of your pamphlet also," he said; "Your brother & myself have expected to see it advertised. What is the title?"[90] Mark Twain, too, must have wondered about the delay, but he waited until January 15 before writing Sheldon to complain that he had not yet seen any proofs. Sheldon answered on January 18 that he had been delayed by the "stereotypers": "It was placed in their hands as soon as the cuts were done & it would have gone on at once, but they had a peculiar font of type which I wanted to use, which was then in use; they promised to send me half of the book in type last week Monday. [I]nstead of that I rec'd one sample page last Thursday." He also admitted that he had not been able to supervise the project as closely as necessary because he had been "upside down moving."[91] Still, Mark

---

[88]Sheldon to Clemens, 22 December 1870, MTP. Sheldon said that he would have given the drawings to "Richardson who is a very good engraver but Stephens insisted that Gulick was *just* the man. They have agreed to make them satisfactory to you."

[89]Sheldon to Clemens, 29 and 31 December 1870, MTP.

[90]Bliss to Clemens, 4 January 1871, MTP. Bliss was simply touching bases with Mark Twain, assuring him indirectly that the pamphlet did not arouse his anxiety.

[91]Sheldon to Clemens, 18 January 1871, MTP. Sheldon began, "Yours of 15th is just at hand." BA1 is not in fact stereotyped; it was electrotyped by Smith and McDougall, 82 Beekman Street, New York City. Sheldon and Mark Twain used the two terms interchangeably.

Twain's complaint had some effect: on the next day Sheldon sent "8 or 10 pages of proof," but he noted, "The stereotyper has forgotten my (your) direction to have each other page a cut. That however can yet be done by simply changing the no on the page." Evidently the page numbers were changed and the pages imposed in the desired order, for the eleven illustrations appeared distributed throughout the text of the sketches, although not invariably on "each other page." On January 21 Sheldon indicated that he thought Mark Twain himself was causing delay: "Why do you not, return the proof sent to you some days since? I fear that it may not have reached you." Sheldon said that to "save time" he planned now to "set up & cast all the balance at once. Any verbal corrections can be made in the plates."[92]

On January 25 Orion wrote to report on a new problem. Bliss had encountered Sheldon on the street in New York; he "at first refused to shake hands, being angry about a neglect to answer a couple of letters," but this petty grievance was soon forgotten in the light of more serious matters. Orion said that the two men had apparently "made it up" when "Sheldon told [Bliss] that the cuts (10 full page) cost him $400, and wanted Bliss to circulate it for him, and he thinks he will do so." But if Bliss's quarrel with Sheldon was shortlived, he now nursed a small grudge against Mark Twain:

Sheldon told him it was to be a 50 cent pamphlet & 75¢ in muslin. Against that Bliss protests. He says that makes it a book. He will not object to a pamphlet at 30 or 40 cents, but does to one at 50¢; and especially to the muslin. He says if you let that be printed in muslin he will not come down on you with the contract, but he will always feel like you haven't treated him right. His company enjoys the prestige of being the sole publishers of Mark Twain, which they use with their agents, and the advantage of this prestige they will lose if a book of yours comes out published by somebody else.

Orion added a mitigating postscript: "Bliss is anxious that my letter should not show any feeling on his part in regard to the Sheldon pamphlet." Nevertheless, Mark Twain certainly took the objection seriously, for on the envelope of Orion's letter he noted: "Jan. 27—71 I wrote She[l]don to-day protesting against a higher price than 25

----

[92]Sheldon to Clemens, 19 and 21 January 1871, MTP.

cents for the pamphlet."[93] On January 31 he telegraphed Bliss: "Have an appointment at Grand Hotel eleven tomorrow can you be there at noon." This appointment was with Sheldon, who had recently occupied new quarters "under the Grand Central Hotel."[94] Mark Twain probably hoped to extract a promise from Sheldon to lower the price of BA1 and to issue only a token number of copies in the offending muslin. Sheldon must have insisted, in turn, that the pamphlet should sell for at least forty cents, and although he agreed to the restricted number of cloth copies, he in fact went on to issue as many as he liked. In 1882 Mark Twain privately threatened to double his royalty on these unauthorized copies: "If I could find out how many cloth-bound books Sheldon sold, I would require him to pay me 25 cents on every one over the 75 copies (he was to bind no more than that.)"[95]

One more matter almost intervened between BA1 and a breathless public. When Mark Twain returned home from his trip to New York (and Washington, D.C.) he found Olivia dangerously ill with typhoid fever. With his wife apparently near death Mark Twain was struck by how "utterly incongruous" it would be for him to appear as a humorist in the *Galaxy* memoranda column, and on February 5 he telegraphed Frank Church to ask him to withdraw the department from the March issue and also to "tell Sheldon to stop the book."[96] After some confusion, the department was withdrawn and the request about BA1 passed along to Sheldon, who received it on February 10. Sheldon answered, "The Pamphlet I can hold a few days if you desire it, but a few samples of it have got out. I might hold the Editors copies back, while the distant orders are on their way by freight lines & they will not reach their destination for some time to come." Then, in an effort to calm Mark Twain's feelings of pending impropriety, he added, "Of course it is universally understood that this book was

[93]Orion Clemens to Clemens, 25 January 1871, MTP. Orion had recently been hired by Bliss to help edit the *American Publisher*, hence his role here as go-between.

[94]Clemens to Bliss, telegram, 31 January 1871, *CL3*, letter 19; "The Galaxy Advertiser," p. 4, following the last page of *Galaxy* 11 (January 1871).

[95]Clemens to Charles L. Webster, 24 September 1882, *MTBus*, p. 201.

[96]Mark Twain's telegram is not extant. The quotations are from Francis P. Church to Clemens, 9 February 1871, MTP. The date of Mark Twain's telegram is given in Sheldon to Clemens, 10 February 1871, MTP: "Your telegram dated the 5th was first seen by me about 2 o'clock to-day (the 10th)."

written long ago & has been in the press for some time."[97] So much for instant publication.

Because the printer's copy for BA1 does not survive, we cannot know what revisions, if any, Mark Twain made on the proofs. As we have seen, Sheldon was eager to have the electrotype plates made as soon as the book was finally typeset, and he planned to make revisions by altering the plates if Mark Twain did not return the corrected proofs before plating began.[98] It is impossible to tell from the copies of BA1 we have examined whether any plate alterations were in fact made. Collation of BA1 with the first printing of "Medieval Romance" in the Buffalo *Express* shows that Mark Twain made only a few revisions in the sketch, probably when he prepared the printer's copy in early December 1870. A secretarial copy of the manuscript for "A Burlesque Autobiography" does survive, but it was probably not used as printer's copy. Collation of the transcription with BA1 shows that a few small revisions were made before the sketch was printed. These revisions, as well as any last-minute changes in the other two pieces, could have been made at any time before the book was printed in late January or early February.

Precise figures on the sale of BA1 have not been found, but nothing indicates that it quite fulfilled Mark Twain's expectations. He made some effort to publicize the pamphlet in December 1870, when he still thought publication was imminent: "I would like it very much if you would put the above item in your column of little floating paragraphs & general notes," he wrote Whitelaw Reid of the New York *Tribune*. A few days later, on December 29, the *Tribune* complied with an announcement that Mark Twain would "publish a burlesque autobiography, in pamphlet form, in a few days, through Sheldon & Co." Mark Twain also volunteered to write advertising copy for Sheldon, who replied to his suggestion on December 29: "Your idea is first rate & it is the very thing that I intended to do. We are accustomed whenever we have a book of any account to set up & print off 100 about like the inclosed & send to every paper with which we advertise.... Suppose you write out the announcement as you

---

[97]Sheldon to Clemens, 10 February 1871, MTP.
[98]Sheldon to Clemens, 21 January 1871, MTP.

would like it . . . & we will set it up & send it out thoroughly. I would like to get up just as much interest in advance as possible."[99]

By mid-January 1871 Sheldon was using the forthcoming pamphlet to promote the *Galaxy*, offering a free copy with every four-dollar subscription. Whether this was part of Mark Twain's "first rate" idea is not known, but in any event there seems to have been a sizable prepublication sale. On February 10 Sheldon told Mark Twain that he could not further delay the pamphlet because of Olivia's illness, explaining that "our orders are very large & our promises & contracts are such that it will be possible to hold it but a few days." On that day Sheldon filed for copyright in his own name, and eight days later —on February 18—two copies were deposited with the Library of Congress.[100]

Official publication was delayed another two weeks: on March 4 Sheldon announced it in the New York *Times*. Evidently Bliss had been persuaded to help distribute the pamphlet (as Orion had mentioned in January), for an advertisement in the first issue of his *American Publisher* boldly trumpeted "Mark Twain's New Book" as the "most humorous . . . published in years." It bragged somewhat deceptively,

One Hundred Thousand Copies

IT IS EXPECTED WILL BE

Sold Within Ten Days.

A more restrained advertisement in the New York *Times* one week later reported "forty thousand copies sold in three days." And the loyal New York *Tribune* reported on March 10 that "orders for Mark Twain's burlesque biography have been received, it is said, to the extent of 50,000 copies, and his publishers expect to sell 100,000. As Twain gets six cents a copy, he may consider his $6,000 for such a bagatelle rather easily made."[101]

---

[99]Clemens to Reid, 26 December 1870, *CL2*, letter 273; New York *Tribune*, 29 December 1870, p. 4; Sheldon to Clemens, 29 December 1870, MTP.

[100]Sheldon to Clemens, 10 February 1871, MTP; copyright no. 1107, Library of Congress, from the report of William A. Moore in the copyright office, 1 July 1975.

[101]New York *Times*, 4 March 1871, p. 5; *American Publisher* 1 (April 1871): 7; New York *Times*, 11 March 1871, p. 5; New York *Tribune*, 10 March 1871, p. 5.

Reviews were relatively scarce, invariably brief, and, with few exceptions, negative in tone. The New York *Tribune* and the Boston *Evening Transcript* made valiant efforts to be amused. BA1 was, according to the first paper,

an effusion of filial piety describing the family tree of his ancestors, and enlivened by certain sentimental reflections of an instructive character. The volume also contains the first romance of the author, which now appears in print for the first time, having apparently been crowded out of the popular weekly journals by the pretensions of less modest writers. Several artistic productions of the pre-Raphaelite school adorn the pages of the work, illustrating the triumphs of modern finance in New-York, and originally intended to accompany a recent article on the subject in the "Westminster Review."

The *Transcript* briefly concurred, saying that BA1 was "crammed with fun, of which the illustrations form no small part. The hits with pen and pencil will be enjoyed by all interested in Erie and other Fiskal operations." But most reviewers could not summon up even that much facetious energy. The Chicago *Tribune* indicated that "as a whole the work is not up to Twain's average of humor, and suggests, perhaps, that the well has been pumped too long." Alluding to Mark Twain's "family tree" (a hangman's gibbet), it suggested that "if capital punishment were the penalty of a poor burlesque, he would soon adorn it, for the Autobiography cannot be called a success." And the editor of *Godey's Lady's Book and Magazine* in Philadelphia was even more severe: "This autobiography does not do justice to Mark Twain's reputation for humor. The necessity for making a book must have borne very heavily on him to compel him to send before the public such a collection of weak jokes and mild witticisms as this. We do not mean to say that it is not funny, and absurd, or that the reader will not laugh at every page, but it does not do full justice to the author."[102]

The Boston *Literary World* specifically attacked the book as a rather transparent scheme on the publisher's part to reap excessive profits. It said with heavy irony:

The honor of this remarkable publication should not be monopolized

---

[102]New York *Tribune*, 10 March 1871, p. 6; Boston *Evening Transcript*, 9 March 1871, p. 1; Chicago *Tribune*, 13 March 1871, p. 3; *Godey's Lady's Book and Magazine* 82 (June 1871): 575. We are indebted to Louis J. Budd for help in locating reviews.

by the author; a large part of it belongs to the gentlemanly and liberal-minded publishers, who have served the public well. See how they have done it. The stereotype-plates and illustrations of the Autobiography cost not far from $400, and for the text—which would be dear at two and three pence—allow one hundred dollars. Here we have $500 as the cost of the book all ready to be printed. The cost of manufacturing each copy—paper, press-work, etc.—could not exceed four cents. The publishers announce that they have sold 40,000 copies. The actual cost of these, including the making of plates, etc., was $2,000; the cost to the public was $16,000, the books selling at forty cents per copy (in cloth at seventy-five cents). This is a living profit, and, considering the dulness of the book-trade, very encouraging.

The reviewer was more direct in his criticism of Mark Twain, saying that his name raised the "suspicion that the work is one of humor; but the book itself affords not the feeblest fibre of corroboration. . . . As to the literary merit of these effusions, they would have had a more appropriate place in some quack medicine almanac. We are sincerely sorry to see Mark Twain, who has done some admirable work, lending himself to a mere money-catching scheme like this."[103]

Mark Twain was anything but indifferent to this sort of criticism. On April 26 he complained to Mrs. Fairbanks that although he was still "pegging away" at the manuscript of *Roughing It*, he expected it to have "no success" because the "papers have found at last the courage to pull me down off my pedestal & cast slurs at me—& that is simply a popular author's death rattle. Though he wrote an *inspired* book after that, it would not save him."[104] BA1 had been less than inspired, and Mark Twain was convinced that no financial reward, however large, would be sufficient to mend the wound to his reputation.

Although the profits from BA1 may well have been substantial, they were inevitably of short duration. Sheldon himself explained on April 4 that "the returns for copyright, after the first settlement, will of course not be large, as a book like this has its main sale at

[103]*Literary World* 1 (1 April 1871): 165. The *Literary World's* estimate of costs was not far wrong: according to the publisher himself the paper-covered copy cost four cents to produce, the muslin-bound one only ten cents (Sheldon and Company to James R. Osgood, 19 October 1882, MTP). Sheldon had bragged in 1871 that the plates cost $400 (Orion Clemens to Clemens, 25 January 1871, MTP).

[104]Clemens to Mary Mason Fairbanks, 26 April 1870, *CL3*, letter 49.

once." Two days later Mark Twain acknowledged this letter and put his finger on yet another problem: "You intimate that the present pamphlet don't give a man his money's worth, considering the price. I feared that that was so, at first—but you said 40 cents was the cheapest it could be sold at."[105] It was an important lesson.

Albert Bigelow Paine reported that "a year or two" after publication Mark Twain "realized the mistake of this book, bought in the plates and destroyed them." The author clearly did realize his mistake but the plates of BA1 remained in existence, if not in use, until 1882. Mark Twain, however, seems not to have received any substantial payment from the book after 1874. In September 1882 Sheldon and Company quietly advertised that the plates would be sold at auction, and James R. Osgood, Mark Twain's publisher at the time, offered to buy them, saying that "it would be better that [they] should not fall into the hands of any cheap shyster." Osgood almost certainly bought the plates and had them destroyed. But Mark Twain's initial impulse was to embarrass Sheldon for alleged nonpayment of copyright. He fashioned an advertisement to be placed in the New York *Herald* "Personals" column: "Will the publishers, Sheldon & Co., furnish to the undersigned a statement of account (now eight years overdue, although several times demanded,) & accompany it with the overdue cash, or will they not? And will they also be warned & make no attempt to sell certain stereotype plates advertised by them, except to be broken up? Address MARK TWAIN, Hartford, Conn." On October 21 Osgood reported that Sheldon also had "about 1300 copies paper, and 50 cloth" on hand, for which he was asking a total of fifty-seven dollars (exclusive of copyright).[106] Presumably Mark Twain, through Osgood, also bought up and destroyed this remaining stock. He never published the provocative advertisement in the *Herald*.

Probably because Mark Twain conceived of BA1 as a pamphlet that he could issue in a matter of days, he made no effort to arrange with the Routledges for simultaneous publication in London, and both

---

[105]Sheldon to Clemens, 4 April 1871, MTP; Clemens to Sheldon, 6 April 1871, *CL3*, letter 45.

[106]*MTB*, 1:433; Osgood to Clemens, 22 September 1882, MTP; Clemens to Charles L. Webster, 24 September 1882, *MTBus*, p. 201; Osgood to Clemens, 21 October 1882, MTP.

they (with BA2) and Hotten (with BA3) soon pirated the little book, although neither undertook to reproduce the cartoons of "The House That Jack Built." Mark Twain made no contribution to either BA2 or BA3, and the textual differences between them are so slight that we cannot be absolutely sure whether both were set from BA1 or one was set from the other. Routledges' records indicate that a printing of 4,000 was received on 4 May 1871 and another impression of 4,000 at some unspecified later date, for a total of 8,000 copies.[107] Hotten's records show that he ordered 5,000 copies of his edition on May 6 and received the sheets on May 15, but 1,000 of these remained unsold by June 1873.[108] The Routledges published sometime in the first two weeks of May and sold their pamphlets for sixpence. Hotten must not have published until late in May and likewise sold his work for sixpence, although he also advertised a more expensive binding for three shillings and sixpence. Hotten described the volume as "a very droll book indeed" and claimed that "readers of this Author's 'Innocents Abroad' will not be disappointed with any acquaintance they may form with the new book."[109] He also advertised his book as the "Author's Edition, containing twice as much as any other," because he included what he doubtless regarded as a bonus: in addition to "A Burlesque Autobiography" and "Medieval Romance" he reprinted "Advice to Parents" and "Train up a Child, and Away He Goes"—two sketches that he believed were written by Mark Twain because they had been published in the Buffalo *Express*, albeit over the signature of Carl Byng.[110]

5. *"Mark Twain's Sketches" (1870–1871)*

The path for a volume of sketches like JF1 but on a "more 'taking' model" was cleared in late November and early December 1870. On

---

[107]Routledge Ledger Book 4, p. 529. BA2 is *BAL* 3595. The Routledges subsequently reprinted the BA2 sketches in their two-volume edition of *Roughing It* (1872) and in JF4b.

[108]Chatto and Windus Ledger Book 1, p. 443. BA3 is *BAL* 3329.

[109]*Bookseller*, 1 May 1871, p. 403.

[110]Hotten's advertisement appeared in BA3. The Carl Byng sketches were first published in the Buffalo *Express* on 31 December 1870, p. 2, and on 28 January 1871, p. 2. Mark Twain denied using the pseudonym "Carl Byng," and the balance of evidence supports this denial: see Jay Gillette, "Mark Twain vs. 'Carl Byng': A Computer-Assisted Test of Authorship," forthcoming.

November 26 Mark Twain apologized to Webb for instituting legal measures the previous January:

I have been very much ashamed of myself several times for getting in a passion & hiring a lawyer & making myself thoroughly uncomfortable when there was no occasion for it—but I hold that a man has *got* to make an ass of himself once a year anyhow, & I am sure I went along intelligently enough the *balance* of last year. I was very sorry, though, that I made trouble with a friend, because that is folly of such a particularly low grade.

On December 10 the JF1 printer gave Webb a full accounting of the copies printed and bound, and by the middle of the month Mark Twain could report that he had succeeded in buying his "'Jumping Frog' copyright back again from Webb." He planned now to "melt up the plates" and begin over again with Bliss. "I gave him his indebtedness ($600,) & $800 cash beside," he told Mrs. Fairbanks, "for <the> his share of the copyright & right of publication. Think of *purchasing* one's own property after never having received one cent from the publication!"[111]

It is likely that Mark Twain completed these negotiations in New York on the same trip that set BA1 in motion. He had originally planned to travel from New York to Hartford to discuss progress on *Roughing It* and the proposed book of sketches, but he returned to Buffalo without seeing Bliss. On December 17 he telegraphed him, "Got homesick. Will come shortly with sketches & manuscript." This trip was delayed until sometime in early January, perhaps indefinitely, but in the meantime Mark Twain set to work in earnest. On December 22 he wrote Bliss again, and his letter was filled with plans for the "real" sketchbook even as he awaited Sheldon's proofs of BA1.

To-day I arranged enough sketches to make <200> 134 pages of the book (200 words on a page, I estimated—size of De Witt Talmage's new book of rubbish.) I shall go right on till I have finished selecting, & then write a new sketch or so. One hundred of the pages selected to-day are scarcely known.

You'd better go to canvassing for the vol. of sketches *now*, hadn't you? You must illustrate it—& mind you, the man to do the choicest

---

[111]Clemens to Webb, 26 November 1870, *CL2*, letter 257; Clemens to Mary Mason Fairbanks, 17 December 1870, *CL2*, letter 263. The accounting, dated 10 December 1870 from S. W. Green, successor to John A. Gray and Green, is in MTP. See note 43 above.

of the pictures is Mullin—the Sisters are reforming him & he is sadly in need of work & money. . . . I think the sketch-book should be as profusely illustrated as the Innocents.

Mark Twain urged Bliss to "make out a contract for the sketch-book ($7\frac{1}{2}$ per cent.)"; and he continued to make a distinction between this project and other, cheaper, sketchbooks: "I think of a Jumping Frog *pamphlet* (illustrated) for next Christmas—do you want it?"[112]

The publisher answered this letter on December 28, adopting an ironic tone: "Yours of 22nd rec'd. Glad to hear you are progressing with the *Books*"—a gentle reminder that *Roughing It*, which Mark Twain had not mentioned, ought to take precedence over the sketch-book. Bliss also apologized for not sending the contracts for this and the Riley diamond-mine book sooner, and promised them the next day. He noted that he would begin to "canvass for Sketchbook as soon as Prospectus is ready for it," which of course could not be done until Mark Twain submitted at least part of the printer's copy. Bliss also agreed to "have Mullin illustrate the sketchbook," and congratulated Mark Twain on retrieving the "Jumping Frog" tale. It was here that Bliss rightly foresaw trouble, and in a nearly incoherent paragraph he suggested using the story in the large sketchbook, urged reissuing JF1 from the old plates, and concluded by reassuring the author that he would publish any pamphlet he wanted. His motive throughout was to retain control of Mark Twain's most famous work to date:

Dont you think Jumping Frog would be a big thing in the sketch book? Seems to me it will do you as much good there as anywhere & pay you back. Think strongly of it, & see if you dont think it will be best to put it there. By the way where are the plates & dont you want the book sold as it is—think we could sell a great many without making a noise—if you dont put it in Sketchbook—*Yes we want it in the pamphlet*, or at least talk it over with you before you let it go, if you use it that way. Are you coming on? . . . Will send Contracts to-morrow. Excuse my past <lies> failures.

Mark Twain was not, however, interested in using the tale in the large sketchbook or in reissuing JF1. Alluding to his current project

---

[112]Clemens to Bliss: telegram, 17 December 1870, *CL2*, letter 262; 22 December 1870, *CL2*, letter 267. "Mullin" is clearly the well-known illustrator Edward F. Mullen: he had recently helped illustrate Albert D. Richardson's *Beyond the Mississippi*, published by Bliss, and Mark Twain wanted him to illustrate BA1 "but didn't know he was sober now & in [the] hospital" run by the charitable "Sisters." Mullen did eventually contribute sketches to *Roughing It*.

with Sheldon, he reiterated his position to Bliss: "If this pamphlet pays, I want <to is> you to issue Jumping Frog *illustrated*, along with 2 other sketches for the *holidays* next year. I've paid high for the Frog & I want him to get his price back by himself. The Sketch Book will be good enough without him."[113] In short, the author regarded his project with Sheldon as an experiment, to be repeated if it turned out profitably. As we shall see, despite his disappointment over BA1 his basic promotional idea of simultaneously issuing cheap sketchbooks and expensive durable ones persisted into 1874 and 1875.

Bliss did in fact forward the contract for the sketchbook on December 29 as he had promised the previous day, and in his covering letter he said, "I mention your altering the old sketches a little to secure a new copyright on them. Would it not be a good plan. You know best, but if you dont do it some *scallawag* may run us opposition you know, by copying most of the work—& throwing it in the track. If the sketches are altered somewhat & a new copyright got it will hold on them pretty strong." Mark Twain no doubt agreed with Bliss's suggestion, but he probably didn't need any excuse to revise the sketches for this collection. On January 3 he told Bliss to "name the Sketch book '*Mark Twain's Sketches*' & go on canvassing like mad. Because if you don't hurry it will tread on the heels of the *big* book next August. In the course of a week I can have most of the matter ready for you I think. Am working like sin on it."[114]

Just two days later he apparently sent part of the printer's copy to Hartford; only the postscript from his letter of transmittal has survived: "The curious beasts & great contrasts in this Pre-deluge article offer a gorgeous chance for the artist's fancy & ingenuity, I think. Send both sketches to Mullen—he is the man to do them, I guess."[115] This postscript alludes to an extract from Mark Twain's long-germinating "Noah's Ark book,"[116] which was never published. The author included the extract (calling it "Pre-flood show") in a list of thirty-

---

[113]Bliss to Clemens, 28 December 1870, MTP; Clemens to Bliss, 3 January 1871, *CL3*, letter 1. Bliss dated his letter "Dec. 29," but it is clear from the context and from the envelope that it was mailed on December 28.

[114]Bliss to Clemens, 29 December 1870, MTP; Clemens to Bliss, 3 January 1871, *CL3*, letter 1.

[115]Clemens to Bliss, 5 January 1871, *CL3*, letter 3.

[116]A project Mark Twain began at least as early as August 1869, when it amounted to "70 or 80 pages" of manuscript (Clemens to Pamela Moffett, 20–21 August 1869,

eight sketches which apparently served as the preliminary table of
contents for "Mark Twain's Sketches" (see figure 19). The two-page
document, now in the Mark Twain Papers, lists thirteen items from
the Buffalo *Express* and ten from the *Galaxy*. In addition, it includes
six items from the *Spirit of the Times,* the *Broadway, Packard's
Monthly,* the New York *Tribune,* the Newark (N.J.) *Press,* and the
New York *Sunday Mercury,* as well as nine that were apparently unpublished: in short, many sketches that were "scarcely known,"
either because they had not appeared in the regular *Express* or *Galaxy*
columns or because they had not been published at all. Mark Twain
listed such things as "Great Land Slide" ("The Facts in the Great
Land-Slide Case," no. 286), which had appeared in the *Express* and
would eventually be made part of *Roughing It* (chapter 34). He listed
"Singular Sagacity" and "Dining w^h Cannibal," parts of two "Around
the World" letters (nos. 267 and 270), the first of which would also
find its way into *Roughing It* (chapter 61). The unpublished material
is less easily identified, but we may conjecture that the four sections
of "P.C.S." were "Pacific Coast Sketches," either extracted from the
Express "Around the World" letters or new reminiscences about the
West. "Tom Leathers in Wash^n" and "Sailor Story" remain unidentified, as does "Fearful Adventure." All in all, Mark Twain was planning a sketchbook that would indeed "give a man his money's worth."
His own calculation at the top of the first page suggests that he estimated an average length of twelve pages per sketch, for a total of 456
pages, doubtless to be "as profusely illustrated as the Innocents."

The nature of the printer's copy for this planned sketchbook is
clear because two of the pieces Mark Twain prepared at this time
have survived: one of them, "Around the World. Letter No. 2" (subtitled "Adventures in Hayti," no. 264) was not demonstrably included
in the preliminary table of contents; the other, "A Ghost Story"
(no. 278), was seventh on the list. Portions of both are reproduced in
figures 20–21. Mark Twain pasted these clippings to loose sheets,
revised them in pencil, and completed the work in his distinctive
purple ink of the 1870s, mostly in the margin. On the first leaf of each

---

CL2, letter 88). In January 1870 he wrote Bliss: "I mean to take plenty of time & pains
with the Noah's Ark book—maybe it will be several years before it is *all* written—
but it will be a perfect lightning-striker when it *is* done" (Clemens to Bliss, 22 January
1870, *CL2,* letter 153). The manuscript is not extant.

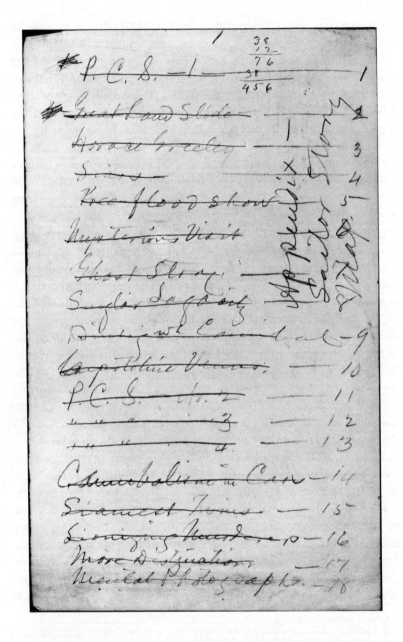

FIGURE 19A. First page of the preliminary table of contents for "Mark Twain's Sketches." The author canceled each title and assigned it a number, presumably after preparing the printer's copy.

1. Unidentified, possibly "Pacific Coast Sketches" from the "Around the World" letters published in the *Express* from October 1869 through January 1870 (nos. 263–270).

2. "The Facts in the Great Land-Slide Case," *Express*, 2 April 1870 (no. 286).

3. "Private Habits of Horace Greeley," *Spirit of the Times*, 7 November 1868 (scheduled to appear in the collection of social and political writings in The Works of Mark Twain).

4. "About a Remarkable Stranger," *Galaxy*, April 1871 (no. 358).

5. Never published, not extant.

6. "A Mysterious Visit," *Express*, 19 March 1870 (no. 285).

7. "A Ghost Story," *Express*, 15 January 1870 (no. 278).

8. From "Around the World. Letter Number 5," *Express*, 18 December 1869 (no. 267).

9. From "Around the World. Letter Number 8," *Express*, 29 January 1870 (no. 270).

10. "The Legend of the Capitoline Venus," *Express*, 23 October 1869 (no. 272).

11. See first entry above.

12. See first entry above.

13. See first entry above.

14. "Cannibalism in the Cars," *Broadway*, November 1868 (no. 232).

15. "Personal Habits of the Siamese Twins," *Packard's Monthly*, August 1869 (no. 237).

16. "Getting My Fortune Told," *Express*, 27 November 1869 (no. 274).

17. "More Distinction," *Express*, 4 June 1870 (no. 307).

18. "The Latest Novelty. Mental Photographs," *Express*, 2 October 1869 (no. 262).

Appendix:

Sailor Story—unidentified.

Map—"Mark Twain's Map of Paris," *Galaxy*, November 1870 (no. 324).

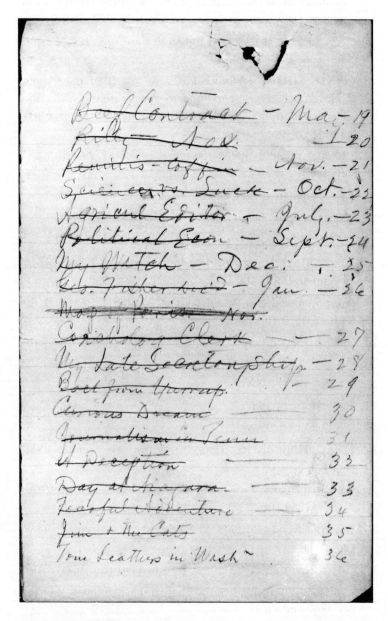

FIGURE 19B. Second page of the preliminary table of contents for "Mark Twain's Sketches." Mark Twain noted the month of publication in the *Galaxy* after some sketches.

ADVENTURES IN HAYTI.

TROPICAL ASPECTS.

AT SEA, OFF PORT-AU-PRINCE, }
October 5.

1869

As I stepped ashore at the above-named place to-day, I was assailed by a swarm of darkies of all ages and all degrees of hilarity and raggedness. But it was a peaceful assault. They only wanted to carry my valise to the hotel.

In the midst of the clamor I felt the valise passing from me. I was helpless. I simply followed it, making no complaint. It was on the head of a bright little darkey who depended solely on his personal comeliness for attractiveness—he had nothing on but a shirt. And the length of time that had elapsed since that shirt was at the laundry was longer than the shirt itself, I should judge.

We wound in and out among narrow streets bordered by small houses scantily furnished, and generally with pigs, cats and parrots and naked colored children littering the dilapidated little front porches; a monkey or two making trouble with all these parties in turn; a glimpse through the open door of an insignificant stock of wares on sale—such as oranges, pine-apples, cocoanuts, bread, sausages, cigars, brooms, herrings, cheap prints of saints ~~carrying their bleeding hearts outside their shirt-bosoms~~—and tending the grocery, a stout wench in parti-colored turban, calico dress, wide open at the breast, cigartie in mouth, no shoes, no stockings. Occasionally we passed genteel houses, entirely surrounded by verandahs, and these verandahs close-shuttered to keep out the heat. In the yards attached to these houses were tall, thick-bodied cocoa-palms, with foliage like a bunch of swamp-flags exaggerated—the cocoa peculiar to the West Indies. And of course in these yards was a world of flowering tropical plants—curious, gorgeous, outlandish-looking things that had the air of being glaringly out of place with no greenhouse glass arranged around them.

FIGURE 20A. The first page of the printer's copy for "Around the World. Letter No. 2" (MTP). The cancellation in pencil is Mark Twain's; Albert Bigelow Paine, however, supplied the penciled "1869" in the dateline.

old man near me and throttle him. I moved away and turned my back—and then I covertly threw my pocket knife out of the window. Now the bill came. It read thus—I translate:

MARK TWAIN to Kingston House   Dr.

To room rent (2 persons)..............	$3,600
" removing baggage to room.............	900
	$4,500

To tradesmen's bill's as follows :

6 bunches bananas.....................	2,760
12 pine apples........................	2,000
10 dozen oranges......................	900
5 boxes cigars........................	92,000
2 baskets claret......................	22,000
2 " champagne	88,000
7 dozen lemons........................	800
1 pair boots..........................	21,000
1 dozen socks.........................	18,500
2 dozen handkerchiefs.................	43,000
	$295,400

Rec'd payment.

Two hundred and ninety-five thousand four hundred dollars ! I read this bill over deliberately six or seven times, and never said a word. Then I said I would step out and get a breath of fresh air.

*   *   *   *   *

I got it—the breath of fresh air. I walked gently around the corner, whistling unconcernedly. And then I glanced back, and seeing nobody watching me, I sauntered toward the American packet ship, at the rate of about eleven or twelve miles an hour. I picked Charley up on the way. We hid between decks a couple of hours, till the vessel was out of sight of land. We were safe. So was the the valise, and the cigars and things—the landlord had them. I trust he has them yet. We have parted to meet no more. I have seen enough of Hayti. I never did take much interest in Hayti, anyhow.

MARK TWAIN.

P. S.—I understand it all now. I have been talking with the captain. It is very simple, when one comprehends it. The

FIGURE 20B. The sixth page of the printer's copy for "Around the World. Letter No. 2" (MTP).

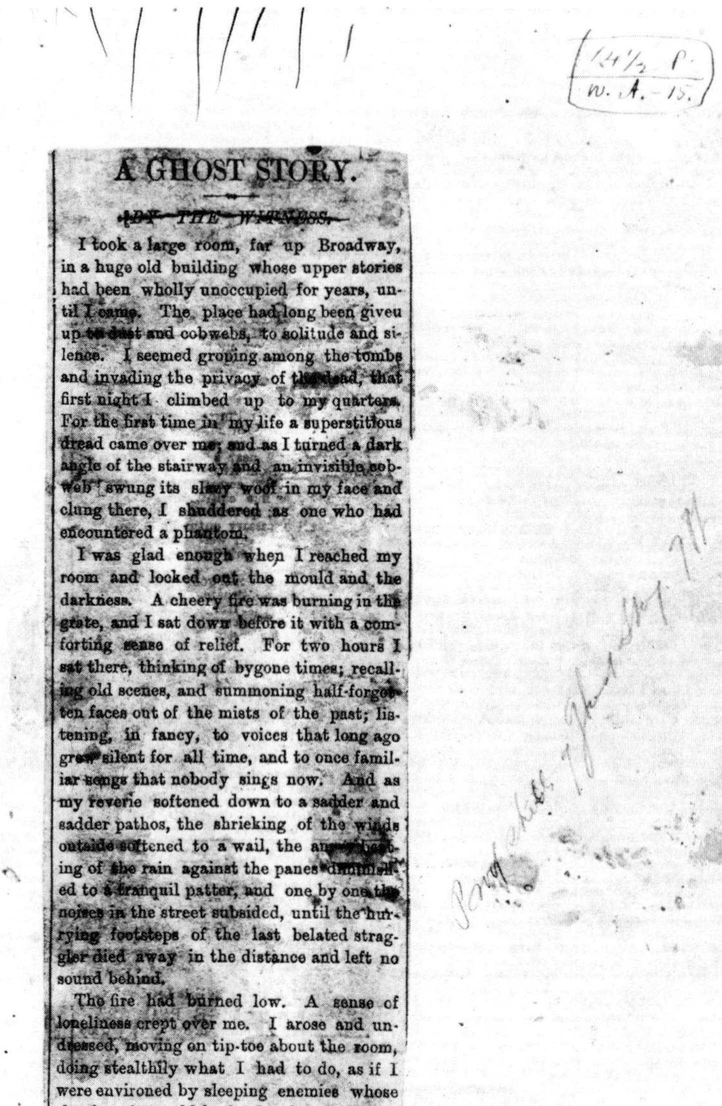

A GHOST STORY.

BY THE WITNESS.

I took a large room, far up Broadway, in a huge old building whose upper stories had been wholly unoccupied for years, until I came. The place had long been given up to dust and cobwebs, to solitude and silence. I seemed groping among the tombs and invading the privacy of the dead, that first night I climbed up to my quarters. For the first time in my life a superstitious dread came over me; and as I turned a dark angle of the stairway and an invisible cobweb swung its slimy woof in my face and clung there, I shuddered as one who had encountered a phantom.

I was glad enough when I reached my room and locked out the mould and the darkness. A cheery fire was burning in the grate, and I sat down before it with a comforting sense of relief. For two hours I sat there, thinking of bygone times; recalling old scenes, and summoning half-forgotten faces out of the mists of the past; listening, in fancy, to voices that long ago grew silent for all time, and to once familiar songs that nobody sings now. And as my reverie softened down to a sadder and sadder pathos, the shrieking of the winds outside softened to a wail, the angry beating of the rain against the panes diminished to a tranquil patter, and one by one the noises in the street subsided, until the hurrying footsteps of the last belated straggler died away in the distance and left no sound behind.

The fire had burned low. A sense of loneliness crept over me. I arose and undressed, moving on tip-toe about the room, doing stealthily what I had to do, as if I were environed by sleeping enemies whose slumbers it would be fatal to break. I covered up in bed, and lay listening to the rain and wind and the faint creaking of distant shutters, till they lulled me to sleep.

FIGURE 21A. The first page of the printer's copy for "A Ghost Story" (Texas). Someone has written, mistakenly, "Proof sheets of Ghost Story" in the margin. The sketch was eventually reprinted in SkNO from this printer's copy.

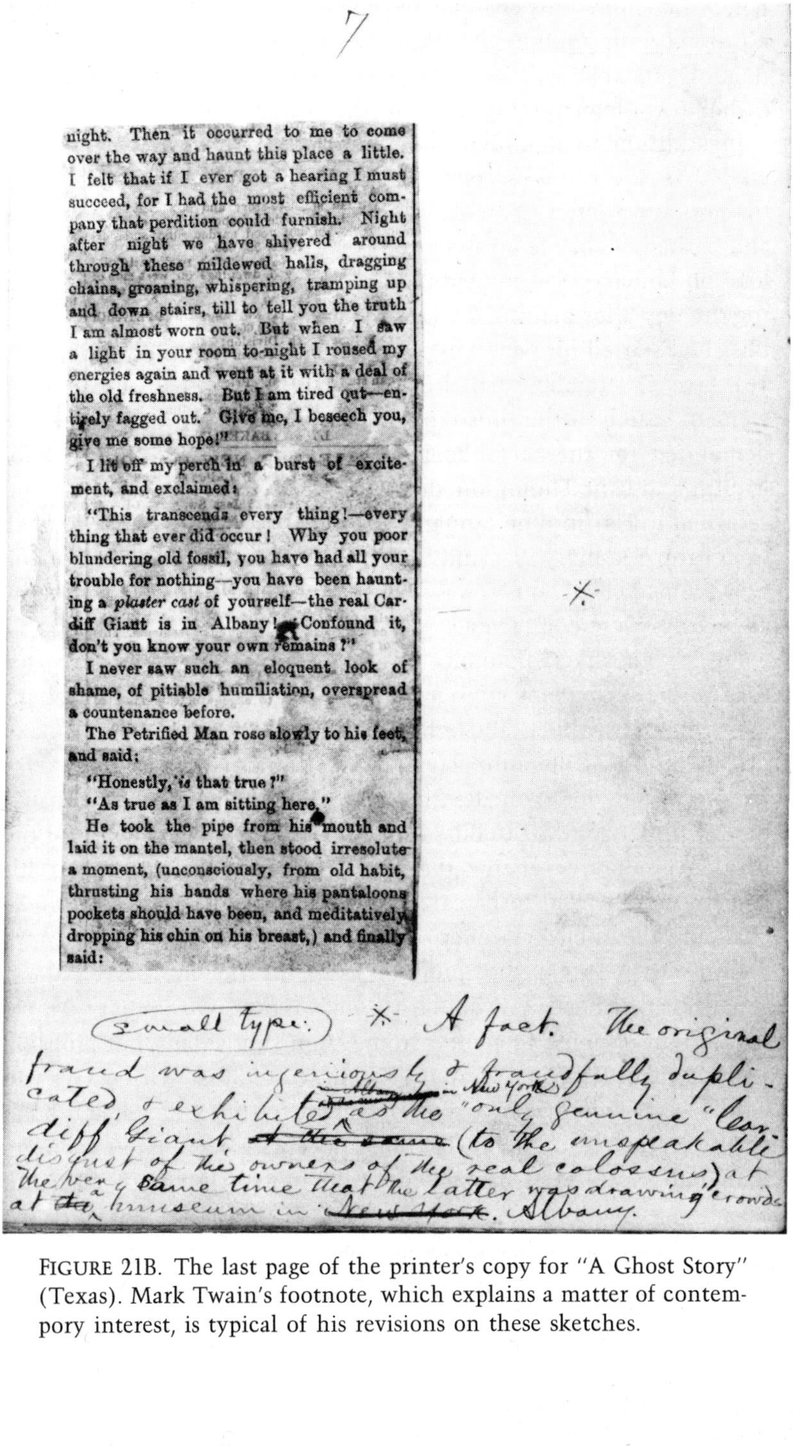

night. Then it occurred to me to come over the way and haunt this place a little. I felt that if I ever got a hearing I must succeed, for I had the most efficient company that perdition could furnish. Night after night we have shivered around through these mildewed halls, dragging chains, groaning, whispering, tramping up and down stairs, till to tell you the truth I am almost worn out. But when I saw a light in your room to-night I roused my energies again and went at it with a deal of the old freshness. But I am tired out—entirely fagged out. Give me, I beseech you, give me some hope!"

I lit off my perch in a burst of excitement, and exclaimed:

"This transcends every thing!—every thing that ever did occur! Why you poor blundering old fossil, you have had all your trouble for nothing—you have been haunting a *plaster cast* of yourself—the real Cardiff Giant is in Albany! Confound it, don't you know your own remains?"

I never saw such an eloquent look of shame, of pitiable humiliation, overspread a countenance before.

The Petrified Man rose slowly to his feet, and said:

"Honestly, *is that true?*"

"As true as I am sitting here."

He took the pipe from his mouth and laid it on the mantel, then stood irresolute a moment, (unconsciously, from old habit, thrusting his hands where his pantaloons pockets should have been, and meditatively dropping his chin on his breast,) and finally said:

(small type.) * A fact. The original fraud was ingeniously & fraudfully duplicated & exhibited as the "only genuine" Cardiff Giant, (to the unspeakable disgust of the owners of the real colossus) at the very same time that the latter was drawing crowds at the museum in Albany.

FIGURE 21B. The last page of the printer's copy for "A Ghost Story" (Texas). Mark Twain's footnote, which explains a matter of contempory interest, is typical of his revisions on these sketches.

sketch he entered his estimate of the number of book pages it would fill along with another number—"W.A. 13" or "W.A. 15"—which remains unexplained, but may have had something to do with an earlier (or a later) arrangement in the sketchbook.

In addition to mounted clippings, several manuscripts were included in the printer's copy. Mark Twain seems to have asked in his January 5 letter of transmittal that at least these unique items, and perhaps all of the printer's copy, be transcribed to protect against loss: on January 25 Orion wrote Clemens that he had "finished copying the day after mailing my last letter to you," and he reported that Bliss had started for New York City the "ensuing Monday" (January 16). Bliss presumably carried Orion's transcription with him, for he went in search of the illustrator whom Mark Twain had repeatedly demanded for the sketchbook. Orion said that Bliss "hunted for Mullin and Lant Thompson, or whatever his name is, two days," but returned to Hartford on January 23 empty-handed. "He is going back to-morrow [January 26] and will find Mullin."[117] The sketchbook now seemed clearly on its way: typesetting could begin as soon as the engravings were completed.

But it seems likely that once Bliss had secured Mark Twain's signature on the sketchbook contract early in January 1871, the publisher's main object was met, and other considerations—timing and maximizing profits—came into play. Bliss was certainly assured that Mark Twain would not soon desert him for another publisher, because he was under contract to Bliss for no fewer than three books. But the furious productive energy that Bliss had thus brought under his control now needed to be carefully guided: here was a situation to challenge the publisher's craft. While appearing to comply with Mark Twain's wish to expedite production of the sketchbook, Bliss was actually sowing seeds of doubt, through Orion. On January 24, apparently in response to a letter from Orion (not extant, but probably written about January 14), Mark Twain wrote Bliss: "Orion says you hardly know whether it is good judgment to throw the Sketch Book on the market & interfere with the Innocents. I believe you are more than half right—it is calculated to do more harm than good, no

---

[117]Orion Clemens to Clemens, 25 January 1871, MTP.

doubt." In fact, Mark Twain offered a new timetable for his three projects:

Suppose we defer the Sketch Book till the *last*. That is, get out the big California & Plains book first of August, then the Diamond book first [of] March or April 1872—& *then* the Sketch book the following fall. Does that strike you favorably? If so write out the contract in that way & forward it. By that time I can write a great many brand new sketches & they'll make the book sell handsomely—& by that time, too, some of the best of the *old* sketches will be forgotten & will read like new matter.

Drop me a line on it.

Orion was likewise asked to respond to this proposal. "About the sketch-book interfering with the Innocents—Bliss says he is going on with the sketch-book, and you will see which is right. The substance is that the new book will outsell the old one, and few people want to buy two books from the same author at the same time."[118] Although Bliss said he was "going on with the sketch-book" (and his pursuit of Mullen indicates that he was), he indirectly argued against it ("you will see which is right"). This subtle discouragement was no doubt motivated by the knowledge that *The Innocents Abroad* continued to sell more than 1,000 copies a month in 1871, and that a sketchbook published at this time would only detract from the continuing sale, as well as from the prospective sale of *Roughing It*. Bliss clearly had nothing to gain by executing all three contracts as rapidly as Mark Twain wanted him to, and he doubtless preferred to see *Roughing It* precede the sketchbook as originally planned. At any rate, the publisher's strategy was totally effective: on January 27 Mark Twain answered Orion's letter by insisting that Bliss put the sketchbook over "till another time,"[119] and this policy was adopted. *Roughing It* became Mark Twain's central literary activity and began to absorb some of the sketches he had planned for the sketchbook,

---

[118]Clemens to Bliss, 24 January 1871, *CL3*, letter 10; Orion Clemens to Clemens, 25 January 1871, MTP.

[119]American Publishing Company Stock Ledger of Books Received from Binderies, 1867–1879, Berg; Clemens to Bliss, 27 January 1871, *CL3*, letter 16. Mark Twain explained *his* reasons for postponing the sketchbook: "My popularity is booming, now, & we ought to take the very biggest advantage of it."

which would never be published just as the author had planned it
in 1870 and 1871.

6. Hotten's Piracies: Eye Openers, Screamers, and Practical Jokes (1871–1872): EOps, Scrs, and PJks Routledges' Authorized Editions: Curious Dream and Mark Twain's Sketches (1872): CD and MTSk

The pressure on the Routledges to work out an effective agreement
with Mark Twain increased late in 1871. On August 21 Hotten bound
his first 3,000 copies of *Eye Openers: Good Things, Immensely Funny
Sayings & Stories That Will Bring a Smile upon the Gruffest Countenance* (EOps). And on October 9 he bound his first 3,000 copies
of *Screamers: A Gathering of Scraps of Humour, Delicious Bits, &
Short Stories* (Scrs).[120] These two small volumes, for which Hotten
boldly claimed "copyright," reprinted most of Mark Twain's contributions to the *Galaxy* (May 1870–August 1871), along with a few
odd sketches from the Buffalo *Express*, the Chicago *Republican*, the
San Francisco *Alta California*, and Hotten's own JF3.[121] The books
were inexpensive (one shilling in wrappers, two shillings and sixpence in cloth), well received, and very popular. The London *Sunday
Times* noted that Scrs was a collection of Mark Twain's "recent and
funniest stories": "The humour of some of these is remarkable. We
have laughed over some of the contents of the volume until tears of

---

[120]Chatto and Windus Ledger Book 1, pp. 445, 451. EOps was ordered on 5 May 1871,
announced in the *Publishers' Circular* on September 15, and deposited with the British
Museum on October 27; see *BAL* 3331. Scrs was ordered on September 1 and advertised
in the *Athenaeum* on October 21 but probably did not appear until November or early
December: the *Booksellers' Record* recorded publication on December 12; see *BAL*
3333.

[121]Hotten's legal claim to copyright was nonexistent, since all of the material had
been previously published in the United States. The title-page copyright notices merely
asserted his moral right to publish (without interference from his competitors) what
he had collected and edited, and he had indeed shown some industry in finding material. EOps included "Journalism in Tennessee" (no. 252) from the *Express*, "Fashions"
(no. 221) from the *Republican*, and Mark Twain's original, irreverent account of the
patriarch Joseph from the *Alta* of 12 January 1868. Scrs included "Baker's Cat" from
"Around the World. Letter Number 5" in the *Express* (no. 267) and "The Story of
the Bad Little Boy" from JF3 ("The Christmas Fireside," no. 148). It also contained
three sketches by Carl Byng, one by the editor of *Cassell's Magazine*, and two by
unidentified authors, all mistakenly attributed to Mark Twain (see Hotten to *Spectator*, 8 June 1872, p. 722).

irrepressible hilarity have rolled down our cheeks."[122] Hotten had printed 21,000 copies of EOps by 20 October 1872, and 19,000 copies of Scrs by December 9. The plates, slightly modified, continued in use long after they were sold to Ward, Lock and Co. on 29 July 1874.[123]

The Routledges probably alerted Mark Twain to Hotten's latest ventures by sending him copies of both EOps and Scrs in late 1871, during negotiations to "simultane" *Roughing It*. The problem posed by these books had little to do with the issue of copyright; rather, it was that Hotten could now advertise seven titles (as he did in both volumes) as the "Works of Mark Twain, Widely known for their fresh and delightful humour."[124] It must have been apparent to the Routledges that if they did not soon take steps to prevent Hotten from single-handedly issuing Mark Twain's works in England, their claim to be the "author's only English publisher" would lose much of its significance. Mark Twain had a corresponding dependence on them: they were his only chance to get fair compensation on any future works that might be republished in England. From this mutual need, we conjecture, an agreement was evidently reached.

The Routledges' copyright edition of *Roughing It* was the first fruit of their patience, and the initial step in a major counterattack against Hotten. The edition was divided into two volumes, called *Roughing It* and *The Innocents at Home*. The first 6,000 copies of *Roughing It* were, according to the Routledge records, printed by 6 February 1872, and 10,000 copies of *The Innocents at Home* by February 28; by February 23 another 4,000 of the first volume had been prepared, and as early as April 12 another impression of 4,000 (both volumes) was called for. The sale was brisk and profitable: within a year of publica-

---

[122]Reprinted in the *Bookbuyer's Guide*, no. 9 (March 1872), p. 20. The *Sunday Times* singled out "An Entertaining Article" (no. 334), "A Reminiscence of the Back Settlements" (no. 331), and "Wit-Inspirations of the 'Two-Year-Olds' " (no. 303), calling them "about as droll as anything we have read."

[123]Chatto and Windus Ledger Book 1, pp. 445, 451; Book 2, pp. 98, 103. The British Museum owns a copy of *Funny Stories and Humorous Poems* (London: Ward, Lock, and Tyler, 1875) printed in part from the plates of EOps (call number 12331.bb.28). *BAL* 3333 notes a copy of Scrs advertised by the same firm in *Publishers' Circular* for 17 August 1875.

[124]The phrase occurs in an advertisement in EOps. The works listed are *Pleasure Trip on the Continent of Europe* (*BAL* 3597); *The Innocents Abroad* (*BAL* 3590); *The New Pilgrim's Progress* (*BAL* 3591); *Burlesque Autobiography* (BA3); *The Jumping Frog, and Other Humourous Sketches* (JF3); and of course EOps and Scrs.

tion in England the Routledges had printed 22,000 copies of each volume.[125]

The strength of the Routledges' position is suggested indirectly by Hotten's reaction. On 3 February 1872, just before the English edition of *Roughing It* (volume 1) appeared, he wrote Mark Twain offering to pay an indefinite amount for selections from it: "I see you have a new book in hand 'Roughing It' will you oblige by MAILING TO ME ON RECEIPT of this some of the proofs—a few chapters. You may depend upon my dealing honourably with you & I will place to your credit whatever is fair & equitable."[126] Needless to say, Mark Twain ignored this request, not only because of his arrangement with the Routledges but because of his growing animosity toward Hotten. Moreover, the Routledges had a number of other cards to play: before the summer was out they had fully matched Hotten's long list of "Mark Twain's Works," and they had also consolidated their position with the author.

---

[125]Routledge Ledger Book 4, pp. 576–577. By 10 May 1879 they had printed 44,000 copies of *Roughing It* and 46,000 copies of *The Innocents at Home* (*BAL* 3335 and 3336). They paid no per-copy royalty, but a flat fee of £18 10s. was given to Mark Twain for each volume (about $185 in all). Because the British copyright was secure, the book was profitable for the Routledges: production costs (including payment to the author, typesetting, stereotyping, printing, and paper—but not binding) totaled about £1,155 in this period. Assuming that the entire sale was in one-shilling wrappers (instead of two-shilling boards), assuming a 30-percent publisher's discount to the bookseller, and assuming £200 for binding and £100 for advertising, we can approximate their profits in seven years: £1,695, or about $8,475. Moreover, in 1882 they published an illustrated one-volume edition for seven shillings and sixpence (*BAL* 3630), and by the turn of the century had begun to issue a sixpence version of the original two-volume edition. By 1900 the Routledges had sold 63,750 copies of volume 1 (*Roughing It*) and 71,000 copies of volume 2 (*The Innocents at Home*), as well as 4,000 copies of the one-volume edition (Routledge Ledger Book 4, pp. 576–577; Book 5, pp. 145, 183; Book 6, pp. 680–681). This was precisely the kind of commercial success that they hoped to achieve through a sound British copyright. When Chatto and Windus offered to buy the Routledges' Mark Twain books in 1892, the latter agreed to relinquish *The Gilded Age* and *Mark Twain's Sketches* (MTSk) for sixty pounds, but added that "Roughing [I]t we don't wish to sell at all" (Edmund Routledge to Andrew Chatto, 2 March 1892, Chatto and Windus files).

[126]Hotten to Clemens, 3 February 1872, Chatto and Windus Letter Book 6, p. 18. Hotten told Ambrose Bierce on July 21, "Three times I have written to Mr. Clemens to gather up his sketches for me, and I had concluded that his great wealth &—as I thought—indifference to anything more than local fame, made him look upon correspondence as a bore—at least I have never had grounds for conjecturing anything else" (Bancroft). We are indebted to M. E. Grenander for alerting us to this letter. Hotten again claimed in September that he had "in three years written thrice to Mr. Clemens, but never received one answer" (Hotten to *Spectator*, 28 September 1872,

Hotten must have sensed the way things were moving. In early March he announced still another unauthorized volume: "Practical Jokes; or, Mirth with Artemus Ward, and other Papers. By MARK TWAIN." Hotten's advertisement was enticingly vague: "The connection of two such names as Mark Twain and Artemus Ward will indicate to the reader the pleasant feast in store for him."[127] The reader, however, had some time to wait. *Practical Jokes with Artemus Ward, Including the Story of the Man Who Fought Cats* (PJks) did not appear until late August 1872. It contained thirty-seven sketches, only seventeen of which were by Mark Twain: they had been drawn from the *Express*, the *Galaxy*, and other newspapers, as well as from the Routledges' edition of *Roughing It* and *The Innocents at Home*. Hotten eventually published 17,000 copies of PJks.[128]

Well before Hotten actually issued PJks, the Routledges had brought to bear the full weight of their prestige as the author's official English publishers. Probably sometime in February or March 1872 they solicited a complete and revised edition of Mark Twain's sketches. The author first alluded to this plan in a letter probably written in late March or early April, in which he turned down an offer from the American publisher James R. Osgood to issue a collection of his sketches in the United States: "Indeed I *would* like to publish a volume of sketches through your house," he admitted, "but unfortunately my contracts with my present publisher tie my hands & prevent me. I have just made up quite a portly volume of them for

---

p. 1237). The Chatto and Windus letter books show that Hotten did write Mark Twain several times in 1872, but record nothing earlier.

[127]*Bookseller*, 2 March 1872, p. 239.

[128]Hotten ordered his first 8,000 copies on 11 June 1872 and received them two days later, but had bound only about 100 of these by June 22. Hotten did not order the necessary paper covers for the bulk of his impression until August 3; PJks was deposited in the British Museum on September 2. The plates were eventually sold to Ward, Lock and Co. on 29 July 1874 (Chatto and Windus Ledger Book 1, p. 229; Book 2, p. 102). Hotten edited the selections from *Roughing It* (which he called "Sending Them Through," "Editorial Skits," and "The Union—Right or Wrong?") rather more heavily than the others, perhaps to disguise his violation of the Routledges' copyright. PJks also contained twenty sketches that Hotten knew were not by Mark Twain. On July 21 he told Ambrose Bierce: "I am rather pained by your note, but am not at all sorry you were the recipient of the 2nd copy issued of 'Practical Jokes.' The little book will be published in paper covers at 1/—, but you had one of a few done up in cloth as gifts. The paper cover will have on the title *By 'Mark Twain & other American Humourists'* wch I believe conveys no other impression than what I intend" (Bancroft). The paper-covered edition did in fact say "By Mark Twain and Other Humourists" on the title page.

Routledge & Sons, London, but I have to leave my own countrymen to 'suffer & be strong' without them."[129] Just how this new Routledge collection was prepared and received sheds some light on the struggle with Hotten and on the republication history of Mark Twain's early sketches.

What Mark Twain called a "portly volume" actually became two volumes, almost certainly at the publisher's behest: *A Curious Dream; and Other Sketches* (CD) and *Mark Twain's Sketches* (MTSk). Both volumes were (according to the title page) "Selected and Revised by the Author." CD contained only fifteen sketches, all of them reprinted in England for the first time; it cost one shilling. MTSk contained sixty-six sketches, including the fifteen new ones reprinted in CD, with the remainder drawn from *Galaxy* pieces and from older pieces already collected in JF1; it cost two shillings. The Routledges received from their printer 10,000 copies of CD on May 8, but only 6,000 copies of the more expensive MTSk on May 10. They paid Mark Twain £18 10s. for each volume—the same amount they paid him for each of the two volumes *Roughing It* and *The Innocents at Home*. Publication must have occurred nearly simultaneously in mid-May 1872, with CD slightly preceding MTSk.[130]

---

[129]Clemens to Osgood, 24 or 31 March or 7 April 1872, *CL3*, letter 161. This letter was written on stationery of the Elmira McIntyre Coal Company; Mark Twain dated it merely "Sunday—1872." The conjectural date of late March or early April is based on a calculation of the time that must have elapsed between the transmission of the printer's copy of MTSk and the receipt of the first printed sheets on May 10. In the case of the Routledge edition of *Innocents*, the time elapsed between the transmission of the printer's copy (June 23) and the receipt of printed sheets (August 1) was about five weeks. Since Mark Twain's letter to Osgood said he had "just made up" the MTSk printer's copy, it seems likely that the letter was written about five weeks before May 10, on either March 31 or April 7, and that the printer's copy was prepared during the month of March while Mark Twain was still in Hartford. The transmission of printer's copy for the Routledge *Innocents* is discussed by Robert H. Hirst in "The Making of *The Innocents Abroad*: 1867–1872" (Ph.D. diss., University of California, Berkeley, 1975), pp. 358–362.

[130]Routledge Ledger Book 4, pp. 586–587. Both CD (*BAL* 3340) and MTSk (*BAL* 3341) were deposited in the British Museum on 8 June 1872. CD sold quite well: 24,000 copies had been printed by 3 March 1881, and almost 43,000 copies by 1 September 1902 (Routledge Ledger Book 4, p. 586; Book 5, p. 397; Book 6, pp. 671, 683). MTSk was less successful: a second impression of 2,000 copies was made on 20 January 1877, bringing the total to 8,000. This stock sufficed until the stereotype plates and cover blocks were purchased by Chatto and Windus on 7 March 1892 for thirty pounds, and that firm issued 1,300 copies of the book from those plates on 19 December 1902 (Routledges' receipt, 7 March 1892, Chatto and Windus files; Chatto and Windus Ledger Book 8, p. 103; Book 9, p. 255).

Although the Routledges conspicuously advertised both books as "copyright" editions, their claim (like Hotten's with Scrs and EOps) had moral rather than legal significance: even with such revisions as Mark Twain made in his texts, neither book could be effectively protected by copyright law. Nevertheless, the Routledges could now advertise six titles of "Mark Twain's Works | Routledge's Editions": JF4b ("With a Copyright Chapter"), *Roughing It*, *The Innocents at Home*, BA2, and of course CD and MTSk. By August 24, moreover, they could list two more titles, "The Author's Edition" of *The Innocents Abroad* and *The New Pilgrim's Progress*, both "Revised by the Author. With a New Preface, especially written for this Edition."[131] Most of these books proved to be profitable for the Routledges, who continued to sell some of them well into the 1900s. But their initial motive for so many simultaneous publications—eight volumes printed or reprinted in 1872 alone—was to please and impress Mark Twain as well as his British public. The Routledges' eight titles now stood as an implicit answer to Hotten, who by 1872 also had eight ostensible titles but could not claim the author's blessing.

Indeed, it appears that the Routledges encouraged Mark Twain to speak out against Hotten's editions—something he was already inclined to do, for he was greatly angered by Hotten's including in Scrs six sketches that the author claimed (and most scholars now agree) he did not write. His discomfort at being saddled with these sketches was acute and quite justified, not merely an excuse for more publicity. For instance, when the London *Spectator* belatedly reviewed Scrs on 18 May 1872, they had high praise for what they termed its "excellent nonsense"—sketches like "The Late Benjamin Franklin" (no. 311) and "My Watch—An Instructive Little Tale" (no. 340). But they thought the book "rather a hotch-potch, and of very unequal merit." "The tales are not all 'screamers,'" they declared: "Some even have a distinctly serious purpose, though put humorously," while "other papers are of a very vulgar type, such as the one 'About Barbers,' 'Dan Murphy,' the 'True Story of Chicago,' and 'Vengeance.' . . . The only piece, however, which seems the result rather of a forced and laboured than a natural drollery is the first, an essay on the nursery rhyme, 'Hey diddle diddle, the cat and the fiddle.'" The *Spectator* thus unknowingly

---

[131]*Athenaeum:* 11 May 1872, p. 604; 24 August 1872, p. 227.

singled out half of the nonauthorial pieces for its dispraise: the last three mentioned were not by Mark Twain. The *Spectator* concluded its review by saying, "In a future edition, we trust Mark Twain will carefully weed out the vulgar papers, and the extravaganzas, and the no-sense as distinguished from the nonsense."[132]

When the Routledges read this review, they sent a letter of protest to the magazine and a copy of their letter to Mark Twain, hoping to underscore both publicly and privately his need for an authorized English publisher. They quoted the last sentence of the *Spectator* review and went on to announce:

Mark Twain, anticipating your suggestion, has prepared for publication a volume of 'Sketches' [MTSk] which will be ready this week. The Author's advertisement, which will be found in your advertizing columns, will explain the "unequal merit" of the papers in the volume called Screamers, many of which he had never seen till he found them fathered upon him in this collection.[133]

The "Author's advertisement" was included in most Routledge advertisements as well as in MTSk itself. In writing it Mark Twain was manifestly prompted by Hotten's piracies and mistaken attributions:

Messrs. George Routledge and Sons are *the only English Publishers* who pay me any Copyright on my books. That is something, but a courtesy which I prize even more is the opportunity which they have given me to edit and revise the matter for publication myself. This enables me to leave out a good deal of literature which has appeared in England over my name, *but which I never wrote*. And, as far as this particular volume is concerned, it also enables me to add a number of sketches which I *did* write, but which have not heretofore been published abroad.

This book contains all of my sketches which I feel at all willing to father.

MARK TWAIN.[134]

The *Spectator* published a brief retraction on 1 June 1872: "We are requested to state . . . that several of the papers attributed to Mark Twain in that volume [Scrs] are not by him, and had never been seen by him till that volume appeared. We understand that a volume

---

[132]*Spectator*, 18 May 1872, pp. 633–634. Two of Mark Twain's own sketches were called "extravagant rubbish."

[133]Routledge and Sons to *Spectator*, 21 May 1872, amanuensis copy, MTP.

[134]*Spectator*, 25 May 1872, p. 670.

of sketches is to be published this week by another publisher, authenticated and revised by the author himself."[135] One week later, on June 8, the *Spectator* also published a reply from Hotten, who defended his selection of pieces: "Nothing has been issued here by me as 'Mark Twain's' which has not already been published in the United States or elsewhere under this signature, or under that of 'Carl Byng,' another *nom de plume* of the same author."[136]

But Hotten also criticized the recently published MTSk in a way that tells us something about how Mark Twain prepared the volume:

I would state that so far from the new gathering of "Mark Twain's Sketches," just issued by Messrs. George Routledge and Sons, being "*revised* and collected by the author," the work consists simply of my own revised editions transposed,—in fact, my little books seem to have been sent to some one in New York, who has returned the "Sketches" intact, but with the arrangement a little altered, and the stories in the "Jumping Frog" volume sorted in to give the appearance of a fresh collection. That the author, Mr. Samuel L. Clemens, has done this one cannot very well believe, as he would not be likely to adopt a London version of his "Sketches," and call it his own; it is not reasonable to suppose he would do anything of the kind.[137]

Nevertheless, collation shows that this is precisely what Mark Twain had done. The convenience of being able to revise his *Galaxy* pieces in book form had overcome any scruples he may have entertained. We have already conjectured that the Routledges sent him copies of EOps and Scrs in late 1871, presumably as a kind of warning. In March 1872 he must have used these books to fill out the "portly volume" of sketches he was preparing for them.

Hotten was sarcastic in his letter, but he was not bluffing: he had gathered the textual evidence to convict Mark Twain of pirating his own pirate, and he used it as the basis of his allegations in the *Spectator*. Hotten had obviously compared MTSk with the edited printer's copy for EOps and Scrs, and he reported his findings in withering detail:

Amongst other fugitive pieces I culled was one from a Philadelphia paper, a most amusing but—as I took the liberty of thinking—rather strongly-worded article entitled "Journalism in Tennessee," and

---

[135]*Spectator*, 1 June 1872, p. 698.
[136]Hotten to *Spectator*, 8 June 1872, p. 722.
[137]Hotten to *Spectator*, 8 June 1872, p. 722.

finding that the fun was just as good with certain forcible expressions left out, I weeded it of such phrases as "not stop to chew a lie," "bumming his board," "hell-spawned miscreant," "[s]teaming animated tank of mendacity, gin, and profanity,"—and I say I weeded out these and many other forcible expressions—and what is strange is that precisely these omissions, with other alterations, occur in this new and so-called "*revised* collection of Mark Twain's Sketches"! There were some paragraphs, too, that I had collected as by "Mark Twain," and to these I affixed headings which I thought sufficiently appropriate. Precisely these headings now appear in the new collection advertised as having been "revised" by the author. For instance, a trifle headed "The 'Present' Nuisance," I thought would be better explained if called "The Poor Editor." This latter heading is given to the article in the new edition issued as "revised by the author."

The same punctuation, the same italics, the same omission of unnecessary lines adopted in my edition, all will be found in this new edition said to be "revised by the author."[138]

Collation confirms everything that Hotten alleged. He wrote the *Spectator* again later that year: "The punctuation, English orthography, and even our printer's errors all appeared in the new 'author's revised edition.' As no denial of my statement has ever appeared in your journal, I suppose its truth will not now be challenged."[139] It never was.

The *Spectator* did, however, answer Hotten's first letter in a brief editorial comment, alluding to a marked book that must have served as part of the printer's copy for MTSk:

All we can say is, that we have ourselves seen marked as "spurious" in what is alleged to be, and we believe to be, Mark Twain's own writing, one of the Essays in Mr. Hotten's edition, and that we are told there are four or five more marked in the same way; and that we know on the same authority (Mark Twain's own handwriting) that Messrs. Routledge's edition is revised by himself, and that he has received some payment for it from the publishers.[140]

In fact, collation shows that Mark Twain revised copies of EOps and Scrs, deleting eighteen authorial sketches as well as the six nonauth-

---

[138]Hotten to *Spectator*, 8 June 1872, p. 722. Hotten may well have seen "Journalism in Tennessee" in a "Philadelphia paper," for Mark Twain's work in the *Express* (where the sketch first appeared) was widely copied by the eastern press.

[139]Hotten to *Spectator*, 28 September 1872, p. 1237.

[140]*Spectator*, 8 June 1872, p. 722.

orial ones, to create part of the printer's copy for MTSk. In doing so he adapted an English edition of his work to his own purposes, and he accepted many substantive revisions and typographical errors introduced by his English editor, John Camden Hotten.

Mark Twain prepared MTSk for the Routledges almost exactly as Hotten had discerned: in most of the pieces taken from EOps and Scrs he caught only a handful of errors; he retained most changes in wording, many of Hotten's titles, and of course the bowdlerized versions of sketches like "Journalism in Tennessee" (no. 252). He also revised many of the sketches, Hotten's scorn notwithstanding. To fill out these selections he took a copy of JF4a (the second Routledge edition of the *Jumping Frog* book, sent to him in 1870 or 1871), revised all but a few of sixteen sketches and deleted the remaining twelve, and then "sorted [them] in to give the appearance of a fresh collection." For most of the fifteen sketches in MTSk which were previously unpublished in England (and ignored by Hotten in his angry *Spectator* letters), Mark Twain probably raided the contents of his unpublished edition of "Mark Twain's Sketches," which included all but three of them.[141] (The amanuensis copy prepared by Orion probably had an unanticipated use here, for it could have allowed Mark Twain to send printer's copy for the twelve sketches to England while retaining the American sketchbook intact.) Of these fifteen new pieces, nine were first printed in the Buffalo *Express*, two in the *Galaxy*, and four others in journals that published Mark Twain more rarely: the Newark (N.J.) *Press*, the New York *Tribune*, *Packard's Monthly*, and the *American Publisher*. Collation shows that Mark Twain slightly revised these sketches—just enough, perhaps, to frustrate the *"scallawag"* whom Bliss had envisioned copying the material and threatening the American copyright. We cannot determine exactly when Mark Twain completed his revisions: for the twelve pieces from "Mark Twain's Sketches" it may have been as early as January 1871, when he completed the original printer's copy for Bliss; for the three other pieces it may have been as late as March or April 1872, when he mailed the new printer's copy to the Routledges. All of the printer's copy—the marked

---

[141]The three new sketches in MTSk not included in the tentative table of contents for "Mark Twain's Sketches" (see figure 19) are "Rev. H. W. Beecher. His Private Habits" (no. 260), "The New Crime" (no. 288), and "A New Beecher Church" (no. 360).

copies of EOps, Scrs, JF4a as well as the new sketches—has been lost. Collation shows that CD, which contained only the fifteen new pieces, was set not from MTSk but from the same printer's copy used for MTSk: either clippings pasted to sheets and revised by Mark Twain, or the amanuensis copy prepared by Orion. This circumstance permits a slightly better reconstruction of the printer's copy for these sketches than can be conjectured for others.

MTSk was indeed a "portly volume" of sketches: some three hundred sixty pages in all, with sixty-six pieces of varying length, ranging in time of composition from "How to Cure a Cold" (no. 63), written in 1863, to "About Barbers" (no. 361), written in 1871. Unlike the contents of the sketchbook Mark Twain had planned to publish in the United States, MTSk included fifteen JF1 sketches; furthermore, it omitted eight pieces that (in the meantime) had been absorbed by *Roughing It*. But drawing on EOps and Scrs it included twenty-three of the original thirty-eight selections. MTSk was very different from the kind of sketchbook Mark Twain had experimented with in publishing his BA1 pamphlet: it contained no illustrations, and it gave the reader a great deal for two shillings (fifty cents). There is some indication that the author feared his readers might be overwhelmed by so large a collection of detached pieces, but in spite of this fear MTSk made a bold claim on the interest of his English public.[142]

Mark Twain did not let the matter of his conflict with Hotten stand thus resolved. When he traveled to England in the summer of 1872 (in part to begin work on his book about English manners, but also to meet the Routledges and to support their campaign on his behalf), he launched an attack on Hotten in the *Spectator*—the first of his many public statements on the problem of international copyright. Citing the "interest of public morality" in the question, he dismissed Hotten's piracies with great bitterness: "I do not protest against" them, he wrote, "for there is no law that could give effect to the protest; and, besides, publishers are not accountable to the laws of heaven or earth in any country, as I understand it." His real grievance—or at least the one he felt most keenly—lay elsewhere:

---

[142]Mark Twain's "Prefatory" to MTSk said in part: "There is no more sin in publishing an entire volume of nonsense than there is in keeping a candy store with no hardware in it. It lies wholly with the customer whether he will injure himself by means of either, or will derive from them the benefits which they will afford him if he uses their possibilities judiciously" (Appendix C3, volume 1).

My books are bad enough just as they are written; then what must they be after Mr. John Camden Hotten has composed half-a-dozen chapters and added the same to them? I feel that all true hearts will bleed for an author whose volumes have fallen under such a dispensation as this. If a friend of yours, or if even you yourself, were to write a book and set it adrift among the people, with the gravest apprehensions that it was not up to what it ought to be intellectually, how would you like to have John Camden Hotten sit down and stimulate his powers, and drool two or three original chapters on to the end of that book? Would not the world seem cold and hollow to you? Would you not feel that you wanted to die and be at rest? Little the world knows of true suffering.

The image of Hotten idiotically drooling unwanted "chapters" into the canon was but one of Mark Twain's unflattering fantasies about the publisher; the other was a direct allusion to EOps and Scrs. He envisioned an imaginary title page with "a picture of a man with his hand in another man's pocket, and the legend 'All Rights Reserved.' "[143]

Given such antipathy, one may well wonder why Mark Twain adopted Hotten's texts, bowdlerization and all. Was this mere expediency, or was there a more deliberate method in Mark Twain's "unreasonable" behavior? A partial answer may be inferred from a manuscript in the Mark Twain Papers—another quite vicious attack on Hotten, probably written in 1872 but never published. In this manuscript Mark Twain reported, as part of his vilification, that "Bret Harte says Hotten not only gives him the benefit of idiotic explanatory notes, but furnishes other notes in which he apologizes for Harte's western indelicacies of speech. Hotten cleanses me carefully before spreading me before the British public, but <I suppose it rather benefits me than otherwise> <I doubt> I suspect he leaves more dirt by contact of his person than he removes from me by his labor."[144] Although Mark Twain revised his words to prevent any compliment to Hotten, the canceled passage shows that the author recognized and endorsed the kind of "cleansing" that Hotten had given him. Further-

---

[143]*Spectator*, 21 September 1872, pp. 1201–1202. Hotten's actual title pages for EOps and Scrs included the phrase "All Rights Reserved," a conventional device to reserve right of translation and republication in countries that shared an international copyright agreement with Great Britain. See Simon Nowell-Smith, *International Copyright Law and the Publisher in the Reign of Queen Victoria* (Oxford: Clarendon Press, 1968), p. 67.

[144]"John Camden Hotten, Publisher, London," Paine 90, pp. 18–19, MTP.

more, Mark Twain's own revisions of the sketches included in MTSk show the same spirit of restraint that Hotten thought necessary before spreading this western humorist "before the British public."

Indeed, the course of Mark Twain's revisions—from JF1 through MTSk, and then later in *Choice Humorous Works* and finally *Sketches, New and Old*—was always toward progressively more restraint. This is a complex phenomenon, but one of its fundamental causes was Mark Twain's extraordinary sensitivity to the kind of audience he was addressing: he was keenly aware that an expression admissible in the American West might be unacceptable to easterners, while something admissible in the East might have to be modified for British and Continental readers. When he was a newspaper man in Nevada, he could be defensively proud of his "vulgar" language. For instance, sometime in January 1864 (while Mark Twain was in Carson City) an unwary compositor on the *Territorial Enterprise* silently altered Mark Twain's "devil" to "d——l," and the author responded in print:

Say—you have got a compositor up there who is too rotten particular, it seems to me. When I spell "devil" in my usual frank and open manner, he puts it "d——l"! Now, Lord love his conceited and accommodating soul, if I choose to use the language of the vulgar, the low-flung and the sinful, and such as will shock the ears of the highly civilized, I don't want him to appoint himself an editorial critic and proceed to tone me down and save me from the consequences of my conduct; that is, unless I pay him for it, which I won't. I expect I could spell "devil" before that fastidious cuss was born.[145]

Yet this defiant stance could not be maintained when Mark Twain sought literary fame in the East and in England. Hotten's "cleansing" was the one welcome part of his editions, and Mark Twain accepted it just as he would other "literary" or "editorial" criticism from friends and colleagues. The list of such critics is long, and in these years includes Mary Mason Fairbanks, Emily Severance, Pamela Clemens, Jane Clemens, Olivia Clemens, Bret Harte, and William Dean Howells. To these we must now add Charles Henry Webb and John Camden Hotten. These critics varied widely in their motives and perspicacity,

---

[145]Mark Twain to Virginia City *Territorial Enterprise*, 14 January 1864, *MTEnt*, p. 139. He referred to a letter of 13 January 1864 (*MTEnt*, p. 134).

but in one sense what they all had in common was a sensitivity to "the language of the vulgar, the low-flung and the sinful, and such as will shock the ears of the highly civilized." As we have seen, Mark Twain initiated the effort to "civilize" his language and humor in JF1, and he was assisted in this step by Webb. We know that in 1868 and 1869 Mark Twain carried out—following the specific recommendations of Mrs. Fairbanks, Harte, and Olivia—a wholesale revision of the *Alta California* and *Tribune* letters for *The Innocents Abroad;* and after he had prepared MTSk for the Routledges in March 1872, he undertook (in May and June) to revise the text of *Innocents* again, deliberately modifying it for a British audience. In all these books he weeded out much of the slang and profanity, and moved the general tone of discourse toward a distinctly more restrained level. His apprentice work, and his "usual frank and open manner," had been left far behind.[146]

7. The Choice Humorous Works of Mark Twain (1873–1874): HWa, HWaMT, and HWb

Mark Twain's attack on Hotten in the *Spectator* was preceded by a visit to the publisher on 7 September 1872. On that day Hotten told Ambrose Bierce that Tom Hood and Mark Twain had just visited him together, pretending that Mark Twain was in fact "Mr. Bryce." "I suppose the joke w^d have succeeded, but I at once brought out my portrait of Mark Twain, & this did the business, altho 'Bryce' intensified his sternness & swore—at least he asseverated—he was of that *ilk* to the last." When Hotten responded to Mark Twain's *Spectator* letter on September 28, he alluded to this hoax and suggested (to defend his reprinting the "Carl Byng" material) that Mark Twain had recently shown a "taste for many *noms de plume*," including "Mr. Bryce." And on October 12, Hotten carried the joke further into the enemy's camp, announcing "Mr. Bryce's Joke-Book. The most won-

---

[146]Of the Mark Twain books published or republished by the Routledges in 1872—*Roughing It*, JF4b, CD, MTSk, and *The Innocents Abroad*—only the first two were not revised for an English audience. But Mark Twain revised the contents of JF4 when he prepared the printer's copy for MTSk in March 1872. And *Roughing It*—the first of his works to be simultaneously published in England—gave him no opportunity to revise because late proofs had to be sent in January to secure publication in early February.

derful Joke-Book ever issued in this or any other country. It is,—well, readers must see it and judge for themselves. The work is placed under the distinguished patronage of 'Mr. Bryce,'—the latest *nom de plume* of that great Humourist, Mark Twain. If the authorities permit it, the work will be entitled 'Awful Crammers!' "[147]

Mark Twain was so troubled by this advertisement—or conceivably by another less facetious advertisement for a collection of his sketches which has not been found—that he offered Hotten his surrender. On November 8 he made a second visit to the publisher and, finding him absent, left a message. Hotten replied the same day:

From the message you left here this afternoon I am sorry to find you are under the impression that I am about to issue *with* your name, a work *not* written by you. You have said some very hard things about me—probably at the instigation of others who hoped to benefit by misleading you, but I do assure you in the friendliest manner possible that *self* respect—apart from my sincere respect for your inimitable talent—would not allow me to do anything of the kind. You have, unfortunately, fallen amongst people who dislike me, people who are jealous of me because I happen to be <a little more> not quite so industrious, not quite so shrewd as they are. These people have misled you, the same as they tried to poison the mind of poor Artemus Ward against me. . . .

The advertisement you have seen—or rather, I suspect, to which your attention has been drawn—refers simply to an elegantly printed volume of your scattered writings that we are preparing. The reason I was not more explicit in my announcement is that other members of the trade watch me as a cat would a mouse but after the frank message you have left here I at once tell you what I am doing, and I can only say that I gladly avail myself of your offer to revise it. I have just telegraphed for sheets, & these shall be with you tomorrow, when you can go over them & let me have back on Monday.[148]

---

[147]Hotten to Bierce, 7 September 1872, Bancroft; Hotten to *Spectator*, 28 September 1872, p. 1237; advertisement in the *Spectator*, 12 October 1872, p. 1316. The attempted hoax on Hotten was discovered by M. E. Grenander. She describes it in her "California's Albion: Mark Twain, Ambrose Bierce, Tom Hood, John Camden Hotten, and Andrew Chatto," which she graciously allowed us to read in advance of its publication. Her article "Ambrose Bierce and Charles Warren Stoddard: Some Unpublished Correspondence" (*Huntington Library Quarterly* 23 [May 1960]: 264–265) also briefly alludes to the hoax.

[148]Hotten to Clemens, 8 November 1872, Chatto and Windus Letter Book 6, pp. 19–20. Hotten wrote on Friday, November 8, and promised the sheets for Saturday, expecting them back on the following Monday, November 11. Presumably he needed to telegraph to Edinburgh where his printer, Ballantyne, had his offices.

The spectre of seeing still more nonauthorial—or perhaps merely "uncleansed"—work republished in England under his name had momentarily overcome the author's loyalty to the Routledges and led him to volunteer to revise and correct Hotten's book.

The volume in question was surely *The Choice Humorous Works of Mark Twain* (HWa), on which Hotten had started work in mid-August 1872.[149] Mark Twain probably never replied to Hotten's letter—he may never have received it—for he was "called home by a Cable Telegram" on the same day.[150] Although Hotten clearly had most of HWa in type by early November, he delayed publication until late March 1873 in order to complete a long biographical essay on Mark Twain, which appeared as the introduction. There is no indication that Mark Twain revised the sheets at this time.[151]

HWa was an immense volume, costing seven shillings and sixpence, in which Hotten gathered together all of the Mark Twain material he had previously printed in smaller volumes. His introductory biographical sketch (40 pages) was followed by the complete, unrevised text of *The Innocents Abroad* (340 pages), which in turn was followed by one hundred seven sketches (240 pages). Collation shows that printer's copy for these sketches was made up in part from JF3, EOps, Scrs, and PJks. Hotten reprinted most of JF3 and EOps, omitted the six nonauthorial sketches in Scrs, and retained about half of the sketches in

---

[149]Chatto and Windus Ledger Book 1, p. 243; see *BAL* 3351. The earliest advertisement for HWa known to us appeared in the Christmas 1872 issue of the *Bookseller* (p. 216), offering a book of seven hundred pages with "Fifty admirable Illustrations": "Admirers of Mark Twain's delightful humour will be glad to get his choice works in a collected form, and produced in a style worthy of their popularity. Some of the illustrations are by the author himself, and many of the stories and sketches will be quite new to English readers."

[150]Clemens to London *Daily Telegraph*, 8 November 1872, *CL3*, letter 229.

[151]Hotten's letter of November 8 mentioned that he was considering "giving a short biography" of Mark Twain, but the sketch he finally did write and publish was quite long and comprehensive. It was subscribed 12 March 1873, and (as shown by a difference in the method of marking signatures) must have been printed sometime after the rest of the book. On March 4 and again on March 18 Hotten asked Ambrose Bierce for information about Mark Twain's biography: "Give me a few particulars about M. Twain's journalistic career in San Francisco," he wrote on March 4. "Was he as poor & as dejected as he says he was in Roughing It. He says he got $12. per week from *Californian*, & that Bret Harte got $20" (Bancroft). The writing and typesetting of the sketch helps to account for the long delay between Hotten's order to print on August 19 and the delivery of sheets on the following March 20. The first 1,500 copies were bound on March 25, and a copy was deposited in the British Museum on April 18 (Chatto and Windus Ledger Book 1, p. 243).

PJks. He also added several sketches from various periodicals, and he quietly reprinted seven of the fifteen new sketches that the Routledges and Mark Twain had "copyrighted" for MTSk and CD.[152]

Hotten received 2,000 copies of HWa in sheets on 20 March 1873, and by late October all but 229 of these had been sold.[153] He failed, however, to see a second impression of his large collection: Hotten died on 14 June 1873.[154] He was succeeded by his assistant, Andrew Chatto, who (in partnership with W. E. Windus) soon approached Mark Twain about the author's original offer to revise and correct the contents of HWa. On November 25 Chatto wrote:

Mr Bierce, Mr Tom Hood, and Mr Stoddard, have all been so kind as

---

[152]JF3 provided printer's copy for twenty-five of its twenty-seven sketches: "Advice for Good Little Girls" (no. 114) and " 'Mark Twain' on the Launch of the Steamer 'Capital' " (no. 136) were reprinted instead from MTSk and Scrs, respectively. EOps provided copy for twenty-six of its twenty-seven sketches; "Introductory" (no. 290) was dropped. Scrs provided copy for twenty-six of its original thirty-three sketches; one had been dropped in 1872 for the second issue; five were omitted because Mark Twain had denied writing them; and one was taken instead from PJks. PJks provided copy for sixteen of its thirty-seven sketches; only "Rigging the Market" among these was not by Mark Twain. To these Hotten added four new authorial sketches: "English Festivities and Minor Matters" (no. 247) and "Information Wanted" (no. 216) from the *Express* and the New York *Tribune* respectively; "A Nabob's Visit to New York," which had been reprinted from *Roughing It* in the *American Publisher* 1 (January 1872): 4; and a portion of chapter 15 of *Roughing It*, dubbed "Mark in Mormonland." He also inadvertently included two nonauthorial pieces, one from the *Galaxy* 12 (August 1871): 285–286, and one still unidentified item called "Mark Twain as George Washington." From MTSk Hotten took only seven of the fifteen new pieces: "The Facts Concerning the Recent Resignation" (no. 217), "My Late Senatorial Secretaryship" (no. 226), "Personal Habits of the Siamese Twins" (no. 237), "The Latest Novelty. Mental Photographs" (no. 262), "Lionizing Murderers" (no. 274), "A Mysterious Visit" (no. 285), and "The Facts in the Case of George Fisher, Deceased" (no. 345).

HWa brought Hotten's list of titles in the "Works of Mark Twain" to nine: *Pleasure Trip on the Continent, The Innocents Abroad, The New Pilgrim's Progress,* JF3, BA3, EOps, Scrs, PJks, and HWa. In some advertisements at this time he even added a tenth: "A Further Gathering of Mark Twain's Delightful Papers," announced as "*Shortly*" forthcoming (advertisement in Charles Warren Stoddard, *Summer Cruising in the South Seas* [London: Chatto and Windus, 1874], p. [10]); but this "Further Gathering" was never published, and may never really have been planned, since Hotten had pretty thoroughly exhausted his material. We may note that the Routledges likewise participated in the competitive listing of titles. By the fall of 1873 they could legitimately add *The Gilded Age* to their list, while they increased their apparent number of titles to eleven by selling two-shilling editions that combined JF4b and CD, or both parts of *The Innocents Abroad* and of *Roughing It*. In December 1873 one could also buy "The Complete Works, 4 vols. bound in half roan" for ten shillings (*Athenaeum,* 6 December 1873, p. 748).

[153]Chatto and Windus Ledger Book 1, p. 243. The British Museum deposit copy is stamped 18 April 1873. The book was announced in the *Athenaeum* for April 12, the *Publishers' Circular* for April 17, and the *Bookseller* for May 1873 (*BAL* 3351).

[154]London *Times*, 17 June 1873, p. 1.

to promise to speak to you about myself as the successor to the business of the late Mr Hotten.

I am sincerely anxious to establish more cordial relations as between Author & Publisher, than have hitherto existed, between you and our firm, and I beg to submit to you a set of the sheets of a volume of your writings, in order that you may (as I understand you expressed a desire to do) correct certain portions of the contents.[155]

Chatto accordingly sent the folded and gathered sheets of HWa to Mark Twain, who was again in London, and the author proceeded to revise and correct them extensively. The corrected sheets served as printer's copy for Chatto and Windus' reissue of the volume, HWb, in early April 1874, and are preserved in the Rare Book Division of the New York Public Library. All of Mark Twain's autograph changes are reported in the historical collations for the present edition, identified by the symbol HWa**MT**.[156] Hinman collation of HWa against HWb

---

[155]Chatto to Clemens, 25 November 1873, Chatto and Windus Letter Book 6, p. 707. Chatto's three allies were all men with whom Mark Twain was already acquainted, and who had some reason to speak well of the new firm, or even of Hotten himself. On 8 November 1872 Hotten had told Mark Twain that he and Ambrose Bierce were "fast friends" and that Hotten had been able to give him "money for material for a little book," *The Fiend's Delight*, published in 1873 (Chatto and Windus Letter Book 6, pp. 19–20). Mark Twain had met Tom Hood in 1872 through the Routledges; but it was Chatto and Windus who posthumously published Hood's *From Nowhere to the North Pole* (1874–1875). Charles Warren Stoddard was Mark Twain's personal secretary at this time, and he too was planning to publish his *Summer Cruising in the South Seas* (1874) with Chatto and Windus. M. E. Grenander has recently provided a detailed account of the influence that Bierce, Hood, and Stoddard had upon Mark Twain in this matter in her forthcoming "California's Albion."

[156]Chatto and Windus continued to bind and sell the unrevised sheets of HWa in late 1873 and early 1874 (*Athenaeum*, 27 December 1873, p. 880). A second printing was ordered on November 12, but was presumably suspended when Mark Twain agreed later that month to revise the book. It is likely that Mark Twain completed his revision by the end of 1873, for on HWa**MT** he criticized the frontispiece as follows: "This is a *libel*. If you want a decent portrait, buy one from the London *Graphic*, published last October or September a *year* ago." The portrait he alluded to appeared in the *Graphic* 6 (5 October 1872): 324. On 23 March 1874 some 2,000 sets of sheets for HWb were delivered, and the first bound copies were ready by April 23; the book was advertised as early as March 28 (Chatto and Windus Ledger Book 2, p. 97; *Athenaeum*, 28 March 1874, p. 415). Thus between December 1873 and March 1874 Chatto and Windus completed the complicated task of altering the original plates, a chore which cost them £16 15s. HWb was a venture that ultimately proved quite profitable for Chatto and Windus, at least in part because they were not required to pay the author a per-copy royalty. By 2 February 1878 they had sold some 6,000 copies: assuming a 35-percent publisher's discount to the bookseller on a retail price of seven shillings and sixpence, that sale alone yielded a gross return of £1,463 (or $7,315). This profit was certainly reduced by the high cost of binding (perhaps £140) and of advertising (perhaps £100), but the book was clearly lucrative, and it remained in print well into the twentieth century, running up some 23,000 copies by 1904 alone. Entries for binding continue until at least 1951.

shows that the printers altered the original plates to incorporate Mark Twain's revisions and corrections: sometimes this meant resetting only a few lines or words on a page, but occasionally whole pages or large parts of pages had to be reset because Mark Twain deleted entire sketches and heavily revised others.

Mark Twain began his revision by reading and correcting Hotten's long biographical sketch. Although he found several passages that he said were untrue ("& would be useless rubbish IF true"), he was on the whole quite favorably impressed. "This is a well written biographical sketch & ought not to be disfigured by this sort of thing," he wrote after canceling an offending passage. "If Hotten wrote it I wholly lay aside the ancient grudge I bore him. However, I did that when he died." Mark Twain had not begun to correct the sketches, however, and his patience was as yet untried.

Mark Twain ignored the text of *The Innocents Abroad*, except to delete five illustrations he considered in bad taste,[157] and concentrated instead on the short pieces. He deleted seventeen sketches: some because they were nonauthorial or too completely corrupted; others because they seemed "juvenile" or "puerile," embarrassing relics of his apprenticeship.[158] The violence of his rejection of early material is remarkable: "A New Biography of Washington" (no. 183) was "rubbish . . . leave it all out." "An Open Letter to the American People"

---

[157]Mark Twain disliked some of the English illustrations for his book (they were not reproduced from the American edition), and asked to have them removed. For instance, he canceled a picture of Christ calming the waters of Galilee which had been captioned "By One of the Oldest of the Old Masters." He noted: "It is hardly a gracious or a reverent thing to make [a] grotesque picture of a subject like this—it is better left out I think."

[158]Only three deleted sketches were actually nonauthorial: Mark Twain simply dismissed "Rigging the Market" with the words "Leave it out"; he canceled "How I Secured a Berth" and explained in the margin, "Leave this out—I never wrote it"; and he likewise rejected "Mark Twain as George Washington," saying "Leave it out—it is not mine." But other sketches that Mark Twain had written were made unacceptable by Hotten's errors and intrusions. For instance, Hotten's extract from chapter 6 of *Roughing It* ("Sending Them Through," Jack's introduction to the story of Moses) had altered the famous phrase "Moses *who?*" to "Moses *what?*" Mark Twain restored the original reading and exploded in the margin: "God damn the hound that altered that." And when he came to "Mark in Mormonland," extracted with many editorial liberties from chapter 15 of *Roughing It*, he tried to restore his original text but soon lost patience: "DAMN these idiotic additions of the asinine editor"; and then later, "God eternally damn the thief that marred & mutilated this chapter." This last extract was omitted from HWb.

(no. 181) was also "rubbish—leave it out." "Washoe.—'Information Wanted'" (no. 75) was "puerile hogwash"; "Origin of Illustrious Men" (no. 193) was "literary vomit"; and "Earthquake Almanac" (no. 122) was "puling imbecility." All five of these had first been collected in JF1. "The Story of Joseph" (extracted by Hotten from an *Alta California* letter of 12 January 1868) was "hellfired rubbish." Even some relatively recent material from the *Galaxy* was found wanting: "A Book Review" (no. 351), for instance, was dismissed as "d—d rubbish—leave it out"; "The Reception at the President's" (no. 325) was also omittable "rubbish." Most emphatically, however, he canceled a sketch that Hotten had titled "On Letter Writing," saying in the margin:

This was simply the prelude to an article that had more sense in it than the editor of this collection ever had in all his life—& with his usual sagacity he has left it out, not being able to believe that sense & humor can possibly dwell together consistently. I fervently hope the said editor is in hell, or will speedily land there. However, this present stuff ought never to have been written & never printed—it is pure unadulterated rubbish—or, as the English say, ROT [*this last in large letters across the page*].

The sketch in question, originally titled "One of Mankind's Bores" (no. 354), first appeared in the *Galaxy:* Hotten reprinted it in PJks, then in HWa, virtually without change. Mark Twain's illusion that an editor was to blame for work that now struck him as embarrassingly youthful may have made the confrontation with his apprentice work more bearable.

Mark Twain also revised the language and scope of pieces that he decided to retain in the collection. "Burlesque 'Answers to Correspondents'" (no. 201) was again shortened, as it had been when he revised MTSk the previous year. Indeed, he sometimes managed to duplicate his changes with uncanny precision,[159] just as he corrected typographical errors, restoring the original word or even—when the sense required it—the original punctuation. He corrected British practices

---

[159]The autograph changes on HWa**MT** should be compared with the changes detected by collation in MTSk, prepared some twenty months earlier. Mark Twain was in both cases revising texts that derived from EOps, Scrs, and JF2, and he often made changes similar or even identical to his earlier ones.

that were always annoying to him: "I say *a* hundred,—not *an* hundred, like [a] d—d fool." Correcting Hotten's "proprietors" to "proprieties," he remarked that "the proof-reading on this book must have been very hurriedly done, or else done by a novice"; and he wrote, then canceled, a more pointed remark: "I hope the new firm has hired a *proof-reader* instead of a shoemaker."

Although Mark Twain confined himself almost without exception to corrections and revisions which affected meaning, he did try to revise the system of paragraphing that had been imposed on one of the sources of printer's copy for HWa, Hotten's earlier collection PJks. His changes reversed Hotten's editing and often restored the original paragraphs. "Make ONE paragraph of this," he noted on page 390 of HWa**MT**; and on the next page asked, "Why is this d—d paragraph split in two?" His notes continue in the same vein throughout the book: "Run in—all one ¶"; "Run this into the preceding Paragraph—I wonder what besotted ass punctuated this edition." His anger gradually increased: "No Paragraph—may God eternally roast the man who punctuated this book." On pages 423–424 he repeated over and over again, "All one paragraph"; "All one paragraph"; "All one paragraph"; and on page 480, "Run this & the next paragraph together. I wish this fool was in hell." Finally, on page 551, he wrote, "I do hope the man is in hell that paragraphed this edition."

Despite his violent criticism of Hotten's editing, Mark Twain could not hope to restore his original texts. "Journalism in Tennessee" (no. 252), which Hotten himself had singled out as an example of his bowdlerizing, was transmitted from EOps through HWa into HWb essentially as the editor had left it. Indeed, in some sketches Mark Twain furthered Hotten's attempts to modify his strong or vulgar language for more fastidious audiences. He deleted allusions to "slobbering" and to the man who "blew his nose on my coat tail." The "spittoon" became a more respectable "cuspidor"; the "blowing of noses" became simply "barking"; and "victims of consumption" became merely "patients." Even the vaguest hint of the scatological was subject to removal: "diarrhoea? dysentery?" became the deadlier but cleaner "cancer? consumption?" He canceled or replaced "vile" several times, along with irreverent allusions to hell or swearing: such words as "infernal," "diabolical," or "cussed" were deleted; "swear" became "rage"; "blasted" became "single"; "cursing" became "raving"; and "d——d" became "hanged."

When Mark Twain retained sketches in HWb which Hotten had originally taken from the *Jumping Frog* book, he often found that they needed more such pruning than later material did—in spite of the fact that he had already gone over them once when preparing JF1. For example, in "The Spiritual Séance" (no. 202) he deleted "or perdition, or some of those places" and changed "infernal" to "disgraceful," "hell" to "Tophet," "damned" to "lost," "perdition" to "the nether world," and "damnation" to "destruction." He made the sketch into a piece that (in the words of the *Saturday Review*) could "be read aloud, without missing a word, by the most fastidious mother to a family circle." The same man who, in the privacy of the printing house, repeatedly wished Hotten in hell, eternally roasting for his absurd punctuation, carefully eliminated such words and allusions from his public, literary utterances.

Chatto and Windus published HWb—"Revised & Corrected by the Author," as Mark Twain wrote on the HWa**MT** title page—in early April 1874. Thus in England there were two contemporaneous editions of Mark Twain's sketches—MTSk and HWb—published by rival firms, both containing numerous corrections and revisions by the author together with the editorial contributions of Charles Henry Webb and John Camden Hotten. Their contents varied slightly (HWb was larger by twenty-four pieces, and of course *The Innocents Abroad*), but each had taken its selection of *Galaxy* pieces from Hotten's EOps and Scrs, and each contained at least some of the newly revised pieces that Mark Twain had also published in CD, as well as independently revised texts from JF2 and JF3. Sketches that Mark Twain had revised for MTSk he often revised again for HWb, making similar, sometimes identical changes. All of the texts suffered the usual deterioration in accidentals: some of the sketches in JF1 were reprinted in MTSk and HWb for the fourth or fifth time. And many of the sketches had been heavily edited by Webb or Hotten, as well as by the author himself. Mark Twain added the final touch to this extraordinary situation the following year: in late 1875 he issued an American edition of his sketches called *Sketches, New and Old*, which drew upon MTSk and HWb for most of its printer's copy.

8. *Mark Twain's Sketches. Number One.*
Authorised Edition (1874): Sk#1

Before Mark Twain went on to produce *Sketches, New and Old*,
however, he made yet another excursion into the realm of the cheap
pamphlet. Shortly after *Roughing It* was published in February 1872,
the author returned to the projected American edition of sketches by
reviewing the printer's copy he had submitted to Bliss in early 1871.
On March 21 he told the publisher that he had at last "sat down in
earnest & looked the new book through," and had decided to stand by
his original decision to leave out the "Jumping Frog" sketch.[160] As we
have seen, the English editions CD and MTSk soon intervened and
siphoned off some of his copy in late March and April. Mark Twain
also spent part of May and June preparing a revised edition of *The
Innocents Abroad* for the Routledges, and shortly afterward decided to
visit England in part to support their efforts on his behalf. Still, on
August 7, he tried to prod Bliss into some sort of commitment to the
American sketchbook: "Hurry up your figuring on the volume of
sketches," he wrote, "for I leave for England in 10 or 12 days to be gone
several months."[161] But Bliss's "figuring" was not soon completed, and
when Mark Twain returned to the United States later that year he was
preoccupied with other matters, chiefly *The Gilded Age*. Three
months after his return, Bliss must have inquired after the sketchbook
and was told: "Can get sketches ready any time, but shall wait awhile,
as I have good hopes of finishing a book which I am working like a dog
on—a book which ought to outsell the sketches, & doubtless will."[162]
The Gilded Age, like *Roughing It* in 1871, now pushed the sketchbook
to one side. Indeed, in January 1873 Mark Twain seemed at least
momentarily content with the English editions of his sketches. In an
autobiographical essay written for Charles Dudley Warner he

---

[160]Clemens to Bliss, 21 March 1872, *CL3*, letter 160: "Don't hesitate about it, but
just *take the Frog out.* What *we* want, is that the book should be *the best we can
make it.* We seriously injure it by putting in the Frog." Mark Twain had not included
this sketch in his original printer's copy, submitted in January (see the table of contents, figure 19). Bliss must have persuaded him to include it at a later time—a decision
the author now reversed.

[161]Clemens to Bliss, 7 August 1872, *CL3*, letter 197.

[162]Clemens to Bliss, 26 February 1873, *CL3*, letter 267. On 16 April 1873 Mark Twain
told Mrs. Fairbanks that he and Warner had been working steadily on the *"partnership
novel"* since his arrival "from England" (*CL3*, letter 290).

remarked, with some pride, that "in England the Routledges & Hotten have gathered together & published all my sketches; a great many that have not appeared in book form here. There are four volumes of these sketches."[163]

In May 1873, Mark Twain returned for a second visit to England, possibly intending to work on his book about English manners, but primarily to see *The Gilded Age* through the rigors of British publication and copyright. Once there, however, he was persuaded by the London representative of the New York *Herald* to write a series of newspaper letters about the Shah of Persia—and this endeavor reignited his old flame, the project of a cheap pamphlet of sketches. On June 18, as he began writing the first of five long letters ("O'Shah"), he told Bliss to "seize them as they appear, & turn them into a 25 cent pamphlet (my royalty 10 per cent) & spread them over the land your own way, but be quick! Don't let it get cold before you are out. I suggest that you disseminate them by means of the news companies."[164] By July 7 he had completed his last letter to the *Herald*, and he now began to consider filling out the little book with additional material. He wrote Bliss:

You can take the Herald letters & put them in a pamphlet along with the enclosed article about the Jumping Frog in French, (which is entirely new) & then add enough of my old sketches to make *a good fat 25 cent pamphlet* & let it slide—but don't charge *more* than 25¢ nor less. If you haven't a Routledge edition of my sketches to select from you will find one at my house or Warner's.

By this time Mark Twain had gone so far as to write a prefatory note, "To the Reader," which deprecated the Shah letters and offered his excuse for republishing them. He said he was concerned about copyright, and he warned his public that he had added to the letters "certain sketches of mine which are little known or not known at all in America, to the end that the purchaser of the pamphlet may get back a

---

[163]"Samuel Langhorne Clemens," pp. 10–11, Pierpont Morgan Library, New York. Mark Twain had completed this sketch by 27 January 1873, when he mentioned it in a letter to Michael Laird Simons (*CL3*, letter 260). The "four volumes" of sketches to which he referred were EOps, Scrs, MTSk, and CD. Hotten's HWa had not yet been published, and PJks was probably too obscure to be counted.
[164]Clemens to Bliss, 18 June 1873, *CL3*, letter 310.

portion of his money and skip the chapters that refer to the Shah altogether."[165]

The Shah pamphlet never materialized as Mark Twain planned it in 1873, but several things about this plan are worth noting. Mark Twain designated MTSk, the only readily available collection of his short pieces, as the source of printer's copy, but he seems not to have been averse to letting Bliss make the selection of sketches on his own. The idea of publishing "a good fat 25 cent pamphlet" with an entirely new sketch included shows that Mark Twain had learned something from his failure with the too expensive—and too thin—BA1, but the resemblance of the new sketchbook to this earlier volume is unmistakable. The insistence on twenty-five cents as the maximum price, the requisite speed of publication, the use of news companies to achieve a spectacular distribution, and the addition of a single new sketch to palliate republishing older material—all these elements are reminiscent of BA1. By July 27 Mark Twain's confidence in the project had waned, and he urged Bliss not to advertise the pamphlet or send it to the newspapers because, he said, he wanted it "to pass unnoticed."[166] The project died a quiet death while Mark Twain spent the rest of 1873 lecturing in England and arranging for simultaneous publication of The Gilded Age, taking extraordinary pains to coordinate the Routledges' edition with Bliss's.[167] As we have seen, in December 1873 he also agreed to revise the sketches in HWa for Andrew Chatto.

The idea of a twenty-five-cent sketchbook persisted into 1874 and, indeed, beyond that year. Mark Twain returned to the United States in late January 1874: he had abandoned the book about England by June 1873[168] and had published The Gilded Age in December of that year, and he now turned his attention once again to an American edition of sketches. On 25 February 1874 he told Mrs. Fairbanks about

---

[165]Clemens to Bliss, 7 July 1873, CL3, letter 324. "To the Reader" is reproduced in Appendix C4, volume 1.

[166]Clemens to Bliss, 27 July 1873, CL3, letter 333.

[167]Despite these extraordinary precautions, which resulted in a secure British copyright for The Gilded Age, the Routledges failed to sell more than 10,500 copies by 1 October 1877. Mark Twain and Warner accordingly split a total royalty of £257—only $1,285 (Routledge Agreement Book A–K, pp. 183–184; Ledger Book 4, p. 765). This disappointing record no doubt contributed to Mark Twain's unhappiness with the firm and his move toward Chatto and Windus.

[168]Clemens to London Evening Post, 25 June 1873, CL3, letter 314. Clemens said that he planned to write it "some day, but not just at present." The book, the idea for which had occurred to him as early as March 1870, was in fact never completed.

his newest scheme: "I am preparing several volumes of my sketches for publication, & am writing new sketches to add to them."[169] He had evidently revived the notion of issuing not one, but a series of pamphlets ("several volumes") reminiscent of Josh Billings' series of *Allminax*. The only result of this plan was a thirty-two-page paper-covered brochure, "Number One" of *Mark Twain's Sketches* (Sk #1). Sk #1 was electrotyped and printed by a now obscure firm, Hutchings Printing House of Hartford, and it was published by the American News Company of New York, sometime in late May or early June 1874. The little pamphlet manifestly failed to satisfy the author's expectations for it, and no "Number Two" was ever issued—although it seems likely that Mark Twain had already begun preparing copy for it in 1874.

Sk #1 is the Shah book without the Shah letters: it cost only twenty-five cents, it was distributed by the news companies, and it contained three new sketches "From the Author's Unpublished English Notes,"[170] in addition to ten items reprinted from the Routledge edition of his sketches, MTSk. Sk #1 was also the fulfill-ment of Mark Twain's ambition, dating from December 1870, to publish a "Jumping Frog *pamphlet* (illustrated),"[171] for among the sketches reprinted from MTSk was a slightly revised version of the author's most famous sketch, illustrated by R. T. Sperry, who also produced the cover design: a cigar-smoking frog sitting underneath a toadstool, contemplating an edition of *Mark Twain's Sketches* (see figure 22).

Sperry also produced eleven additional pictures for other sketches in the collection, but, like the Hutchings Printing House, he too remains obscure. In fact, almost nothing is known about how Sk #1 was planned, what Mark Twain's arrangements with the illustrator and publisher were, what rationale he pursued in selecting material, or even when or whether he read proof. Only a small portion of what appears to be the printer's copy (the manuscript for "A Memorable Midnight Experience") has survived, and there is so little correspon-

---

[169]Clemens to Mary Mason Fairbanks, 25 February 1874, *MTMF*, pp. 183–184.

[170]This phrase preceded three new sketches: "A Memorable Midnight Experience," "Rogers," and "Property in Opulent London." Since all three were written after 1871, they do not appear in the present collection. All sketches discussed hereafter which are not identified by a number in this collection have been excluded for the same reason.

[171]Clemens to Bliss, 22 December 1870, *CL2*, letter 267.

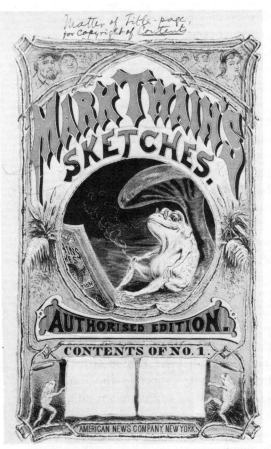

FIGURE 22A. An early print of the cover for Sk#1, sent by Mark Twain to the copyright office on 7 May 1874.

FIGURE 22B. The cover of Sk#1 as published in late May or early June 1874. Mark Twain's publisher has added the contents and several other minor elements not in the early version.

dence about the pamphlet that we cannot even be sure when Mark Twain submitted that copy. The evidence of collation, some scattered documents, and a few letters shed only a little light on this mysterious project.

Mark Twain probably began work on the printer's copy in February 1874, when he told Mrs. Fairbanks that he was writing "new sketches" for the pamphlet series. But none of the new pieces in Sk # 1 was in fact written at this time: all of them came from the abandoned book about England, and had been written in 1872 or 1873. Moreover, Mark Twain did not spend a great deal of time revising the sketches he reprinted from MTSk: only four of these seem to have been revised by him, and these were not extensively altered. Collation shows that he made a few changes in "Depart, Ye Accursed!" (no. 199), "Misplaced Confidence" (no. 296), "A Reminiscence of the Back Settlements" (no. 331), and "Jim Smiley and His Jumping Frog" (no. 119). The overall pattern of cleansing is familiar, but was less severely pursued: "spittoon" became "cuspidor"; "degraded" became "profligate"; "vile" was omitted; and several allusions to cursing chambermaids "in behalf of outraged bachelordom" were dropped. Mark Twain tinkered with the dialect spellings in the frog sketch, apparently altering "wan't" to "warn't," "again" to "agin," and "far" to "fur." He changed "slop-bucket" to "slop-jar" (a delicate refinement), "big funeral" to "lurid funeral," and probably tinkered with the paragraphing as well. We cannot tell whether all of these alterations were made in the printer's copy, because collation of the manuscript for "A Memorable Midnight Experience" against Sk # 1 suggests that Mark Twain probably revised his pamphlet in proof— changing in this sketch, for example, "splendid" to "noble," "generation" to "long year," and "latest novelty" to "latest thing."

We do not know when Mark Twain read proof, but it was almost certainly sometime before May 1, for on that day he wrote William A. Seaver, editor of *Harper's Monthly*, asking him to reprint one of the items planned for Sk # 1 ("Misplaced Confidence," no. 296) in the "Editor's Drawer." Mark Twain had evidently seen the sketch attributed to someone else in a country newspaper and felt the potential embarrassment: "I wouldn't make the suggestion at all," he told Seaver, "but for the fact that I am going to publish my sketches, & if this sketch is already electrotyped it will be too late to leave it out & I shall seem to be stealing from a pauper."[172] Although he remained unclear about the precise stage of production, he seems to have felt that electrotyping was imminent.

Electrotyping may have been completed by early May, but the plate for the cover illustration was not. On May 7 Mark Twain wrote to A. R. Spofford, Librarian of Congress: "I enclose *design of a Pamphlet Cover*, upon which I desire a copyright. Also, the title-page of the Pamphlet—upon the CONTENTS of which I likewise desire copyright." What he sent was, in fact, an early print of the engraved cover, lacking "No. 1" and "Price 25 Cents" in the top margin and (of course) the copyright notice at the bottom, as well as the list of sketches and appropriate page numbers under "Contents of No. 1" (see figure 22).[173] The last stages of production were yet to be completed. Copyright was officially entered on May 9, but it was not until June 4 that two copies of the pamphlet itself were deposited with the Library of Congress.[174] The incomplete title page, lacking the specific sketches to be included, and the month-long delay between copyright and actual publication both suggest that there were unexpected problems with Sk #1. Indeed, on May 10 Clemens wrote Orion that his "pamphlets" were "delayed unreasonably," and that "everything goes wrong & I'm in a never-ending state of harassment." The precise cause of this delay is not known—it could have been any of the things that had plagued the earlier experiment in instant publication, BA1. By May 20 Mark Twain had at least resolved his problem with "Misplaced Confidence": Seaver had written promising to do his best with *Harper's*. Mark Twain replied, "I'm ever so much obliged to you for fixing up that thing for me—& if it don't get into print I will curse other people, not you."[175] Fortunately, no further cursing was required: the sketch appeared in the July *Harper's*, shortly after Sk #1 was published, evidently in time to prevent any misunderstanding about Mark Twain's right to republish it. *Harper's* introduced the piece with a wry explanation, "The Galena editor who published that funny thing about the Sunday-school superintendent's remark to his scholars about the steamer did not remember how good the original

---

[172]Clemens to Seaver, 1 May 1874, University of Wisconsin.

[173]Clemens to Spofford, 7 May 1874, copyright no. 6347 E, Library of Congress.

[174]Report of William A. Moore in the copyright office, 1 July 1975.

[175]Clemens to Orion Clemens, 10 May 1874, TS in MTP; Clemens to Seaver, 20 May 1874, University of Wisconsin.

was, written by Mark Twain, and published three years ago in London."[176]

Mark Twain's attitude toward the illustrations of Sk#1 is not well documented, but he must have been involved with approving what Sperry produced. The author was, presumably, happy to have his own map of Paris reproduced from the Buffalo *Express*, and he undoubtedly approved of two illustrations in "A Memorable Midnight Experience": both were copied from drawings he himself had made in the manuscript. Moreover, we can infer that Mark Twain was proud of the cover illustration, for he showed a strong proprietary interest in it. When he received notification of his copyright from Spofford, Mark Twain wrote back, this time on May 21: "I lately copyrighted, as proprietor, an *Engraved Design for Cover* of 'Mark Twain's Sketches,' & am informed from your office, that I can have evidence of said copyright in the form of a certificate by paying 50 cents more. I would like to have the certificate, & so enclose the 50 cents in this letter."[177]

Still less (if less be possible) is known about the pamphlet's reception by the press, its sale, or even what royalty Mark Twain made on each copy. He probably got the 10 percent he had planned to charge Bliss on the Shah pamphlet, but no contract or letter of agreement has been found. The apparently universal silence observed by the newspapers may indicate that the little brochure was simply too slight to be noticed at all, but this seems unlikely, because similar slight ventures by Thomas Nast were widely remarked upon. The silence may mean, on the other hand, that Mark Twain got cold feet at the last moment and deliberately discouraged reviews, as he had in fact contemplated doing with the Shah pamphlet, which was to "pass unnoticed" without "a copy [sent] to any newspaper."[178] No reviews have been found, and no publishing records have survived. Nevertheless, it seems clear that Mark Twain made less from the sale than he hoped, and that he had at least a temporary change of heart about such projects. Less than a year after the publication of

---

[176]*Harper's New Monthly Magazine* 49 (July 1874): 301. In Mark Twain's original letter to Seaver he had enclosed page 254 from a copy of MTSk, "the London edition of my Sketches," which contained the entire sketch. It had first been published in the *Galaxy* in May 1870; *Harper's* reprinted it from the copy sent by Mark Twain.

[177]Clemens to Spofford, 21 May 1875, Library of Congress.

[178]Clemens to Bliss, 27 July 1873, *CL3*, letter 333.

Sk#1, Mark Twain told Dan De Quille: "Hang it, man, you don't want a *pamphlet*—you want a *book*—600 pages 8-vo, illustrated. There isn't a single cent of money in a pamphlet. Not a single cent. But there's money in a *book*."[179]

Mark Twain carefully copyrighted Sk#1 in the United States, but he made no effort whatever to copyright the contents, even the new material, in England. On 20 June 1874, three weeks after publication, Edmund Routledge wrote him to say that he had "just received and read No 1 of Mark Twain's Sketches which contains 3 papers . . . from your unpublished English Notes." Routledge added that he was "sorry you should thus forfeit your copyright in these papers here, as the result will be that your book on England will be damaged," and he made a generous offer to "buy electros of the cuts of this edition of the Sketches as they appear." Routledge said further that he hoped the author would "arrange this matter for us; but at the same time I hope you will not issue any new work in the States without giving us plenty of time to secure copyright on it here."[180] The Routledges did not reprint any part of Sk#1, with or without illustrations. Having already invested a great deal of time and energy in securing Mark Twain's cooperation, they were perhaps unwilling to offend him with a piracy—but they were also made uneasy by the carelessness he showed about British copyright, a carelessness they rightly understood as a tacit movement toward outright defection.

What the Routledges could not know, and what Mark Twain probably never explicitly told them, was that there would be no occasion to send electros of the illustrations for "this edition of the Sketches" as they appeared, for Sk#1 was the last as well as the first in the series. Three years after publication, on 22 August 1877, some portion of the initial printing evidently remained unsold. William C. Hutchings (presumably of "Hutchings Printing House") told Mark Twain on that day that he had been offered $300 to dispose of "the entire lot of 'Sketches' pamphlets to the Aetna Life Ins. Co.," for which Hutchings was then an agent in New York City. He explained, "They will print their advertisement on the back cover page, as per enclosed sample, (nothing printed on the inside covers,) and circulate the pamphlets at convenience." Hutchings added significantly,

---

[179]Clemens to William Wright (Dan De Quille), 29 April 1875, TS in MTP.
[180]Routledge to Clemens, 20 June 1876, MTP.

"I hope you have no objection to my realizing as above on what is absolutely dead property to me otherwise. It's a small amount, comparatively, but situated as I am at present the $300⁰⁰ will be a perfect God-send."[181]

Mark Twain seems to have made no objection to this plan, and Aetna did indeed buy the remaining sheets and reissue Sk#1 with its advertisement on the cover. Mark Twain's acquiescence in this blatantly commercial scheme suggests that he may well have felt some sort of responsibility toward Hutchings: less than a year after he published Sk#1, Mark Twain set about publishing a book of sketches that was designed to include all but one of the pieces printed or reprinted in Sk#1, effectively reducing its value to zero. This large, fully illustrated American edition appeared in September 1875, and it arose in part out of the belief that Mark Twain had expressed to Dan De Quille: "There isn't a single cent of money in a pamphlet. . . . But there's money in a *book*."

9. *Mark Twain's Sketches, New and Old* (1875): MTSk**MT**, HWb**MT**, and SkNO

Sketches, New and Old (SkNO) was Mark Twain's most ambitious, most thoroughly sifted, and most fully revised collection of his apprentice work. It was also his final one. Alone among the sketchbooks considered here, SkNO became part of the official Writings of Mark Twain which the American Publishing Company began to issue in 1899. It was reprinted several times between 1875 and 1899, and it stood, in the author's lifetime, as the only authorized and widely available edition of sketches written before the author was forty years old.

SkNO may be said to have originated late in 1870 with Mark Twain's plan to publish a collection of his early short work which, as he told Bliss, he wanted "as profusely illustrated as the Innocents."[182] This book, however, had been repeatedly postponed, partly by the demands of two long narratives, *Roughing It* and *The Gilded*

---

[181]Hutchings to Clemens, 22 August 1877, Scrapbook 10, p. 68, MTP. Copies of Sk#1 with Aetna advertisements on the back cover give at least two different totals for that company's assets after 1 January 1877, but it is not known for how long the company reissued Sk#1 in this way.

[182]Clemens to Bliss, 22 December 1870, *CL2*, letter 267.

Age, and partly by the challenge and opportunity posed by Hotten and the Routledges. The American sketchbook had had to compete, moreover, with an alternative plan many times revived: the cheap illustrated pamphlet that Mark Twain never tired of projecting. Nevertheless, such pamphlets were more than an irrational obsession, for they were to some extent designed to avoid an unintended effect of "portly" volumes like MTSk, and even like JF1: the problem of maintaining interest in separate sketches unsupported by any "narrative plank." By restricting the number of sketches, charging a small price, and using ample illustration, Mark Twain hoped to recycle some of his sketches in palatable, profitable doses. When Sk #1 failed to produce the expected financial reward, however, he turned again to the original conception of 1870—not without reservations, and with a rather half-hearted enthusiasm. In March 1875, shortly after completing the printer's copy for SkNO, Mark Twain told his friend Dan De Quille (who was thinking of publishing a sketchbook of his own) what he had learned from several years' experience:

> You see, the winning card is to nail a man's interest with *Chapter 1*, & never let up on him for an instant till you get him to the word "finis." That can't be done with detached sketches; but I'll show you how to make a man read every one of those sketches, under the stupid impression that they are mere accidental incidents that have dropped in on you unawares in the course of the *narrative*.[183]

This method is, of course, the basis of the form of *The Innocents Abroad* and *Roughing It*. The implication of Mark Twain's comments, however, is that he did not regard SkNO as a work of real importance, even as he was in the process of publishing it. Indeed, throughout these months he was far more seriously preoccupied with writing his first long fictional narrative, *The Adventures of Tom Sawyer*.

Mark Twain's interest in an American edition of sketches was stimulated late in 1874 when he began to think of such a book as a way to transcend subscription-house publishing altogether. As early as March 1874 he had become openly disdainful of the "wretched paper and vile engravings" that seemed the inevitable accompaniment

---

[183]Clemens to Wright, 29 March 1875, Bancroft. Clemens added a postscript dated 4 April 1875 to this letter, but he clearly wrote the balance of it on or about March 29.

of subscription books,[184] and in mid-December 1874 he began to seriously consider another way of publishing his sketches. On December 17, shortly after returning from an *Atlantic* dinner in Boston, Mark Twain mentioned to Bliss that he "had a mind to" give his sketches to James R. Osgood.[185] Osgood was William Dean Howells' publisher; he had also published Aldrich, Lowell, and Emerson, and he would soon publish Henry James. Osgood had, it will be recalled, approached Mark Twain with an offer to reprint his sketches in the spring of 1872, and the author had reluctantly turned him down because of his contracts with Bliss. This offer was probably renewed when Mark Twain went to Boston in December 1874, and he set to work in December and January preparing a large collection of sketches—some of them old, some of them unpublished or at least uncollected.

By 11 February 1875 he had gotten "the matter all ready for the press, (index, preface and everything,)" and he frankly broached the idea to Bliss. Although Bliss had treated the first signs of wavering loyalty with restraint—merely arguing in December "in favor of publishing with his company" (as Mark Twain admiringly recalled)— he now moved more forcefully to suppress the revolt, and the author was left to sheepishly explain the result to Osgood:

Concerning that sketch-book. I went to Bliss yesterday and told him I had got all my old sketches culled and put together and a whole lot of new ones added, and that I had about made up my mind to put them in your hands. Whereupon he went to his safe and brought back a contract *four years old* to give him all my old sketches, with a lot of new ones added!—royalty 7½ per cent!

I had totally forgotten the existence of such a contract—*totally.* He said, "It wouldn't be *like* you to refuse to first fulfill *this* contract."

I said, "You flatter me; and moreover you have *got* me. But I won't fulfill it at 7½ per cent."[186]

This contract was, of course, the one Mark Twain had eagerly signed early in 1871, when he anticipated publishing "Mark Twain's Sketches" in the spring. The only concessions he was now able to extract from Bliss were that the book should be illustrated and that

---

[184]Clemens to Thomas Bailey Aldrich, 24 March 1874, *MTLP*, p. 81. The reference is to *The Gilded Age*, which Clemens called "rather a rubbishy looking book."

[185]Clemens to Osgood, 12 February 1875, *MTLP*, p. 84.

[186]Clemens to Osgood, 12 February 1875, *MTLP*, pp. 83–84. The contract is reproduced in Appendix C5, volume 1.

the publisher should pay him a 10-percent royalty, retroactively, when 50,000 copies had been sold. The latter concession had no effect, for SkNO failed to sell that many copies even by 1893, when a cheaper edition was produced by the American Publishing Company under Frank Bliss. Illustrations had always been part of Mark Twain's plan—they had just never been written into his contract, and were not now.

Osgood conceded defeat on February 16,[187] and Mark Twain was then presumably free to give Bliss the sketches he had "culled and put together" for his Boston rival. On February 26 Mark Twain told Warren Choate and Company of Washington, D.C., that he could not agree to sell them the "Jumping Frog" story as they had asked: "I am just on the point of issuing it in book form through my publishers here, along with all my sketches complete."[188] But this was too optimistic: SkNO would not in fact issue from the press until September 1875, seven months later. The long delay between his discussion with Bliss and the production of the first salesmen's prospectuses was caused by several things, but it can be easily explained.

Mark Twain continued to tinker with the printer's copy in February and March: something about a book of sketches inevitably invited this sort of compulsive revision. He probably further revised and culled the material he had already gathered; he made specific instructions to Bliss and to the illustrator; and he added at least one sketch to the contents. For example, on the manuscript of "The 'Blind Letter' Department, London P.O." he wrote instructions about using facsimile letters to illustrate the piece: "Use as many as you think proper, Bliss.—S.L.C." And on the map of Paris (torn from a copy of Sk # 1) he wrote: "Use an *accurate facsimile* of this map, with all its studied imperfections. S.L.C."[189] Sometime in March he solicited the publisher's help in another matter: "From London I sent you a horrible translation (in MS) of the Jumping Frog, from the French.

---

[187]Osgood to Clemens, 16 February 1875, MTP: "And I confess to some degree of delight in finding signs of weakness in so accomplished a business man and successful gambler as yourself: I wouldn't have believed that you could make such a contract, or having made, forget it! But age will tell."

[188]Clemens to Warren Choate and Company, 26 February 1875, collection of Charles Cornman.

[189]The printer's copy of " 'Blind Letter' Department" is at Yale; the copy of the map of Paris is in MTP.

Please hunt it up, if you can, & send to me. I want it for the Vol of Sketches."[190] Bliss found and sent the manuscript that Mark Twain had mailed to him in July 1873, and Mark Twain revised it—changing his imagined audience from Englishmen (whom he had addressed in the original draft) to "anyone," and altering the date of his concluding remarks from "London, June 30, 1873" to "Hartford, March, 1875."[191] He likewise dated the author's preface "Hartford, March, 1875," at least on the copy that was used to prepare the salesmen's prospectus.[192]

Mark Twain probably submitted the completed printer's copy to Bliss in March, and Bliss in turn must have given it to True W. Williams, who had been hired to illustrate the book. Much of the further delay was very likely caused by the time needed to produce some one hundred thirty illustrations, for if production proceeded in a normal way, all the drawings had to be engraved and electroplated before any type would be set or any proofs read. Nor were the pictures the only further cause for delay. On 8 April 1875, some six weeks after he had said he was "on the point of issuing" his book, Mark Twain confided to his old editor and friend, Charles Henry Webb, still another consideration: "It is a mighty tough year for books. The Innocents Abroad & Roughing It, both put together, have not paid me much over $3,000 in the past 12 month. They are old books, they have never had a black eye; I have not lost in reputation—consequently the serious falling off can be reasonably attributed to nothing but the prevailing business prostration." Mark Twain added, however, that he thought "the next 3 months will show a different state of things," and he was therefore "venturing to bring out a new book," something he "could not have been hired to do during any part of the past 12 months, for it would have been a sort of deliberate literary suicide."[193] The depression of 1874–1875 was clearly not over three months after Mark Twain wrote Webb, and Bliss was obviously obliged by it, and by the usual summer slump in sales, to postpone

---

[190]Clemens to Bliss, [March 1875], MTP.

[191]"The 'Jumping Frog.' In English. Then in French" (no. 364). The printer's copy is at CWB.

[192]The author's preface was revised after the salesmen's prospectus was set: both versions are reproduced in Appendix C5, volume 1.

[193]Clemens to Webb, 8 April 1875, *MTLP*, p. 87, corrected from PH in MTP. A large portion of this passage was canceled by Mark Twain before he sent the letter to Webb. We are indebted to Victor Fischer for help in recovering the canceled matter.

publication until the fall—even though most of the substantial work on SkNO had apparently been completed by the end of July.

Since Mark Twain was living in Hartford throughout the spring, and since he did not leave town for a summer retreat at Newport until July 31, he had ample opportunity to work with the illustrator and to read and revise proof for SkNO. But his presence in Hartford meant that he could communicate directly with Bliss and the printing house about business matters that would ordinarily have been discussed in letters: "I only go down town when it is necessary to abuse my publisher," he told Josiah G. Holland on April 29.[194] This unusual lack of documentary evidence leaves us doubtful about precisely when Mark Twain saw proof, but he must certainly have done so. On June 2, for instance, Dan De Quille (who was visiting the author at Hartford) wrote his sister that "Mark is getting out a book which will contain some new and good things, particularly some 'fables for old boys and girls,' where all manner of insects and a few reptiles go out on a scientific exploring expedition, where they meet with and report upon many of the works of the biped man. His 'frog' and other old sketches will be in the book, which will be handsomely illustrated."[195] The allusion here is to "Some Learned Fables, for Good Old Boys and Girls," the longest of the new sketches included in SkNO. It seems likely, therefore, that Mark Twain was seeing proof of this and perhaps other sketches by early June.

Sometime in mid-July the author wrote out the title page of his book:

Mark Twain's Sketches.

[New & Old.]

Now First Published in a Complete
Form in this country.

[Sold only by Subscription.]

Hartford:
The American Publishing Co.
1875.

---

[194]Clemens to Holland, 29 April 1875, TS in MTP.
[195]Wright to Lou Wright Benjamin, 2 June 1875, Bancroft.

At the top of this document he wrote: "Bliss please print this title-page & mail to me for transmission to Washington. S.L.C."[196] Copyright was, in fact, entered in Clemens' name on 20 July 1875,[197] presumably about the time the book had been finally set in type and prepared for electroplating. Eleven days later, on July 31, the author left for Newport, where he remained throughout August and early September, returning to Hartford about September 10. The first copies of the salesmen's prospectus, printed from plates of the book, were received from the bindery on September 3, and the first one hundred copies of SkNO arrived on September 25.[198] In short, Mark Twain's last chance to see proofs for SkNO must have been in late July 1875.

A number of collateral documents have survived which suggest in some detail what Mark Twain did to prepare the printer's copy for SkNO, how he revised proof, and to what extent he and the publisher collaborated on the final selection of material. The manuscript of the author's table of contents as well as most of the printer's copy that he prepared for SkNO have both survived—and from these documents we can now supply a detailed account of Mark Twain's role in publishing this final collection of apprentice work—what he called in February 1875 "all my sketches complete."[199]

The table of contents, which is now in the Doheny collection, affords a wealth of information about individual sketches as well as about the book as a whole: it is therefore reproduced in figure 23. This nine-page list is almost certainly the "index" mentioned by Mark Twain in his 12 February 1875 letter to Osgood: every item in it whose date of composition is known was demonstrably written before mid-February, and the few sketches of unknown or uncertain date were probably written by then. For example, Mark Twain sent

---

[196]Mark Twain's holograph title page is at Yale.

[197]Copyright no. 7619, Library of Congress, from the report of William A. Moore in the copyright office, 1 July 1975. On 15 April 1876, more than six months after publication, A. R. Spofford sent a form letter complaining that the copyright on the book was still imperfect because the two deposit copies "required to be sent to this office within ten days after publication" had not arrived. Clemens nudged his publisher ("Please send these 2 copies at once, Bliss"), and they were deposited on April 20 (Yale).

[198]American Publishing Company Stock Ledger of Books Received from Binderies, 1867–1879, Berg.

[199]Clemens to Warren Choate and Company, 26 February 1875, collection of Charles Cornman.

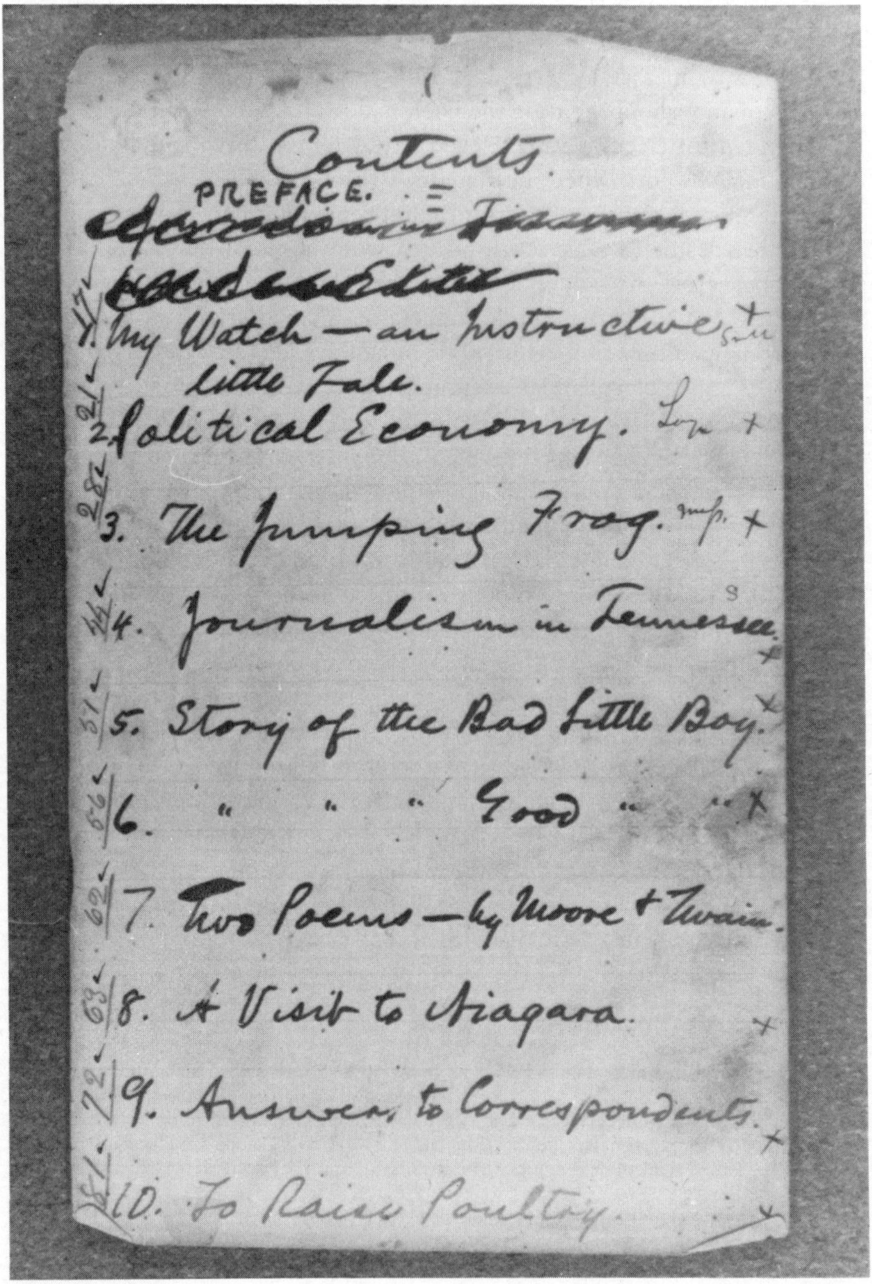
Contents.

PREFACE.

17 1. My Watch—an Instructive little Tale.

21 2. Political Economy.

28 3. The Jumping Frog.

46 4. Journalism in Tennessee.

51 5. Story of the Bad Little Boy.

56 6. " " " Good " "

62 7. Two Poems—by Moore & Twain.

63 8. A Visit to Niagara.

72 9. Answers to Correspondents.

81 10. To Raise Poultry.

FIGURE 23A. The Doheny table of contents for SkNO, page 1.

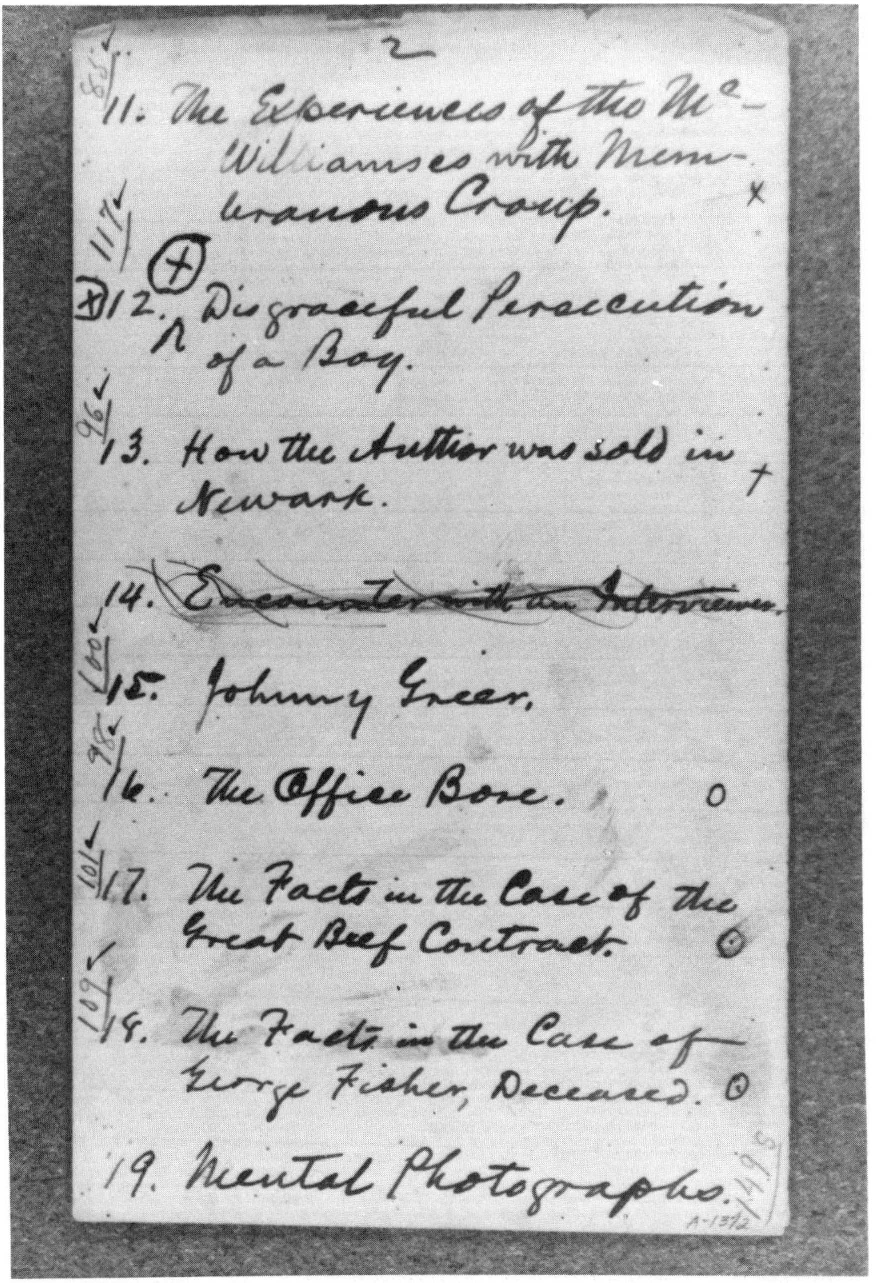
2

85 11. The Experiences of the McWilliamses with Membranous Croup. ×

117 ⊕ 12. Disgraceful Persecution of a Boy.

96 13. How the Author was sold in Newark. +

14. ~~Encounter with an Interviewer.~~

100 15. Johnny Greer,

98 16. The Office Bore. o

101 17. The Facts in the Case of the Great Beef Contract. ⊙

109 18. The Facts in the Case of George Fisher, Deceased. ⊙

19. Mental Photographs. 149

A-1372

FIGURE 23B. The Doheny table of contents for SkNO, page 2.

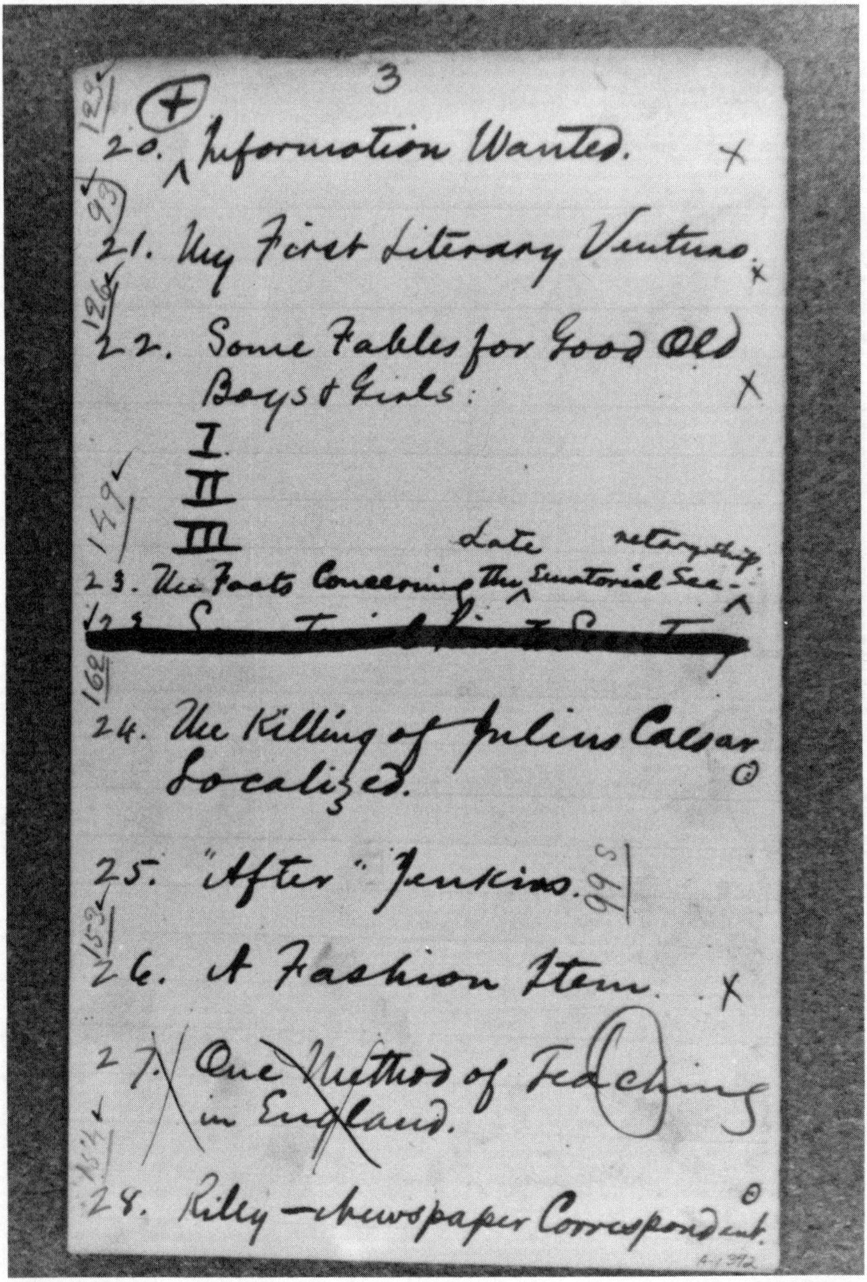

FIGURE 23C. The Doheny table of contents for SkNO, page 3.

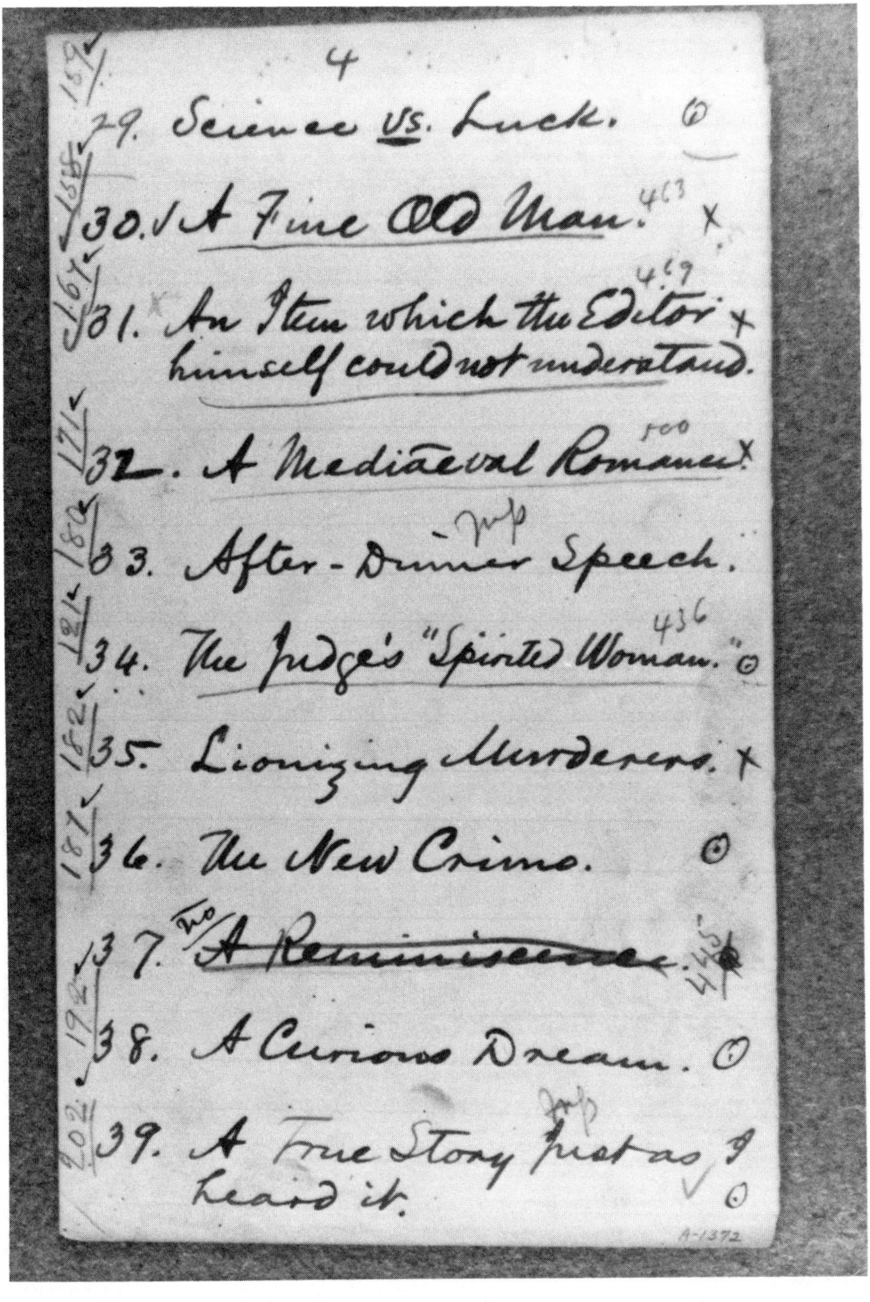

4

29. Science vs. Luck. ⊙

30. ✓ A Fine Old Man. ⁴⁶³ ×

31. × An Item which the Editor ⁴⁶⁹ ✗
himself could not understand.

32. A Mediaeval Romance. ⁵⁰⁰ ✗

33. After-Dinner Speech.

34. The Judge's "Spirited Woman." ⁴³⁶ ⊙

35. Lionizing Murderers. ✗

36. The New Crime. ⊙

37. ~~A Reminiscence~~ ⁴⁴⁵

38. A Curious Dream. ⊙

39. A True Story just as I
heard it. ⊙

A-1372

FIGURE 23D. The Doheny table of contents for SkNO, page 4.

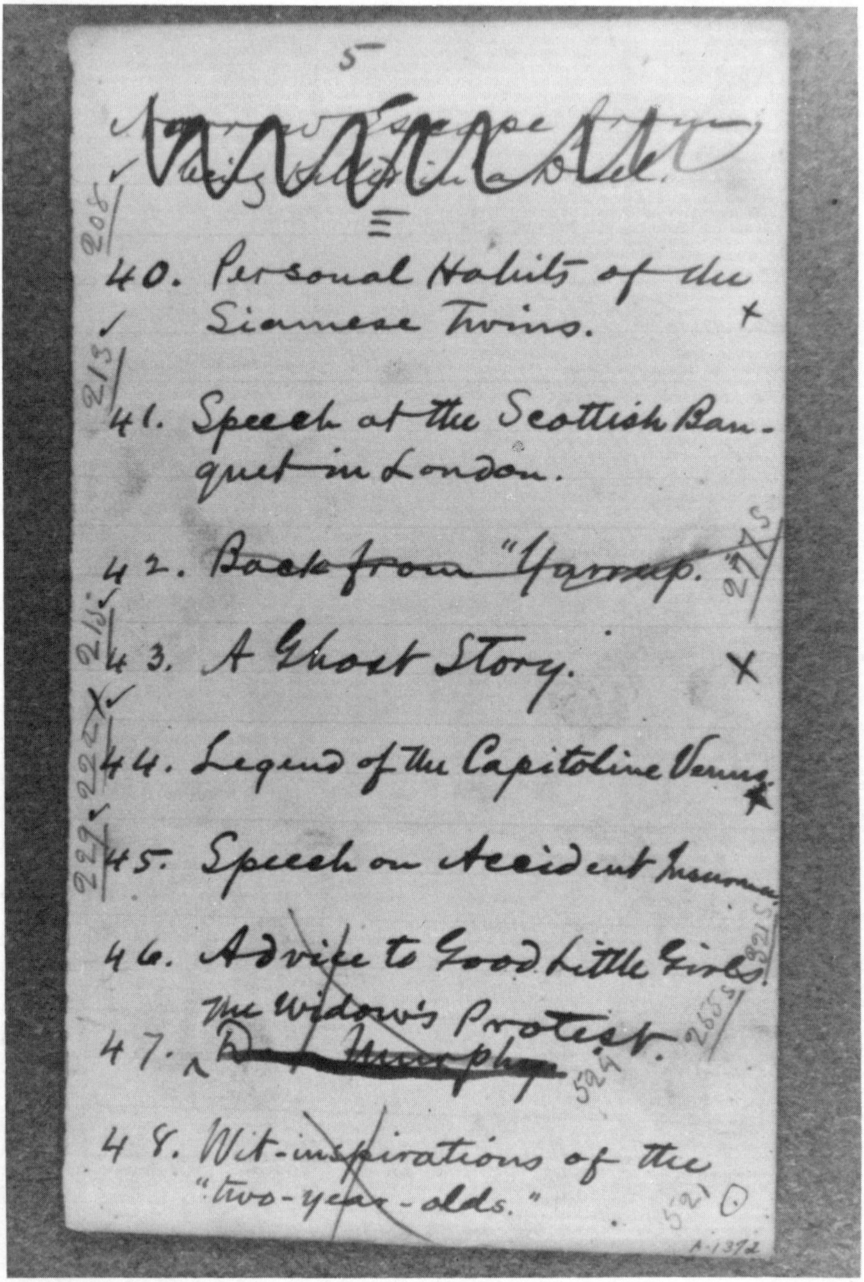

FIGURE 23E. The Doheny table of contents for SkNO, page 5.

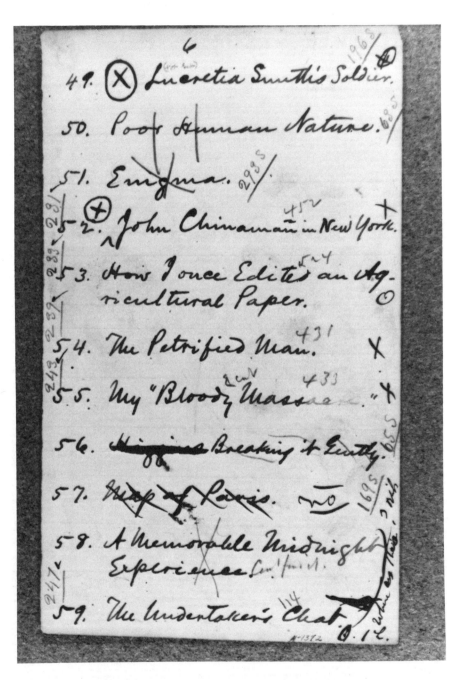

FIGURE 23F. The Doheny table of contents for SkNO, page 6.

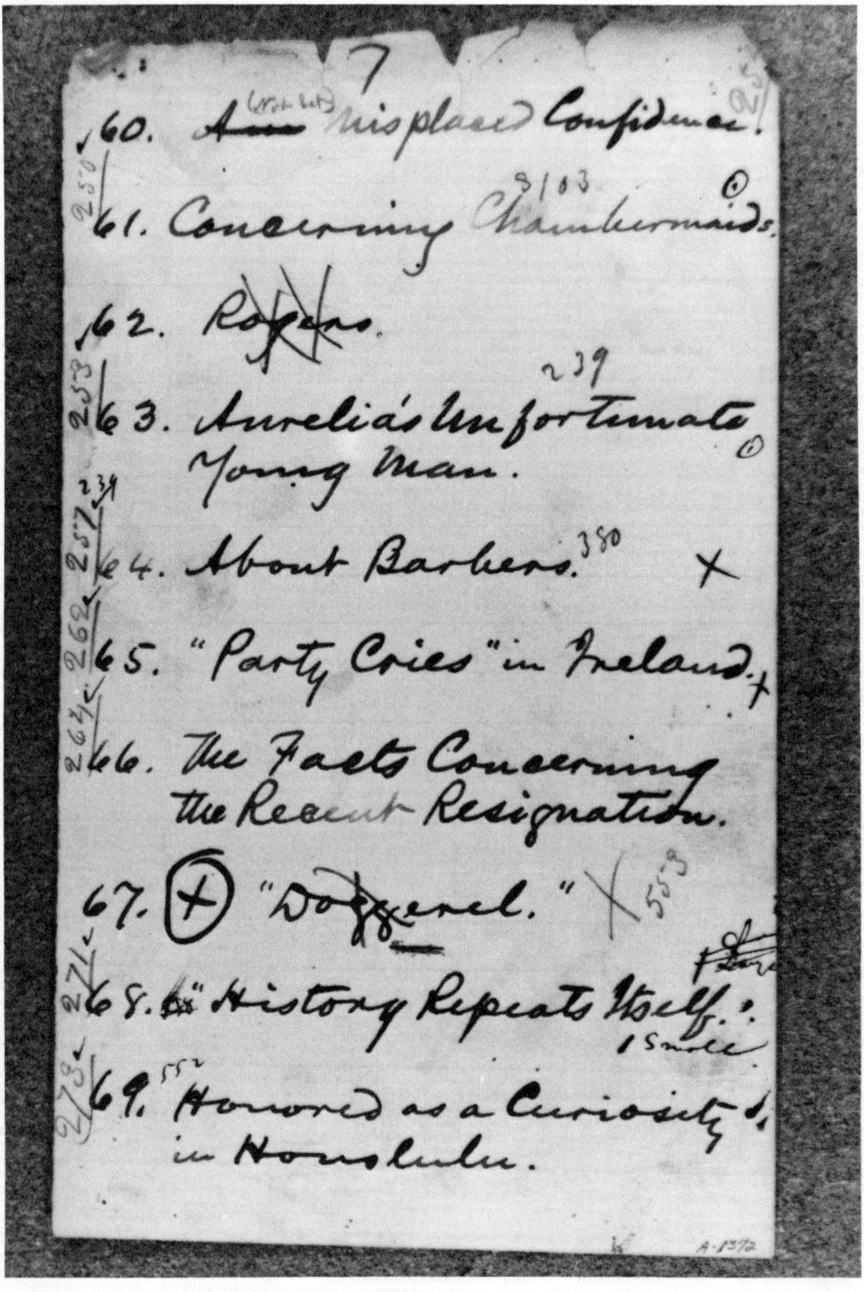

FIGURE 23G. The Doheny table of contents for SkNO, page 7.

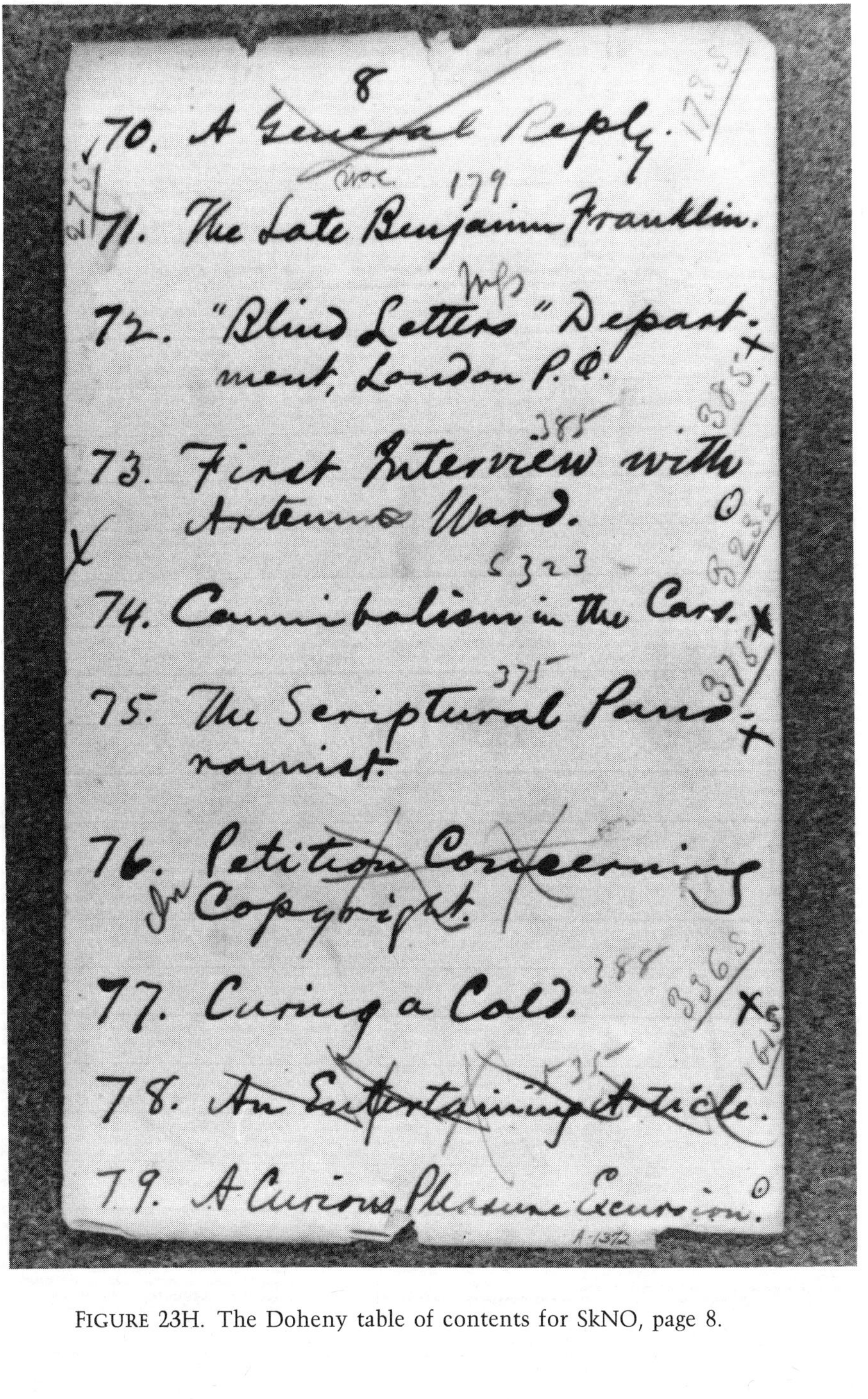

FIGURE 23H. The Doheny table of contents for SkNO, page 8.

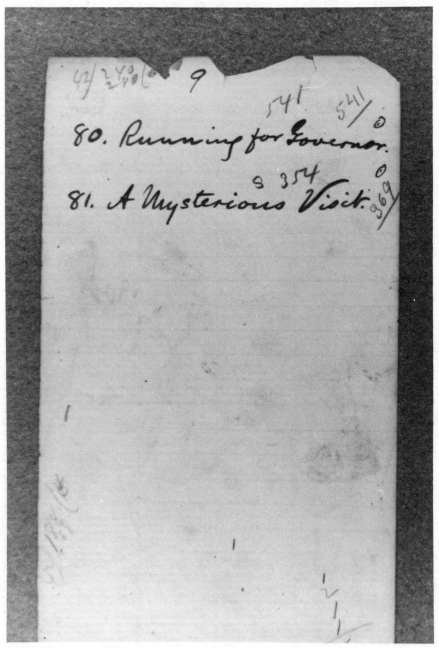

FIGURE 231. The Doheny table of contents for SkNO, page 9.

the first draft of "A Couple of Poems by Twain and Moore" to James T. Fields on 7 January 1875.[200] And he probably wrote "Experience of the McWilliamses with Membranous Croup" soon after his family's frightening but less than fatal experience with this "epidemical & dreadful" disease in mid-January.[201] "Petition Concerning Copyright" was probably written shortly before February 8, when Mark Twain sent a copy of it to S. S. Cox.[202] Even the idea that he had in March of including "The 'Jumping Frog.' In English" (no. 364) would have occasioned no revision of the list, for he had originally entered the Sk#1 version of the story there as simply "The Jumping Frog" (see item 3), the title ultimately used in the SkNO table of contents.

The Doheny table of contents shows that Mark Twain originally planned to offer his publisher a selection of eighty-one sketches, including twelve that had appeared the previous year in Sk#1, fifteen that were either new or uncollected, and fifty-four that had been previously revised and reprinted in two English editions in 1872 and 1874: the Routledges' MTSk and Chatto and Windus' HWb. SkNO ultimately included, however, only sixty-three of these eighty-one selections: between the writing of the list in February and electroplating in late July or early August, eighteen sketches were omitted, for a variety of reasons, and one was inadvertently added, even though Mark Twain had not written it—"From 'Hospital Days.' "[203] Of those

---

[200]Clemens to Fields, 7 January 1875, PH in MTP.

[201]Clemens to Osgood, 13 January 1875, Harvard, TS in MTP.

[202]Clemens to Cox, 8 February 1875, collection of Mrs. Robin Craven.

[203]The following sketches listed in the Doheny table of contents were ultimately omitted from SkNO: "Lucretia Smith's Soldier" (no. 99); "Advice for Good Little Girls" (no. 114); "Enigma" (no. 149); "The Latest Novelty. Mental Photographs" (no. 262); "Back from 'Yurrup' " (no. 275); "Misplaced Confidence" (no. 296); "Poor Human Nature" (no. 297); "Breaking It Gently" (no. 301); "Wit-Inspirations of the 'Two-Year-Olds' " (no. 303); "A Memory" (no. 317); "Mark Twain's Map of Paris" (no. 324); "A General Reply" (no. 332); "An Entertaining Article" (no. 334); "Doggerel" (no. 347); "One Method of Teaching in England" (Paine 90, MTP); "Encounter with an Interviewer" (*Lotos Leaves* [Boston: William F. Gill and Co., 1875]); "A Memorable Midnight Experience" (Sk#1, pp. 3–8); "Rogers" (Sk#1, pp. 13–16). "From 'Hospital Days' " was *not* listed in the Doheny table of contents. It was included in SkNO because Mark Twain had copied out an extract from Jane Stuart Woolsey's *Hospital Days* (New York: D. Van Nostrand, 1868) for his contemplated "Cyclopedia of Humor" (Clemens to Osgood, 16 August 1875, Harvard). Evidently the transcription was shuffled into the SkNO printer's copy, and because it was in Mark Twain's handwriting, Bliss included it. For the result, see below.

included (aside from the nonauthorial piece), collation establishes that thirty-eight were set from a copy of HWb which had been extensively revised and corrected by the author; twelve were set from a less heavily revised copy of MTSk; and thirteen were set from the author's manuscripts and revised clippings. Most of these manuscripts and clippings as well as the marked copies of HWb (hereafter HWb**MT**) and MTSk (hereafter MTSk**MT**) were preserved by Mark Twain. They have been identified for the first time in the course of preparing this edition, and, taken together, they shed some light on the details of production, particularly on Mark Twain's method of preparing the printer's copy.[204]

Mark Twain made his initial selection of old sketches from three— not two—books: HWb, MTSk, and Sk#1. In fact, he probably began by selecting all but one of the thirteen items included in Sk#1: he omitted only "Property in Opulent London" from the Doheny table of contents, and although he listed four Sk#1 pieces there at random (items 3, 17, 42, and 47), he listed eight of them in consecutive order (items 56–63). Most of these sketches had been printed in other collections as well, but two of them—"A Memorable Midnight Experience" (item 58) and "Rogers" (item 62)—could be found only in

---

[204]On 5 November 1875, shortly after SkNO was published, Mark Twain asked Bliss to send him "all of the Sketches that were left out in making it up. I do not want to lose them" (*MTLP*, p. 92). Bliss must have complied by sending Mark Twain the Doheny table of contents, HWb**MT**, and MTSk**MT**, as well as a number of separate manuscripts that had been omitted. MTSk**MT** is now in MTP; HWb**MT** and the table of contents survived in the author's library until they were acquired by the Doheny collection in 1950. Printer's copy for all but five items listed in the Doheny table of contents is extant. "Experience of the McWilliamses with Membranous Croup" and "Some Learned Fables, for Good Old Boys and Girls" are at Berg; "The 'Jumping Frog.' In English" (no. 364) is at CWB; "Speech at the Scottish Banquet in London" and "A Ghost Story" (no. 278) are at Texas; "Speech on Accident Insurance," "The 'Blind Letter' Department, London P.O.," and "After-Dinner Speech" are at Yale; "One Method of Teaching in England" (Paine 90) and "Petition Concerning Copyright" (box 4, no. 5) are in MTP. The manuscript of "A True Story" is at CWB, but SkNO printer's copy was probably tear sheets of the November 1874 *Atlantic Monthly* printing. "A Curious Pleasure Excursion" appeared in the New York *Tribune* of 6 July 1874, and a marked clipping probably served as printer's copy but is not extant. Mark Twain planned to revise tear sheets of the 1875 *Lotos Leaves* printing of "Encounter with an Interviewer" for use as printer's copy; they have not been found. "A Couple of Poems by Twain and Moore" survives only in the early draft sent to James T. Fields (reproduced in facsimile in M. A. DeWolfe Howe, *Memories of a Hostess* [Boston: Atlantic Monthly Press, 1922], pp. 148–149). The original printing of " 'Party Cries' in Ireland" has not been found.

Sk#1, and this fact in itself shows that Mark Twain was working from a copy of that pamphlet. The copy that he presumably marked, however, has not been found, and the revisions themselves cannot be recovered because, as collation shows, the printers did not use Sk#1 to set SkNO. Mark Twain evidently withdrew the copy even before the compositors began to set type, perhaps when he realized belatedly what effect SkNO would have on the sale of Sk#1. Sometime during the course of typesetting Bliss wrote beside "A Memorable Midnight Experience" in the Doheny table of contents: "Can't find it. Where is this? Bliss." This piece was ultimately excluded from SkNO: Bliss could not find it because neither MTSk nor HWb contained the sketch, and he had no copy of Sk#1. "Rogers" was also omitted from SkNO, presumably for the same reason.

After revising his pamphlet, Mark Twain turned for the bulk of his old sketches to the much larger and more comprehensive HWb. Chatto and Windus had doubtless sent him a complimentary copy when they received the first impression from their binder in April 1874. Mark Twain noted on the title page of his 1874 copy (HWb**MT**) that it contained "200 pages" of sketches with "710 words on a page." He proceeded to revise, or to cancel, most of the ninety sketches in the second half of the book (he again refrained from revising *The Innocents Abroad*, which occupied the first half). He made a tentative selection of sketches by this means, excluding pieces that he regarded as too weak to merit republication and material he had republished elsewhere. Brief squibs that Hotten had originally taken from the *American Publisher* or from *Roughing It* ("Sending Them Through," "'The Union—Right or Wrong?'" and "A Nabob's Visit to New York") as well as items that Mark Twain had revised and republished as part of *Roughing It* (the Baker's cat story in "Around the World. Letter Number 5," no. 267; "About a Remarkable Stranger," no. 358; and "The Last Ration," no. 190) were all simply canceled. He deleted several sketches that had first appeared in JF1 ("An Unbiased Criticism," no. 100; and "How, for Instance?" no. 192), and he removed some undistinguished *Galaxy* material originally gleaned by Hotten ("Hogwash," no. 302; "The Tone-Imparting Committee," no. 352; and "The Approaching Epidemic," no. 321). He amalgamated several items into single sketches, directing the compositor, for instance, to "add the article on page 394 to this" and, at another point, to "put this with the lot that begins on page 398." Thus "A Day at Niagara" (no. 241) and "English Festivities and Minor Matters" (no. 247) were made into a single sketch, and "Answer to an Inquiry from the Coming Man" (no. 350) was reprinted as part of a much earlier piece, itself a complicated mosaic of columns from the *Californian* first prepared in the Yale Scrapbook ("Burlesque 'Answers to Correspondents,'" no. 201). Mark Twain canceled sketches that he had presumably prepared already in Sk #1: "Jim Smiley and His Jumping Frog" (no. 119), "Facts in the Case of the Great Beef Contract" (no. 291), and "The Widow's Protest" (no. 304) were all deleted, even after he had begun to revise parts of them.

In addition to making these large-scale revisions, Mark Twain continued the process of cleansing his texts—even though it might seem that he would, by now, find little to alter. He corrected a few spelling errors and a few misprints of his dialect spellings, supplied explanatory footnotes for some topical allusions that could not be removed, struck out adverbs ("excruciatingly" and "infinitely"), tinkered with verb tenses, and removed or modified a large number of allusions to real people like "Sewall," "Skae," "Greeley," and even "N**" (for "Nye"). He pruned away paired adjectives: "grand and awe-inspiring" became "awe-inspiring"; "proper and ample" became "proper"; "thin and ungenerous" became simply "thin." The phrase "it had soured on my stomach" was too vivid, and so it was removed. An allusion to Mark Twain's capacity for alcohol ("I am a match for nearly any beverage you can mention except a whisky-cocktail") was likewise canceled. The barber in "About Barbers" (no. 361) had been described in HWb as "expectorating pleasantly all the while"; he was now no longer permitted to expectorate. Whereas the loafers in "The Editorial Office Bore" (no. 312) were allowed in HWb to "smoke, and sweat, and sigh, and scratch, and perform such other services for their fellow-men as come within the purview of their gentle mission on earth," Mark Twain deleted these details for his American edition of sketches. At one point he had written that the "entire tribe" of Indians "tore all the clothes off" him; he now modestly changed "all" to "half" ("A Day at Niagara," no. 241). He modified his slang in several places that had escaped his earlier scrutiny: "mugs" became "complexions"; "it was rough on the audience, you bet" became "Whe-ew!"; "chaw" became "nibble"; "villain" became "scoundrel"; and "boss" became "head." References to "perdition" were tempered into mere "destruction," and the statement that some event militated "against all my notions of orthodox destruction—fire and brimstone" was dropped, as was another injunction to "go to blazes with it." Finally, after revising a generous selection of material in HWb**MT**, Mark Twain went back over his work and canceled eight pieces he had just revised, including an extensively altered version of "The Spiritual Séance" (no. 202) and four other sketches that he and Webb had first reprinted in JF1. Apparently as a last step Mark Twain also revised the table of contents in HWb**MT**, deleting the titles of thirty-three sketches he did not want republished (at least from this source) and altering many of the titles of the remaining fifty-seven sketches to help the SkNO compositors, who would have to find their way from the sketch title listed in the Doheny table of contents to the appropriate revised material in HWb**MT** or another volume.[205]

Mark Twain must have remembered that the sketches in HWb were, for the most part, duplicated in the earlier collection MTSk— but he also knew that this second smaller volume contained several pieces that had never been included either in HWb or in Sk#1. He therefore scanned the table of contents of MTSk**MT**, eliminating by a brief pen stroke in the margin all but seven of the sixty-six sketches listed there. With two exceptions he did not cancel the texts themselves or indicate in the body of the book that he had already supplied authorized versions in HWb**MT** or Sk#1—an oversight that would cause confusion for the SkNO compositors when they tried to find several sketches in the Doheny table of contents which had been canceled in HWb**MT**. (Mark Twain expected these sketches to be set from his marked copy of Sk#1. Since the compositors never found this copy, they resorted to using unrevised texts in MTSk**MT**.) Mark Twain then listed the seven surviving pieces on the last page of the MTSk**MT** table of contents (see figure 24). By referring to his marked copies of HWb and Sk#1, he now eliminated all but four of these:

---

[205]All of the fifty-seven sketches left standing in the HWb**MT** table of contents were included in the Doheny table of contents, but two of these were combined with other sketches under a single title.

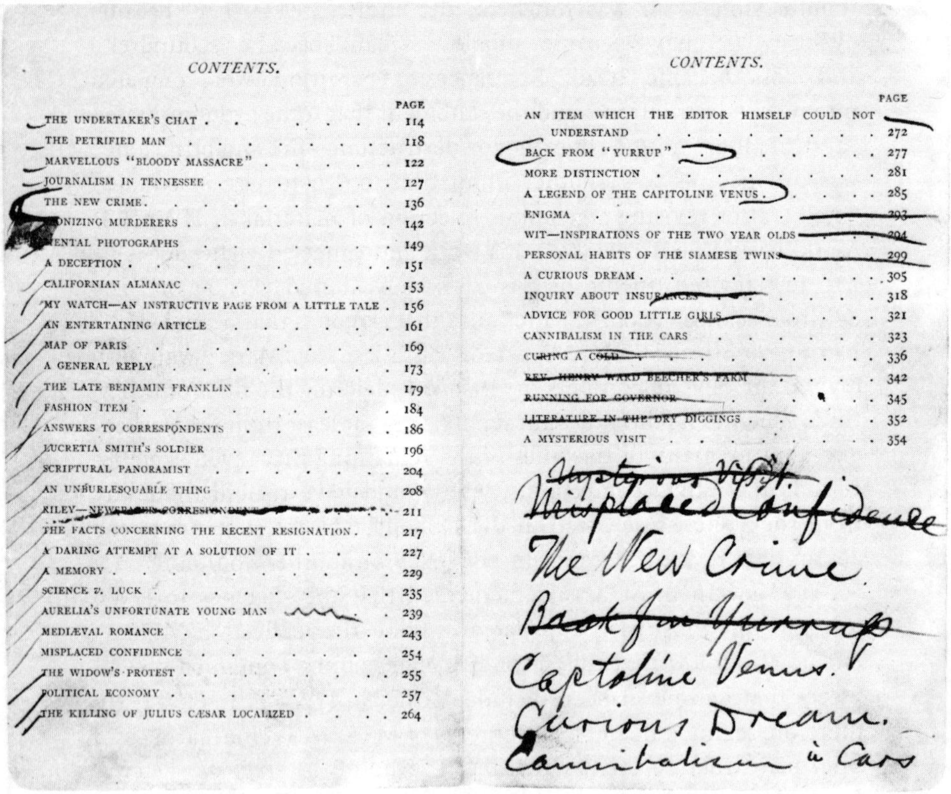

CONTENTS.

CONTENTS.

Mysterious Visit.
Misplaced Confidence
The New Crime.
Back fm Yurrup
Captoline Venus.
Curious Dream.
Cannibalism in Cars

FIGURE 24. The last pages of the table of contents for MTSk**MT**.

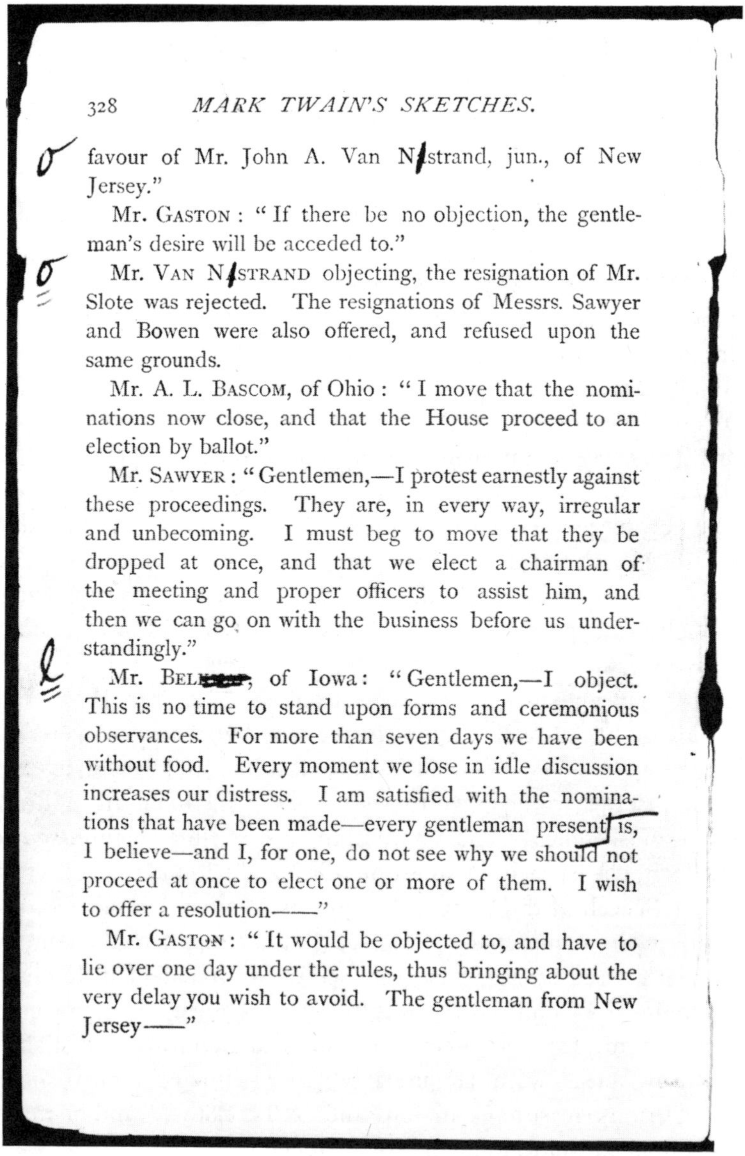

favour of Mr. John A. Van N/strand, jun., of New Jersey."

Mr. GASTON : " If there be no objection, the gentle-man's desire will be acceded to."

Mr. VAN N/STRAND objecting, the resignation of Mr. Slote was rejected.   The resignations of Messrs. Sawyer and Bowen were also offered, and refused upon the same grounds.

Mr. A. L. BASCOM, of Ohio : " I move that the nomi-nations now close, and that the House proceed to an election by ballot."

Mr. SAWYER : " Gentlemen,—I protest earnestly against these proceedings.   They are, in every way, irregular and unbecoming.   I must beg to move that they be dropped at once, and that we elect a chairman of the meeting and proper officers to assist him, and then we can go on with the business before us under-standingly."

Mr. BELKNAP, of Iowa: " Gentlemen,—I object. This is no time to stand upon forms and ceremonious observances.   For more than seven days we have been without food.   Every moment we lose in idle discussion increases our distress.   I am satisfied with the nomina-tions that have been made—every gentleman present is, I believe—and I, for one, do not see why we should not proceed at once to elect one or more of them.   I wish to offer a resolution——"

Mr. GASTON : " It would be objected to, and have to lie over one day under the rules, thus bringing about the very delay you wish to avoid.   The gentleman from New Jersey——"

FIGURE 25. Page 328 of MTSk**MT**, used to set up "Cannibalism in the Cars" in SkNO. Mark Twain made two corrections of the MTSk print-ing and revised "Belknap" to "Bell." The compositor marked the end of a stint following the word "present."

"Back from 'Yurrup'" (no. 275) and "Misplaced Confidence" (no. 296) had already been prepared in his copy of Sk#1, and "A Mysterious Visit" (no. 285) had been revised in HWb**MT**. This left him with four sketches that needed to be typeset from MTSk**MT** because they did not appear in either of the other volumes: "Cannibalism in the Cars" (no. 232), "The Legend of the Capitoline Venus" (no. 272), "The New Crime" (no. 288), and "Curious Dream" (no. 289). He accordingly revised and corrected only these four sketches in MTSk**MT**, making, however, far fewer changes than he had in comparable sketches in HWb**MT** (see figure 25).

In addition to revising these old sketches, Mark Twain had been gradually accumulating new material ever since he had published CD and MTSk in 1872. At least one of these new sketches, "A Ghost Story" (no. 278), had probably been prepared for the original volume of "Mark Twain's Sketches" in 1870–1871 (see figure 21), but most of the new pieces were either manuscripts written between 1872 and early 1875 or clippings of articles and speeches written or delivered in that period. It is clear that this slow accumulation of short writings not readily adapted to a longer narrative was more or less deliberate. On 28 November 1873, for instance, Mark Twain told his English friend G. Fitzgibbon that he had "written a speech" for an occasion just in case he was called upon to give one, but that if he were not so called upon, or were obliged to "curtail it like sin in the delivery," his manuscript would nevertheless "easily find room in a future volume of Sketches as the impromptu speech which I *intended* to make."[206] The speech in question ultimately found its way into SkNO ("Speech at the Scottish Banquet in London," item 41 in the Doheny table of contents): it was set from a clipping of the London *Observer* revised by Mark Twain. "Speech on Accident Insurance," delivered on 12 October 1874, was likewise included, set from a copy printed by the Hartford Accident Insurance Company and slightly revised by Mark Twain. He probably revised clippings or tear sheets of "A Curious Pleasure Excursion" and "A True Story," and he manifestly supplied holographs for five sketches.

Although the new items numbered only fifteen in a collection of eighty-one items, their overall bulk constituted a "mass of matter

---

[206]Clemens to Fitzgibbon, 28 November 1873, *CL3*, letter 360.

which [had] never been in print before,"[207] or at least which had never been collected in a book. The Doheny table of contents shows that Mark Twain planned to scatter these new pieces among the old ones taken from Sk#1, HWb, and MTSk, and it suggests that he carefully ordered the sketches—beginning with his strongest and newest pieces, following these with a section of shorter and weaker pieces, and concluding with another burst of strength in pieces such as "Cannibalism in the Cars" (no. 232) and "A Mysterious Visit" (no. 285).

The final selection from this mass of printer's copy was made jointly by Mark Twain and Bliss; their choice was clearly affected by unforeseen problems like the need to fill out a page, the cost of illustrations, and even accidents at the printing house. Mark Twain controlled the preparation of his printer's copy with some rigor; he did not, or could not, exercise the same sort of control over what Bliss and the compositors did with that copy.

True Williams, the illustrator of SkNO, had probably been given the printer's copy for the book sometime in March 1875. We know little about what he was told to do, or whether Mark Twain exercised veto power over the illustrations he produced—but we do know from his procedure with other books that he tended to participate in this process with great zest. Early in January 1876, when Mark Twain was well along in the production of *Tom Sawyer*, he told William Dean Howells how much he admired Williams' skill: "He takes a book of mine, & without suggestion from anybody builds no end of pictures just from his reading of it."[208]

Whereas Williams himself may have chosen what to illustrate in *Tom Sawyer*, Mark Twain offered some guidance about matter to be illustrated in SkNO. When Mark Twain revised his *Galaxy* reminiscence about the Nevada petrified-man hoax ("A Couple of Sad Experiences," no. 299), he specified in the margin of HWb**MT**: "Make a picture of him." Williams complied. And when Mark Twain submitted the manuscript of "Some Learned Fables, for Good Old Boys and Girls," he made nearly a dozen suggestions and sample sketches for illustrations, in the margin and in the text itself. Williams followed Mark Twain's lead in six separate cases, making, for example,

---

[207]Preface to SkNO, reprinted in Appendix C5, volume 1.
[208]Clemens to Howells, 18 January 1876, *MTHL*, 1:121.

a "picture of procession" as the author had suggested on manuscript page 102, and redrawing the signs that Mark Twain had supplied on manuscript page 68. There must also have been further suggestions from Mark Twain, communicated directly to Williams or to Bliss who, it will be recalled, was charged with deciding how many of the facsimile letters to use for "The 'Blind Letter' Department, London P.O." The point to be stressed here, however, is that Williams complied with Mark Twain's known suggestions, and that he also read the manuscript and produced appropriate sketches for almost every piece included in SkNO. Since these engravings had to be completed before the typesetting began, their very existence must have exerted pressure to include material so illustrated.

The immediate decisions about which of the listed sketches to set in type, and in what order, must have been made by Bliss—sometimes independently, sometimes in cooperation with the author. The Doheny table of contents provides a full record, not always easily glossed, of these individual decisions. Apparently before any typesetting took place, Bliss annotated the holograph table of contents to indicate where the sketches could be found: a few erroneous page numbers show that he referred to the marked tables of contents in HWb**MT** and MTSk**MT** in doing this.[209] He identified these two volumes as "large" (meaning HWb**MT**) and "small" (meaning MTSk**MT**). Accordingly, "65S" and "169S" mean "page 65" and "page 169" of MTSk**MT** (items 56 and 57). When the compositors set a sketch,[210] they knew almost from the start what page it would begin on in the new book: this number they entered in the left margin, probably as they completed each item. As work progressed, Bliss entered brief notations such as "in" (item 76), "not set" (items 49 and 60), or simply "no" (items 37 and 57). These entries were apparently a record of what had been included in SkNO and a way of communicating this information to Mark Twain. The "no" entries presumably indicate the author's veto.

---

[209]For example, Bliss gave "149S" as the page number for item 19 ("The Latest Novelty. Mental Photographs," no. 262): this was an error derived from the MTSk table of contents, which gave the initial page incorrectly as 149 instead of 148.

[210]The compositors for SkNO were Belle, Nellie, and William, who signed portions of the printer's copy, and who would soon help to set *Tom Sawyer*. Their fingerprints are preserved in the ink-stained margins of much of the printer's copy. A careful study of these fingerprints has turned up no significant evidence about compositorial stints.

There was a good deal of room for error in Bliss's system. Moreover, sometimes Bliss supplied page numbers for *both* volumes, as if it were a matter of indifference which text was used; sometimes he supplied no page number. In both cases the compositor was left to choose between HWb**MT** and MTSk**MT** for his setting copy. Usually Bliss failed to specify which book to set from when Mark Twain left a sketch unrevised in both volumes, but because HWb and MTSk evolved independently, their texts are almost never identical. Several sketches that Mark Twain probably revised in Sk#1 for SkNO were in fact set from unrevised printings in MTSk**MT**: since the compositors could not find the marked copy of Sk#1 and Mark Twain had not crossed out the items in MTSk**MT**, they used MTSk**MT** for printer's copy.

Collation of the printer's copy for SkNO with the book itself shows that Mark Twain read at least some of the proof. He further revised the first five sketches and made intermittent changes in some of the later pieces, including the last one, "A Mysterious Visit" (no. 285). The range of these revisions is understandably limited, but they are very similar in intent to those he inscribed on the printer's copy. It is possible, but not likely, that the author deleted some sketches even at this late stage. He wrote Howells on 14 September 1875 that he thought SkNO an "exceedingly handsome book," and added, "I destroyed a mass of sketches, & now heartily wish I had destroyed some more of them—but it is too late to grieve now."[211] This "destruction" probably refers to his original weeding of Sk#1, HWb, and MTSk—as well as to the omission of eighteen sketches listed in his autograph table of contents. But it is conceivable that Mark Twain meant he had recently removed some pieces when reading proof.

Nevertheless, it is clear that Mark Twain's proofreading was not systematic, or at least that he did not read *final* proof of SkNO: the author did not even know that "From 'Hospital Days'" had been included until he saw the completed book. "I saw the first copy yesterday," he wrote Howells, "& about the first thing I ran across was an extract from 'Hospital Days' (page 199)—an entirely gratuitous addition by Mr. Bliss to neatly fill out a page."[212] The inclusion of this

---

[211]Clemens to Howells, 14 September 1875, *MTHL*, 1:99.
[212]Clemens to Howells, 22 and 27 September 1875, *MTHL*, 1:103.

nonauthorial sketch is an extreme example of Bliss's influence on SkNO, but it is clear that he often decided to use very short sketches listed in the Doheny table of contents only when they could "neatly fill out a page." For example, Bliss was confronted with a minor problem in "The Killing of Julius Caesar 'Localized'" (no. 97): when the compositors reached the end of this sketch they were left with an unsightly blank on two-thirds of the last page. Following Bliss's instructions, they clipped the page of proof to the page in MTSk**MT** on which "The Widow's Protest" (no. 304) appeared, marked the proof "166" (for the page number of SkNO), and proceeded to typeset the latter sketch to fill up the blank space (see figures 26–27). It is clear that Bliss decided to include "The Widow's Protest" at this point (it was item 47 in the Doheny table of contents) only because it was convenient to do so: the implication must be that it would have been excluded had no such convenient space appeared for it to fill.

In addition to adding one sketch and deciding the fate of others, Bliss undoubtedly altered a few of Mark Twain's texts simply to make them short enough to fit the available space. Collation of the printer's copy with SkNO shows, for instance, that a number of changes were introduced in proof for "Fashions" (no. 221): "a most" was shortened to "an"; "had been standing" and "had been squeezing" to "stood" and "squeezed"; and "the subject is one of great interest to ladies, and it" to "the subject." "Fashionable" and "of course" were deleted. Nothing in these revisions is characteristic of the author; they were almost certainly the work of Bliss. He had wanted permission from Mark Twain to "cut out a line or an *unimportant paragraph* when needed to make them come out right on pages" in *The Innocents Abroad*,[213] and Mark Twain had not allowed it. With SkNO, however, either permission was not asked or, if asked, was more readily granted. Bliss clearly felt free to revise a text merely to meet the physical and aesthetic demands of the page. Despite the care that Mark Twain lavished on the revision of his sketches, he apparently was not asked to make or approve minor decisions such as these. Like JF1, therefore, SkNO embodies a complex mingling of authorial and

---

[213]Bliss to Clemens, 10 February 1869, MTP. See note 35 above.

nonauthorial choices, both in the selections chosen and in the revisions themselves.

Well before Mark Twain began to read proof he apparently wrote out for Bliss some advertising copy that is extremely suggestive of his anxiety about the quality of his book:

The American Publishing Company of Hartford will shortly issue Mark Twain's Miscellaneous Sketches, complete—both old & new. The book will be a handsome quarto, daintily & profusely illustrated by True Williams. An inspection of the work will show that the growing excellence of subscription-house typography & binding has made one more stride forward in this book. This will be the first complete edition of Twain's Sketches which has appeared, on either side of the water.[214]

We do not know precisely when this was written, but the allusion to "Mark Twain's Miscellaneous Sketches" seems to predate the choice of a title for SkNO, and the effort to praise paper, typography, and illustration likewise reflects the uneasiness Mark Twain felt in January and February 1875 about subscription publishing. SkNO ultimately was not superior in its paper, typography, or illustration— indeed, just the reverse—nor did it incorporate a "complete edition of Twain's sketches" (HWb alone was nearly double its size). Nevertheless, Bliss seems to have taken his cue from Mark Twain's lines, and in copy that eventually appeared in the salesmen's prospectus he boasted of the "artistic illustrations," the "finest of super-calendered, delicate tinted paper," and a "dainty blue cover." More important, he stressed the nature of Mark Twain's audience: "That the pen of our author is not a useless one is proven by the fact that his readers are largely men and women of a highly cultivated class. Scarcely a greater favorite of the Clergy can be named, and Lawyers, Scholars, Merchants, Mechanics and Farmers all read him with undisguised pleasure."[215] As we have seen, Mark Twain undertook to

---

[214]The manuscript of this passage is on a single sheet at the Mark Twain Memorial, Hartford, Connecticut. Bliss wrote what appear to be more notes for advertising copy on the verso, but they are largely illegible. It is not known whether Mark Twain's prose was ever used in an advertisement for SkNO.

[215]Prospectus for SkNO, MTP. Bliss also emphasized that the book would contain the "story of THE FAMOUS 'JUMPING FROG,' as originally written; to which is added a new version with many exceedingly interesting variations."

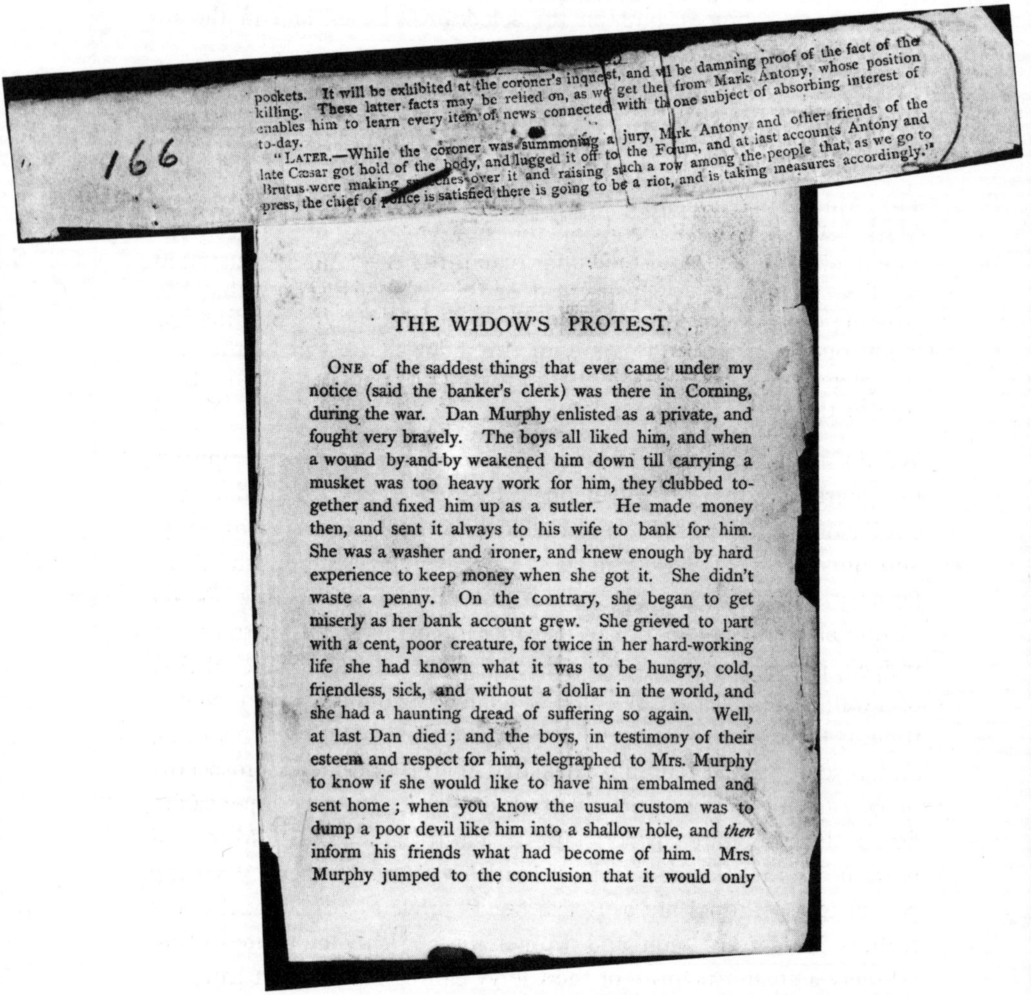

pockets. It will be exhibited at the coroner's inquest, and will be damning proof of the fact of the killing. These latter facts may be relied on, as we get them from Mark Antony, whose position enables him to learn every item of news connected with the one subject of absorbing interest of to-day.

"LATER.—While the coroner was summoning a jury, Mark Antony and other friends of the late Cæsar got hold of the body, and lugged it off to the Forum, and at last accounts Antony and Brutus were making speeches over it and raising such a row among the people that, as we go to press, the chief of police is satisfied there is going to be a riot, and is taking measures accordingly."

166

THE WIDOW'S PROTEST.

ONE of the saddest things that ever came under my notice (said the banker's clerk) was there in Corning, during the war. Dan Murphy enlisted as a private, and fought very bravely. The boys all liked him, and when a wound by-and-by weakened him down till carrying a musket was too heavy work for him, they clubbed together and fixed him up as a sutler. He made money then, and sent it always to his wife to bank for him. She was a washer and ironer, and knew enough by hard experience to keep money when she got it. She didn't waste a penny. On the contrary, she began to get miserly as her bank account grew. She grieved to part with a cent, poor creature, for twice in her hard-working life she had known what it was to be hungry, cold, friendless, sick, and without a dollar in the world, and she had a haunting dread of suffering so again. Well, at last Dan died; and the boys, in testimony of their esteem and respect for him, telegraphed to Mrs. Murphy to know if she would like to have him embalmed and sent home; when you know the usual custom was to dump a poor devil like him into a shallow hole, and *then* inform his friends what had become of him. Mrs. Murphy jumped to the conclusion that it would only

FIGURE 26. A page from MTSk**MT**, clipped to a portion of proof for "The Killing of Julius Caesar 'Localized.'"

pockets. It will be exhibited at the coroner's inquest, and will be damning proof of the fact of the killing.   These latter facts may be relied on, as we get them from Mark Antony, whose position enables him to learn every item of news connected with the one subject of absorbing interest of to-day.

"LATER.—While the coroner was summoning a jury, Mark Antony and other friends of the late Cæsar got hold of the body, and lugged it off to the Forum, and at last accounts Antony and Brutus were making speeches over it and raising such a row among the people that, as we go to press, the chief of police is satisfied there is going to be a riot, and is taking measures accordingly."

THE WIDOW'S PROTEST.

ONE of the saddest things that ever came under my notice (said the banker's clerk) was there in Corning, during the war. Dan Murphy enlisted as a private, and fought very bravely. The boys all liked him, and when a wound by-and-by weakened him down till carrying a musket was too heavy work for him, they clubbed together and fixed him up as a sutler. He made money then, and sent it always to his wife to bank for him. She was a washer and ironer, and knew enough by hard experience to keep money when she got it. She didn't waste a penny. On the contrary, she began to get miserly as her bank account grew. She grieved to part with a cent, poor creature, for twice in her hard-working life she had known what it was to be hungry, cold, friendless, sick, and without a dollar in the world, and she had a haunting dread of suffering so again. Well, at last Dan died; and the boys, in testimony of their esteem and respect for him, tele-graphed to Mrs. Murphy to know if she would like to have him embalmed and sent home; when you know the usual custom was to dump a poor devil like him into a shallow hole, and *then* inform his friends what had become of him. Mrs. Murphy jumped to the conclusion that it would only cost two or three dollars to embalm her dead husband, and so she telegraphed "Yes." It was at the "wake" that the bill for embalming arrived and was presented to the widow.

She uttered a wild sad wail that pierced every heart, and said, "Sivinty-foive dollars for stooffin' Dan, blister their sowls! Did thim divils suppose I was goin' to stairt a Museim, that I'd be dalin' in such expinsive curiassities!"

The banker's clerk said there was not a dry eye in the house.

FIGURE 27. Page 166 of SkNO, which was set from the printer's copy illustrated in the previous figure.

please—or at least not to offend—this "highly cultivated class" by repeatedly cleansing his sketches of slang, irreverence, and other matters regarded as indelicate or improper.

Apparently by the author's design, SkNO was not widely reviewed. Mark Twain felt that *The Gilded Age,* which *had* been widely reviewed, suffered at the hands of the newspapers, and he was not therefore willing to risk the new book in that forum without some sort of insurance. Accordingly, he had Bliss send Howells "advance sheets" of SkNO sometime in early September so that Howells might review it in the *Atlantic Monthly* "before any one else." Howells evidently sent the manuscript of his review to Clemens on 19 October 1875, asking that he return it "with objections" at once.[216] The review appeared in the *Atlantic* for December 1875.

Although Howells had mocked his own review as "awful rot" and had complained about the "difficulty of noticing a book of short sketches," Mark Twain was delighted with his friend's reaction:

That is a perfectly superb notice. You can easily believe that nothing ever gratified me so much before. The newspaper praises bestowed upon the Innocents Abroad were large & generous, but I hadn't *confidence* in the critical judgment of the parties who furnished them. *You* know how that is, yourself, from reading the newspaper notices of your own books. They gratify a body, but they always leave a small pang behind in the shape of a fear that the critic's good words could not safely be depended upon as *authority.* Yours is the recognized critical Court of Last Resort in this country; from its decision there is no appeal; & so, to have gained this decree of yours before I am forty years old, I regard as a thing to be right down proud of.[217]

Howells had, in fact, shown some uneasiness about the selections in SkNO: "In reading the book, you go through a critical process imaginably very like the author's in editing it; about certain things there can be no question from the first, and you end by accepting all, while you feel that any one else may have his proper doubts about some of the sketches." But he was emphatic in noticing "another quality," presumably new—a "growing seriousness of meaning in the apparently unmoralized drolling, which must result from the humorist's

[216]Clemens to Howells, 14 and 27 September 1875, MTHL, 1:99, 103; Howells to Clemens, 19 October 1875, MTHL, 1:106.

[217]Howells to Clemens, 19 October 1875, MTHL, 1:106; Clemens to Howells, 19 October 1875, MTHL, 1:106–107.

second thought of political and social absurdities."[218] As Mark Twain explained to him, this observation was especially pleasing to his wife: "You see, the thing that gravels her is that I am so persistently glorified as a mere buffoon, as if that entirely covered my case—which she denies with venom."[219] SkNO, the long-awaited American edition of Mark Twain's sketches, was clearly designed to counteract the author's image as a "mere buffoon," in part by reprinting texts that had been thoroughly refined by Webb, Hotten, and the author himself.

It is not known what effect, if any, the *Atlantic* review had on other American critics, for no other American reviews have been found. SkNO was briefly noted in at least one English journal, the *Saturday Review*, which five years before had been so uncomplimentary about *The Innocents Abroad*. Apparently all was now forgiven:

Mark Twain's *Sketches, New and Old*, are nearly all capital, and all of them worthy of the author; short and lively, for the most part free from vulgarity and offence, and raising a smile more often than provoking a roar of laughter, but always amusing. This is the kind of book to take up while a patient is waiting for a dentist, a passenger for a railway-train, a client for his patron, or a man for a wife or sister who promised to be dressed in five minutes; and it is good enough to make all of them forget the vexation, and (all but the last) even to forgive it.[220]

The reaction of Mark Twain's friends to SkNO was, predictably, favorable. Thomas Nast wrote to thank Clemens for his complimentary copy and twitted him briefly about "From 'Hospital Days'"; he added that SkNO was "very well got up and makes a very attractive book." Oliver Wendell Holmes likewise thanked Clemens for the "very handsome volume" and reported that he had immediately reread "and rejoiced in my old friend the Jumping Frog and one or two other of the Sketches." Holmes concluded: "I thank you most heartily for the pleasure your stories have so often given me and especially for this most welcome accession to my library with all its humour and its cheerful good-nature and its pictures of life, dressed

---

[218]*Atlantic Monthly* 36 (December 1875): 749–751, reprinted in *MTCH*, pp. 52–55.
[219]Clemens to Howells, 19 October 1875, *MTHL*, 1:107.
[220]"American Literature," *Saturday Review* 41 (29 January 1876): 154.

so prettily that if the books of the season should have a ball it would
be one of the belles of the evening." The Reverend Edwin Pond Parker
reported that he and his family had "read out of the book with exceeding merriment. . . . Your 'gift' is a rare one & a choice one,
and long may you live to exercise it, and make people better through
a whilom forgetting of the griefs & cares & burdens that make life
so heavy & sad."[221] Clemens saved such letters, for he had come to
value private testimony above anything the newspapers might say.

Despite the use of new manuscripts in SkNO, and despite the long
negotiations carried on by the Routledges between 1868 and 1875,
Mark Twain evidently made no effort whatever to secure British
copyright for SkNO. He may have authorized *Information Wanted*—a
reprinting of twenty-two sketches (most of them new material) from
SkNO which Routledge issued sometime in late December 1875 or
early January 1876. But the Routledge account books record no payment to the author,[222] and although *Information Wanted* did carry
the authenticating rubric on its title page—"Messrs. George Routledge & Sons *are my only authorized London Publishers*"—there is
no indication that Mark Twain specifically authorized the book. The
low status that SkNO had occupied from the beginning evidently
combined with Mark Twain's disappointment over the sale of *The
Gilded Age* to make him completely neglectful of the Routledges'
copyright and republication needs. Within a year he had been persuaded that Chatto and Windus would be more active than the Routledges in selling his English edition of *Tom Sawyer*.[223]

---

[221]Nast to Clemens, 9 November 1875, MTP; Holmes to Clemens, 4 November 1875,
MTP; Parker to Clemens, 21 December 1875, MTP.

[222]Evidently 6,000 copies were ordered on 15 December 1875, and an additional
4,000 on 21 April 1876. Another printing of 2,000 was ordered on 12 January 1882, one
of 2,000 on 2 June 1892, one of 3,000 on 9 August 1899, one of 3,000 on 11 March 1901,
and one of 3,000 on 30 May 1902. The total printing in twenty-six years was 23,000
copies (Routledge Ledger Book 4, p. 645; Book 5, p. 150; Book 6, pp. 683–684). *Information Wanted* is *BAL* 3608.

[223]Moncure D. Conway to Clemens, 24 March 1876, *MTLP*, p. 93 n. 3: "I have had
two long sessions with the Routledges, father and son; found them very much opposed
to publishing on 10 per cent commission, but finally willing to undertake it in a spirit
that did not impress me as enthusiastic enough. I am disinclined to let them have
Tom Sawyer." Still it is clear that the Routledges did not regard the lapse over SkNO
as a serious or irreparable break, and when a Canadian collection of Mark Twain's
sketches called "Pilot Life on the Mississippi" was offered to them in 1876, the
Routledges "declined to publish" it and asked to hear from Mark Twain "if such
publication is authorized by you, and if it is, whether or not you will treat with George
Routledge and Sons for their republication" (Edmund Routledge to Clemens, 26 April
1876, MTP).

American sales of SkNO were at first promising, climbing to 23,700 by the end of December 1875. But unlike Mark Twain's three previous subscription books, SkNO fell off precipitously in its second quarter, January through March 1876. The immediate cause of this was, as we have noted, the persistent economic depression. In fact, Mark Twain told Moncure D. Conway on 16 April 1876 that he wanted to postpone publication of *Tom Sawyer* because "whereas the Sketch Book sold 20,000 copies the first 3 months, it has only sold 3,700 the second 3 (ending March 30.) This distinctly means that this is no time to adventure a new book."[224] By the end of 1879 SkNO had sold 32,200 copies—about one-third what *The Innocents Abroad* had sold in a comparable period—and by 1893, when a cheaper one-dollar edition was published, it had still not sold the 50,000 copies that would have raised Mark Twain's royalty to 10 percent. Significantly, when Harper and Brothers republished the book as part of a uniform edition, it sold only 8,000 copies between 1904 and 1907— while *Innocents* sold 46,100.[225]

Mark Twain did not revise the text of SkNO after publication, despite several opportunities to do so. Bernhard Tauchnitz wrote him on 7 February 1883, asking permission to republish "The Jumping Frog." Mark Twain answered on March 1, evidently enclosing a copy of SkNO:

The *Jumping Frog* was a small volume, my first publication, and the chief part of its contents was not worth the printing. Therefore I have broken up the plates and taken that book out of the market. However, a few years ago I took such of the contents as might be worth preserving, including the title sketch, and after adding a lot of new matter, issued the result in a new volume entitled *Mark Twain's Sketches.*

Tauchnitz acknowledged this letter on March 31, and agreed to reprint SkNO in the Continental Series "at a similar arrangement to that which we had about your other former books, as for instance 'Roughing it,' 'Innocents at Home' etc." Mark Twain agreed to this on April 16, and on May 7 Tauchnitz wrote to say that he had requested

---

[224]Clemens to Conway, 16 April 1876, *MTLP,* p. 98.

[225]Sales figures are from two sources: American Publishing Company Stock Ledger of Books Received from Binderies, 1867–1879 (Berg), and a copy of the Harper records (MTP). See also Hamlin Hill, "Mark Twain's Book Sales, 1869–1879," *Bulletin of the New York Public Library* 65 (June 1961): 384.

his "London bankers to make over to you a payment of Four Hundred Mark."[226] The Tauchnitz edition appeared in Leipzig in mid-1883. Like *Information Wanted*, it has no textual authority: the interest of both books lies in their role of popularizing a particular version of Mark Twain's sketches.

Mark Twain did not revise the text of SkNO for the American Publishing Company's "Autograph Edition" in 1899, but he did mark up a copy of the table of contents for SkNO to indicate "Dates of WRIT-ING—& usually of publicat[ion] (to the best of my recollection)." Beside the page numbers for about half the sketches he wrote a date (frequently wrong), and at the bottom of the second page of the contents he added, "I think that the things whose dates I have forgotten were mainly squibs which I put into a 'Department' in the *Galaxy* magazine in 1869-'70—or possibly it was '70-'71."[227] Although Mark Twain made no further contribution to this last lifetime edition, the American Publishing Company's reader, "F.M.," subsequently corrected the texts of the sketches and compared at least some of them with the original *Galaxy* printings.[228]

The original text of SkNO was allowed to stand virtually unchanged throughout Mark Twain's lifetime as the only authorized version of his early sketches. Its publication in 1875 marked the end of the author's willingness to revise and sift this youthful material, but it was hardly the end of the "scissors & slash" method. Even when Mark Twain had transferred his loyalties to James R. Osgood, and

---

[226]Bernhard Tauchnitz, Jr., to Clemens, 7 February, 31 March, and 7 May 1883, MTP. Clemens' letter of April 16 is inferred from Tauchnitz' response of May 7: "I am much obliged for your kind letter of the 16th of April by which you agree with my proposal, concerning your work 'Sketches.'" Clemens' letter of March 1 is quoted from [Curt Otto], *Der Verlag Bernhard Tauchnitz: 1837-1912* (Leipzig: Tauchnitz, 1912), pp. 125-126. I am indebted to William B. Todd for alerting me to this book.

[227]The marked table of contents is at Yale. The publisher evidently used the dates Mark Twain supplied to write brief footnotes appended to the titles of all the sketches in the book. The marked table of contents also contains one clue to Mark Twain's participation in the production of the original SkNO, although it is a clue that must be treated with caution: at the top of the second page the author wrote, "[I don't see] the 'Map of Paris' here, but it's [18]71, I think." He evidently did not recall that this sketch was among those omitted from SkNO, in this case almost certainly because the compositors could not find the copy of Sk#1, where the text was printed.

[228]So-called "editions" of *Sketches, New and Old* which appeared after 1899 were in fact new impressions from the 1899 plates. These new impressions were issued with various names, such as the "Autograph Edition" and the "Royal Edition," and with the imprints of both the American Publishing Company and Harper and Brothers. The copy marked by "F.M." and Frank Bliss is at Yale.

was hard at work on *Life on the Mississippi*, he was laying plans for *The Stolen White Elephant*—a collection of eighteen sketches, including two that had been dropped from the original contents of SkNO.[229] In April 1882 Mark Twain reiterated his attitude toward such sketchbooks: "I reckon I can get the Sketches ready in time, though publishing books don't pay for the trouble of writing them," he told Osgood, adding that of course "this one don't *have* to be written."[230] *The Stolen White Elephant* fulfilled Mark Twain's ambition for an elegant sketchbook (albeit not illustrated), but he returned repeatedly to his interest in a cheaper pamphlet as well. In 1878 he had issued the paper-covered *Punch, Brothers, Punch!*— which contained nine sketches, including his "Fortifications of Paris" (no. 323); the spine of the book advertised it as "Mark Twain's Sketches. Price, 25 Cents." And in February 1885 Mark Twain again toyed with a by-now-familiar scheme: in his notebook he wrote, "Put Jumping Frog &c (25¢, nice cover) in *Union News Co.* at 25¢."[231] Nothing came of this impulse, however, and even though there were later reprintings of SkNO, Mark Twain finally abandoned his apprentice writings as they were preserved in the text of 1875. The history of reprinting and revision which concluded with that book is recapitulated in figure 28 on the following page. American editions and projects appear in the gray area, while Hotten's and Chatto and Windus' editions are on the left and the Routledges' on the right. The entire contents of every edition were not necessarily transmitted in each case, and no single sketch passed through all of the alternative routes of transmission illustrated here.

---

[229]"Rogers," a sketch that originally appeared in Sk#1, and "Encounter with an Interviewer" (items 62 and 14 in the Doheny table of contents).
[230]Clemens to Osgood, April 1882, *MTLP*, p. 155.
[231]*N&J3*, p. 94.

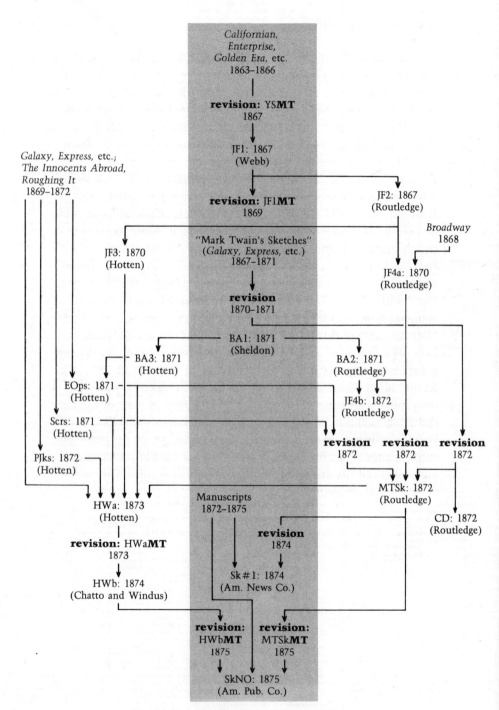

FIGURE 28. History of reprinting and revision.

The Text

Mark Twain could always treat his sketchbooks with exasperating indifference, but he did hold to a remarkably steady purpose throughout nine years of revision and republication. He consistently tried to sift his material for sketches "worth republishing," and he was quite merciless in ruling some material "forever . . . out of any book." What he chose to reprint he always chose to refine, and usually that meant euphemizing what he had written, under more permissive circumstances, in "the language of the vulgar, the low-flung and the sinful." From the earliest tentative revisions in the Yale Scrapbook down through his final destruction of a "mass of sketches" for SkNO,[232] Mark Twain reprinted only what he thought would endure, rejected what he came to regard as too topical or too juvenile, and revised what he did reprint to meet the standards of his eastern and eventually his English audiences. Of the 365 items included in this collection, Mark Twain is known to have revised 130. SkNO ultimately included only 51 of these.

By contrast, the editorial aim of the present collection is to recover, and preserve in their original form, as many of Mark Twain's early imaginative writings as possible—regardless of the author's later opinion of them. Unlike SkNO, this collection includes two dozen items that Mark Twain wrote but never published, many that he apparently never considered republishing, and some that he republished many times only to exclude at last. And, unlike SkNO, the present collection prints the original version of every item, no matter how much or how little the author subsequently revised it. The collection is therefore emphatically not a critical edition of SkNO, or of any other sketchbook designed by the author. Its rationale, both for including texts and for choosing which version to include, is wholly editorial.

There are several strong reasons for preferring Mark Twain's original intentions to his final revised ones in a collection of this kind. Above all, the chronological sequence of apprentice work that is brought together here for the first time provides a unique tool for studying Mark Twain's development as a writer: indeed, not even

---

[232]Clemens to Jane Clemens and Pamela Moffett, 20 January 1866, *CL1*, letter 97; Clemens to Virginia City *Territorial Enterprise*, 14 January 1864, *MTEnt*, p. 139; Clemens to Howells, 14 September 1875, *MTHL*, 1:99.

the author himself ever had so comprehensive a text of his own apprentice work. But to introduce some 130 revised texts into the overall sequence of 365 would destroy its continuity and much of its usefulness. This is especially true because of the timing of Mark Twain's revisions: virtually every item in the collection was completed in its original form by the end of 1871, before the author addressed an eastern and an international audience, but Mark Twain revised portions of them in every year from 1867 through 1875. As we have seen, his motive was explicitly to ingratiate himself with a larger and a less tolerant audience, and the effect of his changes (even when they were quite minor) was to remove the sketch from the continuum of apprentice work that we seek to preserve here. The overall aim of the collection is, therefore, sufficient in itself to compel our decision to reproduce the original version of every sketch.

In addition, we should point out that most of the revised sketches have not been readily available in their original form, even to specialists. The most common source of these sketches, SkNO, is a radical selection, made only in part by the author; its texts are completely corrupted by the hands of Charles Henry Webb, John Camden Hotten, and even Elisha Bliss. The present collection reproduces the only version of these sketches that can be regarded as unequivocally Mark Twain's—the original one. Furthermore, the nature of revision and the complexity of its history both make the choice of Mark Twain's original version the most interesting and the most convenient for the reader. Because Mark Twain and his editors were more inclined to delete than to add material, the reader who is familiar with some of these items from SkNO will find himself encountering whole passages and paragraphs that he had not seen before. But he will not be obliged to fish these passages out of a difficult and forbidding apparatus: they appear in the text as Mark Twain originally wrote them, and the author's later decisions to delete or modify are recorded in the apparatus. Moreover, since Mark Twain sometimes made different decisions about how to revise the same sketch, he produced parallel texts that were altered in similar but not identical ways. The decision to print the original version is the only one that permits us to report precisely how, for example, Mark Twain revised a passage in 1872 and 1873, only to delete it in 1875. Indeed, the reader can reconstruct the revised text of any sketch at any point along the bumpy road from JF1 (1867) to SkNO (1875).

Other editors may well wish to adopt a different editorial rationale. Indeed, the history of revision and republication uncovered in preparing this edition suggests that we do, in fact, very much need a critical edition of SkNO. Readers and students will not want to ignore the selection and revision of sketches which Mark Twain shrewdly if somewhat carelessly offered in that final volume. In addition, there may even be some interest in critical texts for JF1, MTSk, and HWb. This collection presents the data necessary to produce such editions at the same time that it addresses a different and less limited need: to establish and preserve the continuum of Mark Twain's apprentice writings as he first composed and published them.

The present collection is an unmodernized, critical text based upon the theory of copy-text advanced by Sir Walter Greg.[233] It follows Greg in its choice of copy-text but differs from him in its policy of emendation. The copy-text—the document or documents that form the basis of our own text, and from which we depart only in the ways specified in the list of emendations—is always the earliest extant form of the text. We emend that text to correct errors and inadvertencies, but we never emend it to incorporate the author's revisions of his work.[234] All of his revisions are, however, recorded in the historical collations, and from these collations, and the lists of emendations, the reader can reconstruct not only the copy-text, but the revised text at whatever stage of revision seems most useful.

Copy-Text. The labors of a generation of scholars devoted to the bibliography of Mark Twain have helped to identify the earliest extant form of items included in these volumes.[235] The choice of copy-text is accordingly simple.

---

[233]W. W. Greg, "The Rationale of Copy-Text," *Studies in Bibliography* 3 (1950–1951): 19–36, reprinted in Greg's *Collected Papers,* ed. J. C. Maxwell (London: Clarendon Press, 1966), pp. 374–391.

[234]Some exceptions have been made to this procedure. For "Burlesque 'Answers to Correspondents' " (no. 201) and "The Spiritual Séance" (no. 202), both of which Mark Twain took some pains to create from clippings in the Yale Scrapbook, we have reprinted the original sketches as well as the new versions. Likewise, "Jim Smiley and His Jumping Frog" is sufficiently important to warrant including three distinct versions of it (nos. 119, 363, and 364).

[235]I am particularly indebted to the work of my co-editor, Edgar M. Branch. "A Chronological Bibliography of the Writings of Samuel Clemens to June 8, 1867," *American Literature* 18 (May 1946): 109–159, *LAMT,* and *CofC* formed the indispensable groundwork for the present collection. Over the years he has identified, authenticated, and dated hundreds of Mark Twain's early works.

(1) Whenever manuscript has survived, it is copy-text. Only twenty-five items in this collection survive in Mark Twain's holograph, almost always because he chose never to publish them.

(2) When no manuscript is extant, but the first printing typeset from manuscript survives, it is copy-text. About three-fourths of the items collected here are based upon first printings. The reliability of these printings varies somewhat because they range from works set in type by the author on the Hannibal *Journal* to works sent across the continent or the ocean and published without any opportunity for authorial correction.

(3) When neither the manuscript nor the first printing is extant, reprintings of various kinds are perforce copy-text. Of the fifty items collected here which are based on second printings, many are from contemporary newspaper reprintings of the lost *Enterprise*, and a few are from nineteenth-century anthologies and other sources. There is a slightly higher incidence of manifest error and editorial intrusion in such reprintings, which were of course completely outside the author's control.

(4) Radiating texts comprise about ten items in this collection; these survive in more than one independent reprinting of the lost original—usually in two, but sometimes in three or more reprintings. For example, a lost *Enterprise* sketch may survive in two contemporary newspaper reprintings, each of which derives independently, or radiates, from the nonextant original and so may preserve readings not found in the other. When two such reprints share a reading, they provide strong corroborative evidence of what the original must have said. When they differ as to a reading, they pose the necessity of adjudicating between equal authorities. In all such cases, whether there are two or more reprintings to consider, no copy-text is designated because none of the authoritative texts is genetically closer to the original than the other. Instead, all substantive and accidental variants are recorded in a list of emendations and adopted readings, which gives the reading adopted (with its source or sources), the reading or readings rejected (with its source or sources), and any corrections supplied by the editors. Variants are judged according to the majority testimony of the available documents, our knowledge of Mark Twain's habitual practices, and other external evidence. When variants are *completely* indifferent, they are resolved on the basis

of which text appears on the whole to be most like the lost original.[236]

Principles of Emendation. A conservative policy of emendation has been followed for every item in this collection, regardless of the nature of its copy-text. We have emended only what we are satisfied Mark Twain did not write or did not mean to write.

(1) Although we do not adopt his revisions, we do incorporate any corrections he made—a distinction that deserves some discussion because it is not always clear-cut. For example, Mark Twain's alterations of "jolly" to "bully" and of "passed in his checks" to "yielded up his life" were manifestly literary revisions; we have recorded such revisions but not incorporated them into the text. But when, for example, the *Californian* printed "there was a painful negative passing to his sensitive organization," and two years later Mark Twain inserted the word "current" (after "negative") in the Yale Scrapbook, he was apparently restoring the reading of his manuscript, and we have adopted the correction. Similarly, when the *Californian* printed "conferring upon a vice-royalty of itself such an execrable name," and Mark Twain inserted "heaven" (after "of") in the Yale Scrapbook, we have adopted his change as a necessary correction—one that could not have been made without the author's help. On the other hand, when the *Enterprise* printed "all experience teaches us that the best way to ascertain a thing is to find it," and Mark Twain inserted "out" (after "it") in the Yale Scrapbook, he made a change that is arguably a revision or a correction. In this case we have adopted the change as a correction, but the decision is clearly a matter of literary judgment, and it is easy to see how a contrary one might be made.

(2) The most common occasion for substantive emendation of these texts is simple omission of small but necessary words. We emend such phrases as "villainous fire brimstone" (supplying "and") and "not all" (supplying "at") by considering the context. We correct dittography—that is, unintentional repetition ("of the procession of the procession"). We very rarely correct the author's grammar, and we never change his level of usage. We avoid, if at all possible, cor-

---

[236]See Fredson Bowers, "Multiple Authority: New Problems and Concepts of Copy-Text," *The Library* 27 (June 1972): 81–115; Vinton A. Dearing, "Concepts of Copy-Text Old and New," *The Library* 28 (December 1973): 281–293; and G. Thomas Tanselle, "Editorial Apparatus for Radiating Texts," *The Library* 29 (September 1974): 330–337.

recting dialogue or narrative written in dialect. We emend quotations
only when the departure from the original is clearly unintended. We
emend physically defective copy-texts, sometimes of necessity conjecturing as many as four or five words in a line. All emendations
are of course recorded, and each is identified by its source: holograph
evidence like YS**MT**, JF1**MT**, HWa**MT**, HWb**MT**, and MTSk**MT**;
printings that Mark Twain is known to have corrected or for which
he supplied the printer's copy, such as JF1, CD, MTSk, Sk#1, and
SkNO; or the editors of this edition, identified as I-C.

(3) The most common occasion for emendation in the accidentals
of these texts is simple mechanical error: we correct missing or improper quotation marks, commas where a period is required and
vice versa, transposed or dropped letters ("partciular" and "imperturable"), and letters that failed to print clearly or were misset
("hea[r]" and "overlookod"). We also correct misspellings when they
are typographical or unintentional ("thorougly" and "sieze"). We
have preserved unusual but historically acceptable spellings ("ancle,"
"threshed," and "numscull"), as well as the author's somewhat more
idiosyncratic ones ("filagree"). Misspellings in dialect have been
treated as deliberate, and not emended: Mark Twain's fondness for
characters who cannot spell, pronounce, or punctuate began early and
lasted long. Simon Wheeler, the most famous of this breed, can
neither spell nor construct proper sentences, but we are not tempted
to correct him: "Verily, this man *was* gifted with 'gorgis abillities,'
and it is a happiness to me to embalm the memory of their lustre in
these columns."[237] Contemporary editors and compositors were, on
the other hand, less likely to respect the author's spelling in such
cases, and he had frequent occasion to correct them. All variants in
dialect spelling are, accordingly, given the status of substantives and
are so recorded.

Although it is now clear that Mark Twain would have preferred
to correct all the "damnable inconsistencies of spelling"[238] in these
sketches, and that such consistency—whether self-imposed or imposed by compositors and editors—was the prevailing convention of

---

[237]"Answers to Correspondents" (no. 107).
[238]Clemens to Bret Harte, 1 May 1867, *CL1*, letter 130.

the time,[239] no effort has been made here to emend what passed the scrutiny of the author or contemporary proofreaders. In these texts slight lapses occasionally ripple the surface of Mark Twain's remarkably uniform practice, but they remind us that absolute regularity was an ideal not always achieved. Such deliberately limited emendation probably preserves some compositorial lapses, but without a manuscript to guide us, we have preferred to reproduce the copy-text even in its irregularities.

Mark Twain often denounced his printers and editors for failing to respect his punctuation. He knew, he said, "more about punctuation in two minutes than any damned bastard of a proof-reader can learn in two centuries."[240] We have therefore respected the punctuation of the copy-text whenever it is not glaringly deficient. We emend errors or lapses that would cause confusion or that are pointlessly distracting.

(4) The lists of emendation also record a number of instances in which we have been required not to change the copy-text but to interpret it: ambiguous or doubtful readings arising from physical defects in the copy-text (poor inking, tears, folds, ink blots, etc.); alternate readings left standing in the manuscript ("blood-stained dagger/dagger"); hyphenated compounds broken at the end of a line; and dashes following terminal punctuation at the end of a line. Compound words hyphenated at the end of a line in the copy-text are rendered solid or hyphenated according to other occurrences of the word in the same sketch, in other sketches, and in Mark Twain's other works or letters of the period, and, lacking such evidence, according to parallel forms in the same or in other sketches. Dashes following terminal punctuation at the end of a line were used both by the author and his compositors as an easy way to justify that line. Like page numbers or lineation, these dashes are appurtenances of the manuscript or newspaper printing and are not properly included in the text. But because it is possible that Mark Twain intended some

---

[239]For a succinct and unassailable account of this matter, see the textual introduction to the Iowa-California edition of *A Connecticut Yankee in King Arthur's Court*, ed. Bernard L. Stein with an introduction by Henry Nash Smith (Berkeley, Los Angeles, London: University of California Press, 1979).

[240]Clemens to Chatto and Windus, 25 July 1897, CWB.

of them to be set, we record the disposition of all such dashes.

(5) Titles of sketches are those of the copy-text whenever possible, but they may not always be authorial. Any editorial alteration in the words or spelling of the titles is reported as an emendation. Capitalization, terminal punctuation, and line breaks are, however, editorially styled and not recorded as emendations. Thus, while the title of "A Gallant Fireman" (no. 1) appears in the copy-text in capital and small capital letters, followed by a period and a dash, and then by the text, the title here appears in display letters without terminal punctuation of any kind. Some sketches were published without titles; others survive in ways that obscure whatever title Mark Twain may have given them. Whenever the editors were required to supply a title, it is enclosed in square brackets.

(6) Every effort has been made to reproduce the texts without editorial marks. There are no footnote numbers in the text, for example: editorial emendations and notes are given in the apparatus and keyed to page and line; line numbers include all lines except the title. Square brackets in the text are reproduced from the copy-text and are demonstrably or presumably authorial, while square brackets in the apparatus are of course editorial. Ellipsis points in the text, however, are an exception: they are invariably editorial and indicate a lacuna in the copy-text which we have been unable to fill by conjecture. Ellipsis points may represent editorial decisions retained from the copy-text itself, as when we reproduce a partially preserved sketch from a nineteenth-century anthology. If there is any doubt about the editorial origin of such ellipses, a textual note comments on the matter. And when the author himself used ellipsis points in his text, we have adopted the convention of his manuscripts at this time, using asterisks (* * * *) instead of the conventional periods. A few editorial emendations have been required to preserve this convention.

(7) A few mechanical changes from the copy-text are not reported in the emendations lists. Ampersands have been silently expanded to "and" except in business names ("Gould & Curry") and the form "&c." By-lines, signatures, and conventional rubrics (like "By S. L. C." or "For the Journal") have been silently omitted, but when a sketch takes the form of a letter, or when it is a poem addressed to an individual, we retain the dateline, address, and signature but silently

style them. Although extracts are variously rendered in the copy-texts (by indentation, a smaller font, reduced leading between lines, and quotation marks in combination with these other conventions), the present text renders them all uniformly by reduced leading without indentation, but preserves quotation marks when these appear in the copy-text. Internal headings in newspaper letters are sometimes authorial, sometimes not; they are always retained, but have been silently styled in accordance with the design of this edition. Punctuation following italicized words has been styled italic according to the usual practice, whether or not Mark Twain or his compositors so rendered it. The use of an initial display letter followed by small capital letters at the beginning of a sketch is an editorial convention.

Treatment of Variants. All substantive variants that occur in the texts listed under the description of texts, as well as any that occur in printings unique to a given sketch, are recorded in the historical collation for that sketch. In addition, changes in dialect spelling, in emphasis (italics and exclamation points), and in paragraphing are recorded. When Mark Twain demonstrably corrected or revised other accidentals, the full history of such variants is also recorded.

Variants that occur in texts listed as derivative editions are not recorded. Mark Twain revised several copies of his sketchbooks for giving public readings: these revisions are not recorded unless they corroborate other, less certain evidence of Mark Twain's revision.

GUIDE TO THE TEXTUAL APPARATUS

> But that which is most difficult is not always most
> important, and to an editor nothing is a trifle by
> which his authour is obscured.
> —Samuel Johnson, "Preface to Shakespeare"

An individual textual apparatus for each sketch provides everything needed to reconstruct the copy-text and Mark Twain's revisions (whenever any survives). Each apparatus usually, but not invariably, includes the elements described below. A description of texts follows the textual introduction in this volume; it identifies textually significant editions of Mark Twain's sketches and specifies the copies collated and examined in the preparation of this collection. A list of word divisions in this volume, which records ambiguous compounds hyphenated in the present edition at the end of a line, is given at the end of the entire apparatus to facilitate accurate quotation of Mark Twain's texts.

Textual Commentary.   This section gives the copy-text and specifies the copy or copies used; it discusses problems or unusual features of the text; and under a subheading, "Reprintings and Revisions," gives the history of the sketch and characterizes Mark Twain's revisions of it.

Textual Notes.   This section discusses emendations or decisions not to emend: it calls attention to possible errors left unemended in the text, to problems in establishing particular readings, and to variants in the reprinting history which are especially problematic.

Emendations of the Copy-Text.   This section records every departure in this edition from the copy-text, with the exception of the typographical features discussed above. It also records the resolution of doubtful or ambiguous readings. In each entry, the reading of this edition is given first, with its source identified by a symbol in parentheses; it is separated by a centered dot from the rejected copy-text reading on the right, thus:

daguerreotype (JF1)   •   daguerreotpe

A wavy dash (∼) to the right of the dot stands for the word on the left and signals that a mark of punctuation is being emended; a caret (∧) indicates the absence of a punctuation mark; and the symbol I-C follows any emendation whose source is not an authoritative text, even if the same correction was made in a derivative edition, thus:

cold. (I-C) • ∼?
moment. (I-C) • ∼∧

Emendations marked with an asterisk in the left margin are discussed in the textual notes. A vertical rule indicates the end of a line in the copy-text, thus:

footsteps (I-C) • foot-|steps
secret? These (I-C) • ∼?—|∼

Italicized words in square brackets, such as [*not in*], [*no* ¶], and [*torn*], are editorial. Doubtful readings are recorded with the following notation:

Cairo (I-C) • Ca[ ]o [*torn*]		*ir* not present, tear in copy-text
long (I-C) • lon[g] [*torn*]		*g* unclear, tear in copy-text
every (I-C) • eve[r]y		*r* unclear in copy-text
meant, (I-C) • ∼[,]		comma unclear in copy-text
eat; (I-C) • ∼[:]		semicolon unclear, possibly colon
notion. (I-C) • ∼[∧]		space for period in copy-text
saw (I-C) • saw/has seen .		alternate reading left standing in copy-text

Emendations and Adopted Readings. This section replaces *Emendations of the Copy-Text* when the text is established from radiating or composite texts. It records all variants, substantive and accidental, among the relevant texts, which are identified by abbreviations with superscript numbers; the numbers are assigned according to the chronology of publication and do not indicate relative authority of the texts. Thus the following entry shows that three texts agree with each other against a fourth, and the majority reading has been adopted in this collection:

savan (P^{1-2}, P^4) • *savan* (P^3)

And the following entry shows that a compound hyphenated at the end of a line in one text and rendered solid in another is resolved in accord with the two that render it hyphenated:

fore-finger (P^{1-2}) • fore-|finger (P^3); forefinger (P^4)

An entry that rejects all of the radiating texts in favor of an editorial emendation appears as follows:

mixture. (I-C) • ~, (P^{1-4})

Diagram of Transmission and Historical Collation.   These elements appear in the textual apparatus only for sketches reprinted or revised by Mark Twain. We give a diagram every time there is a chain of transmission, and it is essential for reading the entries in the historical collation. A list of the texts collated for each sketch immediately precedes the collation, which records all substantive variants in them. In addition, because Mark Twain is known to have concerned himself with revising emphasis (italics and exclamation points) as well as paragraphing, such variants in accidentals are likewise recorded. When Mark Twain demonstrably corrected or revised other accidentals—spelling, punctuation, and so on—in any of the surviving marked copies (YS**MT**, JF1**MT**, HWa**MT**, HWb**MT**, and MTSk**MT**), the full history of the particular accidental variant is also recorded.

In each collation entry the reading of this edition is given first, followed by symbols for the texts that agree with it; it is separated by a centered dot from its variants, which are identified by the appropriate symbols (given in the list of texts collated). A sample chain of transmission is given in figure 29 to facilitate understanding the examples that follow. Each transmission diagram in the individual apparatuses is essential to reading the collation for that sketch, because although the pattern of transmission is similar for many sketches, it varies in significant ways from sketch to sketch.

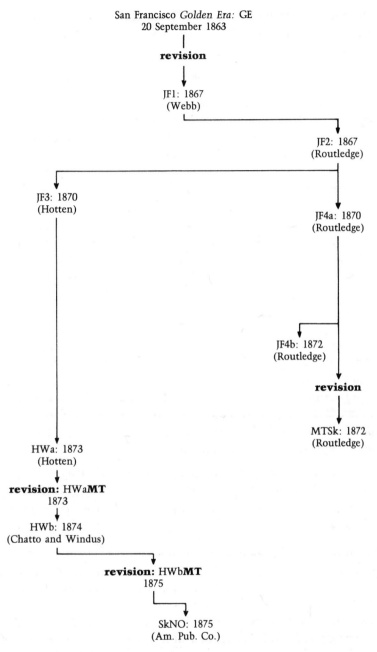

FIGURE 29. Sample diagram of transmission (from "How to Cure a Cold," no. 63).

Symbols joined by a dash (–) indicate that the reading appeared in the first text noted and was transmitted as far as the second. Thus the entry

git (GE–JF4) • get (JF3–SkNO)

indicates that the original dialect word was accurately transmitted from the *Golden Era* (GE) through JF1 and JF2 to JF4; but that Hotten altered it to "get" in his JF3, from where it was transmitted to HWa, then to HWb, and ultimately to SkNO, without being corrected by Mark Twain. A plus sign (+) indicates that the reading appears in the given text and in all printings derived from it. Thus the entry

[¶] If (GE) • [*no* ¶] If (JF1+)

indicates that a paragraph break appears at this point in GE, but not in JF1 or in any subsequent reprinting deriving from it. A more complicated entry, involving Mark Twain's revision, appears thus:

believe I threw (GE–MTSk, GE–HWa) • believed I had thrown (HWa**MT**–SkNO)

Here several complexities are recorded. The reading of the present edition and of the copy-text was, in this case, successfully transmitted from GE through JF1, JF2, and JF4 to MTSk; it was also transmitted from GE through JF1, JF2, and JF3 to HWa. Mark Twain encountered it there and revised it to the variant reading in HWa**MT**, which was incorporated in HWb and subsequently reprinted in SkNO. A still more complicated entry appears thus:

and ate . . . healthy. [¶] After (GE–JF2; GE–HWa) • and eat . . . healthy. [¶] After (JF4); and—— [¶] After (MTSk); and—here is food for the imagination. [¶] After (HWa**MT**–SkNO)

The original reading was transmitted successfully from GE through JF1 to JF2; it was also successfully transmitted from GE through JF1, JF2, and JF3 to HWa. JF4 altered "ate" to "eat" without authority. Mark Twain revised the JF4 text by striking out the passage following "and" and substituting an expressive long dash in MTSk. But when he revised HWa**MT**, he revised differently: he again deleted the matter after "and," but substituted another dash and the phrase "here is food for the imagination." This revision was incorporated in HWb and subsequently reprinted in SkNO.

The historical collation preserves all substantive variants in the texts collated, whether or not they originated with Mark Twain. But the history of reprinting and revision given in the textual introduction permits us to make certain discriminations between variants which Mark Twain certainly made, and those which he could not possibly have made.

(1) Variants that first appear in JF2, JF3, JF4, Scrs, EOps, PJks, and HWa *cannot be authorial.*

(2) Variants that first appear in JF1, CD, MTSk, HWb, Sk#1, and SkNO *may be authorial,* but may also have been introduced by editors or compositors.

(3) Variants for which we have documentary evidence in the form of Mark Twain's autograph changes—YS**MT**, JF1**MT**, HWa**MT**, HWb**MT**, and MTSk**MT** (and a few stray examples of printer's copy in other forms)—*are certainly authorial,* and are so indicated in the collation by the symbol **MT**. Any variant that arises in JF1, HWb, or SkNO can be certainly attributed to Mark Twain when the revision appears first in the marked printer's copy.

The textual apparatus may contain other elements that are more or less self-explanatory. In the items where copy-text is a holograph, we include a section called *Alterations in the Manuscript,* which reports the author's cancellations, substitutions, and revisions. Essential corrections that Mark Twain made as he wrote or reread his work are not recorded: letters or words that have been mended or traced over, or canceled and rewritten merely for clarity; false starts and slips of the pen; corrected eye skips; and words or phrases that have been inadvertently repeated, then canceled.

Special collations are provided when a potentially authoritative text—for instance, a contemporary reprinting of uncertain origin— has *not* been used to establish the present text because it is probably derivative. The variants are recorded as a check on this decision.

R.H.H.
September 1977

University of California at Los Angeles

Description of Texts

The following list identifies and briefly characterizes textually significant editions, impressions, and issues of Mark Twain's early tales and sketches used in the preparation of the present collection. These include editions for which Mark Twain prepared the printer's copy, as well as editions that he did not so prepare but that form part of the chain of transmission. Individual journal printings and manuscripts, and several minor editions that affect only a few sketches, are not included in this list but are of course defined in the textual commentaries. Also excluded, but listed at the end, are a group of editions found to be derivative and without textual significance.

Bibliographical terms used here follow the definitions of Fredson Bowers in *Principles of Bibliographical Description* (New York: Russell and Russell, 1962) and of G. Thomas Tanselle in "The Bibliographical Concepts of *Issue* and *State*" (*PBSA* 69 [1975]: 17–66). Sight collation means the collation of two or more copies printed from different settings of type. Machine collation means the collation on the Hinman collator of two copies printed from the same typesetting or from plates cast from the same typesetting. (The Hinman machine superimposes the images of the two copies on each other and thereby enables the operator to detect even minute typographic differences.)

Following the description of texts is a list of the specific copies of each edition or issue used in the preparation of this collection.

YS**MT** The Yale Scrapbook, which contains clippings from the Virginia City *Territorial Enterprise, Californian,* San Francisco *Golden Era,* San Francisco *Dramatic Chronicle,* Sacramento *Union,* and other unidentified newspapers (Yale). The clippings were published between mid-December 1863 and late October 1866. Many of them were revised by Mark Twain, and the scrapbook supplied most of the printer's copy for JF1.

JF1 *The Celebrated Jumping Frog of Calaveras County, And other Sketches.* By Mark Twain. Edited by John Paul. New York: C. H. Webb, 1867. *BAL* 3310. An authorized American edition. All of the sketches in JF1 were set from newspaper and journal printings— many of them unauthoritative reprints, and most of them taken as clippings from YS**MT**. Machine collation shows no authoritative changes in the plates through 1870, when Mark Twain had them destroyed.

JF1**MT** The copy of an 1869 impression of JF1 revised by Mark Twain (Doheny).

JF2 *The Celebrated Jumping Frog of Calaveras County, And other Sketches.* By Mark Twain. Edited by John Paul. London: George Routledge and Sons, 1867. *BAL* 3586. An unauthorized English edition, set from JF1. JF2 was used as printer's copy in setting both Hotten's unauthorized JF3 and the Routledges' authorized JF4a.

JF3   *The Jumping Frog and Other Humourous Sketches.* By Mark Twain. [Samuel L. Clemens.] From the Original Edition. London: John Camden Hotten, [1870]. *BAL* 3587. An unauthorized English edition, set from JF2. The plates (or duplicate plates) of JF3 were used to supply the text of JF3 in Hotten's *A 3rd Supply of Yankee Drolleries* [1870], listed in *BAL*, p. 246. JF3 served as printer's copy for portions of Hotten's unauthorized HWa.

JF4

JF4a   *The Celebrated Jumping Frog of Calaveras County, And other Sketches.* By Mark Twain. London: George Routledge and Sons, 1870. *BAL* 3319. The earliest issue of an authorized English edition, set from JF2. JF4a contained what advertisements (and perhaps the cover, which we have not seen) called "a New Copyright Chapter," "Cannibalism in the Cars" (no. 232). Mark Twain did not revise the printer's copy for JF4a, but he did use a copy of it to prepare part of the printer's copy for the Routledges' authorized MTSk.

JF4b   *Mark Twain's Celebrated Jumping Frog of Calaveras County And other Sketches. With the Burlesque Autobiography and First Romance.* London: George Routledge and Sons, [1872]. *BAL* 3338. An authorized reissue of JF4a. To produce this reissue, or "author's edition, with a copyright chapter and Mark Twain's Autobiography" (as the cover announced), the Routledges added two sketches to the plates of JF4a ("An Awful—Terrible Medieval Romance" and "A Burlesque Autobiography," nos. 276 and 355). Mark Twain did not revise the printer's copy for JF4b, which is textually identical with JF4a except for the new sketches. Machine collation shows no authoritative changes in the plates through 1900.

BA1   *Mark Twain's (Burlesque) Autobiography and First Romance.* New York: Sheldon and Company, [1871]. *BAL* 3326. An authorized American edition. BA1 served as printer's copy for the Routledges' unauthorized BA2, and possibly for Hotten's unauthorized BA3 as well. Machine collation of BA1 shows no authorial changes in the plates through 1882, when Mark Twain had them destroyed.

BA2   *Mark Twain's (Burlesque) Autobiography and First Romance.* London: George Routledge and Sons, [1871]. *BAL* 3595. An unauthorized English edition, set from BA1.

BA3   *Mark Twain's (Burlesque) 1. Autobiography. 2. Mediæval Romance. 3. On Children.* London: John Camden Hotten, [1871]. *BAL* 3329. An unauthorized English edition, set from BA1 or BA2 with the addition of two pieces not by Mark Twain.

EOps   *Eye Openers: Good Things, Immensely Funny Sayings & Stories That Will Bring a Smile upon the Gruffest Countenance.* By Mark Twain. London: John Camden Hotten, [1871]. *BAL* 3331. An unauthorized English edition. Hotten reprinted many sketches from the *Galaxy* and a few from newspapers. Mark Twain revised a copy

of EOps, which served as printer's copy for portions of the authorized Routledge MTSk. EOps also served as printer's copy for portions
of Hotten's unauthorized HWa.

Scrs   *Screamers: A Gathering of Scraps of Humour, Delicious Bits, &
        Short Stories.* By Mark Twain. London: John Camden Hotten,
        [1871]. *BAL* 3333. An unauthorized English edition. Scrs reprinted
        many sketches from the *Galaxy*, two from JF3, and one from the
        Buffalo *Express*. It also reprinted six sketches that were not by Mark
        Twain; later impressions of Scrs omit the final sketch ("Ven-
        geance"), which was not Mark Twain's. Mark Twain revised a copy
        of Scrs, which served as printer's copy for portions of the authorized
        Routledge MTSk. Scrs also served as printer's copy for portions of
        Hotten's unauthorized HWa.

PJks   *Practical Jokes with Artemus Ward, Including the Story of the Man
        Who Fought Cats.* By Mark Twain and Other Humourists. London:
        John Camden Hotten, [1872]. *BAL* 3342. An unauthorized English
        edition. PJks reprinted sketches from the *Galaxy*, the Buffalo *Ex-
        press*, and *Roughing It;* it included many sketches not by Mark
        Twain. It served as printer's copy for portions of Hotten's unau-
        thorized HWa.

CD   *A Curious Dream; and Other Sketches.* By Mark Twain. Selected
        and Revised by the Author. Copyright. London: George Routledge
        and Sons, [1872]. *BAL* 3340. An authorized English edition. Mark
        Twain prepared the printer's copy for CD by revising clippings from
        the *Galaxy*, Buffalo *Express*, New York *Tribune*, *Packard's Monthly*,
        Newark (N.J.) *Press*, and *American Publisher*. These revised clip-
        pings also served as printer's copy for portions of the authorized
        Routledge MTSk. Machine collation of CD reveals only six minor
        textual variants, none of them authorial, which occurred sometime
        between the 1872 and 1892 impressions.

MTSk   *Mark Twain's Sketches.* Selected and Revised by the Author.
        Copyright Edition. London: George Routledge and Sons, 1872. *BAL*
        3341. An authorized English edition. Mark Twain prepared printer's
        copy for MTSk by revising copies of JF4a, EOps, and Scrs. He or his
        publisher also included the fifteen sketches prepared as clippings for
        CD. The plates of MTSk were sold to Chatto and Windus in 1892,
        who reissued MTSk in 1897. Machine collation reveals only minor
        changes and corrections, none of them authorial. Mark Twain used
        MTSk as printer's copy for portions of the American News Com-
        pany's authorized Sk#1 and the American Publishing Company's
        authorized SkNO.

MTSk**MT** The copy of an 1872 impression of MTSk revised by Mark Twain
        to serve as printer's copy for SkNO (MTP).

HW

HWa   *The Choice Humorous Works of Mark Twain.* Now First Collected. With Extra Passages to the "Innocents Abroad," Now First Reprinted, and a Life of the Author. Illustrations by Mark Twain and other Artists; also Portrait of the Author. London: John Camden Hotten, [1873]. *BAL* 3351. An unauthorized English edition. HWa reprinted sketches from Hotten's own JF3, EOps, Scrs, and PJks, as well as all of *The Innocents Abroad.* It also reprinted seven sketches from MTSk or CD and extracts from *Roughing It,* as well as a few sketches not by Mark Twain. In 1873 Mark Twain revised a set of HWa sheets, and the plates were altered to follow his corrections and produce the authorized reissue HWb, published by Chatto and Windus, Hotten's successors.

HWa**MT**   The set of sheets of HWa revised by Mark Twain and used to produce HWb (Rare Book Room, New York Public Library, *KL).

HWb   *The Choice Humorous Works of Mark Twain.* Revised and Corrected by the Author. With Life and Portrait of the Author, and Numerous Illustrations. London: Chatto and Windus, 1874. *BAL* 3605. An authorized reissue of HWa. The plates of HWa were altered for HWb to follow Mark Twain's corrections on HWa**MT**. Machine collation of HWb reveals no further authorial changes in the plates.

HWb**MT**   The copy of an 1874 impression of HWb revised by Mark Twain and used as printer's copy for SkNO (Doheny).

Sk #1   *Mark Twain's Sketches. Number One.* Authorised Edition. With Illustrations by R. T. Sperry. New York: American News Company, [1874]. *BAL* 3360. An authorized American edition. Sk #1 reprinted ten sketches from MTSk, several of them further revised by Mark Twain, and three sketches not previously published. Machine collation was not performed because no later impression could be obtained.

SkNO   *Mark Twain's Sketches, New and Old.* Now First Published in Complete Form. Hartford and Chicago: American Publishing Company, 1875. *BAL* 3364. An authorized American edition. SkNO drew the bulk of its sketches from copies of MTSk and HWb which Mark Twain revised—MTSk**MT** and HWb**MT**—and the rest of its sketches from manuscripts and revised clippings. Machine collation reveals that in the first impression a new preface replaced that of the publisher's prospectus, which was otherwise printed from the plates of SkNO. Later impressions of SkNO made minor corrections and dropped one sketch ("From 'Hospital Days' ") which was not written by Mark Twain.

DERIVATIVE EDITIONS

The following editions were found to be derivative and without textual significance—that is, Mark Twain played no part in their production, and he did not subsequently revise their texts or anything deriving from their texts. We follow the order of *BAL*.

Beadle's Dime No. 3. Book of Fun. New York: Beadle and Company, [1866]. *BAL* 3309.

The Piccadilly Annual of Entertaining Literature. London: John Camden Hotten, [1870]. *BAL* 3323.

Mark Twain's Memoranda. From the Galaxy. Toronto: Canadian News and Publishing Company, 1871. *BAL* 3327.

Autobiography, (Burlesque.) First Romance, and Memoranda. By Mark Twain. Toronto: James Campbell and Son, [1871]. *BAL* 3334.

A Book for an Hour, Containing Choice Reading and Character Sketches. A Curious Dream, and Other Sketches, Revised and Selected for This Work by the Author Mark Twain. New York: B. J. Such, 1873. *BAL* 3352.

Sketches by Mark Twain. Toronto: Belfords, Clarke and Co., 1879. *BAL* 3384.

Mark Twain's Library of Humor. New York: Charles L. Webster and Company, 1888. *BAL* 3425.

Sketches New and Old, vol. 19 of *The Writings of Mark Twain*. Autograph Edition. Hartford: American Publishing Company, 1899. *BAL* 3456.

The $30,000 Bequest and Other Stories by Mark Twain. New York and London: Harper and Brothers, 1906. *BAL* 3492.

The Celebrated Jumping Frog of Calaveras County, and Other Sketches. Melbourne: George Robertson, 1868. *BAL* 3588.

Information Wanted and Other Sketches. London: George Routledge and Sons, [1876]. *BAL* 3608.

Sketches by Mark Twain. Now First Published in Complete Form. Toronto: Belfords, Clarke and Co., 1880. *BAL* 3624.

Sketches by Mark Twain. Leipzig: Bernhard Tauchnitz, 1883. *BAL* 3632.

Sketches New and Old. Hartford: American Publishing Company, 1893. *BAL* 3651.

Mark Twain's Sketches. Selected and Revised by the Author. A New Edition. London: Chatto and Windus, 1897. *BAL* 3657.

Editorial Wild Oats. New York and London: Harper and Brothers, 1905. *BAL* 3665.

A 3rd Supply of Yankee Drolleries: The Most Recent Works of the Best American Humourists. London: John Camden Hotten, [1870]. *BAL*, p. 246.

Fun for the Million. A Gathering of Choice Wit and Humour, Good Things, and Sublime Nonsense by Jerrold, Dickens, Sam Slick, Mark Twain . . . and a Host of other Humourists. London: John Camden Hotten, [1873]. *BAL*, p. 247.

The Celebrated Jumping Frog of Calaveras County, and Other Sketches. By Mark Twain. Toronto: A. S. Irving, 1870. Not in *BAL*.

TEXTS COLLATED

The following copies were used in machine and sight collations or examined in the course of preparing this edition. In addition, variant readings discovered in collations were exhaustively checked in every relevant copy available to the editors.

JF1 Copies machine collated: 1867 impression (MTP Armes), 1867 impression, variant state with unprinted page 198 (PH of copy at CWB), 1868 impression (Iowa xPS 1322.C4.1868), 1870 impression (University of North Carolina 817.C625.ce).

   Copies sight collated or examined: 1867 impression (MTP Webster), 1868 impression (Bancroft F855.1.C625c), 1869 impression (Bancroft F855.1.C625c), 1870 impression (Iowa xPS 1322.C4.1870).

JF2 Copies sight collated: 1867 impression (PH of copy at Texas), 1867 impression (MTP).

JF3 Copies machine collated: [1870] impression (PH of copy at Texas), [1870] impression, included in *A 3rd Supply of Yankee Drolleries* (PH of copy at British Museum, 12316.cc.27), [1882] impression, George Routledge and Sons (PH of copy at British Museum, 12316.d.34).

   Copy examined: [1877] impression, Ward, Lock, and Co. (MTP Appert).

JF4 Copies machine collated: JF4a 1870 impression (PH of copy at Texas, Clemens 7aa), JF4b [1872] impression, *BAL* "first" (Houghton Library, Harvard University, AL1059.38), JF4b [1872?] impression, *BAL* "third" (MTP), JF4b [1900] impression (Robert H. Hirst collection).

   Copies sight collated or examined: JF4b [1872?] impression, *BAL* "second" (PH of copy at University of Michigan, PS1322.J8.1873), JF4b [1872?] impression, *BAL* "third" (Charles Cornman collection).

BA1 Copies machine collated: [1871] impression (MTP green cover), [1871] impression (MTP brown cover), [1871] impression (MTP purple cover).

   Copies sight collated or examined: [1871] impression (MTP Judd, paper cover), [1871] impression (MTP paper cover), [1871] impression (Berkeley 957.C625.ma).

BA2   Copy sight collated: [1871] impression (PH of copy at University of Virginia).

BA3   Copies sight collated or examined: [1871] impression (PH of copy at Texas), [1871] impression (PH of copy at Yale).

EOps   Copies machine collated: [1871] impression (PH of copy at Texas), [1871 or later] impression (Yale Ix.H251.867ce).

       Copy examined: [1875] impression, Ward, Lock and Co. (University of British Columbia PS1303.W3).

Scrs   Copies machine collated: [1871] impression (Yale Ix.H251.867ce), [1871 or later] impression, without final sketch (University of Indiana PS1303.H834.1872).

       Copies sight collated or examined: [1871 or later] impression, without final sketch (MTP paper cover), [1871 or later] impression, without final sketch (MTP rebound copy).

PJks   Copy sight collated: [1872] impression (PH of copy at University of Illinois, 817.C859p).

CD   Copies machine collated: [1872] impression (PH of copy at Texas, Clemens 86), [1892] impression (University of Chicago PS1322.C74.1892), [1900] impression (Robert H. Hirst collection).

       Copy examined: [1872 or later] impression (Robert H. Hirst collection).

MTSk   Copies machine collated: [1872] impression (MTP), [1897] impression, Chatto and Windus (Bowdoin College PS1319.A1.1897). Copy partially machine collated: [1872] impression, revised by Mark Twain (MTSk**MT**, MTP).

HW   Copies machine collated: HWa [1873] impression (Texas Clemens B33), HWb 1874 impression (PH of copy at CWB), HWb 1877 impression (Texas Clemens B34), HWb 1878 impression (MTP), HWb 1902 impression (McMaster University PS1302.C5.1902), HWb 1922 impression (University of Cincinnati PS1302.C5.1922).

Sk#1   Copies sight collated or examined: [1874] impression (Iowa xPS1322.S47.1874), [1874] impression (Berkeley FILM 4274.PR.v.2.reel C16).

SkNO   Copies machine collated: publisher's prospectus (MTP Tufts), publisher's prospectus (MTP), 1875 impression (MTP copy 3), 1875 impression (MTP copy 4), 1875 impression (Texas Clemens 118), 1887 impression (University of Virginia PS1319.A1.1887), 1893 impression (Texas Clemens 129b).

       Copies sight collated or examined: publisher's prospectus (PH of copy at Yale), 1875 impression (MTP copy 2), 1875 impression (MTP copy 5), 1875 impression (MTP Hearst), 1892 impression (Princeton University 3679.7.382.11).

Textual Commentaries, Notes, and Tables

1. *A GALLANT FIREMAN*

Textual Commentary

The first printing appeared in the Hannibal *Western Union* for 16 January 1851 (p. 3). The original newspaper is not available, so a PH of it in MoHist is copy-text. Clemens may have typeset and proofread the sketch, since he was on the paper's staff.

Textual Notes

62.3   material . . . them] The technical term "material" meant "the Types, Rules, Leads, Quotations, Furniture, and other material belonging to the composing-room" (Thomas Lynch, *The Printer's Manual: A Practical Guide for Compositors and Pressmen* [Cincinnati: The Cincinnati Type-Foundry, 1859], p. 45). Clemens followed contemporary usage—and his own normal practice at this time—in using a plural pronoun.

Emendations of the Copy-Text

62.13   hadn't (I-C) • had'nt

2. *THE DANDY FRIGHTENING THE SQUATTER*

Textual Commentary

The first printing in the Boston *Carpet-Bag* for 1 May 1852 (p. 6) is copy-text. Copies: Boston Public Library; PH in MTP. There is no evidence that Clemens supervised the printing in any way. There are no textual notes or emendations.

3. HANNIBAL, MISSOURI

Textual Commentary

The first printing in the Philadelphia *American Courier* for 8 May 1852 (p. 4)
is copy-text. Copy: PH published by the Antiquarian Booksellers Association
of America (1967). There is no evidence that Clemens supervised the printing
in any way. There are no textual notes.

Emendations of the Copy-Text

67.13   railroad (I-C) • rail-|road
68.11   hang (I-C) • hangs

4. A FAMILY MUSS

Textual Commentary

The first printing appeared in the Hannibal *Journal* for 9 September 1852
(p. 2). The only known copy of this printing, in MoHist, is copy-text.
Clemens may have typeset and proofread the sketch, since he was on the
paper's staff. There are no textual notes.

Emendations of the Copy-Text

70.22   "grabbed" (I-C) • '~"
70.24   discipline (I-C) • disciplin e
70.24   that— (I-C) • ~ — --
71.4   hear (I-C) • hea[r] [*torn*]

[THE DOG CONTROVERSY]

§5. "LOCAL" RESOLVES TO COMMIT SUICIDE

Textual Commentary

The first printing appeared in the Hannibal *Journal* for 16 September 1852
(p. 2). The only known copy of this printing, in MoHist, is copy-text.

Clemens may have typeset and proofread the sketch, since his brother Orion had left him temporarily in charge of the newspaper. The "villainous" woodcuts included in nos. 5 and 6 are reproduced from the original newspaper. As Clemens later recalled in "My First Literary Venture" (no. 357), they were engraved by the author "on the bottom of wooden type with a jack-knife" and inserted into his text. There are no textual notes or emendations.

§6. "PICTUR'" DEPARTMENT

Textual Commentary

The first printing appeared in the Hannibal *Journal* for 23 September 1852 (p. 2). The only known copy of this printing, in MoHist, is copy-text. Clemens may have typeset and proofread the sketch. For the woodcuts, see the textual commentary to no. 5. There are no textual notes or emendations.

7. HISTORICAL EXHIBITION—A NO. 1 RUSE

Textual Commentary

The first printing appeared in the Hannibal *Journal* for 16 September 1852 (p. 2). The only known copy of this printing, in MoHist, is copy-text. Since Clemens was in charge of the paper he may have typeset and proofread the sketch.

Textual Notes

79.22   price!"] Standard practice calls for a question mark instead of an exclamation point here, but the punctuation of the copy-text causes no real difficulty and is evidently deliberate. Compare the same practice at 80.26: "Is-is a-a-that all!"

Emendations of the Copy-Text

79.22   price!" (I-C) • ~!$_\wedge$
80.13   overlooked (I-C) • overlookod
80.34   rind." (I-C) • ~.$_\wedge$

81.5   imperturbable (I-C) • imperturable
81.16   particular (I-C) • partciular

8. [BLAB'S TOUR]

Textual Commentary

The first printing appeared in the Hannibal *Journal* for 23 September 1852
(p. 2). The only known copy of this printing, in MoHist, is copy-text.
Clemens may have typeset and proofread the sketch.

Textual Notes

84.8   Glasscock's] Copy-text "Glascock's" is an error, probably
                caused by the division of the word at the end of a line. The
                island was named for its owner, Stephen Glasscock (see Return
                Ira Holcombe, *History of Marion County, Missouri* [St. Louis:
                E. F. Perkins, 1884], p. 940).

Emendations of the Copy-Text

*84.8   Glasscock's (I-C) • Glas-|cock's

9. "CONNUBIAL BLISS"

Textual Commentary

The first printing appeared in the Hannibal *Journal* for 4 November 1852
(p. 2). The only known copy of this printing, in MoHist, is copy-text.
Clemens may have typeset and proofread the sketch. There are no textual
notes.

Emendations of the Copy-Text

86.7   to-day (I-C) • to-|day

10. *THE HEART'S LAMENT*

Textual Commentary

The first printing appeared in the Hannibal *Daily Journal* for 5 May 1853
(p. 2). The only known copy of this printing, in MoHist, is copy-text. The
poem was reprinted in the Hannibal *Weekly Journal* for 12 May 1853 (p. 1).
Collation shows no variation between these printings, and it seems likely
that the *Weekly* printing is a reimpression of the *Daily's* standing type.
Clemens may have typeset and proofread the poem. There are no textual
notes.

Emendations of the Copy-Text

89.13   Its (I-C) • It's

[THE "KATIE OF H———L" CONTROVERSY]

§11. *LOVE CONCEALED*

Textual Commentary

The first printing appeared in the Hannibal *Daily Journal* for 6 May 1853
(p. 2). The only known copy of this printing, in MoHist, is copy-text. The
poem was reprinted in the Hannibal *Weekly Journal* for 12 May 1853 (p. 1),
apparently from the standing type. No variants occur. Clemens may have
typeset and proofread the poem. There are no textual notes or emendations.

§12. *[FIRST LETTER FROM GRUMBLER]*

Textual Commentary

The first printing appeared in the Hannibal *Daily Journal* for 7 May 1853
(p. 2). The only known copy of this printing, in MoHist, is copy-text. The
letter was reprinted in the Hannibal *Weekly Journal* for 12 May 1853 (p. 4),
apparently from the standing type. No variants occur. Clemens may have
typeset and proofread the letter. There are no textual notes.

Emendations of the Copy-Text

95.2   yesterday's (I-C) • yesterdays'
95.3   (*hell*). Now (I-C) • (~).—|~

§13. [*FIRST LETTER FROM RAMBLER*]

Textual Commentary

The first printing appeared in the Hannibal *Daily Journal* for 9 May 1853
(p. 2). The only known copy of this printing, in MoHist, is copy-text. So far
as is known, there was no second printing in the Hannibal *Weekly Journal*
(compare nos. 10–12). Clemens may have typeset and proofread the letter.
There are no textual notes.

Emendations of the Copy-Text

96.8   there. From (I-C) • ~.—|~
96.9   notice (I-C) • notiec

§14. *TO RAMBLER*

Textual Commentary

The first printing appeared in the Hannibal *Daily Journal* for 10 May 1853
(p. 2). The only known copy of this printing, in MoHist, is copy-text. So far
as is known, there was no second printing in the Hannibal *Weekly Journal*
(compare nos. 10–12). Clemens may have typeset and proofread the letter.

Textual Notes

97 title   Rambler] Copy-text "Bambler" may be intentional, but is
            more likely a simple error caused by the similarity between *R*
            and *B*. Compare "Rambler!" at 97.9.

Emendations of the Copy-Text

*97 title   Rambler (I-C) • Bambler

§15. [*LETTER FROM PETER PENCILCASE'S SON, JOHN SNOOKS*]

Textual Commentary

The first printing appeared in the Hannibal *Daily Journal* for 12 May 1853 (p. 2). The only known copy of this printing, in MoHist, is copy-text. So far as is known, there was no second printing in the Hannibal *Weekly Journal* (compare nos. 10–12). Clemens may have typeset and proofread the letter, which is deliberately mispunctuated throughout, precluding emendation. There are no textual notes.

Emendations of the Copy-Text

98.6   overflowing (I-C) • over-|flowing

§16. [*SECOND LETTER FROM RAMBLER*]

Textual Commentary

The first printing appeared in the Hannibal *Daily Journal* for 13 May 1853 (p. 2). The only known copy of this printing, in MoHist, is copy-text. So far as is known, there was no second printing in the Hannibal *Weekly Journal* (compare nos. 10–12). Clemens may have typeset and proofread the letter. There are no textual notes.

Emendations of the Copy-Text

99.3   fool. (I-C) • ~,
99.12   heels. His (I-C) • ~.—|~

17. *SEPARATION*

Textual Commentary

The first printing appeared in the Hannibal *Missouri Courier* for 12 May 1853 (p. 3). The only known copy of this printing, in MoHist, is copy-text. Since the poem was published in the rival town paper, it is unlikely that Clemens typeset it, although he may have proofread it. There are no textual notes.

Emendations of the Copy-Text

101.4   forever. (I-C) • ~[,]

18. *"OH, SHE HAS A RED HEAD!"*

Textual Commentary

The first printing appeared in the Hannibal *Daily Journal* for 13 May 1853 (p. 2). The only known copy of this printing, in MoHist, is copy-text. So far as is known, there was no second printing in the Hannibal *Weekly Journal* (compare nos. 10–12), but the sketch was widely reprinted by contemporary newspapers (*SCH*, p. 260). Clemens may have typeset and proofread the sketch. There are no textual notes or emendations.

19. *THE BURIAL OF SIR ABNER GILSTRAP,*
EDITOR OF THE BLOOMINGTON "REPUBLICAN"

Textual Commentary

The first printing appeared in the Hannibal *Daily Journal* for 23 May 1853 (p. 3). This was followed three days later by a reprinting, evidently from the *Daily's* standing type, in the Hannibal *Weekly Journal* for 26 May 1853 (p. 2). Although collation disclosed no textual variants between the *Daily* and the *Weekly* printings, slight defects in inking do occur in the copies examined. The copy-text is therefore defined as embracing both printings, the only known copies of which are in MoHist, and the defects in inking are silently corrected whenever one printing is defective and the other is clear. Since the parody was part of Clemens' own "Our Assistant's Column," he may well have typeset and proofread the sketch. There are no textual notes.

Emendations of the Copy-Text

108.1   Bloomington (I-C) • Bloomington's
108.5   verses. However (I-C) • ~.—|~
109.13   short (I-C) • sho[r]t

20. *"JUL'US CAESAR"*

Textual Commentary

The manuscript of this sketch, probably written sometime in 1855 or 1856 but never published, survives in the Jean Webster McKinney Family Papers, Vassar. It is copy-text. The piece is written in brown or black ink on four folios, each page of which measures $6^{11}/_{16}$ by $8^{11}/_{16}$ inches; the text fills only thirteen and a half of the sixteen pages, which are unnumbered. The stationery is cream-colored laid paper with twenty-three to twenty-five horizontal rules, and the first page is embossed in the upper left corner with the words "SUPERFINE LAID BATH" within four braces. Someone, not Clemens, has written "Mark Twain in School when a boy" in pencil across the top of the first page.

Textual Notes

112.21 down street] The idiom is clearly authorial; no emendation is required. Compare the "valiant corporal" who "reeled down street" in "The Guard on a Bender" (no. 138), and Fitz Smythe "jolting down street at four mile a week" in "Fitz Smythe's Horse" (no. 132).

115.14 noticed, one morning,] The copy-text omits the second comma. But since "one morning" is a parenthetical phrase, and since "morning" ends very near the edge of the manuscript page where Clemens may have been unable to supply the necessary punctuation, we have emended.

117.7–8 he had a kind and generous nature, and] Clemens originally wrote "he was kind and generous, and" but he replaced "was" with "had a" and canceled his second "and" before writing "nature, and." In making this revision he inadvertently left the comma standing after "generous" and we have therefore emended.

Emendations of the Copy-Text

111.16 its (I-C) • it's
111.18 its (I-C) • it's
111.24 its (I-C) • it's
113.10 to (I-C) • [*not in*]

113.13	Caesar (I-C) • Ceasar
114.4	ground. (I-C) • ~_∧
115.5	Jul'us's (I-C) • J'ulus's
115.6	its (I-C) • it's
*115.14	morning, (I-C) • ~_∧
115.20	moreover (I-C) • morever
115.21–22	secret? These (I-C) • ~?—|~
115.23	of (I-C) • [not in]
116.14	firemen (I-C) • fire-|men
116.25	yourself? (I-C) • ~.
*117.8	generous (I-C) • ~,

Alterations in the Manuscript

111.7	according] *follows canceled* 'to hear him te'; 'te' *wiped out and* 'ac' *written over it.*
111.12	and the] 'the' *follows canceled* 'got'.
111.16	the manner] 'the' *written over wiped-out* 'his'.
111.17	speaking] *written over wiped-out* 'making'.
111.17	showing] *written over wiped-out* 'show'.
111.18	spending] 'sp' *written over wiped-out* 'pu'.
111.25	been] *follows canceled* 'once'.
112.3–4	(with . . . week,)] *interlined with a caret.*
112.12	in] *written over wiped-out* 'an'.
112.14	their] *interlined without a caret above canceled* 'its'.
112.19	and looking like] *written over wiped-out* 'giving his upper story'.
112.19	giving] *follows canceled* 'and'.
112.21	leaning the] 'the' *written over wiped-out* 'a'.
112.22–23	(on . . . side)] *interlined without a caret.*
112.31	yet] *interlined with a caret.*
112.36	Boston] *written over wiped-out* 'New York'.
112.36	instructive] *written over wiped-out* 'enter'.
113.6	and tell] 'and' *written over wiped-out* 'with'.
113.7	the] 't' *written over wiped-out* 's'; *follows canceled* 'it' *which is in turn written over wiped-out* 'the'.
113.15	then] *follows canceled* 'with'.

113.17	by] *written over* 'un'.
113.18	also] *written over wiped-out* 'con'.
113.21	poet] *written over an open parenthesis.*
113.26	awakened] 'ne' *interlined with a caret.*
113.33	there:—] *colon mended from an exclamation point.*
114.13	enjoyed] *written over wiped-out* 'l'.
114.16	the decree of] *interlined with a caret;* 'c' *mended from* 'g'.
114.16	fate] *written over* 'our'.
114.16	should] 's' *written over* 'c'.
114.19	in action] *follows canceled* 'ac'.
114.23	till] *follows canceled* ' "poetry" '.
114.30	an article] *written over* 'a volume'; 'volume' *wiped out;* 'a' *mended to* 'an'.
115.2	we] 'w' *written over* 's'.
115.6	was] *interlined without a caret above canceled* 'is'.
115.13	ex-poet] *follows canceled* 'ex-'.
115.15	cup on] 'on' *written over wiped-out* 'w'.
115.17	awakened] 'ne' *interlined with a caret.*
115.17	lately] *interlined without a caret above canceled* 'recently'.
115.20	it] *written over wiped-out* 'th'.
115.23	the first] *follows canceled* 'expected'.
115.32	astounded] 'as' *written over wiped-out* 'th'.
115.34	Philadelphia] 'P' *written over* 'p'.
116.1–2	from between her teeth] *interlined with a caret.*
116.2	poor] *interlined without a caret above canceled* 'the trembling'.
116.11	rain bow,—it . . . which,—] *dashes added.*
116.15	a gaudy] *follows canceled* 'with'.
116.22	speech] *interlined without a caret above canceled* 'oration'.
116.31	don't you] 'you' *originally* 'your'; 'r' *wiped out.*
116.31	Ugh] 'U' *written over wiped-out* 'Oh'.
116.31	Ugh! you] 'you' *originally* 'your'; 'r' *wiped out.*
116.35	exclamation] *interlined without a caret above canceled* 'remark'.
117.7	vanity] *written over wiped-out* 'self-esteem'.
117.7	had a] *interlined without a caret above canceled* 'was'.
117.8	generous] *originally* 'generous, and'; 'and' *canceled and comma left standing.*

21. *TO MOLLIE*

Textual Commentary

The manuscript of this poem survives in the memory book of Mary Eleanor Stotts Clemens, which is owned by Dorris B. Schmidt, Lincoln, Nebraska. It is copy-text. Copy: PH from owner. There are no textual notes, emendations, or alterations in the manuscript.

22. *"LINES SUGGESTED BY A REMINISCENCE,* *AND WHICH YOU WILL PERHAPS UNDERSTAND"*

Textual Commentary

The manuscript of this poem, in the autograph album of Ann Virginia Ruffner, is extant but not available for inspection. The first printing, presumably from a transcription of the album entry, in the Hannibal *Evening Courier-Post* for 6 March 1935 (p. 9C) is therefore copy-text. Copy: PH from MoHist.

Textual Notes

123.5   S.L.C.] The signature is placed here on the authority of the editorial comment in the *Courier-Post:* "Sam Clemens signed the verses 'S. L. C.', his customary literary trademark before he became famous under the name of Mark Twain."

123.6–12   Now . . . SAM C.] The *Courier-Post* editor commented that Clemens "added the following lines under the poem, writing an explanatory note, 'long meter' on the margin."

Emendations of the Copy-Text

122.10   thunder. (I-C) • ~∧
*123.5   S.L.C. (I-C) • [*not in*]

23. *TO JENNIE*

Textual Commentary

The manuscript of this poem, reproduced in photofacsimile in the Hannibal *Evening Courier-Post* for 6 March 1935 (p. 9C), is copy-text. Copy: PH from MoHist. There are no textual notes, emendations, or alterations in the manuscript.

24. [*RIVER INTELLIGENCE*]

Textual Commentary

The first printing appeared without title in the regular column "River Intelligence" in the New Orleans *Crescent* for 17 May 1859 (p. 7), which is copy-text. Copies: clipping in MTP; PH from the Louisiana State University Library, Baton Rouge. It seems unlikely that Clemens supervised the printing in any way, because he was serving on the steamer *A. T. Lacey* under Bart Bowen at this time, and the *Lacey* was scheduled to leave New Orleans on May 14 ("River Intelligence," New Orleans *Crescent*, 11 May 1859, p. 7).

Textual Notes

131.6   prophesy] Although Webster's 1828 dictionary gives the noun spelling as "prophecy," it adds that "this ought to be written prophesy." The *Oxford English Dictionary* reports that the "variant spelling *prophesy* is found as late as 1709, but is now confined to the verb." The spelling "prophesy" here (and at 132.24) may therefore be somewhat archaic, but it is not clearly wrong and was evidently deliberate. We have not emended.

Emendations of the Copy-Text

132.8   creature!") (I-C) • ~!"∧
132.16   The (I-C) • "~
132.28   suggest (I-C) • sugggest

25. [*THE MYSTERIOUS MURDERS IN RISSE*]

Textual Commentary

The manuscript of this sketch, untitled but dated 1 August 1859, survives in the Jean Webster McKinney Family Papers, Vassar. It is copy-text. The piece is written in pencil on three folios, each page of which measures $6\frac{1}{2}$ by 8 inches. The paper is embossed in the upper left corner "Damask Laid Highly Finished." The first half of the third folio is missing, creating a lacuna of perhaps four hundred words at 140.32. Because of folds in the manuscript, smudged pencil, and very small handwriting, another lacuna occurs in the first paragraph of the sketch: four or five words are in the manuscript but are not now legible.

Textual Notes

136.4   this usually quiet] Clemens originally began his tale with these words. He interlined the preceding four words with a caret, but inadvertently left the capital letter of "This" standing in the manuscript. We have emended the oversight.

136.13–14   kneed . . . go] The ellipsis points in the text are editorial. Clemens added the last sentence in this paragraph by squeezing it in and writing in very small letters. Four or five words are now illegible.

136.17–18   to wit] Copy-text "to-wit" is the earliest known instance of Clemens' lifelong but erroneous spelling of this shortened form of the phrase "that is to wit."

140.29   murder] Clemens originally wrote, "the porter . . . testified that about two hours before the murder, three men." He changed that by interlining "he saw" above "three men," but ultimately canceled both phrases, and went on to complete his sentence with the verb "was committed." In making these revisions he inadvertently left a comma after "murder" standing in the manuscript. We have emended the oversight.

140.32   must] The ellipsis points that follow here are editorial. The four-hundred-word lacuna is caused by a missing leaf in the manuscript.

140.37   A dagger] These words follow a canceled sentence: "This savors of a connection with the mysterious Lun murders." "Lun" (or possibly "Lin") is not clearly legible here, or in the second and third instances at 141.14 and 141.16. The name may have some significance that was explained in the now missing passage.

141.4–5   * charge ... aiding * * * *] All the asterisks in this sentence occur in the manuscript: they are not editorial.

141.18   blood-stained dagger] Clemens left an alternate reading, "dagger," uncanceled in the manuscript. We have adopted what appears to be the revised choice, but the author himself made no decision.

Emendations of the Copy-Text

*136.4   this (I-C) • This
136.7   the staid (I-C) • [*possibly*] this staid
136.8   *Spaziergang* (I-C) • [*possibly*] *Spaziergaing*
*136.17–18 to wit (I-C) • ~·~
138.22   sidewalks (I-C) • side-|walks
138.25   exclaimed, (I-C) • ~, "
138.29   handkerchief (I-C) • hankerchief
138.33   success. He (I-C) • ~.—|~
139.12   footprints (I-C) • footpints
140.10   watchmen (I-C) • watch-|men
140.20   forehead (I-C) • fore-|head
*140.29   murder (I-C) • ~,
141.4–5   " '* charge . . . aiding * * * *.' (I-C) • "ₐ* ~ . . . ~ * * * *."
141.6   "On (I-C) • ₐ~
141.7–10   " 'This ... houses.' (I-C) • "ₐ~ ... ~."
141.7   took (I-C) • took [*canceled inadvertently*]
*141.18   blood-stained dagger (I-C) • dagger/blood-stained dagger
141.22   been! Yea (I-C) • ~!—|~

Alterations in the Manuscript

136.3   DEAR EDITORS:] *written over* 'Missouri Repub'.
136.4   The phlegmatic depths of] *interlined without a caret above* 'This usually quiet old town have just'.
136.4   old] *squeezed in with a caret.*
136.4   have just] *originally* 'is just now'; 'have' *written over* 'is'; 'now' *canceled.*
136.4–5   been stirred] *follows canceled* 'the scene of a great excitement.'
136.7   the] *written over* 'R'.

136.9   but] 'bu' *written over* 'sa'.

136.13–14   Even . . . often.] *interlined without a caret.*

136.15   small] *interlined with a caret.*

136.18   over] *follows canceled* 'and'.

136.20   records] 're' *written over* 'h'.

136.21   it is reverently whispered that] *interlined without a caret
               above canceled* 'they do say'.

136.23   western] *written over* 'ver'.

136.24   a departed] 'a' *interlined with a caret.*

136.24   Muller] 'M' *written over* 'm'.

137.6   paying] 'p' *written over* 'm'.

137.8   fact] *written over* 'was'.

137.12   Baden,] *comma mended from a semicolon.*

137.13   only] *written over* 'not'.

137.15   want] *interlined without a caret above canceled* 'poverty'.

137.16   The] 'e' *written over* 'is'.

137.24   man] 'n' *mended from* 'y'.

137.31   pretty] 'p' *written over* 'g'.

137.37   went] *interlined without a caret above canceled* 'came'.

138.1   Wahlner's] 'h' *written over* 'l'; *apostrophe and* 's' *added.*

138.2   love] *written over* 'wra'.

138.2   chaste] *interlined without a caret above canceled* 'most
               elegant'.

138.8   acquaintance] *follows canceled* 'dis'.

138.14   Wahlners] *originally* 'Wahlner's'.

138.24   that early the previous evening] *interlined with a caret.*

138.25   three] *follows canceled* 'a faint'.

138.25   exclaimed,] *followed by quotation marks inadvertently left
               standing.*

138.34   the neighbors.] 'the' *written over* 'hi'; *originally* 'neighbors,
               for'; *comma mended to a period;* 'for' *canceled.*

138.36   had] *follows canceled* 'compelled the police to see'.

139.7   abduction.] *period mended from a comma.*

139.11   Katrina's] *follows canceled* 'the abduc-'.

139.17   Wahlner] 'h' *written over* 'l'.

139.20   Wahlner] 'h' *written over* 'l'.

139.21   threats?] *followed by canceled quotation marks.*

139.25   became] *follows canceled* 'folded'.

139.26   murdered] *written over* 'dea'.

139.30	charged] *follows canceled* 'and arrighed'.
140.5	had] 'd' *written over* 'v'.
140.8	—strange] *dash written over* 'fro'.
140.14	their] 'ei' *written over* 'e'.
140.17	flooding] *interlined without a caret above canceled* 'drenching'.
140.25–26	Searches . . . carried on.] *interlined without a caret.*
140.28	At] *written over* 'On'.
140.29	about two hours before] *interlined with a caret above canceled* 'on the night of'; 'the' *interlined following* 'before' *and then canceled.*
140.29	was committed] *follows canceled* 'three men' *which in turn follows* 'he saw' *interlined with a caret and then canceled.*
140.33	paragraph] *first* 'r' *written over* 'p'.
140.37	A dagger] *follows canceled* 'This savors of a connection with the mysterious Lun murders.'
141.7	took away the blameless life of] *interlined without a caret above canceled* 'slew'; 'took' *canceled inadvertently.*
141.8	hath] 'th' *written over* 's'.
141.18	blood-stained dagger] *alternate reading interlined with a caret above* 'dagger' *which is left standing.*
141.23–24	both parties] *interlined without a caret above canceled* 'whom'.

26. [*PILOT'S MEMORANDA*]

Textual Commentary

The first printing appeared without title in the column "Cairo Correspondence" in the St. Louis *Missouri Republican* for 30 August 1860 (p. 4), which is copy-text. Copy: PH from Library of Congress. It is not known whether Clemens in any way supervised the printing.

Textual Notes

145.12	knocked of her] Possibly intended to read "knocked out of her" or "knocked off her." Since the phrase occurs in a quotation, and since it is readily construable as it stands in the copy-text, we have not emended.

Emendations of the Copy-Text

144.2	CAIRO, (I-C) • ~[,]
144.6	Point; (I-C) • ~[:]
144.12	Seven-Up (I-C) • [s]even-Up
144.17	deck. (I-C) • ~[∧]
145.8	34, (I-C) • ~[,]
145.20	board (I-C) • boad

27. [*GHOST LIFE ON THE MISSISSIPPI*]

Textual Commentary

The manuscript of this tale, probably written sometime in early 1861, survives in the Jean Webster McKinney Family Papers, Vassar. It is copy-text. The manuscript is untitled; we have adopted the title given it by Samuel C. Webster when he published the piece in the *Pacific Spectator* 2 (Autumn 1948): 485–490. The piece is written in pencil, in double columns, on two folios, each page of which measures 8 by 9¾ inches; the text fills only five of the eight pages, which are unnumbered. The paper is wove, ruled with twenty-six to twenty-eight blue lines, and embossed in the upper left corner with what appears to be a crown flanked by two lions.

Textual Notes

148.16	Goose Island] Clemens originally wrote "the island" but changed his mind and inserted "Goose" above canceled "the"—leaving "island" lowercase. We have emended the oversight caused by his incomplete revision.
148.20–21	in five minutes afterwards] As in the copy-text. Although the phrase is redundant, it occurs in dialogue and may be idiomatic. We have therefore not emended.
148.28	Then ... when] Clemens originally wrote "The" and canceled it. He then wrote "For when" and left this standing while going on to squeeze in the long phrase cited here. We have adopted his last revision.
148.28	house,] The copy-text has no comma. The word is part of the long phrase discussed in the previous note and appears at the very edge of the manuscript page. Since the sense requires a comma, and since the physical situation may have prevented Clemens from writing one, we have emended.

Emendations of the Copy-Text

148.7	wood-yards (I-C) • wood-|yards
148.15	watchman (I-C) • watch-|man
*148.16	Island (I-C) • island
148.18	Jones (I-C) • Jone's
*148.28	Then . . . when (I-C) • For when/Then . . . when
*148.28	house, (I-C) • ~∧
149.21	hair (I-C) • hair and
150.16	securely (I-C) • ~[,]
150.20	You're (I-C) • Your'e

Alterations in the Manuscript

147.5	Fictitious] *follows canceled* 'The man, Joseph Millard, and I forfeit not confidence'; *Clemens interlined* 'pilot' *above canceled* 'man' *and then interlined* 'referred to,' *with a caret above* 'Joseph Millard'. *He then canceled the whole sentence.*
147.13	himself] *follows canceled* 'th'.
147.21	very] *follows canceled* 'f'.
147.23	reckon] *interlined without a caret above canceled* 'guess'.
148.4	directly] 'di' *written over* 'in'.
148.5	in order] *interlined with a caret.*
148.6	"run"] *follows canceled* 'take'.
148.9	him, on] *open quotation marks before* 'on' *canceled.*
148.10	called] 'ca' *written over* 'm'.
148.16	Goose] *interlined without a caret above canceled* 'the'.
148.18	run] *follows canceled* 'attempt'.
148.22–23	dangers,— . . . darkness—] *originally* 'dangers, . . . darkness'.
148.28	Then . . . and when] *interlined; originally* 'The'; 'The' *canceled and followed by* 'For when'; 'For when' *inadvertently left standing when the interlineation was written to replace it.*
148.33	when he mentioned it,] *interlined with a caret.*
149.9	that moment] 'that' *written over* 'm'.
149.12	sure] *interlined without a caret above canceled* 'certain'.
149.14	pulled] *interlined without a caret above canceled* 'jerked'.
149.15	as] *follows canceled* 'when'.
149.16	from] *followed by an uncanceled caret.*
149.22	apparently] *interlined without a caret above canceled* 'seemingly'.

149.23   alone] *interlined with a caret.*

149.29   heavy] *'h' written over 't'.*

149.35   ghostly] *follows canceled* 'spectre'.

149.37   every moment] *interlined with a caret.*

150.8   *open it,*] *interlined with a caret.*

150.9   disappear] *follows canceled* 'then'.

150.10   and] *follows canceled* 'at'.

150.22   knows!] *exclamation point mended from a comma.*

150.32   oath] *follows canceled* 'othe'.

150.35   "You] *follows canceled* '"And'; 'Y' *mended from* 'y'.

150.35   spoke] *follows canceled* 'mentioned'.

151.3   So] *follows canceled quotation marks.*

151.3–4   foot-board] *'rd' written over 't'.*

151.5   which proved to be a silver watch,] *interlined with a caret.*

151.5–6   detached] *followed by a canceled comma.*

151.6   recent] *follows canceled* 'to be'.

28. *PETRIFIED MAN*

Textual Commentary

The first printing in the Virginia City *Territorial Enterprise* for 4 October 1862 is not extant. The sketch survives in four contemporary reprintings of the *Enterprise:*

P[1]   "A Petrified Man," Sacramento *Union,* 9 October 1862, p. 2.

P[2]   "Petrified Man," Nevada City (Calif.) *Nevada Democrat,* 11 October 1862, p. 2.

P[3]   "A Washoe Joke," San Francisco *Evening Bulletin,* 15 October 1862, p. 1.

P[4]   "Petrified Men," Auburn (Calif.) *Placer Herald,* 18 October 1862, p. 1.

Copies: PH of P[1] and P[3] from Bancroft; PH of P[2] and P[4] from California State Library at Sacramento. The sketch is a radiating text: there is no copy-text. All variants are recorded in a list of emendations and adopted readings, which also records any readings unique to the present edition, identified as I-C.

P[1] attributes the piece to the *"Territorial Enterprise,"* and although it may derive from an unidentified reprinting instead of the *Enterprise,* its publication date shows that it cannot derive from any known reprinting. None of the other reprints listed above can derive from P[1], because they reprint so much more of the text. The publication date of P^2 shows that it cannot derive from any other known reprinting, and its attribution of the item to the "Virginia City Enterprise, of the 4th instant" implies this as its source. P^3 might well derive from an unidentified reprinting instead of the *Enterprise* itself, because it introduced the piece as follows: "The *Territorial Enterprise* has a joke of a 'petrified man' having been found on the plains[,] which the interior journals seem to be copying in good faith. Our authority gravely says." But P^3 probably does not derive from P^2, because, along with P^4, it has a superior reading ("be little" instead of "be a little" at 159.24): it seems unlikely that both reprintings would have dropped the indefinite article independently when copying P^2. Furthermore, since P^3 prints a unique sophistication ("persons" at 159.25), it clearly cannot be the source of P^4. The balance of the evidence favors the supposition that all four reprintings derive independently from the *Enterprise*. Although any of the four could have been copied from a lost intervening printing, this is unlikely for all but P^3. Even if the distance from the original printing is greater than can now be documented, all four printings may still preserve authorial readings among their variants.

Eight additional reprintings of the sketch have been identified in contemporary newspapers, but collation shows that all of these probably derive not from the *Enterprise* itself, but from P^1, P^2, or from each other. These include "A Petrified Man" in the following: Oroville (Calif.) *Butte Record*, 11 October 1862 (p. 4); Visalia (Calif.) *Delta*, 16 October 1862 (p. 3); Red Bluff (Calif.) *Beacon*, 16 October 1862 (p. 2); San Francisco *Herald*, 16 October 1862 (p. 2); Placer (Calif.) *Courier*, 18 October 1862 (p. 4); Eureka (Calif.) *Humboldt Times*, 8 November 1862 (p. 4). All of these derive, directly or indirectly, from P^1. "A Petrified Man in Nevada Territory," San Francisco *Alta California*, 15 October 1862 (p. 1) may derive from the *Enterprise* or from P^2: it shares a problematic reading ("rested" instead of "resting" at 159.8) with P^2, and this may indeed have been the reading of the *Enterprise*. But the *Alta* reproduces too little of the text to demonstrate its independence, and is here treated as a derivative text without authority. "That Piece of Petrified Humanity," Sacramento *Bee*, 16 October 1862 (p. 4), appears to derive from the *Alta* and is likewise treated as without authority.

Clemens considered including this sketch in JF1 in January or February 1867, for he listed it among five alternates at the back of the Yale Scrapbook (see the textual introduction, p. 538).

The diagram of transmission records all known contemporary reprintings, including the derivative texts, but the list of emendations and adopted readings records only the variants among the independently radiating texts.

Textual Notes

159 *title*   *Petrified Man*] Only P^2 gives the title adopted here. P^1 supplies an indefinite article, P^4 changes "Man" to "Men," and P^3 gives

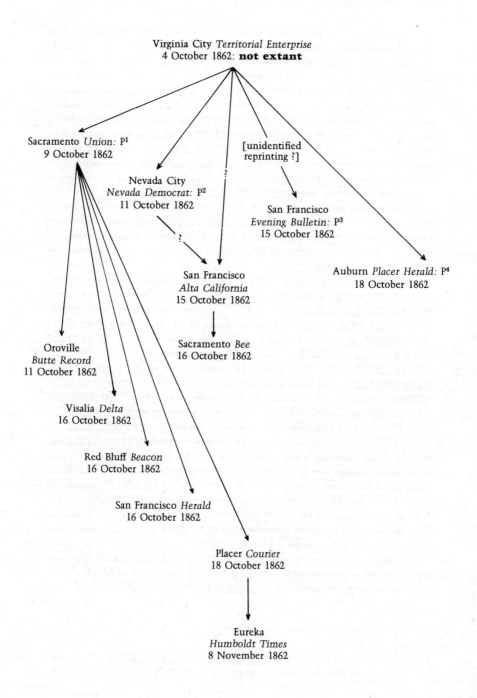

Virginia City *Territorial Enterprise*
4 October 1862: **not extant**

Sacramento *Union:* P[1]
9 October 1862

Nevada City
Nevada Democrat: P[2]
11 October 1862

[unidentified
reprinting ?]

?

San Francisco
Evening Bulletin: P[3]
15 October 1862

?

San Francisco
Alta California
15 October 1862

Auburn *Placer Herald:* P[4]
18 October 1862

Oroville
Butte Record
11 October 1862

Sacramento *Bee*
16 October 1862

Visalia *Delta*
16 October 1862

Red Bluff *Beacon*
16 October 1862

San Francisco *Herald*
16 October 1862

Placer *Courier*
18 October 1862

Eureka
Humboldt Times
8 November 1862

the piece its own title ("A Washoe Joke"). The reading of P^2 is adopted, however, on the authority of Clemens' letter to Orion: "Did you see that squib of mine headed 'Petrified Man?' " (21 October 1862, *CL1*, letter 64).

159.3   has] P^4 prints "had," the tense normally expected here. But the concurrence of three independent printings argues strongly that the *Enterprise* read "has," especially since it is an unexpected reading. The odd sequence of tenses may be part of the strategy Mark Twain recalled in 1870, to "purposely" mix up his description "hoping to make it obscure" ("A Couple of Sad Experiences," no. 299).

159.8   resting] P^2 prints "rested," a reading endorsed by the *Alta*, either because the *Enterprise* so read or because the *Alta* derives from P^2. P^1 does not reproduce the relevant part of the text; P^3 and P^4 both agree in giving "resting." The pattern of the sentence also gives "resting" a slight edge over "rested," for Mark Twain repeatedly combines a simple past-tense verb with a participle: "was . . . leaning," "was . . . resting," "supported . . . pressing," and "closed . . . spread." We have therefore adopted the reading of P^3 and P^4 against that of P^2.

159.11   apart.] The bracketed exclamation point in P^3 is clearly an editorial intrusion in that text. (The brackets in the table of emendations and adopted readings are found in P^3.)

159.24   be little] P^2 is alone in reading "be a little." The sense of the passage shows that Mark Twain means "only slightly less than sacrilege," not "a little bit less than sacrilege." The concurrence of P^3 and P^4 in reading "be little" suggests that they correctly reproduced the reading of the *Enterprise*, and we have adopted it here.

159.25   three hundred] P^2 and P^4 concur in this reading, while P^1 omits the relevant passage and P^3 prints "300 persons." The addition of "persons" makes the sentence read more smoothly, and it is tempting to believe that the *Enterprise* so read. But this has seemed unlikely because P^2 and P^4 independently reproduce the more elliptical reading, as well as the number spelled out instead of in figures—the ordinary practice of the *Enterprise*. We have therefore rejected the reading of P^3 as a sophistication.

Emendations and Adopted Readings

*159 *title*   *Petrified Man* (P^2) • A Petrified Man (P^1); A Washoe Joke (P^3); Petrified Men (P^4)

159.1	A (I-C) • According to the *Territorial Enterprise* a (P^1); The Virginia City Enterprise, of the 4th instant, has the following item: [¶] A (P^2); The *Territorial Enterprise* has a joke of a "petrified man" having been found on the plains. which the interior journals seem to be copying in good faith. Our authority gravely says: [¶] A (P^3); The Virginia City *Enterprise*, of the 4th inst. has the following item: "A (P^4)
159.1	MAN (P$^{1-3}$) • m[]n (P^4)
*159.3	has (P$^{1-3}$) • had (P^4)
159.4–6	owner—which ... defunct. (P^{2,3}) • ~, ~ ... ~. (P^1); ~ (~ ... ~.) (P^4)
159.4	lifetime, (P$^{1-3}$) • life[-]|time$_\wedge$ (P^4)
159.5	ago, (P$^{2-4}$) • ~$_\wedge$ (P^1)
159.5	savan (P^{1,2,4}) • *savan* (P^3)
159.6–16	The body ... exposure," etc. (P$^{2-4}$) • [*not in*] (P^1)
159.6	posture, (P^{2,4}) • ~$_\wedge$ (P^3)
*159.8	resting (P^{3,4}) • rested (P^2)
159.9	fore-finger (P^2) • fore-|finger (P^3); fore[-]finger (P^4)
159.10	eye and (P^{2,3}) • ~, ~ (P^4)
*159.11	apart. (P^{2,4}) • ~.[!] (P^3)
159.12	a profound (P^{2,3}) • [*not in*] (P^4)
159.13	that (P^{2,4}) • ~, (P^3)
159.13	Sowell, (P^{2,4}) • ~$_\wedge$ (P^3)
159.13	City, (P^2) • City$_\wedge$ (P^3); city, (P^4)
159.14	body. (P^{3,4}) • ~[$_\wedge$] (P^2)
159.15	from (P^{2,3}) • frrm (P^4)
159.17	so; (P$^{2-4}$) • ~, (P^1)
159.17–18	discovered, (P$^{2-4}$) • ~$_\wedge$ (P^1)
159.18	him, (P$^{2-4}$) • ~$_\wedge$ (P^1)
159.19	above, (P^{2,3}) • ~$_\wedge$ (P^{1,4})
159.20	him (P$^{2-4}$) • ~, (P^1)
159.21	bed rock (P^{3,4}) • bedrock (P^1); bed-rock (P^2)
159.21	sat, (P$^{2-4}$) • ~$_\wedge$ (P^1)
159.23–26	The opinion ... six weeks. (P$^{2-4}$) • [*not in*] (P^1)
*159.24	be little (P^{3,4}) • be a little (P^2)
159.25	Everybody (P^{3,4}) • Every body (P^2)
*159.25	three hundred (P^{2,4}) • 300 persons (P^3)

[TWO DESCENTS INTO THE SPANISH MINE]

§29. *THE SPANISH MINE*

Textual Commentary

The first printing in the Virginia City *Territorial Enterprise*, sometime in late October 1862, is not extant. The sketch survives in the only known contemporary reprinting of the *Enterprise*, the Oroville (Calif.) *Butte Record* for 1 November 1862 (p. 1), which is copy-text. Copy: PH from Bancroft. There are no textual notes.

Emendations of the Copy-Text

164.10	workmen (I-C) • work-|men
164.20	color. You (I-C) • ~.—|~
164.24	square (I-C) • cquare
165.1	they (I-C) • they they
165.4	intersect. You (I-C) • ~.—|~
165.9	rate. Whereupon (I-C) • ~.—|~
165.29	jail. And (I-C) • ~.—|~
166.8	so to (I-C) • to
166.11	daylight (I-C) • day-|light

§30. *THE SPANISH*

Textual Commentary

The first printing appeared in the Virginia City *Territorial Enterprise*, probably on 12 or 22 February 1863. The only known copy of this printing, in a clipping in the Grant Smith Papers, carton 3, book 4, Bancroft, is copy-text. There are no textual notes.

Emendations of the Copy-Text

168.11	ledge, (I-C) • ~.

31. *THE PAH-UTES*

Textual Commentary

The first printing in the Virginia City *Territorial Enterprise*, sometime between 13 and 19 December 1862, is not extant. The sketch survives in the only known contemporary reprinting of the *Enterprise*, the Marysville (Calif.) *Appeal* for 21 December 1862 (p. 2), which is copy-text. Copy: PH from Bancroft.

Textual Notes

170.6   sage brush] Possibly one word in the copy-text. Since Clemens' almost invariable spelling was "sage-brush," we have resolved the crux as two words, but we have not supplied his customary hyphen.

170.18   half-breed,] The word ends a line in the copy-text, which omits the comma. Since there is space for one between the *d* of "breed" and the right margin, and since the sense requires it, we conjecture that a comma was set but failed to print.

Emendations of the Copy-Text

*170.6   sage brush (I-C) • sagebrush

*170.18   half-breed, (I-C) • ~·~[∧]

32. *THE ILLUSTRIOUS DEPARTED*

Textual Commentary

The first printing appeared in the Virginia City *Territorial Enterprise*, probably on 28 December 1862. The only known copy of this printing, in a clipping in the William Wright Papers, carton 1, folder 120, Bancroft, is copy-text. There are no textual notes.

Emendations of the Copy-Text

173.20   robberies (I-C) • roberies
173.22   hay-wagons (I-C) • hay-|wagons

33. *OUR STOCK REMARKS*

Textual Commentary

The first printing appeared in the Virginia City *Territorial Enterprise* for 30 or 31 December 1862. The only known copy of this printing, in a clipping in Scrapbook 4, p. 14, MTP, is copy-text. There are no textual notes or emendations.

34. *MORE GHOSTS*

Textual Commentary

The first printing appeared in the Virginia City *Territorial Enterprise*, probably on 1 January 1863. The only known copy of this printing, in a clipping in Scrapbook 4, p. 34, MTP, is copy-text. There are no textual notes.

Emendations of the Copy-Text

178.5   riveted (I-C) • rivited
178.7   International. (I-C) • ~,

35. *NEW YEAR'S DAY*

Textual Commentary

The first printing appeared in the Virginia City *Territorial Enterprise*, probably on 1 January 1863. The only known copy of this printing, in a clipping in Scrapbook 4, p. 34, MTP, is copy-text. There are no textual notes or emendations.

36. *UNFORTUNATE THIEF*

Textual Commentary

The first printing in the Virginia City *Territorial Enterprise*, probably on 8 January 1863, is not extant. The sketch survives in the only known contemporary reprinting of the *Enterprise*, the Stockton (Calif.) *Independent* for 14 January 1863 (p. 1), which is copy-text. Copy: PH from Bancroft. The Marysville (Calif.) *Appeal* and the Placer (Calif.) *Courier* reprinted the item, evidently from the *Independent*, on 16 and 24 January 1863 (pp. 2 and 3), respectively. Neither reprinting has any authority.

The *Independent* editor must have omitted the first few lines in the *Enterprise* text, substituting the introduction quoted in the headnote (p. 181). The *Independent's* extract is not intelligible without this explanation. There are no textual notes or emendations.

37. *THE SANITARY BALL*

Textual Commentary

The first printing appeared in the Virginia City *Territorial Enterprise* for 10 January 1863 (p. 3). The only known copy of this printing, in a newspaper at the library of the Nevada Historical Society at Reno, is copy-text. Copy: PH from the Nevada Historical Society. The newspaper has been torn and water stained, which results in an unusual number of doubtful readings. There are no textual notes.

Emendations of the Copy-Text

186.4	the (I-C) • [th]e
186.29–30	stockholder (I-C) • stock-|holder
186.31	everybody (I-C) • everybod[y] [*torn*]
186.32	believe (I-C) • belie[v]e [*torn*]
187.4	was (I-C) • [w]as [*torn*]
187.5	kept (I-C) • [ ]ept [*torn*]
187.6	guests (I-C) • [u]ests [*torn*]
187.6	All the (I-C) • All [h]e [*torn*]
187.7	fare (I-C) • [ ]are [*torn*]
187.8	quadrille (I-C) • [q]uadrille [*torn*]

38. *DUE NOTICE*

Textual Commentary

The first printing appeared in the Virginia City *Territorial Enterprise* for 10 January 1863 (p. 3). The only known copy of this printing, in a newspaper at the library of the Nevada Historical Society at Reno, is copy-text. Copy: PH from the Nevada Historical Society. See the textual commentary for "The Sanitary Ball" (no. 37). There are no textual notes.

Emendations of the Copy-Text

189.8	waters (I-C) • [ ]aters [*torn*]
189.9	of (I-C) • [ ] [*torn*]
189.9	aforementioned (I-C) • aforemen[ ]ioned [*torn*]
189.10	astonishing (I-C) • astonish[ ]ng [*torn*]
189.11	those (I-C) • [ ]hose [*torn*]
189.11	Almack's (I-C) • Allmack's
189.12	our (I-C) • [ ]r [*torn*]
189.12	on (I-C) • [ ] [*torn*]
189.13	our (I-C) • o[ ]r [*torn*]

39. *TERRITORIAL SWEETS*

Textual Commentary

The first printing in the Virginia City *Territorial Enterprise*, probably sometime between 22 and 28 January 1863, is not extant. The sketch survives in the only known contemporary reprinting of the *Enterprise*, the Santa Cruz (Calif.) *Sentinel* for 31 January 1863 (p. 1), which is copy-text. Copy: PH from Bancroft. The *Sentinel* placed the entire piece within quotation marks and altered internal quotation marks accordingly. We have emended back to the original form in the *Enterprise*. There are no textual notes.

Emendations of the Copy-Text

191 title	*Territorial* (I-C) • Teritorial
191.1	THE (I-C) • "∼

191.3   "DARLING (I-C) • " '~
191.7   MADELINE." (I-C) • ~.'
191.8   We (I-C) • "~
191.13   "bubble" (I-C) • '~'
191.14   address. (I-C) • ~."

40. *LETTER FROM CARSON CITY*

Textual Commentary

The first printing appeared in the Virginia City *Territorial Enterprise*, almost
certainly on 3 February 1863. The only known copy of this printing, in a
clipping in Scrapbook 4, p. 11, MTP, is copy-text.

Textual Notes

194.15   who he meant it for] The grammatical lapse is almost certainly
           authorial. Fourteen years later Clemens was still uncertain
           about the words, for he wrote Orion that he called his new
           lecture " 'Reminiscences of Some Pleasant Characters whom I
           have Met.' (If 'whom' is bad grammar, scratch it out.)" (27
           June 1871, *CL3*, letter 64). Since the error is inseparable from
           Clemens' informal, colloquial style, we have not emended.

197.3   duett] Contemporary American dictionaries recognized only
           "duet" and the Italian "duetto," but the *Oxford English Dic-
           tionary* lists both "duet" and "duett." Thus although the com-
           positor may have mistakenly doubled the *t* or dropped the *o*,
           we have not emended.

197.16   Thou hast] Copy-text "Thou has" is probably a compositorial
           error. Since the words occur in a song title within quotation
           marks, and since Clemens intends no gaff here (he is about to
           contrast the other singers with the "squawking" of the Un-
           reliable), we have emended.

Emendations of the Copy-Text

195.4   Governor (I-C) • Gover[n]or
195.6   manner (I-C) • m[a]nner

195.15	house, (I-C) • ~[.]
195.26	life (I-C) • li[f]e
196.1	don't (I-C) • don‸t
196.1	fellow (I-C) • [f]ellow
196.15	entirely (I-C) • ent[i]rely
196.18	than (I-C) • t[h]an
196.28–29	blanc-mange (I-C) • blanc-|mange
196.29	threw (I-C) • [t]hrew
197.16	mother;") (I-C) • ~;"‸
*197.16	hast (I-C) • has
197.23	teeth, (I-C) • ~[,]
198.5	forty-eight, (I-C) • ~-~.

41. LETTER FROM CARSON

Textual Commentary

The first printing appeared in the Virginia City *Territorial Enterprise*, probably on 5 February 1863. The only known copy of this printing, in a clipping in Scrapbook 4, pp. 12–13, MTP, is copy-text. The whole of the letter is not reprinted here; for the omitted section, see *MTEnt*, pp. 56–57.

Textual Notes

201.23	references to allusions] Not an error. Compare the manuscript of *Tom Sawyer*, chapter 3: if Sid "had any dim idea of making 'references to allusions,' he thought better of it."
203.18	permission . . . anyhow] The first six letters of "permission" came at the end of a line, and the last four letters were inadvertently set at the beginning of the line after the one below. See the emendations list.
203.23–24	Miss Mettie Curry] Copy-text "Nettie" is an error, for the bridesmaid's name was Metta Curry, familiarly known as Mettie. Although the error could be authorial, the compositor might as easily be responsible: the *M* and *N* sorts are side by side in the case.

Emendations of the Copy-Text

201.5	Morning (I-C) • Morniug
201.8	town. (I-C) • ∼,
202.9	farewell (I-C) • fare-|well
202.11	fathers, (I-C) • ∼.
202.19	moment. (I-C) • ∼[∧]
203.15	However, (I-C) • ∼.
*203.18	permission was unnecessary, though—I calculated to do that anyhow (I-C) • permis | was unnecessary, though—I calculated to do | sion that anyhow
203.22	preceded (I-C) • pre. | ceded
*203.24	Mettie (I-C) • Nettie
203.24	M. (I-C) • ∼[∧]
203.27	hymeneal (I-C) • hymenial
204.11–12	though. MARK TWAIN. (I-C) • though. [*omitted passage*] | MARK TWAIN.

42. *LETTER FROM CARSON*

Textual Commentary

The first printing appeared in the Virginia City *Territorial Enterprise*, probably on 8 February 1863. The only known copy of this printing, in a clipping in Scrapbook 20, pp. 46–48, MTP, is copy-text. The whole letter is not reprinted here; for the omitted section, see *MTEnt*, pp. 60–61. There are no textual notes.

Emendations of the Copy-Text

207.11	and (I-C) • a[nd] [*torn*]
207.12	writing (I-C) • writi[n]g [*torn*]
207.13	things (I-C) • thi[n]gs
207.22	way, (I-C) • ∼[,]
208.1	and (I-C) • an[d] [*torn*]
208.18	comfortably (I-C) • comforta[ ]ly
208.19	some, (I-C) • ∼[,]
208.29	solitary (I-C) • so[l]itary

208.36   the (I-C) • [t]he
209.5   baritone (I-C) • barito[n]e
209.11   groomsman (I-C) • grooms-|man
209.13   champagne, (I-C) • ∼.
209.26   it. (I-C) • ∼ₐ
209.26–27   it. MARK TWAIN. (I-C) • it. [*omitted passage*] | MARK TWAIN.

43. *SILVER BARS—HOW ASSAYED*

Textual Commentary

The first printing in the Virginia City *Territorial Enterprise*, probably sometime between 17 and 22 February 1863, is not extant. The sketch survives in
the only known contemporary reprinting of the *Enterprise*, the Stockton
(Calif.) *Independent* for 26 February 1863 (p. 1), which is copy-text. Copy: PH
from Bancroft. There are no textual notes.

Emendations of the Copy-Text

211.10   assayers (I-C) • asayers
212.14   ashes (I-C) • asher

44. *YE SENTIMENTAL LAW STUDENT*

Textual Commentary

The first printing appeared in the Virginia City *Territorial Enterprise* for 19
February 1863. A unique copy of the *Enterprise* page containing the sketch
is in the possession of Ruth Hermann (416 Zion St., Nevada City, California,
95959), but is not available to us at the time of going to press. (The sketch,
reproduced from this clipping, will appear in a forthcoming book by Mrs.
Hermann, entitled *Virginia City, Nevada, Revisited.*) The sketch also survives in the only known reprinting of the *Enterprise* in Kate Milnor Rabb,
ed., *The Wit and Humor of America*, 5 vols. (Indianapolis: Bobbs-Merrill
Company, 1907), 5:1818–1820, which is necessarily copy-text. Copy: PH from
Library of Congress. There are no textual notes or emendations.

The source of Rabb's text and the nature of her printer's copy are not known. She may have used for her source *Enterprise* clippings, reprints of the *Enterprise*, or a typescript or transcript made from either of these; the printer's copy itself was probably typed, but may have been identical with her source. For one of the five Mark Twain sketches that she reprints we still have an *Enterprise* printing to compare her text with. The record of her reliability is not encouraging: in "Letter from Carson City" (no. 40) Rabb's text makes at least seventeen substantive errors (omissions and sophistications) as well as twenty-six errors in accidentals. She changes "clatter" to "chatter," "from whence" to "from which," "that" to "its," and "baskets" to "bushels." In addition, she omits the last phrase of the piece entirely. Internal evidence in "Ye Sentimental Law Student" indicates that she made similar mistakes in this piece as well (see the headnote).

45. *A SUNDAY IN CARSON*

Textual Commentary

The first printing in the Virginia City *Territorial Enterprise*, probably on 24 February 1863, but possibly as late as March 31, is not extant. The sketch survives in the only known reprinting of the *Enterprise* in Kate Milnor Rabb, ed., *The Wit and Humor of America*, 5 vols. (Indianapolis: Bobbs-Merrill Company, 1907), 5:1813–1814, which is copy-text. Copy: PH from Library of Congress. The source of Rabb's text and the nature of her printer's copy are not known; see the textual commentary to "Ye Sentimental Law Student" (no. 44).

Textual Notes

222.2   Langton's] The copy-text prints "Layton's," which is an error: the stage to Carson was called "Langton's," and we have so emended. It is barely possible that the *Enterprise* read "Layton's," since Clemens' *y* and *g* could easily have been mistaken for each other. But the overall record of Rabb's texts suggests that the error is hers.

222.22   resistless] Evidently in the sense given by Webster's dictionary (1828): "That cannot be effectually opposed or withstood; irresistible."

222.23   Swayze . . . Derickson] The copy-text prints "Swazey" and "Derrickson," but contemporary documents give the spellings adopted here. The overall record of Rabb's texts suggests that the errors are hers, although the *Enterprise* might easily have been wrong as well.

222.25   satisfaction. . . .] The ellipsis points appear in the copy-text and indicate that Rabb's source had a longer text.

Emendations of the Copy-Text

*222.2   Langton's (I-C) • Layton's
*222.23   Swayze (I-C) • Swazey
*222.23   Derickson (I-C) • Derrickson

46. *THE UNRELIABLE*

Textual Commentary

The first printing appeared in the Virginia City *Territorial Enterprise* for 25 February 1863 (p. 3). Only one copy of this printing is extant. A PH of this unique clipping, in MTP, is copy-text, and is used with permission of the clipping's owner, Ruth Hermann (416 Zion St., Nevada City, California, 95959). There are no textual notes or emendations.

47. *REPORTORIAL*

Textual Commentary

The first printing in the Virginia City *Territorial Enterprise*, probably on 26 February 1863, is not extant. The sketch survives, only in part, in the only known contemporary reprinting of the *Enterprise*, the Marysville (Calif.) *Appeal* for 28 February 1863 (p. 4), which is copy-text. Copy: PH from Bancroft. The *Appeal* evidently reproduced only the concluding portion of the original text. There are no textual notes.

Emendations of the Copy-Text

227.11   Carson (I-C) • Ca[r]son
227.15   me (I-C) • men
228.7   shoulder (I-C) • ihoulder

48. *EXAMINATION OF TEACHERS*

Textual Commentary

The first printing appeared in the Virginia City *Territorial Enterprise*, probably sometime in March or April 1863. The only known copy of this printing, in a clipping in a scrapbook at Yale (Za/C591/ + 1/v.7), is copy-text. There are no textual notes or emendations.

49. *CITY MARSHAL PERRY*

Textual Commentary

The first printing in the Virginia City *Territorial Enterprise* for 4 March 1863 is not extant. The sketch survives in the only known reprinting of the *Enterprise* in Kate Milnor Rabb, ed., *The Wit and Humor of America*, 5 vols. (Indianapolis: Bobbs-Merrill Company, 1907), 5:1809–1813, which is copy-text. Copy: PH from Library of Congress. The source of Rabb's text and the nature of her printer's copy are not known; see the textual commentary to "Ye Sentimental Law Student" (no. 44).

Textual Notes

236.16   poetry. . . . His] The ellipsis points appear in the copy-text and probably indicate an omission made by Rabb, although it is barely possible that the *Enterprise* printing so read.

Emendations of the Copy-Text

237.21   boot-making (I-C) • boot-|making
238.11   station-house (I-C) • station-|house

50. *[CHAMPAGNE WITH THE BOARD OF BROKERS]*

Textual Commentary

The first printing in the Virginia City *Territorial Enterprise*, probably on 7 March 1863, is not extant. The sketch survives in the only known reprinting of the *Enterprise* in Myron Angel, ed., *History of Nevada* (Oakland: Thompson and West, 1881), p. 577, which is copy-text. Copy: first edition from Bancroft. There are no textual notes.

Emendations of the Copy-Text

240.6	Mitchell (I-C) • Mitchel
240.16	speech-making (I-C) • speech-|making
240.19	wholesale (I-C) • whole-|sale

51. *ADVICE TO THE UNRELIABLE ON CHURCH-GOING*

Textual Commentary

The first printing in the Virginia City *Territorial Enterprise* for 12 April 1863 is not extant. The sketch survives in the only known reprinting of the *Enterprise* in Kate Milnor Rabb, ed., *The Wit and Humor of America*, 5 vols. (Indianapolis: Bobbs-Merrill Company, 1907), 5:1814–1815, which is copy-text. Copy: PH from Library of Congress. The source of Rabb's text and the nature of her printer's copy are not known; see the textural commentary to "Ye Sentimental Law Student" (no. 44). There are no emendations.

Textual Notes

243.7	half. . . .] The ellipsis points appear in the copy-text and indicate that Rabb's source had a longer text.

52. *HORRIBLE AFFAIR*

Textual Commentary

The first printing in the Virginia City *Territorial Enterprise*, probably sometime between 16 and 18 April 1863, is not extant. The sketch survives in the only known contemporary reprinting of the *Enterprise*, the Oroville (Calif.) *Butte Record* for 2 May 1863 (p. 4), which is copy-text. Copy: PH from Bancroft. There are no textual notes or emendations.

53. *LETTER FROM MARK TWAIN*

Textual Commentary

The first printing appeared in the Virginia City *Territorial Enterprise*, sometime between 19 and 21 May 1863. The only known copy of this printing, in a clipping in Scrapbook 2, pp. 44–45, MTP, is copy-text.

Textual Notes

252.23   Old, fat, jolly B. C. Howard] The copy-text has a space for a comma after "Old," but no comma appears there. It may have been omitted by the compositor, or it may simply have failed to print. Since the sense requires a comma after "Old" so long as one follows "fat," we have emended.

Emendations of the Copy-Text

250.19   added, (I-C) • ~.
251.11   it's (I-C) • its
251.16   eye: (I-C) • ~[;]
251.18   ain't (I-C) • aint
252.23   shortly. (I-C) • ~,
*252.23   Old, fat (I-C) • ~[ʌ]~
253.14   says: (I-C) • ~[;]
253.14   it's (I-C) • its

54. *"MARK TWAIN'S" LETTER*

Textual Commentary

The first printing in the San Francisco *Morning Call* for 9 July 1863 (p. 1) is copy-text. Copy: PH of clipping from Yale. There are no textual notes.

Emendations of the Copy-Text

256.27   Norcrus (I-C) • Nor-|crus

256.34   Sanfercisco (I-C) • San-|fercisco
257.23   bombshell (I-C) • bomb-|shell

55. "MARK TWAIN'S" LETTER

Textual Commentary

The first printing in the San Francisco *Morning Call* for 30 July 1863 (p. 1) is copy-text. Copy: PH of clipping from Yale. There are no textual notes.

Emendations of the Copy-Text

261.17   wildcat (I-C) • wild-|cat

56. A DUEL PREVENTED

Textual Commentary

The first printing in the Virginia City *Territorial Enterprise* for 2 August 1863 is not extant. The sketch survives in two contemporary reprintings of the *Enterprise:*

P[1]   "A Duel Prevented," Sacramento *Union,* 4 August 1863, p. 2.

P[2]   Untitled extract of the last part of the original in Myron Angel, ed., *History of Nevada* (Oakland: Thompson and West, 1881), p. 292.

Copies: PH of P[1] and first edition of P[2] from Bancroft. The sketch is a radiating text: there is no copy-text. All variants are recorded in a list of emendations and adopted readings. In this case there are no I-C emendations.

P[1] is by far the more complete text, and was ostensibly set from the "Virginia *Enterprise* of August 2d." P[2] reproduces little more than a paragraph from the original text and shows obvious signs of editorial tampering. It begins at 266.14 with three asterisks to indicate the omission of most of the first two paragraphs; it rearranges and conflates two sentences and omits a paragraph break between them; and it omits four sentences without inserting ellipsis points before its concluding sentence.

Despite these deficiencies, both P[1] and P[2] radiate independently from the lost *Enterprise,* and each preserves authorial readings among its variants. Printer's copy for P[2] may have been an *Enterprise* clipping, an unidentified reprinting of the *Enterprise*, or even a handwritten transcript of the original (or a reprinting): it is therefore possible that P² stands at somewhat greater distance than does P¹ from the lost original. We have for these reasons accorded P¹ slight preference when the variants are nearly indifferent. Yet P² clearly does contain two variants that must be preferred on qualitative grounds, as well as one sentence that is manifestly authorial and is not preserved at all in P¹.

The diagram of transmission is as follows:

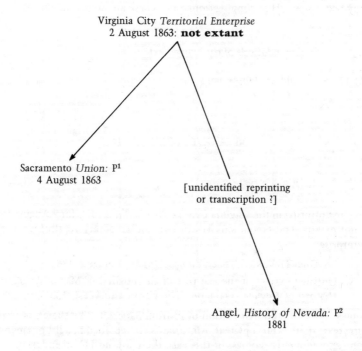

Virginia City *Territorial Enterprise*
2 August 1863: **not extant**

Sacramento *Union:* P¹
4 August 1863

[unidentified reprinting
or transcription ?]

Angel, *History of Nevada:* P²
1881

Textual Notes

266.14   young Wilson] The P² reading, " 'Young Wilson,' " is rejected as
                a sophistication of the *Enterprise*. Compare Mark Twain's style
                earlier in the text (266.3) and in other *Enterprise* printings
                where "young Wilson" is referred to—for example, "Letter
                from Mark Twain" (no. 58).

266.17–18   we . . . half-soled] P² reverses the order of the two clauses as they appear in P¹. P¹ has been preferred because it seems somewhat more like Mark Twain's usual style, and because P² also edited out the paragraph break and changed "then" to "when," perhaps in a general effort to shorten and condense.

266.18   nor] While P² prints "nor," P¹ gives "or," which could reflect the *Enterprise* reading: Webster's 1828 dictionary recommended allowing "neither" to apply its negative force "to both parts of the sentence" by following it with "or." But when the *Californian* printed "either . . . or" in "Answers to Correspondents" (no. 109), Mark Twain altered them to "neither . . . nor" in the Yale Scrapbook, thereby expressing his own practice at this time. We have adopted the P² reading as more like the author's practice, and as potentially the reading of the *Enterprise.*

266.20   and also Deputy Sheriff Blodgett came with] P¹ omits "came" and P² omits "also." Perhaps the *Enterprise* had neither word—that is, the clause may have been elliptical ("and Deputy Sheriff Blodgett with"), depending on the previous verb ("arrived"). If so, the situation might have seemed unsatisfactory to both P¹ and P² compositors, who each mended the matter according to his own lights, adding "came" or "also" to emphasize or repeat the verb. On the other hand, it may be that the *Enterprise* had both words, and that this seemed redundant to each compositor, who then omitted one of the two as he saw fit. The crux cannot be safely resolved on the present evidence, but on balance it seems somewhat more likely that Mark Twain wanted the slightly redundant effect of "arrived . . . and also . . . came," perhaps anticipating the rhetorical device he used in the last part of the sentence, "the battle ground being and lying in Storey county."

266.21   blasted] P² gives "blarsted," an affectation not seen elsewhere in Mark Twain's early writing: we have preferred P¹.

266.30–32   In . . . them.] This sentence appears only in P², where it comes last and follows the one ending "town." (266.23), while P¹ omits it entirely without adding ellipsis points. But P² omits at least one sentence ("And . . . duel.") which must have intervened between "But . . . town." and "In . . . them."—also without adding ellipsis points. Therefore no documentary evidence establishes the position of the sentence in the *Enterprise.* It seems simplest, however, to suppose that P¹ omitted the sentence because it came at the end of the sketch and perhaps seemed superfluous; and that P², which aimed at foreshortening elsewhere, included it precisely because it was the last sentence.

Emendations and Adopted Readings

265 *title*   *A Duel Prevented* (P¹) • [*not in*] (P²)

265.1–266.13 WHEREAS . . . ground. (P¹) • [*not in*] (P²)

266.14   Whereupon (P¹) • [¶] * * * Whereupon (P²)

*266.14   young Wilson (P¹) • "Young Wilson" (P²)

266.14   ourself (P¹) • ourselves (P²)

266.15   horses (P¹) • ∼, (P²)

266.16–17   minute. [¶] Since (P¹) • minute, since (P²)

266.17   then (P¹) • when, (P²)

*266.17–18   we . . . half-soled (P¹) • being neither iron-clad nor even half-soled, we enjoy more real comfort in standing up than sitting down (P²)

*266.18   nor (P²) • or (P¹)

266.19   at last (P¹) • [*not in*] (P²)

266.20   constables (P¹) • Constables (P²)

*266.20   also (P¹) • [*not in*] (P²)

*266.20   came (P²) • [*not in*] (P¹)

*266.21   blasted (P¹) • blarsted (P²)

266.21–22   the . . . county, (P¹) • [*not in*] (P²)

266.22   miserable, (P¹) • ∼∧ (P²)

266.23–30   And . . . material. (P¹) • [*not in*] (P²)

*266.30–32   In . . . them. (P²) • [*not in*] (P¹)

57. [*AN APOLOGY REPUDIATED*]

Textual Commentary

The first printing in the Virginia City *Territorial Enterprise,* probably on 4 August 1863, is not extant. The sketch survives, only in part, in a reprinting of the *Enterprise* in Myron Angel, ed., *History of Nevada* (Oakland: Thompson and West, 1881), p. 293, which is copy-text. Copy: first edition from Bancroft. Three asterisks preceding the first word of the copy-text indicate that Angel omitted a portion of the *Enterprise* text. Paine reprinted the sketch without identifying his source, but collation gives no suggestion that he had access to the *Enterprise,* and he may easily have reprinted Angel (see *MTB,* 1:235). His text is here regarded as without authority. There are no textual notes or emendations.

58. *LETTER FROM MARK TWAIN*

Textual Commentary

The first printing appeared in the Virginia City *Territorial Enterprise* for 25 August 1863. The only known copies of this printing, in clippings in Scrapbook 1, p. 61, and Scrapbook 2, p. 64, MTP, are copy-text.

Textual Notes

272.22   there is] The copy-text has no verb in the clause ending with a semicolon. The author may have omitted his verb or the compositor may have inadvertently dropped it. We have emended by supplying "there is," although other changes might work as well: the emendation is conjectural.

Emendations of the Copy-Text

*272.22   there is (I-C) • [*not in*]
273.4   Messrs. (I-C) • ~[.]
274.9   BATHS. (I-C) • ~∧
275.11   low-spirited (I-C) • low-|spirited
276.3   siege (I-C) • seige
276.4   Co. (I-C) • Co's.
276.18   more, (I-C) • ~.
276.19   machinery (I-C) • machiney

59. *"MARK TWAIN'S" LETTER*

Textual Commentary

The first printing in the San Francisco *Morning Call* for 30 August 1863 (p. 1) is copy-text. Copy: PH of clipping from Yale. There are no textual notes.

Emendations of the Copy-Text

280.27–28   witnesses (I-C) • wi[t]nesses

281.3   considerations (I-C) • consider[a]tions
281.7   shall (I-C) • shal[l]
281.15   spectators (I-C) • spec[t]ators
281.15   Sheriffs (I-C) • Sheriff[s]
281.17   to (I-C) • [ ]o
281.22   defendant (I-C) • defendent
281.27   Dick (I-C) • Dic[k]
281.32   Ellis (I-C) • El[l]is
282.10   classes (I-C) • clases

60. *UNFORTUNATE BLUNDER*

Textual Commentary

The first printing in " 'Mark Twain's' Letter" in the San Francisco *Morning Call* for 3 September 1863 is copy-text. Copy: PH of clipping from Yale. There are no textual notes or emendations.

61. *BIGLER* VS. *TAHOE*

Textual Commentary

The first printing in the Virginia City *Territorial Enterprise*, probably on 4 or 5 September 1863, is not extant. The sketch survives in the only known contemporary reprinting of the *Enterprise*, the San Francisco *Golden Era* 11 (13 September 1863): 3, which is copy-text. Copy: PH from Bancroft.

Textual Notes

290.22–23   grief. MARK TWAIN.] The *Era* printed "grief.—*Mark Twain*," indicating that the sketch was signed in the *Enterprise*, probably in the form of a letter answering "Grub" (see the headnote, p. 288). We have retained the signature, moving it to its standard position, and emended the *Era's* dash and italics to restore the author's unvarying style in the *Enterprise* printings that survive.

Emendations of the Copy-Text

290 *title*	vs. (I-C) • *V. S.*
290.1	HOPE (I-C) • "∼
290.7	ago, (I-C) • ∼[,]
290.8	fairy-land (I-C) • fairy-|land
290.14	be (I-C) • but
290.14	injun (I-C) • ingun
290.22	morning, (I-C) • ∼[.]
*290.22–23	grief. MARK TWAIN. (I-C) • ∼.—*Mark Twain.*"

62. *LETTER FROM MARK TWAIN*

Textual Commentary

The first printing appeared in the Virginia City *Territorial Enterprise*, probably on 17 September 1863. The only known copy of this printing, in a clipping in Scrapbook 2, pp. 78–79, MTP, is copy-text. Only the first half of the letter is reprinted here; for the omitted passage, a review of *Mazeppa*, see *MTEnt*, pp. 78–80.

Textual Notes

294.25	it's] Copy-text "its" is a simple error that does not affect dialect pronunciation. To avoid momentary confusion, we have emended.
294.31	wasn't] Possibly a compositorial error: compare "warn't" at 294.2 and 294.37. Mark Twain disapproved of "deadly inconsistencies of spelling," especially in dialect (Clemens to Bret Harte, 1 May 1867, *CL1*, letter 130). Compare also "agin'" (294.16) and "agin" (294.30). Without a manuscript to guide us, we cannot be certain which of the variant forms Mark Twain preferred, and have accordingly preserved the inconsistency.

Emendations of the Copy-Text

294.9–10	conversation (I-C) • coversation

294.18	ghastly (I-C) • gastly
*294.25	it's (I-C) • its
295.19	circumstances. (I-C) • ~,
295.26–27	nigger!" MARK TWAIN. (I-C) • nigger!" [*omitted passage*] | MARK TWAIN.

63. *HOW TO CURE A COLD*

Textual Commentary

The first printing in the San Francisco *Golden Era* 11 (20 September 1863): 8 (GE) is copy-text. Copies: clipping in Scrapbook 4, pp. 8–9, MTP; PH from Bancroft and from Yale.

Reprintings and Revisions. It seems likely that Mark Twain revised the printer's copy of this sketch before it was reprinted in JF1 as "Curing a Cold," but no evidence in the Yale Scrapbook survives to show which changes he made or what printing (or reprinting) he used: it was probably a copy of GE, although some unidentified reprinting might have been used instead. Mark Twain's facetious allusion to his Gould and Curry stock, as well as his reference to visitors from Virginia City, San Francisco, and Sacramento, were omitted because of their topicality. A few small verbal changes ("So I" instead of "I" at 299.22 and "there" instead of "here" at 303.9) were made, and an indelicacy ("I must have vomited three-quarters of an hour" at 299.35–36) was dropped. The long, angry digression about the narrator's "lady acquaintance" (302.12–28) was also omitted. Since most of the changes were simple deletions, either the author or his editor, Webb, could have been responsible for them. Only one revision seems characteristic of Mark Twain: he probably substituted "I did it, and still live" for "I calculate to do it or perish in the attempt" (303.14).

In addition to these verbal changes, the system of paragraphing in GE was extensively revised: JF1 had only twenty-three paragraphs, while GE had sixty-six. Indeed, there is reason to suspect that the paragraphing of the copy-text had been editorially imposed on the author's manuscript: for more than half the sketch each paragraph contains only a single sentence—a style not characteristic of Mark Twain. Because Mark Twain demonstrably revised the paragraphing of other clippings in the Yale Scrapbook, and because in 1873 he objected to this same one-sentence-per-paragraph system in sketches edited by Hotten, it is tempting to regard the revised paragraphing of JF1 as the author's correction and restoration of his manuscript practice. Nevertheless, we have not adopted the JF1 changes, because they could so easily have been editorial: in the absence of the author's manuscript or of the marked printer's copy for JF1, the paragraphing of the copy-text must be allowed to prevail.

The JF1 text was reprinted in the way the textual introduction describes. Routledge reprinted JF1 in 1867 (JF2), and Hotten in turn reprinted JF2 in 1870 (JF3). Routledge also reprinted JF2 in 1870 (JF4a), and using the JF4a plates reissued the book in 1872 (JF4b). None of these texts was revised by the author, although the compositors introduced several minor errors and sophistications. When Mark Twain prepared the printer's copy for MTSk in 1872, he revised a copy of JF4a, making several changes in this sketch. He continued to remove indelicacies—omitting, for example, his allusion to the fact that he had "acquired a breath like a buzzard's" (301.5–6). He changed "Bigler" to "Tahoe," "lot" to "cargo," "vilest" to "wickedest" (301.8 and 303.4), and he probably tinkered with the paragraphing. He removed the digression about the "negro who was being baptised . . . and came near being drowned" (301.34–302.3), and he dropped a sentence that was a *double entendre*: "I never saw anybody have such an appetite; I am confident that lunatic would have eaten me if I had been healthy" (303.1–2). The MTSk text was not subsequently reprinted.

One year later (1873) Hotten reprinted the JF3 text in HWa. When Mark Twain revised this book for Chatto and Windus in the fall of 1873 (HWa**MT**), he made a number of small changes ("at the Occidental" became "up town" at 303.11, and "Lick House" became "hotel" at 303.10), but he did not delete the baptism anecdote or the allusion to "breath like a buzzard's." He again removed the potentially offensive double entendre about Wilson's voracious appetite, substituting "here is food for the imagination." He tinkered with the paragraphing, deleting three paragraph breaks that had persisted from the first printing in GE: "No Paragraph—may God eternally roast the man who punctuated this book," he noted at one point (299.3). Elsewhere in HWa**MT** he was particularly irate about mistaken paragraphing in sketches derived from PJks; his reaction to this sketch, which derived rather faithfully from JF3, casts further doubt on the authority of the GE paragraphing. All of the HWa**MT** revisions were incorporated in HWb, published in 1874.

When in 1875 Mark Twain came to reprint this sketch in SkNO, he entered the title "Curing a Cold" as item seventy-seven in the Doheny table of contents (see figure 23H, volume 1). The compositors supplied page numbers for both MTSk and HWb, and they or Bliss indicated on MTSk**MT** where the illustrations were to appear in the text of SkNO. But Mark Twain did not revise the MTSk**MT** text, whereas he made five revisions in the HWb**MT** text. Collation confirms that SkNO was set from HWb**MT** and incorporated these revisions: three times the author supplied "City" following the ambiguous "Virginia" (298.16, 299.28, and 303.6), he altered "jes' " to "jis' " (302.2), and restored the paragraph break of GE at 299.31. He made no changes in proof.

The diagram of transmission is as follows:

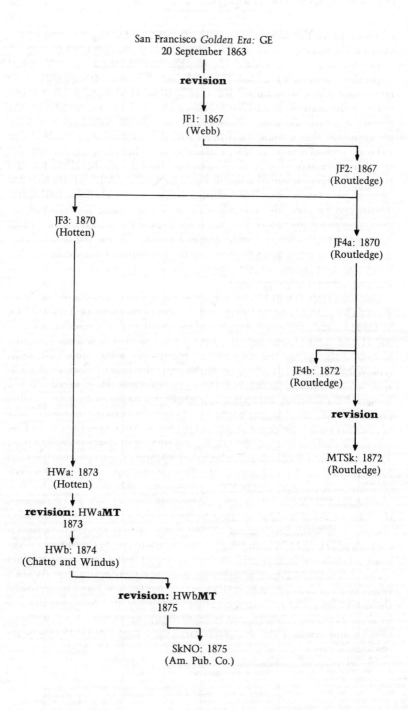

San Francisco *Golden Era:* GE
20 September 1863

revision

JF1: 1867
(Webb)

JF2: 1867
(Routledge)

JF3: 1870
(Hotten)

JF4a: 1870
(Routledge)

JF4b: 1872
(Routledge)

revision

MTSk: 1872
(Routledge)

HWa: 1873
(Hotten)

revision: HWaMT
1873

HWb: 1874
(Chatto and Windus)

revision: HWbMT
1875

SkNO: 1875
(Am. Pub. Co.)

Textual Notes

299.2–7   long. . . . On] When Mark Twain revised HWa**MT** in 1873 he drew a line from "long" to "On" and wrote "No Paragraph— may God eternally roast the man who punctuated this book." Because the paragraph beginning at 299.5 ("I had my Gould and Curry") had been omitted in JF1, it did not appear in HWa, and Mark Twain was therefore making a single paragraph out of three, not four, paragraphs.

299.31   I started] JF1 eliminated the paragraph break here, but MTSk restored it. Since Mark Twain demonstrably restored it again on HWb**MT**, it seems likely that it was he who had restored the reading in MTSk.

300.5   was] JF1 altered this to the more proper subjunctive form "were," and it was so reprinted in JF2, JF3, and all texts deriving from JF3. The compositor of JF4a, however, changed "were" back to "was," a reading that Mark Twain permitted to stand when he revised JF4a for MTSk. This suggests that he was probably not responsible for the correction entered in JF1, and we have not adopted it here.

300.13   scarce,] The copy-text omits the comma, which makes the sentence seem to say that doctors "had from necessity acquired considerable skill in the treatment of simple 'family complaints,'" whereas the context makes it apparent that this acquisition was really that of the "lady who had just arrived from over the plains." We have therefore adopted the comma which JF1 supplied, and which may reflect Webb's or even Mark Twain's correction of the printer's copy.

300.28   Like] On HWa**MT** Mark Twain drew a line between this word and the last word of the previous paragraph ("graveyard") and wrote "Run in." HWb was accordingly altered.

301.25   It] On HWa**MT** Mark Twain drew a line between this word and the last word of the previous paragraph ("was"). He then wrote "Run in," canceled it, and wrote "No ¶." HWb was accordingly altered.

302.2   jes'] Mark Twain altered this dialect spelling on HWb**MT** to "jis'," and the text of SkNO so read. It is tempting to regard this as a correction of the copy-text reading, but in view of the fact that HWb also had "get" instead of "git" and "such" instead of "sich," it is not possible to say that Mark Twain was restoring instead of revising his dialect, for both of these errors were left uncorrected and may even have influenced his decision to change "jes'" to "jis'."

Emendations of the Copy-Text

299.27	until (JF1) • unti[ ]
299.31	I (JF1) • [ ]
*300.13	scarce, (JF1) • $\sim_\wedge$
300.31	was (JF1) • was was
301.11–12	daguerreotype (JF1) • daguerreotpe
302.27	woman (I-C) • women
303.18	them. (JF1) • them.	MARK TWAIN.

Historical Collation

Texts collated:

GE   "How to Cure a Cold," San Francisco *Golden Era* 11 (20 September 1863): 8.

["*Curing a Cold*" in the following]

JF1   *Jumping Frog* (New York: Webb, 1867), pp. 67–75. Reprints GE with authorial and editorial revisions.

JF2   *Jumping Frog* (London: Routledge, 1867), pp. 63–70. Reprints JF1 with few errors.

JF3   *Jumping Frog* (London: Hotten, 1870), pp. 32–37. Reprints JF2 with some errors in dialect spellings.

JF4   *Jumping Frog* (London: Routledge, 1870 and 1872), pp. 57–64. Reprints JF2 with additional errors.

MTSk *Mark Twain's Sketches* (London: Routledge, 1872), pp. 336–341. Reprints JF4 with authorial revisions and corrections.

HWa *Choice Humorous Works* (London: Hotten, 1873), pp. 393–396. Reprints JF3 with few additional errors.

HWa**MT** Sheets of HWa revised by Mark Twain, who made seven changes in this sketch.

HWb *Choice Humorous Works* (London: Chatto and Windus, 1874), pp. 388–391. Reprints HWa with authorial revisions from HWa**MT**.

HWb**MT** Copy of HWb revised by Mark Twain, who made five changes in this sketch.

SkNO *Sketches, New and Old* (Hartford: American Publishing Company, 1875), pp. 300–305. Reprints HWb with authorial revisions from HWb**MT**.

Collation:

298 *title*	*How to Cure a Cold* (GE) • Curing a Cold (JF1 +)
298.4	[¶] The (GE) • [*no* ¶] The (JF1 +)
298.5	[¶] If (GE) • [*no* ¶] If (JF1 +)
298.14	[¶] Let (GE) • [*no* ¶] Let (JF1 +)
298.16	Virginia (GE–MTSk, GE–HWb) • Virginia City (HWb**MT**-SkNO)
298.18	[¶] The (GE) • [*no* ¶] The (JF1 +)
298.24	[¶] And (GE) • [*no* ¶] And (JF1 +)
299.3	[¶] But (GE–MTSk, GE–HWa) • [*no* ¶] But (HWa**MT**-SkNO)
299.5–7	I had … me. (GE) • [*not in*] (JF1 +)
299.8	[¶] On (GE–MTSk, GE–HWa) • [*no* ¶] On (HWa**MT**-SkNO)
299.10	[¶] I (GE) • [*no* ¶] I (JF1 +)
299.15	[¶] I (GE) • [*no* ¶] I (JF1 +)
299.16	[¶] Shortly (GE) • [*no* ¶] Shortly (JF1 +)
299.18	[¶] I (GE) • [*no* ¶] I (JF1 +)
299.19	[¶] Within (GE) • [*no* ¶] Within (JF1 +)
299.21	[¶] I (GE) • [*no* ¶] I (JF1 +)
299.22	[¶] I (GE) • [*no* ¶] So I (JF1 +)
299.28	Virginia (GE–MTSk, GE–HWb) • Virginia City (HWb**MT**-SkNO)
299.29	[¶] I (GE) • [*no* ¶] I (JF1 +)
299.30	[¶] He (GE, MTSk) • [*no* ¶] He (JF1–JF4, JF1–SkNO)
299.31	[¶] I (MTSk, HWb**MT**-SkNO) • [¶] [ ] (GE); [*no* ¶] I (JF1–JF4, JF1–HWb)
299.34	[¶] I (GE) • [*no* ¶] I (JF1 +)
299.35	[¶] The (GE) • [*no* ¶] The (JF1 +)
299.35–36	I … hour; (GE) • [*not in*] (JF1 +)
299.36	believe I threw (GE–MTSk, GE–HWa) • believed I had thrown (HWa**MT**-SkNO)
300.4	[¶] It (GE) • [*no* ¶] It (JF1 +)
300.5	was (GE, JF4–MTSk) • were (JF1–SkNO)
300.6	cheerfully (GE) • [*not in*] (JF1 +)
300.13	scarce, (JF1 +) • $\sim_{\wedge}$ (GE)
300.16	[¶] I (GE) • [*no* ¶] I (JF1 +)
300.21	[¶] I (GE) • [*no* ¶] I (JF1 +)

300.23   [¶] Under (GE) • [*no* ¶] Under (JF1+)

300.28   [¶] Like (GE-MTSk, GE-HWa) • [*no* ¶] Like (HWa**MT**-SkNO)

300.31   [¶] At (GE) • [*no* ¶] At (JF1+)

300.31   was (JF1+) • was was (GE)

300.35   bass (GE) • base (JF1+)

301.2   [¶] Plain (GE) • [*no* ¶] Plain (JF1+)

301.3   [¶] Then (GE) • [*no* ¶] Then (JF1+)

301.4   [¶] Then (GE) • [*no* ¶] Then (JF1+)

301.5   [¶] I (GE) • [*no* ¶] I (JF1+)

301.5–6   result . . . buzzard's. (GE-JF4, GE-SkNO) • result. (MTSk)

301.8   [¶] I (GE) • [*no* ¶] I (JF1+)

301.8   Bigler (GE-JF4, GE-SkNO) • Tahoe (MTSk)

301.8   Adair (GE) • [*not in*] (JF1+)

301.8   It (GE-JF4, GE-SkNO) • I (MTSk)

301.13–15   I . . . while. (GE) • [*not in*] (JF1+)

301.18   [¶] By (GE) • [*no* ¶] By (JF1+)

301.20   [¶] But (GE) • [*no* ¶] But (JF1+)

301.25   [¶] It (GE-MTSk, GE-HWa) • [*no* ¶] It (HWa**MT**-SkNO)

301.33   [¶] I (GE) • [*no* ¶] I (JF1+)

301.34–302.3 Young . . . dis!" (GE-JF4, GE-SkNO) • [*not in*] (MTSk)

302.2   gen'lman's (GE-JF4, GE-HWb) • gen'l'man's (SkNO)

302.2   git (GE-JF4) • get (JF3-SkNO)

302.2   jes' (GE-JF4, GE-HWb) • jis' (HWb**MT**-SkNO)

302.2   sich (GE) • such (JF1-JF4, JF1-SkNO)

302.4–7   Then . . . morning. (GE) • [*not in*] (JF1+)

302.12–28   It . . . anyhow. (GE) • [*not in*] (JF1+)

302.32   [¶] I (GE) • [*no* ¶] I (JF1+)

302.34   [¶] When (GE) • [*no* ¶] When (JF1+)

302.37   [¶] But (GE) • [*no* ¶] But (JF1+)

302.37–303.3 and ate . . . healthy. [¶] After (GE-JF2, GE-HWa) • and eat . . . healthy. [¶] After (JF4); and—— [¶] After (MTSk); and— here is food for the imagination. [¶] After (HWa**MT**-SkNO)

303.1   [¶] I (GE) • [*no* ¶] I (JF1-JF4, JF1-HWa)

303.3   Bigler (GE-JF4, GE-SkNO) • Tahoe (MTSk)

303.4   besides (GE) • beside (JF1+)

303.4   lot (GE-JF4, GE-SkNO) • cargo (MTSk)

303.4   vilest (GE-JF4, GE-SkNO) • wickedest (MTSk)

303.6	Virginia (GE–MTSk, GE–HWa) • Virginia City (HWb**MT**-SkNO)
303.9	here (GE) • there (JF1 +)
303.10	Lick House (GE–MTSk, GE–HWa) • hotel (HWa**MT**-SkNO)
303.11	at the Occidental (GE–MTSk, GE–HWa) • up town (HWa**MT**-SkNO)
303.13	[¶] Each (GE) • [no ¶] Each (JF1 +)
303.13	makes (GE) • made (JF1 +)
303.14	[¶] I . . . attempt. (GE) • [no ¶] I did it, and still live. (JF1 +)
303.17	cure them (GE–JF1) • cure (JF2–MTSk, JF2–SkNO)
303.18	kill them. (JF1 +) • kill them.	MARK TWAIN. (GE)

64. *MARK TWAIN—MORE OF HIM*

Textual Commentary

The first printing of the sketch in this form appeared in the San Francisco *Golden Era* 11 (27 September 1863): 3 (GE), but the main body of the sketch, "Letter from Mark Twain," had already appeared in the Virginia City *Territorial Enterprise* sometime between 21 and 24 June 1863 (TEnt). Printer's copy for GE was undoubtedly made up from a TEnt clipping, perhaps "dreadfully tattered and torn" (309.5–6), plus the author's manuscript for the new prefatory letter from "A Lady at the Lick House." Since none of this printer's copy survives, copy-text for the sketch is double: GE is copy-text for the prefatory letter, while the only known copy of TEnt, now in Scrapbook 4, pp. 42–43, MTP, is copy-text for the remainder. Copy: PH of GE from Bancroft.

Since Mark Twain provided some new copy for the reprinting, he had an opportunity to revise and correct the clipping from TEnt. Seven small substantive variants occur between GE and TEnt, but only one of these seems manifestly authorial, and we have adopted it here. Emendation of misspelling has, for the most part, been forgone: many of the technical terms have no clearly established spelling, and even when those that do are here misspelled, the error must be regarded as an inseparable part of the mock expertise flourished by the "unsanctified newspaper reporter, devoid of a milliner's education" (311.14–15). Punctilious spelling would only interfere with the intended effect.

A number of ambiguities caused by poor inking in TEnt have been resolved from GE, which may have been set from a slightly better copy and so carries the authority of the original.

Textual Notes

308.6   Robergh] Copy-text "Bobergh" is an error, probably composi-
           torial in origin. Contemporary reports show that the man's
           name was "Robergh," and we have so emended.

309.9   ALL ABOUT THE FASHIONS] Copy-text "ALL ABOUT THE LATEST
           FASHIONS" has been emended to accord with GE. It seems likely
           that Mark Twain deleted "LATEST" because his new preface
           made it clear that the fashions described were displayed at a
           party "last June," some three months before.

311.1   guipre] GE renders this "guipure," a more conventional
           spelling. The copy-text spelling is, however, almost certainly
           authorial: compare the same word in "The Lick House Ball"
           (no. 65).

311.31   Mr.] Bad inking in TEnt obscures the first letter of this ab-
           breviation. In our judgment it is an *M*, but GE rendered it as *D*.
           Inking may also have been a problem in the clipping used by GE
           to reprint TEnt, causing the editor or compositor to conjecture
           "Dr." instead of "Mr." On the other hand, Mark Twain may
           have added this touch of mock solemnity in the printer's copy.
           Since the variant is, however, by no means certainly authorial,
           we have not adopted it.

Emendations of the Copy-Text

[*Copy-text from the title through 309.7 is GE*]

308.6   'swell,' (I-C) • '∼,"
*308.6   Robergh (I-C) • Bobergh
308.9   re-unions (I-C) • re-|unions

[*Copy-text from 309.8 through the end is TEnt*]

*309.9   FASHIONS (GE) • LATEST FASHIONS
309.10   SAN FRANCISCO (GE) • SAN [F]RANCISCO
310.1   circumstance (GE) • eircumstance
310.2   headquarters (GE) • head[∧] | quarters
310.9   with (GE) • wi[ ]h
310.11   Solferino (GE) • Sol[f]erin[o]
310.12   graceful (GE) • grace[f]ul
310.17   back-stitch (I-C) • back-|stitch
310.32   maroon-colored (I-C) • maroon[∧] | colored
311.2   head-dress (GE) • head-|dress

311.16	than (GE) • [ ]han
311.24	models (I-C) • mode[l]s
*311.31	Mr. (I-C) • [M]r.

Historical Collation

Texts collated:

GE   "Mark Twain—More of Him," San Francisco *Golden Era* 11 (27 September 1863): 3.

TEnt   "Letter from Mark Twain," Virginia City *Territorial Enterprise*, 21–24 June 1863, clipping in Scrapbook 4, pp. 42–43, MTP.

Collation:

308.1–309.7	"A . . . is! (GE) • [*not in*] (TEnt)
309.9	FASHIONS (GE) • LATEST FASHIONS (TEnt)
309.33	those (TEnt) • these (GE)
310.31	consisted (TEnt) • consisting (GE)
311.24	models (I-C) • mode[l]s (TEnt); modes (GE)
311.25	Bets (TEnt) • Bet (GE)
311.29	Ridgway's (TEnt) • Rigdway's (GE)
311.31	Mr. (I-C) • [M]r. (TEnt); Dr. (GE)

65. *THE LICK HOUSE BALL*

Textual Commentary

The first printing in the San Francisco *Golden Era* 11 (27 September 1863): 4 is copy-text. Copy: PH from Bancroft. In this sketch Mark Twain elaborates the technique used in "Mark Twain—More of Him" (no. 64), enriching his fashion jargon by borrowing from so many other vocabularies (such as mining and farming) that he often approaches nonsense humor. He deliberately calls attention to his inevitable failures of spelling: in describing one dress he alludes to its "maccaroon (usually spelled 'maccaroni,') buttons" (316.32–33)—a rhetorical device designed to assure his readers that his errors for "macaroon" and "macaroni" are intentional gaffes, properly included as part of the blasé pseudocompetence that informs the sketch throughout. As in no. 64, misspelled fashion terms have not been emended.

Textual Notes

314.9–10   trying to get through her head] Evidently in the sense of trying
                to express, despite some difficulty of comprehension or ar-
                ticulation. The idiom is clearly authorial and requires no
                emendation. Compare Mark Twain's usage in the report of his
                speech before the Third House of the 1863 Territorial Legisla-
                ture: "What are you trying to get through your head?"—a
                remark addressed to Mr. Chapin, who seems unable to complete
                his sentence (*MTEnt*, p. 104). A similar phrase ("what he was
                trying to worry through his head") appears in " 'Mark Twain'
                Explains the Mexican Correspondence" (no. 196).

318.14   mashed potatoes] The copy-text reads "washed potatoes."
                Although it is possible to imagine "cauliflower imbedded in" a
                mound of clean potatoes, the likelihood that Mark Twain's *m*
                was misread as a *w*, and the better sense of "mashed," suggest
                the emendation adopted here.

Emendations of the Copy-Text

314.15   postscript (I-C) • post-|script
315.18   Geeminy (I-C) • Gee-|miny
315.33   off, (I-C) • ~.
317.14   S.'s (I-C) • S's.
317.34   straddle-bug (I-C) • straddle-|bug
*318.14   mashed (I-C) • washed
318.36   again. When (I-C) • ~.—|~
318.37   to (I-C) • [ ]o
318.37–38   hurrahing (I-C) • [ ]urrahing

                66. *A BLOODY MASSACRE NEAR CARSON*

                Textual Commentary

The first printing in the Virginia City *Territorial Enterprise* for 28 October
1863 is not extant. The sketch survives in three contemporary reprintings
of the *Enterprise:*

P[1]   "Horrible," Gold Hill (Nev.) *News*, 28 October 1863, p. 3.

P[2]   "Bloody Massacre," Sacramento *Union*, 30 October 1863, p. 1.

P[3]   "The Latest Sensation," San Francisco *Evening Bulletin*, 31 October
          1863, p. 5.

Copies: PH from Bancroft. The sketch is a radiating text: there is no copy-text. All variants are recorded in a list of emendations and adopted readings, which also records any readings unique to the present edition, identified as I-C.

The independence of P^1 is guaranteed by its date of publication: the afternoon of the day the item appeared in the *Enterprise*. Neither P^2 nor P^3 can derive from P^1 because they reprint so much more of the text. It is barely possible that P^3 derived from P^2 instead of from the *Enterprise*, since it appeared one day later. Two superior readings in P^3—"just at" instead of "just to" and "Daney" instead of "Dana" (324.6 and 325.31)—suggest, however, that P^3 derives independently from the *Enterprise*: it seems unlikely that the P^3 compositor could have known to correct the error "Dana" and that he coincidentally shared Mark Twain's preference for "just at" and altered the readings of P^2 accordingly. Although the evidence is not absolutely conclusive, we have conjectured that all three printings derive independently from the lost *Enterprise*, and each may therefore preserve authorial readings among its variants.

Three additional reprintings of the sketch have been set aside as probably derivative from P^2 or P^3. A paraphrase in the Grass Valley (Nev.) *National*, 31 October 1863 (p. 2), might easily derive from P^2; another brief extract in the Visalia (Calif.) *Delta*, 5 November 1863 (p. 2), could also derive from either P^2 or P^3; and the text printed by Albert Bigelow Paine in *MTB* (3:1597–1599) clearly does derive from P^3, not from the *Enterprise*.

The diagram of transmission records all known contemporary reprintings, including the derivative texts, but the list of emendations and adopted readings records only the variants among the independently radiating texts.

Textual Notes

324 title   *A Bloody Massacre near Carson*] P^1, P^2, and P^3 all vary markedly in the title used. Mark Twain's title in the *Enterprise* printing has been conjectured from the following item in the Austin (Nev.) *Reese River Reveille* supplement for 7 November 1863 (p. 1):

> A CANARD.—Some of the papers are expressing astonishment that "Mark Twain," the local of the Territorial Enterprise, should perpetrate such a "sell" as "A Bloody Massacre near Carson," a pretended account of which recently appeared in the columns of the Enterprise. They don't know him. We would not be surprised at ANYTHING done by that silly idiot.

324.7–8   nine . . . five . . . four . . . nineteen] P^1 omits the passage in which these numbers occur, and P^2 renders them as words while P^3 renders them as numbers. We have followed P^2 here and throughout where similar variants occur, for we know from *Enterprise* printings of other material that its usual practice was to spell out numbers. Moreover, where P^1, P^2, and P^3 can all be compared on some of these number variants, P^1 accords with P^2 against P^3. And since P^1 was manifestly condensing to preserve "limited space," the presumption must be that it would not have expanded figures in the original to spelled-out forms.

324.15 About] P^3 has a paragraph break here and at 325.22, but P^1 and P^2 accord against P^3 in both cases. The case against a break is weakened somewhat by the way P^1 combines paraphrase with extract, but the absence of paragraph breaks in P^1 and P^2 accords with the general practice of the *Enterprise,* and we have adopted it.

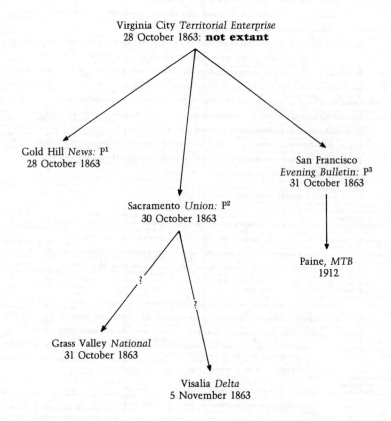

Virginia City *Territorial Enterprise*
28 October 1863: **not extant**

Gold Hill *News:* P^1
28 October 1863

San Francisco
Evening Bulletin: P^3
31 October 1863

Sacramento *Union:* P^2
30 October 1863

Paine, *MTB*
1912

?

?

Grass Valley *National*
31 October 1863

Visalia *Delta*
5 November 1863

Emendations and Adopted Readings

324 *title*	*A Bloody Massacre near Carson* (I-C) • Horrible—(P[1]); Bloody Massacre. (P[2]); The Latest Sensation. A Victim to Jeremy Diddling Trustees—He Cuts his Throat from Ear to Ear, Scalps his Wife, and Dashes out the Brains of Six Helpless Children! (P[3])
324.1–15	From . . . About (P[2,3]) • The most sickening tale of horror that we have read for years, is told in the *Enterprise* of this morning; and were it not for the respectable source from which our cotemporary received it, we should refuse it any credence. The account is given at length, and from our limited space we are compelled to condense it. It is nothing less than the murder of a family, consisting of the mother and seven children by the husband and father, Philip Hopkins, and the suicide of the murderer. The unfortunate family resided between Empire City and Dutch Nick's, and Hopkins has been for some time past supposed to be insane. About (P[1])
324.6	at (P[3]) • to (P[2])
*324.7	nine (P[2]) • 9 (P[3])
*324.7	five (P[2]) • 5 (P[3])
*324.8	four (P[2]) • 4 (P[3])
*324.8	nineteen (P[2]) • 19 (P[3])
324.13	Hopkins' (P[2]) • Hopkins's (P[3])
*324.15	[*no* ¶] About (P[1,2]) • [¶] About (P[3])
324.15	ten (P[1,2]) • 10 (P[3])
324.16	Hopkins (P[2,3]) • Mr. Hopkins (P[1])
324.19	Hopkins (P[2,3]) • he (P[1])
324.20	bore (P[2,3]) • ~, (P[1])
325.1	threshold (P[1,2]) • threshhold (P[3])
325.2	ax (P[2,3]) • axe (P[1])
325.3	committed (P[2,3]) • consummated (P[1])
325.3–4	bedrooms (P[2,3]) • bed-rooms (P[1])
325.6	and (P[2,3]) • as (P[1])
325.7–10	The . . . confusion. (P[2,3]) • [*not in*] (P[1])
325.10	fourteen (P[1,2]) • 14 (P[3])
325.10	seventeen (P[1,2]) • 17 (P[3])
325.12–13	taken refuge, in her terror, (P[1,2]) • sought refuge in her terror (P[3])
325.13	there, (P[1,2]) • ~∧ (P[3])
325.14	mutilated, (P[1,3]) • ~∧ (P[2])
325.14	and (P[2,3]) • and with (P[1])

325.15–21	The ... mind. (P[2,3]) • [*not in*] (P[1])
325.15	girls, (P[2]) • $\sim_\wedge$ (P[3])
325.17	on (P[3]) • upon (P[2])
325.22	[*no* ¶] Curry (P[2]) • [*no* ¶] Mr. Curry (P[1]); [¶] Curry (P[3])
325.22	forty-two (P[1,2]) • 42 (P[3])
325.23	Pennsylvania; (P[2,3]) • $\sim$, (P[1])
325.24	we (P[2,3]) • he (P[1])
325.25	Virginia and Gold Hill (P[2,3]) • Gold Hill and Virginia (P[1])
325.27	stocks (P[2,3]) • $\sim$, (P[1])
325.28	of (P[2,3]) • or (P[1])
325.29–326.5	He ... silence. (P[2,3]) • The stock of this company soon went down to nothing, and the ruined man was driven mad by his misfortunes. (P[1])
325.31	dividend-cooking (P[3]) • $\sim_\wedge\sim$ (P[2])
325.31	Daney (P[3]) • Dana (P[2])
326.4	massacre (P[3]) • massace (P[2])

67. LETTER FROM MARK TWAIN

Textual Commentary

The first printing appeared in the Virginia City *Territorial Enterprise*, probably on 17 November 1863. The only known copy of this printing, in a clipping in Scrapbook 1, p. 71, MTP, is copy-text. There are no textual notes.

Emendations of the Copy-Text

| 328.9 | entirely (I-C) • etirely |
| 328.23 | himself, (I-C) • $\sim$. |

68. A TIDE OF ELOQUENCE

Textual Commentary

The first printing in the Virginia City *Territorial Enterprise*, probably sometime between 1 and 3 December 1863, is not extant. The sketch survives in the only known contemporary reprinting of the *Enterprise*, the San Francisco *Golden Era* 11 (6 December 1863): 8, which is copy-text. Copy: PH from Bancroft. It is clear that the *Era* reprinted only an excerpt from a longer sketch in the *Enterprise*. There are no textual notes.

Emendations of the Copy-Text

332.1	AFTERWARDS (I-C) • "∼
332.10	driveling (I-C) • drivellng
332.12	fell. (I-C) • ∼."

69. *LETTER FROM MARK TWAIN*

Textual Commentary

The first printing appeared in the Virginia City *Territorial Enterprise*, probably on 19 or 20 January 1864. The only known copies of this printing, in clippings in Scrapbook 3, p. 89, and Scrapbook 4, p. 4, MTP, are copy-text.

Textual Notes

337.31   my] Copy-text "any" is probably an error. The two words ("any" and "my") are remarkably similar in Clemens' handwriting, and it is therefore easy to see how a compositor would set one for the other. Either Orion or Clemens himself has corrected "any" to "my" in the clipping contained in Scrapbook 4. We have adopted the emendation.

Emendations of the Copy-Text

334.12	educational (I-C) • aducational
335.9	schoolboy (I-C) • school-|boy
335.32	spit-balls (I-C) • spit-|balls
335.35	shortcomings (I-C) • short-|comings
335.36	headquarters (I-C) • head-|quarters
336.3	swapping (I-C) • swaping
336.26	clap-trap (I-C) • clap-|trap
*337.31	my (I-C, [*possibly*] **MT**) • any
337.37	Miss (I-C) • Mrs.

70. *WINTERS' NEW HOUSE*

Textual Commentary

The first printing appeared in the Virginia City *Territorial Enterprise*, probably on 12 February 1864. The only known copy of this printing, in a clipping in Scrapbook 3, pp. 106–107, MTP, is copy-text. There are no textual notes.

Emendations of the Copy-Text

341.5   old-fashioned (I-C) • old-|fashioned
342.8   ground, (I-C) • ~.

71. *AN EXCELLENT SCHOOL*

Textual Commentary

The first printing appeared in the Virginia City *Territorial Enterprise*, probably on 12 February 1864. The only known copy of this printing, in a clipping in Scrapbook 3, p. 107, MTP, is copy-text. "Winters' New House" (no. 70) and this sketch constitute the first two sections of Mark Twain's letter from Carson City; for a third section, omitted here, see *MTEnt*, pp. 151–152. There are no textual notes.

Emendations of the Copy-Text

345.38   sleight-of-hand (I-C) • slight-of-hand
345.38   foolishness (I-C) • foolishnessness

72. *THOSE BLASTED CHILDREN*

Textual Commentary

The first printing in the New York *Sunday Mercury* for 21 February 1864 (p. 3) is copy-text. Copy: PH from New York Public Library. The printing, preserved in microfilm, is somewhat indistinct and at two points almost completely illegible. Additional copies of the *Mercury* have not been found, but there was one contemporary reprinting in the San Francisco *Golden Era* 12 (27 March 1863): 3 (GE); copy: PH from Bancroft. There is no indication that Mark Twain revised GE, and its substantive variants are clearly editorial or compositorial errors and sophistications. GE is a source for emendation, therefore, only when the copy-text is illegible or very doubtful, and when we conjecture that it preserves the now illegible reading of the *Mercury*.

Textual Notes

352.23–24   boistrous ... harrass] Usually spelled "boisterous" and "harass" by Mark Twain and his contemporaries. The slightly archaic forms of the copy-text, which probably reflect the compositor's preference, are nevertheless preserved here. See also "war-hoop" (352.13) and "reconnoissance" (352.28–29).

354.22   though,] The copy-text omits the comma required by the sense; we have emended to remove a momentary ambiguity.

Emendations of the Copy-Text

351.2   165 (GE) • 1[65]
351.5   time-piece (I-C) • time-|piece
352.5   soothe (GE) • [ ]oothe
352.16   Kerosene (GE) • Kero[s]ene
352.19   come (I-C) • came
352.28–29   reconnoissance (GE) • reconn[o]issance
353.5   she (GE) • [s]he
353.14   two (GE) • [ ]wo
353.18   I'll (GE) • I[∧]ll
353.19   'n' (GE) • 'n[∧]
353.23   of (GE) • o[ ]
353.25   descent (I-C) • de-cent
353.27   doin' nothin' (GE) • do[ ]n' nothin[']
353.33–34   day.) "Hi ... Chinaman!" (I-C) • ∼·∧∧∼ ... ∼!∧
353.33   a (GE) • [*illegible*]
353.34   chances to come in (GE) • [*illegible*]
353.35–36   and ... him.) (GE) • [*illegible*]
353.36–37   "Now ... tail!" (I-C) • ∧∼ ... ∼!∧
354.9   'em; (GE) • 'em[;]

*354.22   though, (I-C) • ~$_\wedge$
354.25   port-holes (I-C) • port-|holes
355.6   brains; (GE) • ~[,]
355.15   to fits (GE) • to fit[ ]
355.25   Johnny. (GE) • ~[,]
356.12   saltpetre (I-C) • salt-|petre
356.13   vitriol (I-C) • vitroil
356.26   recall sad memories of the (GE) • [*illegible*]
356.29   Enough, (GE) • ~[$_\wedge$]

73. *FRIGHTFUL ACCIDENT TO DAN DE QUILLE*

Textual Commentary

The first printing in the Virginia City *Territorial Enterprise* for 20 April 1864
is not extant. The sketch survives in three contemporary reprintings of the
Enterprise, all with the title adopted here.

P[1]   Nevada City (Calif.) *Gazette*, 26 April 1864, p. 1.

P[2]   San Francisco *Golden Era* 12 (1 May 1864): 5.

P[3]   Unionville (Nev.) *Humboldt Register*, 14 May 1864, p. 1.

Copies: PH from Bancroft. The sketch is a radiating text: there is no copy-
text. All variants are recorded in a list of emendations and adopted readings.
In this case there are no I-C emendations.

P[1] precedes all other known reprintings and cannot therefore derive from
them. P[2] cannot derive from P[1] because of the superior reading also found in
P[3], "noble old friend" instead of P[1] "noble friend" (361.14). P[3] cannot derive
from P[1] for the same reason, and cannot derive from P[2] because of three
superior readings: "yesterday" instead of P[2] "Tuesday" (360.2); "one of his
legs" instead of P[2] "one leg" (360.20); and "hash-house proprietors" instead of
P[2] "hash-proprietors" (361.9–10). It is always possible that unidentified reprintings intervened between known reprintings and the lost *Enterprise*, but
even if the distance from the original printing is greater than can now be
documented, all three reprintings appear to derive independently, and each
may therefore preserve authorial readings among its variants.

The diagram of transmission is as follows:

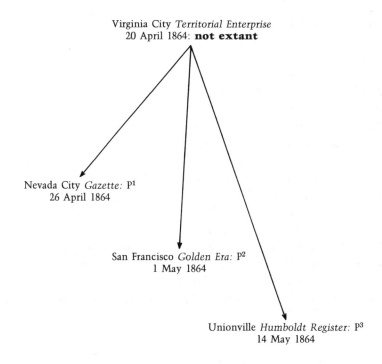

Virginia City *Territorial Enterprise*
20 April 1864: **not extant**

Nevada City *Gazette:* P[1]
26 April 1864

San Francisco *Golden Era:* P[2]
1 May 1864

Unionville *Humboldt Register:* P[3]
14 May 1864

Textual Notes

360.2   yesterday] P[1] and P[3] concur against P[2] in printing "yesterday" instead of "Tuesday." We conjecture that P[2], finding the article in the *Enterprise* for Wednesday, 20 April 1864, altered the text to read "Tuesday," while P[1] and P[3] continued to follow the *Enterprise* reading (and usual practice) in printing "yesterday."

Emendations and Adopted Readings

*360.2   yesterday (P[1,3]) • Tuesday (P[2])
360.5   hour (P[1,3]) • ~, (P[2])
360.6   will, (P[1,3]) • ~. (P[2])
360.6   accident,) (P[1,2]) • ~), (P[3])
360.7   corner, (P[2,3]) • ~∧ (P[1])
360.8   channel; (P[1,3]) • ~[:] (P[2])

360.8   signaled (P[2,3]) • signalled (P[1])
360.11   knee (P[1,2]) • keel (P[3])
360.12   adversary, (P[1,2]) • ~. (P[3])
360.13   yards (P[1,3]) • ~, (P[2])
360.14   will, (P[1,3]) • ~$_\wedge$ (P[2])
360.14   mentioned,) (P[1,2]) • ~), (P[3])
360.15   stomach. His (P[1,3]) • stomach; his (P[2])
360.16   afterwards (P[1,3]) • afterward (P[2])
360.20   of his legs (P[1,3]) • leg (P[2])
361.1   the back (P[1,3]) • his back (P[2])
361.2   rail fence (P[2,3]) • rail-fence (P[1])
361.3   hearse (P[1,3]) • ~, (P[2])
361.6   wouldn't (P[1,2]) • would n't (P[3])
361.9–10   hash-house proprietors (P[1,3]) • hash-proprietors (P[2])
361.14   old (P[2,3]) • [not in] (P[1])
361.15   Brewery (P[1,3]) • breweries (P[2])
361.16   usual. (P[2]) • usual.—[Mark Twain. (P[1]); usual. | 'MARK
             TWAIN.' (P[3])

74. [DAN REASSEMBLED]

Textual Commentary

The first printing in the Virginia City *Territorial Enterprise*, probably sometime between 28 and 30 April 1864, is not extant. The text survives in Albert
Bigelow Paine's *MTB* (1:236), which is copy-text. Copy: first edition in MTP.
The source of Paine's text is not known. There are no textual notes or
emendations.

75. WASHOE.—"INFORMATION WANTED"

Textual Commentary

The first printing in the Virginia City *Territorial Enterprise*, probably sometime in the first two weeks of May 1864, is not extant. The sketch survives
in the only known contemporary reprinting of the *Enterprise*, the San
Francisco *Golden Era* 12 (22 May 1864): 5 (GE), which is copy-text. Copies:
PH from Bancroft and Yale.

An edited version of the sketch, retitled "Information for the Million," was included in JF1, but collation does not conclusively establish the source of that text: it may have been set from the *Enterprise*, GE, or some other unidentified reprinting. Although it is possible that JF1 was set from the *Enterprise* and therefore radiates independently of the GE text, we have not attempted to reconstruct the lost printing from JF1 and GE.

Reprintings and Revisions. The revisions made for the JF1 printing are typical of changes demonstrably made by Mark Twain in other sketches. It is likely that he edited a clipping in the Yale Scrapbook, removing such topical allusions as the joke about the Comstock Lode and the Gould and Curry mine. But his editor, Charles Henry Webb, could also have deleted such topical allusions, and since two new sentences were used to introduce the sketch, and since these do not read convincingly like Mark Twain, all of the variants in JF1 must be regarded as if they were editorial.

The JF1 text was reprinted as described in the textual introduction. Routledge reprinted JF1 in 1867 (JF2), and Hotten in turn reprinted JF2 in 1870 (JF3). Routledge also reprinted JF2 in 1870 (JF4a) and, using the unaltered plates of JF4a, reissued the book in 1872 (JF4b). None of these texts was revised by the author. Presumably when Mark Twain prepared the printer's copy for MTSk in 1872, he deleted the sketch from a copy of JF4a, which formed part of that printer's copy: it was not reprinted in MTSk. One year later, however, Hotten reprinted the JF3 text in HWa. When Mark Twain revised this book for Chatto and Windus in the fall of 1873 (HWa**MT**), he again deleted the sketch, canceling it in the table of contents and striking through the text, saying "Leave out this puerile hogwash" (HWa**MT**, p. 573). The sketch was omitted from HWb, and Mark Twain did not subsequently reprint it.

The diagram of transmission indicates three possible sources for the JF1 text, even though the present edition declines to treat JF1 and GE as independently radiating texts.

Textual Notes

369.19 got the bulge on] Copy-text "got the bugle on" is not necessarily mistaken. But "got the bulge on" is a characteristic phrase of Mark Twain's, and JF1—which may have been set from an authoritative source other than GE, and which may also have been corrected by the author—prints the emendation adopted here.

Emendations of the Copy-Text

367.1   "Springfield (JF1) • ^~
367.2   "Dear (JF1) • ^~
368.30 latitude. It (I-C) • latitude .It

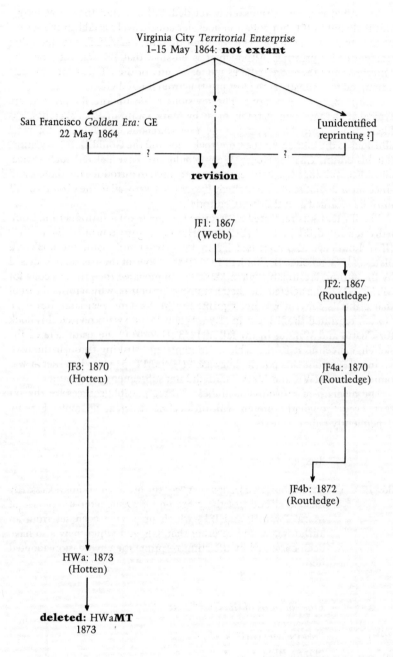

Virginia City *Territorial Enterprise*
1–15 May 1864: **not extant**

?

San Francisco *Golden Era:* GE
22 May 1864

[unidentified
reprinting ?]

?   ?

revision

JF1: 1867
(Webb)

JF2: 1867
(Routledge)

JF3: 1870
(Hotten)

JF4a: 1870
(Routledge)

JF4b: 1872
(Routledge)

HWa: 1873
(Hotten)

deleted: HWa**MT**
1873

369.9   access (JF1) • aceess
*369.19   bulge (JF1) • bugle

Historical Collation

Texts collated:

GE   "Washoe.—'Information Wanted,'" *Golden Era* 12 (22 May
             1864): 5. Reprints the Virginia City *Territorial Enterprise* for
             1–15 May 1864, which is not extant.

             [*"Information for the Million"* in the following]

JF1   *Jumping Frog* (New York: Webb, 1867), pp. 144–152. Reprints
             the text from an unidentified source, possibly the *Enterprise*,
             GE, or another contemporary reprinting; revised by Mark
             Twain or Webb.
JF2   *Jumping Frog* (London: Routledge, 1867), pp. 135–143. Reprints
             JF1 with few errors.
JF3   *Jumping Frog* (London: Hotten, 1870), pp. 108–113. Reprints JF2
             with few errors.
JF4   *Jumping Frog* (London: Routledge, 1870 and 1872), pp. 124–131.
             Reprints JF2 with additional errors.
HWa   *Choice Humorous Works* (London: Hotten, 1873), pp. 573–576.
             Reprints JF3 with few errors.
HWa**MT**   Sheets of HWa revised by Mark Twain. There are no revisions;
             the sketch is canceled.

Collation:

367 *title* *Washoe.—"Information Wanted"* (GE) • Information for the
             Million (JF1+)
367.1   "SPRINGFIELD (I-C) • [¶] A young man anxious for informa-
             tion writes to a friend residing in Virginia City, Nevada, as
             follows: | "SPRINGFIELD (JF1+)
367.1   April (GE, JF1–JF4, JF1–JF3) • *April* (HWa)
367.13   DEAREST (GE) • [¶] The letter was handed in to a newspaper
             office for reply. For the benefit of all who contemplated moving
             to Nevada, it is perhaps best to publish the correspondence in its
             entirety: | DEAREST (JF1+)
367.25   do it (GE) • [*not in*] (JF1+)
368.3   God (GE) • the (JF1+)

368.10–15   (Observe . . . William. (GE) • [*not in*] (JF1+)
368.16   also (GE) • however (JF1+)
368.26   ah, (GE, HWa) • ~! (JF1–JF4, JF1–JF3)
368.28   all winter (GE, JF1) • all the winter (JF2–JF4, JF2–HWa)
369.12   America. (GE, JF1–JF4, JF1–JF3) • ~! (HWa)
369.19   bulge (JF1+) • bugle (GE)
370.2   here (GE) • [*not in*] (JF1+)
370.9   man. (GE) • ~! (JF1+)
370.28   that if (GE, JF1–JF2, JF1–HWa) • that if that if (JF4)
370.29   all (GE, JF1–JF4) • [*not in*] (JF3–HWa)
370.32–36   I think . . . now. (GE) • [*not in*] (JF1+)
371.2   experience. (GE, HWa) • ~! (JF1–JF4, JF1–JF3)
371.15   MARK TWAIN. (GE) • [*not in*] (JF1+)

Line numbers in the following appendix apparatuses refer only to Mark Twain's text and do not include the editorial headnotes or rows of ellipsis points.

A1. SUNDAY AMUSEMENTS

Textual Commentary

The first printing appeared in the Hannibal *Daily Journal* for 10 May 1853 (p. 3). The only known copy of this printing, in MoHist, is copy-text. The sketch was reprinted in the Hannibal *Weekly Journal* for 12 May 1853 (p. 2). Collation shows no variation between these printings, and it seems likely that the *Weekly* printing is a reimpression of the *Daily's* standing type. Clemens may have typeset and proofread the sketch. There are no textual notes.

Emendations of the Copy-Text

376.13   cease (I-C) • ccase
376.14   landsmen (I-C) • lands-|men
376.19   cholic (I-C) • cclic
377.2   all! (I-C) • all! | J.

A2. THE GREAT FAIR AT ST. LOUIS

Textual Commentary

The first printing in the Keokuk (Iowa) *Post* for 21 October 1856 (p. 2) is copy-text. Copy: PH from MoHist. This printing was followed four days later by a reprinting, evidently from the standing type, in the Keokuk *Saturday Post* for 25 October 1856 (p. 2). One variant occurs, at 379.36, a correction adopted here as an emendation of the copy-text. There are no textual notes. The emendation from the *Saturday Post* is designated SP.

Emendations of the Copy-Text

379.11	&c., (I-C) • ~.'
379.24	amphitheatre (I-C) • ampitheatre
379.25	fine (I-C) • fin
379.26	stoves (I-C) • s[t]oves
379.34	In (I-C) • It
379.36	stripes waving (SP) • ns ipeswaving
380.27	gray!' (I-C) • ~!"
380.32	man (I-C) • men
380.34	comes (I-C) • csmes
380.38	gray's' (I-C) • gray's∧
381.3	glimpse (I-C) • glimpsc
381.9	applause. There (I-C) • ~.—|~
381.14	grays (I-C) • gray's
381.15	negro's (I-C) • negroes

A3. [CINCINNATI BOARDING HOUSE SKETCH]

Textual Commentary

The first printing appeared in the Keokuk (Iowa) *Post* for 18 November 1856 (p. 2). We have been unable to examine the original newspaper. A PH of the first printing is therefore copy-text. Copy: PH from the University of Illinois, Urbana-Champaign. There are no textual notes.

Emendations of the Copy-Text

382.4	houses. The (I-C) • ~.—|~
383.13	Blathers (I-C) • B[l]athers
383.34	shouldn't (I-C) • should'nt
384.1	It's (I-C) • Its
384.1	though, (I-C) • ~[,]
384.8	are. (I-C) • ~."
384.10	Silence (I-C) • Sllence
385.23	day, (I-C) • ~;
385.36	ain't (I-C) • [a]in't
386.7	cellar (I-C) • ce[l]lar

B1. LOCAL COLUMN FOR 1 OCTOBER 1862

Textual Commentary

The first printing in the Virginia City *Territorial Enterprise* for 1 October 1862 is not extant. The first item in this column, "A Gale," survives in two contemporary reprintings of the *Enterprise:*

P[1]   "A Gale," Oroville (Calif.) *Butte Record*, 11 October 1862, p. 2.

P[2]   "Washoe Zephyr," typescript of an unidentified reprinting, Grant Smith Papers, carton 1, book 6, Bancroft.

Copies: PH from Bancroft. The item is a radiating text: there is no copy-text. All variants are recorded in a list of emendations and adopted readings, which also records any readings unique to the present edition, identified as I-C.

Both P[1] and P[2] radiate independently from the lost *Enterprise* because each preserves authorial readings among its variants. P[1] was probably reprinted directly from the *Enterprise*. P[2] is a modern typescript of an unidentified reprinting of the *Enterprise*, for it omits the penultimate sentence beginning "There were many guests" (389.5–8). It therefore stands at somewhat greater distance than does P[1] from the lost original, and we have accorded P[1] slight preference when the variants are nearly indifferent. Yet P[2] clearly does contain one sentence that is manifestly authorial and is not preserved at all in P[1], "No one hurt." (389.8). It should also be noted that P[2] attributes the item to "The Enterprise, Oct. 2, 1862," and that while we have concluded the date is in error, the possibility remains that "A Gale" appeared one day later than suggested here.

The diagram of transmission is as follows:

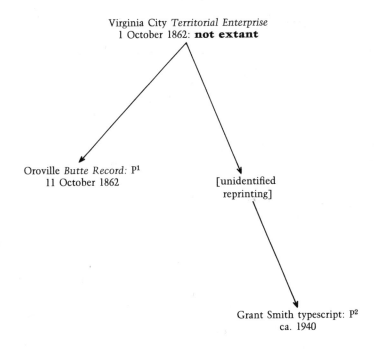

Virginia City *Territorial Enterprise*
1 October 1862: **not extant**

Oroville *Butte Record:* P¹
11 October 1862

[unidentified
reprinting]

Grant Smith typescript: P²
ca. 1940

The second and third items, "The Indian Troubles on the Overland Route" and "More Indian Troubles," survive in the only known contemporary reprinting of the *Enterprise,* the Marysville (Calif.) *Appeal* for 5 October 1862 (p. 3), which is copy-text. Copy: PH from Bancroft.

Textual Notes

389.1   (Sept. 30th)] This parenthetical date is not in the usual style of *Enterprise* local items, but since both P¹ and P² include it, and since Clemens may have been unfamiliar with the paper's style, we have retained it. There is a possibility that the item actually appeared on October 2, as P² indicates, and that it was therefore necessary to clearly identify "Tuesday evening."

389.8   No one hurt.] Unique to P². Because P² omits the previous sentence, however, no documentary evidence establishes the position of the last sentence. We have conjectured that it followed the last sentence in P¹, the sentence omitted in P².

Emendations and Adopted Readings for "A Gale"

389.1   A GALE.— (P^1) • Washoe Zephyr (P^2)

389.1   About (I-C) • They have had windy times of late in Washoe.
             The Virginia City Enterprise graphically describes the con-
             sequent movement in real estate, and says: "About (P^1);
             "About (P^2)

389.1   7 (P^1) • seven (P^2)

389.2   houses (P^1) • ~, (P^2)

389.5–8   There . . . occasion. (P^1) • [*not in*] (P^2)

389.8   alacrity (I-C) • allacrity (P^1)

389.8   No one hurt. (P^2) • [*not in*] (P^1)

389.8   hurt. (I-C) • ~." (P^2)

Emendations of the Copy-Text for "The Indian Troubles"
and "More Indian Troubles"

390.14   are as (I-C) • are are

391.18–19   Mitchell, (I-C) • ~.

391.26   arms, (I-C) • ~.

B2.   *LOCAL COLUMN FOR 1–10 NOVEMBER 1862*

Textual Commentary

The first printing in the Virginia City *Territorial Enterprise*, sometime
between 1 and 10 November 1862, is not extant. The item survives in the
only known contemporary reprinting of the *Enterprise*, the Oroville (Calif.)
Butte Record for 15 November 1862 (p. 2), which is copy-text. Copy: PH
from Bancroft. We have emended out the introductory phrase used by the
Butte Record. There are no textual notes.

Emendations of the Copy-Text

392.1   Mr. (I-C) • The Territorial Enterprise says that Mr.

392.4   Gravelly (I-C) • Gravely

392.6   Kingdom (I-C) • Kindgom

392.9   Comstock. The (I-C) • ~.—|~

B3.   LOCAL COLUMN FOR 30–31 DECEMBER 1862

Textual Commentary

The first printing appeared in the Virginia City *Territorial Enterprise* for 30 or 31 December 1862. The only known copy of this printing, in a clipping in Scrapbook 4, p. 14, MTP, is copy-text. There are no textual notes. The first item is omitted because it appears as "Our Stock Remarks" (no. 33).

Emendations of the Copy-Text

393.11	I (I-C) • J
393.12	Flowery, (I-C) • ~.
393.21	fire-wall (I-C) • fire-|wall
394.24	strictly (I-C) • stric[ ]ly
395.4	Plata (I-C) • Platte

B4.   LOCAL COLUMN FOR 4 JANUARY 1863

Textual Commentary

The first printing appeared in the Virginia City *Territorial Enterprise* for 4 January 1863. The only known copy of this printing, in a clipping in Scrapbook 1, p. 66, MTP, is copy-text. There are no textual notes.

Emendations of the Copy-Text

397.6	to-morrow (I-C) • to-|morrow

B5.   LOCAL COLUMN FOR 6 JANUARY 1863

Textual Commentary

The first printing in the Virginia City *Territorial Enterprise* for 6 January 1863 is not extant. The column survives in the only known contemporary reprinting of the *Enterprise*, the Marysville (Calif.) *Appeal* for 9 January 1863 (p. 2), which is copy-text. Copy: PH from Bancroft. There are no textual notes or emendations.

B6. *LOCAL COLUMN FOR 10 JANUARY 1863*

Textual Commentary

The first printing appeared in the Virginia City *Territorial Enterprise* for 10 January 1863 (p. 3). The only known copy of this printing, in a newspaper at the library of the Nevada Historical Society at Reno, is copy-text. Copy: PH from the Nevada Historical Society. The newspaper has been torn and water stained, which results in an unusual number of doubtful readings. There are no textual notes.

Emendations of the Copy-Text

400.2	house, (I-C) • ~[.]
400.3	used for (I-C) • used [for]
400.15	informed (I-C) • in[f]ormed
400.16	thought (I-C) • [ ]hought [torn]
400.16–17	partition (I-C) • par[ ]tion [torn]
400.18	band (I-C) • [b]and [torn]
400.21	equalled (I-C) • e[q]ualled [torn]
400.21	of (I-C) • o[f] [torn]
400.22	man (I-C) • [ma]n [torn]
400.22	those (I-C) • th[e]se [torn]
400.23	Virginia (I-C) • [Vi]rginia [torn]
400.23	be (I-C) • b[e] [torn]
400.24	emergency (I-C) • e[ ]ergency [torn]

B7. *LOCAL COLUMN FOR 11–21 JANUARY 1863*

Textual Commentary

The first printing in the Virginia City *Territorial Enterprise*, sometime between 11 and 21 January 1863, is not extant. The item survives in the only known contemporary reprinting of the *Enterprise*, the San Francisco *Herald and Mirror* for 23 January 1863 (p. 3), which is copy-text. Copy: Powell Library, University of California, Los Angeles. There are no textual notes.

Emendations of the Copy-Text

401.1   to-day (I-C) • to-|day

B8.   LOCAL COLUMN FOR 19 FEBRUARY 1863

Textual Commentary

The first printing appeared in the Virginia City *Territorial Enterprise* for 19 February 1863 (p. 3). Only one copy of this printing is extant. A PH of this unique clipping, in MTP, is copy-text, and is used with permission of the clipping's owner, Ruth Hermann (416 Zion St., Nevada City, California, 95959). There are no textual notes.

Emendations of the Copy-Text

402.7   labor (I-C) • [l]abor

B9.   LOCAL COLUMN FOR 25 FEBRUARY 1863

Textual Commentary

The first printing appeared in the Virginia City *Territorial Enterprise* for 25 February 1863 (p. 3). Only one copy of this printing is extant. A PH of this unique clipping, in MTP, is copy-text, and is used with permission of the clipping's owner, Ruth Hermann (416 Zion St., Nevada City, California, 95959). There are no textual notes.

Emendations of the Copy-Text

404.11   self-conceit (I-C) • self-|conceit
405.18   couples (I-C) • couple
406.6   Peasley (I-C) • Peasely
406.21   the (I-C) • [*not in*]
406.22   so (I-C) • [s]o

B10.   LOCAL COLUMN FOR 17–26 FEBRUARY 1863

Textual Commentary

The first printing in the Virginia City *Territorial Enterprise*, sometime
between 17 and 26 February 1863, is not extant. The item survives in the
only known contemporary reprinting of the *Enterprise*, the Oroville (Calif.)
Butte Record for 28 February 1863 (p. 1), which is copy-text.   Copy: PH
from Bancroft. The *Butte Record* placed the entire item within quotation
marks; we have emended back to the original form in the *Enterprise*. There
are no textual notes.

Emendations of the Copy-Text

408.1	We (I-C) • "~
408.4	William, (I-C) • ~[.]
408.9	drink. (I-C) • ~."

B11.   LOCAL COLUMN FOR 1–12 MARCH 1863

Textual Commentary

The first printing in the Virginia City *Territorial Enterprise*, sometime
between 1 and 12 March 1863, is not extant. The item survives in the only
known contemporary reprinting of the *Enterprise*, the Oroville (Calif.)
Butte Record for 14 March 1863 (p. 3), which is copy-text. Copy: PH from
Bancroft. There are no textual notes or emendations.

B12.   LOCAL COLUMN FOR 3 APRIL 1863

Textual Commentary

The first printing appeared in the Virginia City *Territorial Enterprise* for
3 April 1863 (p. 3). The only known copy of this printing, in Bancroft, is
copy-text. There are no textual notes. Several extracts have been omitted
from the first item.

Emendations of the Copy-Text

410.5	months (I-C) • ~'
410.24	5th. . . . (I-C) • 5th: [*omitted extracts*]
411.33	pound (I-C) • pou[nd] [*blot*]
411.34	tested (I-C) • t[est]ed [*blot*]
412.8	marvelously (I-C) • [ ]arvelously [*blot*]

B13.   *LOCAL COLUMN FOR 19–30 APRIL 1863*

Textual Commentary

The first printing in the Virginia City *Territorial Enterprise,* sometime between 19 and 30 April 1863, is not extant. The item survives in the only known contemporary reprinting of the *Enterprise,* the Oroville (Calif.) *Butte Record* for 2 May 1863 (p. 2), which is copy-text. Copy: PH from Bancroft. There are no textual notes or emendations.

B14.   *LOCAL COLUMN FOR 27 AUGUST 1863*

Textual Commentary

The first printing appeared in the Virginia City *Territorial Enterprise* for 27 August 1863. The only known copy of this printing, pasted beneath a banner headline and dateline for the *Enterprise* of this date in Scrapbook 2, p. 70, MTP, is copy-text. There are no textual notes.

Emendations of the Copy-Text

416.14	$1,600,000 (I-C) • ₍ₐ₎1,600,000

B15.   *LETTER FROM DAYTON FOR*
NOVEMBER 1863–FEBRUARY 1864

Textual Commentary

The first printing in the Virginia City *Territorial Enterprise,* sometime between November 1863 and February 1864, is not extant. The extract sur-

vives in the only known reprinting of the *Enterprise* in Carl Burgess Glasscock's *The Big Bonanza* (Indianapolis: Bobbs-Merrill, 1931), pp. 122–123,
which is copy-text. Copy: Bancroft. The nature of Glasscock's printer's
copy—whether a clipping of the *Enterprise* or a reprinting, transcript, or
typescript—is not known. Glasscock placed the entire item within quotation
marks; we have emended back to the original form in the *Enterprise*.

Textual Notes

419.15   feasibility. . . .] The ellipsis points are in the copy-text, in-
                dicating that Glasscock had access to a longer text.

Emendations of the Copy-Text

418.1   Eight (I-C) • "~
418.9   Just (I-C) • "~
418.10   "Carlo," (I-C) • '~,'
418.15   We (I-C) • "~
419.3   Mr. (I-C) • "~
419.10–13   "For instance," . . . "they . . . ago." (I-C) • " '~ ~ ,' " . . .
                '~ . . . ~.'
419.15   feasibility. . . . (I-C) • ~." . . .

B16.   LOCAL COLUMN FOR 25–27 DECEMBER 1863

Textual Commentary

The first printing in the Virginia City *Territorial Enterprise*, between 25 and
27 December 1863, is not extant. The item survives in the only known contemporary reprinting of the *Enterprise*, the Marysville (Calif.) *Appeal* for
30 December 1863 (p. 3), which is copy-text. Copy: PH from Bancroft. There
are no textual notes or emendations.

B17.   LOCAL COLUMN FOR 29 DECEMBER 1863

Textual Commentary

The first printing appeared in the Virginia City *Territorial Enterprise* for 29
December 1863. The only known copy of this printing, in a clipping in
Scrapbook 3, p. 60, MTP, is copy-text. There are no textual notes.

Emendations of the Copy-Text

421.4	*Be-hi-me-soi-vin* (I-C) • *Be-hi-me-soi-|vin*
422.4	Dixson (I-C) • Dixon
422.6	Cutler (I-C) • Cutter
422.15	Cutler's (I-C) • Cutter's
422.23	medical (I-C) • medccal

B18. LETTER FROM CARSON CITY

Textual Commentary

The first printing in the Virginia City *Territorial Enterprise,* probably on 12 or 13 January 1864, is not extant. The extract survives in the only known contemporary reprinting of the *Enterprise,* the Gold Hill *News* for 13 January 1864 (p. 2), which is copy-text. Copy: PH from Bancroft. There are no textual notes.

Emendations of the Copy-Text

423.1	Speaking (I-C) • "~
423.13	sack-cloth (I-C) • sack-|cloth
423.17	knees. (I-C) • ~."

B19. LOCAL COLUMN FOR 17–24 APRIL 1864

Textual Commentary

The first printing in the Virginia City *Territorial Enterprise,* probably sometime between 17 and 24 April 1864, is not extant. The item survives in the only known contemporary reprinting of the *Enterprise,* the Jackson (Calif.) *Amador Weekly Ledger* for 30 April 1864 (p. 4), which is copy-text. Copy: PH from Bancroft. There are no textual notes.

Emendations of the Copy-Text

424.13	John, (I-C) • ~∧
424.20	rage? As (I-C) • ~?—|~

WORD DIVISION IN THIS VOLUME

The following compound words that could be rendered either solid or with a hyphen are hyphenated at the end of a line in this volume. For purposes of quotation each is listed here with its correct form.

116.27–28	blockhead
138.14–15	nightfall
151.3–4	foot-board
166.10–11	cork-screw
174.2–3	hay-stacks
186.29–30	stockholder
196.28–29	blanc-mange
208.38–209.1	sourkrout
250.12–13	staircase
260.4–5	bloodshed
325.3–4	bedrooms
341.5–6	dining-room
341.14–15	drawing-rooms
341.22–23	bedrooms
341.23–24	billiard-room
345.37–38	Witchcraft
346.8–9	grandmother
361.9–10	hash-house
379.15–16	knick-knack
397.9–10	to-morrow
406.25-26	school-house

INDEX

INDEX

THE FOLLOWING ITEMS have not been indexed: place names unless the subject of an explanatory note; recipients of letters, when no pertinent statement is made about them; citations and "see" references; fictional characters; the guide to the apparatus and the individual textual commentaries. Works by Mark Twain are listed under their full titles; other works are listed only under their authors' names whenever feasible. When Mark Twain makes a literary allusion without mentioning the author or work, only the identifying explanatory note is indexed; the page-and-line cue of the note will lead to the allusion itself. Daily newspapers are listed under their city of origin, other periodicals under their titles. The abbreviations of book titles used in analyzed entries are explained in the description of texts (pp. 670–673).

600; mentioned in "Jumping Frog" sketch, 30, 527, 529–530

Ward, Lock and Company, 555n, 587, 589n

Warm Springs Hotel, 464

Warner, Charles Dudley, 608, 609, 610n

Warren Choate and Company, 620

Washington Correspondents' Club, 42

Washoe Agricultural, Mining and Mechanical Society, 306, 339, 401, 462

"The Washoe Canary," 387

Washoe City (Nev.), 459–460

Washoe City *Old Pah-Utah*, 493

Washoe City *Times*, 220, 493

Washoe Indians, 406

"Washoe.—'Information Wanted'" (no. 75) ("Information for the Million"), 19, 365–371, 496–498, 605

Washoe Mining and Manufacturing Company, 478

Washoe Stock and Exchange Board, 239–240, 295, 484

Wasserman (S.) and Company, 173, 456

Wasson, Warren H., 197, 461–462

Watson Consolidated Gold and Silver Mining Company, 193

Watts, Isaac, 471

Wayman, John Hudson, 205, 207, 209, 311, 464

Weaver, George Sumner, 445, 446

Webb, Charles Henry ("John Paul"), 29, 33, 489; as Clemens' editor and publisher, 38, 39, 428–429, 503–506, 509–546 *passim*, 556, 598, 607, 637, 654, 656, 670; JF1 copyright dispute, 545n, 558, 572; *Liffith Lank*, 536, 545n

"Webb's Benefit" (no. 141), 33

Webster, Samuel C., 146

Webster (Charles L.) and Company, 674

Wecter, Dixon, 85, 102

Weekly Review, 33, 34, 350, 504, 506

Welch, William, 478

Wells, Fargo and Company, 276, 309, 415–416, 480, 484

Wentworth, "John Doe," 401

Wetherill, Sam, 408

"What a Sky-Rocket Did" (no. 81), 27

What Cheer House, 184, 186, 396

"Where Governor Hoffman Is" (no. 251), 52

"Whereas" (no. 94) ("Aurelia's Unfortunate Young Man," "Love's Bakery"), 55, 521, 526, 557, 612, 630, 638

Whicher, J. W., 231, 468

White, Captain, 403, 482

White, Rev. A. F., 222, 286, 467

White House (Carson City), 397

White House (Virginia City), 259, 261, 270, 298

"White Man Mighty Onsartain" (no. 160) ("Badlam Sharks"), 538

Whitman, Walt, 49

"A Wicked Fraud Perpetrated on Mark Twain in Newark" (no. 234) ("How the Author Was Sold in Newark," "A Deception"), 46, 578–579, 625, 638

"The Widow's Protest" (no. 304) ("Dan Murphy"), 591, 612, 628, 636, 638, 644, 646–647

Wiegand, Conrad, 43

Wightman, A. C., 239–240, 478

"The 'Wild Man' 'Interviewed'" (no. 259), 52

Wilde, Jack, 207, 465

William M. Morrison, 127–128, 130, 144, 449

Williams, General, 397

Williams, True W., 621, 641–642, 645

The text of this book is set in Continental, a typeface adapted for photocomposition from the Linotype font Trump Mediaeval, which was designed in 1954 for the Weber typefoundry by Georg Trump, a renowned German artist and typographer. Continental has been praised for the reserve and distinction of its light, clean characters. For display matter and headings, two closely related fonts were chosen to coordinate well with the text type: Weiss italic (a slightly inclined font with swash capitals) and Weiss Initials Series I (an elegant all-capital font). Both were designed by Emil Rudolf Weiss in 1931 for the Bauer typefoundry. The paper used is P & S offset laid regular, manufactured by P. H. Glatfelter Company. It is an acid-free paper of assured longevity which combines high opacity, for legibility and attractive illustrations, with low weight, for comfortable handling. The book was composed by Advanced Typesetting Services of California on Harris Fototronic equipment, printed by Publishers Press, and bound by Mountain States Bindery.